D0939565

THE APOSTLE

Other books by Sholem Asch
Published by Carroll and Graf

Three Cities
The Nazarene
East River

THE APOSTLE

SHOLEM ASCH

CARROLL & GRAF PUBLISHERS, INC.
New York

St. Peter by El Greco

First Carroll & Graf Edition 1985

Carroll & Graf Publishers, Inc.
260 Fifth Avenue
New York, N.Y. 10001

ISBN: 0-88184-167-6

Manufactured in the United States of America

CONTENTS

PART THREE

PART ONE

Chapter One

FIRST FRUITS

SEVEN weeks had gone by since that memorable day when on the hill of Golgotha Yeshua of Nazareth had been crucified by command of Pontius Pilate. The disciples and followers of the crucified one had left the city and gone into hiding among their own on the Mount of Olives. And now the hosts of the *Ebionim,* the poor, the homeless and forlorn, streamed into Jerusalem up the narrow, winding path leading from the Kidron valley. They came down from the Mount of Olives and up again by way of the Kidron valley into the Akra quarter, the immemorial home of Jerusalem's poor. They slipped through the festive crowds of Jerusalemites and strangers who filled the streets, and their gray, tattered coverings of burlap stood out against the multicolored garb of the holiday celebrants. Their feet were unsandaled, their heads uncovered; their raiment of sackcloth was tied about their waists with girdles of rope. The women among them were not in better case than the men; only to some of them the black veil of widowhood imparted a certain distinction, and there was one whose tall, slender figure and air of stately sorrow brought to the mind of passersby the memory of Naomi returning to her native city from the fields of Moab.

The men were powerful and muscular, their beards and faces covered with the dust of the road. They carried on their broad backs vast bundles of household goods, mattresses woven of bamboo rushes, folded tents, basins, cruses, and baskets of provisions—onions, cucumbers, lettuce, and flat cakes. Clearly they were coming into the city for a prolonged stay.

The hosts of the *Ebionim* attracted little attention. Jerusalem was accustomed to the spectacle of groups of families, and even of entire villages, moving in for a sojourn of several weeks. But no children were to be seen in this throng which moved steadily toward the ancient King David wall opposite the muddy Siloah spring, where the women

3

of Jerusalem's poor came for their water. The cave-dwellings which rose, tier above tier, in the massive wall, were by tradition the refuge of the homeless, and here the *Ebionim* could claim the imprescriptible rights of squatters. Hillel the water-carrier, who was of the companionship, had on one of the tiers his dwelling, in which the Rabbi, whom they now called the Messiah, had eaten the last supper with his disciples.

But there were others besides Hillel the water-carrier who belonged to the *Ebionim* and who had already made their homes in the David wall. They were on hand now to welcome and install the new arrivals. Some of them waited at the foot of the vast ruin and helped the women up the narrow steps to the upper tiers. The men unfolded their tents and pitched them side by side with those of other poor sojourners, on the damp level in front of the wall.

It was the time of the great festival of first fruits, and countless pilgrims were bringing their offerings to the House of the Lord; and since these fruits could only be such as had grown on the soil of the Holy Land, the soil flowing with milk and honey, the great majority of the Pentecost pilgrims were native Jews.

Every province sent the fruits and vegetables which ripened earliest within its borders. There was a rivalry of long standing between the patricians of Jericho, great landowners in the rich Jordan valley, and the poorer Galileans of the north, as to who should bring to Jerusalem the first figs ripened in advance of the season, or a new variety of vegetable, a thornless artichoke, a stringless bean, or some other novelty springing in sacred soil.

A hot east wind blew from the desert and covered with a fine dust the houses glittering in the fierce sunlight. In the streets the dust never settled, but hung in a low cloud about the feet of the countless pilgrims. The city was filled to overflowing; men and women, young and old, sought shelter from the parching heat in the shadows of the arcades which surrounded the houses of the rich in the upper city near the Temple entrance. Others clustered under the awnings of sackcloth or branches which the shopkeepers put up in the great marketplace to keep the sun, the dust, and the flies from their stores of wine, honey, incense, flour, and vegetables. Still others found refuge in the niches between houses in the alleys of the lower city.

And even when it seemed that not another foothold remained in Jerusalem, the crowds of pilgrims continued to pour in and were still absorbed, not without some degree of order. For, according to the custom, the shopkeepers and artisans of Jerusalem waited in the streets for the deputations from their native provinces; and when these approached, carrying their baskets of first fruits, the cry of welcome rose: "Ho, you, brothers of such and such a village, come in peace!" Every group came marching in to the sound of flutes and timbrels; an ox, the sacrificial offering, led the way, its horns adorned according to the means and social status of the deputation, with costly ribbons or with a wreath of olive leaves. The farmers of the neighboring village of Modiin carried the fresh vegetables which were considered such a delicacy in Jerusalem; those that came from remoter areas brought such fruits as would retain their freshness over a longer journey. In the procession of gifts were to be seen yellow sheaves of early wheat from the rich fields of Benjamin, while here and there, from among the sea of rough-woven baskets resting on the broad shoulders of peasants, flashed a fine-wrought golden tray heaped with figs and held aloft in the jeweled hands of a patrician.

The second day of the inbringing of first fruits was the festival of Pentecost, the most joyous of all the Jewish festivals, for it commemorated the giving of the Ten Commandments at Sinai. Many Jews who lived abroad, and who therefore could not bring their first fruits to the Temple, were nevertheless drawn to Jerusalem for the festival. The sacred area was filled with visitors from every corner of the Diaspora, who came to take part in the brilliant ceremonies, to fall on their faces in the Temple courts, to hear the Levites blow the silver trumpets and play on their harps, while they sang verses from the Psalms. In the innermost court of the sanctuary the white-robed Priests stood barefoot, offering up the sacrifices prescribed for the festival. During those hours the whole Temple was a stormy ocean of colors, a pageant of fantastic costumes, and ten thousand faces were lifted eagerly to the light which streamed from the innermost sanctuary. There were Jews from Babylon in long mantles fastened up to their throats, and Jews from Cilicia and Cyrene in cloaks of woven goat's hair; there were Jews from distant regions of Asia, men whose faces were bronzed almost to blackness, whose bodies and limbs were lean and bony, as if the blazing sands had burned away their flesh; there were Jews from Persia and Medea, with long, curled beards and thick-plaited black hair; there were poor Jews from the provinces of Arabia,

5

whose only covering was a white sheet; there were even Jews from Rome, wearing proudly the toga of their adopted city.

On this day of Pentecost, seven weeks after the crucifixion on Golgotha, several men stood in a corner of the Temple court, the center of a crowd of curious pilgrims. It was not their appearance which attracted attention, for their dress and bearing were those of Galileans, familiar figures in Jerusalem: a robe of sackcloth, bony, protruding arms and legs, high heads thickly covered with black curls, tangled beards, flashing eyes. It was what they were relating and their manner of relating it—a marvelous and incomprehensible story told with wild and eager gestures, as if they were feeling the story with their fingers while they told it with their lips.

The principal speaker was a man of middle age, who bore his years like one unaccustomed to them, as if they had come upon him not singly and slowly, but suddenly and all at once. His dense, bristling beard and his close curls were half black, half gray, but his eyebrows, like his eyes, had the luster of youth. His earnest face, furrowed with the marks of labor and tribulation, impressed all beholders with the man's sincerity and truthfulness. But his voice carried even more conviction than his appearance, for though he kept it low, it rang with inspiration. The language he used, a mixture of Aramaic and Hebrew, was barely intelligible to the listeners, most of whom used Greek as their mother tongue; yet, by the intensity of his conviction, by the pressure of his desire to impart his tidings, he compelled not only their attention, but their understanding, too.

He told them an incredible thing: that Yeshua, whom Pontius Pilate had crucified on the Passover before this Pentecost, was none other than the promised Messiah; that he, the crucified one, had risen from death and had revealed himself to his followers and disciples on the Mount of Olives, where they had hidden themselves after his death that they might not be swallowed by the storm. And the speaker went on—amazing his listeners with his learning—to add to his own testimony the corroboration of holy script, quoting verses from the Psalms and from the book of the Prophet Isaiah, which foretold, each in its own place, how the Messiah would suffer and how God would raise salvation for Israel from the loins of King David. This man, this very man whom Pontius Pilate had crucified, was indeed the Messiah for whom all waited. He was the first to have risen from the dead; he had

6

shown himself in the flesh to them, his disciples; he had sat with them, had partaken of food and drink with them; and he had commanded them to carry the tidings to the children of Israel and to all the other peoples, even to the Samaritans, in every corner of the world; he had bidden them say to all and sundry that before many days would pass, he, the Messiah, would come down from heaven, and that the Kingdom of Heaven would begin on earth. He had bidden them go to Jerusalem, which they had indeed done, and impart the tidings to the House of Israel.

The speaker told further how one of the disciples had refused to believe that the stranger appearing to them in the flesh was he who had been crucified by Pontius Pilate. This was how it had come to pass: they, the disciples, were seated together in a garret, and they broke bread in the manner their Rabbi had taught them, and suddenly there was a stranger in their midst, one whom they did not know, and he hailed them with the Jewish greeting, *"Sholom aleichem."*

"His face was the face of a man who had passed through death, and yet he was alive. And he spoke like one of us, and he broke bread with us"—so the doubting disciple had told the story. "He sat among us and was one of us. I looked upon his hands, and I saw where they had been pierced by the nails; the blood was still hardened on the holes, and the wounds were not yet healed. And he took my finger and he thrust it into the wound, and then I knew that it was he, it was Yeshua of Nazareth, who had been crucified by Pontius Pilate and had risen from death, as a Messiah and deliverer for the House of Israel."

Among the bystanders, Jews of Palestine and Jews from abroad, there were some who remembered vividly the strange advent of the Rabbi of Nazareth on the preceding Passover; there were others whose recollection of the incident was vague; but in all of these the passionate speech of the Galilean stirred deep memories of hopes and dreams. It stirred up also the bitter taste of disillusionment and shame. There were still others, however, recent arrivals in the city, who listened wonderingly but did not understand the allusions, and they, inquiring of their neighbors, heard for the first time the story of the high promise and the bitter disappointment.

"So early in the morning, and already so full of sweet wine," said one man.

"Not only with sweet wine, but likewise with the poison of the Evil One," said another.

Then a third voice: "These men do not speak as drunkards do." He that raised the objection was a man of Tyre, as could be seen from his skillfully braided beard.

A learned potter lifted his voice: "So! He sent you even to the Samaritans! Has it ever been heard that the Messiah will come for the Samaritans? Why stop with them? Perhaps he has come for the gentiles, too."

"Yes, for the gentiles too, in the remotest corners of the world," asserted one of the messengers.

"Has it ever been heard that a man shall rise from the dead? Behold, it is written: 'The dead shall not praise the Lord,' and 'those that sleep in the dust shall not praise Him,'" said one man, loudly. He, by the colored girdle round his oddly folded garb, which fell down to his ankles, showed himself to be a member of a Sadducean priestly family. He passed his fingers gracefully through the strands of his beard, and continued: "These men should be driven from the Temple court for spreading such follies among the people." He turned to his neighbor, to explain himself more intimately: "The reward of the righteous man is given him in this life, and the punishment of the wicked is likewise visited upon them in this life. Do not listen to these ignorant Galileans."

During this interchange of views a young man had been thrusting his way swiftly through the throng, until he stood side by side with the Sadducean and face to face with the men of Galilee. He fixed on the latter one fierce and challenging eye, which seemed to concentrate in itself the power of two, for his other eye was almost closed, the heavy lid lying lifeless over the pupil and leaving only a glimmer of white at the bottom. Clearly the young man had heard both the message of the Galileans and the adverse comment of the Sadducean, for, turning from the former with a contemptuous grimace of his tight lips and his thin, hawklike nose, he said:

"No, it is not for their belief in the resurrection that these men should be driven from the Temple court. It is only you unhappy Sadduceans who deny the resurrection. What would our wretched life in this world be were it not for the great life of the world to come? This has been the teaching of our sages!" He darted a glance heaven-

8

ward. "No! They should be thrust forth from this sacred place because they take a hanged man and exalt him as the holy person of the Messiah, whereas it is written in the sacred script: 'The curse of God rests on him that has been hanged!'"

The Galilean leader turned toward those who stood about the Sadducean and the young man, lifted up his arms, and cried: "This was the fulfillment according to the sayings of all the Prophets, who said as with one voice that the Messiah must first suffer. Hear these words of the Prophet: 'We wandered like lost sheep, each of us went his own way; and God put upon him the sins of all of us. He was oppressed and tormented, and he did not open his mouth; he was led like a lamb to the slaughter, and as a young sheep is dumb before the shearer, so he opened not his mouth.'"

"Whence come the words of the Prophets on the lips of these men? I know them, these Galileans!" interjected a bystander, in a baffled tone of voice. "Is not that the fisherman of K'far Nahum, who followed the Rabbi in his life?"

"See how the spirit of God rests on them! They speak like the learned, yet they have never received instruction!"

"Jews!" cried the young man, hotly. "These are misleaders and blasphemers! They have given the name of the anointed of God to a man that was hanged!"

He would have said more, but at this moment he felt a plucking at his elbow. Another young man, evidently his companion, had worked his way to the front of the crowd more slowly. His bearing was, in contrast to that of his friend, sedate and quiet. Tall, graceful, his face framed in a young beard, his curled hair parted and falling on either side of his forehead, he looked like a scion of some rich family of a Canaanite province or of the islands of Cyprus.

"Saul!" he said, gently. "We shall be late for the morning dissertation of Rabban Gamaliel."

"Right, Joseph! You are right!" answered Saul, convulsively. "The babblings of these Galileans will rob us even of our Rabbi's discourse." And, as abruptly as he had thrust his way forward, he now turned and thrust his way out of the throng.

* * *

The two young men who hastened across the court to the arcade where the illustrious Rabban Gamaliel was to deliver his festival dis-

9

course that morning were of the non-Palestinian Jewish community of Jerusalem. The older and shorter of them, Saul, who was all motion and restlessness, as if his veins ran quicksilver instead of blood, came from the famous town of Tarshish, in Cilicia. Following the custom of all pious Jews in the Diaspora, his father had sent him to Jerusalem to sit at the feet of great Rabbis, so that he might learn, together with the Torah, the ways of godliness. His companion came from the rich Sidonian province of Cyprus, famous for its delicious wines, its costly stuffs, its incense, and its copper mines. Descended from a Levitical house, he too had been sent to Jerusalem by his father, in order that he might learn the service of the Levites, and to take part in the Temple ceremonials, such as the singing of the songs of praise on the fifteen steps before the Sanctuary, when the Priests brought the sacrifices. As a further act of piety, his father had bought him a parcel of land in Palestine, so that he might not feel himself a mere sojourner in the Holy Land, and also that he might be able to claim the rights and privileges of one born in Palestine.

Both of these young men had passed their early years in the heart of the gentile world, a world of sin, whoredoms, and despair. They had seen about them, in those years, complete moral chaos, utter bestiality; and they clung now to the one hope in the storm, the Rock of Israel. They had perceived, as they believed from the depth of their hearts, that there existed only one salvation for man, the God of Israel, to whose Temple they had come in order that they might be filled with the spirit radiating from the Rabbis, the sages, and the words of the Torah. And both of them were proud to call themselves disciples of the illustrious Rabban Gamaliel.

In those days a new power had grown up in Jerusalem side by side with the Hasmonean-Herodian dynasty and the hegemony of the High Priesthood: it was the power of the people, focused in the leaders of the Pharisees. As the outstanding representative of the Pharisees Rabban Gamaliel kept a great house, which was frequented not only by Rabbis and pupils but likewise by men of secular and worldly learning and by men of wealth and influence who felt themselves drawn to the Pharisees, such as Nicodemon ben Gurion and the fantastic ben Kalba Shebua. From abroad, too, every Pharisee with sufficient influence and means would arrange ·to have his son, whom he sent to study in Jerusalem, received in the house of the Nasi, the Prince or

Master, the head of the Pharisees. To be accounted of the pupils of Rabban Gamaliel was not only a matter of pride; it was also an important step forward for one who dreamed of a career; it was, further, the guarantee of an education in the best tradition of the great Hillel.

As the two young men threaded their way rapidly toward the arcade of Rabban Gamaliel, he of Tarshish continued the denunciations which his companion had interrupted.

"A Messiah who has been crucified, who was buried, and who has risen from the dead!" he exclaimed, violently. "Where have they learned such things if not from the heathen? What are we? Are we Canaanites, whose Adonis rises from death? Are we Babylonians, whose Bel Marduk dies and comes back to life? Oh, I have seen enough, and more than enough, of these abominations in the city of my birth. It is the way of the heathen. These are the abominations which they would plant in the garden of Israel. Tear them out by the roots, I say!"

"But, Saul, how can you compare those heathen beliefs with what the men of Galilee were preaching? They based themselves on our Prophets. They do not deny our God, neither do they turn from the Jewish way. On the contrary, they call men to repentance, and they prepare for the great day to come. Are you not at all astonished that the words of Isaiah should be so apt for the death of their Messiah? Do not we, too, believe in the resurrection? Is there not something in the words of those men which it would be well for us to ponder, Saul?"

"Joseph!" The older man brought his companion to a halt and fixed on him his one blazing open eye, while his lips tightened ominously. It seemed to Joseph of Cyprus, however, that the half-closed blind eye of Saul was examining him with equal intentness, boring implacably into his secret thoughts.

After a brief pause the companions resumed their way.

"The hope of Israel, the anointed Messiah, one that was hanged!" burst out Saul. "He who will come on the clouds, attended by the heavenly legions, who will harvest the nations of the world and lay them like sheaves at his feet! He of whom King David sang: 'In a little while I shall make the nations of the world a footstool for thy feet!' He whom God has appointed as a light unto the peoples! He, the chosen one of God, who was with Him before the creation of the world! *Him* the gentiles have taken and slaughtered like a sheep, and he did not call the heavenly hosts to his rescue?"

"But did you not hear the man quote from the Prophet Isaiah: 'He was led like a lamb to the slaughter.' And, 'for the sins of my people was he stricken, and he made his grave with the wicked.' Not because he did evil—God forbid!—was he punished, but he freely took upon himself our sins; he bore our sickness, and was smitten with our transgressions."

"You mean—?" asked the young man of Tarshish and stopped again for a moment, keeping his eye sternly on his friend.

"I—I personally do not mean anything. But I do say that the words of the Galileans have put many thoughts into my mind."

There was no more talk between them the rest of the way. In a little while they reached the arcade of the basilica of Herod where Rabban Gamaliel preached that morning. The raised stone seat of the teacher was built into the curve of the wall; the older pupils sat at his feet on low benches, the younger ones stood behind them in a semi-circle. All kept their eyes intently on the speaker. Rabban Gamaliel was a man of slight build, advanced in years, but of majestic appearance. His head was covered, according to the usage of the learned, with a kind of black turban, from which a veil fell backward over his shoulders; the long white beard, reaching down almost to his girdle, framed a grave, wrinkled face.

The discourse he had chosen for this morning of the festival did not deal with the law or with the minutiae of religious observance. It was devoted to the rules of conduct, the principles of human relationships, which had accumulated in the sayings of the Rabbis and which had been woven into the system taught by his illustrious grandfather, the Venerable Hillel. To these rules and principles Rabban Gamaliel added his own commentaries and observations. This was what the two young men heard as they drew near and joined the ranks of the listeners:

"Choose thyself a Rabbi, a teacher, who shall keep thee from the ways of doubt. Man has but a single enemy, and that is his own lack of certainty, because of which he wanders about blindly in the forest of himself. If thou hast doubts, find thyself a teacher and ask of him. Do not persist in paying constant tithes out of doubtful measures. Do not be for ever uncertain as to whether thou art doing thy duty, for God proves the innermost feelings of man; He desires thy good intent; and if thy intent is pure, all is pure; for God desires the goodness of the heart of man. And if thou knowest that there is one who sees thy thoughts, and before whom thou must make an accounting for all thy deeds, thou wilt never doubt. The fear of God will keep thee on the right path. Find thyself a Rabbi and teacher and place thyself under authority."

Saul and Joseph pondered closely these aphorisms, applying them, each in his own way, to the incidents of that day; and as they were returning from the discourse through the tumultuous Temple court, their hearts were stirred by a new restlessness.

"Those were beautiful words our Rabbi uttered today," said Joseph bar Naba. "Man needs a guide, he needs the awe of authority, a thread to hold to, otherwise he is as a lost sheep."

"Not man alone," murmured Saul of Tarshish. "The whole world must be brought under the command and guidance of authority."

They came to the forecourt where, earlier in the morning, they had encountered the preaching Galileans. These were gone; but not so the throng which had heard them. Small groups of Jews, Palestinian and foreign, were discussing the strange tidings they had heard, and a babel of tongues rose from the gesticulating figures. A tall Babylonian in his close mantle lifted his arms to heaven and swayed back and forth as if possessed by a holy spirit.

"Father in heaven!" he called, "can it indeed be that Thou hast sent us Thy deliverer?"

A Persian Jew talked in a dreamlike voice: "I heard with my own ears all that these messengers said. Every day for forty days he appeared to them, exactly as he had been in the life. He sat with them and broke bread with them."

"Look!" exclaimed the young man of Tarshish. "This is what the Galileans have done. The heart of Jerusalem is steeped in longing for the deliverance, even as a woven linen is steeped in oil for the fire at the ceremony of the water-pouring. What will happen if a spark should fall on the drenched heart of Jerusalem?"

"If?" repeated Joseph of Cyprus. "The spark has already fallen. Do you not hear what these people are saying?"

13

Chapter Two

FROM THE ENDS OF THE EARTH

ON that day of Pentecost Miriam, the sister of Joseph bar Naba, had arranged a great reception for the leaders of the Greek-speaking Jewish community of Jerusalem. Miriam was the widow of a wealthy Cypriot wine merchant who had settled in Jerusalem after her husband's death. She had been drawn to the capital by her attachment to her brother and by her desire to provide for her only son an education in the Pharisaic tradition which had governed her father's house. Jochanan—or Marcus, as he was called in the more intimate circle of his Greek-speaking Jewish friends—was inscribed in the study house of the famous Alexandrian Synagogue, and there he received his training in the strictest Pharisaic traditions. For his secular studies his mother kept in the house a Greek philosopher whom she had purchased in the slave market of Tyre and under whom Jochanan, or Marcus, became an adept in the Greek language, according to the custom of his class in those days.

The majority of the Greek Jews lived in the new section of the city which had sprung up on Mount Scopus outside the ancient walls, opposite the Sheep Gate. Accustomed to spacious houses, with gardens and colonnades, they could not find room in the old, crowded sections. The house of Miriam, sister of bar Naba, built in the Cypriot style, resembled a Greek temple; behind it was a garden, enclosed in a peristyle, and here she arranged frequent banquets for the leaders of the Greek-Jewish community of Jerusalem. Her status as a widow and as a member of the Charitable Sisterhood imposed on her, tacitly, a certain modesty in her manner of living; but this obligation was overruled by another, equally tacit but of greater force. She felt it her duty to add to the splendor of Jerusalem, so that visitors to the Jewish capital—especially such as came on festival days—might carry away with them the memory of high culture and magnificent hospitality. Hence the temple-like house, the garden, the peristyle, the appointments, and the innumerable servants.

The day had been hot, and the sun was just beginning to set. Opposite, in the east, darkness was coming up over the hills of Moab. Bar Naba arrived before any of the official guests. Etiquette would have demanded that he take part in the reception, even if his affection for his sister had not inclined him to it. For Joseph was his sister's official protector and guardian, the comptroller of her estate, and her son's spiritual guide. He stood side by side with her now on the wide terrace of the house, with its mosaic floor and its colored hangings. A large ring sparkled on his right hand; a black mantle—the mantle of the scholar—covered his thin tunic.

Miriam was a stately woman in the middle thirties, perhaps a little too heavy for her height, but so graceful in motion that she made an impression of extraordinary lightness. She was clad in black, as befitted her widowhood. A light black tunic rested on her round, youthful shoulders and fell in skillful folds down to her sandals. Her hair was not dressed in the Jerusalemite mode, which called for a vast coiffure and a veil going down as far as the waist, but in the mode of Greek Alexandria, that is, uncovered, drawn back on two sides of a central line and rolled into a ball resting on her strong, feminine neck. A few curls were ingeniously worked on the fringes of her coiffure and hung over her cheeks. Her eyes were unnaturally large, for they had been slit and given a peach form—after the Alexandrian fashion—in her babyhood. Eyebrows and eyelashes were artificially blackened. A refreshing scent of heliotrope, made heavier with a touch of sweet spearmint, breathed from her body.

Joseph had found his sister that afternoon in her private bower, or spice garden, where she spent most of her time. They greeted each other in the exaggerated, stylized phrases then in vogue even among intimates, an echo of the verses of the Song of Songs in a Hellenized setting.

"Greetings, thou comeliest of men! Is peace with thee, my brother?"

"Peace is with me, my sister."

"The shadow on thy face testifies to restlessness of spirit. What cares have cast their shadow over thee, my brother?"

"Today, in the Temple courts, I heard tidings which brought storm into my heart and a trembling to my knees," answered Joseph.

"The Temple courts are the storm nests of Israel. Who can enter

15

them and remain undisturbed? I pray God no revolt is brewing again and that the sword of Edom will not reap a new harvest."

Their conversation, having passed the stage of salutations, took on a more familiar, less stilted tone.

"A revolt?" repeated Joseph. "No. Or, rather, no revolt of the clenched fist. It is a revolt of words, and of the spirit."

His sister smiled. "One of those revolts? The storm of words will easily be laid, if we have only the voice of Jacob and not the hands of Esau."

Bar Naba could not smile with her. "There are times," he said, "when the storm roused by words does not die as easily as the storm which follows on deeds. Many things have happened in the Temple courts and have been forgotten; but words have been said there which will live for ever."

Still his sister would not take him too seriously.

"Let be, my brother. I have news for you which will take the shadows from thy face. This evening we shall have as our guest the happiest of all women, the happiest and most fortunate. Zipporah sent word that she is coming. I am impatient to see what new device she is bringing with her to capture the heart of the comeliest among the men of Jerusalem."

Joseph took his sister's hand. He knew of her concern over his unmarried state, and knew, too, that she had set her heart on Zipporah, daughter of the rich president of the Synagogue of the Cilicians, as a sister-in-law. He was grateful, but he could not give his sister the answer she desired.

"Let her bring all the devices of all the lovely women in the world," he said, "she will not approach the loveliness of my sister."

A faint blush mounted from Miriam's throat to her eyes. She knew that Joseph spoke in earnest and that in his eyes his sister was indeed the loveliest of womankind. But the words, which might have been expected to stir her vanity, caused her no delight. She heard in them the echo of his constant refusal of marriage; every woman she had sought for him had been, in his eyes, utterly unworthy by comparison with her.

"I will seek out the sellers of magic potions, my brother, and ask them for one which diminishes rather than enhances a woman's charms, so that your eyes may rest on others than me."

16

"It will avail you nothing. The moon is comelier shining through a cloud than when the sky is clear."

Miriam placed her fingers on her brother's mouth, for she saw her son Jochanan entering the garden.

The boy too was garbed for the festival; he wore a silken tunic and, thrown over it, a sort of toga which was adorned in the Cypriot style with figures of animals, woven black on white—a style not strictly in keeping with the Pharisaic tradition in which he had been educated. The Greek-speaking Jews had not been able to divorce themselves completely from the customs they brought with them from the lands of their birth; no matter how long they lived in Jerusalem, they reverted occasionally to their native usages, as if they could not wholly refrain from paying tribute to alien gods.

The boy, observing his uncle, started with delight, and remembered only with an effort that according to the law the first honors were due to his mother. He bowed before her, greeted her, and turned eagerly to bar Naba. A moment later Miriam withdrew to supervise the last details of the reception.

There was a great love between the lad Jochanan and his uncle. Fatherless since early childhood, the boy clung to his mother's brother, whom he accepted gratefully as his spiritual guide and teacher and to whom he brought without reserve all the problems which beset his young heart. It was so even at this moment, for scarcely had they exchanged greetings than the lad began to storm his uncle with questions.

"Teach me, my Rabbi and my deliverer," he said, holding Joseph's hand as they walked among the flower beds of Miriam's garden, "is the thing true that was said this morning in the Temple court, that the Messiah has already come, but that we did not recognize him and he was put to death?"

"Who brought you these tidings, my son?" asked Joseph, astonished.

"Certain men of this house who were in the Temple courts this morning heard it from the lips of the messengers. All the servants are speaking of it. Even my Greek teacher, Sadaus, has heard of it."

"The Holy One of Israel will not conceal the truth," answered Joseph, piously. "If this thing is of God, we shall soon witness the

17

great day. And if God has not built the house, then the builders have labored in vain."

"They say that the Messiah had to suffer, for so the Prophets prophesied concerning him. Is that true, my uncle and deliverer?"

"Those men did indeed strengthen their arguments with the verses of the Prophets. But you, my son, must return to your studies. We shall speak of this thing at a more fitting time."

But the lad was not to be put off.

"They say that he is the first to have risen from the dead."

"My son, let not your attention wander from your studies."

"But how shall I think of my studies if the Messiah has come?" asked the lad, excitedly, and, lifting up his arms, he exclaimed: "I thank thee, O God, that thou hast made me a Jew and an inheritor of the hope of the Messiah!"

Joseph bar Naba did not answer, but in his heart he thought: The wind carries the tidings of the Messiah on its wings, and babes and sucklings testify.

Uncle and nephew left the garden and went out on the terrace where the guests were arriving by groups, each group from its synagogue, headed by its president. In the outer vestibule the overseer was stationed with his assistants, to lead the visitors to the terrace entrance.

There came a group of congregants from the Alexandrian Synagogue, headed by their president, Antonius; Philippus, the dignified president of the Cilician Synagogue, brought his group (though they themselves were Cypriots, bar Naba and Miriam belonged to the Cilician Synagogue). Mingling with the Cilician congregants were pilgrims from abroad. There came also Nicanor and Timon, of the Synagogue of Antioch, which is in Syria, and congregants from the Synagogues of Cyrene and Libya. There were even Cappadocians, and visitors from as far as Lystra. Among the Greek-speaking Jews perhaps the most distinguished visitor was the preacher Istephan, whose Greek oratory was the pride of his congregation.

Even among the visitors from abroad there were many faces already long familiar to Miriam and bar Naba. Their father's ships had plied between Salamis, the capital of Cyprus, and the cities of Pamphylia, and many a merchant who had visited them in their island home was now their guest in Jerusalem.

18

Three continents, Africa, Asia, and Europe, were represented in the multicolored throngs pouring back and forth through the alleys and colonnades of the garden. Stateliest among the guests, most dignified in mien and motion, were the wearers of the togas, the citizens of the mistress of the world. In actual fact, it was not always certain either that the wearers of togas were all citizens of Rome or that there were not Roman citizens present who had not chosen to put on the toga. It was definitely known, for instance, that certain men who had all the precious rights of Roman citizenship had elected to come to the reception in the goat's hair mantles of their locality and profession. The young man Saul, his married sister Chaninah, her husband Simon, and their son ben Nechama, as well as others from the city of Tarshish, which had granted Roman citizenship to her inhabitants, did not wear Roman togas but the simple dress of their countrymen.

Following the custom of Jerusalem, the men were received first by bar Naba and his nephew, who directed the servants to bring refreshments of fruit and wine; Miriam presided in another hall over the reception to the women. Later men and women came together in the cool of the evening by the pool and under the cypress trees, where a soft light was shed on them from the lights at the top of the columns. Small, eager groups gathered round the most recent arrivals from abroad, each group seeking news of relatives and friends in the homeland or of public events in remote places. At best the news could not be very fresh; for travel was slow, and whole weeks might be consumed in a journey from a city in Asia, Africa, or Europe to the Jewish capital. Such as it was, it was the best obtainable. Of special interest was the report of the pilgrims from far-off Pamphylia and Lysias. They told that since the Emperor Tiberius had put to death his old favorite councilor, the Jew-hating Sejanus, and had come under the influence of his pious aunt, Antonia, the condition of the Jews in their part of the empire had taken a turn for the better. The Greeks of that region, who had always been jealous of the privileges which the Jews enjoyed in respect of their religion, and who, in the days of Sejanus, had more than once desecrated the Jewish houses of worship, had changed their attitude, which, if it had not become friendly, was at least correct.

"In our country," observed one Jew from the distant province of Galatea, "the gentiles are on excellent terms with us. A new spirit stirs in them. On the Sabbath many of them come to our synagogues to listen to our traveling preachers; and some of them have even taken up the study of our prayers and our Torah."

"Jochanan ben Zadoc!" cried a Jew of Antioch to a friend of his, who was deeply absorbed in a discussion of the prospects of Agrippa for the throne of Judah. "Jochanan ben Zadoc! Come hither and hear what this pilgrim from Galatea has to tell!"

Many others besides Jochanan ben Zadoc left their groups to gather round the pilgrims from Galatea and listened with wonder to their stories of the "righteous among the peoples of the world," or, as they were called among the Greek-speaking Jews, the "God-fearing gentiles."

"In our city of Damascus many women have let themselves be baptized and have entered into the Jewish faith," reported a Damascene. "It might almost be said that every other woman has submitted to baptism."

"In our cities of Iconium and Lykonia many Greeks have converted and have not only submitted to baptism but have let themselves be circumcized."

A pilgrim from the province of Pisidia told how a group of Greeks of the city of Antioch in Pisidia, who had been regular visitors at the Sabbath services of the Jews, had expressed their desire to be converted. The congregation of Antioch had thereupon sent a report to the head of the Pharisees in Jerusalem, who had in turn sent a special messenger to Antioch in Pisidia. The messenger had been able to convert only the women, for the men, hearing that they would have to enter the Abrahamitic covenant through circumcision, had refused, and then had fallen away.

The sarcastic and mocking voice of Saul of Tarshish was heard: "The gentiles are such heroes in the gladiatorial arenas! They will fight with gladiators and even with wild beasts! But when it comes to circumcision their hearts turn to water!"

A Jew of Pamphylia made answer: "It is not cowardice which holds them back from circumcision but their glorification of the human body. From earliest childhood they have been taught the worship of bodily beauty, and it is against their nature to mar its perfection.

20

Many Greeks have told me that if we would only make this one concession, concerning circumcision, they would readily accept the other laws and commandments of the Jewish faith."

"Among us, in Lystra, godfearing gentiles have come to the elders of the congregation, and have asked for concessions concerning the laws of purity of food; they have also asked to be released from the obligation of circumcision. If we would be content with mere baptism, as in the case of their women, they would become Jews."

"And what else? Perhaps they would like us to abrogate all the laws and commandments. They would, it seems, be glad to enjoy both this world and the world to come; they would like their share in the inheritance of Jacob, but without the law of Moses. He who would enter under the wings of the true divinity must bring a sacrifice. He must be holy and pure!" Again it was the young man Saul who had raised his voice, unaware, it seemed, that many of the bystanders felt that it was unbecoming for him to make himself a spokesman in the presence of so many persons of importance. His comrade, bar Naba, who was standing by his side, plucked gently at his sleeve.

"For all that," interposed one pilgrim, "it seems to me that our Rabbis should do something in this matter. The hand of God knocks at the hearts of the gentiles. This is a truth to which everyone dwelling among gentiles will testify. See! There are gentiles who have sent us with money to buy sacrifices for them and to bring them to our Temple. There were many who accompanied us part of the way, together with Jews of Phrygia, and acted as our escort and guard against robbers. And when the time of the leavetaking came, on the shore where we boarded ship, their eyes were full of tears. They sent their prayers through us to the Temple of God, their blessings to Jerusalem, and their submission to the God of Israel."

The words of the Phrygian Jew made a deep impression on the listeners. Other pilgrims took up the theme of his discourse.

"Yes, it is time, and more than time, that something be done for the gentiles. The grace of God has been poured out on them, their eyes are opening to the light of the Torah, and their hearts are drawn to the God of Israel."

"But the Rabbis stand at the gates of the Temple and will not let them enter," said Philippus, the president of the Cilician Synagogue. Had a person of lower standing than his uttered such words, there would have been a sharp retort. Coming from him, they were accepted in silence. But the voice of another pilgrim was heard:

"On my way from Perga in Pamphylia to Salamis in Cyprus I traveled on an Alexandrian ship. One day, wandering about the ship, I came upon the lower deck, where the slaves sit chained to the oars, and I heard a voice which came to me out of the depths of human suffering, out of a world in which there is no more hope: 'Thou blessed son of Israel! I know thou goest to Jerusalem, to the Temple of the one living God! Pray for me to the God of Israel, that he may see my wretchedness and come to my help!' Thereupon I called back into the deep: 'Art thou too of the sons of Israel?' And the voice answered: 'No, I am from the Rhine, and my god is Wotan. But in my need I heard of the God of Israel, and I send my prayer to Him at His Temple, through you!'"

"From east and west we hear the voices of the nations, saying: 'Come, let us go up to the mount of God!' Yes, the God of Israel is knocking at the hearts of the gentiles, even as the Prophet Zachariah prophesied: 'From the going down of the sun to the rising thereof My name is great among the nations. In every place the smoke of sacrifice goeth up, and gifts are brought in My name, for My name is great among the nations, saith the Lord of hosts.' For even those that worship the work of their own hands mean only God: even in their idols they worship the one living God of Israel!" It was the preacher Istephan who spoke, and his voice quivered with exaltation as he lifted up his arms and his face, upon which fell the light of the stars.

There was a moment of silence. Then someone asked:

"What is the special merit in Israel which draws to it the hearts of the nations?"

"It is the holy Sabbath which Israel alone possesses," answered one.

"Nay, it is the belief in the resurrection which Israel possesses," answered another.

"Not that, either," said a third. "It is the coming of the Messiah, of the holy deliverer. The gentiles have heard that Israel awaits him, and therefore they are drawn to us. They too would have a share in the kingdom of heaven."

"Were there not men of Galilee in the Temple today, declaring that the Messiah, son of David, had already come, that he was the first one ever to have risen from the dead, that he revealed himself to them, and bade them come before Israel and spread the tidings to the world?"

"Yes, I have heard something of it. In our synagogue, which is that of the Cilicians, the word was spread," declared the president.

"In our synagogue, too, there was talk of it," added an Alexandrian Jew. "But the bringers of the tidings were simple and ignorant Galileans."

"They were the disciples of the Rabbi in his life, and he appeared to them after his death."

"The word is carried abroad as on the wings of the wind. What do our sages think concerning it?"

"The hour has indeed come for Thee to send thy deliverer of righteousness," cried the preacher Reb Istephan, and lifting his hands he uttered the benediction which the sages had formulated for the God-fearing gentiles: "May Thy compassion be awakened toward the God-fearing gentiles and send unto all of us the reward of those that do Thy will."

*　　*　　*

Later, when the guests had dispersed from the terrace garden of the wealthy widow, bar Naba, the young Levite, still remained seated there, sunk deep in thought. His eyes were fixed on the stars which glittered above him. At his side sat the loveliest of the daughters of Jerusalem, Zipporah. Hand in hand he sat with her, and his eyes were lifted to the dark blue curtain of the sky, which was spread over the great black walls of the hills of Moab. From below came across the night the glitter of the Dead Sea, at the foot of the hills of Moab. The whole world lay wide open to the grace of God, and Joseph bar Naba sat hand in hand with the loveliest of the daughters of Jerusalem, Zipporah.

An urgent warmth breathed out of the night. The plants which had been gathering the heat of the sun all day were overloaded with sweetness, which they spilled out on every hand as if afraid that the desert winds might come and rob them of it; and the body of the night was like a human body which had attained ripeness. The silence was filled with a mute, disturbing hunger. Still bar Naba gazed at the deep glimmering heavens where they bent over toward the desert of Jericho, and he did not know that Zipporah's hand was in his. A long time their hands remained together, and it was as if something flowed from one to the other, stilling the thirst of their youth. But they were aware only of the night, and it seemed to them that they had been drawn into the urgent warmth and silence of the night.

"Why has the gift of prophecy been withdrawn from Israel?" asked Zipporah, suddenly. "Why do not prophets appear to us, as they appeared in the olden days to our forefathers? Wherein are we worse than our forefathers? Why is God silent?"

No one answered her question, nor did Zipporah seem to expect an answer. The sound of her voice was like that of a bell set in motion under water, spreading its tones along the waves. And Zipporah went on talking to herself, more in dream than in waking:

"Sometimes I feel that the time is near when He will pour out His spirit upon all flesh, even as He promised the Prophets. I feel the time is near when prophecy will be renewed in Israel, and He will send His spirit not only to His chosen ones, to the learned and the wise, but also to the simple of heart. And upon us, too, upon us women, the spirit will fall like a refreshing dew. It will cover the whole land, and the scales will fall from our eyes; then we shall see all things in another light, and our hearts will be filled with another spirit. Sometimes it seems to me that I am seized with an incomprehensible strength. I am filled with power as a fruit is filled with ripeness in the summer. Like Hannah, the mother of Samuel, I am drunk, not with wine, but with the power that fills my inward parts, so that they cry out and tear my lips open. Then words issue from my lips, and I know not their meaning and content. They pour out at my lips, as water pours out from a spring. I know that God is speaking through my lips."

"All of us burn with the thirst of the deliverance, and all of us long for the word of God as for a drink," answered bar Naba.

"Like Deborah the Prophetess I long at times to lift up the banner of my people and sing the song of triumph and deliverance. Sometimes the spirit is so strong on me that I believe I can conjure down salvation from the heavens. It fills my heart with the loveliness of the upper worlds, and I hear the beating of wings, though I do not see the angels; and it seems to me that in another moment a door will be opened for me and I will be admitted into the innermost mysteries. And then a voice will issue from the locked wall, and a message will descend from

24

heaven in fiery letters and rest upon my eyes, and I will drink in the fiery script and I will cry out the salvation of all Israel."

Bar Naba was suddenly aware of Zipporah's hand in his, hot as a flaming brand. He looked into the girl's face. Her eyes blazed like the stars which covered the heavens, and like those they sent forth a mystic fire which filled him with bliss and terror.

"Zipporah! How lovely thou art! It is as though Deborah had arisen in thee and thou with thy word wilt light a new hope in Israel!"

"Since when does God have recourse to the help of woman? Only the idol-worshipers have sibyls. Woman is an impure vessel, and the God of Israel will not make use of it. Her heart is painted, even like her lips and her cheeks, and her one desire is toward man." The voice came from a corner steeped in darkness, but its hardness revealed the presence of the young man Saul of Tarshish.

"Did not God make use of Deborah the Prophetess? Was not Deborah a Judge in Israel, and did not God use her as His messenger to Barak the son of Abinoam and prepare a great victory through her prophecy?"

"The times are gone when prophecy lay spread out like a virgin field, for all to plow therein. Today the heavens are closed to us. Israel is in darkness. Only the learned are the eyes of Israel. God speaks today through the mouth of learning and His law. Therefore we must turn with all our strength to the Torah. We must consecrate ourselves utterly to it. Only through the Torah shall we attain to the Holy Spirit," answered Saul, loudly.

Bar Naba withdrew his hand from Zipporah's, and asked:

"By what path shall we reach the Torah?"

"By one path only, the path of withdrawal, separation, and dedication, which is the path of Pharisaism. He who would dedicate himself to the Torah must dedicate himself to it utterly. Let no woman stand between thee and the Torah. The Torah is jealous and demands thy soul in its wholeness. Let thy soul be as a glowing flame, even as it is written: 'My soul longeth for the Torah.' Let all thy manhood be given unto it. This is the prophecy of our time. And how can a woman dedicate herself to the Torah when all her thought is given to the man and all that she does is as an ornament with which to ensnare him? Even the prophecy that is in her she uses as an ornament,

25

like the coloring on her lips, to ensnare the man and take him captive."

In Saul's sharp tone, not less than in the words themselves, there was a clear echo of jealousy. It was a war with the woman for the possession of the soul of his friend. Zipporah rose swiftly to her feet and answered:

"Saul of Tarshish, it is not men alone who can sunder themselves from the world for the love of God. Woman too can conquer and slay all other desire and dedicate her virginity to God. You are right; the spirit of prophecy, too, is jealous, and demands the eternal virginity of the woman. Now I understand the words of the Wisdom of Solomon: 'Blessed is she that is barren and without impurity.' I thank you, Saul of Tarshish. You have spoken well!" And with this she turned from the two young men and withdrew.

Chapter Three

THE PREACHER ISTEPHAN

WHO would have believed that the tidings of the Messiah, which the simple men of Galilee had proclaimed only a few weeks ago in the Temple courts, would have spread with such rapidity over the city of Jerusalem? It was indeed as if the winds were carrying it on their wings. There was no corner of the city where it was not spoken of; and the new sect gained mightily in adherents, not only among the poverty-stricken in the lower sections of Jerusalem where the disciples were settled, but upon the heights, among the Greek-speaking Jews. The good news was proclaimed in their synagogues, and the most famous of their preachers, Reb Istephan, was won over and spread the word of the Messiah from synagogue to synagogue.

It was a hot afternoon in the month of Tammuz, during that time of the year when Jerusalem lies under the skies like a heated lime-kiln. When the day is hottest the Jerusalemites sit in the shadows of their houses, or take refuge in the alleys of the rich houses, or else assemble in the synagogues, where, besides finding surcease from the

26

savage shafts of sunlight, they can refresh their souls with a little learning or with the discourse of a preacher.

It was on such a day that the Cilicians assembled in their synagogue to listen to a discourse on the tidings of the Messiah, to be delivered by the preacher Istephan. Among those who had answered the call were Saul of Tarshish and his comrade, bar Naba.

The Cilician Synagogue was like an alien apparition among the synagogues of Jerusalem. It stood on the rim of the lower marketplace, where the city descended in terraces to the Kidron valley. Its buildings did not, after the fashion of all other synagogues, occupy a central court; instead, they occupied a series of terraces which were planted, in the Asiatic fashion, with rows of cypresses. Thus it was with the synagogue and thus with the halls, which served both as sleeping quarters for pilgrims and as places of assembly and recreation for the Cilician congregation and for Jews of other cities of Asia Minor. The synagogue itself, for that matter, was not devoted exclusively to prayer; it was a place of rest and a hall for discussions. And the institution as a whole might be considered as a sort of mother to the congregation. Every synagogue had its burial place outside the limits of the city, where the bones of its dead congregants, consigned to stone urns, were laid out in rows in catacomblike alleys. Nor was the service of the synagogue restricted, as far as the living were concerned, to their spiritual needs. In the hour of need every congregant turned naturally to the mother synagogue. It might be a local member who had fallen on hard times, a worker who could not obtain employment, a merchant who had lost everything, and it might be a new arrival from one of the home towns who had not a place where to lay his head.

Reb Istephan was the preacher of the Greek Jews. He was not tied down to any one synagogue but was a wandering preacher who might be heard wherever Greek-speaking Jews assembled. He had a great following, and whenever he appeared in the Alexandrian or Cyrenean or Cilician Synagogue, the building was filled to the doors with foreign Jews. It was not only that Reb Istephan was a master in their language; his ways of thought, his ideas, were to their taste. He was, moreover, one of them, having been born in Antioch, where he had passed the greater part of his youth. He had been educated in the Jewish tradition. A deep longing for salvation and deliverance was manifest in his utterances and his works. He was well versed in

27

the sacred script, the Prophets and the Psalms, which he had studied, like many another Hellenistic Jew, in the Greek translations. He had likewise drunk deep of the stormy Jewish-Hellenistic prophetic books, the Wisdom of Solomon, and the Vision of the Sibyls, which had inflamed his imagination and stirred him to burning hope. But his belief in an ethical and universal Messiah, who was to issue for all mankind, was drawn direct from the Jewish Prophets, from Isaiah, Ezekiel, and Amos.

He stood that afternoon in the Moses seat, which was built into the southern wall toward the Temple, his prayer-shawl falling over his dress, a man of some forty-odd years, with a flaming yellow beard and red locks which framed his pallid, shining face. His blue eyes were covered with a misty film of exaltation. His arms were lifted up out of his dress like two blazing torches above the heads of the congregation which packed the synagogue. Through the square orifices in the walls, which served as windows, shafts of the sun entered and fell upon the pillars of the synagogue and upon the multicolored assembly.

Following his custom, Reb Istephan began at the beginning, taking nothing for granted. He told the story of God's covenant with Abraham, of the sacrifice of Isaac, and of Jacob's dream of the ladder; he told them of the election of David, and of the utterances of Isaiah, and came finally to the visions which were recorded in the Hellenistic-Jewish books. It was a terrifying picture of the last days which he presented to his breathless listeners: "The world is being swallowed in the jaws of the wild monster, sin. God has withdrawn His countenance from the world, and the spirit of evil, which He has originally sent to test mankind, now has complete government over it. The children of man have become like the beasts of the field; they hew their little ones into pieces on the stones, fling the quivering fragments into the pits; they turn against the laws of God and nature, the likeness of man is wiped out, species mingles and mates with species. Therefore God will baptize the earth with a baptism of fire. He will send down a storm which will wash away its sin. Behold, the great day is at hand, the day of the great judgment of the eternal God, the mighty King. The wars of Gog and Magog will begin anew. There will be war likewise between earth and heaven, and a rain of fire will be sent down from the clouds. Man and beast will flee from the fiery arrows, they will seek out the

28

caves and the hollows beneath the rocks, but their destruction will not fail to find them, for they will be driven out from their shelters by the Evil One. Stung by scorpions, bitten by wild serpents, they will flee from cave to cave in the wildernesses and forests. A thick darkness will come upon the world, and the sweat of terror will cover men's bodies. And not man alone, but the beasts of the field, too, will run about in dread. The birds and fowl of the air will scream and twitter because of the trembling of the earth, and the fish will leap out of the seas and lakes. The mountains will split and roll their heights into the valleys; the seas will spew forth their waters and drag down into the deeps the monstrous beasts feeding upon man and animal. And wherever the waters of the sea cannot reach, earth herself will open many mouths and swallow those whom the fires of heaven have not destroyed."

The audience heard the dreadful message rolling through the synagogue, and a panic came upon it. The women in the separate galleries were the first to give voice to their fear, and the wailing spread from them to the men in the body of the synagogue below. There were some who wrung their hands, so that the bones of their fingers cracked. The hair stood up on their heads. They smote themselves on the heart with clenched fists, as in a fit of confession.

"Threefold sinners are we all!"

"Sinful! Sinful!"

"Tell us! What shall we do?"

"How shall we save ourselves from the dread judgment day?"

The voice of the preacher rose above the tumult:

"But God will have compassion on the remnant of Israel; He has prepared the cure even before He ordained the affliction. And that is the Son of Man, who was with Him in the heavens even from before the creation of the world. The heavens will open, and in the midst of the clouds shall appear the Son of Man, surrounded by the legions of the angels. When he appears a great silence will descend on the earth. All beasts, good and evil alike, will be seized with fear and will be silent before him. He will bring back the boundaries which were wiped out, and he will send back every spirit and demon to his accustomed and ordered place. A trembling and quaking will come upon the mighty of the earth. They will come before his throne and abase themselves before him, that he might make them his footstool, even as David prophesied

29

concerning him. Then he will awaken the dead from their long sleep, and they will return, each one in his own likeness that is proper to him. For God has created man for all the eternities and has made man in His own likeness. Then He will order eternal peace. He will remove the boundaries between heaven and earth, between this world and the world to come, between death and life. He will abrogate the law, for there will be no wickedness or evil, yea, for goodness will be the natural impulse of creation, and peace will reign upon the earth, even as the Prophet has prophesied: 'The wolf and the lamb shall pasture together, and a child shall lead them.'"

Up to this point the preacher had carried his listeners with him, though toward the end of the speech there were already signs of distress and disagreement. One voice had been raised, to interrupt the discourse with a question, but had died at once. Here and there, on certain faces, there were looks of bewilderment. For a time the magic of his speech, and the sweetness of his tidings, held them all. But as he continued a murmuring could be heard, and his words were repeated in astonishment and resentment: "He will abrogate the law?... Goodness will be the natural impulse?... There will be no more guardianship of the right?... He is the Son of Man, who was with God from before the creation?..."

Then, loud and clear, the challenge came from a corner of the synagogue: "Who is he, this Son of Man, this Adam Kadmon? Whom means he by the King Messiah who is to come?"

"It is the King Messiah who already came, and we knew him not: the righteous man whom we permitted the wicked to put to death, and whom God raised, the first, from among the dead!" cried the preacher, closing his eyes and trembling with ecstasy.

Faces were turned each upon the other, beards were agitated.

"Whom means he then? Which righteous man?" Many voices were raised now.

"Whom can I mean if not the one and only whom God has elected? The righteous man who came to obtain forgiveness for our sins by his death, as the Prophets prophesied concerning him—Yeshua, the King Messiah!"

There was a long interval of amazed silence. Not a breath was heard. Finally one man, who by the colored threads drawn through his earlobes declared himself to be a dyer, lifted up his voice, and as he

30

spoke his gray, dusty earlocks, mingling with his tangled beard, trembled:

"Yea, I saw him, the righteous man, as he fell under the burden of his cross; there was no more strength in him to carry the burden, but the wicked men smote him cruelly; and I went up to him, and it was granted to me to carry his cross for a little space."

"What? He that was hanged on the cross by Pontius Pilate—cursed be his name for ever!—is the King Messiah?"

"He suffered for our sins, even as it is written: 'He shall bear the sins of many.' It was for us that he took these torments upon himself. For us he let himself be bound like a lamb which is led away to the slaughter. He, the righteous one, the Son of God!" the preacher continued to exclaim in ecstasy.

"May thy mouth be stopped up by the serpents and scorpions of the nether world, because of the blasphemy thou hast uttered! Whom callest thou the son of God?"

"The righteous man is called the Son of God!"

"No! It is Israel that is called the Son of God. It is written: 'Sons are ye of your God.' He is our Father in heaven and we are His children."

The preacher took up the challenge: "Are we concerned here with this word or that? What are words? They are as clanging cymbals when their content is withdrawn. No, we have not to do now with a new king, a Solomon or even a David, but with the whole, in all its greatness, with the one and only. What word shall utter him? Where is the name by which he shall be called? Can he be contained and limited in a phrase, a word, an utterance? He pours himself out from all the measures with which ye seek to measure him. This is he for whom you have made supplication. When your throats were stretched out to the knife, it was him that your eyes sought; and now that he is come, you know him not. This is he for whom you have waited so long—the fulfillment of your hope, the reward of your labors, he that justifies all your sufferings and gives meaning to your lives. He it is who affirms all worth and gives issue to all that happens; in him our days are counted; our wandering strikes a path in him; our deeds find an aim in him. Without him all is *tohu u-bohu,* void and formless, an abyss into which we fall, without beginning or end."

"But it is the Almighty and the Eternal of whom he speaks, the

31

Lord of the world! Of whom else can such things be said?" a voice asked through the frightened silence which followed the preacher's words.

"The Almighty is the God of Israel, and His Messiah sits by His right hand. The Messiah is the instrument wherewith the Almighty will judge man. He stands between us and the God of Israel. He knows our sufferings, he knows our nature, for he was among us and is one of us."

"Does God need an assistant? Let him be accursed who says that God needs a helper."

"Shut his mouth for him!"

"Drag him before the Sanhedrin!"

"What say ye? What do ye? He is our preacher!"

*   *   *

Late that evening the two friends sat on the terrace of the synagogue and looked down into the valley of the lower city, whence rose innumerable spirals of smoke from the huts where the wives of the poor were preparing the pitiful evening meal. A black vastness hovered over the valley, spreading out heavy wings which seemed designed to crush the inhabitants of the lower city to earth and to keep them from aspiring heavenward, or from becoming otherwise than the other creatures crawling on the face of the earth. But even under that burden there was an upward surging; the little lights of the homes of the poor sprang out, in defiance of the threat. Up above, on the terrace of the synagogue where the friends were seated, the sky was clearly visible, and the light of the stars played on the mystic pillars of the building. Saul and Joseph had been shaken to their innermost being by the utterance of the preacher, and they sat long in silence. But when the younger of the two was eager to speak, the older contained himself grimly and kept biting his short fingernails. He scarcely made answer when Joseph spoke; it was as though he had drawn a curtain of blackness about himself, in order that none might see the storm that was raging in him. Tears of anger burned on his eyelids, and he seemed to have become shorter, as if he had shrunk in on himself. Such was the condition into which he had been thrown by the message of the preacher. Again and again his companion strove to break through the wall of silence. Saul answered only with a bitter grimace, and his one open eye shone fierily into the night. And then, at length, as though he had finally been able to digest the full meaning of that afternoon's discourse, he broke out:

"But if we are to accept everything that he says concerning Yeshua the Nazarene, we must all fall prostrate before him, and say what was said at the foot of Sinai: 'We will do and we will obey.' We must abandon all the laws of the Torah and all that Moses taught us, and a new order of the world will begin, the order of the Messiah. All the nations will have to come and take upon themselves the yoke of the Kingdom of Heaven. But if this does not come to pass, then all the words that he has uttered concerning Yeshua the Nazarene are written in sand, and all those that repeat them are blasphemers of the living God; they preach apostasy, and they must be haled to judgment before the Sanhedrin."

"But who has said that the King Messiah must be that which the preacher says concerning him—as it were a second Authority, God forbid! The Messiah is sent to us, to Israel, to restore the Kingdom of Israel."

"Not so! Not the Kingdom of Israel alone, but the Kingdom of God for the whole world," cried Saul, fervently. "Touching this point, I am utterly at one with the preacher. On this he spoke like one moved by the divine spirit, and I have never heard one who brought out more clearly the fullness of the meaning of the Messiah. It may indeed be that he crowned him with too much authority, making him almost the equal of God. Yet I say that if he had not applied these words to him that was hanged, if he, the preacher, had not had reference to Yeshua of Nazareth, he would be my brother, my best-beloved brother."

"Of whom dost thou speak, Saul?"

"Of him, of the preacher who gave us the burning vision of the Day of Judgment, and of the coming of the Messiah," answered Saul, his voice vibrant with warmth.

"Do you, too, believe that the King Messiah is, God forbid, a second Authority?"

"I believe with perfect faith that he stands between us and God, and that all the Authorities have been relinquished into the hand of the King Messiah, to loosen the bonds of all that are bound, and to loosen the bonds of the world, and of all worlds, for all time," answered Saul.

"No, no," protested bar Naba, "the King Messiah comes only for Israel, to restore the kingdom, as the Prophets have told us in the name of God."

33

"It is only the little of faith who wait for such a Messiah. I say to you, Joseph bar Naba, that such a Messiah is not worth the price we have paid with our waiting."

"But why can we not be like all the other peoples?" asked bar Naba.

"But *are* we like the other peoples? Have we not been beaten and smitten and humiliated daily for the Messiah's sake? Have we not taken upon ourselves the burden of God, in all love, and again for his sake? Have we not denied ourselves the joys of this world, and still for his sake?"

"But I am weary of carrying the burden of the world; I am weary of being the scapegoat for the sins of others. Is not Israel worthy of being an end unto himself?"

"But I ask you, what is Israel if he is only an end unto himself? He is as a worm under the feet of the nations. But Israel is the light of the world, the star of mankind. And he is not asked whether he wills this or not, for the choice is not with him. He has been elected to this end, even as the Messiah was elected to his, before the creation of the world. He was elected to carry, even like a beast of burden, the yoke of the Torah, until God will send a redeemer of the flesh and spirit of Israel. And then he will bind the nations as the reaper binds the sheaves, and he will bring them into the granary, under the wings of the glory. For such an Israel no price of suffering is too high. Such an Israel is not a worm under the feet of the strong; he is the star of heaven, the pillar of fire which goes before the whole world on the path of redemption."

Bar Naba gazed upon his friend, and in his look there was wonder not unmingled with envy for the other's passionate faith. Nor was it in the words and in the voice alone that Saul's exaltation was manifest. By the light of the risen moon bar Naba saw how the grimness, the pent-up bitterness and resentment vanished from Saul's face when he spoke of the Messiah, their place taken by a glory which transformed him, so that his face became radiant and beautiful.

"And what you have said, Saul, concerning Reb Istephan, that you would hand him over to the Sanhedrin: do you mean that? Would you become an informer? Why?"

"Because he is my best beloved brother," answered Saul, quietly.

34

Chapter Four

THE BREAKING OF BREAD

SINCE the day when he had heard Reb Istephan preach, bar Naba had found no rest for his spirit. Bar Naba had known the Rabbi of Galilee in the life; and the picture of him rose continuously before his eyes. He had seen him in the Temple court, standing in a circle of disciples and pupils, discoursing on the last days. But bar Naba had paid no special attention to him or, for that matter, to many others who seemed to be of his kind. Was there ever a lack of visionaries and expounders of the last days in the Temple courts?

Bar Naba had also seen the Rabbi of Nazareth on that dreadful Friday before the Passover, when he was being hounded through the narrow street toward Golgotha by Roman soldiers with clubs in their hands. Bar Naba had been hastening then to the Temple, to prepare his Passover sacrifice, and he had been amazed and horrified by the scene. Never, so long as he lived, would he forget the man in the white mantle, soaked in blood and sweat, lying prostrate under the cross. Never would he forget the sight of the man struggling to his feet, under the blows of the soldiers, or the way in which he lifted his head, with its crown of thorns. A white, bloodless face ringed by beard and earlocks, eyes filled not with sadness or despair, but with pity, lips contorted with pain—these bar Naba could not forget. An utter sense of frustration and shame descended on bar Naba. There they were, dragging to his death a Jewish Rabbi who had persuaded himself that he was the Messiah, the highest of all powers, the hope of Israel and his expectation: brutal Roman soldiers treading underfoot what Israel held sacred. Humiliated by his own impotence, sickened and inwardly besmirched, bar Naba had fled from the scene. And he had tried since then to tear the recollection of it from his soul. He had hastened to the Temple, he had sought refuge there and renewal of his faith. He had gone once more to the source of strength, to the fount of the ancient belief. No, he told himself: not that which he had seen was the hope of Israel, not that which the Roman soldiers had dragged through the

35

bloody dust. Here was the hope of Israel, here in the flame which rose from the altar to heaven. Loudly and in exaltation bar Naba had sung the verses of the Psalms that day, as he did his Levitical duties on the Temple steps; he had clung to God more strongly than ever. No, he told himself again, that could not be the highest glory which had been abandoned to the base savagery of the Romans; could the lowest and weakest be the highest might? Could the most shamed and humiliated be the supreme Authority?

He had encountered more than once the disciples of the Rabbi. They came to the Temple courts in groups, sometimes in the morning, but more frequently in the afternoons. Their demeanor and deportment did not distinguish them from other, similar groups. At times one of them would deliver a discourse and tell of the wonders their Rabbi had performed in the life, and of his promise to return to them after his death, and of his fulfillment of the promise. They also conducted their own prayers. As a rule they were led by the short, bearded Jew who was known as the first disciple of the Rabbi, Simon bar Jonah, and by his assistant, the broad-boned Jochanan.

One evening, perceiving the disciples before him, bar Naba followed them. When he reached the dwelling of Hillel the water-carrier he was amazed by the multitude which waited there for the disciples. There were such as already belonged to the new congregation and such as waited to be admitted. It seemed incredible to bar Naba that in the short interval since the last Pentecost, when the disciples had first proclaimed the tidings of the Messiah, they should have won over so many souls. Even at a distance from the vast David wall there was a continuous coming and going. Women were at work in the open street, preparing over brick ovens the common meal of the disciples. Men arrived bearing great baskets of flat cakes. Others were bringing their meals out from their wretched dwellings, while still others were preparing meals to be carried away. Certainly these whom bar Naba encountered in the court before the wall belonged to the poor classes of the lower city; he even recognized a few cripples whom he had seen seated at the entrances to the Temple courts, their hands stretched out to passersby. But here and there he caught a glimpse of prominent members of the Greek-speaking synagogues; they were clad in the garb of the poor, and they helped the disciples set the tables for the common meal.

Slowly, and with some difficulty, bar Naba worked his way up to the dwelling of Hillel the water-carrier, where he found the women of the community. One of them was treated with special honor by the disciples, who did not fail to greet her whenever they entered the room: an old, broken woman, seated on a mattress, and supported by another, younger woman. Her gray hair and half her face were covered by her widow's veil. Bar Naba observed how Simon made obeisance before her, and called her "Mother," and after him the other disciples did likewise, though, as bar Naba knew, she was not their mother, but the mother of the Rabbi Messiah. On the bloodless face half hidden by the veil brooded not only her sorrow for her lost son, but the sorrow of all mothers. Her lips were drawn together in a single seam of pain, and the blue veins on her aging throat wove a network which held all the agonies through which she had passed with her son. But in the deep pools of her eyes was reflected neither anger nor bitterness, but only the highest understanding, which issues in forgiveness and compassion. Bar Naba could not look upon that face steadily, so powerfully did it affect him, sending through him a mighty stream of purification and grace.

The woman who supported the mother of the Rabbi was one upon whom age had come suddenly; for her face was young, but her hair was gray, like the down on a dove. The skin shining through the veil was alabaster yellow, and her eyes were filled with a gentle, pious light. Her too the disciples treated with special honor, as an intimate. There was something unearthly about the two women, something not of this life; for their flesh was so transfigured that one would have thought that not two living women but two souls were seated in an embrace.

The great room with the balcony open to the sky was dark and filled with shadows. No lamp was lit. For a long time silence reigned, so that the breathing of the assembled could be heard. Then Simon rose, his face and beard hidden in the darkness and only his eyes shining through. He lifted his arms to heaven and prayed:

"Father in heaven, Thine is the praise and the glory. Thou hast sent Thy Messiah to us, that he might die for our sins, and Thou hast awakened him to life, even as Thou didst promise us through the mouths of Thy prophets. Now send Thy grace and benediction upon us. Open our hearts, that we may perceive Thy truth and that the fear

37

of Thee may dwell in us. Bring us nearer to Thy countenance. Make us worthy to see the coming of Thy elected one in our days. May Thy kingdom begin this day for all eternity. Amen."

"Amen," answered the assembly.

Then Simon raised his arms again and said:

"Remember, Lord, Thy congregation; guard it from evil and make it perfect in Thy love; bring together Thy sanctified ones from the four winds into Thy kingdom, which Thou hast prepared for them. Hosannah to the God of David! He that is holy in belief in thy servant Yeshua, let him be one of us; and he that is not, let him become holy in the belief. Amen!"

Those who already belonged to the congregation, and were called companions, surrounded Simon, Jochanan, Jacob, and the other messengers. Those who were not yet companions stood at a distance, and one of them called out:

"Tell us, what shall we do that we may be received into the holy congregation, and be saved in the Messiah, Yeshua the Nazarene?"

Simon answered:

"Repent and be converted, so that your sins may be wiped out. When the time of the awakening will be sounded by the Lord, He will send unto us Yeshua the Messiah, who has already been preached unto you. Therefore turn unto the Messiah, who has already come, a sacrifice for us and for you, to cleanse us all of our sins and to make us worthy of being accepted into the kingdom of heaven."

Then Jochanan rose and said:

"Let no burden of gold or silver weigh down your souls when you cross the threshold to enter into the keeping of the Lord. Bring with you neither fields nor houses nor any earthly goods, for which the gates of the heavenly kingdom will be closed upon you. Leave your possessions together with your sins on the other side of the threshold before you knock on the door of the heavenly kingdom."

Then it was Simon who spoke again:

"Leave your sorrows for the coming day in the keeping of your Father in heaven: thus it was that our lord and Messiah taught us when he was with us in the life."

"I had a house and a field. I sold them, and here I lay the purse with the gold at the feet of the disciples," said a short, heavy man, in a rich garment, and a ring on his finger, approaching the inner circle.

38

"No, my son, thou hadst neither house nor field. Naked didst thou come forth from thy mother's womb, and naked wilt thou return to the womb of the earth. And when the Lord will awaken thee to the resurrection, thou wilt come with neither house nor field, neither robe nor ring; thou wilt come only with thy good deeds, and they will clothe thee," answered Simon.

"I have no house, and no field, and I bring with me only my limbs and my naked body, and I lay these at the feet of the disciples, that I may be accepted into the bond of the Messiah," said a tall, powerful, half-naked man, who, wearing a girdle of rope, showed himself thereby to be a day laborer.

"My son, neither thy body nor thy limbs are Thine. Thou hast borrowed them from the Creator of all the worlds for the time of thy sojourn on earth. Canst thou make thy body whole again, when it has been broken by age or sickness? Canst thou put back a limb which has been cut off? Nothing is thine, all belongs to the Lord of the world," said Simon.

"Rabbi, I have nothing at all save my sinful soul, which I lay at the feet of the disciples, that I may be received into the covenant of the Messiah!" cried a lame beggar, who crawled forward supported by another cripple.

"My son, my son, thou hast given more than all the others, for thou hast given that which is thine. For nothing is thine, save thy sins. Thy sin is forgiven thee, through the death of the lord. Thou art clean, my son! An acceptable sacrifice is thy soul unto God!" said Simon, placing his hands on the beggar's head.

So they came, one after another, before the disciples, leaving at their feet whatever worldly goods they had. There were between fifteen and twenty of them that evening who were received into the congregation, all of them of the children of Israel.

Bar Naba observed that the great majority of those that came to be baptized in the name of the Messiah were of the poor, many of them beggars who haunted the gates of the Temple courts. Some were Jerusalemites; others were recent arrivals who had been drawn to Jerusalem as pilgrims and had remained there without occupation, and so had joined the ranks of the beggars. But these were not the only ones. There came also men of substance, who wanted to assure themselves of a part in the resurrection which the disciples preached.

Simon approached these newcomers and asked:

"Do you believe with perfect faith that the Messiah whom God sent as a comfort and consolation to His people died for our sins, and that after three days he rose from death, and that he will come with the clouds of heaven, sitting on the right hand of the power, to judge the tribes of Israel, and that he will restore the Kingdom of Israel and purify the world into the Kingdom of the Almighty?"

The neophytes answered in chorus:

"We believe with perfect faith that what thou hast said concerning the lord, Yeshua the Nazarene, is true and perfect."

And now the women of the congregation led forth the female proselytes who were waiting to be received into the faith. At the head of the attendants was Susannah, the mother of the Zebedees. The new converts were brought before the disciples, Simon and Jochanan. Some of the women, who had come accompanied by their husbands, had already relinquished their earthly possessions. Others, who were widows, brought with them nothing more than their widows' veils. The women were asked whether they believed with perfect faith that Yeshua the Nazarene had died for the sins of all men, that he had died and risen from death after three days, and that he would come to judge the world as the Prophets had prophesied. When the proselytes had answered in the affirmative, they were bidden to accompany the women of the congregation to the pool of Siloah, for baptism.

The men proselytes, too, were led forth to baptism. The sons of Zebedee and the other disciples gathered the newcomers for the ceremony. The pool of Siloah was, at this time of the year, little more than a muddy hollow, which the barefoot water-carriers trod, to squeeze out the last drops of water. The proselytes were conducted thither, the men on one side, the women on the other. A beaker of water was scraped from the bottom of the pool, and the disciples repeated these words to the men:

"In the name of the God of Israel and of the Lord of hosts I baptize thee with the baptism of Yeshua the Messiah, and I receive thee into the holy congregation of his believers."

Then the water was poured over the proselyte, and the disciples said:

"Happy art thou that thou hast been judged worthy of this privilege. May we, in thy days and in our days and in the days of all Israel,

40

see the Ancient of Days come riding on the clouds of heaven to begin the Kingdom of the Almighty on earth."

The newly received converts answered: "Amen."

"Our brothers are ye," exclaimed the other disciples, embracing the newly baptized.

The same ceremony was performed over the women proselytes by the women of the congregation.

A multitude of onlookers, most of them denizens of this poor neighborhood, stood about the pool. For them there was nothing new in the scene, for baptism was an ancient usage in Jerusalem and attracted no special attention. Nor was there anything new, either, in the spectacle of the men who rested at the foot of the wall after they had submitted to circumcision.

When the conductors of the ceremony returned to the dwelling in the David wall, they were received by the other disciples with a benediction:

"Blessed be they who come in the name of God and of the lord, Yeshua the Nazarene. Our brother art thou in the lord Messiah, our sister art thou in the lord Messiah," and the disciples greeted the newcomers with the kiss of brotherhood.

The stars had come out in the heavens above the dwelling. The women lit the oil lamps, and the disciples, the new together with the old, stood up, turned their faces toward the Temple, and repeated the evening *Shema*:

"Hear, O Israel, the Lord our God, the Lord is one."

After the evening prayer the disciples seated themselves on the stone floor, while some stretched out a long bamboo mattress which served as a table. There was no distinction now between newcomers and older members of the congregation, but the leading disciples sat at the head, and with them Miriam, the mother of the Rabbi and Messiah, whom Miriam of Migdal and Susannah conducted to her place on a low stool, they seating themselves at her feet. The other women remained standing at the door, behind the curtain; but certain women were allowed to enter, for they carried baskets and pitchers of food, olives, vegetables, and sour milk. A number of the faithful rose to serve. They placed the containers of food on the table, and the flat cakes of bread were brought before the leading disciples at the head. A hollowed gourd with wine, and a cup, were also placed before Simon and Jochanan.

41

Simon acted as the prayer leader. He lifted up the flat cakes, and in a voice which was tremulous with piety, called out:

"Our Rabbi and our lord, Yeshua, the King Messiah of the living God, while he was yet among us, taught us to pray thus to our Father in heaven: 'Our Father, Who art in heaven, hallowed be Thy name. Thy Kingdom come. Thy will be done on earth as it is in heaven. Give us this day our daily portion of bread and forgive us our trespasses as we forgive them that trespass against us. And lead us not into temptation, but deliver us from evil. For Thine is the Kingdom, and the power, and the glory, from now and for evermore, Amen.'"

The congregation answered: "Amen."

"And he taught us, furthermore," continued Simon, "that the table at which we partake of food is an altar of God, and they that sit about it like those who bring a sacrifice. Come, let us therefore change this table of our lord into an altar, and let us bring as a sacrifice unto God our daily bread."

The congregation waited in silence, and Simon continued:

"This was the usage of our lord, the anointed of Jacob, when he was yet with us in the flesh. He took the bread, and broke it into small pieces, and distributed it among us, saying: 'Take and eat, this is my body.' And he took the cup of wine, and said the benediction over it, and gave us of the wine, saying: 'Drink of it, for this is my blood, the blood of the new covenant, which is shed for the forgiveness of many.' And we continue thus in the usage which was his, and we break bread together."

Then Simon took the bread, and broke it into small pieces, and distributed the pieces, saying:

"Even as this bread comes from the wheat which was sown on many hills and which has now been brought together and become one bread, even so, our Father in heaven, do Thou bring together all thy congregation from all the corners of the world, into Thy Kingdom, through Thy servant, the anointed of Israel, Yeshua ben David. For Thine is the power, and Thine is the Kingdom, and Thine is the glory. Amen."

The faithful took the fragments of bread and repeated the benediction.

Then Simon lifted up the cup, poured in wine from the gourd, and lifted the cup, saying:

"See, this is the blood of the new covenant, which was poured out for the sins of many."

Then he made the benediction over the wine, and drank of it, and the cup was passed round for the others to drink. Each of the companions lifted the cup, repeated the benediction silently, and took a sip of wine. Then the cup was passed through the curtain, and the women too made the benediction and drank of the wine.

An interval of silence was observed. Then Simon lifted the wooden bowl which stood before him, took out two olives, and passed the bowl on, and thus he did with the other bowls of food. Each of the disciples followed his example.

Then Simon said:

"Our Rabbi and lord, the anointed of Jacob, when he was yet with us in the flesh, taught us that when we sit at table and break bread together we shall praise and thank God in the songs of David. Therefore let us now do as he taught us."

Another of the disciples responded:

"A song of David. The Lord is my shepherd, I shall not want."

"He leadeth me beside the green pastures," chanted the congregation; and when the psalm was ended, there was another interval of silence.

Then Simon said:

"Our Rabbi and our lord, the anointed of Jacob, while he was yet with us in the flesh, taught us thus: 'If thou bringest thy sacrifice to the altar, and rememberest that thou hast quarreled with thy brother, leave thy sacrifice on the altar, and go first to thy brother and ask his forgiveness, and then return to offer thy sacrifice.' And he taught us further: 'Ye have heard it said that ye shall love your friends and hate your enemies. But I say unto you, love your enemies and pray for those that persecute you, in order that you may be children of your Father in heaven, Who causes the sun to shine alike on the good and the wicked, and Who sends His rain down equally for the just and the unjust."

"Oh, believe them to whom it was granted to hear it from his holy lips; believe the eyes to which it was granted to look at the glory which rested on his face," cried one Jew from a corner, with a heartbroken sigh.

"And something more he taught us," called out Jochanan, of the sons of Zebedee. "When you do charity do it not to the sound of trum-

43

pets, which is the way of the hypocrites in the synagogues and the streets, in order that men may praise them. I say unto you that they have had their reward. But you, when you do charity, let not your left hand know what your right hand does, so that your charity may be secret, and your Father, Who sees in secret, may reward you."

Then another of the disciples lifted up his voice:

"Our Rabbi and our lord, the anointed of Jacob, taught us thus: I say unto you, take no thought for yourselves, what food or raiment you shall have for your bodies. Behold the ravens, which do not reap, neither have they stored up grain in barns, and yet our Father in heaven feeds them. And how much more are you in His eyes than the ravens."

Then one spoke, and another, and a third:

"As our Father in heaven feeds the worms of the earth, as the Writ tells us."

"Who has ever spoken such consolation to us?"

"Indeed, indeed, the Kingdom of Heaven is already with us. It is on the threshold of our door. Why should we take thought for food and raiment? Does not God clothe every blade of grass in the field?"

And one cried out from a corner, in an exalted voice:

"Arise, arise, thou tormented daughter of Zion. The light is here!"

And still another broke into song:

"Blessed be the hour in which he was born!
Blessed be the womb that bore him!
Blessed is the generation whose eyes have seen him!
Blessed be the eyes which await his coming!
When he openeth his lips, he uttereth benediction and peace!
Oh, believeth those eyes to which it was granted to see him!
The utterance of his mouth is forgiveness and pardon for
    Israel!
Happy art thou, Israel, because of what is prepared for thee!"

The crying voices increased in number; they came from every part of the room. Soon the voices merged into a rhythmic chanting, repeating the phrases of benediction over and over again. It was as if the assembly were seeking its way into the utmost intimacy of the Jewish hope and probing the depths of the mystery of the Messiah and of the end of the world. Then, as the exaltation nourished by the chant mounted higher and higher, rhythm of motion was added to rhythm of voice.

Seated on the earth, they swayed their bodies back and forth. Eyes were closed, faces upturned to the ceiling. Again and again they chanted:

"Happy art thou, Israel, because of what is prepared for thee!"

Now the voices of the women began to make themselves heard above those of the men. But it was not words that they uttered; there sounded a shrill crying, a sibilation of half words, a moaning as of doves.

Then Simon spread out his arms, as if he had suddenly perceived someone, and cried:

"Come, thou holy servant of God, thou anointed of Jacob, unto thy congregation, and sit with us at our table. Break bread with us, for thou givest us of thy bread, which is thy body. Come, O anointed one, and bless us and purify us with the grace of thy presence."

Following him, others lifted their arms in welcome, crying:

"Come, O holy servant of God, and sit with us at table."

"Oh, come, oh, come, oh, come!"

And suddenly they were all silent, as if in expectation; and the tall, slender woman who was seated at the feet of the mother of the Messiah, namely, Miriam of Migdal, drew herself up from the earth and lifted up her alabaster-yellow, transparent arms shining in the dimness of the mingled lamplight and starlight. She lifted toward heaven the slender throat covered with a network of blue veins, so that it became taut, like a bowstring, or the string of a lyre. And her head rose higher and higher, till it seemed that it touched the stars:

"*Rabbenu! Rabbenu!* I see thee! I see thee!"

Her voice sent a tremor through the assembly, like the sudden ringing of a harp string, like the sudden crying of a child, like the sudden moaning of a dove. The assembled sat as in stupefaction.

And the woman continued to cry:

"I see thee, my lord, I see thee. The heavens open and thou swimmest forth on a fiery cloud. The cloud is all fire, and thy robe is white, like a white flame. And thy body is crimson, like a crimson flame. And no one can look upon thy face because of its sunlike brightness. Thou swimmest closer and closer to the earth. I see thee, I see thee, lord. Oh, spread out thy grace upon thy handmaid!" And she bowed herself to the earth, and buried her face in her white hair which was spread out upon the floor.

45

"She was the first to see him!"

"Miriam of Migdal!" they whispered.

The vision of Miriam of Migdal was like a trumpet call. Her exaltation passed swiftly into her beholders, and here and there a woman threw herself on the floor, crying:

"I too see him! They are bringing down from heaven a throne of glory on four winged lions. They bear the throne before him through the air. Now I see his robe. His naked feet tread upon the threshold of the earth, and his head is in heaven. And his robe is pure flame, pure flame!"

From the women the exaltation passed into the men.

The first to testify was Jochanan. A deep gurgling issued from his powerful throat, like the sound of the passing of thunder. Then followed a voice, all but unintelligible, ringing like the ram's horn:

"Seven golden candlesticks are burning! A fiery scroll is spread upon the air. There are seven seals upon the scroll. I hear the blowing of a trumpet and an angel weeping and calling: 'Who will open the sealed scroll?' See, see, fiery letters fly out of the sealed scroll! They range themselves between heaven and earth. And now I can read the script, from *aleph* to *tav*.

"And I see a fiery sword uplifted in heaven above the star of Edom!

"Holy! Holy! Holy!"

Then came other words from the throat of Jochanan, and their sound was as of Aramaic, but no one understood their meaning.

Now Simon threw himself on the floor and from his recumbent posture lifted his arms and cried:

"I thank thee and bless thee, thou anointed of Jacob, that thou hast come to our table, and thou hast taken of thy glory and poured it upon thy holy congregation."

When bar Naba came down from the dwelling, he found gathered before the ancient wall a group of men and women of the poor neighborhood. Among them were water-carriers who had come too late that day to obtain water from the pool; there were camel drivers and artisans, weavers and dyers. They stood there, listening to the cries and the chants which came down to them from the dwelling in the David wall. The women had little children in their arms or clinging to their aprons.

And all of them were pressing close to the entrance which led up to the dwelling, and their voices were lifted up, crying:

"Let us, too, enter! Let us approach the holy ones, that they may put their hands upon our children, and bless them."

Chapter Five

STRONGER THAN DEATH

THUS it was, too, in the land of bar Naba's birth: the dead reigned over the living. For bar Naba came from Cyprus, and the god of Cyprus was Adonis. In his ears still rang the lamentations of the women who squatted on the flat roofs with their hair loosened, and smote themselves with their fists on their bared bosoms as they wept for the slaughtered god. Some of them scratched themselves with their nails so that the blood ran down their faces and their bodies. In the days of lamentation for the god every woman was transformed into the goddess Venus-Astarte, who had lost her own dear lover in Adonis; and every woman poured into the lament her own longings, her own unspoken hunger for love. In the evenings they went out with kindled lamps and in the fields, the wood, the gardens, and groves sought the lovely Adonis. But when the springtime came their voices rang with joy, for Adonis was alive again, he was alive with the blossoming of the flowers, with the breath of the wind, with the greening of the fields and the pulsing of the brooks.

It was remote, utterly remote, from bar Naba's mind to associate that which he had seen in the dwelling on the David wall with the abominations practiced by the pagans of his island home. If there was any association at all, it was by contrast; for this that he had seen and experienced among the disciples was the inmost answer to the longings and dreams of *his* soul. He had scarcely left the dwelling than he knew himself to be bound to the disciples with his deepest roots. It was as if the patriarchs of his people had come to him in person, and as if he had been a witness of the highest mysteries of Israel, testifying to the Messiah. He felt that he was now being admitted in fullness to the promise and benediction of Jacob, and he saw his portion in Israel being

47

fulfilled in his bond with the Messiah. He had entered into the tabernacle of peace, and the thirst of his soul was quenched.

In his youth bar Naba had been a prey to cruel and conflicting doubts, which had made themselves a nest in his heart and had preyed on his vitals. Nor had these doubts vanished utterly even when, his first youth behind him, he had stood on the sunlit steps of the Temple of Jerusalem and performed his duties, a Levite of the Lord, intoning the Psalms. Still the old, unanswerable question would recur to him: "The just man suffereth, and the wicked man flourisheth." Why was it that Israel, the chosen people, lay like a bound sheep at the feet of the nations of the world, while they, the idolaters, the worshipers of images of wood and stone, could deal with him as they willed? They could pour out on him all the vileness that was in their hearts, and he lay there, dumb and helpless. If there was such a thing as justice, why was it not made manifest here? All the answers that bar Naba heard, quoted from the sages and even from the Prophets, gave him no satisfaction; they went wide of the mark, like arrows shot from a twisted bow.

With all the fervor of his youth bar Naba had longed for the Messiah and hoped for his coming. At first he had seen in the Messiah only the deliverer of Israel; but slowly the concept had widened in him. He had brooded on the words of the Prophets, he had plunged into the writings of the Hellenistic Jews; and more than these, his comrade, Saul of Tarshish, had given wings to his Messiah and transformed him from a Jewish into a world deliverer.

When he first became acquainted with the disciples of Yeshua his Jewish pride had protested against the idea that the wounded and tortured Jew whom the Roman soldiers had driven through the streets of Jerusalem was the "Ancient of Days," the Messiah whom Reb Istephan preached. But since his intimate contact with them, since he had been with the disciples in the dwelling on the wall and had heard their ecstatic service, had seen them, as he felt, welcome the Messiah into their midst, bar Naba had become drunk with their exaltation. Now, at last, he understood the sufferings of Israel: Israel was the center of the world; God had made Israel the target of His arrows: and because He had chosen Israel to be holy, and thus to personify His will, therefore Israel was sinful. And therefore, far from being ashamed of Israel's suffering, he, bar Naba, should take pride in them, as the sign of the election. Therefore, again, it had been ordained of

48

God that out of Israel should come the world deliverer, who should, even like Israel, take upon himself, in love, all suffering, even death, in order to redeem the world. In this, then, Israel and the Messiah were one: Israel a part of the Messiah, the Messiah a part of Israel. That the Messiah had suffered did not speak against him; quite the contrary, that he had suffered was the proof that he was the Messiah. Yes, that bloody and wounded Jew was the Messiah—and he had come to institute a new order in the world. The blood which had poured from him had justified the sufferings of the Jews, for the sufferings of Israel were the beginning of the agony of the Messiah.

With the passing of days, the two friends, Saul and bar Naba, felt the gulf widening between them; but it was not easy for them to acknowledge the breach. Bar Naba was consumed with the desire to tell Saul of his visit to the disciples. He felt that, in spite of his implacable enmity to them, Saul was apter than anyone else to understand them and even to explain the meaning of certain ritualistic symbols which he had witnessed and could not fathom. But he did not dare to utter a word. The fear of his friend lay on him like an iron hand, and the spirit of his friend oppressed him into silence. Thus, in bar Naba's heart a new struggle went on, this time between the dominion of Saul and the new authority which had been revealed to him.

Day by day bar Naba felt himself ripening toward the final resolve. Since that single visit to their dwelling, he did not miss an opportunity to hear the disciples when they preached in the Temple court. Even when he stood on the Temple steps, in the midst of the service, he could not help thinking that the Messiah might come back any moment, and he, bar Naba, would not be one of the congregation. Yet how he dreamed of that moment, and how he longed for it! He saw himself, a young Levite in the tunic of his service, standing among the others on the Temple steps and greeting with blasts of the silver trumpet the descent of the Messiah on the Temple, at the head of his heavenly hosts. Nor were the heavenly hosts alone in their attendance, for all the generations of the past were also present, with the generation that was now living. Innumerable hosts of souls. All the patriarchs, all the prophets and all the saints—in the train of the Messiah. And bar Naba stands there on the steps leading up to the sanctuary, among the other Levites, those that are known to him and those whom he does not know, souls clad in the white garb of the Levites, and they blow on the silver trumpets and sing the songs of ascent.

Still he did not dare to take the last step. He did not dare to open the door and pass over into the sanctuary for which his soul longed. He was afraid. Before he could open this door, before he could step across the threshold, he had to be certain that he was altogether purified and altogether prepared for the life of the Messiah. What did this mean? That he was prepared to surrender all his worldly goods, to strip himself of all the protection and all the habits which circumstance had till now provided for him, to tear himself out by the roots from today, and to enter a tomorrow which was new—a tomorrow of the Messiah, a tomorrow of many days, a life which was the death of the life he had known till now, the death of the flesh, of pleasure, and of all the fruits of this world. The strong roots of his youth cried out in protest against the demand; and yet, day by day, one root after another seemed to yield before the imperious need of his soul; and with every conquest of himself the pallor increased in bar Naba's face.

Though no word concerning this matter had passed between them, Saul was aware of what was taking place. So they suffered the division to grow in silence, until it could no longer be ignored.

The break came as they were returning together from the study house of their Rabbi. Saul suddenly began to speak as if he were giving words to a conversation which the two of them had been conducting only in thought:

"Do you not see, bar Naba, what is at issue here? It is nothing more nor less than our last hope. Can we permit gross and ignorant Galileans to trample on our sanctity? They turn us into a scandal and a mockery when they associate the hope of Israel, Israel's portion in heaven, with one that was hanged from a wooden gallows!"

"Hanged from a wooden gallows!" The contempt which informed these words gave the last thrust to bar Naba's resolution. He felt that his timidity and indecision made him a partner to Saul's utterance. And suddenly the door which he had not dared to open seemed to swing wide of itself.

Bar Naba stopped dead in his walk, lifted his large, heavily-shadowed eyes to his friend, and said, in firm, decisive tones such as his friend had never heard from him before:

"Saul of Tarshish, I believe with perfect faith that he who was

50

hanged is the King Messiah whom God has sent to us in the midst of our despair. And that he was hanged on the wooden cross is not the disproof but, on the contrary, the proof that he is the Messiah. Like Israel, he took upon himself the sufferings and redemption of the world, even as the Prophets have prophesied concerning him."

The chagrin which descended on Saul was like a visible curtain. He frowned so fiercely that his thick black hair covered the blue veins of his temples. His vigorous lips contracted, and the long, thin, eagle nose which overhung them became paler. Quietly, without looking his friend in the eyes, he asked:

"Hast thou already joined the company of the Galileans?"

"Tomorrow it will be done."

"From tomorrow on thou art my enemy, bar Naba."

And Saul turned and left his friend without a farewell.

*   *   *

The conversation took place on the square in the upper city, not far from the bridge which was thrown across to the entrance of the Temple court; the two friends had come up the slope from the street of the cheese-makers.

For some time bar Naba stood looking at the figure of his retreating friend. Saul did not hasten but walked with thoughtful footsteps over the bridge and turned aside toward the chamber of the Hewn Stones. Bar Naba hoped that his friend would look back; but he was disappointed. When Saul had disappeared, bar Naba went down from the upper city and out through the Sheep-Gate toward the new quarter where his sister had her house. It was not an easy thing to have broken with Saul. It was as if something had been torn out of his life; and though he had been preparing himself for the loss, he stood before it helpless and distressed.

As long as he had known him bar Naba had looked upon Saul as a living exemplar, surrendering himself to the older youth with complete abandon. Bar Naba's character was not marked by great strength. The mild climate of his island home, and the rich surroundings of his childhood, had made him soft and yielding, like a woman. From the moment of their meeting in the Synagogue of the Cilicians, Saul, with his swift, unwavering decisions and uncompromising views, had dominated him. It was with them as it has always been in the Orient, where

51

the friendship of two men, especially in their youth, can often be stronger than the love between man and woman. Bar Naba had looked up to Saul, who not only dominated his friend but became for him an unattainable ideal.

What bar Naba had loved and admired in Saul was his wholeness, and love and admiration had only increased with the passage of time. Bar Naba could not but admit to himself that his hesitation before the door of conversation was due in large part to his unconscious fear of Saul. The break had been hard, the loss was deep, and yet—there was also a feeling of relief, of liberation from a strong and dominating hand which had always been laid on him. Thus, side by side with his sorrow, there was contentment and a sense of heightened importance. He was free now to do as he thought best, and that best was to provide for his own salvation.

Slowly these second feelings overmastered the first; slowly the chambers of his heart filled with undiluted joy; no, not wholly undiluted, for the pain and regret for his lost friend were not wholly abjured. But with every step he took away from Saul the exhilaration of freedom and the joy of his spiritual prospects grew stronger in him.

He felt now that he could not contain himself; he had to share his feelings with someone. The person nearest to him in the city of Jerusalem was his sister Miriam. The intimacy which he felt toward her was, in its way, something that he had never felt for Saul: love and admiration, yes, but these to a degree which created the very antithesis of intimacy. In the presence of Saul, bar Naba had never dared to be himself, but had always striven to appear finer, nobler, and more learned. For Saul he had, as it were, always worn festal garments. To his sister bar Naba showed himself as he was, with all his weaknesses, and notwithstanding that there was not much difference in their ages, Miriam, like all young women who have known sorrow and suffering, displayed a deep spirit of understanding and sympathy.

"Peace is with me, my sister; God has been good to me, all praise to Him," said bar Naba in answer to his sister's greetings, as she came toward him with outstretched arms.

"Your face declares that a heavy burden of care has been lifted from you. Your brow is radiant with happiness. What has happened with you, brother?"

"I have lost a friend and gained a love."

Delight was kindled in the lustrous brown eyes of Miriam. How long she had waited to hear such words from her brother!

"Who is the fortunate one among the daughters of Jerusalem? I will run to her, and bring her home with the music of flutes and cymbals."

"The fortunate one among the daughters," said bar Naba, "is the brightest and most glorious star on the heavens of Israel."

"Brother, you speak today in secret parables. I do not understand you. Let me not wander in darkness any longer."

"The fortunate one among the daughters is my faith in the Messiah. It is the brightest and most glorious star on the heavens of Israel. It is also the last hope of Israel, the reward for Israel's faithfulness as my friend that was, Saul of Tarshish, called it—and it is the chosen one of my heart."

Miriam let her heavy eyelids fall over her eyes.

"But this chosen one you have always had. You have always believed in the Messiah of Israel."

"Until now I have had faith; but now my faith has been justified. It is no longer faith; it is fulfillment, it is reality. The Messiah is reality! He is here, and he moves among us. This is the new, great love which I have won."

"The Messiah is here? Where is he? Who is he? Why do we not hear him? Where is the voice of the messenger on the hills of Israel? Where are the voices and the trumpets? The Messiah is here, and Jerusalem stands where it did, under the guard of Edom's hosts? When did he show himself? Tell me, my brother, speak to me."

"He showed himself to the humble and the humiliated, to the simple and ignorant; it was among them that he lived; they were the first to recognize him. The rich, the strong, and the learned thrust him away," answered bar Naba, exaltedly.

"Do you mean him of whom the men of Galilee speak? Yes, I have heard of him, and of his followers. I know that Philippus, the father of Zipporah, has become one of them. So has Reb Istephan the preacher and others among the Greek-speaking Jews."

"Before many days are past all Israel will accept him as the Messiah. And all the nations of the world will come to the Mount of Zion, and he will begin his Kingdom upon earth," said bar Naba.

"I understand that the bearers of the tidings are common fisher

53

folk, unlettered men; and it is only the poor who join their congregation. Some of my servants, I am told, are of the company. My best perfume mixer, bar Joseph, is definitely of their number; and ever since he joined them he neglects his work. My lovely geranium perfume has withered away, and my tarragon has lost all its sweetness. He says that before long the Messiah will return, and then all leaves will smell like the spices of Paradise. But I understand further that the Rabbis and scholars disregard them completely. How come you to that company? This is a Messiah for the ignorant, not for the lettered."

At this point they were interrupted by young Jochanan, or Marcus, who, hearing that his uncle had arrived, rushed away from the lesson in rhetoric which he was receiving from his Greek teacher and broke into the garden.

Bar Naba sat holding his nephew between his knees, and suffering himself to be embraced by the strong, sunburned young arms which were thrust forth from the tunic. He stroked the boy's curls and earlocks, which hung down delicately over his fresh young cheeks.

"Tell me thy verse, little one. What says the prophet concerning those that walk in darkness?"

"They that walk in darkness have seen a great light," the lad completed the verse.

"There, my sister, is the answer. God has given it through the mouth of your child."

Miriam remained sunk in thought a little while, then, as if to direct the conversation on another subject, she asked:

"And whose is the friendship that you have lost? Do you not know that oftentimes a friendship is dearer and more precious than a love?"

"That of Saul of Tarshish."

"Saul of Tarshish? Ah, that is a pity, a great pity. You once held it of great account."

"For such a love one may well pay not only with the friendship of a friend who was dearer than a woman, but with all the gifts of life. That love asks as its price nothing less than the world."

"And you are ready to pay this price?" asked Miriam, startled.

"I am ready to pay any price," answered bar Naba.

For a while his sister stood in a trance of meditation. Then she murmured: "If that is so, it is a love which is stronger than death. It is a true love, and may God guide you in it, for it comes from a pure

54

fount, the fount of your heart." And drawing close to bar Naba she placed her cheek on her brother's head. "Such a love merits the envy of women."

Bar Naba made as if to depart, but his young nephew clung to him, and pleaded:

"My Rabbi, my deliverer, take me with you on the path you have chosen. I have listened to every word which has passed between you and my mother, and I want to have my share in the great love you have found."

"You will follow that path, and your mother will follow it, my son, for there is no other path." And bar Naba took the ring which he wore on his finger and gave it to his nephew.

"Joseph," cried Miriam, in astonishment. "What are you giving him? Your family ring?"

"I shall not need it any more, sister; neither will Jochanan need it when he comes to us. For among those whom I go to join there are no separate families. There is just one family, which is the congregation of the Messiah of righteousness. Peace be with you, my sister."

"Peace go with you, my brother."

That same day bar Naba sat in the field which was his possession on Mount Scopus, in Jerusalem. The field consisted of an olive grove, whose trees protected the dense alleys of a vineyard. Bar Naba sat before his house, among the columns of the facade, and looked down upon Jerusalem, whose terraces set with whitewashed houses cascaded from the hills into the valleys. Jerusalem was dozing in the heat of the midday hour. Like a flock of sheep in a green meadow, the towers and walls and palaces of the city rested at the foot of the Temple mount among the soft, shadowed green of the summits of cypress and olive. Bar Naba's glance wandered from hill to hill, from tower to tower, from wall to wall, from the House of God to the Kidron valley, and his heart was filled with a benediction for Jerusalem. It was for him the city of peace, the city of eternal happiness, for it had found the bond between man and God. He loved Jerusalem and the life of Jerusalem. And like a Nazirite, a man vowed unto God, who pauses for an instant before he enters on the terms of his sacred oath, he let his mind flash back over the joyous days of his young manhood and the gracious gifts which the city had brought him. He remembered the gay festivals, the floods of pilgrims, the singing of the Jerusalemites, the strength of

55

their young men, the loves of their daughters. The secrets of his youth, which he had kept to himself, came back to him like guests in a swift procession of farewells. He looked down on the gardens and remembered the happy assemblies of the young people of Jerusalem which he —like all the other wealthy young men of Jerusalem—had been wont to call together on the solemn Day of Atonement, when the city was filled with pilgrims, and on the day of the New Year of the Trees, the fifteenth day of the month of Shevat. Those two days of the year were specially set apart for the assembling of the young sons and daughters of Jerusalem, so that they might get to know each other and choose their brides and bridegrooms. He could still hear the shy laughter of the daughters of Jerusalem, as they stood ranged along the alley of cypresses—one girl by each tree. The young men would pass, and the girls would lift their eyes to them and say: "Look not, young man, upon gold or silver, nor upon beauty in these maidens; look only upon the good families from which they spring, so that they may bear thee worthy sons." He recalled the mating festivals, as he had arranged them for the members of his synagogue; when his sister had thrown open her house for the representatives of the Cypriot pilgrims, he had arranged receptions for the youth in his garden. Every cluster of vine, every cypress alley, every bed of flowers recalled now to his memory the laughter which had echoed about them. He remembered also banquets he had given on his little estate to the young Levites and Priests with whom he had participated in the services of the Day of Atonement. On those evenings his garden rang with song, repetitions of the sacred music which had filled the Temple in the day. The joy of youth seemed to burst in waves from the vine clusters, the rose bushes, and the cypress groves, where the young people hid themselves in pairs. And all this lay now on the other side of the threshold; it was closed to him, locked away for ever, sealed with seven seals.

His eye fell on the farther end of his field, where the landscape descended toward a valley and the round hillocks of sand began, like drifts of snow. The hillocks ran into each other, descended into successive depths. Above them brooded the fiery sky, and in it blazed little blue clouds; one would have said they were ethereal oil lamps, sending forth a hot smoke of interweaving cloud. A grim and merciless spirit was spread out on the reaches of the sand hills, a self-enclosed spirit, hard with the hardness of stern justice, unsoftened by a touch of grace or pity. This was the desert of Judaea, baking in the stifling heat, and falling down, down, toward the great, clear eye which lay at the bottom of the abyss. That was the Dead Sea. Beyond the Dead Sea lay the limit of the world, Sodom, and the eternal, sandy walls of Moab. They flickered and danced in the flames of Hell.

There was the boundary, the boundary of space, and also of time.

Bar Naba clapped his hands together. The steward of his house— an old Canaanite, who bore the name of Eliezer, the servant of Abraham, and whom he had inherited from his father as steward and teacher, even as Abraham had given his Eliezer to Isaac, together with the inheritance of camels—appeared before him. Bar Naba began to speak:

"Eliezer, my guide, as a father hast thou been to me. Thy son knows it, and thanks thee."

Eliezer bowed his gray head and answered:

"Why is this day exalted above other days, that my lord speaks thus to his servant?"

"There is no lord, and there is no servant, Eliezer. There is only one Who is above us, and it is He Who reigns in heaven. The time has come for me to say farewell to my household. Call its members together, and call also the scribe, that he may write out the manumission for all my servants."

"Is my lord going on a far journey, to kingdoms beyond the sea, that he has come to this resolve?"

"I am going on the nearest journey on which any man can go; I am going by the path of God and of his chosen one, the Messiah. By that path all of us will travel, all the children of man; some sooner, others later."

"My lord, I do not understand."

"Go, do as I bid thee, Eliezer."

When the servants had assembled in the hall of pillars, bar Naba addressed them.

"There is only One whom it is proper to call lord, and that is the Lord of heaven and earth. From this day on, all of us are freemen. We are free in God and in His Messiah." And bar Naba ordered the scribe to write out the terms of manumission on ostrakons, one for each servant.

The scribe did as he was bidden. He took an earthen pot and broke it into fragments; then with the writing implement which he had hanging from his neck, and which consisted of a slender pencil dipped in a blue dye, he wrote on each potsherd the name of a slave, and the date of his manumission. Then bar Naba went through the rooms of his house and brought out whatever he possessed in the way of raiment and money. These he distributed to the slaves; together with the ostrakons on which their liberation was entered. The slaves received the gifts and the deeds of manumission in silent wonder, not daring to question the acts of the master.

When, passing along the row of his slaves, bar Naba came to his little Egyptian dancing girl, she bent her supple body before him in a deep bow, hid her face in the hem of her master's robe, and covered his feet with her dark, perfumed hair.

"I do not want to go out in freedom. I love my lord; I will follow him and drink the dust of his footsteps like the waters of a living well."

Her master laid his fingers on her shadowy, anointed shoulders and said:

"There is only One who is worthy to be called lord, and He is God." With that he took a golden chain which it was his custom to wear at banquets, and added it to the deed of liberation which he handed the girl.

Thus he did with all his servants, sending them away one by one. When he had made an end, he said to the faithful steward of his house:

"The earth belongs to God. Eliezer, my guide and father, go down into the city and sell my field, which is my portion and my possession, to some merchant, and bring me the price, that I may place it at the feet of the disciples. As for what is left in the house, of furnishings and raiment, take it for thee, my faithful friend and steward, that thy old age may be free from the fear of want."

Incomprehensible as these words and actions of his lord were for him, the old man went about the strange business with a stony face and a heart oppressed by care. He left the estate on the hill, went down into the city, and found a buyer. Before the evening had fallen he returned with the purchase money.

Bar Naba took the bag of gold, said his last farewell to the steward, and left the house without once looking back.

He went straight to the dwelling in the David wall, and there he found assembled all the disciples, with bar Jonah at their head. A line of suppliants, seekers for admission into the new congregation, had already formed; and bar Naba took his place in the line.

When his turn was reached, he placed the bag of gold at the feet of Simon, and said:

"This is the price of my earthly possessions, which I bring and lay at your feet. All that I possess now is the soul which God has put into my body, and I bring that to you. Take it, I beseech you, and make it of the sacred congregation, which calls on the name of God, which waits for the coming of his righteous deliverer, Yeshua the Nazarene, according to the message which he left with you."

Then Simon bar Jonah took Joseph bar Naba of the house of the Levites and baptized him in the name of God and of His Messiah, Yeshua the Nazarene, and received him into the congregation of the faithful, and called out to him:

"Our brother art thou."

And Joseph bar Naba was on that day one of many who let themselves be baptized in the name of Yeshua of Nazareth, for it was a day of plentiful harvest for the workers in the field.

Chapter Six

KHAIFA THE ROCK

IT was being bruited about in Jerusalem that the disciples of the Messiah, who came every day to the Temple courts and proclaimed his tidings, had received from him the power and authority to heal the sick, to bring ease to the heavy of heart, and even to drive out evil spirits. The authority had been given to all the disciples, but the greatest share was possessed by the sturdy fisherman of K'far Nahum, Simon, who was the first among them. The rumor spread first among the poor of Jerusalem and passed thence to the chain of beggars who waited daily about the vestibule of King Solomon in the Temple court, to the real or pretended cripples who crowded about the doors through which visitors and pilgrims passed.

It chanced one day that as Simon and Jochanan passed by the Vestibule of King Solomon, a man thrust himself forward from out of the throng of cripples. He could not walk, but had to drag himself forward on his knees. He lifted up toward Simon his bearded face, on which supplication was written, but whether it was supplication for bread, for money, for healing, or for something higher, for his soul, no one could tell. And it may have been that he begged for all of these things, for the supplication on his face was endless. It was as if all the winds of God and all the shadows of the night had passed across his face. His supplication was compounded of an infinitude of supplications, which started out dumbly from his distended eyes, together with his tears.

In Simon's heart the floodgates of pity were opened, and pity poured through all his limbs and body. Pity descended on him and seized him, as if it were a wild beast. And now it was Simon's face, that simple fisherman's face with its heavy lines and scars, with its sad eyes and tangled beard, which radiated supplication. Simon called out to the cripple:

"Look at us!"

The cripple's eyes became even more distended. There spread over his features an expectation of bliss and of good tidings; and he gazed intently from one to the other, from Simon to Jochanan, from Jochanan to Simon. Thirst was written in his eyes; it was as if they were sucking in the features of Simon and of Jochanan. And from Simon's eyes, as in response, there looked forth immeasurable faith, to quench the thirst of the other. So they gazed at each other, and the beggar became drunk with Simon's look. He lost his will and delivered himself into the hands of him whom he believed in as his helper; he opened his mouth, as if he wanted to shriek out something about the marvelous and unnatural change that was taking place in him, and he stretched out an eager hand toward the wells of pity which shone in Simon's eyes.

"Silver and gold I have not," said Simon in a deep, hoarse voice, "but that which I have I give thee. In the name of Yeshua the Nazarene, arise and walk."

The beggar seemed to be stupefied, as if the words had been hammer blows delivered on his head. He still kneeled before Simon, and his face remained fixed on Simon's.

60

But Simon bar Jonah stepped forward, took hold of the cripple, and with his powerful hand lifted him toward himself; and the legs of the cripple, which were paralyzed, and did not dare to believe in themselves, did not trust themselves to support the weight of the body, obeyed the will of Simon, which broke through into the flesh of the beggar and became his will. The cripple tottered and swayed on his thin legs, which were now stiff, like drawn wires. He stood there like a newborn calf, swayed right and left, thought he would fall any moment, but did not fall; he stood, and took a few paces forward.

All this took place at the hour when the Priests were bringing the afternoon sacrifice, and in the courts was heard the blowing of the silver trumpets. The Levites on the steps which led to the entrance of the Women's Court began to sing their Psalms; and the multitudes which had come to the Temple in order to pray at the time of the sacrifices threw themselves to the ground, pressed their faces into the marble floor of the court, and murmured the prayer of the coming of the Messiah:

"And as to the seed of the House of David, Thy servant, cause it to blossom soon, and lift up his heart with Thy help, for we await Thy help every day. Blessed art Thou, O Lord, who upliftest the horn of salvation."

Through the silence which lay like a covering of peace and protection over the congregation, there rang a sudden cry:

"Hosannah! Hosannah!"

The congregation prostrate, absorbed in prayer, would not look up, but still the voice kept ringing through the silence, taking a higher pitch:

"Hosannah! Hosannah!"

Then, the prayer ended, the worshipers looked up, and faces still illumined with prayer were turned, one upon the other, questioningly.

"What is it? What has happened?"

"A miracle! A miracle from heaven!"

A number of men came running into the court.

"The Galileans who assemble in the vestibule of King Solomon, and who preach of the Messiah who has come, and of the forgiveness of sin through the death of their Messiah, have performed a miracle, in the name of their Messiah!"

"How? What? Where?"

"Nehemiah the cripple, who begs at the gate of the court, has been healed in the name of the Messiah."

"Who performed the miracle?"

"There were two of them, disciples both, Simon and Jochanan, who come every day with their companions and converts to pray here. Simon, the short, heavy man with the tangled beard, he was the leader in it."

"In whose name did you say they healed?"

"In the name of Yeshua, the Messiah of Nazareth. So they call him."

"My Rabbis! Teach me! Who is this Yeshua of Nazareth, whom they call the 'Ancient of Days', and 'King Messiah'? Who is he? Where is he?" These words came from a half naked man who walked about, in his girdle of wild beast skin, among the multitude; his bronzed face was that of a man of the wilderness. "I am of the disciples of Jochanan. We dwell in the wilderness of Judaea, and we wait for the Messiah. And now we hear them say that the Messiah has already come. Who has seen him?"

"Ignorant men of Galilee say they have seen him; the kind that say 'sibboleth' for 'shibboleth' because they cannot even speak aright."

"Is it not the Yeshua who was hanged from the cross this last Passover? Ah, I knew it at once. I knew that something would come of that. I once heard him teach here, in the Temple, and I saw by his face that he brought that with him which—well, I know not—I have always waited for him. And now, thank God, we have lived to see the hour."

"Who knows! It may indeed be that the time has come."

"O God, O Father in heaven, it would indeed be time."

Meanwhile the crowd had grown more dense round the threshold of King Solomon's Vestibule, where the miracle with the cripple had occurred. And now a procession of beggars and cripples, of the lame, the paralyzed, the blind and the half blind, set out from King Solomon's vestibule toward the Court of the Women, where the mass of the worshipers was assembled. At the head marched the cripple on whom the miracle had been wrought, a big raw-boned man with vast eyebrows and a beard that fell over his chest like an apron. As he marched he waved in the air the crutches on which he had supported himself during all the years that he had been seen begging in the Temple courts. Around him and behind him swarmed the multitude of beggars and cripples in their tattered burlap coverings, their naked bodies showing through the rents: a procession of swollen bellies, watering and suppurating eyes, twisted limbs. Tapping with their staves on the stones of the court, they cried, as they performed a grotesque imitation of a dance:

"Hosannah! Hosannah in the name of the son of David!"

"Hosannah in the name of the anointed of Jacob!"

A blind man who had become separated from the procession, and who seemed to be under the impression that the division of the Kingdom was taking place there and then without him, shouted, desperately: "I want my share, my portion, in the Kingdom of Heaven! I am a son of Israel, of the tribe of Naphthali, and I have been waiting long for the coming of the Messiah."

A dense circle formed round Simon and Jochanan. It consisted not only of beggars and cripples but of regular worshipers in the Temple and of the pupils of the famous Rabbis who had their open schools in the courts—Rabban Gamaliel, Rabbi Jochanan ben Zachai, and others. Before long an enormous throng engulfed the two disciples. And there was a furious babbling of voices, in which one question recurred insistently: Who was he whom they proclaimed as the Messiah and in whose name they had performed the miracle?

Simon cried out:

"Men of Israel! Why are you filled with wonder by this thing that has happened, and why do you gaze upon us as though the miracle had come to pass through our power? Not we have performed it, but the name of Yeshua the Messiah through us."

No sooner had Simon proclaimed these words and exalted the name of his Messiah than the crowd began to dissolve. The listeners hastened away from the spot as if they feared to be caught in association with the new doctrine. Simon lifted up his eyes and saw approaching Alexander of the House of Fabi, the overseer of the Temple, surrounded by Temple guards.

Alexander of the House of Fabi was notorious for the savagery of his discipline. His appearance was of a piece with his reputation. The thick, heavy ringlets of his hair covered his naked back, and as he walked they danced and seemed to hammer his flesh. In front the twisted plaits of his beard beat similarly on his naked breast. His massive legs,

63

which seemed to be poured of metal, came out alternately from under the folds of his priestly garments, and he walked with iron footsteps, casting a terror into all beholders. On his chest hung the tablet of his authority, by virtue of which he could take prisoner any one who transgressed against the laws of the Temple courts; and in his hand he carried a whip, whose multiple thongs were loaded with iron weights. Behind him, in a double row, marched the guards. Like him, they were naked to the waist, and the locks of head and beard hung down on their flesh; like him, too, they carried in their hands whips with many thongs. As they drew nearer to the multitude about the disciples, Simon bar Jonah grew visibly paler. His eyebrows quivered, and his voice grew weaker. Still he continued to proclaim the tidings.

Simon bar Jonah was a son of Israel. For him, as for all the sons of Israel, the High Priest was the ruler over Jewry, the supreme authority, the anointed one, of the line of Aaron. The fear of the High Priest had passed into his blood with the tradition of countless generations; and in the heart of the simple fisherman a bitter struggle now went on. Deep was his faith in his deliverer; deep also was his dread of the authority of the High Priest. His knees seemed to melt under him, and as on the previous occasion, when he had been held by the servants of the High Priest near the fire, while his Rabbi was being tried, his tongue began to stammer, and the ground heaved under his feet. He would have liked to flee, as the others were doing. But broadshouldered Jochanan, standing behind him, laid a heavy hand on Simon's covering of burlap, brought his bristling beard close to the other's ear, and growled angrily:

"Simon bar Jonah, wouldst thou deny the lord a second time in the hour of trial?"

A quiver of shame passed through Simon. His heart contracted, his eyes wandered. Then he came to. It would not happen again. No; this time he would not deny him.

Simon bar Jonah remained standing at his post, though his limbs were like water. His eyes were covered with mist, but he looked back steadfastly at the Temple overseer.

"By whose authority dost thou this thing?"

"By the authority of my lord and savior, Yeshua of Nazareth, who has risen from the dead."

"Meanest thou the Yeshua who was hanged on the eve of Passover? Meanest thou that blasphemer? Take them! They shall answer for it to the High Priest!"

Instantly the guards seized Simon and Jochanan, pinning their arms behind their backs.

Voices rose from among those who had not fled at the approach of the overseer.

"By what right, and in the name of what law, do they lay hands on Rabbis in Israel who preach the resurrection?"

"They have neither said nor done anything against the laws—for our Rabbis teach the same."

"The sons of Eli hate all those who preach the resurrection. Knowest thou why?"

"Nay, why?"

"Because they alone of all the house of Israel will remain for ever in the depths of hell."

"Alas for the chains of the sons of Eli, which are heavier on our necks than the bonds of Edom!"

The loaded whips of the guards began to fly about the heads and shoulders of the protesters; the two prisoners were thrust forward toward the dungeons of the Temple, which were outside the gates, next to the Hall of the Sanhedrin, by the chamber of the Hewn Stones.

The hour was too late for the holding of a trial, and Simon and Jochanan were held prisoners till the next day. In the darkness of the long hours of that night Simon was aware of a great inner light. He remembered that Elijah the Prophet had been a prisoner in the dungeons of the Temple; and other prophets, too, had been confined here because they had dared to proclaim God's truth against the mighty. All through the night Simon prayed:

"O Father in heaven, even as I believe in Thy holy servant, in the deliverer whom Thou hast sent to us in our poverty; even as I have seen him with the eyes of my flesh and the eyes of my spirit; even so do Thou strengthen me, so that I may be able to serve him in all purity. When Thou wilt place me face to face with the mighty, to bear witness for Thy holy servant, put Thy mantle about me to shield me from the piercing glance of the strong. Fill my heart with faith as the grape is full of softness. Let the strength of Thy truth be in the light of mine eyes, that they may be as steel against the sharp arrows of their looks. O Lord, let the shadow of Thy holy servant fall upon me. When Thou

65

lettest me be brought to judgment, grant that I feel the presence of Thy holy servant, in order that I may bear faithful testimony to the truth which Thou hast made mine eyes to see and my hands to feel. Strengthen me, O God, and make me worthy to serve Thy servant in truth and love. Amen!"

In the morning Alexander the overseer placed his report before the Chief Officer of the Temple, Jochanan, but the latter did not think the matter of sufficient importance to bring it to the attention of the old High Priest, Chanan, who was charged with all incidents occurring within the Temple precincts. Nor was he inclined to make an issue of it before the present High Priest. Actually he was more amused than indignant and found the story both ludicrous and insignificant: a couple of gross, illiterate Galileans had persuaded themselves that one of their countrymen was the promised Messiah and had risen from the dead. This was nothing to make the foundations of the Temple tremble, and Jerusalem could still sleep safely. Many "Messiahs" had arisen; they had flourished for a few days, then they had vanished, never to be heard from again. This Messiah, too, would die the natural death of oblivion.

Despite Jochanan's resolve to dismiss the matter, it somehow came to the attention of the old High Priest, Chanan, who was however in full agreement with Jochanan as to the importance of the "dangerous criminals" who had been arrested by the Temple overseer.

"And those Galilean boors, who scattered like mice when their Rabbi was in danger, now gather round him when he is safely dead?"

He was wholly in agreement with his son, the Chief Officer of the Temple, that it would be an error to arouse interest in the matter. The word "Messiah" was like a bellows, capable of fanning a spark into a raging fire, and fire was not something to be played with. The Galilean louts ought to be called in, given a thorough talking to and warned never again to mention the name of their Messiah in the sacred precincts. With that they should be sent packing. A regular trial and judgment was out of the question. Indeed, if anyone was to be brought to trial, it ought to be the Pharisees, who were responsible for all this nonsense about resurrection.

Meanwhile it was bruited about in the household of the High Priest that the Temple Overseer had thrown into the dungeons the men of Galilee who had performed a miracle in the name of their Rabbi. The news created considerable excitement among the servants and officials of the priestly household, for nearly everyone remembered the man whom the Roman soldiers had seized and brought to be tried in the court of the High Priest. When the hour came for Simon and Jochanan to be led from the dungeons to the inner office, a crowd assembled, and one of the servant girls pointed to Simon and cried out loudly:

"There he is! That's the one who swore by everything he held holy that he had nothing to do with the man. That was the time when he stood with us, warming himself at the fire. And now that his Rabbi is dead, he preaches in his name!"

Simon bar Jonah recognized the servant girl's voice. The lids fell over his eyes, he felt a sudden tug at his heart, and he said inwardly:

"Lord of the world! Be with me in this hour!"

The High Priest, who was submitting to the ministrations of his Syrian hairdresser, was, for all his contemptuous attitude, curious to see the Galileans. He therefore sent word that the proceedings should not open before his arrival.

Old Chanan was quite certain that the simple fisher folk who had scattered in terror when their Rabbi had been arrested would fall on their faces in the presence of the High Priest, confess their sins, and promise never to repeat their blasphemies. There the matter would end. For this reason he had raised no objection to having the High Priest present. The Chief Officer, for his part, had objected on the grounds that such a gathering of the supreme officials would impart an artificial importance to the incident. But the old High Priest, and the High Priest in office, had their way.

But to the amazement of the supreme officials, and no less that of the Overseer, Alexander, and the attendants, the Galileans were not overwhelmed by this assembly of the hierarchy. For one instant only Simon bar Jonah seemed to lose himself. His knees were seen to tremble, and everyone expected that he would fall prostrate before the High Priest. But the next instant he had recovered. Instead of stammering and confessing, he looked back steadily at the High Priest and admitted in a loud, clear voice that he had been the instrument of the miracle performed the day before in the Temple court, and that the power had been that of Yeshua of Nazareth.

"Yea, in the name of my lord, the savior of Israel, Yeshua of Nazareth, whom we delivered into the hands of Edom and who on the third day rose from the dead."

The face of the High Priest became pale to the roots of his beard,

67

which still glistened with the oil poured on it by his hairdresser. Old Chanan drew down his thick white eyebrows over his eyes and tugged with one hand at his beard. The Chief Officer of the Temple, Jochanan, became very earnest. Chanan ben Chanan, the youngest son of old Chanan, who was also present, bit his upper lip. Only Alexander, the Overseer, responded at once. He lifted up his hand, as if to slap Simon bar Jonah, and cried out:

"Is this your answer to the High Priest?"

But the blow did not fall, for in that instant Alexander caught the glance of old Chanan. The High Priests looked at each other in silence. They were at a loss for words; the situation had not developed according to their expectation.

"Take the men out," commanded old Chanan.

The guards approached and conducted Simon and Jochanan into an adjoining room. The Priests remained silent, like images on their stone seats. Finally the High Priest spoke up:

"There are but two ways before us. Either we act with firmness and tear out this evil by the roots, that is, destroy these men for daring to proclaim as the Messiah one whom we found guilty of blasphemy; or else we release them and thereby give them permission to continue their agitation. If we do the latter, we tacitly confess to having committed a miscarriage of justice in handing over to the executioners a man who was utterly innocent."

"Confession or no confession," said one of the former High Priests, Eliezer, "it will be so interpreted by the people. Worse than that, we shall have displayed weakness."

"Nay, nay, you go too far," interrupted old Chanan. "Our only punishment is to expose these Galilean boors to ridicule; and, better still, to shame them to themselves, by showing them how foolish is their illusion concerning this Messiah of theirs. But it must be done with wisdom; with one hand we must thrust them from us, with the other draw them closer. Let this be my task. Bring in the men!"

When Simon and Jochanan stood again before the High Priests, old Chanan ordered the guards to leave the room. Then he turned upon Alexander, the Temple Overseer, in pretended indignation.

"By what right, and on the basis of what law, have these innocent, honest, and godfearing men been arrested and held prisoner?" He turned to Simon and Jochanan. "You are free, good men!" Then he turned back to Alexander and commanded him furiously to withdraw.

Simon and Jochanan stood paralyzed before the semicircle of High Priests. The sudden change in the attitude of their judges bewildered rather than reassured them. They did not dare yet to take old Chanan's words literally. They waited, and old Chanan continued:

"Sit down, good men, sit down among us, and we will talk this matter over at our ease. Not that, God forbid, we have aught against you. On the contrary, we rejoice that God has given you this power of prophecy. No doubt it is the place you frequent, the Temple court, which is responsible for the high privilege. We have heard, too, that you strengthen the spirit of the people, bidding them tread the path of righteousness. There is but one matter which divides us: that you do these things not in the name of the God of Israel, but in the name of one Yeshua the Nazarene, whom you call the Messiah. Now this no one can approve. You are pious and godfearing men, and you know well that all things come from the living God of Israel. Promise me, good men, that you will heed my words." And old Chanan stretched out his hand to Simon.

Simon was silent a moment, gathering together his thoughts. Then he lifted up his big, childlike eyes and looked at old Chanan and at the High Priest.

"Now tell me, even you," he said, "is it proper to turn one's back on God's command and to listen to the speech of men? We have received our command from God."

This was by no means the reply which old Chanan had expected. For a few moments he lost his poise. He looked sternly at the Galilean fishermen, trying to discover whether the answer had been given in all sincerity or whether it was a cunning countermove. But he could read nothing in Simon's face, which was open and naïve, like that of any man of Galilee. The childlike eyes were fixed on those of the old High Priest.

"God's command?" he repeated. "God's command to do what?"

"To spread the tidings of the Messiah in Israel."

"And through whom was this command of God delivered to you?"

"Through the Messiah himself, when he revealed himself to us after his death."

"After his death?"

"Yes, for God raised him up from death."

69

One of the Priests muttered impatiently to old Chanan: "But do you not see that you are dealing with stupid and ignorant folk, who do nothing but babble of resurrections?"

And another Priest added: "We have the Pharisees to thank for this—the harvest is of their sowing."

"Tell me, good man," said old Chanan smoothly to Simon bar Jonah, "are you not he who denied your Rabbi in the presence of the servants and maidservants of my household, when he, your Rabbi, was on trial before us?"

"Yes, I am he," answered Simon, still keeping his eyes on the old High Priest's face. "I was weak in the lord and failed him in the hour of his need. But I have prayed to God to strengthen me in the faith, and God has heard my prayer and has given me the power to stand with unshaken spirit in the presence of the High Priests."

The High Priests—those that had held office, he that was holding office now, and those that were in line for office—gazed intently at the fisherman. But Simon did not shrink; and still they did not know whether this was the fearlessness of simplicity or the boldness of cunning. Whichever it was, they felt keenly that the scene could not be prolonged, for with every passing minute their standing fell lower and lower with their own servants.

"You may go, good people," said old Chanan, and his voice was still even and friendly, at least on the surface. "You are free, both to preach and to continue in your good deeds. But bear in mind what I have said. Do not mention again the name of that man, or we shall be compelled to take measures against you, and it would not be to our liking to deal harshly with honest, pious, and godfearing people such as you are. You will remember, will you not?"

"We shall do as God has commanded us," answered Simon bar Jonah, from the door. "For it is not proper to place man's command above God's."

*   *   *

When Jochanan and Simon came out of the High Priest's office, Simon fell on his knees, lifted his arms to heaven, and exclaimed:

"I thank Thee, O God, for the strength Thou gavest me in the hour of trial."

When he stood up he observed that he was facing the masonry of

70

the well. This was the spot where, on that memorable night, the servants had made a fire, and he had denied his Rabbi.

Chapter Seven

SAUL OF TARSHISH

TWO souls lived side by side in the heart of the young man Saul, and they struggled for the mastery, even as Jacob and Esau had struggled in the womb of their mother, Rebeccah.

Saul had passed his childhood and boyhood in Tarshish, in the modest home of his father, who had been a goat's hair weaver. From his earliest years he had known that he lived on a little island set in an ocean of paganism, sinfulness, and despair and that whatever was fine, decent, purified, and bound up with God was to be found in his father's house, in the little street of the Jews, and in the house of God, the synagogue. He had studied, as a little boy, in the school attached to the synagogue and had absorbed at an early age the Torah of his people, the Pentateuch, the Prophets, and the other sacred books. He had been deeply affected, even then, by the utterances of the Prophets, and his mind had been filled with fiery visions of "the end of days." But the tumultuous life of the city of Tarshish had not left him unaffected; for it had poured past him through a thousand channels, roaring about his father's house and about the little workshop of the weavers. Greek had been Saul's second mother tongue; and though his father had seen to it that the boy should grow up an adept in the lore of the Jewish people, he had not neglected his secular studies but had also engaged a special teacher of Greek literature. Thus Saul grew up, as many Hellenized Jews did in his day, with a thorough knowledge of the books and culture of the surrounding world; and as he grew into young manhood there arose in him, in spite of his contempt for the idol-worship of the gentiles, and even in the teeth of it, a grudging admiration of their serenity and wholeness of spirit, their joy of life, and their feeling for the beautiful.

71

Tarshish was something more than the city of the goat's hair weavers. Gleaming like a jewel in the green plain under the shadow of Mount Taurus, Tarshish was the crown of the province of Cilicia. The waters of the Cydnus, fed by the melting snows of Mount Taurus, connected the rich little inland province of Asia Minor with the Mediterranean. Great rafts of felled trees and galaxies of ships carrying wheat, oil, wine, and fruits floated down the river. The sails of a score of cities floated on the Cydnus, and in the streets of Tarshish could be heard the jargons and dialects of a score of countries. The city was full of craftsmen from the Greek islands, Egyptian cooks and dancing girls, Assyrian perfume mixers and magicians, Sidonian merchants, and Roman legionaries, officials, scribes, and tax-gatherers. But above all, there were philosophers, teachers, and their pupils.

For Tarshish was not simply a city of labor and commerce. It ranked with Alexandria and Rome as the city of scholars and thinkers. To Tarshish came the youth of Asia Minor in quest of knowledge. Every school of thought was represented there. Since the days of Athenadorius, who had been the teacher of Augustus, her academies had been famous for their courses in arithmetic, rhetoric, and astronomy. There too were taught the loftiest moral codes, the systems designed to ennoble human life and help it achieve the highest degree of perfection.

There was nothing lacking which might contribute to the happiness of the people of Tarshish. In addition to earthly and divine riches, they possessed also that highest of mortal privileges, the freedom of the city of Rome. Ever since the time of Pompey the Great, Tarshish had been part of the Roman Empire, and her inhabitants enjoyed the supreme protection of Roman citizenship. Julius Caesar had confirmed Pompey's decree, and it had never been challenged since that day.

But neither the earthly riches of Tarshish, nor the wisdom of her teachers, nor the privilege of Roman citizenship, could provide her inhabitants with the one highest happiness which man can know, that which binds him to the ultimate principle of life and guides him along the path of light into eternity: they could not provide him with faith.

The days of Tarshish were like the days of a drunkard, and her nights were the nights of harlots.

All the moralistic teachings of her sages did not place upon her inhabitants a single binding obligation; philosophers and pupils alike were pulled along in the stream of whoredom and sin, in the Syrian idol worship of Sardanapalus, the abominations of the Baal of Canaan, and the filth of Ashtoreth.

By day the Greek sages preached the highest morality, the virtues of modesty, continence, and simplicity; they taught the Stoic law of contentment with the bare necessities of life; they taught that the soul of man is part of the essence of the gods and that it was man's duty to flee from the nothingness of earthly existence in order that his soul might be united with the divinities. But without a God and without a Torah the words of the Greek sages were as empty as the clashing of cymbals. Tarshish was a melting pot in which the unrestrained dissoluteness of the Orient fused with the refined viciousness of the Greeks. The Greeks and Oriental gods had entered into a conspiracy to drown the spirit of man in an ocean of limitless depravity. About the body of the young man Saul had swirled, like a poisonous miasma, the clouds of incense which went up from the groves, the gardens, and the temples, from the baths, from the banquet halls of the rich, and from the sour-smelling drinking places of the poor, where orgies like those of Sodom and Gomorrah were repeated nightly. The image of man, created in that of his Creator, was defiled by the removal of the boundaries of sex; men, crazed with drink, and painted like whores, wandered about the streets. The orgies spared neither man nor woman, neither the old nor the young. Children were pulled into the torrent of profligacy. And all this was practiced not by ignorant Canaanitish Phoenicians, but by the followers of Plato, by the pupils of the Stoics, and by the preachers of the morals of Facedonius.

The young man Saul walked the sunny streets of Tarshish, and one question tormented him insistently: Why had God created Jews *and* gentiles? Wherein were the gentiles guilty if God had not revealed Himself to their forefathers, had not made a covenant with them, and had not bestowed on them a Moses and a Torah? He knew, indeed, that the Messiah would be a second Moses, who would come to the gentiles with the offer to make them Jews: and either they would accept or be doomed to eternal hell. But where was he, this Messiah? Why was his coming delayed?

Young Saul was for ever anticipating the great event. The hope of it had penetrated him so deeply that he looked upon his whole life

73

as a preparation for the coming of the Messiah and even as an instrument for its hastening. The studies of his boyhood in the holy books had been for him the beginning of the redemption. In those days he had conceived this redemption as being associated only with his own people; but with the years he had accustomed himself to think of a Messiah for all the world. His understanding of the gentiles, the love which—sometimes to his own terror—he discovered in himself for them, led him to believe in a Messiah who would cover, as with a mantle, all the nations. So closely was the hope of the world intertwined in him with the hope of the Jewish Messiah, that the latter gradually took on the aspect not simply of an earthly liberator but of a divine redeemer. The Messianic passages in the Books of the Prophets, in the Book of Daniel, and in the Judaeo-Hellenistic literature, worked incessantly on his imagination. No, he decided; not simply a Messiah for the Jews, but a Messiah who would change the whole order of the world.

To the vision of such a Messiah he dedicated his life. He was aware of certain feelings which he dared not give reign to; of certain thoughts which he dared not think through. Afraid of them himself, he did not breathe a word of them to others. They were the inmost secret of his life, binding him, from boyhood on, to the Messiah. They were born of his passionate desire to witness, and indeed to hasten, the redemption; they were born also of his love for his fellow Jews and of his compassion for the gentiles, whom he saw engulfed in bottomless vileness. And the substance of these feelings, half acknowledged, half repressed, and of these thoughts which he dared not think through, was this: that he had been dedicated in his mother's womb to the approaching Messiah.

Very early in his manhood he began to mold his life consciously in the spirit of his exalted vision of his destiny. He took certain religious vows and practiced secret fasts. Like a Nazirite, he sundered himself from the surrounding world, spending his nights as well as his days in the study of sacred and secular books. He denied himself the ordinary luxuries of life and persistently ignored the hints of his parents that it was time for him to take a wife to himself and to build a house of his own. It was as if he had given himself wholly to God. His health, which had never been too good, suffered from the severe discipline of the vows which he imposed on himself. Very often he would work himself into a condition of ecstasy which resembled a trance; he would fall down, and foam would break out on his lips. His parents were terrified by the recurrence of these incidents, but they could not persuade him to alter his manner of life. This was his decision, and no one could swerve him from it.

He began to speak of Jerusalem and of his need to go there, so that he might sit at the feet of Rabban Gamaliel and drink from the purest source of Jewish lore; he spoke of the Temple, where he would feel himself close to the heart of Israel and the word of God. Here, indeed, he struck an answering chord in the heart of his parents. What Jewish father or mother in the lands of the dispersion did not dream of having a son studying in the Holy City? Who would not be proud of a son enrolled among the students of the illustrious Rabban Gamaliel?

With her own hands his mother wove for him his shirts and his student's mantle; lovingly she packed his bags when the day came for his father to go up with him to Jerusalem on one of the pilgrimages. Nor would Saul arrive in the Holy City a complete stranger. His father had a letter of introduction to the Chief or Prince of the Pharisees, and a married sister of his had her home in Jerusalem.

Very soon after his arrival in the Holy City, Saul made the acquaintance of Joseph bar Naba. The two young men were drawn to each other by their common language, their common education in the Jewish-Hellenistic literature, and, above all, by their common faith in the coming of the Messiah. But it was not an equal friendship. Joseph bar Naba under the dominion of Saul was like clay in the hands of the potter. Almost before he knew it, he had changed completely in the matter of his Messianic dreams; for him too the Messiah was transformed from a deliverer of the Jews into a deliverer of mankind.

On the one hand, the wealthy, aristocratic young man of Cyprus was overwhelmed by the disciplined bearing of Saul; on the other hand, Saul found in bar Naba the one spirit to whom he could pour out all his dreams and visions of the Messiah. It was a friendship which endured until the day when bar Naba declared that he had found his Messiah.

For Saul the break was even more painful than for Joseph, and he vented his bitterness and disappointment on the "disciples" who had robbed him of his friend. For among the students of Rabban Gamaliel, bar Naba alone had been prepared to put up with the harsh ways of Saul and to endure patiently his overbearing spirit. Love gave him patience and taught him forgiveness; and when he went out of Saul's life, the latter perceived how few there were among his fellow students to whom he could turn for friendship. For Saul was regarded in the school as a hard man, one who "was quick in the kindling of his anger and slow in forgiveness." He was known widely for his obstinacy; when Saul of Tarshish had made up his mind on any question, it was useless to try to change him. In argument he was passionate and unregardful of the feelings of others. They applied to him, sardonically, the verse: "All my limbs shall praise the Lord," for in debate— if that could be called debate in which Saul of Tarshish participated— he spoke with hands and feet and eyes.

But if they could not love Saul of Tarshish they admired and respected him. No one had ever challenged the purity of his motives. Whatever Saul of Tarshish did or said was in the name of heaven; he sought nothing for himself. In his heart blazed the fire of a great love for the God of Israel, for the people of Israel, and for its redemption. Saul was compounded of nothing but faith. Nor was faith for him merely an abstraction, even as God was not for him a divine Father of purely unimaginable form. Faith was for Saul, very often, an apparition in the flesh, a daily experience. Faith in a heavenly Father was the only possession of worth, and for its sake alone the burden of life was endurable. He did not think of faith as something apart, a separate refuge for himself, a reward, or a promise of reward, for his righteousness. He desired neither glory nor praise. Only in God the Father did all life possess meaning and suffering its justification. Life for its own sake was not worth the tribulation it entailed; it consisted, in itself, of a chain of torments, individual and general, physical and moral, a chain of innumerable links. The only enduring happiness it afforded lay in the bond with a heavenly Father.

Companion Saul was not only a powerful preacher; he was one who subjected his own body to the disciplines he preached. He had known the torments of the flesh from his childhood on. A malarial disease had fastened on his bones and like a hidden leech ate into their marrow. His bones became soft, his blood watery. No word of complaint ever passed his lips, even to his nearest friend. It was a point of pride with him to bear his affliction like a secret gift from God, for "he whom God loves He punishes," said the Holy Script, and the sages taught, "Afflictions are God's bestowals upon his saints." Yet Saul knew that in nurturing this pride he was committing a mortal sin which might cause him to fall to the lowest level. So he fought with his pride too; and he would have liked to expose his sorrows to others, in order that he might lower himself in their esteem. But he could not bring himself to do it. The pride which locked his lips against his companions was his second nature.

His physical torments did not cause him to diminish by a hair's breadth his determination to outdo the most disciplined of his companions in his submission to the rules and ordinances of the House of Hillel. He did not permit himself the luxury of sleeping on a soft bed or of lying down on a bamboo mattress under the covering of a roof. The brief hours of the summer nights he passed in the courtyard of the House of Study; winter nights he slept on a hard bench in the dormitory. Weekdays his food consisted almost entirely of flat cakes of bread, a little fruit, and a few olives. His drink was water. Very rarely did he touch wine. Most of the time he was under the secret vows of a Nazirite, taken for one reason or another. But often his behavior betrayed his secret and brought him into conflict with his teacher. The taking of Nazirite vows of abstention was against the spirit of the House of Hillel, and Rabban Gamaliel reproved his pupil sharply. "Those who multiply vows," he said, "multiply sin. They transgress against the commandment: 'Ye shall care greatly for your bodies.' And do not play the saint too much, for playing the saint leads to pride of spirit, and pride in a saint is like a worm in a sweet apple. He who takes many vows considers all others sinful." It was told of Saul that his Rabbi's reproof was not without its effect and that it prevented him from going out into the wilderness and joining the Essenes, a plan which he had contemplated for some time. It was one of the very rare instances, in Saul's life, of submission to outside influence. But Rabban Gamaliel could not persuade Saul to take himself a wife, as nearly all the other companions had done. This was Rabban Gamaliel's constant advice to his pupils, that they marry young, in order that they might have "bread in their basket," also that they might not be haunted by the desires of the flesh, which were an impurity in themselves and a hindrance to the study of the Torah. "Two things are good for a man to do in his youth, to take himself a wife and to choose a path for himself," he taught them. But Saul had answered him: "I have already taken to wife the eternal virgin, God's Torah, and along whatever path God will choose to lash me, that path will I follow."

In spite of these words, Saul had chosen, if not a path, at least an occupation. For while his fellow students paid lip service to the ideal of following a handicraft but lived either on public charity or the gifts of their kinsmen, Saul provided for his modest needs by pursuing the trade of a goat's hair weaver, which he had learned in his native town. Two or three times a week he hired himself out to a fellow countryman, a tent-maker, who had his workshop in the Kidron valley, under the wall on the road to the Mount of Olives. This work Saul did at the expense of his studies. Every student was supposed to know the verses of the Hebrew text by heart. But there were also many laws and ordinances of later formulation which had never been written down but were transmitted by word of mouth and also had to be learned by heart. There were customs and regulations which had come down with the spoken tradition; there were parables and aphorisms in which these customs and traditions were embodied. The studies of Rabban Gamaliel's pupils covered every branch of life, and there were not hours enough in the day for a mastery of the complete subject matter. Saul could not keep pace with the curriculum, because of the time he lost at his trade, but he could not be persuaded to seek an easier way, such as the other students had found. He regarded the earning of his bread by the labor of his hands as an important principle, perhaps the most important principle of the moral life. For, being dependent on no one other than himself for his daily bread, he was free to act and speak as his conscience dictated, and this he considered more essential to the moral life than training and knowledge. In matters which concerned Saul's conception of the moral life no compromise was possible, not even under the pressure of his honored teacher.

But he derived from his obstinate pursuit of a trade one advantage which was denied his fellow pupils. He learned the ways of life, not from the theory of laws, but by contact with the reality; he saw at first hand the hills and valleys which confront man and the winding paths which life must follow. He came in daily contact with the very poorest of the poor. He saw men and women, and even children, prepared to sell all that they had—their strength—for a morsel of bread; but there was no buyer. He saw women who gave away the adornment

God had meant for them, the locks of their hair, to the hairdressers, to adorn the heads of others. He saw the outworn bodies of old laborers thrown into the street, like garbage. The young man Saul knew the meaning of life. He knew that for the poor man there was no hope save in the life which lay beyond death, when the Messiah would call him forth from his grave.

But the hope of a life after death, and of a righteous redeemer, was given not only to the children of Israel. Saul found many aliens in Jerusalem, slaves and freedmen, of Askelon and Sidon, and even Samaritans, who had reached—God knew by what paths—the lowest depths of the lower city, and in them too burned the hope of a Messiah King. They had heard from some Jewish neighbor of the resurrection; or perhaps they had learned it from the lips of some preacher, that and the kindred gift of the Messiah, which made up the inheritance of Israel; and they pleaded for a share in the inheritance. They wanted to come in under the skirts of the mantle. For what had these people else? What did they possess apart from their bodies, which hungered when they were in health, and rotted when they were sick, and were thrown out like the carcasses of animals in death, to be eaten by the flies in the daytime and by beasts in the night.

In the outer circle there is cold, trembling, and gnashing of teeth, and all of them yearn for the inner circle, for the tent of Israel, for the fire where they may warm their souls and by which they may see a comforting faith.

Saul the student listened intently when he heard these, the forlorn and abandoned, the friendless and betrayed, speak of the Messiah. More than once he had discussed the matter with his fellow workers at the loom. More than once he had overheard little groups whispering of it in the dark corners of the synagogues. Donkey drivers and camel drivers gathering round the waters of Siloah had this hope on their lips, and Saul had caught it, again, from the lips of the washerwomen kneeling by the Kidron stream, fed by the waters of Hezekiah's Pool.

But Saul also knew how deep in the people the Galileans had planted the roots of the false new faith, that the Messiah had already come. The Messiah had come, and the earth was still steeped in sin! The Messiah had come, and Israel still lay like a chained sheep at the feet of Edom! What was there to do but drive out from the vineyard of God the foxes which were devouring its grapes? These men, who were deluding the people with a false hope, were an abomination in Israel. Deceivers they were, preying on the pitiful longings of their people.

Nor had they spread their net of deceit only among those who dwelt in the darkness of ignorance! They had reached out for the best in Israel. Saul's friend bar Naba, tender-hearted and susceptible, had fallen into the trap and was lost to him. Parched with thirst, he had gone to them, and they had given him of their poison to drink. And many others were in his case, fellow countrymen of Saul's, students, and for that matter teachers, too, Reb Istephan, and the gentle-spirited Philippus, of the Cyrenean Synagogue, and Timon, the pure of heart, who had always longed for the redemption, and Nicholas, the gentile convert, saintly and scholarly. Day by day the number of victims grew, among the learned no less than among the simple folk, and the Rabbis stood by and did nothing. Day by day the evil increased —Jews who had blasphemed against the principles of the Jewish faith, offering up prayer to a man who had been hanged on the cross. Where was a new Phineas, to defend the honor of God with fitting zeal?

Saul did not keep these furious thoughts to himself.

The Study House of the Master, or Prince of the Pharisees, together with the courtyard, was on the street of the cheese-makers, which sloped downward from the upper city. Like all such institutions, the Study House consisted of a group of buildings, while at the center of the level court there was a water cistern surrounded by a fence. Stone benches were ranged about the cistern, for the convenience of students and visitors, and on these, one hot afternoon, a few men were seated, discussing the extraordinary incident—it had set all Jerusalem by the ears—of the followers of the new Messiah who had been arrested by the Temple Overseer and then released by the High Priests.

"Once they were brought before the court of the Priests and the High Priest himself was present, they should have been pronounced guilty and wiped out." It was Saul of Tarshish who spoke, and every word fell with the distinctness of a hammer blow.

"But wherefore should such bloody sentence be delivered against them? Is it because they believe in the resurrection?"

"No!" answered Saul, in a ringing voice. "Not because they believe in the resurrection, but because they preach a false Messiah. They proclaim one that was hanged. And concerning such a one it is written: 'The curse of God rests upon him.' "

"Who shall count the number of the Jews who have been hanged upon the cross by Herod, and of those whose suspended bodies have lined the roads of Judaea by the orders of Varus? Wilt thou say that the curse of God rests upon them, too? Do we not know that they were saints, and that they died to sanctify the Name? Ah, Saul, let thy portion in the world to come, and mine too, be no worse than theirs. Now bethink thee of their Rabbi, and of what they say concerning him, that he is the Messiah. He was not tried by a Jewish court, nor found guilty by one. The Rabbis were not present at his trial. In our eyes he must be accounted as a newborn child for sinlessness. And if there is truth in what his disciples say, namely, that he rose from death, then this is surely proof that he died without the stain of sin. If there is truth in the saying that on one that is hanged rests the curse of God, then I tell you that the saying does not apply to such a one. On the contrary, a Jew who died thus must be accounted among us as a martyr and a saint. He died untouched by the shadow of guilt; he died for the sanctification of the Name."

"But I say that for these very reasons the liberation of the disciples will be a calamity for all the generations to come. For no sooner will the common people know that these disciples stood before the High Priest and yet were set free than they will flock to them to listen to their doctrine. They will gather in, from this time on, souls without number."

"But if their cause is just, why should they not?"

"But seest thou not whither this thing leads?"

"And because of what thou fearest wouldst thou condemn Jews to death, against the laws of the Torah?"

"For the greater glory of God and of His holy Temple," cried Saul.

"And I say that for the greater glory of God and of His Torah they have merited life," answered the first student.

The students shrank away from Saul.

Chapter Eight

RABBAN GAMALIEL

IN the household and among the followers of the High Priest it soon became evident that it had been a mistake to liberate the disciples of the Galilean—the more so since the High Priest himself had lent the dignity of his presence to the proceedings. All sorts of stories were current in Jerusalem, and their gist was that Simon, the simple fisherman of K'far Nahum, had stood up daringly to the High Priest himself and had come off none the worse for it. The unpunished courage of Simon was interpreted as proof that the Galileans were not only sure of the truth of their tidings, but were protected by higher powers. And if this was the case, did it not mean that there was some deep significance in what they proclaimed? Who could tell, then, how far their message carried?

Regretting the leniency which had been shown the Galileans on the occasion of their first arrest, the High Priest now issued orders that if the blasphemers appeared again in the Temple court, they were to be arrested again, and imprisoned, not in the Temple dungeon, but in a special fortress in the heart of the city.

The Galileans duly appeared in the Temple court, and the High Priest's orders were obeyed, but the incident did not pass off smoothly. It was manifest that the preachers of the new doctrine had made an impression on the masses, for a large crowd of the poor attempted to prevent the arrest, and there was an unseemly scuffle. More remarkable, however, was the fact that a number of learned Pharisees, occupying covered porches in the Temple court, raised their voices loudly in protest, while several Priests actually joined the crowd which interfered with the guard in the execution of its duty.

But all this was as nothing compared with what followed. The morning after the second arrest of the Galileans, Jochanan, the Chief Officer of the Temple, was astounded to receive from the Temple Overseer the report that Simon and Jochanan, who had been placed under lock and key in the special prison, were at large in the courts, preaching their dangerous doctrines again. How had they escaped? Had they secret sympathizers among the priestly guards themselves? An immediate investigation was ordered; the guards naturally denied any complicity in the escape. Driven into a corner, they suggested that a miracle had taken place: a band of angels had descended and freed the Galileans. For the High Priests this suggestion was infinitely more dangerous than the breach of discipline which they suspected. But as the culprits could not be identified, the High Priests contented themselves with warning the guard sternly to make no mention of angels and miracles, particularly as the Sadducean doctrine denied the existence of angels. This injunction was as futile as the investigation. With lightning speed the miraculous version of the liberation spread through the masses in the Temple court and in the city. It was fostered by the Galileans themselves, and it was caught up eagerly by a miracle-hungry populace. The standing of the Galileans was immeasurably strengthened, and it became obvious that a third arrest, unless carried out with the utmost skill, would meet with such opposition as the High Priesthood did not dare to provoke.

But a third arrest had to be made, and it was ordered. The guards were instructed to wait until the evening, when the preaching Galileans were leaving the Temple court and the crowds of their followers had dwindled to a handful of men. Swiftly and silently the disciples were surrounded and spirited away almost before their companions were aware of what had happened. This time Simon and Jochanan were thrown into the prison-room on the premises of the High Priest's court; a double guard of picked men was thrown about the prison. The Small Sanhedrin would be convoked with the least possible delay for action against the Galileans.

The High Priests were under no illusions as to the opposition which they would meet, in this procedure, from the Pharisaic leaders. But old Chanan warned them that without the presence of the Prince of the Pharisees, Rabban Simon ben Gamaliel, the trial would fail of its effect; whereas if Rabban Gamaliel could be persuaded to participate and to lend his authority to a negative judgment, the new movement would receive a death blow. An invitation was therefore dispatched to the Rabban Gamaliel to attend the next session of the Small Sanhedrin, which was to try the men of Galilee on the charge of blasphemy committed in the Temple court.

The invitation was no sooner received by the Master than the entire household was apprised of it. Rabban Gamaliel sent for Rabbi Nicodemon and the rich man Joseph Arimathea, both of whom, it was known, had been acquainted with the Rabbi, Yeshua of Nazareth: and he closeted himself with them in the special office of the Master of the Pharisees, which was located above the cedar roof covering one of the alleys of pillars in the Temple court. There he interrogated them closely concerning the Rabbi of Galilee, asking what manner of man he had been, how he had conducted himself, what he had taught his followers, and also what had happened at the trial. All this the Master needed in order that he might be able to pass judgment on the men who now declared that the Rabbi of Galilee was none other than the Messiah.

Among the pupils of Rabban Gamaliel none was so passionately interested in the incident as Saul of Tarshish. His fellow students were amazed and startled by the feverish manner in which he discussed the forthcoming trial, and more so by his transgression of the rules pertaining to these situations. For whenever a Pharisaic teacher was called in to pass judgment on someone accused of a crime, it was permissible for his pupils to say something in defense of the accused; it was not permitted to them to join in the prosecution. But Saul did more than aid the prosecution, as it were, among his fellow students; he carried on what amounted to a public agitation against the Galileans. He visited the synagogues of the Greek-speaking Jews, he spoke to the merchants in the public squares, he dared to assail the followers of the Galileans in the very Temple court. But his principal activity was concentrated on the vast household of the Master, with its many departments. He even went so far as to approach those fellow students of his whom the Master had charged with the preparation of material for the forthcoming trial. This was regarded not simply as tactlessness but as a direct breach of discipline.

When the day of the trial came, Rabban Gamaliel did not ask any of his pupils to accompany him, as he had a right to do under the law. The fact was that Rabban Gamaliel refused to admit that what was about to take place could be called a trial. The procedure did not correspond to the Pharisaic definition of a regular trial; for instance, no witnesses were to appear against the Galileans. Rabban Gamaliel ruled that he was attending not a trial, but a simple investigation. He was therefore attended by none of his students, and he only permitted a number of scholars to accompany him, as a matter of dignity. Saul of Tarshish, who had hoped to be among the pupils present at the trial, was bitterly disappointed.

He remained behind in the Study House, nursing at least the hope that his Rabbi would take up the right attitude toward the blasphemous Galileans and lend his prestige to their condemnation.

In this hope, too, he was bitterly disappointed. And not only disappointed, but amazed and frightened. The "trial" had ended with the vindication of the disciples, and the entire school of Rabban Gamaliel, with the exception of Saul of Tarshish, interpreted the outcome as a triumph for the Master and the Pharisees over the High Priest. Still more, they regarded it as a great demonstration of religious freedom, a reaffirmation of the principle that every son of Israel had the right to preach whatever he wished and to interpret the sayings of the Prophets after his own fashion, so long as his utterances remained within the framework of the Jewish laws and the Jewish constitution. Every Jew was a freeman in respect to his relationship to the divinity, and no one had the right to interpose himself between a son of Israel and the God of Israel. This was how they all felt, with the exception of Saul, who saw in the liberation of the Galileans a frightful danger to the Jewish faith. To him it seemed like the end of all things. A sharp knife had been delivered into the hands of the Evil One, and the edge of it was being applied to the thread which bound Israel to his Father in heaven. Saul of Tarshish rebelled openly against the action of his teacher. And then, suddenly, Jochanan the scribe, the secretary to the Master, brought a message to Saul. The Master had conferred upon Saul the privilege of service—Saul was to attend Rabban Gamaliel, and wait upon him, the following morning.

It was an honor as signal as it was unexpected, to be called out of turn to serve one's teacher. Saul was astonished and puzzled, but he obeyed with delight.

He prepared himself for the service according to the rules and traditions of the institution. He rose before sunrise on the appointed morning, bathed his whole body in an earthen vessel, and anointed himself with oil, a luxury which he very rarely permitted himself. He combed his hair and beard, straightened out the tangles of his earlocks, put on fresh linen, and covered himself with the black mantle

85

which was the uniform of the Jewish scholar. Then he rubbed his hands with a special salve, to take out of them some of the roughness they had acquired at the loom, bathed his eyes in a lotion, and hastened to the door of his Rabbi's house, arriving there before the hour of the morning *Shema*.

The house of Rabban Gamaliel reflected his double dignity as the Master of the Pharisees and as a descendant of the Royal House of David. The house itself was large, the appointments rich, in accordance with the ancient saying: "Fine vessels and ornaments enlarge the spirit of man." But the Master himself paid little attention to the opulence of his surroundings, which had more to do with the important public functions and receptions which took place in the house than with his personal tastes.

When Saul appeared at the door of the great hall, the roof of which was supported by marble pillars between which the light of day was breaking in, there came to meet him an old man, whose face was overshadowed by vast white eyebrows and covered in part by the long white beard which reached down to his waist. The Master did not have his beard anointed and curled, in the manner of the High Priest, but followed the custom of the Pharisees in letting it grow naturally. But the care and cleanliness of the body was also a law among the Pharisees; a scholar was enjoined to pay the utmost attention to his personal appearance, since he was the representative of the Torah. The Master's beard, though it was neither curled nor anointed, had been combed with extreme care, so that every silver thread seemed to lie separately on his breast. His body was covered with a finely-woven black mantle, and on his head he wore, as the insigne of his rank, a covering of black silk. The Master walked with a stoop, as if laden with invisible burdens, and though he had not yet reached his seventieth year he looked like a man in the eighties. Old age had come upon him prematurely, so that he had long borne the name of "Venerable." Rabban Gamaliel came toward Saul with outstretched hand, in obedience to the Pharisaic injunction to be first in greeting.

"Peace be to thee, my beloved pupil, Saul of Tarshish, and peace be to the whole House of Israel."

"Peace unto thee, my Rabbi, and unto Israel," answered Saul, bowing before his teacher.

"I did not send for thee, my beloved pupil, throughout all these days while the trial was pending of the followers of the just man who was done to death by Edom. I did not call thee before me because I knew of thy opinions concerning his disciples, who have declared him to be the Messiah. I feared the pressure of thy will on mine, being, as I was, one of the judges. But I desired to see thy face once more; therefore with the ending of the trial I sent for thee, to come and attend on me, and rejoice me with thy presence."

"I too have desired to see thy face, my lord and Rabbi," answered Saul, bowing again.

"Thou art a faithful son of our father, Abraham; may there be many like thee in Israel."

When Rabbi and pupil had thus exchanged formal greetings, a servant came forward and handed over to Saul the "instruments" of his service, the garb of white Sidonian linen and the cruse of oil. Bearing these, the signs of his distinction for that morning, Saul accompanied the Master to the bath house. When the ceremony of washing and anointing was over, Saul helped his Rabbi to put on the white linen garment, and went back with him to the large chamber set apart for the Master. There they repeated together the morning *Shema*.

The prayer completed, Rabban Gamaliel received a messenger, the overseer of his household, who reported to him:

"The wants of all the members of thy household have been satisfied. Thy servants have eaten their morning meal. Thy beasts have been led to drink, and their bins have been filled with fodder."

It was only after this report that the Master sat down to his morning meal, which consisted of a few olives, a light salad, a morsel of bread barely large enough to justify the benediction, and a cup of fig wine to strengthen him.

The purpose of the formal "service" which was bestowed as a special honor on a student was to create more intimate personal contact than was possible elsewhere and to afford the student an opportunity to observe the daily conduct and bearing of his teacher. A secondary purpose, though an important one, was private instruction, not of the sort delivered before the group, but by way of conversation, in which the Rabbi, having perhaps some correction to urge upon his pupil, would make use of a parable, or an everyday incident, to hint indirectly at his object. Very often such instruction might be impersonal, or, even if personal, universally applicable, and the student would afterwards repeat proudly and reverently the words which his teacher had uttered to him in the privacy of the "service."

A servant came forward with the wine cup, and as Saul was filling it for his Rabbi, an insect began to circle round the rim. Fearing that it would fall into the wine, and thus throw a blot on his "service," Saul swiftly and skillfully caught the insect with his free hand, crushed it, and flung it away. Rabban Gamaliel, who was already seated at his sparing meal, called out:

"Saul, Saul, make good the damage thou hast done the Creator."

Saul paused in astonishment and said:

"Teach me, my Rabbi, what thy words mean."

"Does not a creature belong to Him that created it?"

"Assuredly, my Rabbi."

"Then thou hast inflicted damage on the Creator in that thou hast destroyed one of His creatures. Hasten, then, to make good the damage."

"But how, my Rabbi, can I make alive that which is dead? Am I co-equal with the Lord of the world?"

"Then let no man ever cause such damage as he cannot make good again. And if it is true concerning one of the trivial creatures, an insect which lives but a moment, that if we have killed it we cannot bring it to life again, how much truer is it of the highest of the creatures, which is created in the image of God, and into which God has breathed a soul. Who, then, dares to take it upon himself to destroy a man? Bear this in mind always, Saul: do no damage which thou canst not make good."

"But may it not be, Rabbi, that I was myself but the messenger and instrument of the Almighty, who sent me to destroy the insect because its time had come?"

"The Lord has many instruments and messengers, all prepared to do His will. Therefore let a man choose from among the purposes of the Lord those which confer benefit and bring peace to the world; let him leave the other purposes of the Lord to others."

"Teach me, my Rabbi. What are 'others'? Are we not a part of the whole? And if there is aught to be done, no matter what its nature, why should I leave it to my friend to do? Wherein am I better than he?"

"The sages have taught us that God sends the good through good men and the bad through wicked men. Therefore let a man say to himself: 'I am the instrument of God to fulfill His attributes on earth,' even as it is written: 'Ye shall make yourselves one with Him.' What do these words mean? How shall man make himself One with God? By uniting himself with God's attributes. Even as God is good, so shall man be good; even as He brings peace, so shall man bring peace."

Here the conversation ended, for now the Master repeated the grace after meals and set forth on his day's work.

Saul accompanied Rabban Gamaliel while he made the round of the various offices of his institution. Then teacher and pupil proceeded to the special office of the Master, above the cedar roof in the Temple court.

Here was already assembled a group of scholars and teachers of the Pharisees whom the Master consulted regarding questions directed to him by the Jews of the Diaspora, the Jews of Babylonia, of Persia, of the remote Greek islands, and even of Macedonia and Rome. All of the questions pertained to religious procedure. That morning there was adopted, with little debate, the resolution to intercalate an extra month in the calendar, so that the festivals should revert to the regular cycle and the Jews of all parts of the world observe them at the same time. Jochanan the scribe, secretary to the Master, was already seated at the table, his parchments and papyri spread out before him. He took the bronze stylus out from behind his ear, dipped it into a box of dye, and wrote as Rabban Gamaliel dictated:

"To our brothers in the east, in Babylon, to our brothers in Medea, and to all our brothers in the dispersion of the children of Israel: let peace be with you for ever. Know that it has been found good in the eyes of the sages, to increase by one the number of the months of this year . . ."

Saul listened carefully to the words which his teacher dictated, and his heart was moved. Here, from this little room, from this table, the Master spoke to the Jews of the world, in all their exiles, the exile of Babylon, the exile of Medea, which was in Persia, and the others. The threads went out to Asia, to Macedonia, to the Greek islands, to Egypt, to Rome, and they return to this point, this office above the Temple court, whence the spiritual sustenance of Israel flowed out. All Israel was knit as it were into a single body. The scene sank deep into Saul's memory.

"All Israel prays for you to our Father in heaven," continued Rabban Gamaliel. "I send you my benediction from the place of holiness; and all the sages who are with me send you their benediction; also my disciples send their benediction of peace."

Outside the office the messengers already waited to carry the missives of the Master to the scattered communities of Israel.

It was only when he had completed his day's schedule of labors that Rabban Gamaliel was able to devote another interval to the student in service. This occurred between the afternoon and evening prayer; the rest of the day would be taken up by the dinner, at which it was customary for the Master to entertain important visitors.

Resting on his couch in the office above the Temple court, tired with the day's work but mindful of his duty, Rabban Gamaliel addressed himself to the young man who stood ready to serve him:

"Saul, my beloved pupil, what is the path that a man shall choose to walk in?"

"My Rabbi, hath not the harp of Israel, King David, sung: 'I have chosen for myself the way of righteousness'?"

"What is the righteousness of man, my pupil? It is written: 'Only God is righteous in all His ways.' The righteousness of man is a short garment. If it cover him to the thighs, his legs are still naked. The righteousness of man is one-sided. 'God seeks the heart of man.' Only the heart can always guide us along the right path, for the heart is our eye in the darkness."

"If that be so, my Rabbi, wherefore has God given us laws and commandments? If the chief guide be the heart, why can we not follow the heart alone?" asked Saul.

"Saul, my pupil, consider what God desires of us, He Who spoke and the world was. Is He—forfend the thought!—like a king of flesh and blood, who rules over us by strength to obtain from us gold for his armies? Nay, my son; the laws and commandments which God has given us were meant for our good, to help us in our search for the right path. Man is a creature like all the creatures of the earth; his inclination from within is toward evil. But God granted him this much of His grace, that He created him in His image, and breathed into him a spark of Himself, the pure soul, that man might be ennobled and lift himself from the circle of beasts toward the higher worlds of the heavens, and of the Divinity. He has set posts and markers for him on the way, in the form of laws and commandments. But not the laws and commandments are the chief thing; we are the chief thing. The laws and commandments were created for us, not we for them; and they have but one purpose, to purify us and train us till we can unite our hearts with God and with His will; for the Torah consists but of a single sentence, that sentence which the Venerable Hillel, whose name is given to our school, taught to one of the heathen. For there came one of the heathen to Hillel, and asked to be taught the whole Torah in the time that a man can stand on one leg. To which our teacher replied thus: That which thou desirest not to be done unto thee, do not unto another. That is the whole Torah. The rest is commentary.'"

That which the disciple Saul of Tarshish learned from Rabban Gamaliel on the day of his service sank deep into his soul, like a seed, to bear fruit in time to come. But in the hour of the planting, Saul was not aware of it. He went home heavy of spirit and disappointed.

Chapter Nine

THE TWO MIRIAMS

WHEN it was known that the disciples had been tried before the High Priest and had been released, and further, that the Master of the Pharisees himself, Rabban Gamaliel, had delivered himself of this opinion: "It cannot be known, perhaps the thing is of God. We cannot therefore fight against them, for it might happen that we should be fighting God"—when all this was known the belief in the Messiah not only became permissible in the eyes of the pious, but the disciples themselves rose to new importance among the people. Legends were widely told concerning their power; there was the miracle which Simon had performed with the lame man in the Vestibule of King Solomon; there was also the story of the angels who had liberated the imprisoned disciples. Many miracles were also remembered which their Rabbi, the Messiah, had performed when he lived in the flesh.

The chamber in King David's wall, where the disciples and the women had made their home, drew toward itself multitudes of the afflicted. In the yard below there was a ceaseless wailing and screaming. The sick, the halt, the lame, the possessed, filled the whole area about the waters of Siloah; and whenever Simon appeared he was followed, as his Rabbi had been, by a host of cripples. They laid the sick down in his path, so that at least his shadow might fall on them. Cripples crawled after him in the dust, lifted up toward him their withered limbs, crying: "Simon, Simon, heal us in the name of Yeshua the Messiah."

Meanwhile the Greek-speaking group in the new congregation was increasing not only in the matter of number; when bar Naba joined the disciples he already found among their followers many cantors and higher synagogue officials of the wealthy and powerful Greek colony. These included settlers from his own island province of Cyprus, Libertines, Cyreneans, Cappadocians, and representatives of the Greek islands, as well as members of the popular Greek-speaking synagogues of Jerusalem, such as the Alexandrian. Istephan and Philippus, and other well-known figures among the Greek Jews, were already of the congregation. The increase in numbers and weight led to a demand for special representation in the "serving at the tables."

This was a matter of the utmost importance.

The Essenes and Pharisees practiced a strict code in regard to the "table," that is, in regard to the question as to who could and·who could not sit with them at meals and break bread with them. The same procedure had been instituted by the new companionship. Only he could be admitted to the meal who was a full-fledged "companion."

The table, which in the Jewish tradition was regarded as an altar, and the breaking of bread, which was regarded as a sacred service, were the supreme symbols of comradeship and companionship. At the tables companions sat only with companions. The divisions and prohibitions extended not only to gentiles; brothers in the flesh who were not of the companionship could not break bread with their own. The sexual looseness which defiled the masses of the godless and the ignorant added hygienic force to ritual law; self-respect and prudence dictated the utmost caution in permitting newcomers to dip their fingers in the common food bowls. The ignorant man and the outsider were automatically suspected of sexual impurity; the touch of their hands made food ritually unfit for consumption; their breath was impurity. When a man had been admitted to the table, and had broken bread, he was subject to a severe regimen of cleanliness both in the matter of food and in his general deportment.

The new companionship was similar in all respects to the old ones, except that it believed that the Messiah had already come and would soon return. In the breaking of bread in common the new companionship saw its highest mystic symbol—an act of communion with the righteous redeemer. They were extremely circumspect in admitting newcomers to the common meals, which were called the "serving at the tables."

Until this point the right to admit anyone to the "serving at the tables" was restricted to the twelve disciples whom the Messiah had appointed in accordance with the number of the tribes, eleven of them by his direct authority and the twelfth by lot and the Holy Ghost. These alone had the right to accept new members in the companionship and to perform the ceremony of baptism. The increase in the membership of the new congregation made it impossible to hold the common meals in one place, which hitherto had been the home of Hillel the water-carrier in the old David wall opposite the waters of Siloah; the congregation therefore instituted common meals in the various homes of wealthier members, who for this special purpose were absolved from the duty of selling their earthly possessions. Wherever the common meal was held, one at least of the twelve disciples was present, and he it was who conducted the service. He decided who might and who might not be admitted to the table. This "serving at the tables" absorbed much of the time of the disciples. Disputes early became an evil in the new congregation, and the disciples alone possessed the authority to settle them. Thus they soon found themselves prevented from preaching the gospel of the Messiah, and accepting new companions, which could not be practiced by others. It was clear that something would have to be done.

Simon bar Jonah, the leader of the disciples, was confronted by a difficult problem. He could not but admit that the Greek-speaking companions were right in maintaining that if the tidings could be spread in the Greek-speaking synagogues there was prospect of a rich harvest. His simple fisherman's sense told him that the net should be thrown deepest where the haul was likely to be greatest. On the other hand, the authority to spread the gospel had been transmitted only to

93

the twelve by the Messiah, and he did not know whether he had the right to transfer this authority to others.

Simon bar Jonah was a man of the people. He was not strong in the law. He had his faith and his mission, and these sufficed for him. Whenever he was thrown into doubt as to any course of action, he retired within his heart and put the question to his faith. He did this in simple words, even as he had done in the night of his imprisonment, when he had prayed to his lord Messiah to strengthen him for the hour when he would stand before the High Priest. Thus it was always with him; there was an inner door which the power of his faith opened for him. Not always did he perceive the face of his lord shining upon him with the light of heaven, and not always did he hear his voice. But always after prayer he was aware of clarification, a grace which made the crooked paths straight before him and threw upon them the illumination of understanding and peace. This condition of clarification, which came upon him when his heart was filled with humble bliss, when his eyes were given sight, and his resolution became clear, he regarded as a visitation of the Holy Ghost. In this condition he strove to imagine what the King Messiah desired to have him do in the relevant matter, and what the King Messiah himself would have done. Regarding the difficult problem of the transmission of authority, then, Simon consulted his faith.

The night before he had to issue his decision on this important matter, Simon bar Jonah stood in a corner of the disciples' home, where his Rabbi had broken bread with them before he went forth to become a sacrifice. About him, on the floor, the disciples were fast asleep, each man covered with his mantle. Simon lifted up his beseeching eyes to the deep blue, star-sown skies; he humbled his heart before his lord and prayed.

The next day he called together the Greek-speaking Jews and bade them—according to the usage of all the synagogues of Jerusalem —draw lots among themselves for "cantors" and "beadles" or "servants."

It also became clear to the new companionship that no matter how they were to be prepared for the return of the Messiah of righteousness —who could reveal himself at any moment—it was necessary to take into account the needs of the hour. The giving up of all earthly possessions, which came very hard to many, was also a great obstacle to the growth of the companionship. In this connection, too, something would have to be done. The belief in the Messiah was attracting all classes of the population, the rich alike with the poor. Men and women went about unoccupied, living on the charity which the congregation was able to distribute as a result of the sales of possessions. Simon perceived that the things of God had to be administered even like the things of man. He remembered that in the old days, when he was a fisherman of K'far Nahum and had gone forth in his little boat after fish, he would take into account the storms that came over the waters of Kinereth; he would not venture forth blindly with his nets, but would wait for a quiet moonlit night; now, in his new mission, he would have to use the same forethought. Even though the Messiah might be standing on the threshold, he must guide his congregation as prudently as he had guided his boat on the lake.

And thus, when Miriam, the sister of bar Naba, joined the companionship shortly after her brother, Simon did not insist—as he had insisted in the case of bar Naba himself and other wealthy newcomers—that she sell her estates and the great house which she had in the new quarter of Jerusalem. Rather than let these fall into the hands of the speculators who haunted the home of the disciples, he decided to keep them as the common property of the congregation. Members of the congregation or companionship worked the estates—the well-tended vineyards and olive groves—and lived on them as a single community. Miriam's great house was particularly useful to the congregation. It gave accommodation to a large number of companions; likewise it had vast rooms for the holding of prayers and for the common meals.

Thus the rich house of Miriam became a home for the more intimate members of the family of the Messiah; for the women whom the disciples had brought with them from Galilee and for others who were sent for to join the congregation in Jerusalem.

The first one to be moved to the new quarters was Miriam, the mother of Yeshua. She was becoming weaker from day to day. Charged with the care of Miriam the mother were the two women who had come with her from Galilee, Susannah, the mother of the Zebedees, and Simon Khaifa's mother-in-law. The disciples regarded the mother of the Messiah as the mother of all; for of her who had brought the Messiah into the world it might be said that she had brought them all into the world. Accompanying Miriam the mother was Miriam of

Migdal, who had been the first to see the Messiah in the spirit and who had therefore taken on, among the disciples, the character of a prophetess. She was often possessed by the Holy Ghost, pronounced tidings and spoke in tongues. She too was wasting away with the passing of the days; her skin was becoming finer and more transparent, and her face seemed to be transformed into two great eyes, deep blue stars which alternately flamed with inner fires or shone through a veil of tears.

The two women, Miriam of Migdal and Miriam the widow, sister of bar Naba, were drawn together from the first day, like two sister souls which had lost each other and were now reunited after many years. Miriam the widow reawakened in Miriam of Migdal her ancient love for incense plants and sweet oils which had never died in her, but had merely slept; she needed but to find herself among the flowers and delicate shrubs of the garden and her old passion would return to her. She began to interest herself again in salves and ointments, and she instructed certain perfume mixers among the companions to grind and mix the roots and flowers of plants according to her secret recipes, as she had done in days long past to give pleasure to the many that loved her, and then to her lord and redeemer. She used the preparations now for her own body, to make it ready for the bridal canopy of the life to come, upon which she believed she was to enter very soon.

The two Miriams often sat among the shadows of the cypress alley, when the ripening jasmine poured its sweet perfume on the air and the mint its bitter perfume; and Miriam of Migdal told Miriam the widow of the days when her lord and redeemer, the savior of righteousness, had been among them in the life. She told her of the days when love had failed her and she had longed for a higher and eternal love; how she had heard the call of the man of Nazareth, whose good name had come to her like the perfume of a sweet oil; and how she had left her many lovers and her powerful protectors and her rich house and had gone to him in K'far Nahum, and had heard that he was sojourning in Naim; how she came to the house of Simon the Pharisee, in the city of Naim, and saw her lord seated at the end of the table which was by the door, and knew him at once to be the lord; and how she had fallen at his feet and begged forgiveness for her sins, and anointed his feet with her sweet oils and dried them with her hair.

Then she would undo her plaits, and in spite of her body's frailty

96

her hair was thick and heavy as if weighted with gold, and there went out of it the faint echoes of old, extinguished perfumes, the pure and delicate breath of lilies mingled with young lilac, spreading upon the air the spirit of spring. The echoes of the extinguished perfumes were like little thunder clouds which appear suddenly on a pure, clear blue sky; they awakened memories of what had been . . . but her hair had been privileged to touch his feet . . . and, closing her eyes, she took handfuls of it and washed it against her pale, delicate parchment-like skin.

Miriam the widow bent down, lifted a strand of the snow-white hair and pressed it piously to her lips.

Miriam of Migdal told, further, of the days when she and the disciples had followed their lord and savior through the hills and valleys of Galilee; of the Sabbath they had passed together in his mother's house; of the entry into Jerusalem; and of his last days.

Young Jochanan, called Marcus, the son of the house, sat at the feet of the two women. He listened hungrily to Miriam's descriptions of the life and acts of the King Messiah, and wrote them down on the tablets of his heart.

Chapter Ten

THE ZEALOT

THE spirit of Saul of Tarshish was aflame with jealousy for the Lord. Neither the wise and learned words of his teacher nor the lash of his own conscience were of avail; it was something stronger than his own strong will, his iron character, and his rigid discipline—a power which ravened in him like a wild beast, driving him to pour out his fury on the new companionship. For since the companionship had broken like a wolf into his own flock, of the Greek-speaking Jews, and destroyed his closest friend, Joseph bar Naba, the jealousy for the Lord which burned in Saul was made hotter by a jealousy which was personal.

97

But the ideal of the Messiah was the all-in-all for Saul, and he could not, under any circumstances, have remained indifferent toward those that called themselves the congregation of the Messiah. If he could not be of them, there was but one alternative, to cleanse the soil of Israel of them. The wider the acclaim they won, the more steadfast became his rage. And news of their triumphs reached him day after day; he could not have escaped from it, for he encountered it on every hand. Greatest of all was their success in his own congregation of the Greek-speaking Jews; and he, Saul of Tarshish, was left standing outside.

It chanced one day that he was seated at his loom in the workshop of Eliezer, the weaver of goat's hair. The house lay in the deep part of the Kidron valley, where the law had concentrated many trades, outside the city proper, such as tanning, pottery, and tent-weaving. In spring and autumn, when the waters poured down from the city into the valleys which lie on three sides, the courtyard which was Eliezer's workshop would be flooded. But on this day, in the midst of the hot summer, the earth in the courtyard, like the remainder of the valley, which was covered with green in the spring, was parched and withered. The people who lived in the Kidron valley moved, throughout the summer, among dense clouds of dust. Under the scanty protection of bamboo mattresses the men in the workshop sat, half naked, in a foul confusion of camel hair and heaped goatskins. Others were occupied in the spring; they stamped about in the half-dried bottom, to squeeze out the last drops of water for the washing of the skins or the carding of the hair. At the looms under the bamboo the weavers worked the camel and goat's hair into tents, and among them was Saul, listening to the utterances of his fellow workers on the decision which had been given by Rabban Gamaliel at the trial of the disciples. Some of them expressed satisfaction with it; others were of Saul's opinion.

"No one has reported seeing these men of Galilee, or, as they call themselves, the messengers, do anything, God forbid, against the Torah," said Reuben the lame, whose crippled body, like a fish half in water, was covered to the waist by a heap of goat's hair. "On the contrary, they are always to be encountered in the Temple, and they pray there, like all other Jews, for the coming of the redeemer."

"But they say that the redeemer has already come," cried out Samuel ben Eliezer, a hairy man who was known to all as a great zealot. Whenever there was a disturbance in the Temple, Samuel ben Eliezer was sure to be in the midst of it. The city authorities always kept an eye on him. He was a giant of a man, a Samson. His face was almost hidden by his vast beard. He lifted up in his muscular arms the entire structure of a tent and thrust out his face, on the visible parts of which there was a multitude of scars, left there by swords and spears in the many revolts in which he had played a part. His nose was broken, his jaw hammered to a side, and one eye was closed. He opened his twisted jaws, in which one half of the teeth were missing, and roared ironically:

"A man who went like a lamb to the slaughter, and let them hang him on a cross—*he* the deliverer of righteousness who shall redeem us from the hands of Edom? If thou art the Messiah, show us what thou canst do against Edom, the oppressor of Israel! As for the accounting of my sins, leave that to me and my Creator!"

"I, on the contrary, am glad that one has come who can forgive sins. I need it," said Nathanyah, a young weaver of evil repute. He was known throughout the valley as a great sinner. The strength of his youth attracted to him the women of the valley, particularly the widows, who were very numerous. He had been in the habit of taking one woman after another, leaving them to look after themselves, while he himself spent his days in the taverns. Finally, on a complaint, he was handed over to the authorities. He was scourged and released, and this happened many times; at one point he was in danger of being sold as a slave, for the authorities had it in mind to use the money so obtained to purchase releases for the widows, who could not live with him until they were provided with such documents. In the end, however, they condemned him to work for Eliezer the weaver; his wages were turned over to the court, which was paying off a release for a widow whom he had married and then divorced. There had been a rumor at one time of his being caught with a married woman, for which the penalty was death. Now this Nathanyah, hearing of the forgiveness of sins, was greatly contented. He turned his face and perfumed beard in the direction of the women who were working at the other end of the court, some grinding grain, others extracting the oil from seeds, still others kneading dough, and cried out:

"Women, women, do you hear? I can sin now as much as my heart desires. There has arisen a righteous redeemer who forgives sins."

"May thy mouth be stopped with dust for the mockery it utters," said one of the men. His breast was so thickly covered with hair that it looked like a second beard; a rope about his waist held up his tattered covering of sackcloth. This was Joseph, the porter, who carried the completed tents from the workshop to the storehouse. "I was a slave, and he whom you mock redeemed me."

"Was he so rich, when he was alive, that he could redeem thee?"

"Rich? Yes, he was very rich. Not in gold, but in the wisdom of God. He redeemed me, not from the ropes of my labor, but from the ropes of sin, which were tighter on my body than these are now. They were on my throat, like serpents and scorpions; I could not breathe because of them. With the words of his mouth he redeemed and liberated me and made me a free son of Israel."

"I heard him preach in the streets of Jerusalem. Pearls they were, pure pearls, that poured from his lips. He was the comforter of all that were heavy-laden and oppressed," said a little man who lay almost wholly concealed in the mound of goat's hair which he was carding.

"His disciples testified before the Sanhedrin that he is the King Messiah, whom God raised up to be His right hand."

"I say that is blasphemy."

"Yes, and the Sanhedrin sentenced them to the lash for it."

"I heard tell that they took the punishment with joy and thanked God that it was granted them to suffer and be humiliated for his name."

"But there must be something in him, I say, if men believe in him so."

"It is not blasphemy, it is idolatry to say of a man of flesh and blood that he is the helper of God. Does God need a helper?" cried Zadoc, of the following of the House of Shammai, speaking up for the first time.

Saul knew Zadoc and had been waiting to hear what he would say. If the popular saying that "the sage lies in wait like a serpent to take his revenge" had any application, it was to Reb Zadoc, the zealot. There was even something about his appearance which suggested the serpent. He was long and lean, as if he had been kneaded and drawn out as the baker draws out his dough, and all his life and energy had become concentrated in his head. He was all head: a slender backbone and a head to which was attached a fiery red beard. He was by nature a silent man; he would listen long to the discussions before throwing in

100

a word, but the word was brief and pointed. As became a disciple of the House of Shammai, he not only preached but exemplified in his life the severe religious discipline of his teachers. He was so scrupulous in the matter of ritual purity that he lived in isolation. Were it not for the Sabbath, he would never have partaken of cooked food, for no vessel was pure enough for him, no meat was *kosher* enough, no bread sufficiently certain to be made of grain out of which the proper Temple tribute had been paid. He nourished himself for the most part with roots and vegetables, and his wasted body showed the effects. Faithful to the injunction of the sages, he followed a trade, but most of his time was spent standing at a lectern in the study house of the Shammaites, where he had his dwelling, and where, day by day, he listened to the fiery harangues of the disciples of his school. On his face, too, there were countless scars, come by in the riots and revolts which were so frequent in the Temple court.

"Rabban Gamaliel was present at the latest trial; he heard what they had to say, yet his decision was to set them free. Only the Priests sentenced them to the lash," said someone in defense of the disciples.

"There are many today who trample God's garden, and no one forbids it," answered Zadoc. "Woe unto Israel! The vineyard of God is desecrated, and they who are set as its keepers slumber."

"Where is the desecration?" asked one.

"I will tell you," answered Saul, swiftly. "Go to the Synagogue of the Libertines, and in the place of the preacher stands one by the name of Reb Istephan; you will hear him say that which will make your ears tingle."

Herod and Zadoc suspended work. The clatter of their looms ceased while they fixed their eyes on the young man Saul, who kept his head bowed over his labor.

"Yes," repeated Saul. "Come with me this Sabbath, and you will hear him say, concerning the Holy One of Israel, that which has never been said before. And this in the Holy City of Jerusalem, which God has made the abode of His Glory, the Temple."

Another spoke:

"Is it any wonder that the yoke of Edom lies so heavy on the neck of Israel? For we have thrown off from it the yoke of the Lord. The word of God has become a mockery. The fence of His garden has been leveled, and whosoever desires enters and tramples on the vines."

"If the great ones are silent, must the little ones be silent too?" asked Saul. "Have not our sages taught, 'Every Jew is responsible for every other Jew?' Everyone of us here is responsible for the garden."

"I hear words!" shouted Herod from his loom. "We are all responsible. Moreover, the sages have also taught: 'Where there is no man, be thou a man.'"

"Aye! 'Strength and triumph shall come to the Jews from an unexpected place,'" added Zadoc the zealot.

"Hear us, thou," said Herod to Saul. "Take us with thee this Sabbath to the Synagogue of the Libertines. Let us hear what this man has to say concerning the Holy One of Israel."

"I too will go," called Zadoc.

"Count me a third," cried Nathanyah. "Perhaps I shall have a hand in a good deed, and my sins will be forgiven me."

"Strength and triumph shall come to the Jews! Strength and triumph shall come to the Jews!" The words rang in Saul's mind when he returned that evening to the study house of his Rabbi, and his thoughts would not rest. Zadoc the zealot, and Herod, and Nathanyah, who was a sinner, and who could expiate his sins in an act of zeal for the Lord. And there would be others. There would be others.

*　　*　　*

In the Synagogue of the Libertines were assembled not only the members of that congregation, but many that belonged to the Synagogues of the Cyreneans and the Alexandrians. For on this day, between afternoon and evening prayer, Reb Istephan was to preach again, to the Greek-speaking Jews, on the return of the Messiah. It was known in the city that Reb Istephan had been specially entrusted with the duty of bringing the tidings to the Greek-speaking Jews; and there came enemies as well as friends to listen to the sermon; or, one might better have said, to participate in the dispute, for of late the sermons of Reb Istephan had attracted much attention, favorable and adverse, and they were attended by many learned men who, armed with the Jewish law and skilled in the Greek language, came for the purpose of refuting him.

Among these were Saul of Tarshish, and with him were, from among those who had promised to attend, Zadoc the Shammaite and Samuel ben Eliezer.

The synagogue was filled to the doors, the congregation overflowing on to the terraces which descended toward the valley. On the pulpit, before the Ark which contained the Scrolls of the Torah, stood Reb Istephan, draped in his prayer-shawl. His red beard shone fierily in the afternoon sunlight which broke in between the pillars of the synagogue. His arms were lifted toward heaven, and with a passion which his followers had never observed in him before, he spoke again that day of the preparation for the coming of the Messiah, of whom the Prophets had prophesied.

Close to the preacher, like a servant or bodyguard, stood the Levite of Cyprus.

Joseph bar Naba was of those men who must always be attached to a guide or teacher. There was a need in him to look up to someone, to honor and follow him. Once it had been Saul of Tarshish, whom he still honored in his secret thoughts; but when Saul left him he had looked for a new master and had found him in Reb Istephan. In one sense the preacher was nearer to him, because of his belief in the Messiah; but in another sense he was remote, for Joseph had need of a leader whose character was wrought iron, like Saul's, and this he did not find in Reb Istephan. Still, he had observed the rule laid down by Rabban Gamaliel and chosen himself a Rabbi and guide. He now followed the preacher to all the synagogues where he delivered his message. Now, between afternoon and evening prayers, on this Sabbath, he stood close to Reb Istephan, and looked up longingly at the flaming face emerging from the covering of the prayer-shawl.

From his corner Saul observed his one-time friend stationed below the preacher. He observed the hungry eyes turned up toward Reb Istephan. Those eyes, which had so often been turned toward him, were filled with such childlike faith, such unbounded devotion, that Saul experienced, against his own will, a pang of bitterness. This personal touch, fusing with his pure zeal for the faith and his hatred of the new sect for the sake of God alone, Saul of Tarshish knew to be unworthy, and he tried to deny it. But his efforts were vain, for his longing for the friend of his youth was too strong in him.

The voice of the preacher, ringing out over the assembly, became deeper and more impassioned. His red beard seemed to send out a light of its own as he stood there on the pulpit, swathed in his prayer-shawl, while from his lips poured verses from the Books of the Prophets to prove that Yeshua the Nazarene, tortured and slain, was the true Messiah; he, the Messiah, had taken these sufferings upon himself not because, God forbid, he had lacked the power to save himself—the hosts of heaven were at his command—but because it had been so decreed by God, even as the Prophets had prophesied; he had taken the sins of the world upon himself in order that the world might be purified and prepared for his return. Reb Istephan's voice, heavy, metallic, powerful, cast a trance over the multitude in the synagogue.

Then another voice, a harsh, protesting voice, broke in. It was the voice of Zadoc the Shammaite:

"Children of Abraham! How long will ye stand by and let alien feet trample the garden of the Lord?"

The spell was broken; fists were lifted toward the preacher.

"Hale him before the Sanhedrin!"

"He has blasphemed the Name of God!"

While the tumult was growing, Saul of Tarshish pushed his way forward and clambered to the pulpit. He gesticulated at the excited throng and at the top of his voice asked for silence, making the demand first in Greek, then in Aramaic. But it was the pallor in his face, the earnestness of his gestures, which wrought on the audience more than his words. Silence was gradually restored.

"I would ask the preacher a question." And Saul turned again toward Reb Istephan. "Your Rabbi, when he was still alive, said that he would destroy the House of God in three days, and build another house. Do you also believe that your Rabbi can destroy the Temple?"

"What is the House of God?" answered Reb Istephan. "Is it, God forbid, a house which sustains idol worship? Is our God a god of wood and stone, who, when his house is destroyed, perishes with his house? What house is there that our God needs for his support? What space can enclose Him? Within what boundaries shall He be confined?"

It seemed that these words of the preacher were not without their effect. The audience became silent and attentive. But Saul interrupted the preacher.

"We would have your answer! These people, to whom you bring the tidings of your Messiah, have a right to it. Is it or is it not true that your Rabbi said that he could in three days destroy the House of God, and build another in its place, for which the Sanhedrin sentenced him to death?"

"If my lord, the King Messiah, said it, then it is a holy truth, for the power has been given to him," answered Reb Istephan, firmly.

"You have heard!" cried Saul. "You are witnesses, that here and now, in a holy place and on the Sabbath, the preacher said that the Temple, the pride and glory of Israel, in which the Divinity has its abode among us, shall be destroyed."

"We are witnesses!"

"Reb Zadoc! Reb Samuel!" cried Saul. "Come. We have learned that which we desired to learn."

"Drag him before the Sanhedrin!"

"Not on the Sabbath! The Sanhedrin has long arms; they will find him."

With this Saul of Tarshish and Zadoc the Shammaite and Samuel, son of Eliezer, left the synagogue.

*   *   *

When Saul left the Synagogue of the Libertines, he separated himself from Zadoc the Shammaite and Samuel, son of Eliezer, remaining silent with a third companion, ben Chanan, the son of his sister. To him he said:

"Ben Chanan, take me to thy house."

"His nephew understood him without further explanation.

There were certain signs by which Saul of Tarshish recognized the beginning of the onset. . . . All day long he had felt it gathering above him, like a storm cloud. A fiery circle was pressing against his temples, an increasing darkness was shed upon his eyes. Nevertheless there was within him a bright stirring, as though a new soul were being poured into him. Saul of Tarshish hated this condition, which made his footsteps uncertain, and deprived him of self-control, turning him over to a power over which he had no influence. . . . And yet he longed for it, as a man longs for the warm, encircling arms of a beloved wife. . . . It was with him as though he were being sped beyond the limits of this world and entering into another which knew no limits and no boundaries; a world in which there was neither yea nor nay, only an infinite space of blazing brightness, through which he fell for ever . . . and continued to fall . . . through infinite time. . . . In that condition the impossible became possible . . . he dreaded to enter into this world, as a man dreads to cross the threshold of the unknown, as a man dreads to cross the threshold between life and death. . . . Yet he was drawn irresistibly toward the threshold, and the nearer he drew to it the more powerful became the attraction of the unknown, of the infinite, of the limitless, of the impossible-possible. He had been fighting against the pull of that condition all day long; he fought against it now as he hastened toward the house of his sister. He stumbled rather than walked through the narrow streets of Jerusalem; his limbs obeyed his will and memory when he himself could no longer direct them. At last he reached the door of his sister's house, but he could go no further. There the condition fell upon him, as if it had been a murderer lying in wait, and flung him to the ground.

Saul stretched out his body stiffly. His eyes became glazed. A thin foam broke out on his lips.

His nephew took off his mantle and laid it over Saul's face, to conceal it from the gaze of passersby.

In the midst of his seizure Saul beheld an angel of the Lord cleaving the air in downward flight toward him. The angel sank, feet downward into the earth, and only the upper half remained visible, but that upper half was blinding white, as though it were all fire within, covered by a human skin. The angel lifted his wing-arms to heaven, as if in prayer, and the face of the angel, which shone with divine fire, was likewise upturned, and on it rested a vision of eternal grace, as if the eyes of the angel had penetrated to the Glory....

When Saul came to he marked, as always after one of his seizures, that he had for a time lost the power of sight. In the darkness which surrounded him he saw, in recurrent visitations, the angel which he had beheld during the seizure, and he wondered greatly over the meaning of the vision....

Chapter Eleven

THE STONING

IN due course Saul of Tarshish appeared before the Chief Officer of the Temple, bringing with him his two witnesses, Zadoc the Shammaite and Samuel, son of Eliezer. At his instigation the two witnesses deposed that on the previous Sabbath, being in a sacred place, they had heard Reb Istephan, preacher to the Greek-speaking Jews, declare that his Messiah, Yeshua the Nazarene, would abrogate the law of Moses, and would destroy the Temple, building another upon its place.

Jochanan, the Chief Officer of the Temple, never took the slightest step without first consulting his father. He bade the accuser and witnesses wait in the office, while he sent a messenger for old Chanan.

In the presence of the former High Priest, the witnesses formally repeated their charge; but to their astonishment Chanan did not betray, either by word or gesture, any symptom of rage. He only sighed, and said, with a despair which had lost its pain and become almost indifference:

"Yes, yes—a sinful generation; and because of our sinfulness we can do nothing against those who are digging at the foundation of our sanctity. Our hands lack the power."

Young Saul of Tarshish was astounded by these words; his companions even more than he.

"The Sanhedrin!" he exclaimed. "The sentence of the High Priest!"

"The Pharisees sit in the Sanhedrin and proclaim that every son of Israel is free to preach as he thinks fit concerning God and the Torah. The sentence of the High Priest depends on their decisions."

"Is the vineyard of God open to every passerby, then?" asked Saul, hotly. "Can he who will enter and tread the vines under foot? Have we not been taught by Moses our teacher: 'And ye shall burn out the evil from your midst'?"

"Go, put that question to thy Rabbi, Gamaliel, and ask him further what he did in the case of those other men who preached similarly in the courts of the House of God."

"I know," muttered Saul.

"The fathers have eaten sour grapes and the teeth of the children are set on edge; one unclean sheep will cause the whole flock to sicken. One sins, and the wrath of God is poured out on all the congregation. Thus it is, until there arises a Phineas who takes it upon himself to execute the vengeance of God," said the old High Priest, significantly.

"Tell us, what is to be done? We cannot stand by and see the continual desecration of the sanctities. Who knows how far this will go?"

"Oh, we know only too well how far it will go. Think you that such words are uttered only in the Synagogue of the Libertines? They are repeated daily in Temple courts. And from here they will be carried abroad to all the settlements of the Jews, so that soon the cry will be heard: 'The Lord God of Israel has abandoned His House in Jerusalem.' If that be so, they will ask, wherefore should we make these pilgrimages, so costly and so dangerous? And they will bring their offerings and sacrifices not here, to Jerusalem, but to gods nearer home," continued old Chanan.

"I say we must stamp upon this fire before it spreads!" cried Saul.

"How, then?"

"Let my lord the High Priest listen, and I will tell him how," interposed one of the scribes of the Sadduceans, one Herod, an interpreter of their laws.

"What is thy counsel?"

"The words of the Torah are clear: 'And the hand of the witnesses shall be the first against him.' The meaning of these words is exactly as written: those who heard with their own ears the blasphemy shall carry out the punishment. Whatever the law says, yea or nay, their obligation is clear, and if they do not discharge it they are themselves blasphemers."

"Is this the law of the Pharisees?" asked Saul of Zadoc the Shammaite.

"The commandment 'The hand of the witnesses shall be the first against him' is a commandment of action, and not of refraining from action. In a commandment of action thou canst not invoke the saying of the sages: 'Withhold and do not.' This is what the Pharisees teach: Every commandment of action must be carried out."

"If that be so, we know what we have to do."

" 'The hand of the witnesses shall be the first against him!' " exclaimed both witnesses.

"Not too hastily, young man!" said old Chanan, addressing himself to the impetuous Saul. "We must be prudent. Let there be no disturbance in the streets of the city, lest the powers hear of it, God forbid, and interfere. I counsel that you go first among the congregants of the synagogues where the blasphemy is preached, and awaken among them the spirit of zeal for the Lord, so that they take the matter in their own hands. The God of Israel needs many Phineases, even like yourselves. Alas for our sins! There are many to follow the ways of Zimri, few to follow the ways of Phineas. God grant that your numbers multiply in Israel."

With these equivocal words old Chanan dismissed Saul and the witnesses.

*　*　*

The utterances concerning the Temple which Reb Istephan had permitted himself, in a house of worship, had sent a wave of horror through many of his listeners. The Greek-speaking Jews were, as a group, more jealous of the Temple institutions than the Palestinian Jews themselves. They knew, from first hand observation, the evil of idol-worship, the abominations and unmentionable foulnesses which flooded the pagan world; and they regarded the House of God in Jerusalem as the only island upon which the scattered Jews of the world could take refuge from the universal flood of defilement. There was no other bond between Israel and God. The Greek-speaking Jews could not imagine a continuity of Jewish life in the midst of the heathens without this central place where the tradition, the inheritance of the patriarchs, was concentrated, and whence it radiated to the ends of the exile. Many of them had abandoned their homes, relinquished worldly advantage, comforts, old habits of luxury, in order to make their homes in the vicinity of the Temple. And now there arose one, in their midst, who spoke of the destruction of the House of God. It was not difficult for Saul of Tarshish to find a multitude of Greek-speaking Jews prepared to carry out his plan.

Two days after the complaint had been lodged with the Chief Officer of the Temple a crowd of Jews brought Reb Istephan to the court of the High Priest. Half dragging, half carrying the preacher, they hastened through the streets, young Saul of Tarshish at their head, and by his side the two witnesses, Zadoc the Shammaite and Samuel, son of Eliezer. They had pulled Reb Istephan down from the pulpit of a synagogue, in the midst of a sermon on the Messiah, and they haled him, without an instant's delay, before the Sanhedrin. But this Sanhedrin was not the great assembly of scholars which had its sessions in the "Chamber of the Hewn Stones." It was the Little Sanhedrin, which met in the house of the High Priest. The Little Sanhedrin could always be convoked at a moment's notice, for it consisted only of the Chief Officer of the Temple, who spent most of the day in his office, and two or three scribes and interpreters of the law, charged with various duties in connection with the administration of the Temple. Not only was this "Sanhedrin" without the power to decide issues of life and death; it had not even the right to conduct a formal investigation of such issues.

Those of the crowd who, dragging Reb Istephan with them, were able to push their way into the room, were amazed to find assembled, as though in expectancy of the event, all the members of the House of Chanan. There was no need to send for anyone. The crowd relinquished Reb Istephan to the guards, who placed him before the Priests, and the witnesses, Zadoc the Shammaite and Samuel, son of Eliezer, proceeded at once to testify: they had heard the preacher state that Yeshua the Nazarene would destroy the Temple and would abrogate the law which Moses had handed down at Sinai.

Their deposition made, the High Priest addressed the accused: "Is this which the witnesses testify concerning thee the truth?"

The preacher, still intoxicated with the passion of the sermon from which his accusers had dragged him, did not try to defend himself. Instead, as though he were resuming the sermon where it had been interrupted, he launched again upon his theme. He spoke of the beginning of things, of Genesis and the patriarchs, then of the Five Books of Moses, of the Kings and Prophets, showing that all had been only a preparation for the coming of the Ancient of Days, the King Messiah. The crowd listened impatiently; the witnesses were restive and interrupted the preacher several times. But the High Priest was patient. He bade the guards keep order and signaled to the accused to continue. So far there was not a single passage in the sermon which could awaken the resentment of the listeners. The preacher rehearsed the tradition, after the manner of all other preachers. Only when he came to speak of King Solomon and the Temple, he departed suddenly from the accepted narrative and inserted his own variation.

"But the Eternal does not dwell in temples built by the hands of man. Even as the Prophets have said: 'The heavens are my abode and the earth is my footstool. Where is the house which you would build for me? saith the Lord God. Have not my hands made all things?'"

Though this was a quotation from the Prophets, and the accused had not made a single adverse allusion of his own to the Temple, his listeners, remembering his previous sermons, caught the implication of his deviation, and the office was filled with an indignant shouting:

"He blasphemes the Temple! We will not listen!"

"Stone him!"

The High Priest stilled the clamor with a gesture. And now the accused suddenly changed his tone, passing from explanation and exposition to denunciation. He lifted up his eyes to the High Priest and to the other judges, and pointed with his white hands at the mob which pressed on him:

"Ye stiff-necked ones! Ye uncircumcised of heart and ear!"

This word "uncircumcised" was perhaps the most offensive he could have used. For in this context it meant that not the pagans were uncircumcised, but they, the Jews.

Despite the gesticulations of the High Priest, the crowd broke out again into angry cries. Several shouting men tried to break past the guards to lay hands on the preacher. But he, raising his voice, still made himself heard:

"You have always rebelled against the Holy Ghost. Even as your forefathers did, so do you."

"And who art thou?" yelled one. "Art thou a bastard? Are not thy forefathers even our forefathers?"

The accused ignored the interjection. "Which of the Prophets," he went on, "did not your forefathers persecute? And they slew those who prophesied the coming of the Just One, to whom—"

"But which of the Prophets did we ever slay? What slanders are those which he heaps upon our forefathers and upon us?"

"To whom," continued Reb Istephan, resolutely, "you have become traitors, and whom you have murdered."

This was more than the crowd could stand.

"To the stoning place!"

" 'Let the hand of the witnesses be the first against him!' " These words, issuing suddenly from the lips of Saul of Tarshish, fell like fierce sparks on dried tow. The crowd roared approval. But still the preacher continued:

"You received the Torah from the hands of the angels, but you have not kept its commandments holy."

"Who is he to reproach us?"

The accused no longer looked on the bench of the High Priests, or on the tumultuous assembly, on the angry faces, on the clenched fists and quivering hands which were stretched out toward him. He looked upward, and the sunlight of the late afternoon fell on his red beard, his red earlocks and his white face. The autumn sky—it was the month of Elul—shed downward a flood of brightness which broke in a thousand reflections on the golden thresholds and golden gates of the Temple, so that the courts, and the place of the trial, were submerged in a sea of gold. And the voice of the accused, ringing louder and louder, quivered with a mixture of fear and purest ecstasy. His hands shot forth from his ripped garment, reaching toward heaven; the hands were white as snow in the sunlight, and they were lifted far above the heads of the dense throng.

"Now I see the heavens open, and I see the Son of Man standing at the right hand of God."

He said no more. The next instant a white body was swimming in the air, above black heads and bearded faces and clenched fists. A chorus went up into the air:

"The hand of the witnesses shall be the first against him!"

The High Priest called for peace, but no one listened. The guards, which should have kept the preacher from the hands of the mob, were no longer there. They were not even within calling distance. The Overseer of the Temple, Alexander, cowered behind a curtain. The High Priest reiterated vainly:

"Wait: it is against the law!"

"Wait! We have not yet issued sentence!"

But no one was sent to find the guards, and no effort was made to hold back the fateful procession. At the head of it marched Saul of Tarshish. His hair, his earlocks, his beard, were twisted into a single tangled mass; his body swam in the perspiration of a strange agony. But he maintained his place at the head of the procession. Behind him strode the witnesses, lean, withered Zadoc the Shammaite, with the snake head, and broad-boned Samuel, son of Eliezer; and behind them followed the roaring confusion of hands, heads, beards, with a half-naked white body swimming in the midst.

"The field of stoning" lay outside the city. It was not really a field; it was a pit on the summit of a hill. Around the sides of the pit lay heaps of stones—the soil of Jerusalem and of the countryside nearby was sown with rocks. The bottom of the pit was not visible because of the stones which covered it, stones which had been thrown into it in the course of executions, stones on which there were, here and there, flecks of dried blood.

The clothes were ripped off the accused; a multitude of hands flung him down into the stony pit, and a voice cried:

"Witnesses, come forward and do your duty. Fulfill the commandment: 'And the hand of the witnesses shall be the first against him!'"

Zadoc the Shammaite stepped forward. Samuel, son of Eliezer, stepped forward. Saul of Tarshish, too, made an effort to step forward, but an inner command, stronger than his own will, held him back. He remembered what Zadoc had said at the time of the formal accusation: that according to the Pharisaic tradition it was not possible to invoke the saying, "Withhold and do not" in the case of a commandment of action. But he remembered also that this was the Shammaite interpretation of the tradition, while he, Saul, belonged to the House of Hillel, which took a milder view.

"'Two witnesses shall establish a thing,'" he said aloud. "Two witnesses suffice."

Zadoc the Shammaite and Samuel, son of Eliezer, threw off their mantles of burlap. Tattered and wretched these mantles were, but the garment of the poor is precious to them.

"Who will guard the garments of the witnesses?"

Saul bethought himself. No, he could not take advantage of the Rabbinic saying: "Withhold and do not." He could not remain a passive bystander. He cried out that he would guard the mantles of the witnesses.

He sat down on the bundle of garments by the edge of the pit, and saw the first stones fly down on the condemned man.

White body covered suddenly with blood . . . another stone . . . then a rain of stones . . . naked hands uplifted . . . still a rain of stones . . . white, bloody body kneeling . . . falling . . . rising . . . a half body dipped in stones, and a half body rising naked out of the sea of stones. The last rays of the sun falling on the white body, making patches of silver amid patches of blood. . . . Then two naked hands, like silver wings, uplifted toward the sun, a white face lifted to the sky, a high voice, the ringing, metallic voice of the preacher:

"Lord, Yeshua, receive my soul!"

Where had he seen this picture before? An angel, half sunk in the earth, the upper half of the body flickering in white fire, wing-arms lifted up to heaven. . . .

Where had he seen this?

113

In the mind of Saul of Tarshish there was hot confusion. He dropped his eyes. He would look no more. But he could not shut out the voice, ringing still, but dying away:

"Father, forgive them. . . ."

*　　*　　*

As Saul was returning from the execution a strange man attached himself to him and walked with him. Twilight had fallen on the lower city, deepened by the clouds of smoke going up from the fires where the women were preparing the evening meal. The half darkness was dotted with the twinkling lights of oil lamps. Saul did not remember that he had ever seen the stranger before; yet he did not turn round to look closely and make certain. The excitement of the bitter incident, in which he had been not merely an onlooker, but a participant, still held him, and as if to lighten a burden on his conscience he said aloud to the stranger:

"God be thanked, a commandment was fulfilled: 'The hand of the witnesses shall be the first against him.'"

"Yes, but the witnesses have forgotten the second half of the verse," responded the stranger.

"What meanest thou, the second half of the verse?" asked Saul.

"That those witnesses that have borne false witness shall be punished with the punishment which would have been visited on the accused.

"But the witnesses did not bear false witness," answered Saul, angrily. "Didst thou not hear the words out of the man's mouth?"

"That matters not. Thou knowest as well as I that as long as the Court has not issued sentence against him, the accused remains as innocent as a newborn child. They who stoned the child are, then, not witnesses, but murderers!"

The stranger disappeared, leaving Saul alone in the dark, narrow little street.

Saul stood looking at the shadows which had swallowed up the stranger. He was certain now that he had seen him before, but he could not remember where or when.

Chapter Twelve

THE PARTING OF THE WAYS

THE picture which Saul had seen with the eyes of his spirit became indistinguishable from the one which he had seen with the eyes of his flesh, and thenceforth the face and hands of the stoned preacher pursued him relentlessly. The very night of the execution he was driven to visit once more the "field of stoning." It did not for an instant occur to him that the "sentence" carried out against the blasphemer and misleader had been an unjust one or that it had served any but the divine purpose; what filled him with restlessness was the utter self-certainty of the proponent of the wrong. He saw the ecstatic face of Reb Istephan, he heard the cry with which he relinquished his soul to the highest authority: "Father, forgive them!" According to report these were the very words which their Rabbi had uttered when he was dying under the tortures of the heathens. Like him, the disciples who had stood before the High Priest were ready to die for the sanctification of the Name. The preacher had so died. But could a blasphemer and misleader die thus?

And if he could, if all of them could, whence the source of their strength? What were the springs which fed them? To give up life for the cause of God was the highest achievement of which man was capable, the highest condition to which he could attain; it was the fulfillment of the great commandment: "And thou shalt love the Lord with all thy soul." But how could he, Saul of Tarshish, admit that—God forbid this a thousand times—these men drew their strength from the fount of true holiness? That could not be. He knew that abomination and evil had their own world of authority; the Evil One possessed powers which he distributed among those who ranged themselves with him. One saw that clearly in the men who fought with beasts, or with each other, in the arena, the gladiators; or in those men who carried out upon their own flesh the operation of castration in the presence of the idols, as he had seen more than once in his native town. There was no doubt about it; evil had its gifts of power to distribute, too. But this being so, what was the distinguishing sign, how could one tell whether self-sacrifice came from the true sanctity or from the fount of evil? Whither were his thoughts leading him? He repeated harshly within himself: in no wise, under no circumstances, could he that was hanged on the cross be the Messiah. It followed therefore, without possibility of denial, that all these men drew their strength from the power of evil. Of this, then he was certain. But why was there this restlessness in his heart? Why could he not sleep? What was it that drove him in the night through the dark, narrow alleys of the lower city and out through the Dung Gate beyond the walls? He was not wandering forth in obedience to his own will: an irresistible need impelled him to seek confirmation—as though he needed confirmation!—of the justice of that which he had done, impelled him to clamber up the hill which held, like a cup of death, the pit reserved for the stoned.

When he reached the summit, and looked down into the hollow, he started back.

Below, in the dimness among the stones, little points of light moved to and fro, flickering wicks of oil lamps. Dark forms swam hither and thither; a murmur of voices came up to his ears. Then some torches were lit, and Saul beheld men lifting up the body of the stoned preacher which glimmered like white parchment in the uncertain light of the lamps and torches.

The throng grew larger and larger; the lights became more numerous. To his amazement Saul perceived that the participants in the rites did not consist merely of followers of the Messianic movement to which the dead man had belonged; for he recognized a number of important leaders of the Scribes and Pharisees. Rabbi Nicodemon was there, attended by a number of pupils; so was Joseph Arimathea. There were even colleagues of his own, pupils of Rabban Gamaliel, carrying oil lamps. The intimates of the dead preacher had already lifted the body out of the pit; but they still searched among the stones, and those of them which were stained with the blood of the stoned man they lifted up, too, to bury with him. And they did all this sorrowfully and piously, not in shame and fear; they acted as men act at the burial of a great saint who has given up his life for the sanctification of the Name.

Saul drew his mantle up over his face, in order that he might not be recognized, and mingled with the funeral procession. He listened

116

to the murmuring voices, and he heard praises of the dead man being uttered not only by his companions in the faith, but by the Scribes and Pharisees; they were joining freely in exalting the death of the blasphemer and misleader as the death of a saint, a pure and holy death; and they were condemning the act of execution as an act of murder. And Saul asked of himself: "If this be so, where is the example which we intended to set with the death of the blasphemer? Has he not become an example of the very contrary of that which we sought? Has he not brought strength to those whom we would weaken?" There were many in the train who envied the dead man. And when the procession reached the place of burial, there were funeral orations, in which the stoned preacher was openly and publicly called a saint, a martyr, one who had achieved the supreme end of man. His death, they said, was a testimony to the coming of the Messiah; in the manner of his death he had been privileged to drink from the same cup as the Messiah—the cup of sorrow and suffering; there was no higher privilege reserved for man. Who could doubt, they asked, that he had mounted at once all the rungs of the ladder of holiness, to find lodgment under the wings of the Glory?

"Blessed art thou, Rabbi, that hast acquired this privilege," they called out.

But it was not in the nature of Saul to be intimidated by the words and thoughts of others. What happened this night was that he understood, or seemed to understand, for the first time, the vastness of the danger which was represented by the new sect; for if sages and teachers and prominent Rabbis could permit themselves to participate in the funeral of a blasphemer, and join in the eulogies which were uttered for him, then it was indeed ill with Israel. The zeal of the Lord was strengthened that night in Saul; he was convinced, more than ever, of the justice of his cause. Heaven and earth would have to be moved, but the fire which had been lit by the men of Galilee would have to be extinguished.

But when Saul rose the next morning, betimes, as was his habit, and hastened to the school house in the court of the Master, he found himself as one who had been thrust forth from the congregation of Israel. No man answered his greeting of "Peace." No man approached him or suffered him to approach. The friends of yesterday turned their faces away, and those that had known him knew him no longer. He stood alone in the corner of the study house, saying the morning *Shema,* and behind him he heard voices:

"This morning we say the *Shema* in the company of a murderer."

Saul did not respond. He did not respond when, a few moments later, one of the pupils asked loudly, clearly, whether it was permitted to say the prayers together with a murderer. Not for a single instant did Saul's faith in himself waver. Being certain that in his action he had been moved by no personal feelings toward the dead man and had had in mind only the divine will, he was certain that he was utterly in the right. Let the heavens and the earth tremble, let bands of angels bear witness against him, there was no power which could divert him from the path which he had chosen. Saul was not a man of wavering spirit; it was yea or nay with him. He was prepared to take upon himself the insults and humiliations which were now his lot. He saw in them the test which God had ordained. God was trying him, but his heart was strong; he was worthy to bear the spear of Phineas and oppose a forehead of bronze to the mighty, even as the Prophets had done.

"For Thy sake I will bear all things. I shall make my body a target for their arrows, that Thy will may be done," he prayed in his heart, and he was filled with exaltation.

But Saul, with all his strength, was in some measure dependent on men. There was need in him of a comradely atmosphere. Powerful though his convictions were, they were not enough to fill his solitude. Heavenly joy could not wholly replace the warmth of a living heart, of an understanding ear. Therefore Saul threw himself swiftly into the task of creating some sort of group for himself, however small, in the midst of which he could take human refuge. He needed but a foothold; he needed but a single hand to take in his; and like one who feels the waters closing over him he grasped at those about him:

"But hear me to the end, disciples of my Rabbi!"

In vain. He had but to approach a man, had but to address him, and the other hastened away.

He ran from group to group, sought to hold on to friends and acquaintances; his lips poured out explanations and vindications, his face was filled with supplication. He humbled his proud and obstinate heart; and his self-love bled. Throughout it all, his convictions remained firm, but no one would listen to them; no one answered. He had become like an unclean thing, like a leper.

Bathed in the sweat of his agony, which made his garment cling to his body, and sent runlets trickling down his beard, heartbroken, but utterly secure in the rightness of his cause, he sought refuge in a corner of the study house, covered his face with his hands, and prayed:

"Thou knowest, O Lord of the world, that it was not for my honor, and not for the honor of my father's house, that I did that which I did, but only for Thy Name's sake, and for the sake of Thy holy Torah."

The brief prayer restored his inner balance. When he turned from the wall, his eyes shining, his face aflame, he beheld before him the overseer of the study house, who, without giving greeting of peace or responding to Saul's greeting, delivered a message:

"Saul of Tarshish, thou art bidden to appear before thy Rabbi." With which he turned, without the farewell of peace.

Saul found Rabban Gamaliel waiting for him in the large lecture room, which was empty. Unattended by anyone, Rabban Gamaliel sat on "Moses' seat," from which he delivered his lectures. This complete absence of attendants was in itself a rare and portentous circumstance. The Rabbi's face was pale and weary, the face of a man bowed under a double load of years and sorrows. His eyes were red with sleeplessness. His frail body was covered by a black mantle.

To Saul's salutation Rabban Gamaliel responded with a cold nod, so that Saul was almost frozen in his place near the door. But Rabban Gamaliel motioned him to approach.

Without greeting, without offering his hand, the Rabbi began:

"It has been reported to me that my pupil took part in the slaying of the just man, Reb Istephan, the preacher of the Greek-speaking synagogues, without the sentence of the Court."

"My Rabbi and my lord! The sentence was ratified by witnesses, according to the words of the Torah: 'Two witnesses shall establish the thing.' And the witnesses were those who stretched out their hands against the man of sin, even as we are enjoined by Moses: 'The hand of the witnesses shall be the first against him.' "

On the Rabbi's lips trembled the verse from the Psalms: "And to the wicked man God saith: What dost thou, calling upon my law?" But he gave utterance only to the first half, interrupted himself, and proceeded in anger:

"Without the sentence of the Court the slaying by the witnesses is not a good deed, but murder! And all those that had part in it are murderers!"

The blood left Saul's face. He tried to frame an excuse, but the words of his Rabbi continued to fall on him like hammer blows.

"I know; it is for my sins that God has punished me through thee. When God has reason to punish a teacher, he does it through his pupils. I have lain awake all night and sought in vain what transgression of mine has been so heavy as to merit such a calamity. But God is just and His deeds are just, and surely I have earned this affliction."

Silence fell between Rabbi and pupil. It was the sign that now Saul could withdraw. But Saul had not the strength to move. His head had fallen lower and lower under the weight of his Rabbi's utterances. Still sunk in thought, he did not even hear when Rabban Gamaliel clapped his hands, as a sign that the interview was at an end, and the overseer, who had been waiting on the other side of the door, entered. But before he sent Saul away, Rabban Gamaliel spoke once more:

"I am afraid for thee, Saul of Tarshish. The path which thou hast chosen for thyself is narrow and perilous; the abyss lies on either side of it. Know that those who fall into it are never again lifted up. Thou hast sore need of the help of heaven. I will pray for thee, that God may open the sources of love in thy heart. For on this narrow and perilous path of thy choosing there is no light, there are no signs and guide posts. All the lights are darkened, all measures confused, good and evil are indistinguishable. There is but one thread for thee to hold on to: 'Thou shalt love thy neighbor as thyself.' That thread alone can guide thee back. Hold fast to it; it may yet save thee."

The closing phrases of Rabban Gamaliel's admonition were not audible; they were washed away by the tears which welled from his eyes and rolled down over face and beard.

Saul lifted up his eyes, which had become two great, flaming wounds, into which fell the tears rolling down his Rabbi's face.

These were the last words Saul ever heard from his Rabbi; this was the last glimpse he had of him, before he set out on the long and dangerous road of his life.

Chapter Thirteen

DAY OF ATONEMENT

A ROYAL caravan winds its way through the streets of Jerusalem, and all the inhabitants of the city, young and old, rich and poor, have abandoned their homes to look on the wonder. The flat house-tops are black with spectators, who hang, like clusters of grapes, from the walls and towers, or overflow, like waters in the autumn, the alleys and lanes and niches. There is not a foothold, a vantage point, which is not occupied; and the sound of the city, too, is like a roaring of waters. Countless hands hold aloft branches of palm and of olive; there is a tumultuous waving of green, a roaring of welcome, as the caravan moves with regal dignity toward the upper city.

What is this marvel? It is the wealth of the East on pilgrimage to Jerusalem. Who has ever seen the like in the way of embroidered camel-coverings? The sunlight sparkles on the golden latches and the silver chains and on the purple weave of tapestry. In the riding basket which rocks at the head of the procession sits none other than Queen Helena of Adiabene, which is on the banks of the Tigris. For weeks now the caravan of camels and donkeys has been traveling across the wilderness, drawing ever nearer to the holy city, whither the Queen of rich Adiabene comes to the House of God, to bring her offering to the Holy One of Israel, for Whose sake she has cast aside the idols of her native land. All know that in this she was preceded by her son, King Isotis, who not only embraced Judaism publicly but endangered life and throne in submitting to the ritual of circumcision. And this is his mother, Queen Helena, who undertook the long and burdensome pilgrimage to the place where God has made His earthly dwelling, so that she might bow down in worship before Him.

Her face is unveiled for the Jerusalemites to see, and her lovely black eyes wander with startled glances over the crowded roofs, whence the countless branches of palm and olive greet her. She is dressed in black, according to the Persian style; about her camel there is a heavy guard of ringleted eunuchs, who hold back the throng; behind her follows the train of her attendants. But the eyes of Jerusalem's multitudes are not fixed on these, the ladies of the Queen's court, in their multicolored Arabian shawls, and not on the armed slaves carrying silver-tipped sticks. They are drawn to the heavy-burdened camels and donkeys, with their barefoot attendants: these are the treasures of the East, of Asia and Arabia, brought as offerings to the Temple. But the choicest of the offerings are not the bags of golden dinars and silver drachmae, and not the gold-and-purple-woven tapestries which attendants carry like unfurled banners behind the Queen. Something else sets the heart of Jerusalem a-flutter: the little jars, wrapped in soft silks as new-born children are wrapped in swaddling clothes, and carried as tenderly as new-born children, the little jars which, it is reported, are filled with the most marvelous oils and unguents and perfumes of Arabia—all a gift for the House of God. The people on the roof-tops point and murmur in each other's ears: the legendary myrrh and frankincense of the Arabian wilderness; the oil of Helbonah; more precious than gold, rarer than the costliest stones, are the dried roots of spice plants, which will be burned on the golden pans of the sanctuary, or be ground and mixed with oil for the eight-branched candelabrum. Joy and hope shine on the faces of the Jerusalemites; it is the Queen of the East who comes to bow down in the Temple before the God of Jewry. "Israel is not orphaned!"

The caravan halts before the Temple entrance. The first camel crouches, and the eunuchs lift the Queen out of the riding basket. She is little, this Queen, and she walks with rhythmic steps, like the daughters of Greek Macedonia from whom she is descended, as her name, Helena, testifies. They tell, concerning her, that before she turned her heart to the God of Israel, she married, following the custom of her land, her brother, King Manobaz. Now, for the sins committed in ignorance—which are not sins—she comes to purify herself before the altar of God.

She has stepped down from the riding basket, and at a signal from her the ladies of the court approach and take off her sandals. Her shimmering white feet tread with little singing steps on the bronze and yellow weave of the carpets which her servants spread out at the entrance to the Court of the Gentiles, on the northern side, by the Vestibule of King Solomon. She draws near to the beautiful gate of the Court of the Women. Assembled before the steps, the leading figures in Israel and the authorities of the Temple await her. But she will see no one, she will greet no one, until she has bowed down before the invisible God for Whose sake she has made this long journey. Closer by the gate stand the "noble and pious women of Jerusalem," carrying perfumed veils, which they throw about the Queen, hiding her face from the gaze of all. They put into one of her hands two twin doves and into the other a branch of incense; these she must bring as the offering of purification before she can enter the Court of the Women. But as she approaches the threshold, the Queen, her face hidden in the veils, falls upon her knees, and touches the earth with her face; then she rises and passes over the threshold. The men who throng the Court of the Gentiles, seeing the Queen of the East prostrate herself at the entrance to the Court of the Women, lift their voices in a great cry of exultation. They behold in this the fulfillment of the tidings of the Prophets: "And the gentiles shall seek out Thy light, and the kings shall seek out the rays of Thy brightness."

Such was the coming of Queen Helena of Adiabene to Jerusalem. On that day Saul of Tarshish was among those who stood in the Court of the Gentiles and saw the Queen fall on her knees and touch with her forehead the threshold of the Court of the Women; and his heart was filled with joyous pride. A thousand times he repeated to himself, like one who stills a hunger for faith with sacred words, the words:

"Let Thy Glory be revealed, and let the nations of the world see Thy light and stream toward it; for Thou alone art the sole living God, and Thy Torah is the Torah of truth."

* * *

Saul of Tarshish withdrew from the authority of his Rabbi, but he entered beneath no other. He remained without a teacher. He did not repent, or think for one instant that he had cause to repent, of the act which had separated him from his Rabbi. He was still certain of the rectitude of his cause. *He* was certain and unshaken; it was only his heart which was not certain. His heart trembled, and his mood was dark. He was still haunted in the nights by the vision of the angel; he still saw, in half dreams, the eyes of the stoned preacher and the hands lifted to heaven. But whatever he saw, whatever he felt, it was unthinkable that "they" were in the right. For if this were so, he was a murderer; and more, he had lifted up an ax and struck at the root of

123

Israel. If "they" were right, it was the end, the utter end, for him. And so all the learned and pious words of his Rabbi, the parting words which had fallen on him like millstones, availed nothing to swerve him from his path.

But he needed to be fortified in his heart; and like one who seeks for ever to convince himself again of that concerning which he is already convinced, he found in every incident on his path the confirmation of his views. This, for instance, the pilgrimage of Queen Helena to Jerusalem: was it not a sign that the nations had seen the light? He meditated deeply on the significance of the occasion:

"And the nations shall see thy righteousness, and all the Kings, thy glory; and they will call thee by a new name." The Kings of the East were beginning to come and the Kings of the West would also come in due course.

Let a thousand Rabban Gamaliels direct their reproaches at him— he would not give up the struggle against those who would abrogate the law of Moses. There was none beside himself filled with the zeal of God; therefore he would endure though he would perish in the flames. Had not the sages said: "Where there is no man, do thou be a man"?

"For Thy sake I will not be silent, and for the sake of Jerusalem I will not hold my peace, until her righteousness shall shine forth like a light, and her help shall burn like a flame."

And now the Day of Atonement was drawing near, a day which Saul considered propitious above all others for the stirring up of the passions of the zealots and of their hatred for the disciples; this by reason of the unusual sanctity and solemnity of the festival, and by reason, likewise, of the leading role which was played in its celebration by the High Priest.

On this Day of Atonement the new High Priest, Jochanan, of the house of Chanan, was to perform the sacred ritual for the first time.

The long governorship of Pontius Pilate had come to an end. His recall was in no way connected with the crimes which he had committed against the Jews, but was precipitated by a complaint which the Samaritans lodged against him in Rome. Vitellius, the imperial legate in Antioch of Syria, sent Pontius Pilate back to Rome; or, more exactly, to Capri, where Tiberius was staying at the time. With him went also the High Priest Joseph, from whom his younger brother-in-law, Jochanan of the house of Chanan, purchased the exalted office.

During the eight days preceding the festival, the High Priest was confined to a special chamber in the Temple, and in case of some untoward incident which might incapacitate him, another High Priest was held in reserve. These eight days the High Priest spent in the company of the oldest scholars of the Sanhedrin, who read the Sacred Books to him, and instructed him in all the minutiae of the service. On the day preceding the festival, the scholars of the Sanhedrin relinquished their charge to the old members of the Priesthood. He was led into another chamber, where he bound himself by the most solemn oaths to conduct the ritual in accordance with the ancient and accepted tradition; and so moving was the occasion that always the High Priest wept, and the old men wept with him. He was not permitted to sleep through the night which ushered in the Day of Atonement, but had to listen to the reading of the Sacred Books; and if he nodded, the young Priests in attendance roused him by snapping their fingers in his ears. Nor was the city quiet throughout that night; it was accounted a meritorious act to stay awake from the evening before till the morning of the Day of Atonement; the Temple court was open, and the tumult of preparation for the solemn festival, dinning in the ears of the High-Priest, helped likewise to keep him from falling asleep.

When the first shimmer of dawn appeared in the sky, the High Priest was led forth to begin the ceremonials in the court.

A curtain of fine woven linen was suspended between the High Priest and the congregation, and behind the curtain the High Priest was bathed and sanctified.

On every other occasion in the year, the High Priest had the right to perform the services in the Temple, but the privilege was turned over to the regular Priesthood; on the Day of Atonement none but the High Priest could perform any part of the ritual.

When the High Priest had been bathed, and his hands had been anointed, the golden robes were brought: the coat with the golden bells and pomegranates, the hat, the golden plate with the twelve jewels on which were inscribed the names of the twelve tribes. Then the High Priest, fully clad, was led forth to perform the daily service of the Temple; to bring the daily sacrifice, and to fill with the smoke of incense the Sanctuary, carrying the burning spices on golden shovels. This completed, the High Priest took a cruse of oil, entered the Sanctuary again, and attended to the golden candelabrum.

125

In the court the congregation looked between the curtains at the preparations of the High Priest; but when he entered the Sanctuary none might see him but the attendant Priests, and at that moment the congregation fell upon the ground in silent prayer.

And now the great moment was approaching. The High Priest, again purified and sanctified behind the curtain, and wearing, not the golden robes, but the linen raiment which, it was believed, had come down from heaven, was led by the Chief Officer of the Temple and by the oldest members of the Court to the two goats on which he cast lots: one "for God," the other "to Azazel." The two goats were young, strong, and washed white; they were of the same size; both had crooked horns like distorted branches of a tree; for one of them was reserved the privilege of giving its blood for the sprinkling of the corners of the Holy of Holies; the fate of the second was to be laden with the sins of Israel, and to be thrown down a slope of rock to wander away into the wilderness of Judaea. When the High Priest placed his hands on the white goat destined for "Azazel," and confessed the sins of the people, the congregants threw themselves again to the ground and confessed likewise. A legend was attached to this supreme moment of the ritual: it was said that even if the court was so filled with worshipers that there was not room for a needle, yet, when the people bowed down and confessed its sins, there was a sudden and miraculous space about each man, so that none might hear the confessions of his neighbor. Now the High Priest, carrying the shovels on which the incense burned amid the glowing charcoal, entered the Holy of Holies. The congregation became breathless, and the beating of a multitude of hearts could be heard; for now the representative of Israel, the pleader before the Throne of Grace, had entered the most sacred place in the world. Within that enclosure of the Holy of Holies there was not a single object. Of old, in the time of the First Temple, it had contained the Tables of the Law, with the fiery Ten Commandments which Moses had brought down from Sinai. But though the Holy of Holies was now utterly empty, it was built about the stone upon which Abraham, at the command of God, had been prepared to bring his only son, Isaac, as a sacrifice. Upon this stone the High Priest placed the burning incense when he addressed himself to the Almighty in a brief prayer for his house and for all the sons of Israel.

Without, in the courts, the congregants lay with their faces pressed to the marble floors. It seemed to them that in the air above them hovered the cherubim, making a shelter of their mighty wings. Hearts trembled, and eyes overflowed with tears. They could hear the voice of the High Priest making the count as he sprinkled the blood on the walls of the Holy of Holies: One, one and one, one and two, one and three, one and four; and then invisible rays came forth from the Holy of Holies, and upon them the hearts of the congregants were drawn into the service which the High Priest performed. For in that moment they were lifted out of themselves and became one with the High Priest, who stood within, confronting God for all of them. And in that moment all the bitternesses which were felt throughout the year against the High Priest were forgotten and forgiven; all barriers between him and the people were dissolved; whoever he might be, and whatever he might have done, he was now, in the Holy of Holies, the son of Aaron, the inheritor, in direct line, of the Priesthood; he was the delegate of Israel to the Lord, bringing the prayers of Israel before the Holy One.

And among the congregants, pressed close in that enormous throng, his face hidden against the cold marble, lies Saul, the young man of Tarshish. What thoughts now traverse his heart, what pictures unroll before his closed eyes! Does he not feel himself now bound to the core and navel of his people? He sees the stretches of the wilderness; he sees Moses descending from Sinai bearing the Tables of the Covenant; he sees Aaron the Priest before the Ark to which the Tables are consigned; vision succeeds vision; the eyes of his spirit pierce through the mists of the past—deeper, ever deeper. He sees the beginning, Abraham, the father; Isaac, the son, the only son, the long denied, the much prayed for, the tenderly loved, lying bound upon the sacrificial stone—that same stone upon which the High Priest has now placed the glowing incense. Israel remains the eternal offering to God, His first fruit, His first testimony. And that is why Israel is the elect among the peoples. The election was not bestowed upon him by the free grace of God; he bought it with his life's blood, which he offered upon the altar of God. Thus it was that God spoke to Abraham after the offering: "Because thou hast done this thing and hast not withheld thy son, thine only son, therefore in blessing I will bless thee, and in thy seed shall all the nations of the earth be blessed; because thou hast obeyed my voice."

And yet Israel lies bound like a sheep, not upon the altar of God, but beneath the feet of the world's peoples. They tread upon him. Four hundred years, God said to Abraham, his children should suffer slavery under Pharaoh, and then He would draw them forth with a mighty hand: such was the teaching of the Rabbis. The four hundred years are never-ending; they multiply, they continue, and the blood of Jacob's children, shed by Edom, streams as far as the gates of the Sanctuary: and help comes not yet.

Fire glows in the brain of Saul; a blazing wheel revolves in his head, making it strain away from his shoulders, as though it were ready to fly heavenward. His gross body lies on the earth, but his spirit seeks the heavens; it would penetrate to the inmost circle, seeking an answer to the mystery of Israel's pain and suffering, Israel's election not to the blessing, but to the curse. In a flash the answer comes to him. It is not true that God has cursed Israel; God has blessed Israel, blessed him with sorrow and tribulation and pain, which he must endure for the salvation of the world; in this bed of sorrow and pain the Redeemer will be born, the Adam Kadmon, the primordial man, who will come with the clouds of heaven, he whom God created before the world was, the healing for the wound, the liberation before the exile began, he who will bind the beginning to the end, the end of all ends, who will be in the great day of eternal life, in the Kingdom of Heaven.

Are they not purifying the High Priest again now, and putting back upon him the golden robes, one by one, that he may go forth and slay the ram for the sacrifice—that ram which appeared in the bush when Abraham was about to put the knife to Isaac's throat and an angel held him back?

The ram has long, curled horns. It is from these that the *shofar,* the ritual trumpet, is made. And the purpose of the trumpet of ram's horn, when it calls, is to remind us of the sacrifice of Isaac. It is the ram's horn which will be blown when the Messiah will come.

The trumpet of the Messiah!

He hears it now—the great pealing of the eternal Redeemer.

But no! Those were not trumpet peals which Saul heard in his waking dream, as he lay with his face on the stone floor of the Temple court; those were the cries of exultation with which the High Priest was greeted as he issued from the Holy of Holies. And now the people, according to the custom, accompanied the High Priest toward his home. The vast court was in a joyous tumult; strangers greeted each other warmly, friends embraced, a single spirit of happiness and affection bound them all into a congregation of the Lord—Priests, Levites, children of Israel, Pharisees, Sadducees—it was all one. The young Priests—the "blossoms of the Priesthood"—marched ahead of the High Priest; immediately behind him walked the notables of the city of Jerusalem and the leading members of the Sanhedrin. And he himself, the young High Priest, accompanied by the Priestly hierarchy, his old father, Chanan, his brother Eliezer, former High Priests, moved in the midst of song toward the palace which was his home. He was the elected of his people, its representative not only before Edom but—and this first of all—before the Lord: he was the son of Aaron the Priest.

All the gardens and orchards of Jerusalem were filled that night with youth, with joy, with dancing and singing. Young men and young women wandered, with the verses of the Song of Songs on their lips, among the cypress alleys and the vineyard beds. The youth which had come to Jerusalem for this festival, from all the ends of Palestine, and from countless cities and provinces of the Diaspora, made the acquaintance of the youth of Jerusalem. It was arranged thus: row by row the young girls stood, and the young men walked between the rows, looking, seeking their destined ones.

But that night of *Yom Kippur* Saul walked alone in the tumultuous streets of Jerusalem. He did not frequent the gardens where his comrades, the pupils of his Rabbi, were at that hour seeking brides among the daughters of Jerusalem. He was locked within himself; his lips were tightened into a thin line, his eyes were sealed in dreams. The fiery wheel was still spinning in his head. One thought pursued him now: from his mother's womb he had been destined for God. Yes, he saw it now. A curse rested upon him, as it rested upon all Israel, not to partake of the joys of youth, but to dedicate himself to the cause of God. The curse of the divine election rested on him. Today, for the first time, he dared to say it openly to himself: he was chosen for God: his life was one great sacrifice for the cause of God.

What was the cause of God? Who was the spokesman of it? Who had the right to speak of it, to command for it? Certainly not his Rabbi, Rabban Gamaliel. His Rabbi was, like every other Rabbi, an interpreter of the law. The right to speak in the name of God, to issue commands in the cause of God—and the right to be obeyed by every Jew—belonged only to one, and he was the legitimate representative of the Jewish people, not in the presence of Edom but in the presence of God: he who held in his hand the supreme authority, and had held it from the beginning: the son of Aaron, the High Priest.

The morning which followed the Day of Atonement, Saul made his way to the chamber of the Chief Officer of the Temple; it was now occupied by Theophilus, the third son of old Chanan. Saul stated briefly that he wished to serve the High Priest in the Temple.

The oldest of the High Priests, old Chanan himself, accepted his offer. He remembered the young man, he remembered his spirit of zeal for the Lord; and he repeated what he had said once before:

"Because of our many sins, there are few Phineases among us these days. The honor and glory of the Temple are trodden under foot, the Priesthood is shamed—and there is none to play the Phineas for her. Thou art a true son of Abraham, Saul of Tarshish. May thy like multiply greatly in Israel."

Chapter Fourteen

REB JACOB BEN JOSEPH

FROM the cleft of the rocks where, like a traveler ensconced between the humps of a camel, lies the quiet little town of Nazareth, there came forth one morning a young man. He was tall of stature, lean, with a face bronzed by the sun. Without a bundle at the end of his stick, clad only in a tattered covering of homespun, with tattered sandals on his naked feet, he strode upon the clayey earth which the dew had moistened in the night. The rainy season was not yet over; the earth was still drinking in with a thousand mouths the living waters which God sent down upon it. The road wound among the rocks as it descended toward the valley which, from the heights, could be seen spread out like a green lake colored with innumerable growths. Far off the little earthen houses stood up to the fresh morning sun, and the peace of God rested upon the scattered villages and hamlets. The young man's heart was filled with benediction for the habitations of the children of God, and he cried out:

"How goodly are thy tents, O Jacob, thy tabernacles, O Israel!"

Some years had passed since his older brother had set out by the same path, which leads from Nazareth, the modest townlet in the cleft of the rocks, to K'far Nahum, which is set like a jewel in the shore of Lake Kinereth. But not K'far Nahum was his destination. He was making for the Jordan valley, which winds southward to Jericho, whence the road leads upward through the wilderness of Judaea to Jerusalem.

The road was not new to him. He had been this way more than once. He had often visited the Essenes in the wilderness of Judaea, and he had linked himself with them. Returning to Nazareth, he had followed his father's occupation, that of carpenter, and had been the support of his father's family after his older brother, Yeshua, had departed on his mission. But in his mother's house he lived altogether after the manner of the Essenes. He was scrupulous about the cleanliness of his body; he never touched meat, but sustained himself only with green stuff; he broke bread only with his companions of the sect; and he remained a Nazirite, abstaining from the taking of a wife. Very rarely did he go up to Jerusalem to bring a sacrifice to the Temple, for, with the Essenes, he laid emphasis on the words of the Prophets which said that what God desired was not sacrifices, but clean hands and a humbled heart. He therefore gave himself up greatly to prayer. Like the Essenes, he despised worldly goods, made his lot with the poor, and was forever pondering the ways of God and of His Torah. But he believed above all in good deeds.

During the early part of his stay in Jerusalem he concerned himself little with the leadership of the congregation. This he left to the direct disciples of the Messiah, to those who had been closest to him when he had lived in the flesh, namely, Simon and Jochanan. He did not preach the gospel, he did not win new souls for the congregation, and he did not perform any miracles. His time was given to the Temple courts, and to prayer. He could always be seen in a corner, among the poor; and most often prostrate upon the ground, his face buried in the stone.

Reb Jacob ben Joseph soon became friendly with these men, for, like them, he would spend entire days in fasting and prayer in the Temple. His name became known among the Rabbis and the Pharisees of Jerusalem as that of a most devout man and a most charitable. He went far beyond the prescription of the law, and his charitable spirit was boundless. When he came mornings to the Temple courts, he would carry with him sacks of flat cakes from the common fund to distribute among the poor. For this reason he was always encircled by a crowd of the poor. When the disciples preached the tidings in the Temple court, Reb Jacob would stand among the listeners, a lean, towering figure, clad in a sackcloth covering which was tattered but scrupulously clean; every drop of fat had been drained from his body by his innumerable fasts; a rope was tied about his waist, and the ritual fringes dangled at his feet. He stood with head lifted heavenward, so that all that could be seen of it was the prematurely gray beard and, below it, the lean, stringy neck, stretched out as if for sacrificial slaughter. As he listened, or prayed, convulsive tremors would pass through his body, and those that beheld him then were filled with the fear of God. It was known of Reb Jacob that not only was he a man of charitable deeds, and a man of prayer, but one who observed every detail of the law as it had been propounded by the Rabbis. Such was his reputation among the learned and pious that he became a shield and buckler to the disciples and the congregation. They said of him, among the sages: "There can be no evil in their congregation if Reb Jacob has joined himself to the disciples."

Two mighty powers Reb Jacob had brought to Jerusalem from his father's house in Nazareth: a godfearing piety which expressed itself in his close observance of all the minutiae of the law and a deep feeling of justice for the poor and oppressed, for orphans and widows, and for all those who earned their bread in the sweat of their brow. It was this closeness to the poor laborer which had awakened in him his contempt for wealth and his dislike of the rich; and his enmity for the powerful landowners was rooted in what he had seen of their pitiless exploitation of the day laborer in the fields about Nazareth. Notwithstanding the stern laws of the Torah, which bade every man feel for his fellow, and love him; notwithstanding the stern Mosaic prohibition against the taking of usury—and, for that matter, against the severe interpretation of the "loan," for it was written: "If thou at all take thy neighbor's raiment to pledge, thou shalt deliver it to him by the time the sun goeth down; for that is his covering, it is his raiment for his skin: wherein shall he sleep?"—notwithstanding all this, Palestine, and Galilee in particular, was covered by the network of the money-lenders,

132

who ground the faces of the poor, often took away their little patrimony, and sometimes even sold men into slavery for the payment of debts. More than once Reb Jacob—like his brother Yeshua before him—had witnessed scenes of oppression and ruthlessness which had made his blood run cold. His contempt for the rich had taken deep root in him in his earliest years.

Therefore Reb Jacob had preached to the poor, to the laborers, bidding them bear in patience the yoke of suffering until the coming of the Messiah, who would remove all inequalities and injustice. He had done more; he had healed the sick and the fallen; not by the performance of miracles, but through the application of remedies which he had learned from his mother. He knew how to prepare certain unguents for bruises and boils; he had his recipe for the grinding of roots and herbs, to be put into a plaster. It was a common thing in Israel that a family should have preserved, from out of the far past, the secrets of certain remedies, the pressing of oils, the preparation of plasters, the extraction of the essence of cactus roots and other plants. Sometimes these traditions were handed on from generation to generation together with the genealogical tables and were transmitted orally from age to age.

Such was the case in the family of Reb Jacob of Nazareth, who had learned and stored up all the knowledge of herbs and cures which had come down from forgotten ancestors, and who brought his skills with him when he came to Jerusalem. No sooner had he joined the congregation than he made it the beneficiary, as the poor of Nazareth had been, of all that he was able to perform as a healer. However, along with this, he sought to institute, in keeping with his Essenean teaching, a far severer watch over the tables and the "serving at the tables" than had been observed until then. He was extremely scrupulous as to whom he would sit with at the breaking of bread. He went so far that he annulled the conversion of many companions who had come into the congregation. It was true that they had baptized in the name of the Messiah, and that they believed in him; but Reb Jacob was not satisfied with their observance of the laws of purity, and denied them access to the tables, which was equivalent to annulment of their conversion. In the majority of instances these were Hellenistic Jews, who had been accustomed to the usages of their native provinces and did not take naturally to the laws of purity of food. Reb Jacob also demanded that those who joined the new congregation should be observant of the law in all its complicated details and that they should go beyond the law in their devotion. He demanded that they bestir themselves early in the morning and go to the Temple; that they pray long; that they observe the Sabbath with all the rules which had been worked out by the Rabbis; that they avoid all physical contact with gentiles and even with ignorant Jews who did not know the laws of purity. He was also set on restoring to the congregation the former practice which had been introduced by their first teacher, namely, the selling of all his earthly possessions by every new member, and the turning over of the proceeds to the common fund—a practice which Simon bar Jonah and the other disciples had suspended on grounds of convenience. Reb Jacob was dissatisfied with the laziness which reigned among many of the believers, who did nothing but wait for the return of the Messiah. He demanded that all the companions, the women not less than the men, who were entitled to sit at the tables, should follow the usage of the Essenes, and go to work, become day laborers, each at his or her trade, and bring the day's earnings to the common fund, out of which all companions were fed, whether they worked or not. He demanded further that the companions withdraw from the houses of the rich, and from the work there, and go down into the lower city again, to live among the poor. He himself set the example, making his home in the David wall, in the chamber which the disciples had first occupied, and which he considered the center of the congregation.

One day this man stood in the Temple court, his lean and lofty body, like a straight flame, wrapped in a white sheet, from the bottom of which protruded his naked, bony feet. His hair cascaded in tangled, uncombed locks upon his shoulders, and his beard rested in the same neglect on his breast, bearing witness that he was under the vow of a Nazirite. To his belt, which was a pack-carrier's rope, he had tied a hollow gourd, in which he kept his special unguent for the healing of boils and wounds. He was addressing a group of men as ill-clad as himself, men whose bodies were covered with burlap and among which there was not, save for their ritual fringes, a single whole garment. The colored threads which they wore either in the pierced lobe of the ear or wrapped round their earrings, the sewing-thread which was passed through their wretched coverings, the porter's ropes which they wore about their loins, but, more than these, their starved and unwashed faces, proclaimed them to be workers in search of employment. In the Temple court every trade had its customary place where the workless assembled waiting for someone to hire them. For this reason there were always on hand in the court, and, to a greater extent, in the "Street of the Gentiles," groups of workers many among whom lent a ready ear to the inflammatory speeches which were heard there so frequently. But the man in the white sheet was uttering words wholly devoid of rebellion, or of protest, or even of complaint. He spoke of the poverty of his listeners, but not as if it were a curse, but rather a gift from the Lord. Poverty, he told them, was God's highest bestowal, for only in poverty did man attain to an understanding of God. Man, he said, is purified in trial, learns to account himself of little worth, learns to love his neighbor who is in the same condition as himself. It is not, said the speaker, in complaints against anyone, or in rage, that a man will find relief from need; it is rather by taking on himself these sufferings in love, as a gift from God: thus he will reach the highest grace and perfection and inner peace. He warned them against the sins of the tongue: "If any man among you seem to be religious, and does not bridle his tongue, but deceives his own heart, that man's religion is vain. Pure religion and undefiled before God the Father is this: to visit the widows and fatherless in their affliction, and to keep unspotted from the world." He spoke to them in parables: "See, we put bits in the horses' mouths, that they may obey us, and we turn about their whole body. Behold also the ships, which, though they are great, and are driven by strong winds, yet they are guided by a little rudder, as the pilot wills. Even so the tongue is a little part of the body, but when it is not controlled, it can be as a little fire which kindles a whole wood." Therefore he taught them to restrain their bitterness. He spoke in other parables of beasts, which are tamed and made harmless; even so, he said, man must tame his nature. And yet this man, when he came to speak of the rich, could not put a bridle on his own tongue, and words escaped him which were full of poison and death, and he cursed men who were created, as he himself recalled, "in the similitude of God." "Hear me, my dear brothers," he said; "has not God chosen the poor of *this* world to be rich in faith, and heirs of the kingdom which he promised them that love him? But you that are rich, weep and howl for the miseries that shall come upon you. Your riches are corrupted, your garments moth-eaten. You have lived in pleasure and have been wanton." Then, recovering himself, he dwelt on the guilt of all, in which he too had his share. "We did not know the just man when he was still among us in the life," he said, and followed this with the promise of the return as a reward for the poor. And he spoke of their Rabbi as being one with Job and the Prophets, an example of patience in suffering. "See, we count them happy who endure," he said. "You have heard of the patience of Job, and you have seen the end of the lord, and how the lord is full of pity and mercy." He taught them further to take to heart the example of the lord, and not to swear by heaven or earth. "Let your yea be yea, and your nay nay." He enjoined them to love one another, to help one another in the afflictions which come upon men, and to pray for one another. "Cleanse yourselves of all filthiness and of all superfluous wickedness and receive with meekness the planted word, which is able to save your souls."

In those days there was an increase of interest in the sermons concerning the Messiah among the pious Jews, particularly, however, among the Pharisees. There were many among the workers who were of the Pharisees, or who stood under their influence. And Reb Jacob, whom they began to call Reb Jacob the Just, drew to himself many of the disciples of the Pharisaic Rabbis. His sermons contained nothing which was not in complete harmony with the teaching of the Rabbis. What was new in Reb Jacob's sermons, however, was the hope of the redemption, which he declared as an already accomplished thing for the poor.

"Since the days of Amos the Prophet, we have not heard such words in Israel," said one worker, swaying his body back and forth as in the act of prayer.

While Reb Jacob was still preaching, there came running toward him a woman in a torn sackcloth robe. Her eyes, filled with pain and terror, stared out through her tumbled hair at the holy man. With arms protruding from her robe she pushed her way through the group of workers and scholars, threw herself at the feet of the preacher, and cried:

"Rabbi, Rabbi, in the name of the Messiah, heal my child!"

Reb Jacob suspended his sermon, ran down the marble steps, and helped lift up the woman.

"Where is thy child? Lead me to him."

In another moment he was following her, leaping with naked

feet, like a goat, down the slopes which led to the Kidron valley; and after the holy man streamed some of his disciples. They came to the courtyard of a poor weaver, and when Reb Jacob entered he saw, lying on a heap of leaves, a boy of some twelve years, his young body shaking with convulsions.

The mother wrung her hands and poured out her bitterness: "I tell thee, thou holy man, it is an evil eye which has been cast upon him. He is my only one. I bought a talisman for two *prutos* from the blind woman who sits in a corner of the marketplace, but it helped him not. For it lost its virtue, and evil Lilith has cast her eye on my only one."

"He ate sour, unripe grapes," was the explanation which a woman standing by the child offered to Reb Jacob.

Reb Jacob stooped and tore from the boy's neck the talisman, which was a potsherd with some words scratched upon it. Spitting out, and uttering the words, "Accursed be the filthy thing," he flung the talisman away. Then he poured out upon his hand some of the oil in the gourd at his belt, rubbed it on the child's stomach, took his stand by the child's head, and closed his eyes. His face became pale. He stretched his neck upward, placed his hands on the child's head, and murmured a prayer.

In a few moments the courtyard was filled with mothers, dragging or carrying children. Each one of them wanted the holy man to place his hands on her child and bless him. Then poor neighbors implored him to come to their homes, where the sick lay and could not stir forth. Reb Jacob went with his gourd from one dark hole to another, squeezing the drops out of his gourd, relieving the pain of the sick, and warming their hearts with his pious words. Wherever he came, he left behind him consolation and hope.

Thus it was with Reb Jacob: his deeds and his utterances lifted him, without his seeking it, to a place of leadership. When he spoke of the Messiah, the oppressed heard the promise not of a rising sun which would shine alike on the rich and poor, the bad and the good, but of a smiting rod, which would free them of their sufferings and humiliations; their wounds would be healed, they would be led out of the naked streets under a protective covering; their bodies would be clothed, their empty stomachs filled. The wealthy oppressor would be punished, and they, the oppressed, would be uplifted.

They said of him, again and again: "Who has ever comforted

137

us as he does? Surely it is a second Amos who has risen for us."

And Reb Jacob stood like an Amos in the midst of the people, a pillar for the poor and abandoned. He drew the mantle of the Messiah over their nakedness. Messiah was no longer an angel, who was known to be present, but who was revealed only to the few, the elect; he was not of the beyond, of the after life. He was the here and now; he was life as they lived it every day; he knew their needs; their poverty was his poverty, their wretchedness was his. He would come for them; he would execute vengeance on the wealthy, and exalt the poor.

And he, Reb Jacob, was among them and of them. He lived with them in their misery. There was no man so sunk in filth and wretchedness that Reb Jacob would not wash the filth from him with his own hands, and with his own hands apply the oil to his sores. In the old dwelling place of the disciples he slept on the floor, among them, leaving himself uncovered to place his raiment on the festering body of another. Nothing could disgust him, nothing turn him away, where one of his brotherhood was concerned. He went about with his oils and salves among the crowds by the Dung Gate, where the human scourings of Jerusalem were assembled—among putrefying bodies, withered limbs, the stink and decay, and he applied his remedies, washing the sores of the afflicted and binding them up. He demanded but one thing—the *inner* cleanliness of man. Let his companion in the faith be outwardly foul, his hands and face covered with the dirt of his labor, it mattered not; he could dip his fingers in the same bowl with Reb Jacob. But if he considered one innerly unclean, then, though the body was washed and perfumed, and the fingers sparkled with rings, Reb Jacob would not touch him, as he would not touch a reptile.

So it came to pass that all those companions who conformed to the law of the Pharisees, poor Priests, Jews of Palestine, accepted in all love the leadership of Reb Jacob. And in the end the leadership was accepted by those who had led till now, the disciples who had received their appointment at the hands of the Messiah himself. For grace and the law were with Jacob ben Joseph.

Among the High Priests, who kept a close watch on all that happened among the disciples, it was soon realized that it would be wholly inadvisable to lay hands on the following of Reb Jacob; for it was clear that any act of repression would awaken the anger of the Pharisees and stir up the masses of the populace. But as against this, it was easy to move against the Hellenistic, Greek-speaking element in the new sect; their position was weak and could be stormed without difficulty. They had not the support of the Pharisees, for it was known that they were not strong in the law.

At an assembly of the High Priesthood, which was held long enough after the death of Reb Istephan for the response of the populace to have crystallized, old Chanan said: "We must do after the manner of the Roman captains; we must seek out the weakest side of a fortress for the attack." And in this spirit instructions were issued to Saul, who was told that he could attack the Greek-speaking Jews, but not to lay hands on the followers of Jacob.

"We have nothing against those who stay within the limits of the law—let them believe in the Messiah or not," said old Chanan to Saul, when he authorized him to arrest those among the members of the new sect who transgressed the law. And dismissing him, he quoted a verse from Holy Script:

"Lay not thy hand upon Jacob!"

Chapter Fifteen

QUICKSANDS OF CONSCIENCE

O FATHER in heaven, Thou Who probest the souls of men, open a little ray of light for me into the bottomless darkness of the human heart, in order that I may penetrate for an instant into its mysteries; send one swift beam for me into the depths, in order that I may see, as in a flash of lightning, the forces that wage war for the possession of a man's soul. For who can pierce, who can weigh, who can even grasp the dark things which lie, involved like demons in an abyss, in the coils of the mind of man? What were the powers which worked in the young man of Tarshish that he might carry out the work of the Evil One? Was it not as though all the stages of man, from the crawling thing of the unremembered past until the latest achievement of his spirit, had all been reborn in him, in simultaneous transmigration? Was it not as though each of them brought with it its own fury, to drive him upon the path of his mission? Storm upon storm seized upon him in never ending succession; he was the battleground of a struggle between good and evil. What is good and what is evil? Who has ordained their boundaries? Where is the measure which shall determine their limits? Where is the proof and touchstone which can transcend the helplessness of man?

Saul of Tarshish became a strange and sinister figure in the life of Jerusalem. He surrounded himself with a bodyguard made up of the darkest elements of certain obscure African and Asiatic Jewish communities, in which he kindled a fanatical hatred of the new sect. He persuaded his followers that they, in aiding his enterprise, were rendering the highest service to God. One of his lieutenants was one-eyed Judah of Pumbedita, a manumitted slave, a Goliath of a man, with a split upper lip and limbs which bore upon them the marks of the chains he had once worn. Another lieutenant was Zebulun of Damascus, who gathered about him a band of manumitted slaves of the Synagogue of the Libertines. Zebulun was a little man, but his body was close-knit and powerful, like that of an ox. The life of Zebulun of Damascus had known all things. He had been the leader of a robber band—one of those bands which were made up of the shattered army of Judah the Galilean. He had been captured by the Romans and condemned to the galleys. One day when his ship was anchored in the port of Haifa he inspired his fellow slaves to a sudden revolt and broke his way through to freedom. The name of Zebulun of Damascus was a by-word in Jerusalem.

Besides these, there were the men who had followed him from the loom, the men whose fanaticism Saul had hammered into hard relentlessness: the pious Samuel, son of Eliezer, and the zealot, Zadoc the Shammaite. To season his band, Saul obtained from the High Priest a number of official guards, Levites in white aprons and high hats; their knees were naked, their feet sandaled; on their breasts hung the tablets of the Temple authority. They carried whips and copper-tipped staves, and a trembling seized upon the Jerusalemites at their approach. And Saul traversed the city with them. He was to be seen in the Temple court, on the streets, in the synagogues of the Greek-speaking Jews.

With the help of his guards he broke at will into the homes of members of the new sect.

But against those who were of the following of Reb Jacob he could do nothing, for it was not an offense against the law to believe in the Messiah or in the resurrection. The legitimation of the Priestly guards was confined to those who offended against the accepted commandments. Saul was, moreover, careful not to bring charges of such a character as involved the death penalty, for that would have meant a convocation of the Sanhedrin, on which the leading Pharisees sat; worse, it would have meant the intervention of the Roman authorities. He therefore limited his accusations against the Greek-speaking followers of the new sect to such transgressions of the law as called for nothing more than the lash, sentence to which could be issued by the minor Priestly court. But even such transgressions could not be charged to the following of Jacob and Simon, which was composed of scrupulously pious Jews observant of all details of ritual. As against these, however, the men of the new sect who were drawn from the Greek-speaking communities, and who were known for their laxity in the ritual, offered a wide field. For that matter, the Greek-speaking Jews who persecuted the new sect were equally lax, but their transgressions were ignored, and the severity of the band was directed solely against those who were suspected of leanings toward the disciples.

His eyes glittering with excitement, the sweat trickling from the tangled locks on his temples, Saul would enter a synagogue, wearing under his cloak the tablet of the High Priest. He would enter alone. His men would precede him, singly, scattering among the worshipers, entering into conversation with them, or listening to conversations already in progress. If they heard anything which might be interpreted as derogatory in the slightest degree to the dignity of the High Priest, or which lacked in the proper reverence for the Temple, or which seemed to carry the faintest echo of the sermons of Reb Istephan, they gave the signal to Saul, who thereupon ordered his guards in from the outside. The suspect was seized on the spot and carried off to the Temple court. There he was imprisoned and beaten by the guards until he confessed to transgression of the law. The trial and condemnation followed with little formality. The extreme penalty within the jurisdiction of this court was "the lash." But "the lash" had many interpretations. Or the punishment of the lash could be imposed a second time.

For repetition of transgression, or for the contumacious refusal to perform one of the laws, an offender could be lashed until he cried out: "I am willing."

Among the followers of the Messiah the name of Saul of Tarshish became overnight synonymous with that of the Angel of Death. Its terror preceded him, like clouds preceding a thunderstorm. When his shadow fell on the stones of the Temple court, there was a whispering and scattering. The Greek-speaking disciples hid themselves in their homes and in their tomb vaults. They dreaded to appear in the Temple or in the synagogues, lest they come within reach of the shadow of Saul.

Therefore Saul pursued them and sought them out in their homes. He knew well the ways and practices and habits of the Greek-speaking Jews. He knew hundreds of them in person. He did not have to wait for his guards to tell him which of the Greek-speaking Jews were likely to have fallen under the influence of Reb Istephan; for, besides his own recollection and instinct, he had the help of informers. Jerusalem was a city of many divisions, both between the Palestinian Jews and the Jews from abroad and within the separate communities themselves. In the days of Saul's bitter activity a new instrument of hatred was placed in the hands of men, and whosoever among the Greek Jews had a grudge against another, he had but to point him out as a member of the new sect. The daytime was not enough for Saul; he descended on suspect homes in the night, dragged away the father, or mother, or both, destroying the family. It was the prison, the Priestly court, the lash—and on top of these the gratuitous beatings administered by the guards. Saul looked on at the beatings and sometimes lifted up his own hand against an old man, as if he wanted to spit out of his soul the last drops of his wickedness and cruelty.

And how was it with the Pharisaic Rabbis and leaders? How was it with the Master of the Pharisees? They looked on in utter amazement at the terror which the High Priest had instituted through the hand of Saul. And when the Master protested to the High Priest, old Chanan answered him piously, playing the while with his long, white beard.

"We do not, God forbid, persecute anyone for his belief in the Messiah; much less for his belief in the resurrection. We bring to judgment only sinners in Israel, such as would destroy the law; it does not matter whether or not they are of the new sect. As long as one insults the Temple, or blasphemes against the commandments of Moses, we ask not whether or not it is in the name of a false Messiah. We do your work, Pharisees!"

Technically, the defense of the High Priest was perfect. The Pharisees could only express their ironic amazement at this sudden zeal on the part of the priesthood for the Pharisaic traditions.

And Saul? Saul was drunk with jealousy for God, unable for an instant to restore the balance of his mind, to admit any possibility that the disciples might have some point of justification for their views. "It is unthinkable that we shall leave it to time to decide whether this thing is from God or not," he said, remembering the view which his teacher, Rabban Gamaliel, had expressed in this connection. No, the decision was to be made now; if the thing was of God, it merited immediate acceptance, and he, Saul, was now on the side of the Demon. But if it was of the Demon, then could he, Saul, or another, stand by and watch the desecration of the supreme sanctity of Israel? The evil must be torn out by the roots, cut away like a wild growth on living flesh. But this cutting away, it seemed to him, was being done on his own bleeding flesh.

In one of the cells of the Temple dungeons Saul sat one day, his wild hair falling over his face and shoulders like a black foam; for Saul was under Nazirite vows, having sworn, on the day he entered the service of the High Priest, neither to cut his hair nor to touch wine until he had wiped out the new sect from among the Greek-speaking Jews. Before him stood one Joseph Nikator, a dyer, whom Saul's men had just seized at his caldron and dragged away. Saul knew Joseph well. They had often prayed together in the Synagogue of the Cilicians. Joseph Nikator was a young man of twenty-four, a widower, the father of two children. He was a day laborer, employed by a fellow countryman in the dyers' section of the valley. His learning was not of a high order; he could barely say his prayers in Hebrew, and he spoke a Greek corrupted by many local Aramaic expressions. But Joseph was deeply pious. He rose early every morning to attend synagogue before he went to work, and he did not return to his home till late in the night; for he was devoted to his congregation and a willing worker for it. Joseph was also given somewhat to fantasies and loved greatly to listen to the sermons of the traditional preachers. He believed in the Messiah and expected his coming hourly. Saul had met Joseph not

143

only in the synagogue but during the hours of work. For the dyers' court where Nikator was employed stood side by side with the court of the goat's hair weaver who was Saul's countryman. Saul had found delight in the simple, unshakable faith of Joseph Nikator, a faith which was derived from the patriarchs, not from the philosophers, a faith which shone in Joseph's big, childlike eyes. And Joseph, for his part, found in Saul a help in time of trouble. For the life of this simple child of the people had been visited by many storms. His wife, with whom his soul was closely knit, died, leaving him to bring up the two little ones. Work was not always obtainable, and Joseph was too proud to apply to the public charities. Therefore he would often remain in his pitlike dwelling in the valley, hungering together with his children. Yet he never broke into rebellion or complaint. His bearing was always joyful, and he found happiness in every stray beam of sunlight. Saul often visited him, and derived a deep pleasure from his simple talk, which was fresh and pure with his faith in his Father in heaven. Later, however, it was known that Nikator had fallen under the influence of the powerful preacher, Reb Istephan. Now he stood before Saul, surrounded by the guards with the loaded whips; his face was swollen and streaked with wounds; the blood trickled down on to his bared breast and the remnants of his sackcloth garb. Saul's eyes, peering through the tangles of his hair, were fixed sharply on the childlike face of the accused. The two Tarshishites observed each other in silence.

"When did you last bring your sacrifice of purification to the Temple?" asked Saul.

"A long time ago, before the Messiah revealed himself," answered Joseph Nikator in a quiet, matter-of-fact way.

"Before the Messiah revealed himself?" asked Saul.

"Yes, before he showed himself to the disciples, and the pure martyr, Reb Istephan, had not yet given us the tidings, or drawn us into the company of the believers."

"And from that time on you have not sinned and have not felt the need to bring a purification sacrifice to the Temple?"

"From that time on my purification offering has been the Messiah redeemer, who was tormented and died for our sins, which he took upon himself, as we have been taught by our teacher, Reb Istephan."

Saul bit his upper lip and felt the sweat of his anguish dampening his brow. He clenched his fists, feeling himself lost for a moment. Had

144

it been a scholar, or one of the prominent members of the Greek-speaking community, who had confronted him with these words, he would have known what to do. He would have watched with harsh joy the man's punishment and been refreshed by the spectacle. But these childlike words, this innocent expression, known to him so well from the past, disarmed him. For it was in the same tone, with the same expression, that Joseph used to answer Saul's questions about his faith in God the Father. It was the same unshakable, rocklike, enduring foundation laid by the generations. How was he to begin destroying it from beneath the feet of the accused?

"Nikator!" he cried. "Nikator, my friend, my dear friend! Do you not know that for refusing to fulfill a commandment you may be given the lash until you cry out 'I am willing'?"

"Saul, my brother, what can you do to me if my Messiah has already come? And what can happen to me if my share in the Messiah and my portion in the Kingdom of Heaven are prepared for me in every way? Who can do evil against me any more when my soul is knit into redemption by the Messiah redeemer?" asked Nikator, lifting his eyes to the roof of the chamber.

"But Nikator! Nikator! This is idol worship which your hand encloses!" cried Saul, his patience deserting him and his body beginning to tremble.

"No, Saul, my brother, this is not idol worship which my hand encloses. It is the tradition of my fathers and the covenant of the Patriarchs. They have not deceived us with a false Messiah; this is the true, the only Messiah, promised us by the Prophets, in the name of God."

"Take him away," shrieked Saul. "He blasphemes!"

Later that day Saul stood by when the servants of the High Priests laid Nikator across the threshold of the court, and their lead-weighted whips fell upon his naked back. . . . One, one and two, one and three. . . . Saul watched and saw one bloody welt after another springing up on the naked flesh. Not a moan, not a sigh, escaped the young man's lips; he surrendered his body in love to his tormentors, taking the lashes in joy of his faith. . . . Only now and again a murmur came from him, words of the Psalms, "Into Thy hands I deliver my spirit." . . . And now the lead-weighted lashes seemed to be falling on Saul's naked soul, and with every blow he clenched his teeth, as though he, and not the prostrate Nikator, felt the burn of it. Saul was aware of a wild impulse

145

to throw himself on his knees, to cover with his eyes and lips the wounds springing out on the white flesh. He knew that the longer he watched, the greater was the harm he did himself; he knew that the foundations beneath him were being shaken. Yet he stayed at his post, and drained the bitterness of the cup which he himself had filled. He drained it with regret, with horror and with certainty, as though he needed to take this punishment upon himself. . . .

That night he lay on the hard and narrow bench which was his bed, in the upper room of his sister Chaninah's house, and spoke in his heart:

"Lord of all the worlds, take pity on me! Everything is in Thy hand, except the fear of Thee. Thou hast taken the children of man and thrown them, like wild beasts, into a dark and tangled forest, and Thou hast said to them: 'Feel your own way through the labyrinth to the light of the sun!' How can we, Father in heaven, when Thou hast delivered the same powers and authorities to the good and the wicked, and the powers war with one another, and the authorities mingle and are confused, so that boundaries cease, and our hearts incline this way and that, while we are inclined to sin from our birth? Father in heaven, open for me but one ray of light, narrow as a needle! For it cannot be, Father, that thou makest me, without reason, to drink the blood which my hands shed. Thou knowest my heart and my secret thoughts, and Thou knowest that I do all but for Thy Glory and for Thy holy Torah. For what have we on this earth but Thy teaching and Thy laws? Father, help me in my wretchedness, for I have built all upon Thee, and to Thee I have confided all. With Thee I am the defender of Thy Torah; without Thee I am a sinner lost for ever!"

His nephew, ben Chanan, who slept near his door, heard Saul's groaning, rose from his bed, and came to him.

"Uncle Saul, what ails thee? I hear thee weeping."

The sound of the lad's voice brought a sudden change in Saul. A flood of certainty uplifted him. "What avails it," he asked, "to tear the fruit down, piece by piece? A great ax must be lifted against the whole tree, and the fruit will perish with it. Not the little ones are guilty, but the great ones who are their misleaders. It is the great ones we must destroy!"

He rose early the next morning and set forth, Judah of Pumbedita on one side, Zebulun of Damascus on the other, his guard following, for the Temple court. There he found the disciples at prayer by the side of

146

the King Solomon Vestibule. In one group stood Jacob ben Joseph, Simon bar Jonah, Jochanan and Jacob of the Zebedees. A second group stood in another corner of the court. They were not preaching at this moment; they were saying the morning *Shema,* for this was the time of the morning offering on the altar. When Saul drew near to them they did not interrupt their prayers; they did not see him. Saul withdrew to a little distance. He saw before him Jews at prayer, Jews engaged in the same devotions as all other Jews. How could he lift his hand against this tree, which was rooted in Israel? These disciples were Pharisees, like himself. He did not dare to lift a hand against them.

"Lay not thy hand on Jacob!" the High Priest had said to him.

He left, commanding his men to follow him.

"Our authority is only over those who destroy the law and desecrate the Temple," he said to his men, and led them in the direction of the Greek quarter.

There was nothing for it, then, but to pluck the fruit piece by piece, and to this he set himself with renewed fury.

New sources of energy, which he had not suspected in himself, were released. He rested neither by day nor by night. His ear was ever open for reports, and wherever suspicion pointed he went with his guards, dragging the sinners from their homes, flinging them into the Temple dungeons.

While his energy carried him, it was well with him. But the few hours which he spent on his hard, narrow bed were hours of torment. There was no peace for his spirit, and the time which should have been given to repose was the time of torment for him. Drops of anguish were pressed out of his soul by the vise of his conscience. Over his bed hovered strange clouds in the shape of writhing bodies. That which he looked on by day, the ripped and bloody flesh agonizing under the lashes of his guards, returned to him in the nights. But he heard no sound, for there was never a sound of complaint or of rebellion; silently, in love, they accepted their suffering, as if it were a precious gift. And these whose bodies visited him in his sleeplessness were not the bodies of men strong in learning, but the bodies of ordinary weavers, perfume mixers, dyers, sandal makers, the victims of the poverty of the Kidron valley, the lowest stratum of the Greek-speaking Jews. They were barely able to read, they were weak in the law, their code of observance was slender and uncertain. These Jews, who stood near the doors of the

147

Greek-speaking synagogues of Jerusalem, who filled the marketplace with their crying as they offered their wares to passersby, who bowed their bodies before the looms, who dabbled their hands in the caldrons of dyes, these simple Jews whom he knew so well and loved so deeply—where had they found this strength? Whence did they derive the endurance to suffer so much for a false Messiah and a lying hope?

Chief among the ghastly visitors in the night was the face of Joseph Nikator, the dyer who belonged to his own synagogue and whom he had given up to the tortures of his guards. The open, friendly face, the eyes that seemed to seek protection, to look for someone's superior strength and wisdom to hang on to: the spirit that had been for Saul the very symbol of the virtues of Israel: this pursued him dumbly. What were the powers that moved Saul now? Were they of God or of the Demon? But no! It was impossible, a thousand times impossible, that he had tortured and flayed an innocent soul. Oh, how much sweeter it would be for him if he could let his own body be tortured for the cleansing of Israel!

Joseph Nikator gave him no peace. Saul decided at last to go in search of him, to speak with him, to convince him, with all the arguments at his disposal, that he was wandering on a false path, that he had been misled by others, that he could still be saved, if he would but listen to Saul. For it seemed to Saul, in the nights, that Joseph Nikator's soul was his own soul and that in rescuing him he would be rescuing himself.

Forsaking his companions and guards, Saul went down into the Kidron valley. Knowing that, if he were recognized, a panic of fear would fall on the populace and the word of his coming would run before him, he wrapped himself in a black mantle, and keeping his face covered he asked his way from court to court, seeking the dwelling of Joseph Nikator.

He found him at last. Joseph Nikator lay under a canopy of branches supported by four upright poles. His shattered body was stretched out on a pile of burlap. Near him stood an earthen cruse with water for his refreshment; and at his head sat a neighbor, black as the earth, half-naked, dipping a rag into a ewer of oil and applying it to the welts on Nikator's back. Elsewhere, in the shadow of the canopy of branches, two little children played. There was no one else about.

When Saul unfolded his mantle and sat down near the feet of the beaten man, the neighbor recognized him. With a wild yell the half-naked figure sprang to its feet and fled from the booth.

But Nikator betrayed no fear and not even astonishment. He looked at Saul as though he recognized him with difficulty; then his face was distorted as by a smile of pain, and in his eyes pity was written.

"Joseph Nikator, I have come to you to ask your forgiveness for having put you to the lash," said Saul.

"I forgave you long ago, Saul," said Joseph, with his childlike smile.

"Is there no anger in your heart against me? It was for your good Nikator."

"I know you meant it so. I accepted the pain of it with love."

"It was to make you turn from evil ways, which wicked men have tempted you to follow, and to have you return to your Father in heaven."

"You are right, Saul. I am a sinful man. God punished me for my own good. God is just, and His judgments are just."

"To have you return," continued Saul, "from following the path of belief in a false Messiah."

"No, Saul, the Messiah is a true Messiah. God has seen our poverty and He has taken pity on us and has sent us a redeemer, to help us."

"How can he help you if he could not help himself?" asked Saul.

"Saul, Saul, the Messiah took pain upon himself in order to feel on his own body our suffering and our need, in order to be as one of us—shamed and crushed. And in order to take our sins upon himself, he drained to the dregs the cup of our shame and wretchedness. Thus it was that Reb Istephan taught us while he was yet in the life."

These words were like scorpions in the ears of Saul.

"Let the tongue be stricken dumb which utters those blasphemies! God's chosen one shamed and beaten by the rod of Edom, even like one of us?"

"Saul, Saul, I am not as learned as you, but do you not see that if the Messiah is to save each one of us, even the lowest of the low, he must go down to the depths of hell and lift out thence the souls which have fallen into it? Now nothing more can happen to us, even though we should fall into the pit of death, for in the lowest depths stands the Messiah, with outstretched arms, and lifts up the fallen souls. What can befall me, I ask, and whom shall I fear, if the arms of the Messiah are wide open to receive me? 'Yea, though I walk in the valley of the shadow of death, I fear no evil, for Thou art with me.' That is why the Messiah yielded himself with love to the blows and insults of Edom."

Saul sat dumfounded. There was no way of talking with this man, no conceivable way of guiding him. For this that he heard from the lips of the dyer had neither wit nor logic in it, and was so alien to all that he had learned as the law of Moses that there could be but one answer : punishment, the lash, the uprooting of the weed by main force. But he was weary of doing this. This man who lay before him was now so covered with the evil growth that he was beyond redemption. All that Saul could do now was curse, curse the misleaders : and this he now did.

"Cursed be the mouth which whispered these falsehoods into your ears ! Cursed be those who brought the poisonous weeds into the garden, making your soul a prey to the Evil One. You have put yourself beyond the pale of the community, you have lost your portion in Israel. Return, return, Nikator, before it is too late." And Saul stretched out his arms to him.

"Saul, Saul, I will pray to God to open your eyes, in order that you may see the great light which has come to us in our darkness."

"You will pray for me? I am your enemy, and I have beaten you, and will beat you again, until you will perceive the Evil One whose net is spread out for you, and who has dug a pit for your feet. Until you return to the God of Israel, I am your enemy, Nikator."

"The lord taught us to love our enemies, to bless those that curse us, to do good to those that use us despitefully, and to pray for all those who persecute us for his sake."

"Which lord? Which lord?"

"The lord who is the servant of God, the Messiah."

"To do good to those that persecute you?" asked Saul, wonderingly.

"Yes, so that we might be children of our Father in heaven, who sends His sun to shine on the evil and the good and sends down His rain for sinners and saints."

Saul fled from Nikator's presence shaken to the soul, filled with rage against himself and against his former friend. What was this? He had come to an ordinary, simple Jew to teach him, to exhort, to enlighten; to make it clear that all that he, Saul, had done was for the sake of heaven; and in the end he had cried out that he was his enemy and would punish him again and again; and then the "sinner," the beaten man, had turned upon *him* with enlightenment, had declared that he had nothing against his tormentor, that he loved him, and would pray for him, because thus he had been taught. Saul was shamed in all his depths by the action of this simple man, who had so disarmed him that he had been unable to answer and had been driven to rage and bitterness. But who was this whom he had called "the lord"? Who had he been who was able to implant such love in the hearts of the simple that they were ready to be thrust out of Israel for his sake? Who was the man who had spread such teachings among the broken of spirit that they could stand before the learned and disarm them with the sword of their faith? Who was he who had sent such a light into the dark pits of the poor? Who had given the strength of rocks to the shattered? Who was he whose fall had been interpreted as the supreme victory, whose weakness was seen. as unconquerable strength, whose humiliation had been crowned with the glory of the Messiah? Who was he? Who?

That night Saul had a dream. He saw once again the form which had appeared to him so often before, the form of the fallen angel whose body was half sunk in the earth and whose breast and face rose from the heap of stones. But it was no longer an angel, for arms had replaced the wings, and the face was clearly that of Reb Istephan, as he, Saul, had seen him for the last time, kneeling naked, half buried in stones, his flesh covered with running blood. The body shone, dazzling white, and on it the rivulets of blood marked their clear paths. The hands were spread out to heaven, the face was upturned, the lips murmured a prayer. But now the stones were no longer stones; they had become transformed; they were human heads, human faces, and all of them so near, so familiar to Saul. . . . They were the heads and faces of Jews whom he saw often at prayers, at the reading of the Torah, in the marketplace; faces which he loved; faces with big Jewish eyes, with trembling beards, with fluttering earlocks above necks stretched out ready for the sacrificial knife in the name of God's commandments; faces which reminded him of Nikator's, with its childlike, wide-open eyes, in which burned the unquestioning faith of Jews; lips, wounded, fainting lips, on which hovered a smile of blissful hope; faces which had looked on everything, had seen the end of all ends, and had become peaceful, because all questions had been answered for them, all hopes fulfilled; faces which dissolved in the last dissolution of union with God as they were caught up into the eternal clarity of grace; faces he had seen so often of late, being flung across the threshold of the prison, before the punishment began. Then, finally, all the stones which had become faces bore one likeness, and the likeness was that of Joseph Nikator . . . one heap of faces on the field of stoning . . . and among them was sunk the body of the angel—no—of the preacher, Istephan, whose arms and face were lifted to heaven, whose lips murmured a prayer, the prayer for all of them, opening the path into the heavens, carrying thither their cry of hope, and their obedient response, We will do and we will obey.

Chapter Sixteen

THE BRINK OF THE ABYSS

WHEN he awoke, a thousand fiery points were pressing against his temples, his forehead, and his neck. He felt as though a sharp-toothed adder had forced its way into his bones and was feeding on the marrow. There was a black abyss in his heart, the abyss of lowest hell, and into this abyss everything was falling, everything that had been as firm as the rocks—falling with him. His little nephew, ben Chanan, had to bring him a cup of honey wine to strengthen him, to put some warmth into his limbs; for the color of his face was like that of a spleen, and his eyes were glazed, as with a growth.

And yet he bestirred himself, met his guards at the appointed time, and set out feverishly on the hunt for new victims.

God, or the Demon, had chosen his heart as the battlefield between himself and mankind; God, or the Demon, played a wild game with him, danced before his eyes, and flung him, like a ball, from certainty to doubt and from doubt to certainty; God, or the Demon, delighted in mocking him. Saul was at times strongly inclined to believe that it was the Demon, the very same Demon, indeed, who had cast a spell of false hope and vain belief on the victims of his persecution. The Demon stirred up in them a mad ecstasy of faith, so that they endured all suffering but still clung to him and took him for the Holy One of Israel.

This same Demon was making mock of him, dancing before him, flinging him about like a ball, luring him into pits of doubt. But Saul would resist! He would stand up like a man to the messenger of evil, and with the help of the God of Israel he would overcome him!

He redoubled the zeal of his activities. He closed his ears to the pleading voices of the sinners, his eyes to the sight of their pain; he closed his heart with seven seals to the thought of doubt. Oh, he knew that they all took their sufferings upon themselves in the spirit of love. But there were a few of them who repudiated their affiliation with the companionship and turned back with healed and restored hearts to the God of Israel and His Torah. The great majority, and they the simplest and most ignorant, still clung to the Demon and obeyed him in all his devious ways.

It often happened that his path almost crossed that of the disciples. He would arrive at the home of a victim barely an hour after they had paid a visit; the dust on the threshold still bore the imprint of their sandals. Chief among them was the pious, eternally praying Jacob ben Joseph: Saul still felt in the air the odor of his oils and unguents and heard in the replies of his victims the words of consolation which the disciple had planted there. Saul knew well, from the reports of his spies, that Jacob ben Joseph, Simon, and Jochanan were making regular, secret rounds, entering the wretched homes of their followers and strengthening them against the persecution. But unless the transgressor was of the Greek-speaking community, Saul was as impotent against him as against the disciples themselves.

Saul now decided that the time had come for him to stretch out his hand against the leaders of the Greek-speaking group, instead of against the little ones. A number of the leaders had, as he knew, fled from the persecution, leaving the little people to bear its brunt. He determined to seek them out. Philippus, the friend and comrade of the dead preacher, was first on his list. He lived in a great house on the Street of the Cheesemakers, not far from the entrance to the upper city. The house stood on a slope and was distributed over several terraces. The lowest terrace consisted of the cemented courtyard, in the center of which was a water basin set about with cypress trees and a peristyle. The sleeping quarters were on this terrace, and a flight of steps led to the next level where the living quarters were. On the uppermost terraces there were many low, flat-roofed rooms; these were the quarters of the women.

When Saul came into the quiet, well-tended garden court, he found no one. The chambers of the men were emptied of all furniture, except for an occasional bamboo mattress or a low-legged table or a stone grinding pot or an open wooden box containing manuscripts. In one place a mantle hung on the wall. But Saul encountered not a single person. As he issued from the men's quarters, he suddenly perceived, on the steps leading down from the uppermost terrace, Zipporah, Philippus's oldest daughter. She, seeing Saul and his men, stood still. She was dressed after the manner of all the women followers of the sect, in the sackcloth garb of the poor. She no longer wore her hair in piled-up braids, Greek fashion, but had let it fall back on her neck and shoulders, under a hair-veil which also covered her face, according to the usage of the women of Jerusalem.

"They whom you seek are not here, Saul," said Zipporah, in a singing voice. "Only the women of the house are left. Carry out your work, Saul, we are ready."

"My work?"

"Command your men to take us prisoner; you have done it with others."

"Prisoner? Take whom prisoner? The men are gone."

"Us, the women."

"The women! Who pays any attention to them?" he quoted the Aramaic phrase of contempt current in Jerusalem.

"Are we any better than the women of the poor, the women whom you have dragged to the court of the High Priest, Saul? Why do you not arise, Saul, and carry out your mission?"

"I have told you—women do not count. 'The mind of women is light.' Today it is one thing with them, tomorrow another." He turned to his companions. "Come! The men have fled, leaving the women's clothes behind."

"Saul, you do not perform your task honestly! There are some whom you flatter!" Zipporah called out.

Saul did not answer her. Outside, he said to his followers: "Women are a race apart." Nevertheless Zipporah's words rang in his ears: "You do not perform your task honestly!" In his heart he knew that she was right. Yes, he played favorites. It was the first time it had happened; but he could not bring himself to drag Zipporah and her mother and sister to the Priestly court. But why had he done it with

154

other women, with the wretched, ragged women of the lower city? He could still hear their lamentations, their moans; he could still see their hair flung over their bodies, those weak, defenseless bodies. But when it came to the rich, the mighty, those whom he knew, it was another matter.

"Who art thou, Saul, and what art thou?" he asked himself. "An oppressor of the poor, or the avenging messenger of God, holy in zeal for His honor and His Torah?"

But the accusation had gone deeper than Zipporah had realized. Saul had come to this house in order to arrest Philippus because his conscience would not let him rest. He had suspected that Philippus had left the city; Philippus had ceased to appear in the synagogue; therefore he had gone to look for him in his home. But there was another, whom he had seen in the company of the disciples, and him he did not seek out. His authority extended over bar Naba, for bar Naba was of the Greek community. It would be a very light matter to subject bar Naba to cross-examination, to find him guilty of transgressing one of the laws, and to have him condemned to the lash. Him he could have beaten as he had had the others beaten. Yet Saul had avoided bar Naba. He knew that in the home of bar Naba's sister were assembled the women whom the disciples had brought with them from Galilee; he knew that the disciples were frequent visitors there, that the common meals of the companionship were held there. He avoided bar Naba not because he was afraid of him, but because he had not the firmness to stand face to face with his former friend, whom he had not talked to since their separation. He avoided him because in the inmost chamber of Saul's heart a whisper ran about, and the purport of it was that bar Naba was the just man, and he, Saul, the wicked one; that bar Naba was the persecuted and he, Saul, the persecutor. Saul feared to put the issue to the test, dreading in advance to look in bar Naba's eyes. But he could no longer evade the challenge, and he resolved on the spot to meet it. He must prove to himself that he was in the right. The law was on his side, the truth was on his side; he could bring the weight of both to bear on his friend. And if he secretly entertained feelings of respect for his friend's enthusiasm—arising, perhaps, out of love—all the more reason for the final test. Yes, it might well be that he envied bar Naba's swift acceptance of an ideal and his capacity to surrender to it his youth, his joy, and his love. Bar Naba had much to give. He was

155

young, he was filled with the joy of life; he was not like Saul, who despised joy and had denied his own youth. Goodness and gaiety had radiated from the face of bar Naba and had surrounded his body like a brightness and a warmth, attracting young and old. The loveliest daughters of the land had dreamed of him as their chosen, and the wealthiest families had sought his hand. Saul remembered well, only too well, the joyous assemblies in bar Naba's vineyard. All this bar Naba had surrendered freely, laying his youth like a burnt offering on the altar of his faith. Saul could not help it if he yielded to a certain admiration and envy. This was the reason for his evasion of any encounter; and precisely this was the reason, after Zipporah's taunting reproach, for meeting the issue at last. Bar Naba would be the touchstone of his sincerity, bar Naba would help him determine, once and for all, whether the work he did was of the Lord or of Satan.

From the house of Philippus he hastened with his guards toward Miriam's house, toward the house in which he had so often been a welcome guest.

He found there neither servant nor overseer to welcome him in the vestibule, as in former days. The gate was opened for him by a girl, a member of the household; and when she perceived Saul and his men, she let out a scream of terror and fled toward the inner rooms. Quite without thinking, Saul restrained his men from entering; and in a little while bar Naba came out, accompanied by the boy Jochanan.

Saul recognized his former friend with difficulty. Was this the graceful and elegant bar Naba, whom he had always seen of old in his tunic of delicate linen, in the flowing black mantle, with the flashing ring on his finger? Was this the bar Naba whose presence had been a shining and a singing? The man coming toward Saul had the aspect of a Nazirite; his body, wrapped in sackcloth, was lean, not slender; his hair hung down like a mat; a wan face peered out from behind the wild growth of beard. The two men confronted each other wordlessly. Their eyes grappled in mid-air, and on Saul's face there was something which betrayed a terrified weakness.

"Peace be to your coming, Saul, my brother," said bar Naba, and stretched out his hand.

" 'There is no peace for the wicked, saith the Lord,' " answered Saul, and turned his eyes away.

"I pray for you, Saul, that God may help you to see whither the

156

false promptings of your will have led you! Saul, my brother, awaken!"

"The prayer of the wicked is like incense on the altars of idol worshipers," retorted Saul. "And I am no brother to those who eat of their sacrifices."

"I will not cease from praying for you, Saul, my brother. And when you have awakened and have perceived how far down the path of evil your steps have taken you, do not fly in terror to the valley of death, but find the strength to cling to the horns of the altar, so that you may return to your Father in heaven. For I know, Saul, that you do not do these things out of wickedness, but because you have been misled by evil counselors, who have persuaded you that this is God's work. Saul, Saul, awaken, and realize that this is the work of Satan, not of God!"

"Is this how thou speakest to the messenger of the High Priest? Villain!" yelled Zadoc the Shammaite.

"Villain!" shouted Judah of Pumbedita, after him.

"And this is how we deal with villains!" yelled Zebulun of Damascus, and lifting up his whip smote bar Naba with it across the cheek.

Before Saul could gather together his thoughts, which the words of his former friend had thrown into the utmost confusion, he saw the blood start out from bar Naba's mouth and pour down on his sackcloth mantle; and bar Naba, the proud bar Naba, the friend of his early manhood, did not answer with angry words, but turned his other cheek to the Damascene, smiled sorrowfully at him out of the great eyes which Saul knew so well, and said:

"The lord taught us that if one smite you on the cheek, turn him also the other."

"Yes, we have heard it!" shouted Zebulun, and lifted his whip again.

But now he felt on his arm the hot, sharp fingers of his leader.

"Thou son of wickedness! Are we bandits?"

And without glancing at bar Naba, Saul said to his followers:

"Let us go from here. The blows of your hands have spoiled the work of God." And he led his men forth. But as he marched out at their head he heard bar Naba's voice behind him:

"Saul, Saul! I knew it! You are my brother!"

Now Saul was certain of one thing: he was a flatterer and had not the right to continue in God's work.

157

From that moment Saul of Tarshish wandered blindly about, like a poisoned man. Bar Naba had poisoned him, slain him, defiled his strength. He tried to carry on, but as often as he confronted one of the followers of the disciples, he saw before him bar Naba turning the second cheek to Zebulun of Damascus. Yes, others had done it before, carrying out the instructions of their Messiah, but Saul had not paid attention to it until he saw it done by bar Naba: bar Naba, the proud, the beautiful, his friend, standing with bloody mouth, turning his cheek to the smiter. And he heard Zipporah's voice: "Saul, you do not perform your task honestly! There are some whom you flatter!"

Yes, he was a hypocrite, a flatterer, and could not continue with his mission.

Two or three days he wandered with his band about the streets of Jerusalem, his heart torn by conflict. Then he formed a new resolution: in Jerusalem he flattered and spared, he played favorites,. he had too many friends among the sinners. He would ask to be sent elsewhere, to some place where he knew no one and was known to no one. Then, between him and the followers of the disciples there would be nothing save the law of God, and he would win back to his old strength and self-certainty.

The opportunity soon presented itself.

The believers among the Greek-speaking Jews of Jerusalem had scattered from the city because of their terror of Saul. They fled to the provinces, to Samaria, to Galilee, to the seashore, to Safad, to the Sharon valley, and to the Shephela, the lowlands to the south of Joppa. They even fled outside the borders of Palestine. In the Jewish settlement in Antioch, of Syria, and elsewhere, the tidings were spread of the return of the Messiah. The field was wonderfully ready for the seed. Everywhere the coming of the Messiah had been momently awaited. The disciples of Jochanan had penetrated to many Jewish communities, baptizing many in the name of Jochanan. In a large number of cities companionships had been formed in the spirit of the Essenes, who lived in separation, following strict laws of purity and preparing for the Messiah. Now, when the Greek-speaking believers, fleeing from Saul's persecution, came into these various places, they found it easy to organize small congregations. Word of this development reached the circles of the High Priest, occasioning much concern; and in particular the High Priest was disturbed by the reports from Damascus of Syria.

Damascus was perhaps fruitful soil for the Messianic tidings. The city contained a large number of gentile converts, mostly women, for whom the Rabbis of Damascus made conversion to Judaism especially easy. It was said that the majority of the women of Damascus had baptized to the Jewish faith. With the men it was not so easy, but crowds of the unconverted, "righteous among the gentiles," besieged the synagogues on the Sabbath. In Damascus, too, a congregation of the new sect was formed. The High Priest learned, to his alarm, that the disciples of the new sect were gaining new converts daily among the Greek-speaking Jews, and numbers of gentiles had joined them. It was resolved, at a session of the hierarchy, to send a plenipotentiary to Damascus, with authority to arrest the leaders of the new sect and to bring them to Jerusalem for trial. The relations between the High Priest and the Nabataean King in Damascus were excellent. The Arab ruler was often in Jerusalem, where he was a guest in the palace of the High Priest, and where he brought his offerings to the Temple. The Ethnarch would understand the danger represented by the rebellious sect, for it would be made clear to him that the blasphemous attitude of its leaders to the Holy Temple would corrupt the piety of all the Jews of Syria if it were allowed to go unchecked. There was no doubt in the High Priest's mind that the ruler of Damascus would co-operate in the arrest of the blasphemers and turn them over to the messenger. If any doubt existed, it had to do with the choice of the messenger, for the man to be entrusted with such a mission had to be one consumed with zeal for the cause.

When the decision of the hierarchy came to Saul's ears, he wasted not a moment, but hastened at top speed to the chamber of the Chief Officer of the Temple, and in a voice which shook with eagerness and despair, cried out: "Send me to Damascus!"

The request was transmitted to the High Priest, and the High Priest concurred at once. That same day letters were addressed to the heads of the synagogues of Damascus. The hand of the High Priest was powerful and far-reaching: everywhere Jews were recognized as a separate people, and the High Priest was recognized as the legal representative of the Jews: he had the right to order his Jewish subjects to appear before him in Jerusalem.

The letters were sealed and handed over to Saul: he was armed with the authority to arrest at his discretion any Jew of Damascus and to bring him to the High Priest's court.

By whatever path it traveled, the news of this disposition came to the ears of Reb Jacob and the other disciples, and they were terrified by the prospect of Saul's descent on the young congregation of Damascus. Seated at the common meal, with Reb Jacob at the head of the table, they sighed for their brethren in the faith, the men, the women, the children, delivered into the hands of the persecutor, Saul of Tarshish. The very name was a harbinger of calamity. Eyes dropped, faces were pale, and hands trembled. Here and there, however, other emotions were betrayed, not fear, but anger and contempt; particularly was this so among those of the believers who had known him in the school of Rabban Gamaliel. The Pharisees among the believers, and their numbers were considerable, felt themselves shamed and humiliated at the mention of Saul's name, as their forefathers were once shamed by the mention of the golden calf.

"Who knows what will be now with the holy congregation of Damascus? I have heard that among the letters he carries, there is one addressed to the ruler of Damascus, who is a friend of the House of Chanan; and the ruler is prepared to deliver the saints to the slaughter," said one.

"To think," said another, "that this same Saul was once a pupil of Rabban Gamaliel, a disciple of the mild Hillel."

"Let us pray for the peace of the holy congregation in Damascus," said one of the older disciples. "Let us pray that He protect them from the hand of the oppressor, from the hand of our enemy, Saul of Tarshish."

"Did not our lord teach us to pray for our enemies?" responded Reb Jacob ben Joseph. "Come, dear brothers, let us all pray for the young man, Saul of Tarshish, that God may be merciful to him and turn his heart to the good."

And Reb Jacob, at the head of the table, and the disciples and brothers, following him, bowed their heads and prayed for the soul of Saul of Tarshish.

"Lord of the worlds, Thou Who art the father of all souls, have compassion toward the soul of the young man, Saul of Tarshish. Lift it from the nethermost depths into which it has fallen. Open his eyes, that he may see the light of Thy Holy servant, Yeshua the Messiah, whom Thou hast sent to us as comforter. Turn his heart to the good, in order that he may recognize and eschew the evil which he has done; and be compassionate to him in the hour of his repentance; strengthen him then, that he may not fall into despair and sin, but rely on Thy grace, and find strength in Thy faith; and bring him back upon the path of Thy teaching. Amen."

The women on the other side of the curtain repeated word for word the prayer which Reb Jacob ben Joseph offered up for the soul of Saul of Tarshish.

Chapter Seventeen

THE ROAD TO DAMASCUS

THE messengers of the High Priest, with Saul in their midst, press forward on the road to Damascus. There is a great emptiness in Saul's heart, but he presses forward. The Temple guards placed at his service by the High Priest ride on little asses; Samuel, the commander of the guards, is mounted on a camel. Saul's own men, Judah of Pumbedita, Zebulun of Damascus, and Zadoc the Shammaite, are on foot, like Saul himself, though he has been provided with a camel. Saul prefers to walk. He carries on his breast, suspended by a purple thread passing round his neck, a wax tablet on which has been engraved with a stylus his letter of authorization from the High Priest: "Be it known to all, that Saul, bar Reb Baruch, of Tarshish, which is in Cilicia, who is also called Paul, has been appointed and authorized by the High Priest, and is hereby vested with the right to arrest and bind and deliver to the men of the High Priest any of the Greek-speaking Jews who fail to fulfill or who actively oppose the law of Moses, in order that they may be brought to trial in Jerusalem." The tablet bears the signature of the High Priest and of the Chief Officer of the Temple; it is attested by the scribe of the High Priest and stamped with the Seal of the High Priest.

The young man Saul marches forward, weighted with authority, to fulfill his mission in Damascus. His eyes are red from the dust of the road and from nights of sleeplessness. It is three days since he took boat at Tiberias, crossed Lake Kineret, and set foot at Gederah on the soil of the heathens; three nights he has slept in the open, avoiding the

161

pollution of the tents of idolators. For all this time he has been in the ten cities of the gentiles which Pompey the wicked took away from the Jews and settled with Greek idolators. Onward from Caesarea Philippi he avoided the cities and villages, which was easier for him in the Arabian half wilderness than among the thickly settled Diaspora.

The Greek gentiles Saul knew from his native land. But the semi-barbaric Arabs of the Hauran, who dwelt in stony caves or in artificial holes in the ground, and who imitated the Greeks in their own formless, undisciplined, savage Oriental way, were strange to him and filled him with horror. He kept his men in the open for the nights, in some cleft of the rocks, every man spreading out on the ground the little bamboo mattress which he carried in a folded bundle and covering himself with his mantle. Their food, like Saul's, was dry food: flat cakes, olives, dried cheese, figs and other fruits. They did not enter the inns and eating places of the gentiles, for the food was impure. Saul and his men were so wearied by the journey that when they wound their way down into the hot lowland which lies between Mount Hermon and the oasis-like, thickly covered landscape of Damascus, they reeled in their walk like drunkards. Ever since they had entered the sandy, stone-strewn wastes of the Hauran they had not breathed air but dust. Their mouths and nostrils were filled with sand, and there was sand in their throats and their lungs. Their teeth ground upon dust. And as it was within, so it was without their bodies: their faces, necks, breasts, beards, and ears were black with dust. Here, in this wild country, their mantles could not protect them from the sand. But when they came to the deepest part of the lowland, which was like a caldron of stone, the rays of the sun smote them like bundles of spears. Behind them towered the heights of Hermon, which seemed to hold concentrated upon the pit below the accumulated heat of the sun. There was no tree, no bush, no place of shadow; there was no shelter from the sun or from the running waves of sand; and though the morning was little advanced, the rays of the sun seemed to fill the air with tongues of flame. The air became more metallic; it pressed at a million points on the skin of the marchers.

So, driven by sandstorm and by fire-rain, Saul and his men stumble forward toward the refreshing oasis which awaits them in the vicinity of Damascus. They see it like a chimera, appearing and disappearing as in a mirror, far off. They see the springs which flow together and fall into the Abana. The oasis is so close that they seem to catch the sound of murmuring waters among the thick groves. But their feet also seem to be fastened with chains to the stony road, and their exhausted bodies scarcely move forward. It is as though they will never cover the distance which separates them from the springs. The closer the vision is brought to the eye, the farther the reality is from their feet. They have emptied the two skins of water which the donkey carries, part for drinking, part to wash their eyes. The camel with the large load lingers at the end of the procession, ready to fall under the burden which the shafts of the sun press down upon it with double strength. And at the head of the procession, leading, insistent, calling up his last energies, strides the young man Saul.

These are his last reserves of energy. His feet move under him mechanically. That emptiness in his heart with which he set out from Jerusalem has not diminished, as he hoped it would. It has grown deeper and sharper. Whither is he going? What is he about to do? Begin once more the work which he could no longer continue in Jerusalem? But those same faces which confronted him in Jerusalem, forcing him more than once to look away and cast his eyes to the ground in shame and pain, will surely confront him in Damascus. Faces of simple men, big eyes which utter as with a cry the power of faith. Only a few of them will deny that they have had dealings with the men of the Messiah. The greatest part—and not the worst part, either, Saul knows—will cling to their Messiah and accept in love the torments visited upon them. They will not cry out, they will not defend themselves, they will only turn on him their big eyes and in the forgiveness shining from them they will turn back upon him, upon Saul, the tortures he inflicts upon them.

And who is *"he"*? For the hundredth time Saul repeats this question. Who is he whom they have crowned with the name "Son of God"? Neither Abraham nor David nor Moses have been called "God's son." Until now it is only the Jewish people as a whole, the chosen people, the people of the eternal hope, which has been called the son of God. It is a thought, an ideal, the Torah, daughter of heaven. But how can they apply to a man, to a single individual, who was not a King, who was not a Solomon to whom the Lord said: "Thou wilt be a son unto me, and I a father unto thee"—who was plain flesh and blood, one whom

163

Edom had tortured like a slave, hammered him to the cross—how can one say of such a one that he is God's son? Who is he?

And yet, perhaps—perhaps they are right, the simple and the blind —and perhaps because he is the highest fulfillment he took upon himself the basest sufferings, let himself be slain like a slave in order that he might justify the supreme election. If this is so, what am I doing here on the road to Damascus?

The mad question shakes him like a storm. He sets his teeth and grinds them together. A shudder passes through his veins, as if they were the tensed strings of a fiery instrument, plucked by an invisible hand. No! It is because he will prove the contrary that he is now on the road to Damascus!

He masters himself, and his footsteps become firmer, more defiant. But not for long. There is no peace of soul for him. He finds himself asking again: "But what am I doing here? How did I set foot on this road? Why did God choose me to be his instrument of doom and punishment? And what is there in my hand to prove that I, who work cruelty, do the work of God, while they, who submit to my cruelty lovingly, do the work of Satan? Suppose it is the opposite? Perhaps it is I who am cutting, as with a sharp knife, the thread which binds Israel to salvation. Oh, God, what am I thinking? Who am I? How come I here?"

Suddenly he sees before him the face of Reb Istephan and the faces of all his victims; they come in a stream against him, to block his path, to hold him back: and they cry out: "Saul, Saul, thou art one of us. Why dost thou persecute us?"

"O God, help me!" he screams suddenly, and the men marching behind him are dumbstruck with astonishment.

Meanwhile Saul does not notice that they have at last crossed the line between the desert and the town, that their feet now tread the oasis which surrounds Damascus; they are in the midst of trees, bushes, vineyards, vegetable gardens, little woods of date trees, apricots, pomegranates, citrons; and there is about them a sweet, refreshing rush of waters, which fill the air with delicious odors. Like thirsty hinds, Saul's men throw themselves down on the banks of the rivulets half hidden under overhanging bushes. The first thing they do is wash their throats, with a loud, spitting gurgle; then they wash off their eyebrows and beards the thick accumulations of desert dust; they plunge their hands

164

and legs into the water, and renew themselves in its coolness and sweetness. This land! It is the paradise which Adam inhabited before he ate of the Tree of Knowledge.

And now the road which leads to the walls of Damascus begins to fill with travelers. They pour in upon it from a hundred little by-paths; camels laden with merchandise, donkeys festooned with skins of honey-wine, earthen jars, woven stuffs, silver dust and with iron dug up in distant countries; camels carrying beams of cedar, donkeys with loads of incense and spices, of washed sheepskins, with colored cloths from the shores of Tyre and Sidon; there are also single drivers of camels and asses, Arab bedouins, with their big, colored tents folded into bundles, with their household possessions towering high up between the humps of their camels; slaves carrying the palanquin of their lord, with heralds before, and heralds at the sides, to keep the road clear. Men and animals, caravans and individual travelers pour in from the bypaths upon the road which leads to the gate of the city, and to the Street that is called Straight.

A shepherd driving his flock along the road sets up a cloud of thick dust and a stink of unwashed wool about Saul and his men. True, they are no longer out in the wilderness, or in the depression of the Hauran, and the sun rays do not beat down mercilessly on them; but here the air between the high green palisades is swollen with dampness, which pours like molten lead through the pores of their skins and makes their limbs heavy with a poisonous heaviness. Here, in the midst of the luxurious greenness of the oasis, Saul feels a weariness taking possession of him, like an imposed authority. He tries to assert himself, but a thousand blazing wheels revolve about his head; a thick mist gathers about him. He reads the portents only too clearly—he knows them from of old. . . . He reads them with terror, but not without eagerness. Now as always when the "condition" comes down on him, he tries to fight it off, even though he knows himself to be impotent against it. His limbs become soft, they are covered with some strange fabric woven about them by an invisible spirit. It is another will than his own that is about to take command, and Saul trembles with fear, and yet is drawn toward it by the sweet, mystic charm which radiates from it. He struggles, he exerts himself to maintain the alertness of his nerves, to drive off the alluring sleepiness which descends on him with warm enfolding arms.

165

The world is suddenly quiet, as though the Angel of Silence is hovering above it on widespread wings. The leaves and branches of the trees have stopped rustling, they have stopped breathing through their green pores, they are motionless, as if they were not blossoming things, but dead images. The air has been burned out of space. Everything falls back into the ancient silence. Only above, high up, a thick black cloud appears, a little cloud, no bigger than a man's hand. And suddenly the colors of the world change, and become fixed in their new radiance. It is as though the face of the universe were unveiling itself, throwing off, one after another, the accumulated developments of all the epochs and returning to the first light of creation. The plants blossom in a green which is not of this world. Color and shadow are interwoven. The shape of the plants is not of this world. Between the towering, unfamiliar trees, in the deep, unfamiliar gloom of color, paces, with quiet footsteps, the spirit of God. . . .

It often happens thus in these Oriental parts, toward the end of the summer, when the rains are about to begin. The handful of cloud expands with terrifying swiftness, until it covers the whole sky. Then the winds are unloosed, and a million storm demons take hold of the four corners of the world. The heads of the trees clash together, the waters of the rivers are agitated and heave against their banks; and the fury breaks on the stretch of land which lies before Damascus. The flock of sheep, cowering, trembling, is sent by the fierce wind among the camel caravans, the donkeys, the travelers. There is one huge, roaring confusion, in the midst of which can be heard the tinkle of smashed vessels. Bales of wool tumble on cruses of oil; asses, donkeys, and men are flung together. Everyone snatches at something to hold on to, seeks shelter. Rocks come plunging down on the road from the surrounding hills, men throw themselves with faces to the ground. Some call out on their gods, others lift their hands to heaven. The terror of God is upon the earth.

It lasts but an instant. The storm is gone. Once more the world is quiet, expectant.

No, the storm does not dissolve in a cloudburst of rain, as might be expected. No. Terrible shafts of light begin to break up the gigantic cloud, and to pierce through to the world below. At first they come singly; but soon they multiply, are gathered into bundles, become like slanting pillars of solid light, which have been broken from the mass of heaven by a gigantic hand. Eyes are dazzled. A new fear seizes the earth. The donkeys break away from the road, scatter over the fields; the camels sink to the ground. Men kneel again. Now there are no longer pillars of light slanting down from heaven; now it is one burst of light which inundates the world from end to end.

At the edge of the road lies Saul, as though a mighty hand had flung him down. About him stand his companions, paralyzed with amazement. His face is turned up to the open sky, his eyes are open, foam breaks out on his lips. His companions hear Saul's voice. He is speaking with someone. They catch a few words. They know he is seeing a vision. They are terrified by the dread occasion of which they are the witnesses.

Before Saul's face stands a man. A man who is spirit and flesh and blood. He is taller than any man Saul has ever seen. Yet he is not a giant; he is an ordinary man; a Rabbi, in prayer-shawl and phylacteries; with great eyes, mournful yet radiant, filled with faith and love, eyes such as Saul has often seen among the disciples. His beard and earlocks are black, interwoven with gray. A man, not an angel; clothed in white, as for the Sabbath. Even in his present condition Saul's thoughts are clear enough for him to recall that God created man in His own image. Therefore he who stands before him in the likeness of a man may be a spirit of the Lord. But he stretches out his hands to Saul, and the sorrow on his face is a human sorrow. His eyes are filled with tears, in the midst of which swim the brown pupils. His lips are distorted in pain, as though all the anguish of the world had passed into him. He stretches out his hands to Saul, and the unhappy voice is that of a simple man who suffers, even as Saul has seen so many suffer:

"Saul, Saul, why dost thou persecute me?"

In the voice Saul hears the silent protest of all those whom he has tormented; in the face of the man, in the expression of pain on the thin lips, he sees all the pain of all those whom he has caused to suffer.

The men standing about Saul hear him ask:

"Who art thou, lord?"

Saul hears the reply:

"I am Yeshua of Nazareth, whom thou persecutest."

The men standing about Saul again hear him ask:

"Lord, what shall I do?"

Again Saul hears the reply:

"Arise and go to Damascus. There it shall be told thee what thou hast to do."

Saul starts and awakens. The vision is gone. But not the image alone has disappeared; the world has disappeared with it. Where is he? He is in the midst of darkest night, darkness on every hand, darkness above and below. His companions ask him what he has seen, with whom he has spoken. He does not answer; he sits, silent, helpless, blind, near the gates of Damascus.

His companions give him a cup of pressed date wine, and comfort him. They tell him he has lost his strength, and that is why his eyesight is gone. When his strength returns, his eyesight will return with it. Some of them say, however, that he has been blinded by the fierceness of the light. They too were dazzled into blindness, but their sight has returned. Saul hears them, and he does not answer.

They lead him forward, Zadoc the Shammaite supporting him on one side, Samuel, son of Eliezer, on the other. They lead blind Saul into Damascus. Travelers on the road come over and ask them who the blind young man is whom they lead.

"He has seen a vision on the road and has become blind."

They are not astonished. They understand. Such things happen daily. But the young man Saul is exalted in the eyes of his companions.

They reach the Street which is called Straight. They know of an inn which is kept by a Jew. They enter the courtyard, which is filled with towering camels and little donkeys. From the low arches of the inn issues, with the smoke of the tripods, the heavy odor of damp wool and of camel dung. Saul's companions hire a little room on the upper floor. There, on a bamboo mattress stretched on the ground, they lay down the blind Saul.

And there he lies, young Saul, in the upper room of the inn, with closed and blinded eyes. About him is darkness and eternal night. He cannot rise, he cannot take a step, without help. The world about him is like the nethermost abyss of Hell, and he is still falling, falling, without hope of ever reaching the bottom. There is nothing to hold on to, there is nothing which recedes from him, or draws nearer to him, as he falls. But his heart within him gives birth to a point of light. It is as though the light of day has shrunk to a single point, and the

168

point has found lodgment in his heart, whence it sends out its rays. Now he will have to walk in darkness, and his only guide will be the rays of light which stream from the bright consciousness in his heart. This will have to be, from now on, his measure and his support in all things.

His companions are impatient. They are for seeking out the heads of the synagogues and reporting to them what has befallen the chief messenger of the High Priest, who carries with him the authority to arrest and send to Jerusalem all who have left the Jewish path and followed after the false Messiah. Saul does not let them go. No! In two or three days he will be well, his eyesight will be restored to him. Then he will report to the heads of the synagogues. Meanwhile he lies there, blind Saul, and waits for the sign which was promised him on the road to Damascus, the revelation which would make clear to him what he was to do. There is nothing but this before him. Therefore he continues to wait. In a dark and soundless world he lies, waiting, like one dead, refusing to eat or drink.

Meanwhile his companions try to help their blind leader. They bring to him exorcists, they bring healers, men who cure blindness with salves, men who cure it with incantations, and who drive out evil spirits with magic, who pierce through the darkness with mystic stones and miraculous roots. Nothing avails. Saul remains blind. Finally they bring a certain old man, Chananyah, who has been healing the sick of late in the name of a certain saint. Chananyah is known in all Damascus as a pious and godfearing Jew who observes the law in all of its details. No suspicion attaches to Chananyah, the pietist.

It is now the third day that Saul has been lying on the bamboo mattress in the upper room of the Jewish inn. His body is withered from the three-days' fast, his face is taut. His blind eyes are turned up at the ceiling, and he repeats in his heart:

"Whence cometh my help?"

Reb Chananyah stands in the doorway and asks for the young man of Tarshish, Saul by name. There he is, lying on the floor. He has had a vision on the road to Damascus and has become blind. Canst thou cure him?

"Leave me alone with him," says Chananyah. "I have something to say to him."

They withdraw from the room, and the old man is alone with

169

Saul. He draws near to Saul, seats himself by him on the floor, takes his hand in his.

They stay silent a long time, blind Saul and the seeing old man. He knows well, this old man, who it is that lies before him. Word reached them from the congregation in Jerusalem: "Know that there comes to Damascus these days one Saul of Tarshish, armed with the authority of the High Priest to take fast all those who call upon the name of our lord, Yeshua." Chananyah also knows what Saul has done in Jerusalem to those in the faith. He knew also, before the men told him, that Saul had had a vision on the road to Damascus, for he too, old Chananyah, had had a vision and a dream concerning Saul, who was coming to Damascus in the name of the High Priest. In the dream he was told what he had to do. And Saul lies there, and old Chananyah has been called in to heal him. But Saul, too, knows who sits by him. For the name of Chananyah had been sent on to Jerusalem by the spies of the High Priest. He is one of the leaders of the congregation of the faithful. On the way to Damascus Saul had had it in mind that Chananyah would be the first to be seized and sent to Jerusalem. And it is Chananyah who sits by him now, having come to heal him of his blindness. Is this, then, the sign, is this what he was bidden to await in Damascus, the revelation of what he was to do? Saul's heart beats fast, his lips tremble, and his hand trembles in the old man's hand. And suddenly repentance and regret overwhelm him. He sees with his blind eyes the depths of the abyss in which he has been plunged by the spirit of envy. Were it not for the vision on the road, this gentle, loving hand which holds his would now be loaded with chains. Saul cannot see the old man's face, but he feels warmth and love and understanding streaming into him from the hand which encloses his, the hand which he would have twisted and bound, till its veins burst and the blood gushed forth, this hand which fondles him, caresses him as with loving lips, this hand like so many other hands which he, Saul, has put to the torture. And suddenly there rise before him all the beaten bodies, the welt-covered backs, the bleeding faces, which he has looked upon. He sees them, he sees all his victims, and he sees nothing else. "God! Is there any help for me?" No, no, let him remain for ever blind; he will lie there, and he will not eat or drink, he will lie there until he withers away in his blindness. Those were his thoughts until the coming

170

of this miracle, the second half of the vision, the command and the promise, the decision! He lies in agony, praying, and his body trembles like a leaf.

"And how did this blindness come upon you, Saul, my brother?" he hears the old man ask.

"I had a vision, Reb Chananyah, on the road."

"A vision, brother Saul?"

"Yes."

"And what did you see in the vision?"

Saul's eyes start out of their sockets; he stares about the room as though he could see, as though he would make sure that he is alone with the old man.

"There is none here but you and I?"

Saul sits up on the mattress, his blind eyes fixed on vacancy. They are wide open, and it seems to him that they are blind only to this world of ours; but he can see that which no one else can see. He lifts his arms to heaven:

"I saw Yeshua the Nazarene, he whom you call lord!"

He cries this out, falls back again upon his mattress and buries his face in his hands. The room is filled with a groaning and a lamentation, a weeping without tears.

"I know it, brother Saul," says Chananyah.

"You know it? You know it?" He sits up again, feels with his hands for the old man's knees, and burrows his blind face into them.

"Yes, I know it, as I know that you came to Damascus with the authority of the High Priest, to take prisoner the faithful, as you did in Jerusalem. And the lord showed himself to you on the road."

Saul lifts his head from Chananyah's knees. He strains his eyes, which swell and become injected. The will to sight tries to break through the wall which imprisons it. But the passion of repentance descends on him like a storm and shakes him from head to foot.

"Chananyah! Do you believe there is forgiveness for my sins and salvation for my soul?" he cries, and the cry comes more from his blind eyes than from his lips.

"Saul, do you not understand that the God of our fathers has chosen you, that you might know his will, that you might see the just man, and hear his voice? For from now on you will be a witness and testify to all men concerning that which you saw and heard. And now, why do you delay? Arise, and baptize yourself, wash yourself of your sins and call on the name of the lord."

And old Chananyah placed his soft, warm living hands on Saul's eyes.

A violent trembling came over Saul, as though all the storms were concentrated within him now, and in that instant the scales fell from his eyes. A hot flood of tears broke through the stoniness of his heart, burst upward toward his eyes, and washed away their blindness. Saul stared about him. Joyous, sun-drenched, the world lay before him; and beside him stood old Chananyah, his old face shining with grace and forgiveness. He fell back to the earth and was silent.

Saul was baptized that day. Then, with the letters of the High Priest to the heads of the synagogues still in his possession, he stole secretly out of the gate of the city and set out, all alone, on the road to the wilderness.

Chapter Eighteen

METAMORPHOSIS

THE young man Saul plunges on through the world, marches day and night, alone. The stretches of heaven above, the oceans of sand beneath, and he between them. The fiery tongues of the sun have licked the flesh off his body and drawn the blood out of his veins. His body, a bundle of bones and nerves, half-wrapped in a sheet which wind and sand have reduced to tatters, his body, which peers out from the covering in a score of places, is black, scorched, withered, and shrunk, skin drawn tightly over ribs. The scraggy legs support thin hips and a strengthless belly worn out by hunger and thirst. The long hands, pitifully thin, like the hands of a starved child, lean on a bamboo staff, while his feet sink at every step into the pathless sands. His neck is like a twist of cords. Only his head has grown bigger, a great, pear-shaped head, with a great expanse of forehead sweeping downward. Brown wisps of shaggy hair stick out from under the tattered head covering and mingle with his earlocks and with the beard which covers his narrow jaws. In the pear-shaped head two eyes are set; the good, seeing eye flames with a sickly light, malarial, terrifying. The face, the lower half of which is folded in the headdress, is black as coal, and covered with a layer of sand. And a layer of sand lies on the eyes. The sand-laden wind penetrates everywhere. His throat is stopped up with sand. His pores are filled with it. He is drunk with sand. His senses are dimmed by it.

Nearly three years have passed since the day of the vision before Damascus. These three years, which he has spent in loneliness, remote from the congregation of Israel, have laid on him the marks of three decades. His hardened face, streaked and ploughed like the carapace of a turtle, would be the face of an old man, were it not for the one flaming eye, the youthful, nervous twitch about his tightened lips, and the strange radiance of his wide forehead, which has remained obstinately young. His stooping back, inclining almost toward a hump, has known the full weight of that which he has taken upon himself; and even now his feet, like the hoofs of a camel, sink deep into the sand, as though the load which he carries would press him into the depths of the earth.

Where has Saul been? What has he done through these years? On the day of his flight from Damascus he was still wrapped in the mist of his vision. His eyes had recovered their sight, but his mind was dazed with the blow which had fallen on it. He was aware of a mortal need for solitude and rest. He had but one desire—to find again the self which he had suddenly lost. When he stole out of the gate of the city it was without a plan, without direction; he fled aimlessly, asking only to be free from thought, to feel no will. It so happened that the road he took led to the second city of Arabia, Petra, the capital of King Artos of Arabia. Arriving there, he bethought himself that his name was unknown in these parts, and he sought out a Jew who gave him employment at his trade. He did not reveal himself to the Jews of Petra, not even to those who were of the new congregation concerning which reports reached him. He wished to be alone. He was careful to observe all the Jewish laws, and on the Sabbaths he went to the synagogue, stationing himself at the door. No one knew who the young man was. Petra was a city of the gentiles. In the streets of the cave dwellings hewn out in terraces on the cliffs which make up Petra, there were Moabites, Edomites, Midianites, Amalekites—all the

173

peoples which had inhabited Sodom; and the city was, in fact, another Sodom. An unclean city. They that dwelt in it were like the idol which they worshiped. An echo of the culture of Greece had reached them, and they sought to imitate the manners of the Greek population of the Decapolis. Their chief god was the Semitic Baal-Shamen, whom they had transformed into an Asiatic Dionysus, the god of fruitfulness and joy. His symbols were the grape cluster and the wine cup. And as the god was, so were his services. A never ending series of Bacchic festivals accompanied the worship of Baal-Shamen, to whom they attributed the most abominable forms of sexual intercourse. The emblems of these revolting perversities were engraved on all the sacred utensils, or given form in them. The oil lamps were in the shape of sexual organs. Every cruse, every dish, every seat, every wall, was covered with representations of Sodomitic rites; even the tombs were not free from them.

In the city of drunkenness, of unbridled and savage appetites, of debased Hellenistic-Asiatic manners, Saul lived alone in the little Jewish community, pursued his trade, and kept to himself the secret of his vision. He lived apart, waiting for restoration after the storm through which he had passed. Slowly he began to emerge, and it seemed to him that he was finding his way back to himself.

But when his recovery had reached a certain stage, he was thrown, by his own recovered strength, into a new paroxysm of fear. For he was able again to perceive his nakedness. He saw himself standing amid the ruins of his own being. There was nothing left to him but the vision on the road to Damascus. The rest was a wilderness, in which he wandered with the weight of his misdeeds hanging about his neck. And as to the vision, though he could not doubt the reality of it—for this was his last hold on life—he could not find peace in it either. On the contrary, it was the starting point for new torments and terrors. "For if the vision was a true one"—and he knew it had not been otherwise—"then my whole life has been one great sin." Young in years, he had already committed so much evil, shed so much blood, brought so much anguish upon the world!

There was a time, during the awakening of his conscience in Petra, when Saul was in danger of sinking into the depths of that abomination from which there is no return. It was as though the Demon were making his last effort to gather under his authority the soul of the young man, before the gates of the orchard of light could be opened to him; and this effort took the subtle form of a moral despair, a torment of the conscience, which dimmed his mind and almost loosed his hold upon the thread which he held in his hand. He said to himself, again and again: "If I have done so much evil till now in the name of good, what proof is there that the good which I hold today is indeed the true, the last measure? Perhaps a day will come when I shall be given another measure, according to which the thoughts I cling to now, and the deeds I contemplate, will be as evil as those of my past. Who, indeed, is man that he should undertake to penetrate to the final truth? We are nothing but passing shadows. We are begotten by a drop of filth, and all that is within us, thoughts, deeds, truths, which we call the good, are foul and putrid with this beginning. And if this be so, why should we not live as the heathen do, after the nature of the drop of filth? Why should we not quench every lust which is born of it? For I am a stinking pot, which will be broken. We claw upward toward heaven, we make search of the deeps, but the unknown is sealed away from us with seven seals."

And it chanced that one evening Saul was pulled along in a triumphal procession of idolaters—a riotous throng of men and women who, bearing aloft palm branches and torches, went with the clashing of cymbals and loud singing, dancing half naked to the music of flutes, toward the steps of the city god. Baal-Shamen, the giver of youth, renewal, and joy. A lithe, dark-eyed, brown-skinned Arab girl darted toward Saul and drew him into the circle of the dancers. He partook that night of the meal of sheep flesh and goat flesh from the altars of the idol, and gave himself to the dancing, the music, and the drunkenness of the ceremonial. He woke in the morning on the temple steps, and his head was in the lap of the idolatress, and he was tormented by the question whether he had not in the night defiled his body before Baal-Shamen.

Often, in the moments of his despair, he remembered the practice of the learned, and he conjured up the image of his teacher, of Rabban Gamaliel; and he recalled the words of warning which had been uttered at their parting: "Saul, I fear for thee. I will pray God for thy soul. The road thou hast chosen is narrow and perilous." Now Saul could understand how clear had been his teacher's vision. Narrow and perilous was the road, and he was in imminent danger of the abyss.

But it was not in Saul to yield to such temptation. He perceived that the temptation had arisen from the irregularity which had come into his life ever since the vision. Was it not high time for him to put some order into his soul? But as he meditated on this undoubted truth, he began to see that order in his soul would have to be preceded by unification, and unification was as yet impossible, for the vision before Damascus had brought a division into his life, and the two halves could not be joined together. One of the two halves would have to be deleted and sacrificed. He resolved that it was the first half which was to be destroyed; the only salvation for him was his faith in the new and second life to which he had won through.

The old life was one mass of sin. He had stained it with the blood of innocent men and women whose spirits had been finer, lovelier, and more godfearing than his. In the old life he had sown pain and harvested regret. The rivers of tears which he had caused to be shed, the pain he had caused to be endured, the lives he had shattered, built up a leprous growth over the whole of his first life; and there was only one cure, one salve, one healing water: faith in the Messiah. For in the new faith he would not be responsible for what he had done in the old faith, just as the idolaters of Petra were not responsible for their worship of Baal-Shamen. Their inmost desire was to worship the true and only God, and their sacrifices to Baal-Shamen were sacrifices to the true God. There were no such things as false gods; Baal-Shamen was not a false god—he was simply a piece of stone. There was but one God, the true and living God. But they of Petra did not know of it, and therefore they were sinless. All that which he, Saul, had done before the vision had been done in the way of error. He could therefore look upon it now as if it had not been. He had been born again in Damascus. He was within the orchard now, and all that which had been outside the orchard was no more for him.

The new faith was the thread which would lead him out of confusion and dissolution. He had been on the brink of disintegration, and if not for the thread in his hand he would have yielded and plunged in. Therefore he clung to the thread now with his life, with all his strength.

Had he not seen the face of the lord? Had he not heard his voice? Had he not seen that form which had been buried and had risen again to life? Had he not heard him say: "Arise and go to Damascus; where it shall be revealed to thee what thou shalt do"? Had he not been told in Damascus that God had chosen him as an instrument and intended great things with him? To him, to Saul, who had persecuted the congregation, and had gone to Damascus on a mission of destruction, to him, the sinner, the lord had appeared in a vision and chosen him as his instrument.

Did that not mean that whatever he had done until Damascus had been forgiven him? Had not the lord washed him with fiery water in the baptism which he had accepted in the name of the lord? Was he not now as a new-born child which in its mother's womb had been consecrated to God as an instrument of the Messiah?

Why, then, was he afraid? Why did his heart tremble? See, he told himself, every care is gone. The rays of my faith fall like those of the sun on my heart and drive away the clouds from before my face.

Then it came to pass that the young man Saul found the sun, and was strong, filled with life as a ripe grape is filled with wine. What evil could befall him now? Whom had he to fear if he had been cleansed in the eyes of the lord, if he had been chosen as an instrument of the Messiah?

Faith in the Messiah became the personal salvation of Saul of Tarshish, the liberation from the bonds of sin, the renewal of his birth. This faith his heart longed to bring to all men; but the word of God had left him.

Days became weeks, weeks mounted into months, months slipped by into the sea of the past, and Saul was still excluded from the table of God, dwelling in a world of gentiles, without a sign, without direction. There had been a lightning flash: the vision of the form of the savior had descended on him, he had been lifted up by the hair of his head, he had been set down where he was—and there was no second sign, no word of what he was to do now.

The tragedy of faith is that it bears not its own security within. In the eternal, ceaseless, downward rush of a man's life there is nothing for him to lay hold on save the faith which burns in his heart. Out of its flames a man may weave a fiery rope for himself, to cling to. The road to Damascus had been illumined for the young man Saul by a lightning flash. The road from Damascus he had to build for himself.

And the Demon lay in wait for him and did not relinquish all his power over him. In those days Saul was forming a resolution to take himself a wife, and to raise a family, as all men do. The people of the city reminded him that it was time for him to marry, and he himself was inclined to do so. It was as though he sought to escape from his destiny. He was reluctant to assume the yoke which was prepared for him. He was in rebellion against his call. "Why should I not, like all others, plant one blade of grass in the garden of God, why should I not enjoy His grace, His sun, His rain and dew, and be at peace? Is it not arrogance of spirit and sinful pride to seek to be unlike all others, to delude myself with the belief that I am destined for higher ends?" Who was he, and what was his father's house? But against these thoughts, too, Saul strengthened himself. Was he, in simple truth, like all other men?

Throughout his confusion he knew that the message had been intrusted to him, and he would carry it. Sooner or later a countenance would reveal itself to him, and the sign and direction would be vouchsafed. For Chananyah had told him that this was God's word: "Saul shall suffer much for My name." He was prepared to suffer much, to bear the burden in love. In the secret places of his heart he had always known that he had been consecrated to this purpose from his mother's womb. Now he saw why he had sanctified his body and refused to defile it with a woman. "A childless woman who had not brought forth, for she had not defiled herself." Yes, he would be eternally childless in the flesh, in order that he might be eternally fruitful in his mission for the Messiah.

And Saul burned to set out on his mission; but there came no sign.

It was then that he resolved to betake himself to the wilderness and to descend toward Sinai, the mountain of the Torah, where God had revealed himself to Moses.

Sinai had always drawn toward itself the religious spirits who hungered for the divine spirit. Among the Essenes, and among other sects of enthusiasts, it was believed that the mountain was peculiarly apt to inspire visions. For this was the mountain which had been chosen from among all others for the giving of the Torah; and tradition declared it to be the purest of all mountains, the center of sacred inspiration. The divine spirit brooded over it because it had never been made unclean with idol worship like the other mountains. The idolaters had not been able to get a foothold on it; it had been protected from false gods and reserved and sanctified for the God of Israel. For it was said that it was not only the Torah which was given on Mount Sinai; all prophecies, all visions, all Torahs which were to be granted to man had already been given on Sinai and were hidden there. Like a powerful mother-breast Sinai fed all that hungered for the truth of God. The Essenes were drawn to it; the disciples of Jochanan were drawn to it. And therefore Saul resolved to repair to it, to dwell in its shadow in sacred solitude, as a Nazirite, in order that he might be visited by the divine spirit.

He attached himself one day to the caravan of a rich Arab merchant who was taking a cargo of spices from Arabia to a port on the Red Sea. He accompanied the caravan as far as the sandy plateau where the foothills of Sinai began, and there he left it.

On the roadless slopes he encountered here and there withered, half-dead Nazirites who dwelt in caves, Essenes, disciples of Jochanan the Baptist, and members of a brotherhood of Damascus, the Sons of Moses, who also believed that the Messiah had come, and who awaited momently the beginning of the Kingdom of Heaven on earth, for which they were sanctifying and preparing themselves. Shadows of men they were, hollowed out by the hot winds and the cold storms which raged alternately, by day and by night, on the plateau. The black tatters on their bodies barely sufficed to cover their shame; hair and beard were wildly matted. Under perpetual Nazirite vows, they sometimes passed whole weeks without food; and when they ate it was either the roots of the cactus plant, ground in hand mills, or dried and pressed dates, or parched wheat grains; they drank the dew, which they collected painfully, drop by drop, in cruses, using most of it, however, for purification. They passed the days in prayer and meditation; and in the night they stared up from their sandy caves at the heavens, reading the stars for their destiny. Often a wailing and howling would go up from the black caves, a calling, a crying in tongues from such as were possessed of the Holy Ghost.

For months Saul lingered on the slopes of Sinai. He fasted and mortified his flesh, seeking to bring down the Holy Ghost by strength of will. But there came no sign, no hint, no revelation. Indeed, because of the weakness of the body, the spirit was weaker within him. He ceased to think and analyze. His self vanished, carried away in a torrent of involuntary, fruitless, and hysterical exaltation which reduced him, as it had reduced others, to an unintelligible babbling. He was intoxicated and could not command his senses. But Saul hated this condition. He attached very little importance to the babbling that passed for "tongues." The center of his world was his "I," his conscious, firmly-founded, clear-thinking "I," which measured, judged, and defined. Whatever was done without his "I" he ignored. He would not acknowledge his participation in that from which his brain was absent. His brain was his "I." Even in his visions he did not abandon his "I"; for he always saw himself as a part, an important part, of the vision. He had been too long a pupil of Rabban Gamaliel, he had been schooled too long in the tradition of the Pharisees, in the discipline of the House of Hillel, to surrender himself to the confusion of hysteria and exaltation which was induced by the privations of the body. He remembered what had been told in the house of his Rabbi concerning the Venerable Hillel. The opponents of Hillel, disputing with him a certain point of the law, sought to move him by declaring that they had the support of voices from heaven. But the old teacher would not be impressed; he answered that the Torah had been given to mankind, not to the angels, and therefore it was Hillel and not the angels who would decide what was right and what was wrong. Saul placed such emphasis on the "I" that even in the vision on the road to Damascus, his first question had been: "Who art thou, lord?" Even in the vision he insisted on knowing who confronted him, with whom he was dealing, to what authority he was asked to bow.

Here, on the slopes of Sinai, he was in a company of visionaries; they achieved "the ascent of the soul" daily; daily they saw heavenly faces, heard heavenly voices. Here too Saul did not yield up his mind. But here, more than elsewhere, he felt himself devoid of the Holy Ghost. For *his* converse with the Holy Ghost Saul needed alertness of the mind, freshness of the senses; for his Holy Ghost wrought on him through the instrumentality of his brain.

Therefore he decided to withdraw from Mount Sinai. He longed again for human habitations; he longed for the place where his new life had begun. Had he not been told that it was in Damascus that the revelation of his mission would be vouchsafed him?

He went down to the foot of the plateau and attached himself to a caravan bound for Damascus. Bound to his girdle was the gourd of water, and at the end of the staff which supported his footsteps in the track of the camels was a bundle of dried dates. Thus he traversed the desert again. And let it not be thought—though many have said it— that the desert has but a single countenance. Sometimes the desert looks like the surface of a great, calm sea, ruffled by the cold; little

waves of sand overlap each other, like the scales on the body of
Leviathan. Sometimes the desert breaks into storm, and then caves are
hollowed out on its surface, and hills rise upon it. At such moments
the withered body of Saul crouched, rising and falling as on the deck
of a ship; his eyes were closed, his mouth covered by the end of his
headgear, Then the desert storm would die away. The sandy wastes
rolled gently under the sun, the wind wrought symmetrical arabesques
on their surface, like a mysterious script. Then Saul would come to
fields of the dead, tombs of the wilderness. The sand took the shape of
withered bones of man and beast. The generation of the wilderness—
the first generation of the liberation from Egypt—had passed this way;
their skeletons were sown beneath the sand. Here and there they protruded, as if seeking once more the heat of the desert sun. It seemed to
Saul that he could hear a lamentation: "Moses, Moses, why didst thou
leave us in the wilderness?" Far off to the west there was the subdued
murmur of the Israelites moving onward. The Ark of the Lord is carried before the host; Moses and Aaron are there, sowing the sand with
the bones of the dead of the wilderness. And then the sun set. The
heavens were flooded with blood and fire, as if some tremendous sacrifice were being offered to God. The sand waves below caught fire from
the flames above. Far off, on the horizon, the field of sun and the field
of sand ran together and mingled. Long black shadows rose slowly and
settled on the desert road. Saul came upon a place which it had been the
thought of God to make into an oasis, but the thought had not been
carried to completion. In this place there had no doubt been a little
water, in the far-off past. Fantastic shapes of cactus, drawf palms,
crippled plants of many shapes, doomed at their birth, led a half life
here. Flooded by the sand, shaken by the storms, they seemed to cry
out of the sea of sand for help. There, among the crippled plants,
Saul took his station in the night. Human habitations could not be far
now. By the wailing bark of the jackals, by the howling of other creatures, audible in the distance, Saul knew that they were approaching
the rim of the desert. He lay down on the ground, his face turned
westward, toward the Temple, and said his evening *Shema*. Then he
let a few drops of water fall from his gourd upon his hands. He washed
and partook of the pressed figs in his bundle. He praised God before
the meal and after it. Then he sought out a place among the dwarf
plants, where he could lie down, certain that no beast could approach

without waking him up by the rustling of its footsteps. He lay with his face to the stars which were springing up in the heavens. His sheet was so ripped and worn by the winds that it could no longer cover his body.

Alone between heaven and earth Saul lay there, and his spirit held converse with heaven, as in a dispute. The whole universe had concentrated into a point and had become his adversary, who stood by him and disputed with him. It was as though Saul himself were outside the boundaries of the world. He could perceive it before him, seize it, enclose it in his hand.

This world, this universe, was a creature, even like himself. And who was the Creator of both of them? God, Whose Glory fills the universe. Could he but seek Him out, there in the inmost veil of heaven, confront the Unchangeable, uncover the Undiscoverable! On this night his thoughts were clear and fresh. His mind worked like a well-balanced mill. Saul passed the seed of his experience once more through the millstones of his mind. What had happened to him? He had had a vision. In this vision the Messiah had revealed himself to him. This was the treasure which he held in his hand; on this treasure he was building everything.

Who the Messiah was he had known till now from the Books, from the Prophets, from the Book of Enoch, the Wisdom of Solomon, the Sibyls—and from his own inspiration. He knew that the Messiah was the unknown, the inconceivable, withdrawn from the understanding of man; he was the unimaginable, who would come with the clouds of heaven, surrounded by the heavenly hosts, to judge the world, having been with God before the world was created.

The unimaginable and incomprehensible had, then, unveiled itself to him. He had heard the voice, he had seen the form. And he, Saul, now belonged to him for all the eternities. But was it indeed the unimaginable one who had revealed himself to him—the Messiah? If that was so, Saul asked himself for the hundredth time, why, to Saul's question, "Who art thou, lord?" had he answered, not "I am Yeshua, the Messiah," but "I am Yeshua, whom thou persecutest?"

"What," asked Saul, "did he seek to let me know by that answer? What was the purpose behind it? If he, the Yeshua whom I persecuted, is a part of the Messiah, then it means that the Messiahship begins not with his coming on the clouds of heaven, but with the persecuted

Yeshua. And the Yeshua who will come with the clouds of heaven is one and the same Messiah, in his wholeness, the Messiah who lived with us and we knew him not; it is the Yeshua who went about among us, taught us, performed good deeds for us, was tortured and died on the cross. If this be so, then the earthly Yeshua is as important a part of the faith in the Messiah as the Yeshua who will come with the clouds of heaven."

Only now did he perceive, as clearly as he saw the stars above him, that Yeshua the tortured one, the persecuted and martyred one, the crucified one, was a part of the faith in the Messiah. And thus the Messiah was not only the unknowable and unimaginable and incomprehensible; he was likewise the known and imagined and comprehended, that which had been upon earth with man. "We saw him with our eyes, we heard him with our ears, he walked among us, not *a* Messiah, but *the* Messiah, who is contained wholly in the person, in the individual, whose name was Yeshua.

"And who is the Yeshua who was born of woman, a man like myself who is yet the Messiah? Who is he?

"He is the unknowable and unimaginable and incomprehensible, who was with God in the heavens before the world was created."

The thoughts of Saul were clear and fresh, the wheels of his mind spun smoothly, like wheels of a mill driven by a steady stream. His senses, his heart, the intuition of his spirit, were alert, working vigorously, driving forward ceaselessly toward the ultimate truth.

He had seen a light in darkness, a flash of illumination; and he turned his faculties swiftly in that direction.

"And who was the incomprehensible Messiah who dwelt with us?

"He cannot be merely the created, such as I am, such as the stars are. The created is comprehensible. See, I am bounded in my nature, even as the stars are. Only the idolaters believe that the stars are creative gods, and therefore they worship them. But we know that there is but one living God, who created the stars, as he created me, and created this whole world about me. They are all ordered in their motions according to a system which is the wisdom of God. Wisdom directs the motion of all creatures, wisdom determines the order of the world. It fills all God's creation, as water fills a running stream. Therefore it is that wisdom is called the daughter of heaven. It is the nature of God, the radiation of God, which is also understanding, and nothing can exist without it. Without it everything is false and deceptive, and must fall to pieces, for it is the part of divinity which works in creation, and without the divinity nothing can be.

"Wisdom is the ordered regulation of divinity. The Messiah is the redemption, the lifting of creation to its highest perfection, to its ultimate purpose, that for which God conceived it; it is the end of days, the fulfillment of the task which was in the mind of God in the act of creation. And for this alone the creation took place. The Messiah is this part of the divinity in creation. His purpose is perfection, redemption, the highest level of salvation.

"And if this be so, then the Messiah is the higher will of God. He is higher than wisdom, for wisdom is but the present condition of creation. The Messiah is the supreme objective of creation, its striving for perfection, for liberation from the earthly nature; it is the being bound to divinity not in wisdom, which can be achieved only by laws and commandments, by provision and arrangement and system, but in the nature of God, which is possible only through redemption. Messiah is the supreme effort of the universe. Without him the creation has neither sense nor purpose. He is the reward and the last achievement. He is the thread which binds all creation to the divinity.

"Thence it follows that the Messiah is the Son of God, and not, like wisdom, only the daughter of heaven touched with the nature of God; he is the Son who bears with him our liberation from nature and our unification with God. Through him we become like the angels; through him we arise to eternal life; through him we are redeemed from our imperfection and achieve highest perfection—with the grace of redemption.

"But if this be so, then Yeshua, the persecuted one, he who lived with us, he who came from the poor, nameless town of Nazareth, who preached in the Temple court, who was not recognized in his earthly life, he who was seized and bound, smitten and shamed, he who bore the anguish of the cross, this Yeshua is the Messiah, the highest radiation of the divinity, God's redemption for the universe, the higher will and the higher wisdom, the Son of God. He is the chosen one, the divine higher power which is the supreme purpose of mankind and of the whole universe. Only through him do man and the universe acquire the meaning of their existence—and that is the achievement of perfection in redemption. He is the redemption of God, the radiation of God's highest will."

And now Saul knew what had been the purpose of his flight to the wilderness. This was the revelation for which he had waited. The Messiah showed himself to him and spoke with him, not through a form, but through a voice; and this voice did not come from without; it was within him, within Saul, the utterance of the Holy Ghost which he had called up with his mind.

In the starry night of the wilderness Saul thought he could see Yeshua of Nazareth; he filled, like a spirit, the entire space of the world. He stood upon earth and his head was in the heavens. Thus Saul thought, and he saw the ladder of Jacob's dream. It was on such a night that Jacob had seen the ladder which stood on the earth while its topmost rungs rested in heaven and had seen the angels ascending and descending. Heaven and earth are linked in an uninterrupted bond. The ladder, said Saul to himself, is Yeshua the Nazarene, who was born in Nazareth and died in Jerusalem. Upon this ladder we mount to heaven. And Saul resolved to bring the tidings of Yeshua of Nazareth as a gladness to all men.

By the light of the stars he saw his own black, withered body, and a verse came into his mind: "He gave his body to the smiters."

Saul of Tarshish knew what his body would have to endure for the sake of the tidings.

"I will consecrate my body to Yeshua of Nazareth, even as I have consecrated my soul to him. Was I not created in my mother's womb for God?"

Chapter Nineteen

THE FORETASTE

OUTSIDE the little fence before Chananyah's house stood a desert dweller, his face burned black by the sun, his naked body half covered by a ragged sheet. The thick tangles of his hair fell over his face. With the end of the long bamboo stick which he carried in his hand he

185

tapped on the low, dust-eaten gate of woven palm branches. None of the passersby in the lively street recognized, in the man of the desert, whose thin legs seemed barely able to support his weight, the young man Saul of Tarshish. He was not recognized, either, by the master of the house, who thrust his massive, silver-covered head through the opening above the door.

When Reb Chananyah, perplexed by the sight of the stranger, opened the door, the exhausted, withered body collapsed in the wide-open arms of the old man. It was only when Reb Chananyah looked more closely and observed the pear-shaped outline of the skull, which was almost breaking through the cracked skin, that he knew the apparition from the desert to be Saul. Reb Chananyah paled, remembering that the Ethnarch's men were still looking for Saul. They had never given up the search for him; and on several occasions they had sought him in Reb Chananyah's house.

But this was not the time for thought. Reb Chananyah called to his wife, who lived with him in the tiny, low-roofed clay house. Between them they carried Saul within, closed the door behind them, and laid him on the floor. When they had refreshed him with a cup of milk, they covered him over with skins, so that a neighbor who chanced to look in should not see him.

A little later, Saul opened his eyes and came to; he began at once to talk of the Messiah, of Yeshua the Nazarene, who, he said, was the Son of God.

"Of these things we will speak when thy strength is returned," they said to him. "In the meantime, rest, and be at peace."

That evening Reb Chananyah went to synagogue for evening prayer, according to his rule, for his absence would have been noted, he being always the first at morning and evening prayer. But he said no word to anyone concerning his visitor.

Reb Chananyah and his wife kept Saul in concealment for several weeks, tending him carefully, nourishing him with milk and vegetables; for Saul was so weak, his body was so burned by the desert sun, that he could scarcely stand on his feet. Reb Chananyah treated the black, cracked skin with unguents and from day to day increased carefully the quantity of goat's milk which he gave him, as well as the ground vegetables which he and his wife prepared; for Saul could scarcely digest even the little food they gave him on the first day.

No sooner had he regained enough strength to be able to walk, than he pleaded to be taken to the Sabbath service in the synagogue. "I have great tidings for the House of Israel," he said. "The spirit was with me in the desert, as it was with Father Jacob, when I slept under the stone. I have seen Jacob's dream. Now I understand the dream of Father Jacob, the dream of the ladder."

Reb Chananyah did not understand him and believed that Saul still spoke in a delirium.

"Thou canst not go to the synagogue, thou canst not show thyself to the people of Damascus, for thou art known here, and it is known, too, with what purpose thou camest here. Certain of the men who came with thee, to bind us and carry us to Jerusalem, have remained here. When thou wentest forth from Damascus the government made a search for thee in the city. They were here, too, in this house. By now the thing is almost forgotten, but if thou art seen in the synagogue and heard preaching there, they will remember, and thou wilt surely be slain."

"Naught can befall me," answered Saul, tranquilly. "Didst thou not tell me thyself that the lord appeared to thee and spoke to thee concerning me—that he had chosen me as an instrument, to carry his word to the nations and to kings and to the House of Israel?"

"Yes, that was told me when the spirit was on me," answered Chananyah.

"Then, how can anything happen to me before the words of the lord have been fulfilled? Who can do me evil? Who can slay me, destroy me, or undo me if I am the instrument of the lord? No, nothing can happen to me."

Reb Chananyah looked at Saul in astonishment, for Saul's face was like a sheet of flame in his exaltation.

"If thy faith is so strong in thee, go with the power of thy faith and fulfill that which the spirit has told thee, and may God be with thee in all straits," answered Reb Chananyah and fell silent out of the fear which Saul's faith cast upon him.

* * *

With his unshakable faith in his mission Saul not only won Reb Chananyah's consent to his appearance in the synagogue, but moved the old man to negotiate for him. Reb Chananyah went to see the head of the synagogue and persuaded him to invite for a sermon the coming Sabbath the young Rabbi who had just returned from Mount Sinai and who was often visited by the spirit. Chananyah did not lose sight of the fact that the situation was fraught with great danger for Saul, since no one had forgotten with what mission he had originally come to Damascus; he foresaw also the possibility that Saul's sermon would only embitter those members of the new sect who remembered Saul's reputation in Jerusalem. They would not take the conversion to be sincere. But Reb Chananyah was as under a spell when it came to Saul; and he carried out his request to the letter. And when the Sabbath arrived, he accompanied Saul openly to the synagogue.

The great synagogue of Damascus was not a building in a single style, intended from the beginning as a synagogue. It was a cluster of buildings which had accumulated in the course of time. The Jewish community of Damascus had, with God's help, grown so rapidly that the addition of buildings had never kept pace with the needs of the congregants. It was not so much by the influx of the children of Israel that the community had grown, as by the conversion of gentiles. The population of Damascus consisted of diverse elements, and the Jewish religion had many followers among the gentiles; or half-followers, for, without ceasing to bend the knee before their own god, they came on the Sabbaths to the synagogue, to hear the reading of the Torah, which was translated in the vernacular. Most of the women of Damascus had converted, and they too came on the Sabbath to the synagogue, together with the Jewish women. There was much heart-burning and jealousy among the men on this account, and the Priests of the temple of Baal-Shamen were careful to play upon these feelings. The pressure of Jew and gentile—that is, of the "godfearing gentiles"—increased from year to year, so that the synagogue authorities were compelled to add new buildings, hastily constructed of stone, or of wood, or even of baked clay; until the original synagogue looked like a mother hen sitting on a brood of chicks.

On this occasion, as on all others, the synagogue was jammed with worshipers, who overflowed from the main building into all the adjacent buildings. The worshipers in every section of the synagogue kept a close eye on the beadles, who transmitted the signals, after the utterance of a benediction or a sanctification, for the response of "Amen!" When the week's portion of the Pentateuch had been read—

twice in the original Hebrew and once in translation—the head of the synagogue rose from his built-in stone seat by the Ark, mounted the pulpit and called out:

"Today there is among the worshipers a young Rabbi who has just returned from Mount Sinai, where he fasted and sought the secrets of the word of God. He brings us a word of comfort. Let him arise here, and speak as the spirit directs him."

From his place near the door, where he stood side by side with Rabbi Chananyah, Saul came forward. He wrapped himself in a prayer-shawl which one of the cantors gave him and stationed himself between the head of the synagogue and the chief judge of the synagogue court.

Many of the congregants, indeed, most of them, had heard of the young man Saul who some years ago had come from Jerusalem with a mission from the High Priest and then had disappeared, but few knew his face, and these only among the intimates of Reb Chananyah. When the assembled worshipers saw the pallid, sun-scorched young man, with his high, pear-shaped head swathed in the prayer-shawl, instinct told them that something unusual awaited them. A breathless silence descended. The men looked at each other dumbly, and there was a questioning in their eyes.

It was from the preacher himself that they learned who he was. He did not begin his sermon in the accepted fashion, with a verse from the part of the Pentateuch which was read that Sabbath. He began by speaking of himself:

"I am a Pharisee of the Pharisees. I sat at the feet of Rabban Gamaliel, at the time when there awoke in me, as I thought, the jealousy of God against those who praised Yeshua of Nazareth, saying that he was the King Messiah."

"Saul! It is the young man Saul!" A murmur of astonishment ran through the synagogue. "Saul of Tarshish, who persecuted the new sect in Jerusalem and was sent for the same purpose to Damascus."

And one believer murmured to the other: "He bound the faithful like sheep and dragged them to the slaughter."

"And that was his purpose in his coming here with the letters of the High Priest."

"Silence, brothers. Let us hear what he has to say in defense of his misdeeds."

"Yes, for his past misdeeds, and for his present misdeeds, too," cried a man angrily, opening wide his wind-reddened eyes.

"Silence! Let us hear!"

The young man before the Ark addressed himself to the congregation. He told in simple, straightforward language what had happened to him: how he had been on the road to Damascus, where it had been his purpose to take fast the faithful; how he had had a vision in which the form of the lord, Yeshua the Nazarene, had appeared to him; how he had been blind for three days, and how, when he had recovered his sight, he had fled, leaving his companions behind him. He told them how he had wandered in the wilderness and had come to Mount Sinai and had meditated on all that had befallen him; and how the spirit, which was woven of his own thought, had come upon him as he was returning through the wilderness to Damascus; and how he had seen clearly the ladder of Jacob our Father, in a dream in the night, and had known that the ladder between earth and heaven was Yeshua the Nazarene, and had known further that this Yeshua, whom they had thrust away from them when he was still in the life, was the Son of God, the Father, who had sent him as a salvation to the world.

And Saul, thus speaking, was seized with exaltation when he left his own story and touched on the lord Messiah. Even if the lord Messiah had been crucified in weakness, he was still alive in the power of God. He was the only one who gave meaning and justification to our life, for he was the redemption, the fulfillment of the creation, the promise which God had given through the mouths of the Prophets. He would come and resurrect the dead, for without the resurrection life had no meaning and discipline was purposeless.

Now there were many among the worshipers who were of the believers; and more than once their own Reb Chananyah had stood before them, where Saul was standing, and had preached to them of Yeshua the Nazarene. But even those who were not numbered among the believers had never been inclined to accuse Reb Chananyah, who was known as a godfearing and pious Jew, incapable of transgressing the law or in any way committing blasphemy against the Jewish faith. That Yeshua the Nazarene had freely, of his own will, died on the cross for the sins of all, and would soon return on the clouds of heaven, was believed by many, both such as had formally accepted the faith, that is, had been baptized in the name of the Messiah, and such as had not been baptized. All this which the young man preached was not new in Damascus and created no excitement. What did, however, create a storm among the worshipers, was the statement of the preacher that Yeshua the Nazarene was not only the King Messiah but the Son of God. For he went on to say that just as there could not be anything without God, for "the world is filled with His glory," even so there could not be anything without Yeshua the Nazarene, for he was the personification of the redemption, the significance and the purpose of creation. And this being so, then Yeshua was not merely as a god; he was a second Authority; he was more than that, for Yeshua made whole and filled with significance the work of God. And who was saying this? A man who but yesterday was persecuting with all the means at his disposal those who believed that Yeshua was the Messiah; a man who but yesterday had come with letters from the High Priest to this same city of Damascus, to take prisoner the faithful. He stood there now, preaching things unheard of till then in Israel.

They would not let him go on. The fire which was kindled in the eyes of the chief officers of the synagogue awakened an answering fire in the hearts of the worshipers. It was not only among the pious Jews, it was among the faithful, those who had learned from Reb Chananyah that Yeshua was the Messiah, that brows were knit in bewilderment and discontent. They had never heard such words issuing from Jewish lips. A noise of disputation went up from among the worshipers. It was not as in Jerusalem; no fists were raised at the preacher, no hands were stretched out to drag him down from the pulpit. But there were dismay and discontent. The head of the synagogue rose, signaled for silence, and declared:

"With the permission and authority of the head of the synagogue court and of the other elders, I bid Saul of Tarshish to be silent, and I withdraw from him the privilege of preaching in the synagogue."

The congregants dispersed that morning sadly, with heads down; they felt as if they had been present at the worship of the golden calf.

*   *   *

It was high time for Saul to be gone from the city. He had not ceased to give utterance to his views on the King Messiah, addressing himself to anyone who would listen. The elders of the synagogue had not only forbidden him the use of the pulpit; they were even considering seriously whether Saul should not be haled before the court and sentenced to the lash. If they refrained, it was because they were reluctant to attract greater attention to the matter. Saul therefore spoke to little groups, or argued with scholars. Nor did he hesitate to speak to simple, ignorant people, if they only gave ear. The congregation divided into two groups, one in agreement with him, the other in disagreement; and the division extended beyond the Jews to the interested gentiles, who were thrown into confusion by the dispute. Everywhere they spoke about Saul, for he was active throughout the city. In vain did Reb Chananyah plead with him to consider his own safety and consider likewise the safety of the little congregation of believers in the city, which had until now lived at peace with the other Jews, no one making a distinction between those who believed in the Messiahship of Yeshua and those that did not believe in it: all were equally members of the Jewish congregation. But Saul was like a storm wind. He was here, there, everywhere. He would spring up suddenly in the midst of a little group in the synagogue or at the side of a group of workers in the marketplace, or among a handful of merchants. With all of them, buyers and sellers, weavers, camel drivers, pack-carriers, he plunged into argument concerning the Messiah, who was the Son of God. Quarrels broke out in the streets and inns, and even in the homes. To all the warnings which Reb Chananyah uttered, Saul had one reply: he belonged to the lord, and as long as the lord needed him here, in this life, no evil could befall him. And if evil should befall him, if he should indeed be slain, it would be proof that the lord needed him in the other life, for the lord was the lord not only of the living but also of the dead.

It did not take long for rumor of the disturbances to reach the ruler of the city, and in governmental circles they recalled the letters which had been sent by the High Priest in Jerusalem to King Arotus concerning the young man Saul and his disappearance. King Arotus, a close friend of the High Priest, had forwarded the letters to the ruler of the city, instructing him to search out Saul and take him prisoner. But they had searched the city in vain. Now they learned that Saul had returned, and the order was issued anew for his arrest. Moreover, he was, according to report, the center of the disturbances which had become a plague to Damascus.

Guards were sent out to seize him, but they did not find him. They looked for him among the believers, they lay in wait for him at the doors of the synagogue. Saul came no more to the synagogue, and he was not seen among the believers. Nor did he appear any more on the street and in the marketplace. Who had warned Saul of the secret renewal of the order for his arrest? No one knew. All that was known was that Saul had vanished.

The guards came to the house of Chananyah and searched it thoroughly. They searched the houses of other believers. In vain.

But they were determined that if Saul was not already gone, he should not leave the city a second time; he should not steal away, as he had done the last time from the men he had brought with him out of Jerusalem.

Now it happened that there was present in Damascus, in those days, Zebulun of Damascus, who had been one of the lieutenants of Saul and one of the messengers of the High Priest. To him, of course, Saul was well known, and should he once set eyes on the hunted man, that would be the end of the search. No matter what disguise Saul assumed, no matter how he had changed, he would not deceive Zebulun of Damascus. Zebulun sought out other men who were familiar with the features of Saul and stationed them at the gates of the city. Whoever left Damascus in those days was closely scrutinized, sometimes even stripped. Even the women were examined, lest their garb, and their hair, should be nothing more than a disguise. The watch was so strict that the authorities were certain of apprehending their man if he should attempt to leave. But if he had not left, then he was still in the city. Where was he hiding?

On its eastern side, the wall of the city of Damascus ran through a little olive grove. At the foot of the wall, within the city, there were niches, hollows, and arches which had been occupied by poor oil-pressers, vegetable dealers, camel drivers, and shepherds. The wealthy oil mills, on the other side of the gate, were worked by the streams which ran like a network through the rich, fruitful woods about Damascus. Under the wall, on the inside, were only the poor oil-pressers, the wheels of whose mills were turned by a donkey or by a blind slave. To these pressers the small farmers brought their sacks of olives to be ground and pressed. In front of the wall there were great heaps of olive-kernel slag, which was sold as fertilizer. In the daytime the place was noisy with the braying of donkeys, the neighing of camels, the bargaining of the farmers and the pressers, the chaffing of merchants. At night silence reigned around the niches and hollows at the foot of the wall. Only the modest little oil lamps, sending up their slender spirals of smoke, testified that this was a human habitation.

Among the oil-pressers who had their own niches here was a young man named Zachariah ben Elijah. All day long he dragged the sacks and baskets of olives to the mill, drawing forth from it cruses and skins of pressed oil which he loaded on waiting donkeys. His body, and the sheet about it, were greasy with oil; and not only these, but the hole which he inhabited, the vessels, the mattress, were saturated with oil. The baskets piled on each other dripped oil. There, among the baskets and cruses, covered with a greasy rag, lay, all day, Saul of Tarshish.

For the first time he felt what he had made so many others feel; for the first time he knew what it meant to be in danger for the sake of Yeshua the Messiah. There was no fear in him. He knew that none had power over his life as long as he had not fulfilled his mission. But for the first time he knew what it meant to be hunted, he who had so long been the hunter, to be the sheep, he who had so long been the wolf. It was an experience which clarified and exalted. Under the filthy covering which concealed him, Saul felt himself uplifted. He had achieved the privilege of being hunted and persecuted for "the love of the God who is in the King Messiah."

One night two powerful arms lifted him out of his hiding place and deposited him in a basket which was filthy with the thick ooze of olive waste. Zachariah also handed him a cake of bread and a gourd of water and vinegar to sustain him in the desert. Then he covered the basket over with leaves, so that it looked like a basket of olives about to be carried to the mill, bound the load on his shoulders, and set forth. He knew a place where the wall passed through a lonely grove. Thither he made his way, bent under his burden. When he reached the spot he climbed to the top of the wall, and thence lowered the basket down with a rope. "Now bind the basket on thy back, Reb Saul," he said, "and if the watchers about the wall stop thee, say thou art carrying thy load of olives to be pressed in the great mills outside the city. God be with thee, Reb Saul."

But on the other side of the wall Saul encountered no one. He stepped forth into the deep blue night, and looked up at the stars which he had known so well in the desert. Whither?

The answer came of itself. Was there any road for him to take but that which he had come by the first time?

To Jerusalem, then! To Jerusalem, to those whom he had persecuted, and to whom he would join himself now! To Simon bar Jonah!

He turned his footsteps in the direction of Mount Hermon, whose majestic white head, illumined by the stars, was visible in the night.

Chapter Twenty

"I WILL SEND THEE"

SAUL stood under the heavy shadow of a great cypress tree, waiting till someone would come through the gate of the house of Miriam the widow, on Mount Scopus, in Jerusalem. He knew only too well what a paroxysm of fear his presence would call forth among those who lived in this house. His cloak, stained with oil, blackened by the earth, ripped by the wind, left patches of his stringy body exposed. The sandals on his feet had burst their seams, and the knobby ankle bones looked like gnarled roots of olive trees, and like the roots of trees they were covered with a layer of dust. Saul stood and waited. It was the hour before dawn in the late summer. The green about him had been scorched and withered by the sun, and Saul's body and limbs had about them the same singed look as the landscape. He had made the journey from Damascus to Jerusalem on foot, sleeping mostly in the open; in the cities it was between the pillars of some rich house, or in some camel drivers' inn under a roof of woven straw; in the fields it was under the open sky, or in the booth of a vineyard watchman. Good people had taken compassion on him; a stranger would not die of hunger among Jews. One had given him a cake of bread, another a plate of green vegetables, a third a cup of water. He had not had the time to pause and earn something at the trade in which he was skilled. He was in haste to reach Jerusalem. He paused in no place, except for sleep, and pressed onward through all his waking hours until he reached the gate of the house sheltering the leaders of the community which he had persecuted. Now he stood and waited till someone would come forth. With the first glimmer of dawn his friend bar Naba, kingly under the garb of the poor, for his covering of sackcloth had not changed his bearing, appeared at the gate; tall and graceful as a palm tree, it was as if he were still swathed in Tyrian linen, with flashing rings on his fingers. With him walked his nephew, the lad Marcus. As they approached they talked earnestly. And how tall the lad Marcus was now—almost as tall as his uncle! They passed, without noticing, the man under the cypress.

"Joseph bar Naba! Joseph bar Naba! Thou noble one!"

Uncle and nephew stared and looked round. They beheld the beggarly figure in tattered garb, in burst sandals. It was no new sight for them. They came by the thousand to the home of the disciples. Bar Naba sought hastily in the bag which was tied to his girdle to put something into the outstretched hand of the stranger.

More than once Saul had stretched out his hand on the road for a piece of bread. He had not regarded it either as a humiliation or a sign: all Israel are brethren, and there is a place under every roof for the wanderer. But this gift from the friend of his youth awakened in him a confusion of emotions. First there was a pang at his heart, a stab of pain; but this was followed by a strange sweetness; the humiliation did him good, purifying him through shame. He felt that this incident was not without meaning; it was not an accident, either, but had been intended for his edification. His eyes brightened and his heart was filled with joy.

"I thank thee, O lord, that thou hast humbled my spirit," he whispered. And he added: "The lord has been gracious to me."

Bar Naba stared at the man, who stood there with the coin in his open hand, looking into his eyes.

And suddenly Joseph's eyes were flooded with tears. He opened his arms, fell upon the neck of the beggar, and cried out ceaselessly:

"Saul, my brother! Saul, my brother! Saul, my beloved brother!"

"Is Saul of Tarshish worthy to be your brother, Joseph bar Naba, after what he did to you and yours?" asked Saul.

"But you have never ceased to be my brother."

"Not even when I persecuted the faithful?"

"Not even then. For I knew you would come to us. I knew that

196

your footsteps were on the path which leads to us, even when you struggled so hard against it."

"The lord was stronger, and overcame me."

"Yes, we have heard. There were messengers from the congregation of Damascus who told us all that happened to you."

"Joseph bar Naba, the lord came to me, he descended on me like a fierce wind and took me by the hair and carried me off, as an eagle carries a young lamb, as a fisherman takes a fish in his net."

"We are all fish to be caught in the net which is spread out by his messengers."

"But Joseph, my hands are stained with the blood of his messengers. Can you forgive me for what I have done?"

"Who are we to hold you defiled when God had declared you clean?"

"Joseph, my brother," said Saul, weeping in the arms of bar Naba.

Between them Joseph and his nephew led Saul into the house.

In the courtyard of Miriam's house stood the little apartment which was used by Simon bar Jonah, and his wife and mother-in-law; these two women tended Miriam, the mother of Yeshua, and Miriam of Migdal, who were both ailing. Jacob ben Joseph was still living in the old dwelling of the disciples, in the David wall, with those of the believers who had come from the ranks of the pious Pharisees.

When Saul had been washed, rubbed with oil, fed and clothed, Joseph bar Naba asked himself what was to be done with his friend, whose name was still a by-word and a terror among the faithful. Meanwhile, Saul asked after Simon Khaifa, whom he was eager to converse with as one who had been with the lord when the latter was still living. Bar Naba sent word cautiously to Simon bar Jonah regarding the arrival of Saul and his desire to speak with the first of the disciples. Simon bar Jonah, like the others, already knew of Saul's conversion and of his disappearance into the wilderness. He received the news of Saul's arrival in the city with mixed feelings. Assuredly he rejoiced that Saul had seen the error of his ways and had turned his heart to the good; no doubt the lord meant greatly with him, to have appeared to him in a vision and chosen him as an instrument—as Chananyah, of the Damascus congregation, had reported to Simon. Yet there was need, at the moment, of great care. His presence in Jerusalem would have to be kept secret for some time. The memory of his deeds was still fresh in the congregation, and they would not trust him. It was therefore decided to keep Saul in the house for a time, and not to let him go forth.

Joseph bar Naba led Saul before the middle-aged but already graying Simon bar Jonah, whose strong face, with its deep folds, bore the marks of the sufferings through which he had passed in his ministry. The young man, sunburned but pale, bowed deeply before the fisherman, and called him teacher and Rabbi:

"I have come," he said, "to sit at the feet of the first of the disciples, of him who was the first among men to serve our lord when he was among the living."

"How wonderful are Thy works, O Lord," answered Simon bar Jonah. "Blessed be the God of Israel who has wrought this miracle in thee, Saul of Tarshish. Much must thou have merited to have seen our lord face to face. We have heard of all that has happened with thee, and our hearts have been filled with joy. A beloved brother art thou to us, Saul." And Simon bar Jonah rose and embraced Saul and gave him the kiss of peace, to which Saul responded by kissing the shoulder of his Rabbi.

"A witness art thou to the lord, Saul of Tarshish," continued Simon bar Jonah. "The mouth which cursed him is now filled with blessing; the hand which smote the disciples now heals them as with sweet oils. Chosen art thou of the lord, Saul of Tarshish. Therefore let our lips never remember again thy deeds, which have been wiped out by grace. But hear me; many among the believers are nevertheless embittered against thee, and their hearts are hot. Stay thou therefore with us until they have been prepared for thee. And as the spirit instructs us, so will we do with thee."

"May God reward with double measure all the congregation for the kindness thou showest me, teacher and Rabbi," said Saul.

Simon bar Jonah sent for his wife, and, pointing to Saul, who stood before them with bowed head, said: "A brother has come to us, one who was far from us and is therefore doubly dear. Go, wife, prepare a bed for him, and set the table, and give him what food we have. Our brother Saul will be with us as long as he stays in Jerusalem."

But when two or three days had passed, and Saul had heard what Simon had to tell concerning the lord, the pupil who had come to sit at the feet of the Rabbi turned teacher. Saul unfolded to Simon his own ideas concerning the nature of the lord, as they had come to him during his sojourn in the wilderness, the ideas which he had propounded in Damascus.

The fisherman listened, and his mind became confused. Simon of K'far Nahum was fixed in his ways—the ways in which he had been brought up from childhood, the ways of Moses and the Prophets, which his lord had not changed, but merely set in a new light. They were the ways of Israel, the tradition which had been given him in his childhood, and which his faith in the lord in no wise altered. For, as he saw it, the gentiles could find salvation in Yeshua only through acceptance of the faith of the Jews. The advent of the Messiah meant that the nations would come to the mount of the Lord, as the prophets had foretold, and would walk in the ways of Jacob; that, or they would cease to be. The lord was God's instrument for the redemption which He had promised to the Jews. But what was this that Saul was saying—that the gentiles, the uncircumcised, were also children of Abraham by reason of their faith? And what did he mean by the strange words "Son of God, in heaven, on earth and in all the worlds"?

"These are hard things to understand, brother Saul," he said, perplexed. "When our lord was with us in the flesh, he taught us this: 'Sooner shall heaven and earth pass away than the law be diminished by a jot or tittle.'"

"But even though our lord was with us in the flesh," answered Saul, "and performed miracles, and taught the Torah to his disciples, we cannot look upon his miracles, and upon his teaching of the Torah, as we would upon the miracles and teachings of another Rabbi, a Rabbi of flesh and blood; for even in the flesh our lord was spirit, and we cannot judge according to the flesh."

This was too much for the simple, aging fisherman of K'far Nahum, and for the moment Saul refrained from pressing his views. It occurred to him that Simon bar Jonah was not the man to understand him; it would be better to address himself to the more learned Jacob ben Joseph, the brother of the lord, whose reputation for wisdom and piety was familiar to Saul. But this would have to be arranged, for Saul was being concealed from the disciples. There were but four who knew of his presence in Jerusalem: Simon, Simon's wife, bar Naba and Jochanan. After some days Saul persuaded bar Naba to advise Jacob ben Joseph of his arrival and to urge upon him to come to the house.

Late in the night Jacob ben Joseph came up from his dwelling in the David wall, and scarcely had he entered and exchanged greetings than Saul plunged excitedly into his views on the Messiah. The Messiah, he said, was a universal might, a radiation of the divinity, the personification of the divine redemption; the Messiah was the Son of God, with power to bind and loosen not only on earth, but in heaven too; he was the authority delegated by God to order the worlds in justice; by his death he had destroyed sin, and likewise the law, which created sin.

Reb Jacob listened closely and was astonished by these strange words. He answered at last.

"I understand thee not. Wouldst thou have it that the Messiah came to fill out and complete God? Only the idolaters believe that their gods can be improved. The Messiah came to fill out and complete man, and to prepare the world for redemption. As for God, we know: 'He is Who He is.' And it is written: 'The beginning of wisdom is the fear of God.' And in what thou hast said, Saul, I hear not the fear of God."

"All this," answered Saul, "was true until the coming of the lord. Until his coming it was proper to fear God, who expressed Himself in law. But the Messiah has liberated us from fear. He gave us a closer kinship to God. From now on we serve God in love."

"These are fine words, Saul; and it is true that God Himself bade us love him. Is it not written: 'Thou shalt love the Lord with all thy soul and with all thy might'? But love of God is not a sounding cymbal. Love of God is expressed in deeds. For who are we that we should be able to love God? Can we conceive His being? Can we comprehend His nature? Has anyone seen Him? Has anyone touched Him with his hand? The idolaters love their gods, because they have molded them of gold or silver, or hewn them out of stone, and they love the treasure which is their own work. But we hold no treasure in our hands, to be loved thus. We have only the law, which was given us by Moses on Sinai; and we can love God only in obeying His will, in fulfilling His commandments, in serving Him with all our heart. Love of God is not an empty sound, and it is not as the love of man for man. The expression of our love is the fear which fills us and our obedience to His will."

"This," responded Saul, "is but a faith in the deeds of the law, which are sown with stumbling blocks, rocks upon the road which leads to God. The Messiah has brought us a new faith, which is love."

Jacob ben Joseph did not answer. For him the young man Saul existed no more. He turned to Simon bar Jonah, who was seated in a dark corner of the room, trying hard to follow the dispute, and said:

"Saul of Tarshish shall not preach these things in the synagogues. Would he destroy the peace which our congregation has, God be thanked, been vouchsafed of late?"

"No, Saul will not preach in the synagogues," answered Simon. "It is not his intention. Brother Saul has not shown himself to the disciples, and his presence in Jerusalem is known but to us."

*   *   *

Brother Saul did not preach in the synagogues before the congregations, for the pulpit was denied him. But the secret of his presence ceased to be a secret. He could not stay hidden any longer, but issued forth and preached to all who would listen. He appeared in the synagogues of the Greek-speaking Jews, and argued with them, whether or not they were of the faithful. Everywhere he proclaimed that the Messiah was the Son of God. Those who encountered him stared openmouthed. Was this the man who, only a few years before, had persecuted the faithful, dragged them before the High Priest's court, condemned them to the lash, not for such daring views as he now expressed, but for mere belief in the Messiah? Was this the man who had taken a hand in the stoning of Reb Istephan, and who had set forth for Damascus to destroy the congregation there? Since those days the deep wound in the Greek-speaking community, which had been divided into believers and non-believers, had been healed. The congregation was once more united; no man watched and spied upon his fellow; no one was punished for believing in the Messiah. They said: "When he will return a second time, with the clouds of heaven, we shall see whether this is the true Messiah, or another." But now the disputes which Saul launched divided the congregation again; and wherever he appeared there also appeared unrest, enmity, and anger.

Moreover, there were secret suspicions concerning him among the faithful. They remembered his past, they remembered what suffering he had caused them, and their memories caused them to doubt the sincerity of his conversion. His strange gospel of the Sonship of the Messiah wounded their deep-rooted Jewish feelings, and they asked themselves whether this was not a trick of his to destroy the congregation. And even those who did not question his sincerity mocked him. A phrase became current among the faithful: "Saul went forth to find

201

asses and found the Kingdom." The fact that Saul was not accepted by the heads of the congregation made him an outsider, both among the Greek-speaking Jews and among the others. The believers knew that the disciples had not put their hands on Saul and that they had forbidden him to speak in the synagogues in the name of the new congregation. Thus his words were without effect, except that they called forth bitterness, disputes, wranglings, and even fights.

Such was the resentment kindled against Saul in the Greek-speaking synagogues—he did not show himself in the other synagogues—that his life was endangered. Among the worshipers there were some of the men he had taken with him to Damascus and had abandoned after the vision; and they took counsel how to avenge themselves on the man who had, as they believed, betrayed them. There was talk of killing him.

The disciples were greatly disturbed. They feared a renewal of the persecutions on the part of the Priesthood. Jacob ben Joseph, in particular, was angered by the actions of Saul, and he said to Simon bar Jonah:

"Saul must be sent away from Jerusalem. They will not listen to a man who preaches that for which he persecuted them only yesterday. Let him begone."

Simon too was of the belief that unless Saul left Jerusalem the peace which the young congregation enjoyed would be shattered.

But Saul would not be persuaded. Had not the lord shown himself to him? True, that had been but once, and since that time the lord had left him in darkness. There had not been a second vision to explain to him the nature of his mission. But he could not forget that night in the desert, when he had seen so clearly the meaning of Jacob's ladder. This much, he said to himself, he must bring to the House of Israel.

The House of Israel would have none of him. The House of Israel listened only to those who were recognized and accepted. The House of Israel was bound with the thongs of the law. Then Saul asked himself: Is there not a great world outside of Israel? Are there not other peoples which wait, even like Israel, for the redemption? Is not God the God of the gentiles, too? And had not the lord said to his disciples, when he appeared to them: "Ye shall be my witnesses to Jerusalem and to Judaea and to Samaria, to the ends of the world"? Yes, to the ends of the world!

Meanwhile the bitterness against Saul grew from day to day. It chanced once that he was in the Synagogue of the Libertines, and when he began to talk of "the Son of God" he was surrounded suddenly by men whose eyes were filled with fury, and one of them exclaimed:

"Saul of Tarshish, didst thou not hale men before the High Priest for less than this? Didst thou not stone one, and were we not thy helpers?"

Saul looked up, and beheld the witnesses who had carried out their own sentence of death against Reb Istephan.

"Didst thou not say then: 'The hand of the witnesses shall be the first against him'? Come, shall we not execute the same sentence upon thee?"

But before they could carry out their intention, Joseph bar Naba appeared, accompanied by a group of the faithful. From that time on bar Naba was always with Saul.

And still Saul would not leave the city, or cease from preaching, until he had been given a sign. He felt that he had been appointed the guardian of the true belief, and he would not move until he had been relieved; not though he was rejected by the disciples and by all their followers. He stayed in the house of Simon bar Jonah, but knew that the latter housed him out of pity, not having the heart to turn him out of doors. It was a bitter time for Saul. His life became a burden to him. There remained to him only his faith in the lord, whom he believed himself to be serving with all his heart. But the waters had come up to his soul, and he waited in anguish for the sign.

One day he was in the Temple court, stretched out in prayer, his face buried in the stone. And he prayed thus in his heart:

"Thou holy servant of God, our lord and master, show me thy face. Let me hear thy voice, as thou didst once on the road to Damascus. Reveal thy will to me, for I stand forlorn in my ignorance."

And as he ended this prayer, his heart was suddenly filled with a strange joy. He lifted up his head and looked about him. The House of God shone in the sunlight, surrounded by the children of Israel kneeling in prayer. Ecstasy took hold on Saul, and a fire burned in him. He looked up toward heaven and saw an intenser blue blazing in the blue depths; and out of that core of light someone emerged with slow footsteps. He heard a voice echoing in the chambers of his heart:

"Arise, and hasten away from Jerusalem, for they will not accept thy testimony concerning me."

Saul did not lose himself in the vision. As always, he retained the clarity of his mind, for he knew that the vision was a message, and he must read it aright in order to know what was expected of him. He called out:

"Lord, thou knowest how I persecuted those that believe in thee. Thou knowest that when they shed the blood of thy witness, Istephan, I was there and was as one of the slayers, for I guarded the clothes of those that slew him."

Then Saul bowed down again, and hid his face once more in the stone floor of the Temple court. And the voice spoke again:

"Get thee hence, Saul, for I will send thee far away among the nations."

*   *   *

Now he had found it. Now he knew what was expected of him. When the disciples heard that he was willing to leave Jerusalem, they sent him to Caesarea. His friend bar Naba accompanied him part of the way.

"The words of the lord will be fulfilled," said Saul. "Until then I shall wait in suffering."

"Until then I will pray to God that the fulfillment come soon," answered bar Naba.

The two friends exchanged the kiss of peace. A long, long time bar Naba watched Saul as he rode away, the dust rising under the quick, quiet footsteps of the little ass.

PART TWO

Chapter One

ALEXANDRIA

THE house of the wealthy Alabarch of the Jews of Alexandria in Egypt did not stand in the densely populated Jewish quarter of the delta. It faced the government house, the *Regio Judaeorum,* on the outskirts of the Jewish quarter, where the great circle of pillars enclosing the city ended on the shore of Lake Mareotis. The air of Alexandria, which was celebrated throughout the empire and had been praised by many a Roman poet, was at its clearest and freshest here, for the waters of the lake, streaming in from the Nile, brought with them the sweet odor of green fields. The great arched windows of the Alabarch's house, fronting the pillars, shone with innumerable lamps of glass and earthenware, hanging by silken cords from the capitals of the columns.

A great host of harbor workers in holiday garb was assembled at the foot of the stairs. They were Jews, who had come in from the delta to bring their greetings to the Jewish king, Agrippa. The leading members of the Jewish Senate were gathered in the house of the Alabarch. Even the brother of the Alabarch, the philosopher Philo, who seldom went abroad, had left his library to pay his respects to the new king. For Agrippa, who had been imprisoned by the Emperor Tiberius, had been released and exalted by the Emperor Caligula, and instead of iron chains he wore the golden chains of kingship. He was on the way to Palestine, where he would replace his brother-in-law, Herod Antipater, assuming the title of king; and he had paused in Alexandria to pay a visit to the Alabarch, who had lent him great sums of money during the years of his waiting. The king had not intended to let his presence be widely known in this city with its vast Jewish population; he had left his ship outside the harbor and had been rowed to land in a little boat. But certain of the workers had seen, at the prow of the row-boat, the banner with the cluster of grapes, the emblem of the Jewish people. The news spread as on the wings of the wind, and the delta was emptied. The porters left their baskets of wheat on the quayside, the perfume merchant his stand in the marketplace, the potter his oven, the weaver his loom, the money-changer his table, the housewives their pots, and the children their schools. The whole delta was there, in festive garb, carrying countless flags with the emblem of the cluster of grapes: the women with flaming scarlet headdress, their arms naked, their eyes ringed with cosmetics; the men in burlap. Wealthier Jews came, too, from other quarters, wearing mantles of Sidonian linen, blue-striped, their hair glistening with oil. Their women wore golden chains; their hair was woven into coils and flashing with unguents. They came with little cymbals in their hands, and before the arched windows they clashed their cymbals and chanted: "King! King!"

Agrippa was forced to show himself several times. But to the disappointment of the populace he was not clothed in scarlet, and not even in silver, the symbol of rule; nor did he carry a scepter. He came out, the Alabarch at his side, wearing a Roman toga, his thin, pointed nose twitching with irritation, his eyes hidden under his frowning brows. But he permitted himself a gracious smile in response to the tumultuous salutation. Agrippa, the courtier, could not for a moment forget his aristocratic origins, his friendship with Caesar, and his high connections in Rome. He could not for a moment forget that after all he was making a great sacrifice in leaving the capital of the world, where he was in the foremost rank, an intimate of the Caesar, to take over the rulership of an obscure little Asiatic kingdom. As yet, however, he was not the King of Judaea, that center of the world for all Jews. He was only a little Tetrarch of Galilee and Petra. But standing there, he put on the wearied look which the mighty think becomes them in the presence of the poor of the earth. The tumult of joy became louder, more sincere, when his wife appeared. She was known for her piety and for the influence wielded over her by old Rabban Gamaliel. It was known, too, that she alone could hold her husband in check and that she did her utmost to maintain his interest in the Jewish masses. It was hoped that because of her Agrippa would turn out to be a good king, for the Jews made great demands of a king, especially one who was of their own blood. The anointing of a king made him, among the Jews, a symbol of the Messiah, and the honoring of him was part of the ritual law. Agrippa was not the legitimate heir to the throne and not in the direct line of descent; but the Jews forgot the Herodian-Edomite side of his ancestry and remembered only that he was descended from the Hasmoneans, that in his veins ran the blood of the unhappy Queen Miriam, bloodily done to death by her savage husband, Herod. The Hasmoneans were accounted of the Davidian line, and therefore, in a sense, Agrippa was legitimate, belonging to the great dynasty which incorporated the highest hope of Israel—the hope of the Messiah.

The Jewish masses of Alexandria, assembled before the house of the Alabarch, simply would not disperse. If anything, their numbers increased. The street was packed from end to end, and the harbor was dead. Flags, processions, songs, cymbals—a riot of jubilation had broken out in Alexandrian Jewry. In vain did the Alabarch send out his servants to remind the mob that there were others than Jews in Alexandria. There were Greeks, there were Egyptians, and it was foolish and dangerous to arouse their envy by such demonstrations. And since this argument fell short of its purpose, the servants of the Alabarch invoked others: after all, this Agrippa was at least as much a Herodian as a Hasmonean. Gradually the mob became quieter. Shouting "Hail! King! King!" was all very well, but it did not fill the stomach. The workers went back to the harbor, the shops, the marketplaces. There remained only the chronic idlers who lived for such occasions: they lingered before the façade of the palace and continued to cheer hoarsely for the new Jewish king.

Within the palace the proceedings were calm and dignified. When Agrippa had greeted the leading members of the Jewish Senate of Alexandria, he withdrew, together with the Alabarch and a few of his intimates, to the library. The Alabarch and his friends were anxious to hear the latest news from the imperial capital and Agrippa's views on the outlook under the new Caesar. It was known that Agrippa was closely bound to the most important figures in Rome and particularly to the members of the mighty Julian family, with whom he had, in fact, received his early upbringing. Agrippa was therefore considered one of the most influential figures in the Empire, particularly under the new régime. In the eastern territories of the Empire his views and decisions would be of immense importance. There came to the house of the Alabarch, in addition to the Jewish Senators, the leading scholars of the Academy of Alexandria—the so-called "Museum"—hoping for some tangible evidence of the traditional Herodian attachment to the sciences. There came also high officials of the city government, partly in hope of gifts, partly in hope that the new king would pledge himself to donate some striking edifice to Alexandria. There were present the leading officials of the world's greatest library. All these had assembled to hear the latest news from the capital of the Empire; and there was wanting only one man, the Governor of Alexandria, the local representative of the Caesar—Flaccus.

Why was Flaccus absent? There were various surmises. Perhaps he had expected an official invitation from Agrippa. Perhaps he was indicating by his absence that he knew Agrippa's visit to be informal and unofficial. Perhaps he was unwilling to pay homage to the new king. And perhaps it was the coldness of the relations between the Governor and the Alabarch. But perhaps, again, the matter was without importance. It was known that Flaccus's days as Governor of Alexandria were numbered. When Caligula had already been proclaimed Emperor by the legions, Flaccus, ignorant of the death of Tiberius, had still agitated in Alexandria against the son of Germanicus. There was no love lost between the new Emperor and the Governor of Alexandria, and the failure of the latter to appear at the reception for Agrippa was a matter for surmise, but nothing of importance. None but the Governor stood to lose by this piece of tactlessness, and Agrippa felt himself too powerful to take the matter to heart. Despite his ostensible attitude of indifference toward the plebs which had hailed him, Agrippa was pleased by the popular reception. About him were the leading figures of Alexandria, his friends, his family, his son Agrippa and his lovely daughters, who had accompanied him on the journey. Was not Veronica the most charming princess in the world? Was not every eye in that assembly fixed blissfully upon the gracious, lissome form of young Antelope, who sat at her mother's feet, the multicolored lamplight playing on her glorious head of hair? Childlike, innocent as a new-born child, she sat there, a king's daughter, and bride of the Alabarch's son.

Suddenly there was the whisper of a new tumult in the street. The servants hastened through the palace courtyard, their bare feet slapping on the smooth stones. The gates of the palace were closed hastily. Some of the guests went to the windows and saw in the half darkness a gathering of crowds. There was a sound as of rushing waters. The servants, returning, reported that the Alexandrians were assembling again, and this time not the Jews, but the Greeks and the Egyptians. New voices were audible from without, and the flicker of torches was cast through the windows on the ceiling. There was a clashing of cymbals, a wailing of flutes. What was this?

The distinguished guests became uneasy—all but the king, who retained his calm bearing. His face took on again that look of boredom and disdain with which he had favored the cheering Jews. He had learned well the manners of the Imperial court: the great never betrayed emotion in the presence of the masses. They did not even betray interest. And looking on the king, the Alabarch composed himself, and imitated his indifference. But it was otherwise with the guests; they could not refrain from asking each other what this tumult portended.

As if an answer to their curiosity, the mob set up a shouting, in which separate words were audible. They were calling the king; not in Greek, which all Alexandrians, Jews or gentile, understood, but in Chaldaic, the tongue of the poorest of the poor in the city, the tongue of the aliens, who came to the Egyptian capital from the Arabian and Syrian provinces in search of labor.

Only now did the Alabarch send out his servants to discover the meaning of the tumult. But it was no longer necessary. The guardian of the gate came running in and reported that a mob of Greeks and Egyptians had taken the famous city buffoon, Karabas, had put a prayer-shawl on him, had crowned him with a crown of papyrus, had put a scepter into his hand, and had brought him to the gate of the palace. They were dancing about him now and shouting lustily: "Maron! Maron!" The roar of their voices came clearly into the library: "Maron! Maron!" And looking out of the window, the Alabarch beheld the mob surrounding the buffoon, gesticulating in grotesque imitation of Jews, yelling with a Jewish accent: "Oy, oy, Maron! Maron!"

There was no doubt about it now. The Greeks and Egyptians had assembled to insult the new Jewish king. The Alabarch consulted the captain of the guard, who reported that it would be folly to attempt to disperse the mob. The guards had barely been able to shut the gates. Isidorus, the priest, was in the crowd, egging it on. The Alabarch paled. This was rebellion! Had the Governor of the city been informed? He was told that even now messengers were on the way to the Governor's palace. Meanwhile the leading gentiles of Alexandria, the chief librarian, the rector of the museum, and others, were withdrawing quietly from the room, without a formal farewell. Before long there remained only the Jews.

The yelling of the mob became louder and louder. New masses poured into the square. Soon there was a screaming as of individuals being tortured. The mob was breaking into Jewish homes. Men and women and children were being driven into the street. The glare of the torches paled as flames began to light the sky.

But where was the Governor? Was it not his duty to preserve order in the city? Where were the legions, the might of Rome? Did not the Governor know what all this meant? The second greatest city of the empire in revolt: law and order flouted: where was the Governor?

Aristobulus, the king's brother, the only member of the family on friendly terms with the Governor, burst into the room. His face was white. He reported that the Governor had refused to receive him: instead, he had sent word that he, the Governor, could do nothing against the just indignation of the Alexandrians. For the time being he was still, Flaccus had said, the Governor of Alexandria; it was for him to decide what was right and what was wrong. This had been his answer to all of Aristobulus's transmitted admonitions and warnings. Something, then, was wrong in the Empire of Rome, the Empire which stretched from Babylon to the western ocean, from the African waste to the banks of the Danube—something was wrong in the Empire which was founded upon law. If a Roman Governor refused to maintain order, if the Pax Romana ceased within the borders of the Empire, what was there left in the world? This was what the Alabarch asked, and found no answer. Mankind would fall back into savagery, people would rise against people, slaves would rise against their masters, and the Empire would dissolve and melt away. No, no, it could not be. This was the mad, last desperate act of a Governor who knew himself to be condemned to death. Flaccus accounted himself a lost man, and this was his revenge on the Jews.

Meanwhile new and frightful reports poured in. The mob had thrown off the last restraints. Broadswords, undoubtedly stolen from the arsenal with the connivance of officials, had been distributed, and a massacre had begun in the Jewish quarter on the delta. It seemed as though the Alexandrian mob was preparing to carry out the plans of the agitator Apion, whose insane pamphlets had been ignored by the Jews, but not by the non-Jews. With the mob mingled city officials who declared that the Governor was in sympathy with the rioters. Jewish women were being dragged out of their homes and through the streets to the theaters, where they were being compelled to eat the flesh of

212

swine. Something had to be done: but what? What if the Governor, the official representative of Rome, was with the mob?

"One thing we must not do," explained the king. "We must not set ourselves against the legions, lest Flaccus be provided with the excuse that he was defending the soldiers of Rome."

Word was sent out at once, in the name of the king, the Alabarch and the Senate, to the Jews, that they were under no circumstances to attack any official, or any legionary. They were not to shed blood, not to defend themselves, but to rely on the clemency of Caesar and the justice of Rome. The Caesar would restore their rights and punish the rioters.

Yes, the king, who had grown up in the shadow of Rome, was certain that the foundations of the world were supported by the law and order of Rome. This that was happening about him was a foolish and trivial incident, the act of a criminal bent on self-destruction. Did not he, Agrippa, know who the Caesar was? Had not the two of them, Gaius and Agrippa, talked together, when they went on the hunt, of the time when Tiberius would die and Gaius would take his place? Did not Agrippa have with him the golden chain which the new Caesar had bestowed on him, in exchange for the iron chains which the old Emperor had forced him to wear? Had not Bernice, the mother of Agrippa, been the most intimate friend of the mighty Empress? Were not the privileges of the Jews a sacred right in the traditions of Rome, ever since the days of Julius? Was not he, Agrippa, himself a part of the Empire, and had he not been officially recognized by the Senate? No, he would not let himself be swept off his feet by the insanity of an official who, in his last desperation, was taking revenge for his impending fall on the people of Agrippa.

For all of these reasons Agrippa suppressed, as became a king educated in the ways of Roman nobility, any signs of vulgar excitement. He patted Veronica's head and sent the women off to their apartments, to lie down and rest, to whatever extent the tumultuous night would let them rest. He himself, however, remained in the library, together with the old philosopher, Philo, and a few members of the Jewish Senate; for, in spite of his assumed indifference, the king was far from being at ease. To this spoiled princeling, whose whole life had been a gamble and who was accustomed to staking on a single throw of the dice huge sums of money which he had borrowed or extorted from his friends, life had only one meaning—power; happiness was for him the smile of the mighty and the opportunity to share their authority. Yet he could not but be aware, particularly at this moment, of the insecurity of his position, backed as it was not by the might of Rome but by the Jews —a futile and impotent people. What was there for him to rely on? A few words dictated by the Caesar and inscribed on a bronze tablet. To-morrow another Caesar could recall the appointment; and in the mean-time any higher Roman official could laugh in his face—as Flaccus, for all the transience of his power, was doing tonight.

On such foundations was reared the edifice of his kingship. What was it worth? And thinking again of the people whose king he had become, he remembered that the Jews, at least, had never accepted, as the foundation of their strength, the promise of Rome. The Rabbis in Jerusalem—this much he knew—looked elsewhere for their security. The grace of God, and His promise, was what they built on. He under-stood now whence his people had drawn the courage to stand up to Rome. Rome was a human thing, uncertain and deceptive: not so the law of God, which the Jews obeyed. That was why the Jews had dared to rebel against his grandfather and to despise him for his subservience to Rome, for his rational, worldly political attitude. The Jews did not build on Rome, but on Jerusalem.

But what was he thinking? What fantastic conclusions were these? Agrippa started back in dismay. If he had lost faith in Rome, he was naked indeed. No, no, he would not let himself be completely unsettled by a meaningless riot. Tomorrow the incident would be over, the day after tomorrow it would be forgotten.

Meanwhile, however, the rioting went on; the roaring of the mob became louder, the flames spread and reddened the sky. So far they had spared the palace of the Alabarch; no doubt they had received their orders. Or was it the strong guard about the palace? And if it was the latter, how long would the mob respect it?

Had not his wife, then, always been right? As often as he had re-turned from an audience with the Caesar, radiant, almost speechless with joy, she had quoted at him a verse from the Sacred Books of the Jews: "Put not thy trust in princes." He said to himself: "Perhaps I shall do well to give ear to the words of the Rabbis in Jerusalem." It seemed to him that he was learning more this night than he had learned before in all the forty years of his life.

But there was another in the room who was learning much from the events of this night: the famous scholar and philosopher Philo, the brother of the Alabarch.

Philo was at this time past his sixtieth year, but his appearance was that of a man in the seventies. He had acquired a permanent stoop from bending over manuscripts; but his face, for all the evidence of the years, was filled with light. His white locks, running into his earlocks and beard, completed a circle of silver, in the midst of which shone his great eyes. He sat in a corner, keeping his own counsel. He was not accustomed to the company of the great, whom he had always avoided. Several times his brother sought to draw him into conversation, but without success. Relay after relay of bad news was brought into the room, but Philo said nothing, though the deepening of the furrows on his massive brow and the bitterness in the lines about his mouth betrayed what was taking place in his heart. He was not afraid; he trembled neither for his own life nor for that of his companions, believing, as he did, that both he and they were in the hands of God. If God had decided that these lives had reached their term, it was well; and if not, no power could prevail against him. Nor was it wickedness as such that frightened him. He believed, as he taught, that evil was a transient thing, goodness eternal. For goodness, not evil, was the nature of God. God had created first the spiritual world of ideas, which were the intermediaries between the world and God. Spirit ruled the world; the spirit might be overshadowed for a moment by evil, but it was bound to emerge again. What disturbed Philo now was quite another matter. He believed that Judaism and the Jewish law, as they had been revealed by the greatest of the Prophets, Moses, were the highest wisdom and the highest love that God had given to the world. Only this wisdom, becoming an effective force in life, could bring to mankind the peace of God. But what, asked Philo, availed the wisdom and love of God, if these blessings had been entrusted to a weak, persecuted people, to pitiful, insecure human beings who were being swept away in a storm of ignorance, defilement, and depravity?

In this soul, anchored as it was in God, the frightful incidents of that night awakened feelings not of revenge against the gentiles, but of pity. Evil was in reality non-existent, for nothing existed without God, and God was all goodness. That which men called evil was only ignorance and blindness. Destruction had to come down, not upon the sinners, but upon that which was called sin. What did it avail that the Jews were a peculiar people, chosen of God to serve Him and to drink of His living waters, if the world was evil because of its ignorance? God's wisdom must cover the world as the waters cover the sea. The Torah of God must become the portion of all mankind. The Logos, the directing wisdom, which God had appointed as His first Son to rule the world with love and justice for all, must become the redemption of the whole world, not merely of the peculiar people.

It was not as he had believed till now; the *idea* which had been incorporated in the peculiar people, which had been chosen and trained to this end, could not be the embodiment of the will of God. That embodiment would have to emerge in the universally effective *power* of the Logos, a power expressing itself not in thought, but in action, the responsible directive in the ways of men. The Logos in action, not the Logos in thought, was the wisdom of God. And therefore the wisdom of God could not be the privilege of individuals, or of a peculiar people, as the idea was; it had to become the redemption of all humanity, as only through the Logos in action could love and justice be brought to humanity.

This was the philosophy on which Philo meditated in that night of terror.

* * *

Behind the Alexandrian riots there was a history of agitation, connivance, and neglect. The Jews themselves had paid no attention to the evidences of the gathering storm. They had not taken seriously the activities of Apion, the grammarian, the writer of scurrilous pamphlets; and the authorities, far from attempting to suppress him, had given him their tacit backing. The Jews of Alexandria felt secure in their position and history. They had been brought to the city by its founder, Alexander, who wished to replace Tyre, which he had destroyed. The Jews of Alexandria had taken the place of the Phoenicians as traders. The ships which dropped anchor in the harbor of Alexandria were owned by Jewish merchants, who exported great cargoes of grain to the imperial capital. The workers in the harbor were all Jews. What would

216

Alexandria be without the Jews? Who cared, then, if Apion reviled them in unmeasured language, and Isidorus, the priest in the Temple of Isis, preached against them? Was it not known that Isidorus had transformed the Temple of Isis into a public brothel and that he collected vast sums from the hordes of women who served as prostitutes? Was it not known also that Apion was a common thief, who had once been sold as a slave for his crimes? What, then, asked the Jews, could result from the slanders of such men?

And so they decided to ignore the agitation against them, on the ground that every answer would only attract more attention to the libels. But the agitation bore fruit. The riots which began on the night of Agrippa's visit lasted for weeks. Agrippa left secretly for Palestine, but as long as Flaccus remained in power, the mob, tacitly or overtly encouraged, roamed the streets of Alexandria—slaves, freemen, workers, merchants—and did as it pleased. One section after another of the Jewish quarter was attacked. Drunken crowds dressed in the garments which they had stolen from Jewish homes went from street to street. Day after day the most brutal excesses were committed with impunity. Here one saw a terrified group of Jews, their clothes ripped from their bodies, sweat and blood pouring down their faces, being driven from outlying quarters into the delta ghetto. There one saw a Chaldean stargazer standing in the midst of a circle of admirers, a heap of stolen goods at his feet: clothes, vessels, furniture, a couch adorned with ivory, a mantle of Sidonian linen, pots of earthenware and metal.

Throughout the weeks of rioting the Alexandrian theater was filled with spectators, for the spectacles which were enacted had not had their like in the history of the city. The Greek and Egyptian aristocracy attended, and watched Jews being flung into the arena to become the playthings of their tormentors. The faces of the Jews were smeared with a mixture of wine and honey, and lumps of swine meat were forced into their mouths. Aristocracy and plebs alike yelled with glee as the Jews, old and young, men, women, children, fought, turned their heads away, screamed, and writhed with loathing as the forbidden meat was thrust between their teeth. Members of the Jewish Senate were not spared. Indeed, these were subjected to special treatment. They were stripped naked, thrown across benches, and lashed. And the delighted mob, never wearying, continued to howl: "Maron! Maron!"

In between these brutalities, actors entertained the spectators with obscene parodies of Jewish life. One appeared in the arena wearing an ass's head: he was supposed to represent the God of the Jews; others, in Jewish costume, came before him and bowed down to him. The ceremony of circumcision was enacted several times, to the special delight of the women spectators. And from time to time "serious" speakers descended into the arena, and harangued the Alexandrians on the baseness of the Jews: Apion was there, and Isidorus of the temple of Isis, and others.

During those days Philo the philosopher, leaving his ivory tower, went among the people, exhorting and encouraging. Flaccus the Governor published an edict withdrawing from the Jews the rights which had been guaranteed them by the Roman Senate. Philo assured his people that the edict was without power and that it would be abrogated by Rome; the rights of the Jews would be restored. He pleaded with the Jews to offer no armed resistance; not only was it useless—it would only lead to greater excesses in Alexandria and would compromise their cause in Rome. He said: "The prudence of the individual is the protection of the people. As long as our enemies do not attack the root of Israel, which is planted in God's earth, no individual Jew may do that which might endanger the existence of his people." He urged them to be patient, to endure; the storm would pass, God's justice would prevail, their rights would be restored. "Of what use is it," he asked, "to throw oneself into the waves of a raging sea? The wise captain pilots his ship carefully, avoiding the crests of the waves. He waits for the storm to subside, and thus he finally comes to port. Therefore let no Jew commit any act of desperation. We must accept these calamities as the will of God, and wait for the better time."

But there was worse to follow. From Rome came the news that the wild and dissolute young Caesar, Gaius, better known as Caligula, had proclaimed himself a god and had commanded the peoples of the Empire to place his image in their temples and to offer him sacrifice, as they did to Demeter, to Tike, to Nike, to Eros, to Zeus, Apollo, Astarte, Aphrodite, and the others. All the peoples of the Empire obeyed—with the exception of the Jews. A transformation was suddenly wrought. They who had submitted to every cruelty and indignity with the meekness of lambs became, in the defense of their sanctity, like lions. Even Philo, the man of extreme prudence, was for resistance. He bade the Jews suffer a thousand deaths rather than prostrate themselves in worship before an idol, even if it were the image of a living king. "This," he said, "strikes at the root of Israel, and when the root is in danger, accept death; let them slay you, but do not throw a pinch of incense on the altar fire. It is kingship which is divine, and not the king. The kingship is of God, but the king is compounded of dust and ashes, even as we are."

And now the Greeks of Alexandria had a new weapon against the Jews. Apion proclaimed that the Jews were blasphemers; they were eternal aliens who would not do homage to the gods of their country. Religion and patriotism were invoked; the Jews were both the enemies of the gods and the enemies of Caesar. But neither Apion nor the Greeks nor the Egyptians had their way. When a mob appeared before the great Alexandrian synagogue, dragging an image of the Caesar which they intended to install before the Ark, the Jews, who had suffered the long pogrom without counter-attacking, closed the doors of the synagogue, flung themselves on the idolaters, and drove them out of the Jewish quarter.

And now even Philo realized that the time for action had arrived. Old as he was, a stranger to public affairs, Philo agreed to head a delegation to Gaius Caligula, the Emperor. At the same time a delegation of the Alexandrian Greeks likewise proceeded to the capital of the Empire, to present their side of the story.

Chapter Two

DIFFICULTIES OF DIVINITY

DURING the first two years of his reign the Emperor Gaius Caligula was indulged and petted by the Roman mob just as he had been indulged and petted in his childhood by the Roman legions during his father's wars. His outrageous whims were regarded by the plebs as the charming fancies of a spoiled only child. He had hardly assumed the purple before he began to display his longing for the fantastic and extraordinary; he did everything to attract attention, except venture on the field of battle, and all his "exploits" were confined to Rome. No Caesar had ever possessed such a palace as Gaius Caligula built himself on the Palatine hill. The modest residence of his predecessor was completely eclipsed by the vastness of the new Caesar's edifice, which, with its endless rotundas, basilicas, arches and windows took up a quarter of a mile of frontage on the northern edge of the Palatine. He pulled down the famous homes of distinguished men of the past, those of Cicero, Crassus, Catiline, and others; he did not hesitate to remove from his path the sacred altars of the Vestal Virgins. He threw a bridge across from his palace to the Temple of Jupiter on the Capitoline hill so that—as was later revealed—the Caesar, declaring himself a god, might be able to visit his brother Jupiter without having, like any ordinary mortal, to climb down the side of the Palatine and up the side of the Capitol.

The masses, far from begrudging him these costly fancies, were delighted by them. They did not cease to applaud even when he began to betray obvious symptoms of lunacy. On a sudden impulse, he once caused to be collected in the port of Baia all the ships which brought grain to the heart of the Empire from Asia and Africa; he then commanded that a pontoon bridge, three and a half miles long, be constructed on the water from Baia to Puteoli, so that he might be able to drive across the sea on a chariot, fulfilling the obscure prophecy of a woman soothsayer. The result of this piece of insanity was, of course, a famine in the city of Rome, which depended on the provinces for its supplies. With pinched faces and empty bellies the Romans streamed out to enjoy the remarkable spectacle of a Caesar driving his wild horses over the sea: for the Roman mob was at least as hungry for circuses as it was for bread.

The Senators perceived too late what calamities they had stored up for themselves and for their country by their spineless indulgence of the young prince; but they could not arrest the process which they had set in motion, and they went on competing with each other to win the favor of a ruler under whom Rome and the Empire were being driven to ruin. They had called forth the demon: they were now unable to exorcise him. Distrustful of each other, they continued to worship the "divinity," and to feed him with gifts. The provinces were squeezed dry to enable Caligula to fulfill his wild fancies.

On a certain day not long after the completion of his palace on the hill fronting the Capitol, a special activity was to be noted in the vast area covered by the vestibules, basilicas, and garden courts of the Caesar's home. Long lines of deputations consisting of the most prominent citizens and the priestly hierarchy of the great provinces waited to prostrate themselves before the new god, and to bring him their offerings.

The priests of Egyptian Isis, in long, hornlike headgear, and short aprons covering their sexual organs, had deposited their offerings and had withdrawn from the Forum. German horsemen, guarding the entrance to the Forum—this was their special privilege since the days of Augustus, who had entrusted to them the security of the heart of the city—then admitted a deputation from the city of Ephesus, priests of the famous Diana who had come to worship the new divinity. It was Caligula's pleasure to present himself to each deputation in the guise of the god of its locality. Appelus, the Askelonite actor, helped the imperial buffoon with the make-up, and Helicon, the drunk and dissolute Egyptian priest, instructed him in the mysteries of the various divinities. Gaius Caligula kept on changing his costumes, like a cheap actor in the circus. He put on a golden beard which was to present him in the identity of Zeus for a Greek deputation; he removed that, and put on the female garments of the goddess Isis, for the benefit of an Egyptian delegation. And now he was being clad in the stiff costume of hammered silver—a dazzling cover of scale armor—which was to transform him into Diana of Ephesus. It was anything but a comfortable garb; the upper part of the costume consisted of multiple breasts, which swung against his body and raised bruises on his flesh; the lower part of his body was tightly encased in a narrow silver skirt, which pressed on his thighs and hindered the motion of his legs, so that he could neither walk nor sit down nor even bend over. He had to stand there like an image poured in one mass of metal. But Gaius Caligula took his duties as a god very seriously; no discomfort was great enough to prevent him from discharging his high obligations.

Of all the representations which the god Caligula had to appear in, perhaps this of Diana of Ephesus was the most difficult and exacting. It was not only the matter of his physical transformation. Diana of the Ephesians was a great goddess of many mysteries, many secret words, and many significances. Upon her legs were engraved esoteric

221

signs which only her priests could read, but which Caligula had to learn, too, in order that he might properly fulfill the role. Helicon instructed his master-god in the content of the mysterious inscriptions.

"Oh, great god Gaius! Know that when the goddess Diana of Ephesus moves her many mother-breasts, she causes the milk of her divine desire to flow into those who behold and worship her. And if Diana can so move to ecstasies of passion her worshipers, how much more thou, incomparable god? Do thou fill the breasts of Diana with thy virile strength, and move them mightily, let those that behold thee be driven into madness of lust, for thou art both man and woman, thou art the giver of passion, like Venus. Move thy breasts, and sound with them the music of thy divine character, which embraces within itself all the beauties and lusts of woman."

But "the breasts of Diana" were not cool, soft woman's flesh; they were metallic globes which were a burden on the flesh of the Caesar.

While Helicon instructed Caligula in the inner secrets of the goddess, Appelus directed him in the matter of deportment: thus and thus the goddess held her hands, thus and thus she stood, to emphasize her goddess charms:

"O thou mighty god, Gaius Caesar, thou who hast come down from heaven to bless us with thy glorious form! What goddess can compare with thee in the graciousness of thy deportment, and in the melting tenderness of thy smile? If thy divinity will indeed condescend to bestow its presence on the pious pilgrims of Ephesus, thou wilt surely rouse to jealousy, with thy conquering smile, the great and proud goddess who waits for them at home. For them, for the pious Ephesians, this will be ample reward after the long and painful journey they have made in order to bow down before thee. Smile, thou god Gaius, hold thy hands thus upon thy hips; for, even as thou art mightier in manhood than Zeus and Jupiter, so thou art more alluring in womanhood than Venus. For like the supreme gods, thou art hermaphroditic. Smile, great god Gaius, smile!"

But Apion, the Greek grammarian from Egypt, who had come to Rome at the head of a deputation bearing complaints against the Jews, outdid both Helicon and Appelus in the fulsomeness of his flattery:

"Who dare mention Jupiter in the same breath with the god

Gaius?" he asked. "To whom do they compare thee, thou god of men and gods? Silent, dumb, terrified, the gods lie before thee. Oh, what a trembling came upon them when thou didst appear, when thou camest to take government over heaven and earth! I have traveled much, great god, I have been in all the cities of the Greeks; and nowhere have I seen the image of a god which approaches thee in manhood, or of a goddess which approaches thee in beauty. Ah, would that Homer were alive today, so that he might sing of thy divinity, of the power of thy muscular arms, of the strength of thy neck, and of the softness and sweetness of thy hips! Not in vain do they tell us that Jupiter has grown gray on the Capitol, and that Aphrodite in all her temples lets her head sink upon her breast. Envy of thee eats them, great god Gaius. Thou needest not even command them, mighty Gaius! No sooner did the numberless subjects of thy provinces see thy likeness, than they hewed off the heads of gods and goddesses, to place thy head upon their shoulders. In all the temples of thy Empire thy statue stands, an ornament. Thou art the master god of all the gods of Rome, and all bring sacrifice to thee, fall before thee on their faces, perform for thee, upon their altars, the fitting mysteries. The women of thy Empire sleep with the image of thy divine body in their arms on the thresholds of the temples. The men must disguise themselves, imitate thy attributes, when they desire the favor of their wives. Thou embodiment of all gods and all divinities! Thou art the god of love and the god of fertility; thou art the god of valorous strength and the god of beauty. But alas for the blasphemy which is committed on this earth! All thy peoples serve thee in terror and awe, save for the accursed Jews, who insult thy divinity and refuse contumaciously to obey thy commands: the Jews, who will not admit thy radiant image into their temples, their synagogues. They disperse with violence thy obedient officials and pious worshipers who bring thy image to the doors of their synagogues!"

Gaius's face darkened. He was exhausted by the burden of his goddess-garb; he was exhausted by the ceaseless torrent of adulation to which he had been listening. His narrow forehead, on which the perspiration held down the locks of his hair, wrinkled suddenly, and his eyes turned to slits. A weary grimace of discontent passed over his face, disturbing the beholders, and disturbing most of all the little Greek, Apion, who had been received during Gaius's rehearsal of his role as Diana, for the god was extremely busy, and had to transact imperial business in the midst of his divine occupations.

Apion, a shriveled, undersized figure of a man, resembling a raisin which had lain too long in the sun, was a master of many languages; he was a master, too, in the wordless language of gestures and grimaces. He understood that somehow his calculated accusation had miscarried, he had touched the god Gaius in a tender spot. But he did not know wherein he had erred. Surely it could not be in his remarks against the Jews. He had been careful, too, in preparing his approach by a long and highly seasoned introduction of flattery. And at this point he was helpless. He did not know what other attributes and virtues to ascribe to the god Gaius: he had used up all his collection of high phrases. He had put Gaius above Zeus and above Jupiter. What was there left for him to add? In desperation, he turned now to his most beloved subject, the great poet, Homer, on whom he had lectured in many Greek cities. He began once more to bewail the ill-timed season of Homer's appearance on earth. If the singer of the Odyssey could be reawakened from his slumbers, and if he could be aided by the mighty Virgil. . . .

Both Helicon and Appelus made signs at the perspiring, loquacious little Greek, to stop speaking about Homer. Apion stood like one forlorn. He did not quite understand what the signs and gesticulations meant, until the Caesar-god himself burst into speech.

"Hold thy tongue, thou foul little toad!" And Gaius's cold blue eyes seemed to Appelus to flash like swords. "Whom dost thou choose as the fitting singer of my deeds and my divinity, my name, my victories, my crossing of the Rhine, my chariot-driving on the sea? Whom dost thou choose? The wretched, limping rhymester whom they call Homer? That babbling, grating, unskilled word-cripple whose books I have ordered thrown out of all libraries? How much more glorious is my beloved horse, my Incitatus, how much more poetry there is in the music of his neighing, when he receives his food in a golden bin; how much better he sings my fame, than thy Homers and Virgils! Mention not their names, if thou wouldst not have the skies darkened with my thunderstorms!"

Apion's face became a clayey gray. His dull little eyes sank deeper into his head. His heart beat furiously, for he knew himself to be standing on the brink of the abyss. Instinctively he grasped at the new line, took his cue from the Caesar's allusion to his beloved horse, Incitatus, and began a new song:

"O mighty god! What mortal can compare to divinity, even when that divinity takes on the form of an animal? Thy horse, thy great Incitatus, can be compared only with the sacred cow of the Egyptians. How wise, and how benevolent it was of thee to make thy horse one of thy priests, to bring before thee the prayers of all horses, and their submission to thy divinity. How profound is thy wisdom, Caesar, in making Incitatus a Senator of Rome. Surely he is entitled to that position not less than a human Senator, for he represents horsedom in the Senate. But Incitatus is something more than a Senator and a priest of horsedom; he is divine, too. For it is known that even as the gods are heavenly, and are of a divine nature, so too are the beasts and animals whom the gods use. Incitatus is the god of horses even as thou, great Gaius, art the god of men."

Soothed by this praise of his beloved horse, Caesar relapsed into content, and his face assumed its familiar expression of satisfied pride, the cover to his inner emptiness. Apion pressed forward, not to lose the advantage of the moment, and returned to the purpose of his mission—the punishment of the Jews of Egypt:

"Mighty god! What joy came upon the nations when they learned the tidings of thy divinity! We of Egypt put Isis our goddess in second place, to make room for thee. For thee our hearts beat, great god! None, none, doubts thee, none questions thy divinity, thou older brother of Jupiter. None, I say, except the Jews. Oh, who can wipe out the disgrace of their blasphemy and their impiety? Hear, thou god, of the desecration committed against thee. When we brought thy divine image to their great synagogue of Alexandria, accompanied by the symbols, and by the music of our priesthood, having provided ourselves, too, with an ancient he-goat and a slaughtered swine divided into three parts, as an offering for thee, the Jewish rabble came out against us and fell upon thy innocent worshipers. Three days and three nights they rioted and slaughtered. And whom do they prefer above thee, great Caesar, to whom do they attribute divinity instead? Hear me, thou god: it is well known that, in their temple in Jerusalem, there is a place which they call the Holy of Holies. No man is permitted to enter it. Only once in the year their High Priest may enter and proffer prayer. Knowest to whom, to what, the prayer is offered? Hear me, thou god. To an ass's head, which hangs upon the wall of their Holy of Holies. This they worship! This they prefer to thee!"

"An ass's head?" murmured the Caesar, in astonishment. "I had heard that their God was neither to be seen nor heard."

"It is even as he tells thee, great Caesar!" declared Helicon, the expert in religious mysteries. "O thou mighty god and Caesar, it is high time that thou, the brother, the elder brother, of Jupiter, shouldst bestow thy divinity upon the Jews, too. Command them to put an end to their barbarous idolatry, even if it be to a God whom no one has heard and whose appearance none knows. Great Caesar: the God of the Jews is envious of thee. He dreads thy divinity, and He has instructed the Jews to ignore thee. Do thou show the Jewish God how much mightier thou art than He. Command the Jews to place thy statue in the Temple of Jerusalem. Whom is it more fitting that they should worship there, in the great temple, than thee, the greatest of the gods, Gaius?"

Thus, urgently seconding the petition of Apion, Helicon whispered into the ear of Caesar. And Caligula, disguised in his Diana role, sweating under the weight of her robes, suffering under the impact of the swinging, metallic breasts, listened, and was aroused; this was a challenge to his delusions of divinity. And he issued his order to Petronius, Proconsul of Syria, concerning the Temple in Jerusalem.

*   *   *

Weeks lengthened into months, and still the Jewish delegation pleaded in vain to be admitted to the presence of the Caesar. They followed him at a distance, whenever he issued forth, they lingered at the doors of his palaces. In the end, wearying of their importunity, Caligula commanded them to be brought in. The audience took place in the midst of a consultation which he was holding with his architects on the subject of certain changes in the lay-out of his mother's gardens on the bank of the Tiber. For the most part, Caligula was so busy with his affairs as a divinity that no time was left for the conduct of the government. And even when the pressure of his divine occupation relaxed, there were human weaknesses which took precedence over the Empire. High among these weaknesses was his passionate interest in new buildings. From time to time, somewhere in between his godly and human preoccupations, he managed to squeeze in a little governmental business.

226

When the Jewish deputation was admitted, Caligula was surrounded by architects, engineers, gardeners, and other specialists who were submitting their plans. With eyes fixed on the plans, Caesar listened to the petition of the Jewish delegation, who rehearsed before him the constitutional rights which the Jews had enjoyed in Alexandria since the days of the founder of the city, Alexander the Great. They recalled that the great Caesar Julius had confirmed them in the possession of these rights; that the confirmation had been repeated by Augustus and by Gaius Caligula's predecessor, the Emperor Tiberius. They discussed their position in the greatness of Alexandria, their contribution to its commerce and industry, their share in the famous Alexandrian institutions of learning, and their rootedness in the history of the city. But the Caesar had his eyes fastened all this time on a grandiose plan which one of the specialists had submitted: a great hanging garden on the banks of the Tiber, supported on pillars of wood, a garden which would seem to be floating in the air, as was altogether becoming for the Caesar-god. Suddenly Caligula interrupted the leader of the deputation:

"But tell me, why won't your little Jews eat swine meat?"

"Our laws have forbidden it from the most ancient times. This practice of ours does no harm to anyone—certainly it does none to the swine," answered Philo.

This was a little too daring. One did not jest with the Caesar. But fortunately the Caesar had not paid any attention to the reply; he had plunged immediately into a discussion of the hanging garden. And then, when it seemed that he had completely forgotten the presence of the delegation, he blurted out another question:

"But tell me, why won't your little Jews offer me sacrifice?" And he said this not with outraged majesty, but rather with the pouting playfulness of a spoiled child. And then, in the next instant, as though he had bethought himself of what he was saying, he turned pale with rage. His head began to tremble on his thin neck. "Am I not god enough for you?" he squealed. "All the nations have recognized my divinity—all, except you!"

Philo perceived there was only one path before him—that of courage. He answered: "The Alexandrians also worship animals, like the crocodile and the cat. But we, the Jews, are not as the Egyptians. We have received from our fathers the tradition and duty of the One living God. Yet we have three times brought sacrifice upon our altars for thy

227

happiness, and our priests have prayed for thy welfare in the Temple of Jerusalem. These were the three occasions: when thou wert proclaimed Caesar, when thou wert cured of thy sickness, and when thou didst return in triumph from thy expeditions to Germany and Britain. On each of these occasions we offered up sacrifices in our Temple for thy peace and prosperity."

"Yes, yes, sacrifices *for* me, but no sacrifices *to* me. You preferred to offer your sacrifices to a God whom you neither see nor hear. Neither do you know what his deeds are. Has he conquered the Germans? Has he crossed the wild sea to the land of the Britons and conquered them? Where are his victories? Is it such a God that you prefer to me?" And Caligula forgot, in turn, his engineers and architects and gardeners. He drew himself up to his full but not very impressive height. "Oh, you diminishers of the gods! Blasphemers and unbelievers! How long will you continue in this stiff-necked obstinacy against my divinity? And to think that Agrippa is my dearest friend, bound to me by many gifts, and by the memory of our childhood years. Hear me, you Jews! Drive me not too far! I would still believe"—here he turned with altogether unexpected pathos to his entourage, and indicated the Jews to them—"I would still believe that these men are not guilty. They are to be pitied. They are foolish rather than wicked."

With that he gave the signal for the withdrawal of the delegation, and the Jews left without having had their petition even considered.

This was not the end, however. A few weeks later the Jewish delegation was bidden to attend the Caesar at Puteoli. As Philo and his companions entered the city, they were met by a Jew of Palestine, a man whose bulging eyes seemed about to leave their sockets and whose face was as yellow as ancient parchment. His clothes were stained and tattered, like those of a man who had not yet washed from himself the dust of his journey. He told them that he had just arrived from Palestine, at the head of a delegation of Palestinian Jews; and he brought news with him the like of which had not been heard by any generation of Jews since the beginning of the world. Gaius Caligula had dared to do that which no other Caesar had even dreamed of: he had ordered his image to be placed in the Holy of Holies in Jerusalem, and he had commanded the Syrian Proconsul to occupy Acco with an armed force, ready to descend on Jerusalem if the Jews did not obey.

Chapter Three

THE TIDINGS REACH ROME

NO one remembered when the Jews had first settled in Rome. It was known that in the time of the Jewish Kings, the Hasmoneans, when the latter signed a pact of eternal peace with the Roman Senate, the Jewish population of Rome had been suddenly increased by numbers of merchants, who dealt in Palestinian grain, figs, spices, and oils. Later there was an influx of Jews from Alexandria, the harbor through which the grains of Asia and Africa passed to Rome. The city of the Caesars, the city of Senators, soldiers, slaves, and idlers, produced nothing. From every part of Italy the demoralized population streamed toward the capital, leaving the fields to be worked by slaves—Gauls, Britons, and Germans—under the rule of corrupt overseers. The fertility of the soil declined from decade to decade, and Italy became more and more dependent on the spoils of the provinces. The Jews of the capital early became active in the vital transfer of supplies. Long before the time of Julius, they organized a congregation in Rome. When Pompey brought back to Italy great numbers of Jewish slaves, taken in the siege of Jerusalem, and put them up for sale in the Italian market, the congregations of Rome and Alexandria were able to ransom large numbers of them. In any case, it was known that Jews did not make good slaves. Their faith interfered with complete service; and in particular their obstinate maintenance of the Sabbath and of the food laws prevented them from becoming perfect house servants. As against this, however, the Jews were noted for their intelligence, their adaptability, their skill in commerce, and their international relations: for a net of Jewish communities was spread throughout the entire Empire and beyond. They were, then, excellent commercial agents, stewards, and managers, in which capacities they were highly appreciated by the practical Romans. It came about that many Romans did not wait to have their Jewish slaves taken off their hands but manumitted them of their own accord and raised them to positions of trust. Within a few years the Jewish slaves whom Pompey had brought to Rome in chains had become so

229

powerful an element in the city that the great Cicero was afraid to attack them openly in the Forum, and when he had occasion to mention them unfavorably he would lower his voice. The Jews took an active part in the elections and agitated for their own candidates among the Roman masses. They were a definite power both locally and internationally, so that the Caesar and the Senate were compelled to reckon with them. Nor were their activities confined to any special lines. They were bankers; they were also spice and perfume sellers in the streets of the city; they were merchants, peddlers, actors, smiths, weavers, dyers, sandal makers. They displayed a high degree of skill as oil-mixers, for many of them had brought family recipes with them from their native land, and the oils of the Jews became very popular among the Roman matrons.

The Jews of Rome had a quarter of their own on the right bank of the Tiber, a densely populated, swarming quarter, with tenement houses towering roof to roof above the narrow alleys, and with innumerable windows belching forth the thick smoke from the tripods on which they distilled their oils. Sweet savors of cinnamon, delphinium, and attar of roses hung heavy on the air—the savors which had so irresistible an attraction for the patrician women of Rome. (Other work which, unlike the delicate distillation of the perfumes, did not have to be done within the confines of a room, went on, after the fashion of Orientals, in the alleys, or on the garbage heaps in the small courtyards, the homes being used only for sleeping. They were all to be seen outside: the goldsmiths with their charcoal braziers, the sandal makers, and the weavers.) The women poured the oils into little vases, mixed the salves and unguents, and carried them in baskets to the homes of the wealthy Roman matrons. But the Jewesses of Rome spread something other than cosmetics, shawls, and sandals among their Roman clientele: they spread their belief in the One living God and in the sanctity of the Temple in Jerusalem; and more than one Roman matron found herself drawn to the exotic faith of the Easterners, with its mystic power, its strange and original institution of the Sabbath, its spiritual security, and its unshakable belief in the after life; more than one Roman matron neglected the services of the Capitoline Jupiter to pay tribute to the strange God in the distant and sacred Temple of Jerusalem.

On the day when it became known that Gaius Caligula had ordered the desecration of the Holy of Holies by the introduction of his image, a cry of lamentation and despair went up from the Jewish community of Rome. This was not just one of the calamities to which Jews in the Diaspora had become accustomed; it was the end of the world. On that day all work ceased in the Jewish quarter. The wealthy Jews who had their shops on the Campus Martius suspended business. They closed the banks, the offices, the perfume depots, and fled to the Jewish quarter on the right bank of the Tiber. They gathered in the synagogues. The weavers had left their looms, the goldsmiths their braziers, the bakers their ovens, the sandal makers their lasts, the potters their wheels—all of them assembled in the synagogues. Even the Jewish politicians, whose activities were conducted among the Roman masses and who were always to be seen about the Forum, congregated that day in the Jewish quarter. No Jewish woman ventured into the aristocratic districts with her perfumes and love philters. And among the crowds there could be seen, here and there, old people, not Roman by birth, but immigrants from Jerusalem, who were following the ancient custom of their native land and were going about with ashes in their hair in sign of mourning. In the streets, from open windows, from courts, rose a ceaseless wailing of women's voices.

When evening came the great synagogue, named in honor of Caesar Augustus, was filled to overflowing. Rich and poor, old and young, indiscriminately, were jammed into the building, which was illumined by countless oil lamps and candelabra. The walls were streaked with runlets of condensed vapor, the air was heavy with a mixture of sweet essences and of sour perspiration. On that evening all bodies had become one body—the body of the Jewish people in exile, waiting to hear the report of the Alexandrian delegation to Caligula.

Actually the delegation as such, including the Alabarch of Alexandria, had been placed under arrest; only Philo the philosopher had been allowed to go free. He stood now, a broken old man, in the pulpit of the synagogue and addressed the assembled Jews of Rome. Only his body betrayed the effect of his sufferings. In these last weeks he had aged by as many years. Pallid, frail, stooping as if under the weight of a physical burden, the tear sacs under his eyes swollen unnaturally, his white hair tinged with yellow, he bore himself as calmly as when, from the window of the Alabarch's house, he had watched the Alexandrian mob storming the Jewish quarter. That evening, in Alexandria, he had

231

felt that the Jewish people was one body with innumerable heads; this evening, in Rome, he felt this truth again. Israel could not be wiped out, because it was one body composed of innumerable individuals. Individuals could be slain; but not Israel. He had said to himself, during the Alexandrian riots: my body is a part of the whole; though they slay it, it will live on in the other bodies, for my blood will be in their veins, the blood of the patriarchs; my faith will be there, my hope and my aspiration.

But this which had come to pass in Rome was different. Not individual Jews were in peril but Israel as such. What did it matter to him now whether the Jews of Alexandria had their rights restored to them or not? If Israel went on living, the Jews of Alexandria would go on living, with or without rights. And if, God forbid, the Caesar were to have his way, then the Jewish community of Alexandria would assuredly perish, even if it had all its rights restored to it. And this is what he preached to the assembled Jews of Rome:

"Brothers, and men in Israel. That which the Caesar desires he will never fulfill. Even though we shall be called upon to sacrifice our lives to the faith, we shall not turn back. Even though we die, death with honor is better than life with shame: for after they will have desecrated the Temple they will wipe out the word 'Israel' from the annals of mankind. There is nothing else that we can expect as the result of our opposition; but let the expected happen, and let us die a glorious death in defense of our laws. And yet the last measure of hope must not be denied us. Let us repose our hope in God the redeemer. He has protected us in the past; perhaps this time too He will find us worthy. Let us then bear witness for Him, and let us show the world that Israel alone among the peoples stood firm in the day of trial and refused to dishonor the name of God by bowing down before a creature of flesh and blood, which lives today and tomorrow is in the grave. Let us have this trust in the justice of God; remember that there is no faith without trust. And even though we should not live to see the vindication of justice, let us, dying, trust that God's word will triumph, and that the peoples will remember us as the faithful witnesses of the living God. They will remember us as the only people strong enough in God to die for Him. Faith in God must lead us to a forgetting of ourselves. We must be filled with the madness of God and let the whole world know of Israel's folly and madness in God. Let the whole world learn from

232

the madness of Israel and be filled with it. For then the spirit of God shall cover the earth as the waters cover the sea. Then the glory of Israel shall be made manifest to all eyes; then the peoples will stream to the hill of God and bow down before Him, and they will know that Israel guarded the light of God not only for his own salvation but for the salvation and redemption of the world. It is not for our own sakes that we treasure, like the pupils of our eyes, the sanctity entrusted to us but for the sake of all the world, whose inheritance it shall yet be."

An interval of complete silence followed the address. Two of the cantors supporting him, Philo walked with uncertain footsteps to the place of honor which had been reserved for him, the Moses seat cut out in the wall next to the Ark. When the Archant, the head of the synagogue, asked if any congregant wished to question the speaker, no voice was raised.

There were no questions, and no comments; but much was written on those faces, many of them clean-shaven, after the fashion of the Romans. And most of the congregants were not only clean-shaven, and habited like Romans; their names were Roman, their lives were steeped in the tumultuous ways of the world capital. But all of them were prepared to fulfill literally the admonition of the speaker: "Better to die a thousand deaths than to desecrate our sanctity." It was this that could be read on the somber faces, and in the staring eyes under the frowning brows.

Among the worshipers assembled that day in the Caesar Augustus Synagogue were also certain pious gentiles. They were in the habit of attending Sabbath services, listening to the Jewish preachers, the cantors and the readers of the Torah—which in this place was used in the Greek translation. Silent and awed, they had heard, from their places near the wall, the appeal of Philo—better death than betrayal of the God of the Jews. They trembled at the defiance cast in the Caesar's teeth. Did not these men know, they asked themselves, that for such defiance the punishment was to be thrown to the wild beasts in the arena or to be nailed to the cross? And the hearts of the gentiles melted with dread of the God of Israel, who could pour such a power of faith into the veins of His believers.

One of the houses in the Jewish quarter, on the right bank of the Tiber, was more agitated than the others. Externally, the house differed in no wise from its neighbors. Windowless and doorless, like a mausoleum, with holes which admitted the sunlight and permitted the inhabitants to crawl from brick-walled room to brick-walled room, it was less a home than a night shelter. The families which it housed spent their days in the open, by the city gates, on the bridges, and in the squares. Men and women sat on the ground by little tables which displayed their wares—perfumes, magic herbs, silverware. In the rooms, or rather, holes, there were rolled up mattresses, tripods, and a few other light household possessions. The tripods were used in the evenings for the preparation of the main meal, and at sunset dense clouds of smoke billowed from the houses, so that the walls were covered with a thick mantle of black.

This pent-up life of the Jewish quarter had its good as well as its bad side. Every woman knew what was cooking in her neighbor's pot; the most trivial, as well as the most intimate, affairs of every inhabitant were public property; and the whole vast household became like a single family. Private life there was none, since all lived perpetually among a crowd of witnesses. The odor of cooking passed from room to room, together with peaceful conversation or loud curses. Rome's underground system of canals did not extend to this area. On weekdays the district was fetid enough, but on the Sabbaths and festivals, when especially rich meals were prepared in the windowless rooms, the air was unbearably rank. Some measure of relief was obtained by the use of incense, burned in braziers, and of unguents smeared on the body.

With all this went the joy of a common faith that bound together, in loving brotherhood, all the inhabitants of this house, drawn though they were from the most diverse provinces of the Roman Empire.

The soul of the house was a certain young couple which had only recently migrated to Rome from one of the cities of Asia. The man's name was Aquila, the woman's Priscilla, shortened affectionately by all who knew her to "Prisca." Husband and wife, but the wife even more than the husband, were beloved by the inhabitants of the house and, indeed, of the entire Trans-Tiber district. Aquila had brought with him, out of his home in Pontus, a trade which was then new to Rome, though long established in Asia, and that was the weaving of clothes and tents out of fine goat's hair. The peculiar virtue of this material was that, while it was as dense as felt and proof against rain, it was much lighter and more elastic than felt. Tents and mantles of washed and combed goat's hair were a novelty in Rome, and within a short time Aquila established a small industry. He had brought with him a modest capital, with which he set up a weaving factory in the Jewish quarter. His employees, Roman Jews who lived in the same house with him, near the Synagogue of the Hebrews, worked on an open campus, under a canopy of reeds. In addition to his trade, Aquila had brought with him a little store of Jewish learning; he could interpret the Holy Script and even quote some of the verses in the original Hebrew, which he had learned in the *cheder* of his native city. This was enough to give him considerable standing among the Jews of the Trans-Tiber quarter. Soon after his arrival he was elected an elder of the Gerusia, the Synagogue of the Hebrews, and then promoted to the position of one of its heads.

But greater than his influence, both in the house and in the Trans-Tiber quarters, was that of his wife, Priscilla. She knew the names and the personal affairs of everyone who lived in the huge house and of nearly everyone in the quarter. She knew, for instance, of the calamity which had overtaken Alexander the sausage maker, who occupied a den on the lowest floor, from which there poured forth perpetually the dense, acrid fumes of his occupation: she knew that Alexander's wife had fallen sick and was in need of rubbing oil. She went at once into the little room, where the paralyzed woman lay, moveless as an image, among the heaps of raw, fly-covered meat, and with her own arms applied the oil to the woman's body. She knew that from the room of Zadoc the mason, whom they called Justus, no evening smoke had gone up for two days in succession, which meant that Justus, his wife, and his three children were starving, for Justus was a man well on in years and could not find employment at his trade. Before the end of the second day Priscilla was in the room with a basket of bread and a promise that her husband would take Justus into his factory. A newcomer, she had already founded a Sisterhood of Pious Women in the Synagogue of the Hebrews. "Daughters of Jerusalem" was the name she chose for the Sisterhood, and its special function was the care of poor women in childbirth. Every member of the Sisterhood was pledged to visit the homes of the poor; when a poor woman was brought to bed with child, the member of the sisterhood had to remain in the house, not only to take care of the new mother, but to attend to the needs of the family, and to do the washing and the cooking. A second Sisterhood created by Prisca founded an orphanage in the vicinity of the Synagogue, and a third was occupied in visiting the sick and providing dowries for poor brides. There was not a charitable work in the district in which Prisca did not have a hand, and before long it was understood in the district that wherever a needy case arose, the first person to be notified was Priscilla.

But above all Priscilla was known for the hospitality of her home. Whatever strangers or travelers chanced into the Synagogue of the Hebrews were the guests of Aquila and Priscilla. Their home became a center not only for chance visitors but for all the inhabitants of the neighborhood. On Sabbaths and festivals it was the common practice to assemble there. Everyone brought his own modest meal with him, and all sat down on the mattresses and listened to tidings of the Holy City and of the Temple brought by travelers from Palestine. Here too the meetings of the elders took place, here the funds were raised to be sent to Jerusalem and the pilgrims appointed. On certain festive days the Jewish scholars of Rome would assemble at the table of Aquila and Priscilla; then there would be learned talk, interpretation of texts, discussion of the salvation to come. And the greatest marvel of all was that among the speakers who quoted this or that verse from the Sacred Script, and found a hint of deliverance in this or that prophetic saying, was the hostess herself. For, as happened more than once in Oriental countries, the wife was more learned in holy lore than the husband, and in this instance more learned than the majority of the men who made up the congregation. Priscilla was the daughter of a scholar, and she had heard for many years the talk of scholars in her father's house. She knew by heart many verses from Isaiah and Amos and others of the Prophets who had foretold the tidings of the Messiah. This, it appears, had been a favorite theme among her father's friends. Nor was she a stranger to the legends and the laws. She was therefore able to participate in the discussions of the learned in her home. This was the less remarkable among the Jews of Rome and of the Diaspora generally, where the position of woman was nearer to equality with that of the men than in Palestine itself. Priscilla's learning and, still more, her activity in the charitable work of the congregation, gave her the right to the title of Mother of the Synagogue, the equivalent of that enjoyed by her husband as a Ruler of the Synagogue. She was privileged to attend the sessions of the elders and the Rulers of the Gerusia, and to take an equal share in the direction of all its affairs.

Where did this woman find the sheer physical energy to discharge the multiple obligations she had assumed, as an official of the synagogue, as an organizer of charities, as the mistress of a household which was a hospice for strangers and travelers? Her appearance belied the suggestion of strength implicit in her many activities. She was of moderate stature, perhaps on the shorter side. Her face was a long and delicate oval. Her black, shining hair was drawn back, in the Alexandrian fashion, and formed into a knot. But there was great power in her eyes, the lids of which she touched, in the manner of Asiatics, with cosmetics, to accentuate their lines. She had small ears, a long, straight nose, small, full lips and an energetic chin. Her throat was long, and of womanly whiteness, rising in fine lines out of a superbly lifted bosom. But what distinguished Prisca from all other women was the magnificent power of her hips, which seemed to be poured of Corinthian bronze and to be filled with immeasurable energy. All the inexhaustible strength of this otherwise delicate female frame was concentrated in those hips, which were built to support the weight of a Hercules. Bursting out of the close-wound black dress which covered her body, the hips of Priscilla had been predestined, one would have said, to send forth a mighty generation of sons into the world. But if this was indeed their original destiny, that destiny had been frustrated. Prisca was childless, and all the energy which should have gone into the bearing of a line of heroic sons had been diverted into her charitable and public activities. But she not only radiated strength: she attracted it, too; and it was this remarkable capacity to render and to extract service which made her the center of the vigorous life of the congregation.

Since the hour when the calamitous tidings arrived from Jerusalem, Priscilla had known no rest. She was in continuous motion, encouraging the men to organize themselves for resistance against any attempt to introduce the image of the Caesar into the synagogues. The Jewish congregation of Rome set watches at the gates of the synagogues, and Priscilla made the rounds like a commander. Strangely enough, since the order concerning the Caesar's image had been published, the numbers of the gentile visitors in the synagogues had increased, and the bitterness spread to the non-Jews. Likewise the latter envied the Jews because they alone had dared to stand out against the acceptance of Caligula as a god. Nor did Priscilla neglect to play upon these sentiments of bitterness and envy. In particular she addressed herself to the women and stirred up in them a mingling of resentment against the decree, and of new devotion to the God of the Jews.

"Look you, it is not to the Caesar alone that you will have to offer sacrifice and not before his image alone that you will have to prostrate yourselves. Has he not a sister, Drusilla? Her too he has declared a divinity, the sister of Venus. And we know too well what the relations are between Drusilla and her brother," said Priscilla to Lucina, the wife of Procopius, the swordsmith, who was a frequenter of the congregation.

"That whore!" exclaimed Lucina, contemptuously.

"And the Caesar has other sisters, whom he has associated to the divinity. Whomever the Caesar takes to his bed, she becomes a divinity."

"And these shameless creatures we must honor as we would honor our own children. This is the command!" said another woman.

"The Jews are the only ones who know how to give due reverence to their gods."

The Roman women who had taken the baptism brought their husbands to the Jewish quarter and showed them the guards at the entrances of the synagogues—men prepared to let themselves be thrown to the wild beasts in the arena for the sake of God.

Then it came to pass that many Romans linked themselves with the Jews who guarded the synagogues and when other Romans came near, with the images of the Caesar, helped them to beat off the attacks.

The desperate obstinacy of the Jews made a profound impression on the pious gentiles. They came in ever larger numbers, not only to the Sabbath services but on Friday evenings too, in order to be witnesses of the preparations for the Sabbath and to see them light the candles for the evening feast.

Is not the Sabbath the day of God? Is it not the day on which Jews throughout the whole world stretch out their hands to each other, across mountains and seas, and become united, or rather show their union, being, all of them, branches of the great tree of Israel whose roots are in God's earth? Always and everywhere the Jews ceased from labor on the evening of Friday, to assemble in their synagogues and in their illumined homes, to the amazement of the gentiles, who could not understand how men wasted one day in seven, doing no work thereon, but passing the hours in prayer and in exalted communion with their God. At all times, in all places, this had been the sentiment of the gentiles; but now and here, in the days of Caligula and in the city of Rome, the response was strongest. Once, in days gone by, when the Jews had been more pious, they had suspended work on the afternoon of the sixth day, and had streamed homeward into the Jewish quarter from every part of the city. This was true not only of free-born Roman Jews, old inhabitants of the cities, but even of the half-free and of the slaves; and no power had been able to break them of this practice of resting on the seventh day and of resorting to their synagogues. They came to the Jewish quarter bringing with them provisions, earned, or even begged, to pass God's day in the traditional manner. The rich brought baskets of tuna fish, caught in the Tiber, whose waters were fed by the Cloaca Maxima. But the more pious ones would not eat of this fish, which had the taste of swine meat, and was a favorite dainty with the wealthy Romans. The poor brought baskets of vegetables from the various Campuses of the city, or little salted fish, which they fried in a coating of dough. From the openings in the huge Jewish homes on the right bank went up an odor of onions and garlic. The gentiles were wont to make fun of the Jewish taste for these vegetables, but they were attracted by the appetizing smell. On Friday afternoons there went up from the dens of the Jews the tumult of their Sabbath preparations, the mingled noises of cooking and washing and scrubbing. Then, when evening fell, the tiny candles, modest wicks burning in flat earthen dishes, starred the darkness, and all Rome knew that the Jews had begun the celebration of their Sabbath.

On this Friday Priscilla prepared for the Sabbath with a special degree of devotion. There would be present an unusually large contingent of guests. She had invited, in addition to the workers in her husband's factory, almost half of the membership of the synagogue. All this in honor of the visitor who had arrived with strange tidings from the Holy City.

Every Jew who came from Jerusalem was a welcome guest among the Jews of Rome, who were eager to hear the latest reports concerning the city and the Temple. This visitor from the homeland had appeared in Rome a few days before, and had presented himself at the synagogue. He had been of those who had reported to the Roman Jews of the Caesar's decree to place his image in the Holy of Holies in Jerusalem. But he, alone among the delegates, had spoken of something else, had given a hint of fantastic tidings which sent a thrill of

239

hope through the community, tidings which men did not dare to accept as reality, lest they be defiled; tidings which were only dreamed of in moments of Sabbath exaltation: tidings that the Messiah had revealed himself, and that the redemption had begun.

He did not declare these tidings openly; he did not make them the subject of a sermon in the synagogue. He did not possess the authority to make public proclamation of the tidings; but he was of those who believed that the Messiah had come, who had been baptized in his name, and who fulfilled the commandments which he issued when he was among the living; he was one of those who lived in the hourly hope that the Kingdom of Heaven was about to begin.

Already there was some talk concerning this visitor among the Jews of Rome. They spoke of him, not openly, and not in the rich synagogues, like the Augustus Caesar, or that of the Alexandrian Jews, but secretly, in the little prayer houses of the poor. There was a whispering, a hinting, and a spreading of rumors. And with lightning speed it became known that what the stranger had brought with him from Jerusalem were the tidings of the coming of the Messiah.

Priscilla and Aquila, too, had heard of this extraordinary man, and they begged him to come to the Synagogue of the Hebrews for that Friday evening. As always, a visitor to the Synagogue of the Hebrews was a guest in their home, and it was for this man's sake that Priscilla had made special preparations and had invited to her home half the membership of the congregation. She hoped that before such an assembly the stranger would speak openly and in detail concerning the Messiah and the new brotherhood of believers which was springing up in every part of the Diaspora.

All the lamps were lit that evening in Priscilla's home. The mattresses of goat's hair were spread on the floors. The Jews did not eat after the manner of Romans, half reclining on low couches around the table; at least, only the rich Jews imitated the gentiles in this practice. The poor retained the habits of the homeland. They sat on the mattresses which were spread on the floor; the oldest and the most honored ate from a low table. The others, the younger and the less prominent, stood around the walls, the women in the doorway. On the table was spread a white, newly washed sheet, a custom introduced by the Jews. On the sheet were placed a few oil lamps, the light of which was reflected from the jar of Roman glass which held the red date wine.

Near the jar stood the goblet of the master of the house. The table was laden with the dishes which the women had prepared, the vegetables, the fried fish, the rolled cakes. The master of the house made the Sabbath benediction, using his own goblet, on the sides of which were depicted the pillars of the Temple, and a candelabrum: this goblet was always buried with the householder, to testify for him that he had observed the sanctities of the Sabbath. The benediction ended, the assembly partook of the common meal. This was followed by the singing of certain verses from the Psalms. Finally the visitor, who sat at the head of the table next to the father of the synagogue, began to deliver his tidings of the Messiah.

Andronicus was the name of the visitor—a Greek name; and Greek was his mother tongue. But for all that he was a Jew of Jerusalem, and Jerusalem was written on his features, Jerusalem spoke from his garb and from his gestures. He was one of the *Ebionim,* as the believers called themselves ever since Reb Jacob ben Joseph had taken over the leadership. He was one of the oldest members of the congregation, and it had been granted him to hear the Messiah himself preach in Jerusalem while he was yet among the living.

"Be it known to you, brothers in Israel," he began, and his body swayed back and forth like a reed of the sugar cane in the wind, so that his beard and his earlocks swung this way and that, and his whole body was like a singing flame, even as it is written: "All my bones shall praise the Lord." His eyes were closed in ecstasy, and his face was pale, but with the pallor of a cold, white, inner fire. "Be it known to you, brothers in Israel, that the holy Messiah of the God of Jacob came to us, but because of our manifold sins we knew him not. We were not worthy of the knowledge, we were not prepared for his Messiahship. Therefore the just man was delivered into the hands of the gentiles, who did with him according to their will. They put him to the torture and inflicted on him sufferings beyond the imagination of man: even as the Prophets had prophesied concerning him: 'He turned his cheek to the smiter and stretched out his body to be beaten.' And he died for our sins, as it is written: 'He bears the sins of many.' Know, further, that all this was ordained by heaven, for our sakes, that he might atone for our sins, and that through his sufferings we might be raised from death, and win redemption, even as the holy Prophets have prophesied. And of his own will he took death upon himself, in order that he might be a pure offering for all of us. But know this too, that the just man lives, even as it is written concerning him, and he is with God in the heavens. And he showed himself to his disciples; they saw him, even as we see each other here. And he sent them to carry the tidings of his advent to the world, and to prepare the world for him. For salvation will come suddenly, even as the Prophets have testified: 'A voice is heard in the wilderness: Prepare ye the way; and the voice of the messenger is heard on the hills.' Therefore we must be prepared, for the redemption will come like lightning at midday. And all that we pass through, all that we hear and see this day, is but the warning of his approach. The Evil One grows stronger and rages against us; Ishmael puts forth all his strength, issuing in the form of the Caesar, who would exalt himself above the Lord of the world and wipe out the name of God from the earth; wherefore he commands that his image be placed in the Holy of Holies and calls upon us to bow down before him. I say these are but the travails of the Messiah, for the redemption stands on the threshold; it knocks on the door and pleads for admission, even as the wisest of all men has sung: 'The voice of my beloved calls, open, my sister, my bride.' And these words were written of the Messiah, who knocks upon our doors. Therefore we must be prepared for the day when the Messiah will come with the clouds of heaven, and the heavens will open, and the legions of the Lord of Hosts will descend to earth, and the Messiah will ascend the judgment seat to judge the living and the dead. Then he will call together his flock, and the dead will rise from their graves, even as Daniel prophesied, 'some to eternal life, some to eternal death.' "

A shudder of awe passed through the assembly. The listeners began to sway back and forth with the speaker. A breath of the Holy City had passed through them, and it was as if they were once more in the house of their Father.

"What must we do to be worthy of admission into the Kingdom of Heaven?" asked Reb Zadoc, one of the fathers of the synagogue.

"Ye have heard," resumed Andronicus, "that Jochanan came, and called us into the wilderness of Judaea, and baptized us and called us to repentance. Know, then, that Jochanan was the voice coming from the wilderness, according to the prophecy: 'A voice shall be heard crying in the wilderness.' Jochanan was Elijah the Prophet, who came bearing the tidings. After him came the Messiah, the pure and holy one, the Messiah of the God of Jacob, Reb Yeshua of Nazareth, who, though he was born of a woman, was yet an angel messenger of the Lord. Therefore let everyone who desires to be saved and to enter into the Kingdom of Heaven be baptized in the name of the Messiah, and let him believe with perfect faith that Reb Yeshua of Nazareth, who died for our sins and was the first to rise from the dead, as the twelve disciples have testified, with Simon bar Jonah at their head, is indeed the just Messiah. We must be a holy people: we must love our enemies, we must forgive those that do evil unto us, we must be as little children, we must purify our hearts, removing from them all uncleanness and all sin, we must cling to him, and be made one with him and part of him, even as his holy disciples have taught us: for they teach that when they feasted together at the Passover feast, before the just went up to be sacrificed, he broke a cake of *mazzoh,* and gave them all to eat, saying: 'This is my body.' And he took a goblet and made the benediction, and gave them to drink, saying: 'Drink, this is my blood.' What shall we understand this to mean? It means that all who believe in the Messiah must become a part of him, must live in purity and holiness, even as he lived. Thus we are taught by his disciples, to whom it was granted to learn at the holy source."

Then the Jew Andronicus of Jerusalem went on to tell of the doctrine which the Messiah had taught in his lifetime and of the deeds and wonders which he performed and of the prayers which he composed; he went on to tell of his death and of his resurrection and of the martyrs of Jerusalem. The congregation sat in mortal silence while the visitor spoke of the brotherhood of the *Ebionim* in Jerusalem, and of Rabbi Simon bar Jonah, whom they called "the rock," and of Jochanan, and of Rabbi Jacob ben Joseph, the brother of the lord, and of all the other holy ones. He told them of the persecutions which the congregation of the faithful had had to endure in Jerusalem and of the death of the first witness, Istephan, who had died with the name of the Messiah on his lips. "And all those who believe in the Messiah must be prepared to offer up their lives as testimony, and to suffer even as the Rabbi had suffered, according to his words: 'They must drink of my cup.'" Then he told them of a certain young man, Saul by name, who had persecuted the faithful in Jerusalem, and had gone for that same purpose to Damascus, and the Messiah had appeared to him on the road. He told them further of the marvelous things which God had wrought with the gentiles, in that He had opened their hearts to the word of God as it had been preached by the Messiah: them too the Messiah had taken into the Kingdom of Heaven. And he had enjoined his disciples to carry the tidings to the remotest corners of the world. Thus it was, indeed; the tidings of the Messiah were spreading now, and before long they would be as the spirit of God, covering the earth as the waters cover the sea.

And now, word having passed through the various dwellings in the house regarding the words which were being spoken in the home of Aquila and Priscilla, groups of Jews began to enter. They left their own Sabbath feasts, some bringing along cruses of wine and pots of boiled meat. They stole in silently, and the place was filled with Jews— filled so that body was locked with body, limbs were intertwined: eyes, great, dark flashing eyes, were massed upon the speaker; eyes which were damp with tears of hope, eyes which broke into lightning flashes of ecstasy; one great, intense body with innumerable faces—straight noses, crooked noses, black beards, yellow beards, shaven chins, shining foreheads, foreheads which were smooth and foreheads which were wrinkled, long, stringy throats, short, stumpy throats, Jews standing, silent, dreamy, meditative, their spirits wandering in alien worlds— and on some faces a tender smile of belief, on others a hovering shadow of doubt and bitterness. And other faces there were, with neither belief nor doubt written upon them, but a silent, far-off longing.

In most of the earthen lamps the last drops of oil had long since burned away. Here and there a wick still flickered and danced before the final extinction. Thick shadows lay upon the room; faces and bodies were fused into one heavy darkness. And still from the white-covered table rose the quiet voice of Reb Andronicus:

"And the Messiah lifted his eyes to his disciples and said: 'Blessed are ye, the poor, for yours is the Kingdom of Heaven.' Therefore they are called the *Ebionim*, the poor. Furthermore, the Messiah taught them: 'Be ye merciful, as your Father in heaven is merciful. Judge not, lest ye be judged. Accuse not others, that you may not be accused. Forgive, that you may be forgiven.' "

All night long Andronicus sat with the Jews in Priscilla's house, and before the Sabbath dawned, the first congregation of the Messiah, the congregation of *Ebionim,* had been founded in the city of Edom, which is Rome.

On the Sabbath there could be no baptism; the ceremony was therefore delayed until the next day.

In the early hours of Sunday a gay company of young Roman aristocrats, returning from a banquet, all of them staggering with drink, all of them crowned with olive wreaths, beheld a strange spectacle at the Pontus aqueduct. A group of men and women, clad in white, stood shoulder deep in the water. A man with a long gray beard and dangling earlocks, like one of those who in the daytime hung about the Roman bridges interpreting dreams for a couple of copper coins, was baptizing the males, while a woman leader was baptizing the females, to the accompaniment of murmured words.

It was a damp, wintry morning. Dull, leaden clouds were rising over the Tiber and blanketing the city.

"Rome is filled with alien and sinister faiths. Look!" cried one of the revelers, pointing to the men and women steeped in the waters of the aqueduct. "Jews!"

Another answered: "Our Roman matrons have taken a fancy to the God which the Jewish women sell them together with their Oriental cosmetics. I tell you that the conquered will soon be masters of the conquerors; before long the Romans will be passing every seventh day in idleness and turning up their noses at a savory piece of pork."

"It's high time something was done about it," returned the first. "Our Empire should have one god and one Cacsar. Come! We will sacrifice a suckling pig to the god Gaius."

Chapter Four

THE STIFF-NECKED PEOPLE

THE bronze and copper smiths of the Roman Empire, the workers in metal and the sculptors, were confronted with a perplexing artistic problem. How were they to transmute the feeble, effeminate outlines and expression of the Caesar into the mighty image of a Jupiter, fit to be placed in the temples of all the provinces, without at the same time sacrificing every resemblance to the mortal original? It was not for nothing that little Gaius, the spoiled darling of his father's camp, had been nicknamed "Caligula" by the soldiers—a diminutive from *caligae,* the boot of the Roman foot soldier. Everything about Caligula was suggestive of the soft and miniature: he was short of stature, his forehead was narrow, his cheeks tender, his nose curved. The outstanding characteristic, if one might so put it, was his receding chin. This, together with the dangling lower lip and the little, blinking eyes, reduced the artists of the Empire, entrusted with the production of the imperial-divine images, to despair. The sculptors of the city of Sidon had, of course, the same problem as the others, complicated, however, by the local stylization of all their art forms. The statue which they finally turned out for the adornment of the Holy of Holies of the Jewish temples in Jerusalem had a typical Asiatic cast of features: the nose was that of the god Moloch, flat and broad, and the Asiatic head reared on a thin slender neck—in this last detail they remained faithful to Caligula's picture—produced the effect of a caricature.

Petronius, Proconsul of Syria, an aesthete and a man of classical education, first saw the statue when he arrived with his legions in the harbor of Ptolemaeus, and it was with the utmost difficulty that he repressed an explosion of laughter. The hideous face on top of a comical neck which rose out of a gigantic Jupiter-body, the mixture of decadent Roman and repulsive Asiatic, was too much for him. He naturally said no word to anyone in his entourage, in part because he was certain that any disrespectful utterance would certainly reach the ear of the Caesar, and in part because he had learned from his predecessor in office, Vitellius, of the obstinacy and inflexibility of the Jews, and he had no intention of encouraging them in their refusal to admit the statue to their Temple. Concerning their opposition to Caesar's command he had already heard from various sources, but he was astonished and disturbed to learn that they had abandoned their fields and, under the leadership of Aristobulus and Helius, the brothers of King Agrippa, were streaming en masse toward Akko, accompanied by their scholars and Priests. At first he was inclined to think that the Jews had received a description of the grotesque image of the Caesar-god and that they were coming to him to protest against the indignity of being compelled to lodge the monstrosity in their beloved sanctuary; and in his heart he could not but sympathize with them. He was already revolving in his mind a compromise solution. Since Agrippa, the Jewish king, was an intimate of Caligula's, perhaps he could prevail on the latter to withdraw the hideous Sidonian statue and substitute for it one of the masterpieces of Phidias or of Praxiteles which Caligula had brought from Athens to Rome. After all, the Temple in Jerusalem was one of the most famous sanctuaries in the Roman world. Perhaps he, Petronius, would win the gratitude of the Jews if he obtained for the adornment of their national shrine a work of art worthy of their venerable religious tradition.

Akko was a port on the frontier of Phoenicia, a city built in the Herodian style of Caesarea: white marble steps and white marble buildings enclosing a forum on which stood a temple and the Governor's house. A flood of men, women, and children, ten thousand of them at a moderate computation, had poured in from the Jewish countryside, and still they continued to arrive, contingent after contingent. They were of all classes; many were barefoot and clad in sackcloth. They had left their wooden plowshares in the fields. All of them were in mourning, some had sprinkled ashes on their heads. They chanted songs of lamentation, high, nasal melodies, deep gurglings from the back of the throat, filling the air with doleful sound. The Syrian Greek inhabitants of Akko came out upon their thresholds and gazed in astonishment on the wailing throngs. The voices of the women rose highest into the cloudless skies, but a deeper sorrow and a more implacable resentment glowered in the eyes of the men. Their brows were drawn, their faces furrowed. An atmosphere of tacit fury and hidden insecurity filled the little harbor. A great many of the men carried scythes and shepherd's staves, formidable weapons in the hands of an enraged multitude. The starved and wiry bodies, the tense faces, hinted of desperate resolution.

Petronius was a skillful Roman administrator, not devoid of a sense of justice, which he associated with Roman law. For him Roman order and the Roman peace were divinities to which he brought a boundless and unquestioning worship.

As was often the case with the Roman Proconsuls, this traditional sense of justice endowed him with a certain degree of insight into the local customs and traditions of the populations he was sent to govern, and it was a principle with him to avoid, wherever possible, outraging the sensibilities of his charges. But when all was said and done, he was first and foremost a Roman soldier, and a challenge to the Emperor's edict had to be met squarely. He looked at the throngs streaming into the city. Despite the staves and scythes which some of them carried, he knew their intentions to be peaceful; so much was obvious from the fact that they had brought their women and children with them. Moreover, their spokesmen were the brothers of King Agrippa, who, like Agrippa himself, had been educated in Rome and were accounted the friends of Rome and of the Caesar. For all that, he neglected no precautions. He stationed his legionaries, fully armed, at strategic points about the forum and the marketplaces, strengthening them with bands of mounted German auxiliaries. Only when he was certain that he had the situation well in hand, and that his men were ready, at a signal, to hurl themselves upon the masses, did he admit the spokesmen to his presence, to hear why the peasants had left their fields, the city dwellers their workshops, to assemble in Akko.

Suspecting as he did that the Jews had been outraged by the unspeakable ugliness of the image which it was proposed to introduce into their Temple, he was even ready to treat with them regarding the substitution of an acceptable work of art for the monstrosity which had been produced by the craftsmen of Sidon. He was, indeed, somewhat surprised that a description of the image should already have reached the Jews; but this mild astonishment was swept away by something resembling stupefaction when he heard that the Jews were in no wise concerned with the unworthiness of this particular image and its inadequacy both in respect of their Temple and of the majesty of the Caesar-god, but that they would under no circumstances permit any likeness of a man of flesh and blood to desecrate their sanctuary. Such a proposal, they told him, was contrary to their faith, and they were prepared to lay down their lives rather than permit it to be carried out. For this, and for no other reason, had they come in such multitudes to petition the Proconsul.

He listened in silence, his blue, steely eyes fixed on the faces of the spokesmen sitting before him. He was at a loss for words. These men spoke Latin, like himself; they wore the Roman toga, even as he did. They had been educated, like himself, in Rome, and among his superiors, for Aristobulus, like Agrippa, had been brought up in the household of Caesar Augustus and in his childhood had been the playmate of the Caesar's children. And it was this Aristobulus who was uttering words which were incomprehensible to a Roman. It was against *their* law, the Jewish law, to place any image in the Jewish sanctuary. But what sort of law was this which constituted open defiance of the law of Rome and threatened the Roman peace? What sort of law was this which differed from the laws of all the other nations which acknowledged the rule of the Caesar? There was not a single nation which had not been grateful to accept the Caesar as a god and delighted to place his image in their pantheons, to offer sacrifice to him and to address their prayers to him. Their gods had manifested no jealousy; on the contrary, they had regarded it as a compliment to be considered a brother-god of the Caesar. Only the Jewish God was too jealous to admit another to share his honors. Petronius remembered now all the fantastic stories told him by his predecessor and by others, concerning the inexplicable obstinacy of these Jews, these eternal trouble makers, and he asked himself whether they had not, after all, been in the right.

He had to call up every precept of Roman discipline, he had to remind himself of his importance as the representative of Rome, to prevent himself from losing his temper. Dissembling his fury, he asked the deputation in a quiet tone of voice:

"Is it because the statue produced by the Sidonian masters is unworthy of your great Temple that you refuse it admission? If so, I shall intervene personally with the Caesar and ask him to send a statue produced by the best of the Greeks, a statue covered with gold from head to foot. For I have heard that your God is a great lover of gold"—he smiled ironically—"and I hope that, with the help of your king, Agrippa, we shall persuade the Caesar to treat your God with the dignity which you regard as his due."

"Though Caesar were to send us the Capitoline Jupiter, covered with gold from head to foot, or the great Zeus of Athens, we would not admit the image into our Temple."

The Roman paled, and his blue eyes flashed.

"Am I to take this as a declaration of war on Rome? Is it for this reason that you have assembled your multitudes here in Akko?"

"No! We do not desire war with Rome. But we cannot transgress our law, which forbids us to recognize as a god a man of flesh and blood and to place his image in our Temple."

"I am here to fulfill the decree of Caesar; my commands do not issue from *your* law. I do not need your permission. I have my legions."

"The people will oppose them."

"Your people will war upon Rome?"

"If our people cannot war upon Rome, it can at least die for its God and for the law of its God."

"Hear me! I have been in many lands, and until now I have seen people die only for the Caesar and for the laws of Rome. I have not seen people die for their gods and for their laws."

"You will see it here, in Judaea."

"I am here to carry out the Roman law, not the law of Judaea."

With this the interview ended, and Petronius issued a command to a waiting legionary.

The Caesar-image had been in Akko for some time. It had been brought by boat from Syria, and it lay on a wooden platform mounted on six wheels. The Jews had not yet seen the image, for it was draped in Sidonian linens, like a mummy. Now, on the command of Petronius, the linens were unwound from about the image, which was slowly lifted into position and fastened, erect, with ropes. The bronze head, covered with gold leaf, flashed in the sun. The Jews closed their eyes, in order not to behold the abomination. But when the centurion gave the order to start the platform rolling toward Jerusalem, a terrific cry of lamentation went up from the vast assembly. The storm of wailing spread from the quay to the forum, from the forum to all the open places. And now a wall of living flesh suddenly formed about the platform and about the embannered legion which accompanied it. Like sheep huddling against a storm the Jews pressed themselves together in the path of the monster. Every exit from the quay was closed; there was not room for the passage of a single human being.

The first wave of armed legionaries, headed by the mounted Germans, burst upon the wall of the living flesh. It yielded, but it did not break. Wherever an opening was formed, a mass surged forward to close it. In vain did the mounted Germans force their horses against the solid mass of men, women, and children. In vain did the legionaries press forward, hewing blindly. Where one fell, a dozen took his place. Like a rock in the midst of a raging flood the wall of flesh and blood withstood the fury of the onslaught. There was no attempt at defense. They fell where they stood. Only a great wailing, a gurgling of pain and desperation, went up.

Petronius stood on the terrace of the government house and looked on. To him all this was sheer madness. He had never, in all his long and varied career, seen the like of it. No, these men had definitely not come out to wage war on Rome, or to oppose their obstinate wills to Rome's laws as such. They were not defending themselves. No hand was lifted against the legionaries. It was incomprehensible. If at least they would fight, if they would defy the Roman law actively, he would feel justified in giving the command for a general massacre. But this was different; this was something not so easy to cope with as open rebellion. He realized, to his utter amazement, that the representatives of the Jews had spoken no more than the simple truth when they said that their people would suffer complete annihilation rather than admit the image of their Caesar-god to their Temple.

It occurred to him suddenly that if he persisted, if he carried out to the letter the imperial decree, he would have to drag the image into an empty and abandoned Temple. There would be no Jews left to do homage to Gaius the god. There would be no Jews left to worship the new divinity or to offer it sacrifice. For these fanatics would let themselves be slaughtered to the last man, and the land would be left desolate. He had received reports that throughout the length and breadth of Judaea no work was being done. Those who were not now in Akko were on the way, or they were assembling in the towns which lay on the route to Jerusalem. It was a baffling situation. Caligula had sent Petronius down from Syria to install the divinity in the Temple of the Jews; but if there were no Jews there would be no Temple of the Jews, and the image would stand in an empty ruin gathering dust. What Caligula wanted was to be worshiped in a living shrine. To induct the sacred image into an abandoned temple in a depopulated land would be the greatest insult of all to the majesty of the divinity.

What was to be done? Slowly Petronius came to the conviction that there was nothing for it but to wait with his enterprise until he had advised the Caesar of his extraordinary dilemma. It was the only way out. Enough damage had been done to the prestige of Rome and the dignity of her law.

Side by side with the rage and even disgust which this exhibition of senseless and suicidal obstinacy had evoked in him, there grew now a feeling akin to admiration. *This* was devotion to a god! And the wonder of it was the more incomprehensible to him when he reflected that

251

the God for whom they offered their naked and defenseless bodies to the swords of the legionaries had in no way exalted them above their neighbors. On the contrary, their God had abandoned them to the fury of their enemies; and as far as he, Petronius, could tell, the only reward they reaped for their incomparable faithfulness was misery. They were oppressed by the strong, despised by their neighbors; on top of it they bore a heavy burden of capricious laws. And yet—they were prepared to die for this God! What was the secret of the indestructible bond? What hidden bliss streamed out of the mysterious divinity to inspire such fidelity? For that there was a kind of bliss, an indescribable and incomprehensible bliss in their adoration, was undeniable. No other god in the Roman Empire, neither Capitoline Jupiter, nor Zeus of Athens, nor Diana of Ephesus, nor Isis of Egypt, commanded the obedience which was offered this unknown and invisible God of the Jews. Who was He, who could plant such adoration and faith in His followers, such certainty that in relinquishing this world they were only acquiring another and more significant world? Was it possible that they had the answer to the question which had so long and so often tormented him, the question of what lay beyond the veil of death? Petronius was afraid to pursue further the thread of his thoughts; he was even more afraid of that which his eyes were now looking on.

"Halt the procession of the god Gaius!" he commanded suddenly. And to his astounded entourage he said, as if to explain himself: "The Caesar sent me to Judea to place his image in the Temple in order that the Jews might worship him. The dead cannot worship!"

And to the Jews he called out:

"Begone to your homes! Return to your occupations! I shall send a full report to the Caesar. I would rather pay with my own life than take upon myself the responsibility and the sin for the destruction of so many lives offered up in the name of your God—and mine!"

The officers clustered about Petronius stiffened and became paralyzed at these astounding words. The Jewish spokesmen stood silent and open-mouthed. But from the mass in the square an ecstatic shout went up:

"Hosannah! Hosannah!"

And again it rolled through the city: all despair, all bitterness was gone. Joy, exultation, and triumph filled the air, and the masses in the streets and squares of Akko flung themselves to the ground in adoration and hope.

"Hosannah! Hosannah!"

Petronius turned a dumb, bewildered look on the Jewish spokesmen. The latter pointed skyward and said:

"For three months now not a drop of rain has fallen in the land. The latter rain, which was due three months ago, has been withheld. And now look, Petronius, and see what thy pious words have moved the Lord to do."

The worshipers lying on the ground lifted up their heads, and the Romans looked upward too. The sky which had been, until a few minutes before, a dazzling blue, sending down merciless shafts of fire and light, had suddenly darkened. The sun was covered by a gigantic mass of leaden, rain-bearing clouds. And yet, as though they were conscious of being the bearers of blessing, the clouds unfolded without any sign of storm. Slowly, like caravans of laden camels, they marched across the sky. A little wind, breathing the freshness of hope, passed across the assembled masses, and the first gentle drops fell on the upturned faces of the Jews, and on the massive, bronzed heads and shoulders of the Roman legionaries.

"Hosannah! It is the latter rain!"

It was a miracle and a sign! With the latter rain would come better and happier days. The latter rain would wash away not only the dust accumulated on the soil, but the sins accumulated in the hearts of men.

A sigh of confidence went up: "From now on everything will be better!"

"God has heard the pious words of a gentile, and they have found favor with Him!" said the Jews to one another.

253

Chapter Five

KHAIFA BREAKS THE BARRIER

GAIUS CALIGULA was killed by the Roman aristocrat Chaerea, and there was no one to mourn his passing, except the Germanic guards who, under the leadership of a gladiator, made an unsuccessful attempt at a rebellion. Bleeding from a hundred wounds, the corpse of Caligula, brother of Jupiter, lay in the gutter like the carcass of a mad dog. The news of his death arrived in Palestine before Petronius received the command to commit suicide because of his failure to carry out the imperial decree concerning the image and the Jewish Temple. Caligula's successor, the timid Claudius, assumed the purple with the direct assistance of Agrippa, the Jewish king; for Agrippa had extensive connections in Rome, and carried on an active agitation among the senators and the army leaders in favor of his friend. Claudius had been so terrified by the mad reign of Caligula—who had left scarcely one member of his family alive—that he had to be coaxed out of his hiding place to ascend the throne. But he remembered with gratitude the services of his boyhood friend, Agrippa, and treated him as one of his most intimate councilors. He not only made Agrippa's title of King formal, but enlarged his territories and returned to him all the provinces which had belonged to his grandfather, Herod. Claudius went further: he extended his graciousness to the people of Agrippa. He openly declared himself the friend of the Jews; he restored the privileges of the community of Alexandria and punished with a heavy hand those who had been responsible for the pogroms which had resulted, in Alexandria and in other cities, from the refusal of the Jews to admit the statue of Caligula into their places of worship. He reaffirmed all the rights which had been granted the Jews by Julius and Augustus, proclaimed full tolerance for the Jewish faith, and instructed the governors of the various provinces to protect the synagogues and to permit no attempt to introduce into them either his statue or the statue of any other Caesar.

The exaltation of the Jewish king, Caesar's friendliness to the

254

Jews, the re-establishment of the rights and privileges of the Jewish people, and the proclamation of the sanctity of their synagogues called forth among the Greek peoples of the Empire a resurgence of the old envies and rancors. Again the cry was heard, and this time louder than ever before, that the Jews, in refusing to worship the local gods, were demonstrating that they were aliens everywhere. But on the other hand, the extraordinary steadfastness in the faith which the Jews had manifested in the days of the persecution produced its own effect in the hearts of the more pious among the gentiles. They regarded the reaffirmation of the rights of the Jews as a reward for their devotion to their God. The hideous death of the Caesar-god, which put an end to the persecutions which threatened the existence of the Jewish people, was hailed as a miracle; and side by side with the wave of renewed hostility there was a wave of admiration and of wonder. The Jewish synagogues were now being frequented by ever larger numbers of gentiles, godfearing men and women who were attracted by the mysterious bond between this heroic people and its God.

The first one to carry abroad the tidings of the risen Messiah, and to preach him to the gentiles, was Philippus, the head of the Cyrenean Synagogue. Fleeing from the persecution of Saul, he went first to Samaria, and when Jacob and Simon and Jochanan, the leaders among the disciples, heard in Jerusalem of the souls which Philippus had won for Yeshua the Messiah among the Samaritans, they raised no objections, but on the contrary rejoiced that their lost brothers in the faith, the Samaritans, were returning to the fold of Israel. For they argued that, in accepting the Messiah, the Samaritans accepted by implication the Prophets. They saw, in this conversion of Samaritans, the finger of God, the beginning of the unification of all Israel, the sign of the approaching Kingdom of Heaven. Simon bar Jonah and Jochanan of the Zebedees, the pillars of the Messiah, went up to Samaria to lay their hands on the heads of the converts and to bring them under the wings of the Holy Ghost.

But Simon bar Jonah, noting the power of the spirit in Samaria, and the ecstasy which came on the converts at their common meals, was not satisfied with this harvest alone. From Samaria he began to visit the surrounding towns, some of which were entirely Jewish, while others were of a mixed population. He went down to the city of Lud. Lud was a completely Jewish town, nestling in the green fields of the

Sharon valley. From Lud he went to Joppa. Joppa had always had a mixed population of Jews and Greeks, for it had been a harbor town from its immemorial beginnings. Here Simon stayed with a certain tanner who, because of his trade, had his house outside the city limits. The tanner had been the first of the inhabitants of Joppa to join the new faith. By the time of Simon's arrival there was already a tiny community of believers, all of them Jews, of course, and Simon greatly strengthened their spirit. There was a great harvest ready for the reaping in Joppa. But Simon's eyes and heart were fixed on Caesarea, a city in which the non-Jewish element was larger than even in Joppa. Joppa and Caesarea were not far from Akko. The Greeks of Joppa and Caesarea had been profoundly impressed by the unforgettable demonstration of Jewish faith which had occurred in Akko, and they were equally impressed by what they regarded as the reward which the Jews had won for it from heaven. In both of these mixed towns the rumor of the risen Messiah, and of the hopes associated with him, was widespread among the non-Jews, and a spirit of unrest and awe came on the gentiles, so that not only the townspeople, but many members of the Roman garrison, were deeply affected. One of the latter, a centurion by the name of Cornelius, became "a pious, godfearing gentile." He did much for the Jews of his city, and his name was mentioned with respect and affection by the Jews of Caesarea. Such was the case, too, with the centurion of K'far Nahum, whose son had been healed by the Messiah and who had built a synagogue for the Jews. Of all these things Simon bar Jonah knew. He knew from the Jews of Joppa of the strong inclination of the gentiles of their city to enter the congregation of the believers; but he also heard that the greatest obstacles to the fulfillment of their desire were the circumcision and the laws of *kosher* food.

Now since they were eaters of unclean foods, it was impossible for any right-thinking Jew to sit with them at one table or even to house with them under one roof. The law was that if a gentile so much as touched any food, whether it was honey, or bread, or wine, the food became unclean and could not be eaten by Jews. But on the other hand, the common meals were the most powerful instrument of the faith possessed by Simon bar Jonah: it was at the breaking of bread that he told of the life, the deeds, the saying, the death, and the resurrection of the Messiah; it was at these assemblies that the spirit came upon him and his listeners, that visions were vouchsafed and the gift of tongues manifested itself. But how was Simon bar Jonah to bring down the Holy Ghost upon the gentiles, and thus gather them into the fold of the believers, if he could not sit at table with them and could not break bread with them?

Simon bar Jonah sat one day in the house of Simon the tanner, outside the city, and looked out on the waters of the Great Sea. It was toward the evening, and the time was summer. Far off, in the faint mist which lay on the sleeping waters, he saw the masts and the many-colored sails of the ships of Caesarea and Akko, of Tyre and Sidon and Cyprus, anchored in the harbor of Joppa. Simon bar Jonah was an inland man, though he had grown up by the waters of Kineret. He had fished hitherto in quiet, inland waters, and now the sight of the Great Sea awakened in him a longing to visit remote countries. "How great is Thy world, how countless Thy wonders," thought Simon. "These waters, O Lord, lead to distant places. They wash the shores of half the world, they reach the peoples of the islands. They enter, through channels, the heart of many provinces. And in all these islands and cities and provinces there live men who have not heard the name of God and know nothing concerning the Messiah redeemer. They worship idols which are the work of their hands, they worship sticks and stones, or they are deceived by star-gazers and soothsayers." He himself, Simon bar Jonah, had of late encountered in Samaria a certain man known as Simon the Magician, who had offered to purchase for a certain sum the right to distribute the Holy Ghost, which he had taken for a sort of magic. This Simon the Magician went about with a certain whore by the name of Helena, concerning whom he told the poor, credulous Samaritans that she was the mother of all that lived, the mother, even, of all the gods. And as Samaria had its Simon Magus, so all the other cities had their deceivers and women idols. All these were waiting to be delivered from the bonds of false-hood by the word of the true Messiah. They longed inwardly for the tidings. Simon bar Jonah had read it in their faces, he had seen it in their eyes. How eagerly some of them came to the synagogues, to refresh their souls with the message of the living God! Why was the road made hard for them? Had not God created all men and all women? Did not God desire salvation for all mankind? Had not the lord himself, when he had appeared to them, said: "Ye shall be witnesses for me in Jerusalem, and in all Judaea, and in Samaria, even to the ends of the world"?

Simon bar Jonah stood up and looked out more intently across the waters of the Great Sea. It seemed to him that a voice came out of the waters: "Come to us! We beat on the shores of distant lands, where hosts of men and women wait, hungry for the redemption." And Simon bar Jonah asked himself whether it was for nothing that God had made him a fisherman. He had begun his calling in small inland waters, but was not the sea which covered half the world waiting for him now?

"What shall I do," asked Simon bar Jonah one evening of Simon the tanner, "if the Holy Ghost descends on us only at the time when we sit together and eat the lord's body and drink the lord's blood?" The two men were seated together on a rock overlooking the sea and partaking of their frugal evening meal, dipping their bread in the bowl of soup which Simon the tanner's wife had brought out to them. "What shall I do if the gentiles eat all manner of unclean things and are themselves unclean and if the Rabbis have forbidden us to sit at table with them?"

"The Rabbis have forbidden not only eating together with gentiles but even eating together with Jews who are ignorant and unobservant of the law," answered Simon the tanner. "Yet thou sittest with me, who am a tanner and am so befouled by my trade that, as thou knowest, my wife has the right to divorce me if I did not declare to her, before the marriage, what trade I followed. Thou sittest here with me, thou who art a man of learning and the first of the disciples of the Rabbi Messiah; thou breakest bread with me and eatest from the same bowl, and no other man of learning would do this."

"The lord, the holy Messiah, also sat at table with simple and ignorant people; and not only with such, but with publicans, yes, even with women of sin, if they had repented. There was not a soul in Israel fallen so low that my Rabbi would not sit at table with him. Nay, the lower the man had fallen, the dearer he was to my lord. For he said that not the hale need a physician, but the sick. Therefore he did not avoid the company of sinners and publicans. Yet I never saw him sit at table with gentiles, with such as eat all manner of unclean things," answered Simon bar Jonah.

"Teach me, my Rabbi," said his host. "Hast not God created the heavens and earth and all that is between them? Can there be a thing which God created which is unclean and an abomination? I am a simple man, and I am not skilled in the scriptures; yet I ask myself always: Who is the man who can make unclean that which God created?"

Simon bar Jonah was thrown into confusion by the straightforward question. Until this moment he had not encountered it and had not searched his soul for an answer. Brought up in the Jewish tradition of *kosher* and unclean foods, he had always taken it for granted that there were foods which were permissible and foods which were impermissible. It was in the order of nature.

All that night Simon bar Jonah stayed awake, revolving the problem in his mind. He tried to imagine what the lord would do in his place, how the lord would act if he saw all these gentiles longing for admission to the Kingdom of Heaven and excluded from it by the wall of the law. Surely, he said to himself, the lord would remove the barrier, he would open wide the gates of the Kingdom to the gentiles. These were the words which the lord had uttered: "The law and Prophets have been given until the time of Jochanan. And from that time on the Kingdom of God has been declared, and everyone can enter." What did this mean but that everyone who sought admission would have the gates opened for him? But had not the lord also said that heaven and earth would pass before one jot or tittle of the law would fall away?

He who had seen the lord daily, and had observed all his deeds, he, Simon bar Jonah, was certain in his heart that the lord would have accepted the gentiles into the Kingdom of Heaven. He remembered with what special love the lord Messiah had gone in to the son of the centurion of K'far Nahum and brought him out of his sleep of death. He remembered how the lord Messiah had dealt with publicans, and with fallen women, and with Canaanites. Had the lord ever thrust anyone from him? Had not all men and women been equally his children? And Simon bar Jonah also recalled the parables he had heard from the lips of the lord, especially the one concerning the son who was lost and who returned. Yes, yes, the lord would have accepted the gentiles as a dove takes her little ones under her wing. But this being so, why should his disciples do otherwise? Had he not given them the power to bind and to loosen on earth? "That which you bind upon earth shall be bound in heaven, and that which you loosen upon earth shall be free in heaven."

So debating with himself, Simon bar Jonah decided nevertheless that he would do nothing until he had been given a sign from heaven. And as always when he stood as it were before a wall, he declined to act according to his own insight. He considered himself but an instrument in the hands of the lord, and the lord would instruct him through the Holy Ghost, which would visit him in the likeness of a countenance or through the sound of a voice. For this he waited now; and he had been waiting since his arrival in Joppa, refraining meanwhile from winning new souls for the holy congregation. He spent most of his time walking to and fro along the seashore, watching the fishermen cast their nets into the deeps. And once he drew close to a group and looked intently at the contents of the great net which they were hauling in.

He saw there an astounding variety of creatures, of things that swam and things that crawled and crept, such as he had never seen in all the years of his fisherman's life by the quiet waters of the Holy Land. He had not even known that the sea was so full of creatures, even as full as the dry land. As the net flattened out on the sands he beheld fish that were shaped like stars and glowed like stars, while others were as black as the deepest hour of night. Some of them had blown-up bellies, and the fat oozed out of them like the slaver oozing from the snout of a swine, and there were such as actually had swine snouts. But there were also creatures in the form of miniature flying horses and others with long, glittering bodies, slippery as snakes. There were fish with huge, overlapping scales, bearded and bewhiskered fish, and fish with saillike fins. And there were insects in the likeness of gigantic spiders, with prehensile claws which brought to mind the claws of tormenting demons of the nether world. Creatures there were which in no wise resembled living things; they were like dumb, dead growths, covered with mail and gluey feathers; there were creatures the size of a man's finger, with transparent skins through which could be seen the repulsive working of their vitals; and there were others which called to mind petrified plants, but the moment they were touched they opened enormous jaws. And all this hideous agglomeration squirmed and rolled in a slimy thickness. The men and women of Joppa came out to the shore and bought everything from the fisherman. They split the oysters and the other sea-creatures between two rocks, and lifted them to their lips, so that the living ooze ran down the chins and breasts of the eaters. Simon bar Jonah was filled with a retching disgust, and in his heart he gave thanks to God for having made him a Jew and given him a law which divided him from the other peoples, bidding him eat only the clean animals and fowl and fish, so that his body might remain sanctified.

Yet, meditating on these matters, he was aware of bitter and oppressive doubts. He had compassion on the gentiles, from whom God had averted His countenance; but he also said to himself: "Is it not written in the Holy Script that God beheld His creation and He saw that it was good?" If God had created these horrors of the sea, how could they be unclean? Also he heard again and again the words of his master: "The law and the Prophets have been given till the time of Jochanan; and from that time on the Kingdom of God is preached, and everyone can enter." His heart was ground between the upper millstone of his pity for the gentiles and the nether millstone of the law of Moses. His head was heavy; the heat of the day had dried the air into lifelessness. Simon bar Jonah longed for coolness, for clarity of spirit, for illumination of the heart. He was weary and hungry, and when evening drew on, the time of the late afternoon *Shema,* he withdrew into the upper chamber set aside for him in the house of Simon the tanner. He lay down on the floor, his face in his hands, and prayed long and earnestly. He prayed for clarity of spirit and illumination of the heart. He prayed as he had always prayed when he was tormented by doubt. This time his prayer united him once more with his Rabbi, the Messiah, and of a sudden, in the midst of his intense supplication, his heart was flooded with joy and with awareness of the presence of the Holy Ghost. His limbs became light, his eyes were opened. It seemed to him that the heavens divided above him and light poured down upon him as from a vessel. The whiteness of crystal was all about him. It seemed to him that a great table descended from the heights, and on its radiant cover stood an enormous dish in which swam about four-footed creatures and birds and sea beasts, some of which he knew and many of which he did not know. Crawling things were there, too, such as he had seen in the net of the fishermen. And he heard a voice: "Rise, Simon bar Jonah! Rise and kill and eat."

Terror held the heart of Simon bar Jonah as in a vise. Was this a dream or was it a waking and true vision? Where was he now, in Joppa or in the city of Shechem, where Simon the magician had conjured down a table from heaven? Was it the Evil One who stood behind the vision, to test him, or was this the sign from the lord which he had prayed for? He called out: "Nay, I have never eaten that which is unholy or impure!" Then the voice rang out sternly: "That which God has made clean, make not thou unclean!"

Had he not heard these words before rising out of the confusion of his heart? Had he not been meditating on this throughout the nights? Perhaps, then, it was his own voice which re-echoed in him now. Simon bar Jonah repeated desperately: "I have never eaten that which is unholy or impure!" And again the voice rang, more sternly, more imperious: "Arise, Simon, and eat! That which God has made pure, do not thou make impure!" And thus it was, once, and twice, and three times.

There was no doubting it now! It was the sign from heaven! That which his heart had told him, that which had made him shrink back in terror was the will of God. He stretched out his hand to the food, which was no longer impure food. God had created everything, everything was pure, everything was permitted. He stretched out his hand. But as he did so everything vanished and was not.

He lay with his face to the floor.

Later, when he came down from the upper chamber, he was told that certain men had come, asking after him. They were messengers from Caesarea, the city of the gentiles. This was what they told him:

"Cornelius the centurion, the gentile, a just and godfearing man, whose name is held in esteem by the Jews, was visited by an angel of the Lord, and bidden to send for thee, who art to come to his house, in order that he, Cornelius, may hear thy words."

Now there came upon Simon bar Jonah the clarity of spirit which he had prayed for. It was the will of God that he should sit at table with gentiles, in order that the Holy Ghost might descend on them. This was the final proof that he was never again to call any man unholy or unclean.

Simon bar Jonah went up to Caesarea with the messengers and with certain companions from Joppa. He came into the house of the gentile Cornelius, for he understood now that God regarded no people as His favorite, but accepted every people which feared him and walked in the paths of righteousness.

From that time on he preached the word of God to the gentiles and acquainted them with the tidings of the Messiah. He gave them assurance that everyone who believed in the Messiah would share through him in the remission of sins.

The gentiles who were assembled in the house of Cornelius the centurion were filled with divine exultation. Together with the Jews present at table they experienced the visitation of the Holy Ghost, and to the amazement of the Jews they spoke, there and then, in tongues.

Then Simon bar Jonah, seeing all this, called out:

"Can any man forbid the water that it shall not baptize these men?"

And he directed that the men should be baptized in the name of the lord, even though they had not entered into the covenant of Abraham.

And this was the first time that gentiles were admitted to share in the Messiah without first passing into the Abrahamitic covenant; and it was done by Simon bar Jonah according to a vision which he had seen and a voice which he had heard from above.

Chapter Six

SAUL WAITS

THE waters of the river Cydnus are level and peaceful in the sunlight. The ships at anchor in the harbor are bright with decorations, and each flies the emblem and the name of the land of its origin. The tumultuous port is at rest. The population of Tarshish is out on the streets, from the wealthy merchant, fresh-shaven and draped in fine linens, to the barefoot slave in burlap, with the tablet bearing his owner's name hung round his neck; from the gaily attired daughters of respectable families to the alluring dancing girls who walk about with clashing cymbals, the signs of their profession; from the students of the academies in their sober togas to the naked youths of the stadium.

It is festival time in Tarshish, the festival of the chief god, Sandan. A huge pyre has been erected on the quay. Here, on this pyre, the celebrants will offer up in flames the tree belonging to the last year, after which the tree belonging to the new year will be planted, for the festival is that of the new year for the great god Sandan. The earth is green again, and a thousand bushes of myrtle and laurel and evergreens bloom on the banks of the river. Above the city towers the mass of Mount Taurus; eternally white, harboring cities and villages on its gigantic shoulders, it dominates half the country. Here, from the banks of the Cydnus, Mount Taurus has the aspect of a young athlete frozen in motion, the lower part of his body wreathed with eternal cypress and splashed with the blood-red blossom of oleander.

Rivers of color mingle in the streets, robes of cinnamon brown and violet and purple, heads crowned with wreaths of laurel and flowers. From the waves of color rise the sounds of flute and cymbal and drum. A vast procession, in which each participant carries the uprooted trunk of a young, blossoming tree, accompanies the image of the city god. Following the ancient ritual, the worshipers plant the trunks anew about the temple of their god and create a fresh-blooming garden as the background to the many-colored fleet in the harbor. When this ceremony is ended, there pours out of the Stadium a host of young men, Adam-naked, ready for the athletic contests. The new year festival is the festival of the reborn god, who issues together with the earth out of the night of the winter. Sandan renews himself in young life, and he must be worshiped in competitive games and sports in the famous Stadium of Tarshish. Men and matrons and girls look on the assembled athletes, on the rolling chest muscles, the indrawn stomachs, the hardened buttocks from which the curving backbones rise upward, the massive shoulders, the powerful knees, the sharp-hewn ankles, and a jubilant cry goes up from ten thousand throats. In vain do the priests swing their bells, in vain do the women wave their veils; the eyes and hearts of the Tarshishites are fixed on the bodies of the young athletes. The air rings with a single cry:

"Adonis! Adonis! Adonis!"

Among those who came out from the city to attend the festival of Sandan, and to watch the athletic games, was Saul. Unlike the majority of the Jews of Tarshish, he had not taken refuge on that day in the closed courtyard of his home or in the synagogue, in order not to witness, even by accident, the abomination of the idol worship. Saul wanted to see and hear everything. He wanted to know everything that the inhabitants of Tarshish, which he regarded as his own city, delighted in, and in what manner they worshiped their local god.

For seven years Saul had been waiting. Seven years had passed since that exalted moment when he had lain with his face pressed into the stone floor of the Temple court, since he had seen the lord in fire and light, and had heard the voice: "Arise! I will send thee to the gentiles!" Every day of these seven years he had waited for the vision which would usher in the fulfillment of those words. There had been no vision, no voice, no sign; no word had come to him, either from on high or from below, either from Jerusalem or from any other place.

Throughout all this time he had held himself in readiness, prepared at a moment's notice to enter upon the fulfillment of his mission. In order to perfect himself for the work to which he knew he was destined, he even enrolled in the famous academy of Tarshish, defying the injunction of the Rabbis. He studied by night, for during the day he continued in the exercise of his profession, and earned his bread by weaving mantles and tent coverings of goat's hair. His teachers at the academy were philosophers famous in Athens, and he had even joined the company of a number of young Stoics, with one of whom he had formed a close friendship. It was a peculiar gift of Saul's to be able to attract younger men toward himself and to awaken in them a deep and indestructible devotion. In Jerusalem he had had the intense, the unforgettable affection of bar Naba; here, in his home town of Tarshish, he had tied to himself, with an eternal bond of devotion, a young Stoic of the academy, Titus. In order to discourage the development of any inclination toward the opposite sex, Saul had consistently refused to entertain the idea of marriage, to the deep distress of his parents and the disapproval of the elders of the local synagogue, who regarded this vow of celibacy as a transgression of the Jewish way of life; for it was an injunction of the sages that by the age of eighteen every Jew ought to have taken a wife to himself. Unshakable in the conviction that he had been consecrated to a mission, Saul reserved himself entirely for his life's work. Was he not an instrument of the Lord? Had not the Lord snatched him up, as a lion snatches up a kid?

The celibacy which was the expression of his consecration endowed Saul with a special capacity for winning the friendship of men.

Young Titus, of the academy of Tarshish, was one of those who had been fascinated by Saul's dominating personality. He was a Greek by birth, a native of Antioch, who had come to complete his education at the famous schools of Tarshish. At the time when he first encountered Saul he was completely given over to the doctrines of the Stoics. Like all his comrades he had regarded the moral and philosophic system of his great teachers as a private possession and ornament, the privilege of the "chosen" intellectual, in no way connected with the life of the mass of humanity. But inevitably his association with Saul had influenced his outlook. The latter spoke freely to him concerning the God of the Jews and His Messiah, and Titus felt the strong pressure of Saul's faith in a life of purity and love and faith. He struggled against it, driven as he was by a pagan spirit and a youthful, passionate nature which refused to accept the bonds of the Jewish spirit.

At this moment, as the two of them joined the throng which awaited the opening of the competitive games, as they looked on the naked athletes and heard the ecstatic shouting of the Tarshishites, they were deeply aware of the difference in their sentiments, and they could not help urging their views on each other.

"Look, Saul," cried young Titus, his dark eyes, aflame with enthusiasm, turned upon his older companion, whose beard had become thinner with the years, and upon whose head a bald patch showed. "Look at the perfection of the human body, the instrument of Eros. Look at the beauty of its lines, at the singing harmony of its motions. Why do you say that Eros belongs to the fleeting moment, is a thing doomed to fade and disappear? Can not Eros bring infinite bliss? Is not Eros too independent of external circumstance, being within you and of you? Eros is all that you possess, and no one can deprive you of him. He slumbers in the deepest recesses of your heart, he comes to you in the darkest hour of night, bringing you the grace of his love. He is the only consolation of the slave, for in him even the slave is free. And when one body desires another and in desire mingles with it, as river mingles with river, there is life's utter perfection. Desire, the one master of life, radiates from the visible and invisible Eros, pours into man's veins like ichor, swells the flesh and makes it fruitful, washes over it like a storm, encloses it in the intimacy of fulfillment. Who, then, can put bounds to Eros and challenge comparison with his power?"

Saul listened patiently to the pagan outburst of his young friend, and a smile of forbearing affection played about his eyes. Like an elder addressing himself to a wayward child he answered:

"Your Eros, dear Titus, is like a blind beggar, who holds a stone in his hand and takes it for bread. For, if that which he holds be bread, it is only the bread of the vile flesh. With the fading of the flesh Eros fades, and with its death he dies. He dies continually with us, as the stream of time carries us toward the grave. But we are not merely our flesh, and we are more than worms. Seen in the body, we are here for a moment; we pass through life as a ship passes over the waves; we vanish, like a breath; we wither like the grass, which, when it is dried, the wind scatters abroad. But seen in the spirit we are eternal. And therefore we live, not according to the flesh, but according to the spirit. It is in the spirit that we are born to eternal life. And there is only one gateway to the birth of the spirit—faith in the only and living God and in His Messiah who brought us salvation. In faith we live eternally, for we live in the spirit."

Titus looked at Saul wonderingly.

"But is not my flesh life too? Is not my flesh subject to unalterable laws? Is there not an eternal logic in the structure of my body? And what are these laws, this logic, if not life?"

"Your body," answered Saul, "is subject to the laws of human life, which have in them the nature of destruction and death. Thus it is, too, with the logic which regulates your life—it is the logic of destruction and death. But the laws which regulate eternal life and are of the logic of the spirit proceed only from God and are revealed only by His Messiah, who triumphed over his body, triumphed over destruction and death, becoming pure spirit. Only through faith and the higher logic does our body find communion with the spirit and our life acquire worth and meaning. Without this spirit there is nothing but a great emptiness."

Still Titus looked uncomprehendingly at his companion:

"I do not know what you mean by the 'higher laws' and the 'higher logic.' What proof have you that such 'higher' categories really exist? Can you prove to the sense, or to the senses, that such a logic as you speak of is a reality?"

"I cannot prove it to your sense, for your sense too is earthy and part of our base and vile physical being. The higher logic is revealed to a higher sense—and that responds to the voice of God speaking in your heart."

"I have never heard that voice."

"You will hear it when God will take compassion on you."

"Till then, Saul, let me live by the light of my lower sense, for as often as I hear you speak I begin to lose faith in it."

Later in the day the two friends found themselves in one of the little booths which were erected for the festival along the banks of the river. Above them were leaves of blossoming myrtle, olive, and evergreen. Gay and tumultuous, the throngs poured about them. Innumerable fires had been kindled, and over them, in tripods, food was being prepared, sheep flesh and goat flesh, lobsters, young boars' heads, calves' kidneys, pheasants, doves. The people lay at ease under the trees and bushes. On every hand there went up laughter, singing, the music of flutes, the ringing of cymbals.

Saul and Titus had sought out a quiet eating place somewhat aside from the main throng of celebrants. Titus ordered his favorite dish, roast pork liver, and a jar of sweet wine. Saul kept him company at the meal. Still adhering strictly to the Pharisaic laws, he would not partake of forbidden meat, but he had by this time so far relaxed his orthodoxy as to sit at table with his gentile friends, and he no longer felt a revulsion at the sight of unclean food. Titus, knowing that his companion still followed the dietary laws of his religion, tactfully forebore from inviting him to share his meal. Close by the two friends, under a bamboo shelter, sat a number of Stoic students, who by this time seemed to be devotees of Bacchus rather than of Zeno.

One of the innumerable beggars who hovered thick as flies around the eating places approached the young roisterers. There were some beggars who practiced their profession under the pretense of selling love philters. Others had nothing to offer but the sight of their crippled limbs or their sores, which they uncovered less with the intention of awakening compassion—a feeling generally unknown among the gentiles—than of arousing disgust, so that the eaters would hasten to get rid of them by flinging them a piece of meat or a copper coin. This beggar, however, posed as an interpreter of dreams. Stationing himself near the drunken students, he began to'whine:

268

"O thou free son of a free father! In the drawn brows above thy lovely eyes I perceive that Fortuna visited thee in the night and breathed into thy ear a dream which thou seekest in vain to interpret. Tell me thy dream, and I swear to thee by the great god Sandan that in exchange for a slice of roast pork mixed with lobster dipped in oil, and a stoup of wine, I will so interpret thy dream that the wrinkles will disappear from thy brows and the daughters of Tarshish, who are as ripe with love as the almond trees with fruit, will fall into thy manly lap. Only yesterday I interpreted a dream for a slave of Tyre, and today I encountered him on the street with the tablet of his manumission on his breast: he was accompanying his former lord in the festival. Tell me thy dream, and let thy countenance be enlightened." The tattered interpreter of dreams was not addressing any one of the students in particular. He spoke into the air; for he was blind and could only guess who was seated before him.

"Do you not know," called back one of the young revelers, "that the life course of a man lies not in the hands of the gods, but is predestined, according to the doctrine of the great Epicurus?"

"By thy wise speech I know thee to be one of the philosophers of mighty Athenadorus," replied the beggar. "Thou speakest to a colleague, a philosopher of the groves of Plato. Brother philosopher, fill my empty stomach, which has understanding but for one thing—bread."

"Brother beggar, if thou art a philosopher thou surely knowest that there is no condition in which the philosopher cannot find happiness. So our thinkers have taught," said another of the students, and sucked lustily at the claw of a lobster. "The pain of hunger is but a condition; thou art in the condition of hunger, and I am in the condition of satiety. Disturb not the harmony of my condition by dragging me into the sphere of thy condition." Wherewith the student put down the empty claw and picked up another.

A third called out:

"What will it profit me if I give thee today a dish of succulent pork seasoned with frog-sauce fried in oil, and a stoup of wine mixed with honey, for which thy withered throat longs, even if I add thereto half of this lobster, whose white flesh still retains the fresh tang of the sea, so that it delights my tongue and freshens my virility as only the fat meat of lobsters can? What profit, I ask, will be mine if I give thee part of this roast goat's liver which lies before me, and I cannot make use of it because of my satiety? Wilt thou not be a-hungered again tomorrow? Wilt thou not be suffering still, and will I not be but prolonging thy suffering? Am I not logical, my friend? If thou art a philosopher, as thou sayest, and as I have not the right or even the inclination to doubt, thou must freely admit that if I were to give thee the pheasant which the cook has just placed before me, on a soft bed of egg-cakes, so that it squats there, adorned again with all its feathers, waiting until I will bring up from my stomach what I have eaten till now, in order that it may find room, thou must admit, I say, that if I were to place this bird, the fat of which bursts through its tender, roasted skin, in thy trembling hands, I would be doing myself an injury in giving thee what is mine; and surely thou desirest not to be the cause of my suffering."

Titus had stopped eating. His eyes were fixed on the neighboring table. Suddenly he rose from his place, approached the blind beggar, and drew him away from the mocking crew:

"Come," he said, "sit at my table. Thou shalt have thy fill of tender pork, and of sweet wine mixed with honey, for which thou longest."

The beggar, suspecting that this was but a continuation of the game, held back awhile. But, approaching the table, he smelt the good food with flaring nostrils, and threw himself on it with the fury of a starved beast.

The Stoics at the second table, amused and astonished by the issue of the little comedy, commented audibly on the action of Titus, agreeing among themselves that this young man undoubtedly had been infected with the queer faith of the Jews, a faith which preached the sharing of one's bread with the hungry and needy.

"The number of defections from our home gods grows from day to day. An alien faith corrupts our city, and it is time the city fathers did something concerning it."

Saul and Titus remained silent. On the way home Saul asked his friend:

"What caused thee to do it?"

"To do what?"

"Give thy supper to the blind beggar."

"I know not."

"Art thou not of the opinion that the Stoics at the other table did well, according to the logic of our thoughts?"

"Surely they did well, according to logical thought."

"But thou didst not act according to logical thought. Why?"

"I know not, I tell thee. A passing mood, a touch of contrariness."

"Nay, brother Titus, it was neither a passing mood nor contrariness. Thy action was true to the higher logic of which I spoke to thee before, the logic of the spirit, according to which the Jews alone have lived till now. But since the coming of the Messiah the whole world will live in the birth of the spirit within which all of us are brothers."

"Tell me more, Saul. I feel I am beginning to understand," said Titus.

"No, not to understand, brother Titus, but to live it in your feelings, as in a new birth—a new-born child in the spirit of the Yeshua Messiah."

* * *

No father could have watched more tenderly over the footsteps of a little son than Saul over those of Titus. From that evening on he accompanied his friend everywhere. He waited for him outside the doors of the temple when he went to do service before the idol. He waited for him outside the door of the rubbing chamber of the gymnasium, to which the young men went after their baths. Saul entered neither the temple, nor the baths, nor the rubbing chamber; but he made no effort to dissuade his friend from continuing his accustomed practices. He used no pressure. He only waited, knowing that his young friend was moving step by step toward the new life and the new doctrine which he, Saul, offered him. For his friend's sake Saul surrendered many of his own practices and imperiled his position in the Jewish community. For the elders of the synagogue murmured against his addiction to gentile company. It was known that he sat at table with gentiles, and there were some who asserted that he went into their temples. All this Saul endured—and more; for the discontent with him spread from the community into his own home. Saul's father no longer lived; his mother, who had reposed such high hopes in him when she sent him forth to the Holy Land, was heartbroken by the strange turn in the life of her son. She wept for the disaster which had come over Saul, she wept because he would not take a wife and found a house in Israel, like all other Jews; she wept because he talked like a sick man, asserting that he had seen the Messiah in a vision and that he was waiting for a miraculous sign; and meanwhile the years were passing, and his life was coming to nothing. The other members of the household regarded him as a lost soul, and had it not been that he still had his trade with which to support himself, he would have been forced to leave his mother's home and to hunger among strangers. Saul endured everything because he felt that this pagan youth, this gentile, Titus, was the touchstone of his belief that the gentiles could accept the faith of the Messiah. In Titus he was testing the gentile world: one drop in the ocean, nothing more, but in this one drop all the laws of all the waters of the ocean were implicit. There was something more in the relationship: Titus was for Saul his child of the spirit, the soul which he was bringing into the fold of the Messiah.

By day and by night, taking time from his work, he accompanied Titus about the city, waited patiently at the doors of the temples and gymnasium, walked with him in the cool shade of the academic groves or by the swarming quays. Gently, by degrees, he fed him with the truth as a little child is fed with milk; gently, by degrees, he nourished to wakefulness and strength the purer instincts in his young friend, playing especially on the instinct of compassion, the one most native to Titus. But always Titus was puzzled by the fact that this same instinct did not show itself in others and that he had not been aware of its existence in himself. But the instinct unfolded surely. Saul taught him not only to give charity, but to love his brother, to understand the heart of the stranger, to be patient and forbearing and loving even with his enemies. So Titus ripened in the spirit until he was ready to accept the tidings of the Messiah.

Then Saul told him of the Jewish patriarchs, of the covenant which God had made with Abraham and his descendants; he told him of the descent into Egypt, of the exodus, of the giving of the law at Sinai, and of the promise revealed through the Prophets. Finally he came to the fulfillment of the promise in the Messiah, Yeshua.

Late one evening, on a green field under the white shadows of birches by the quiet waters of the river, Saul spoke to his young friend of that memorable Friday in Jerusalem: he drew for him the picture of the Roman soldiers driving on the road to Golgotha the elected of God, bent under the weight of the cross, his white robe stained with blood and the sweat of his anguish; slowly he described the last agonies, the death, the resurrection, and the appearance to the disciples. Then he reached his own part in the unfolding story, his refusal to believe, his persecution of the faithful, and the vision on the road to Damascus.

"He seized me," said Saul, "as one seizes a pot and shatters it. He shattered me and put me together again. Now I am his instrument, his servant, waiting for the word of command which will send me out on my mission, according to his promise to me in Jerusalem."

"And I am thy servant, Saul. Take me and command me as thou wilt."

"Nay, not my servant, but my brother, whom I have won in Yeshua the Messiah."

Chapter Seven

THE CALL

THE quiet light of little earthen oil lamps brooded in the dwelling room of Saul's home. In one corner Saul was seated over his "parchments," and in the opposite corner his mother was drawing the threads from her spinning wheel. From the lamps behind them the shadows of mother and son were thrown gigantically across the room, over household utensils, jars, and mattresses, on the white-washed walls. The mother's face was unnaturally long, as though care and sorrow had drawn it out to write their records there. The tear-sacs under her eyes were swollen with much weeping, and her nose, like her son's, overshadowed the lower lip, but was even longer than his. She worked unceasingly, with her thin, heavily veined arms, at the flaxen thread issuing from the spinning wheel, but her plaintive voice, mournful and insistent, floated across the dim room:

"A Rabbi in Israel: this was what thy father, and I, expected thee to return from the Holy City: a Rabbi accompanied by his disciples, an ornament to our latter days. And thou camest back a lonely and forlorn man. They took away from my house a young blossoming tree and have given me in its place a withered thorn bush. Thou wert the pride

273

of the seed of Ephraim, the hope of our family, and see what has become of thee. Thou art thrust forth from the congregation of Israel, and even in thine own sect thou art not beloved. Thou art the companion of heathens, the word 'unclean' is cast at thee behind thy back, and thou sittest like a mourner in thy celibacy—waiting, waiting, for ever waiting. What art thou waiting for, my son?"

Saul swallowed in silence his mother's reproaches. He felt her pain and understood her longing for some earthly fulfillment through her son. What could he do? He rehearsed in his heart the words of the lord: "Who is my father, who are my brothers?" But she who sat in the opposite corner was flesh of his flesh, bone of his bone, and his heart overflowed with pity. He answered, from his corner:

"Mother, thou knowest well the reason for these things. It was not I who chose the road to Damascus; it was God who set me upon it. Can I leave the road upon which my feet have been set by God, even for thy sake, mother?"

"Forget, my son, forget. An evil dream it was which visited thee on the road to Damascus. An evil spirit took possession of thee, and it blows hot and cold in thee and makes thy heart restless."

"Mother, thou speakest against that which is of God, God forgive thee."

"I repeat: an evil spirit has taken lodgment in thee. Return, my son, return. Return, and place thy forehead on the threshold of the synagogue, and ask forgiveness. Bethink thee; thy name and the name of thy family will be cut off from the tree of Israel. Thou alone remainest of thy father's sons, the oldest, the heir. I will seek out a wife for thee. Beget children, raise up thy father's house again in Israel. Why should I be accursed among the mothers in Israel?"

Saul, who confronted all others in the consciousness of his strength, was still a child in the presence of his mother. Her sorrow unmanned him. He rose from his place, went over to his mother, and, bending down, said:

"I owe thee the honor which the law has enjoined upon children to their parents. My love and obedience are thine, but my life belongs to the lord. In thee I was formed for him. I will implore God to open thy eyes, so wilt thou see that the instrument thou hast created is destined for His work, and thy sorrow shall be turned to joy."

That night Saul lay awake in his corner, and prayed:

"Lord of the world, take pity on her! Thou hast cast me out like an unworthy vessel. The waters have come up to my soul. Take me out of the torment of my useless waiting."

When he rose, before dawn, he was bathed in sweat. He sought to begin this day as he had begun the day before and all other days. He washed his hands, repeated the morning *Shema,* and took his portion of bread, to carry with him to his place of work like any other day laborer. But he did not go to the weaver's factory. He went instead to the quayside. For it was springtime; the branches were covered with blossoms, the trees were adorned as for a bridal ceremony. It was the season of the year when the Jews sent their pilgrims to Jerusalem and came out to the waterside to see them off. But perhaps it was not the desire to witness the departure of the pilgrims which carried Saul that day in the direction of the port. His heart was heavy-laden; but behind the pain of the burden a sweet hope was stirring: every branch on every bush had its time of blossoming, and his time would come too.

The ships plied busily between Antioch and Tarshish. A little canal connected the waters of the Orontes, on which Antioch stood, with the port of Seleucia. Thence it was a short distance to Tarshish, a day's journey in fair weather. Jewish merchants of Antioch arrived with every boat. From them Saul would gather news of the community in Antioch, where the numbers of the faithful increased from day to day. Many gentiles, who had already been converted to the Jewish faith, joined themselves to the new congregation. Similar reports reached Saul through Phoenician merchants, through Cypriots and others. There came messengers from Jerusalem, bearing the great tidings. He alone stood without, as though, God forbid, he had been thrust forth from the congregation. All had forgotten him.

He walked to and fro on the quays, as he had often done on such days. Like a stranger cast up from a shipwreck on an abandoned shore he wandered about, waiting for the ship that would bring him the sign.

In the evening, when he returned from work to his mother's house, he found a man waiting for him.

At first sight of him, it seemed to Saul that he was looking, not with the eyes of his body, but as in a vision with the eyes of his spirit. For though only seven years had passed since the friends had last seen each other, bar Naba was as a stranger. A mysterious spiritual beauty shone from his face, as though the divine Glory rested on it. The trim little beard which Saul remembered had been replaced by a great black growth, forestlike, secretive as the night. It was not combed and oiled, but wild, descending like a dark cascade upon the black mantle; equally wild and unkempt were the thick locks of his head. But as the mystery of the night slept in his locks and beard, even so the lovely openness of the day shone in his eyes—eyes which seemed to have fathomed the meaning and purpose of the world and to have unlocked the riddle of life. To those eyes everything was simple and straightforward. Belief in God and in His chosen Messiah flooded the eyes of bar Naba with childlike confidence and joy.

Very different was the impression which Saul made on his boyhood friend. Bar Naba beheld before him a young man who had suddenly become old. Of the thick head of hair nothing was left but a fringe about a large bald patch. The head was still mighty, as of old, but weighted with all the sorrow of the world. The eyes gave forth the hot light of a frustrated longing, and the fallen cheeks spoke of years of patient waiting. Something about the fringe of hair suggested a crown of thorns.

A long time the two men stood staring at each other, speechless, then suddenly they fell into each other's arms.

"Saul, my brother!"

"Joseph!"

"I have come to take you with me to Antioch. The holy community of Jerusalem sent me, to strengthen the hands of our brothers there. But you are fitter for the task, for God's spirit rests on you."

"Joseph, my brother! I knew you would come. The lord, who chose me and set me apart, has sustained me till this day."

The two friends sat up the whole night, hand in hand, and told each other how they had fared during the seven years of their separation. Saul was eager for every detail of the growth of the community in Jerusalem. He asked after Simon bar Jonah and wanted to know the names of those who had most strongly opposed him when he returned from Joppa and Caesarea; how Jacob ben Joseph had taken the matter of Simon's vision; what they of Jerusalem had done to strengthen the hands of the congregations which Philippus had created in Samaria.

Bar Naba went on to tell of the new persecutions visited on the congregation of Jerusalem by King Herod Agrippa, and of the death of Jacob, brother of John, of the Zebedees. Herod Agrippa had not forgotten the chains which he had worn in prison in the time of the Emperor Tiberius; he had not forgotten, either, the pogrom which he had witnessed in Alexandria. A change had come into his character, if not into his way of life. At home, in his provincial palace, he conducted himself like a proud Roman aristocrat, that is, like a heathen; he instituted gladiatorial combats, and even fights between men and beasts, in the arena. In no respect did his manners differ from what they had been in the heyday of his Roman period. But as against this, whenever he came up to Jerusalem he conducted himself like a pious Pharisee. He became a zealot for the faith; ignorant of its contents, ignorant too of conditions in Jerusalem, he laid his heavy hand on the purest of the pure, on the disciple who lived in poverty, innocence, and devotion, on Jacob, and had him slain. Herod Agrippa had also taken Simon bar Jonah prisoner, but Simon had been rescued by a miracle: God had thrown a heavy slumber on the prison guards, and an angel had led Simon forth to freedom. Joseph recited the miracle at great length. On one occasion, he told, they had been assembled at the house of his sister Miriam and were astounded to learn that Simon was knocking at the gate. They had been almost certain that Simon was dead. Ever since the sudden and public death of Herod Agrippa the congregation had lived at peace. The holy ones of Jerusalem interpreted his death as a punishment from on high. Now no one troubled the believers in Jerusalem. The Sages, the Scribes and the Pharisees, seeing that the believers obeyed all the commandments of the law of Moses, had made peace with them, and many of the Pharisees now sat at table with them. For the gospel was spreading; some of the Pharisees had entered the faith; they sat together with Jacob, son of Joseph, and with Judah, his brother, and they helped direct the congregation in the spirit of the Pharisees. This, however, led to internal dissensions in the congregation; for the new converts from the Greek-speaking Jewish communities and from among the gentiles could not submit to the heavy yoke of the laws which the Pharisees placed on the neck of the community. Because of this severe discipline there were many gentiles—and for that matter no small number of Jews—who could not enter the congregation of believers. And they had even quarreled with Khaifa, that is, with Simon bar Jonah, when he returned from his visit to the seaboard cities, and they learned that he had gone into the homes of the uncircumcised and had broken bread with them.

A flicker of bitterness passed across Saul's face. He asked:

"And what says Khaifa, he into whose hands was delivered the direction of the congregation? How does he stand in this matter? Is he firm in his interpretation?"

"Sometimes he speaks thus and sometimes otherwise. When he is with the gentile converts and with the Greek-speaking Jews, he agrees with them; and so much the more, of course, when he is in a city mostly gentiles, such as Caesarea. But when he comes to Jerusalem and hears the words of Jacob ben Joseph, of Judah, of Simon the Zealot, he agrees with them in making heavier the discipline of the law which he himself had made lighter elsewhere."

"One that carries water on both shoulders," muttered Saul.

"God forbid!" answered Joseph, trembling for the reputation of his Rabbi, whom he held in deepest reverence. "I tell thee, Saul, Khaifa is the only one that holds the congregation together; he is the rock on which everything stands, and the lord chose him to play this part. Or, if thou wilt, he is the fire which fuses the different parts into a unity. Night and day he is troubled for the unity of the congregation. That is why he sometimes makes the law easier and sometimes harder, according to circumstances; but whatever he does, it is for the good of the holy congregation, for his heart is filled with utter love for the lord, and he would see all men gathered into salvation. He was compassionate toward the gentiles and sought to ease their path to the Kingdom of Heaven; but he is insistent on this one point, that they shall be bound to the God of Israel, and shall observe His laws. Whatever Simon bar Jonah does has the warrant of the Holy Ghost, for the peace and blessing of the lord rest on him." Speaking of his Rabbi, Joseph bar Naba warmed into a natural enthusiasm; at the same time he conveyed the intimation that all within the congregation owed obedience to Simon bar Jonah. Saul understood the hint and was silent. He knew how to be silent when necessary.

The next morning Saul came before his mother, made obeisance, and said:

"Mother, the lord has called me. Peace be to thee, my mother. Pray to God that He attend my footsteps, so that thy tears shall be dried by a great joy."

"Whither goest thou, my son?" asked his mother, her eyes fixed on his face.

Saul returned her look steadfastly, and it seemed to him that he now saw his mother's face in the light for the first time. It was as if the course of the coming years of his life were suddenly revealed to him. Her skin quivered, as if pain and sorrow had set up vibrations in her blood. The face of Saul's mother consisted of nothing but cords and muscles, hillocks and valleys, folds and wrinkles—paths leading by strange detours into remote, unknown places. It was like a world on whose uneven stretches a mournful spirit was shed from her swollen eyes. Here Saul beheld, as with the eyes of prophecy, the storms and tribulations which he would encounter on the long road which awaited him. In the weeping voice echoed all the terror of her heart:

"Whither goest thou, my son?"

"I go by the road which God has appointed for me," he answered. "Peace be to thee, my mother. God grant that this countenance, which many have shamed, shall be honored by many."

He took with him upon the road the remembrance of her face.

Chapter Eight

AMONG THE GENTILES

BAR NABA, Saul, and Titus took boat from Tarshish to Seleucia, a day's journey. The commerce on this short sea route was heavy and well regulated, for the ships which came from Cyprus to Tarshish called at the port of Seleucia on the way back. From Seleucia they passed by the short canal to the Orontes and the city of Antioch. The river Orontes was accounted unclean by the Jews; unlike the Cydnus, the river of Tarshish, which swarmed with the ships of a dozen nations, the Orontes was largely a pleasure resort, foul with the abominations and lusts of idolaters. The winding banks were covered with cypress and laurel and set with many gardens dedicated to gods and goddesses whose eunuch priests clashed their cymbals at passing boats, calling on the travelers to descend and worship in the hidden groves. The most famous of the temples stood on the river bank at a distance of five miles from the city. Within it stood a gigantic image of Apollo. The Temple of Apollo was surrounded by woods of laurel, cypress, and myrtle, and in the woods were the groves and caverns of various idols. Men, women, and children burned incense on the altars and abandoned themselves to licentious rites. Here, on the water's edge, was the central gathering place of the "consecrated women" of both sexes, who sold their bodies on the steps of the temple; they lay around the altars waiting for pilgrims to come and do reverence to the idol, and the small fee of their sacred prostitution was collected by the priests.

The ship on which Saul and his companions traveled was filled with pilgrims to the Temple of Apollo. When it dropped anchor there descended from it a host of men and women; and the latter were of all ages, from young virgins to ancient crones. All of them, men and women alike, had come to offer their bodies to the idol. Such Jews as traveled on the ship covered their eyes that they might not see the abominations which were being performed in the groves and stopped up their ears, that the sound of the cymbals and the tumult of the crowd might not reach them; or else, more offended by the waves of incense which rolled out over the river, they held their noses. So, stopping their senses as best they might, they spat out three times and repeated the formula: "Let the abomination be laid waste!" Saul and bar Naba did like the rest. For all that, Saul insisted that he and his friend go down at this spot with the pilgrims, to witness the abominations of the pagans. Bar Naba had lived so many years in Jerusalem that he had forgotten what the gentiles were like, though he had been brought up among them in Cyprus, and Saul wanted him to remember.

Scarcely had they set foot on the sin-steeped soil than they were enveloped by the heavy reek of death and lust which issued from the idolatrous service. Whatever God had created here, on the blessed banks of the Daphne, was radiant with sunlight and earthly perfection. The laurels and cypresses, shaking their laden branches side by side, sent out their pure odor. The oleanders, modest as brides, swayed their heads gently. The green meadows were dappled with sunlight and set with refreshing color patches of various bushes and beds, violets, lilies, jasmine, and crimson poppies. And this blossoming paradise had been transformed into a swamp of whoredom and sin. Women with tumbled hair and naked breasts stretched their arms to passersby and offered them their diseased bodies with the repulsive smiles of harlots. The rank smell of putrefying flesh, of open sores, beat from the bodies of many women, mingled with the sickly-sweet perfume of oils; they lay under the trees, the human cast-offs of human beastliness. The sharp odor of aromatics and the bright colors of cosmetics could not conceal the underlying corruption. And like these women there were men in women's clothes, washed with perfumes, raddled with cosmetics, who invited passersby to the embrace of death. They called to the pilgrims, stretched out their arms, and grinned affectedly. A sickness which convulsed his vitals came upon bar Naba. He tried not to see or hear or smell and hastened his footsteps in order to pass the more quickly through the horrifying scene. But Saul slowed down his footsteps, and compelled him to look well on the ways of the heathen.

For this same reason, in order that his companion might learn into what condition the heathen had fallen, Saul took bar Naba to see the pillared alleys of the corso of Antioch. The great corso stretched across the city from the Golden Gate to the river bank. Shadowed by trees, the pillars held between them innumerable images of kings and gods. Antiochus Seleucus had built the corso, and it had been extended and enlarged by the Jewish king, Herod the Great, who had been prodigal in his gifts of building to alien cities. Day and night the corso swarmed with idlers, and the empty tumult of the pleasure seekers echoed among the white shadowed pillars from end to end of the city.

Antioch, the third city of the Empire, produced nothing. She had not the energy and industriousness of Tyre and Sidon or the commerce and scholarship of Tarshish. Erected by the Seleucid kings to dominate this part of the world, from Syria to the Babylonian deserts, Antioch housed the officials and soldiers who were grouped about the person of the Proconsul. To these had been attracted a mixed Asiatic population in search of an easy livelihood. Swindlers, jesters, circus masters, magicians, sellers of magic potions, peddlers of exotic goods— these dominated in the civilian population of Antioch. There was also a heavy contingent of slaves, upon whose shoulders rested the burden of providing for all these idlers and intrigants. In addition to the regular residents there were hosts of provincials circulating about the court; some of them sought relief from the oppression of local tyrants, others negotiated concessions, such as the farming of taxes or the collection of road tolls. On every hand there were officials, centurions, procurators. Thus the city was filled with inns and amusement places, chiefly for the nights; innumerable prostitutes, representing all lands and nations, haunted the streets and inns. Seen from without, Antioch was a city of superb beauty, with its great palaces, its incomparable corso, and its famous hanging gardens on the bridges of the Orontes. But perhaps the greatest attraction of Antioch was the dissolute worship of the goddess Athorgetis, the Astarte of Antioch, an Asiatic Aphrodite who was the glory of the capital of the Seleucids; her ritual had a special charm for the sexual appetites of the Antiochians, who were Oriental more than Greek.

The wide alley of columns and statues is bathed in brilliant sunlight against which stand out the shadows cast by the swaying cypress tops. From the summit of Mount Ciliphius a cool wind blows, bearing with it the perfumes of evergreens, of modest violets, and of refreshing jasmine. A coolness spreads also from the surface of the Orontes and with it the distant shouts of the boatmen. In the shadows of the alleys lazy bodies are stretched out. So weary are the idlers that they have not even the strength to smile at the rhymes and antics of the comedians who, in their fantastic masks, parade before them, hoping to collect a few copper coins for bread and wine. Nor do they hear the boasting of the snake-charmers, who carry their baskets of snakes and their flutes. They do not respond to the appeals of the soothsayers and Chaldaic star-gazers, who sell their prophecies for a measure of boiled lentils. The only sound which can stir them out of their lethargy is the clashing of the copper dishes of the sellers of sour wine and rose water, who sit in their little shadowed booths. But very rarely will a man lift his head out of the lap of his companion, even though his throat is parched for the taste of wine.

Suddenly there comes from the distance the subdued sound of drums and the rhythm of marching feet. The sound draws nearer, becomes clearer and louder. Here and there a dreamer wakes and looks around. Now, above the roll of the drums and the beat of the footsteps, is heard the clashing of cymbals. A wild throng of women, half-naked, leaping and dancing as if possessed, comes pouring across the bridge. The slumbering idlers start up, stirred at last by the oncoming storm. In the midst of the mad dancers the awakened sleepers catch glimpses of a little donkey, covered with silks; it is being led by a band of eunuch priests whose naked bodies are smeared with cosmetics of all colors. On the back of the donkey rides the goddess Apuleus, half woman, half fish. Before the donkey march the priests, in two lines; they are naked save for short aprons. They march in rhythm, with zigzagging footsteps, to the sound of the drums. And suddenly the tumult is stilled. The donkey has come to a halt in the midst of a circle of naked eunuch priests. The men and women who have been sleeping under the columns are wide awake and alert. Some still sit, others have risen to their feet, but all eyes are fixed on the goddess and the eunuchs which encircle her. The drums begin to beat again, softly and slowly at first, then louder, faster, more insistently; and as their rhythm changes, the rhythmic movements of the priests change with it. The beating rises to a wild climax, the dancing of the priests becomes frenzied. And now something happens. One of the dancing priests lifts a naked arm to his mouth and tears open a vein, so that a stream of blood gushes forth. Another priest follows suit. A third bends down, lifts a fold of his belly to his teeth, and tears the flesh open. Here and there a sword flashes in the hand of a priest. He points it at his own flesh, drives it in, and a fountain of blood is released. It flows down over his apron, which in a moment becomes crimson. Now the censers begin to smoke around the goddess, so that she peers out through a cloud. The naked priests, their bodies gushing blood, dance in and out of the cloud. The drums beat, furiously, ceaselessly, the feet thunder on the blood-stained green earth. And once again there is sudden silence.

"Who among you desires to sacrifice his manhood to the goddess?"

"Who of you would unite himself with the great goddess who grants eternal life?"

"Who of you would unite himself with the goddess who is the universal mother, the bringer of fruitfulness?"

A young lad has risen to his feet. He has the build of an athlete, with a powerful, arched chest. He stands there confused, still a little shy. The idea is working in his head. His companions sitting on the grass shout their approval and encouragement:

"Come! Offer up thy manhood to the goddess!"

And the drums begin their rhythm again, slow at first, hesitant, doubtful. They speak to him, draw him into their wordless, muffled circle. They beat faster, they rise to a fury of thunder, they call to him louder and still louder. A eunuch priest approaches and thrusts his dripping knife into the lad's hand. And suddenly the belt is ripped open

283

there is a flash of steel, and the lad flings the flesh of his lost virility at the feet of the goddess.

A rain of copper coins falls into the metal tray. Women tear the ornaments from their necks, their noses, their fingers, their ears, their arms, their legs, and throw them toward the donkey. Some rip the silken veils from about their bodies. Others bring forward bundles of incense which they purchase from the dealers accompanying the goddess. Still others offer doves, measures of flour. On the instant a young pig is slaughtered, and after it a sheep and a goat. The smell of frying meat, of oil, of baking flour, goes up from the tripods which are erected around the goddess. Men snatch at the sacrificial flesh and at the wine flasks. And as the day draws to an end women pass from man to man, the assembly dissolves in an undistinguishable fury of drunkenness and lust.

This was the city to which bar Naba had called Saul.

Saul turned to his friend and indicated the beastly animal ferment under the trees. Saul's lips were drawn tight, and two flecks of foam broke out at the corners. He spoke in a paroxysm of rage and bitterness:

"The world is carried away by a flood of abomination! Men have become worse than the beasts of the field in their fleshly lusts. They squirm like vermin in the filth of their whoredom. . . . This would be the end if God had not taken pity on the world of mankind and sent it His Messiah, to cleanse it in his baptism and to bring it under the yoke of the Kingdom of Heaven. I hear the voice of the lord calling to me: 'Take pity on these people, and bring them the tidings of my advent. Carry the news from end to end of the world, so that there shall not be under the heavens a single people which has not heard the name of the one living God and of the Messiah whom He sent, a comfort and a salvation for man.' "

Bar Naba stared at his friend. He recognized the old, passionate zeal; once it had burned in hatred, but now it burned in love and devotion to the man of sorrow.

Chapter Nine

ANTIOCH

IT was in the nature of things that the tidings of the Messiah should spread at once from Jerusalem to Antioch. From the earliest times there had been a considerable Jewish settlement in the Syrian capital, which was often spoken of as half Palestinian. A lively commerce connected the two cities, and the new faith had scarcely arisen in Jerusalem before it was brought to Antioch, which became the center of the first congregation of the Messiah in Syria.

On the right bank of the Orontes, in the midst of the ocean of sin which was Antioch, there existed a little island with a life of its own—a life which stood under the sign of the Kingdom of Heaven. The Jewish community of Antioch clustered about the great synagogue, famed as the repository of certain of the holy vessels of the first Temple at Jerusalem. All Jews of Antioch belonged to the synagogue, whether they followed the Mosaic law or believed that the Messiah had already come; and this was true of converts to the faith also.

It was impossible that Antioch, or any other city, should consist exclusively of idlers. There were other inhabitants besides those that spent their days lounging in the gardens and their nights in drunkenness and fornication. Antioch had to be fed and housed, as well as amused. A constant flow of food and raw materials converged upon the city from all the provinces of Asia Minor: wheat, vegetables, linen, ores, pottery, wines, honey—all those necessities which Antioch herself did not produce. Long caravans of camels, donkeys, and mules bearing stone and wood for the builders came through the mountain passes, the foodstuffs arriving mostly by ship.

The right bank of the river was the workshop of Antioch: from this district the coppersmiths, perfume mixers, potters, weavers, and sandal makers issued daily into the streets and markets of the city; here slaves and freedmen stood in the open air under canopies of woven leaves and carried on their work; the shopkeepers, withdrawn into the shadows of their booths, chaffered loudly with their customers; the

285

money changers clashed their trays to attract attention to their tables.

But the crowds were thickest, the noises loudest, on the bank of the river. Here some of the incoming boats dropped anchor, and long rows of naked men, stooping like beasts of burden, carried the bales and bundles of merchandise from the quay to the warehouses. The sweat pouring over their bodies glittered in the sunlight. Here and there little canals extended from the river, enabling other boats to bring their cargoes into the yards of the warehouses.

It was in one of these yards that Saul found himself on a certain day in the company of bar Naba, who had brought him thither. Entering, the friends beheld a crowd of workers gathered about two figures, one a short, black-bearded Jew, with brown skin and glittering Oriental eyes, the other a towering gentile. Both of them were speaking to the assembled workers on the same theme—the Messiah who had risen from the dead and had brought salvation to all that believed in him.

The messengers greeted the preachers with the word "Shalom"—Peace! In a little while Saul found out where he was. This was the warehouse yard of the rich Jewish merchant, the first citizen of Antioch, Menachem. Concerning this Menachem, who had been brought up in the court of Herod, the Tetrarch of Galilee, it was already told that he had joined the brotherhood of the believers, and the report had served to raise the standing of the brotherhood in the eyes of the Jewish community of the city. Many Jews had entered the brotherhood, which met with little opposition on the part of the other worshipers. A number of prominent gentiles, too, had accepted the new faith, but for the time being kept their conversion secret. The two preachers whom Saul encountered here for the first time were Simon, the Jew, whom they called "Niger," and Lukas of Cyrene, the gentile, a convert. They were active among the Jews and gentiles of Antioch and had won over many souls, particularly among the gentiles who frequented the synagogues. They also went out into the markets and the warehouse yards and preached to the workers during their rest periods. On these grounds Simon and Lukas began to be called "Prophets," a title which had come into currency again among the new believers, the Jews themselves no longer using it.

Mingling with the slave pack carriers in the warehouse yard of the wealthy Menachem were also certain workers from neighboring streets. It was the evening hour. The slaves had been released from their la·-

bors, the free workers and shopkeepers had closed their booths and stalls. Some of them had not heard the gospel preached before. But they had heard fellow workers, Jews and non-Jews, and the latter even more than the former, speak frequently of "the anointed one," the rumor of whose advent had spread into all the corners of laboring Antioch, among the forges and smithies, among the weavers and potters and pack carriers. On this evening, they had been told, Jewish messengers would arrive from the Holy City, sent forth by the mother congregation to preach the tidings of the Messiah.

Before these, slaves and freedmen, Jews and gentiles, Saul preached that evening as one who had been sent direct to them by him who was the comfort of the poor and oppressed:

" 'Come, all you that are weary and heavy laden!' The Messiah is the bringer of consolation and the help of all sufferers. There is no pain, no anguish, no oppression, and no degree of slavery which the Messiah did not feel on his own body. All this he took upon himself freely, that he might in his own suffering redeem those that are in bonds. The anointed one himself was tortured on the cross for all that are poor and oppressed, and God lifted him up to life on the third day; and he sits at the right hand of God, the protector of all that suffer. And when he lived on earth he taught men to love each other and help each other. And those who make a bond with the anointed one shall be beyond the reach of evil, for they will be sure that no matter what happens to them on earth they will be lifted up by him when they come into the world beyond. He will awaken them from death, and they will find again their eternal life in the midst of their own beloved ones."

"Will he bring me together with my wife Vespa?" called a naked, blackened slave from out of his corner.

"Where is thy beloved Vespa, brother?" asked Saul.

"I know not where she is now. We lived together in peace, in a little house by the sea. We lived on what my net brought out of the water. And one day we were seized by the government because of a rebellion on the island, and we were placed on the slave market. I was purchased by my master and brought to Antioch. What became of her I know not."

"She too will hear of his name. She will turn to him, and pray to him, even as you do, and both of you will unite with the Messiah. And no matter how far you will be from each other, you will be united in

287

him. And he will bring you together in eternal life, when you will come before him. Be sure that thou wilt find her. She will be waiting for thee at his side."

These were words which slaves understood.

Within a few months after Saul had begun to preach in the synagogues, the workshops, the warehouse yards and the marketplaces, to Jews and gentiles, the congregation of believers in Antioch was fused into perfect unity, so that no differentiation was made between circumcised and uncircumcised. Such a consummation was more easily to be expected in Antioch than in any other city, for Jews and gentiles had dwelt here side by side from the earliest times, and it needed only a common ideal to bring them together in unity.

The faith penetrated to all levels of the population, to the rich and poor, and even more to the poor. In the slave quarter around the port the legend arose of a man of God who had descended from heaven to earth and had taken upon himself all the pains and sorrows of mankind. He had endured everything, until he was tortured to death, dying like a slave on the cross, so that he might feel in his own body all human pain, and redeem all human beings from the sins which they had committed in ignorance until his coming. The God-man, or, as they began to call him, the Son of God, had risen to life on the third day after his death, and he was now in heaven as well as on earth; he was wherever pain was to be found; and all who believed in him were redeemed from their sins, becoming like new-born children. And though their bodies still remained enslaved, their souls were freed from sin, and they were bound to him in the highest glory in heaven. The Messiah would soon reveal himself on earth, and he would ascend the judgment seat to judge all mankind: then there would be no more masters and no more slaves, no strong and no weak, no ruler of people and no ruled people: there would be only the saved and the lost, those that believed in him and those that did not believe in him. All that believed in him would share the highest good in an eternal life of peace, of glory, of everlasting fullness of satisfaction, united with those from whom they had been torn in life; those that did not believe in him would be lost forever. And the belief in the Messiah kindled hope in hearts that had been extinguished, bringing light where darkness had seemed complete and immovable.

And before long scenes unknown before in the history of Antioch became a commonplace.

Along the corso, under the trellis of roses strung from column to column, the panders to the lusts of Antioch walked offering their wares. There were Chaldaean star-gazers, Aramaic magicians, African snake charmers. Arabian harlots danced to the rhythm of drums, showing the supple lines of their dark-glancing bodies. The young idlers of Antioch, sated with every lust, exhausted by every perversity, looked on in boredom, or wearily approached the dancing women, felt their bodies, and pushed them away with cynical remarks. Across this confusion of whoredom, folly, and mockery, weltering by the river, marched a group of the "faithful." They were a familiar sight by now, easily distinguishable from the rest of the population. Their clothes were of sackcloth. The men and women did not use dark cosmetics for their eyes or bright cosmetics for their lips and cheeks. They did not drench their bodies in exciting or oppressive perfumes. They did not anoint their hair or curl their beards, but let them grow freely. It was known, too, that the "faithful" took no part in the open games and ceremonies or in any of the city celebrations; they were not to be met in the temples; they were absent from the sacrifices and the orgies. The sight of the "faithful" was particularly infuriating to the wicked element of the city, which included many of the wealthy idle young men who haunted the corso by day and the houses of assignation by night. Now, when this procession of sober-clad men and women, whose eyes were modestly fixed on the ground, drew through the corso, one young buck, making an obscene and contemptuous gesture, cried out:

"Here comes the anointed!"

For some reason or other this particular word caught the fancy of the bored idlers. A score of them imitated the obscene gesture of the first, and shouted derisively:

"The anointed! The anointed!"

From that day on this was the title of mockery current in Antioch for the believers; wherever they appeared, the street rang with the cry: "The anointed!"

When Saul heard of the new fashion, he said:

"God Himself put the word in their mouths. We are indeed the anointed. Even as our lord the Messiah was anointed by God to wear the crown of thorns and to bring salvation to the world, even so are we anointed to suffer for his name and to live a life of purity and holiness in our faith. Our lord is called the anointed Messiah, and we call ourselves the anointed."

Thus the believers took up the word "anointed" and made it a title of honor. From that time on they called themselves "Christians" and "anointed ones."

The power of Saul was great in his sermons and greater still in his actions. He was, to begin with, himself the model of all that he preached. From the day of his arrival in Antioch he earned his daily bread by the labor of his hands. He never applied to the charity funds either of the congregation of believers or of the general Jewish congregation, as other preachers were wont to do when they arrived in a city. He asked nothing of any man. He found employment at his trade and earned enough for his modest needs. This had a double effect; it raised him in the eyes of the congregation, and it confirmed him in his feeling of independence. He was free to speak as he thought right, even to the Cantors and Prophets of the congregation. His personal attitude in matters concerning the Jewish ritual was so correct that even the strictest Pharisees of the Jewish community of Antioch could find no fault with him. He preached the lightening of the discipline for the gentiles, but he himself gave full obedience to the law. He was scrupulous in the observation of the laws and kosher and non-kosher food; the Sabbath he regarded as a sanctity, and he preached the sanctity of the Sabbath to gentiles as well as Jews. Particularly strong was the impression made by his prayers. Though he did not call himself "Prophet" or "Elder," and though he did not bring forth ecstatic utterances at the common meals, he wrought mightily in prayer, and his supplication was so intense, so passionate, that often he fell in a faint in the midst of his devotions. He made no resolution, took no new step, without first praying long and earnestly in the privacy of his room, his face pressed against the floor, calling upon the Name of God until his heart was illumined by understanding. Often Titus, who shared his room, would wake up in the middle of the night, to see his companion stretched out rigid on the floor and to hear him calling insistently and passionately on God, until the ecstasy of his supplication drew the soul out of him and he lost consciousness. Then Titus would approach him, lift him on to the mattress, and strengthen him—if Saul was not then under the vows of a Nazirite—with a sup of wine. For every resolution concerning the guidance of the congregation there were hours of agonizing prayer. But once the resolution was fixed in his mind, there was no changing him; it was then as if he had received clear instructions from above, through a divine voice.

In those days there was much talk in Antioch regarding a famine which was expected in Jerusalem and the whole of Judaea. The fields of Judaea were parching in the sun. The latter rain had delayed so long that the grain was withering away, and a time of bitter hunger was approaching for man and beast in the Holy Land. Queen Helene of Adiabene, the devoted convert to Judaism, had sent her agents to Egypt and Phoenicia, to buy up stores of wheat and figs for the population of Jerusalem. The Jews of Antioch, and the congregation of the Messianites, or Christians, were greatly concerned for the fate of the Holy Land. Messengers arrived from Jerusalem, and the first to bring direct news of the impending calamity was a wandering Prophet by the name of Agabus. The Jews, who had been accustomed from of old to send their taxes, tithes, and offerings to the Temple, at once set about collecting money; but the gentiles in the congregation were not wholly accustomed to the giving of charity or to sharing their bread with the needy. Here Saul perceived a golden opportunity to implant in the uncircumcised among the believers a stronger understanding of the virtue especially associated with the patriarch Abraham—that of compassion. Saul therefore went about preaching of the hunger in Jerusalem to gentile believers, slaves and freedmen alike. He exhorted them to spare something from their meager daily rations, earned in the sweat of their brow and sometimes under the lash of the overseer, for "brothers" whom they had never set eyes on, of whose existence they had been unaware but a little while ago, who dwelt in a strange and distant city— the hateful Jewish city of Jerusalem. He spoke to them of the love which the Messiah had preached, and of pity, an emotion still new to them. He told again how Yeshua, the Messiah himself, had submitted to all the sorrows and dolors of the world, for strange people whom he had never seen, for the unborn, for Jews and gentiles of his own land and of all lands, taking them to his heart and binding them to himself in eternal love. And thus all who were united in the faith of the Messiah were no longer strangers to each other. "Though you have never seen them," he pleaded, "they are your own brothers, brothers in the blood which Yeshua offered for all of us, brothers in the spirit which binds us each to each. For all of us have died in the sins of our lives hitherto, and we are born again in the spirit, in love and the faith of the Messiah; and therefore not they are your brothers and sisters who are such to you in the blood, but they who are brothers and sisters in the spirit. By the pity and love which you manifest toward them you bind yourself to them in Yeshua the Messiah. You make true his words and you testify to him in your deeds." And Paul represented to them that the love which they bore to one another was the mother in their rebirth. "In the birth your new lives are forever renewed; all believers will be woven into a single community, one in body and spirit, by the love you bear one another in Yeshua." And if one of them died, he went on to teach, he did not die, but continued to live in the congregation of the Messiah. Then, when Saul beheld how the gentiles, side by side with the Jews, took out the last copper coins which were their food for the morrow and which they held in little sacks suspended around their necks—took them out and threw them into the common fund; when he beheld how poor women brought their last cruses of oil to sell, or even cut off their hair; how the slaves brought part of their daily rations, the lean cakes which were their only food, and put them at the feet of the messengers; when he beheld all this, it was to him a sign that the offering of the gentiles was acceptable to God and that the compassion which awakened in their hearts had made them children of Abraham. And to bar Naba he said: "Arise and see how the water of the baptism which the gentiles have taken in the name of the lord has been changed into blood."

When the offerings had all been collected, the elders of the congregation of Antioch, Simon Niger and Lukas the Cyrenean and Menachem, chose Saul and bar Naba to carry the gift to the holy ones in Jerusalem.

In Jerusalem bar Naba brought Saul before the assembly of the elders of the congregation, before Jacob ben Joseph and Simon bar Jonah and Jochanan of the Zebedees. And he told them of the work that Saul had done in the community of Antioch: how he had drawn the hearts of the gentiles to the God of Israel through Yeshua the Messiah, how he had trained them in the virtue of Father Abraham, the virtue of compassion, and had inducted them into the ways of the lord. Then bar Naba laid down the bags of money which had been gathered from among the gentiles, and said:

"Here is the proof that for the gentiles too the gates of salvation have been opened."

When the elders of the congregation of Jerusalem beheld the wonder which God had wrought with the gentiles, they rejoiced and said that of a surety God had taken pity on the gentiles and had given purpose to their life. Nevertheless, they did not put their hands on Saul, and they did not invest him with authority. But they sent bar Naba back to Antioch, with Saul under him. Bar Naba also took with him Jochanan, called Marcus, his sister's son, for the lad had now grown into manhood. And the three of them set out for Antioch.

Chapter Ten

FROM SAUL TO PAUL

WHEN Saul and bar Naba returned from Jerusalem, the congregation of Antioch said: "Surely God has now opened the gates of salvation to the gentiles. Let us therefore act accordingly. Come, we will place our hands upon our brothers, Saul and bar Naba, and invest them with the authority, and send them to other cities, to bring the gospel of the Messiah first to the Jews and then to the gentiles, even as the lord himself commanded: 'There shall not be a corner of the world whither the Name of the God of Israel and of the Messiah of Jacob shall not have reached.'"

Then the leaders and pillars of the Antioch congregation, Simon, whom they called "Niger," and Lukas the Cyrenean, and Menachem, went into solemn council; they fasted and prayed for sanctification of their act, and being convinced it was conformable to the will of God, they put their hands on Saul and bar Naba and sent them out to the cities of the gentiles, to bring the tidings of the Messiah first to the Jews and then to the gentiles.

The messengers took with them Jochanan-Marcus to serve and assist them in their holy work.

After long meditation and prayer the messengers and their servant made the last preparations for the journey. They decided, on bar Naba's plea, to make their first call at Cyprus, for bar Naba was eager to bring the gospel to his homeland.

At Antioch the elders accompanied them to the ship, and the messengers sailed down the river to a certain point where they debarked again and made their way on foot to the port of Seleucia.

Here they stand, then, by the water's edge in Seleucia, three Jews waiting for a ship to take them over to Cyprus: bar Naba, tall and stately, his black beard falling half way down the front of his black mantle; Saul, frail and restless, with his vast head atop of his slender neck, with the strands of his beard falling on his chest; and the young man Marcus, on whose soft beard and earlocks still rests the pious breath of the Holy City. Marcus's blue, crystalline eyes are covered by smooth eyelids, which he has closed in meditation; his face shines with his consciousness of the solemnity of the moment and of the high privilege conferred upon him, who has become the servant of the messengers of the Messiah in their most sacred mission. He turns away to busy himself with the bundles of provisions—Jewish-baked cakes, dried cheeses, pressed figs, a cruse of honey, and a gourd of soured goat's milk —so that the travelers might not be compelled to have recourse to unkosher foods between their contacts with Jewish communities. Marcus also carries one extra garment, and an extra four-cornered ritual fringe-shirt for each of the travelers, and a few manuscripts, parchment, and papyrus, of certain of the Holy Books, Isaiah, Psalms, and Daniel.

About no other port in the world are the waters as stormy as at Seleucia. In the center of the city an inland basin has been hewn out for the safe anchorage of vessels, and a short canal connects the basin with the open sea. The city itself lies in a hollow, with vast imprisoning walls on three sides. The tremendous heights of Mount Corypheus stretch along the coast, till they mingle with those of Mount Cassius, and on clear days it is even possible to glimpse on the horizon the white summit of Taurus, on the side of Tarshish. Within the narrow sea corridor enclosed by the cliffs there is eternal warfare between the sea and the rocks. Furious, green-crested, the waves hurl themselves against the immense cliff which shelters the entrance to the canal and the harbor. The waters, flung back repeatedly by the granite guard, gather themselves again, roaring, and renew the assault. Saul stands on an eminence and watches the ceaseless battle between the sea and the rock. No matter how often the sea is repulsed, it does not give up the siege of the powerful breast which stands like a sentinel between it and the port. Ever and again the howling waters seek renewed strength in the bosom of the deep, and one wave gathers up the pent force of the wave that went before, adds it to its own, and proceeds again to the eternal assault. Dashed into a million ribbons of foam, it retreats, to transfer its energies to the wave that takes up the quarrel behind it. Undiscourageable, fed by immeasurable will power, the sea continues to shout of certain ultimate victory. And to Saul it seems that he has seen the curtain lifted for a moment on the image of his own years to come, and he says in his heart: "From this day on my life shall be like that of the assaulting ocean."

The ship bearing the messengers to Cyprus tossed about like a cockleshell on its way to the open sea. Soon there unrolled before them the panorama of the Syrian coast; they beheld the full outline of the hills enclosing Seleucia and the green forests which crowned them. Far off they caught the glitter of the Orontes, winding seaward through the woods. This was their last glimpse of Syria, and Syria was still in a measure the homeland. Straight roads led on solid earth by way of Lebanon to the Holy Land. Syria belonged to Greater Palestine. The tidings of the Messiah had traveled by the straight, royal road from Palestine to Syria. Now, turning, they beheld the open sea and the open path to all the lands of the world, the lands of the gentiles. They beheld, emerging from the faint white mist on the horizon, the green outlines of Cyprus. The gospel had already been carried to the island by those who fled from Jerusalem at the time of persecutions about Rabbi Istephan; but it had been offered only to Jews. Now the gospel was being brought to the gentiles of Cyprus.

The messengers and their servant sit huddled together on the deck, and as is the custom of Jews traveling by sea, they repeat from memory verses of the Psalms and of Isaiah bearing on the promise of the Messiah. Neither the captain nor the sailors are astonished by the sight of these men swaying back and forth and murmuring to themselves. It is a familiar sight. Now and again a gentile makes a mocking observation, about them or about Jews generally. The three travelers ignore it. They are alone on the sea, a little island on the boat. From Seleucia to Cyprus is a journey of a few hours—and soon the ship scrapes against the salt-encrusted quay of the great Phoenician port of Salamis.

In Salamis there are, God be thanked, many Jews. They trade chiefly in salt, in oils, and in the famous wine of the island. Some of them export the copper ores of Cyprus to Tyre and Sidon, Corinth and Achaia. The first thing the travelers ask for, as they set foot toward sunset in the swarming harbor, is the road to the synagogue of the Jews. They hope to reach it before sunset, so that they may repeat there the evening *Shema*. Bar Naba has many distant relatives in Salamis, but he will not seek them out. From this day on the synagogue is his home, and his relatives are all those who call on the Name of the living God and acknowledge His Messiah. By the Synagogue of the Cypriots, which bar Naba remembers out of his childhood years and where he once prayed with his father before he left for Jerusalem, there is the little hospice for traveling Rabbis, for messengers from Jerusalem, who came to collect money for the ransom of captives or for the Temple. The messengers of the congregation of Antioch, traveling in the cause of the Messiah, enter the hospice. There bar Naba and Saul ask after their brothers in the faith: are there such in Cyprus as have received baptism in the name of the Messiah, Yeshua the Nazarene? "Yes," they are told: "There are such here, among our Jewish brothers and among the gentiles, too. You may encounter all of them in the synagogue, on the Sabbath, also on Mondays and Thursdays at the reading of the Torah." They decide, then, to wait for the Sabbath. Meanwhile bar Naba seeks out old acquaintances. They too repeat that there are many on the island who have received baptism. Some among the speakers are of the faithful. Others are still waiting. And when bar Naba urges baptism on them, they say they will wait and consult their Rabbis again. On the Sabbath bar Naba preaches the risen Messiah, at the services. He is given a patient, friendly hearing. But when Saul mounts the pulpit there is a tumult among the worshipers. "Is not this he who persecuted the faithful even to destruction? How comes the persecutor to be preaching the Messiah?" For they have heard his name, and for them the name is flecked with blood. Eleven years have passed; but they have not forgotten that together with the tidings of the Messiah there came to them the report of the persecutions about Istephan; and from that time on contempt and hatred are associated with the name "Saul of

Tarshish." Old wounds are opened among those who have received baptism in the name of the Messiah; there is anger, disillusionment even, among those who have held back from baptism. Jewish believers and gentile "anointed" feel the same concerning him. They do not let him speak, but interrupt him at every verse. They were ready to hear the same words quoted, and interpreted in the same way, by bar Naba, but they will not accept them from Saul. The very way he calls them into the faith offends them. The tumult grows in the synagogue until the head of the synagogue forbids Saul to speak further.

Saul sees it now; his very name is an obstacle to his mission for the Messiah. There are men who remember his former sins, which for him have long since been washed away by his tears. They will not let him become that which the Messiah himself destined him to be—a carrier of the tidings. He bethinks himself that he has another name, given him among the gentiles, Paul; but the time does not seem propitious for him to accept the change of name. All that he has done till now was done under the name of Saul. To change names now would mean to disown all his past, so that the name Saul would remain forever steeped in sin. It is this name, Saul, which must be cleansed and made acceptable. And Saul waits for a sign from heaven, to know whether it is indeed the will of God that he shall adopt the new name.

And suddenly the sign came, like a miracle.

The news of the arrival of messengers spread swiftly from end to end of the island, and reached the ears of Sergius Paulus, the Roman Proconsul in the capital city, Paphos; and Sergius Paulus sent word to the messengers to appear before him in the capital.

There was unrest of heart among the gentiles of Cyprus, but more among the educated than among the unlettered. The latter at least believed blindly in the power of their idols and yielded themselves to corrupting sexual orgies in their temples. But the educated and the thoughtful perceived into what depths of moral and physical degradation they were being dragged by the priests, and they sought refuge in heathen wisdom and heathen intelligence. But the wisdom and intelligence of the heathen were like two withered breasts, from which no nourishing milk could be pressed. By the ingenuities of logic and the acrobatics of the schools they could bend the intelligence to any egotistic purpose. With all their intelligence and wisdom they were held fast in the chains of a helpless fatalism, against which they struggled, nevertheless, calling to their aid soothsayers, readers of the stars, interpreters of dreams and portents, exorcists, snake charmers, and the mystic rituals of their idols. The dealers in demonic powers could do nothing to change the destiny of their clients—they could only foretell the evil hour and perhaps enable them to defer it.

Sergius Paulus, Proconsul of Cyprus, was one of those "men of intelligence" who in their private affairs are more prone to enlist the service of sorcerers than that of the intelligence. In moments of indecision he turned not to wisdom which he had learned to respect so highly in the schools of the Stoics, but to Syrian star-gazers. A philosopher of the Stoic school, he was forever surrounded by sorcerers and soothsayers.

It often happened, especially in the remoter Asiatic provinces, that a Roman official would take over by degrees the religious customs of his subjects. Among the idolaters this sort of changing over was not regarded as an act of defection from the home deity, but rather as a sensible and even honorable precaution. Rome granted the gods of conquered peoples complete local autonomy, and a Roman official often acknowledged the god of the people which he was sent to rule. The goddess of Cyprus was Aphrodite. More than once Sergius, the cultured Roman aristocrat, had looked on when a high-born lady of his own circle, the wife of a prominent citizen, covered with a veil, had taken her place on the temple steps, among the other women, so that any passing sailor or merchant could approach her and say: "In the name of Mylitta Aphrodite, I demand thee!" Under penalty of the goddess's wrath every woman of Cyprus had to submit herself at least once in her life in the temple, nor did she dare to leave the precincts until a strange man had demanded her. The money of her prostitution was a sacred offering to the goddess. A worship of this character had nothing in it to attract or convince a cultured and philosophical Proconsul. Though he was prepared to take the dictum of his sorcerers and star-gazers in practical matters, the Proconsul had stayed awake many a night to rack his brains with the question: "What is the purpose of the world and of man?" He had heard of the one living God in whom the Jews believed. And now he heard of a redeemer, an ever-present help, whom God had sent to the world; one who had died on the cross and had come to life again. Messengers of the re-arisen one had arrived on the island. It was told of them that they could heal the sick, exorcise the possessed. Who knew?—perhaps they even had the magic art of bringing the dead to life. Thus thought the Proconsul, and he sent a request—which is to say, a command—that the messengers appear before him.

And so the messengers, bar Naba and Saul, accompanied by Marcus, traverse the towns and villages of the hundred-mile-long island to the capital, Paphos. In their minds is the hope that God is preparing a miracle through them, and the Proconsul of the province will accept the faith, and the name of the Messiah will be sanctified from end to end of the island. And perhaps, on the other hand, the Proconsul may be expecting them to perform miracles. They knew that Sergius Paulus believed in sorcerers and kept a staff of stargazers. The first and foremost of them was—to Israel's shame be it said!—a certain Jew by the name of bar Yeshua, who had crowned himself with the title of Alymas the Sage. He had rejected the law of Moses, which forbade the practice of sorcery, compared it to idol worship and sodomy, and declared that a sorcerer was a child of death, to be slain by stoning.

Jochanan tells the messengers of that sorcerer of Samaria, Simon Magus, who had offered his master, Simon bar Jonah, money in exchange, as he said, "for the secret of bringing down the Holy Ghost upon men." Jochanan had been with his master in Samaria at the time. There they had encountered on the marketplace a gigantic figure of a man, who had stood out by his height and bulk from the other inhabitants of the city. The man's face had been covered by a forest-like growth of hair. About him was gathered a large crowd. This Simon Magus always had with him a certain woman. She stood there now like a stone image, her pale face unmoving, her eyes lusterless. The man performed his magic through the woman. He transmitted thoughts to her without uttering a word. He looked into her face with his black, burning eyes and she fell into a trance. In sleep, at an unspoken command from him, she would begin to move, and to pass through the crowd gathered about them, stopping before this one and that one, uttering their names, revealing acts out of their past and foretelling their future. She could also raise herself in the air while she slept, and hover like a bird. The man, Simon Magus, persuaded the people that she was *Machshavah,* Thought, the mother of all deeds, for thought precedes every deed. He himself, Simon Magus, was God, who directed the thoughts of man. There were many who believed him. He had been a great hindrance in the spreading of the faith in Samaria. Simon bar Jonah had cursed him, but it seemed that the man was able to ward off the curse with his magic. Later, they heard, he had spread his practices beyond Samaria. He had taken on the title of Son of God and had persuaded a great many that they could find salvation by giving themselves to the woman who accompanied him. But he had many disguises and could change his appearance and body at will; sometimes he appeared as a Samaritan, sometimes as a Syrian healer, and sometimes as a Chaldaean mathematician. The messengers were quite certain now that the bar Yeshua—son of Yeshua—before the Proconsul was none other than the Simon Magus of Samaria. Now he had assumed the identity of a Jew and had come to the island to prevent the spreading of God's work.

"Most certainly he is the son of the Devil," said Saul. "The Devil is envious of God, and inasmuch as God has sent His son down to earth to rescue mankind, the Devil has sent *his* son to hinder the work of rescue, and to keep mankind in the bonds of impurity."

In Saul's mind it was clear that he would have to do battle with the son of the Devil, in the name of the son of God, to the death, and to prepare the field for the plow of the Messiah.

On the morning before their appearance at the palace, Saul washed with unusual care, anointed himself, combed his beard, and put on his scholar's mantle. The others did even as he. As Pharisees, they observed the injunction that it is not meet for scholars to appear on formal occasions otherwise than in formal attire; and this day they were to appear before the mighty of the earth.

Sergius Paulus received them in the audience chamber of the palace. When they entered he was seated on the throne, and about him were ranged some of the leading officers and councilors of the province. Along the wall stood the sorcerers and soothsayers. Their leader was in the likeness of a little Jew with a hump, and a hook nose, which protruded from his face as his other limbs protruded under his clothes. These were dyed in many colors and adorned with many designs, Chaldaic cycles and epicycles, pictures of the beasts of the constellations, mystic letters, and every other manner of magical trickery. On his head he carried the high hat of a Priest of the Temple of Jerusalem; over part of his multicolored clothes he wore an apron; but his feet were bare. Ranged about him were his assistants, some Chaldaean mathematicians with cycles in their hands, and a few Syrian healers and black desert Arabs, carrying cactus roots and other herbs in censers.

Though bar Naba was the official head of the delegation, and as such introduced himself and the others to the Proconsul, it was Saul who soon assumed the role of spokesman. To the three questions which the Proconsul formally asked of all newcomers—"What is thy name? Whence comest thou? What is thy business here?"—Saul answered.

"My name is Saul. I am also called Paul, and I am a citizen of Rome. I come from the not unknown city of Tarshish. I am a servant of the living God of Israel. And I carry to men the tidings of His Messiah, who is the salvation of the world."

The first words spoken by Saul produced a profound impression, which the startled bar Yeshua could not but remark. The Proconsul, long accustomed to dealing with swindlers and adventurers of all kinds, had been, in spite of rumors to the contrary, prepared to see in Saul and his companions common sorcerers, after the fashion of his own bar Yeshua, with whom they were prepared to compete on his ground. What he beheld, however, was something else: three men of dignified attire and bearing, without any of the hocus-pocus of the magicians in their speech or equipment. They spoke simply of the living God, and one of them was a citizen of Rome, even like himself, and carried on his breast the bronze tablet, with his name inscribed, assuring him all the privileges of Roman citizenship. What was more, his Roman name was that of the Proconsul himself: Paul.

Bar Yeshua trembled when he heard the name of the living God. This was a sound which pierced him like a polished spear. He knew well that, as a Jew, he was liable to the death penalty for the practice of sorcery; and he did not relish an open conflict with those who spoke in the name of God and His Messiah. Bar Yeshua knew, too, that this was no common test which confronted him, but the decisive one; and he would have need of all his wits and all his tricks to retain his position in the household of the Proconsul. His very life was at stake. With assumed boldness he lifted his hand, to indicate that he wished to say something. Permission granted, he stepped out from among his assistants and approached Saul with outstretched hand, a broad smile on his uneasy features:

"Brother Saul, welcome! Peace be to thee, brother Saul. In the

name of our common art and of all the spirits, greetings!" Then, with
the bow of an acrobat, and an artful gesture of his right arm, he turned
to the Proconsul. "Great Proconsul! We were at one school with this
man, the school of the prophets in Jerusalem, the Holy City. The art of
reading the fates, of driving out evil spirits, of delaying evil decrees of
the high powers, of evading disaster, and of fighting black demons, we
learned from one Rabbi. Rememberest thou not, Saul, the great Rabbi
Abigal, the old man, who held a thousand demons in leash with each
strand of his beard? Rememberest thou not, likewise, the great Rabban
Gamaliel, who was our instructor?"

At this point Saul fixed on the little sorcerer the full fury of his
seeing eye, and said, in Hebrew:

"Who art thou, that permittest thyself to utter the holy name of
my Rabbi with thy impure lips? Let thy speech be taken from thee,
thou son of Satan."

The words "Son of Satan" almost prostrated the little sorcerer.
But remembering what was at stake, he gathered up his courage, and,
with a semblance of high glee, turned to Sergius on his throne:

"What did I tell thee, great Proconsul? I mentioned the name of
our great Rabbi, and he recognized me straightway. He is a brother, a
Jew like myself. Much knowledge did we gather, side by side, in the
school of the prophets, in Jerusalem. We can foresee events, we can
read the stars like an open scroll, and we know when the time comes to
act, and when it is the time to rest. But we have learned more here,
brother Saul, than in Jerusalem. We have enriched our art, we have
strengthened it with the star lore of the Chaldaeans and the healing
principles of the Syrians. We have learned from the sages of the desert
how to grind and mix herbs, and from the wise women of Askelon we
have learned how to avert the evil eye. We have become a great academy
of sages and soothsayers. With us are the greatest masters. Here, for
instance, is the great star-gazer of Babylon. Look at him. And here is
the master of the medicine mixers of Arabia. One mouthful of his potion is enough to bring into the arms of our great Proconsul any
woman he desires—let her heart be closed to all others with seven seals.
Wouldst thou behold something of our art, brother Saul? With thy
permission, mighty Proconsul, I would let our brother see what we have
learned, and ask him to repeat our wonders."

"Show, bar Yeshua!" commanded the Proconsul.

Bar Yeshua ranged his assistants about him in a special order. Then, frowning as in great concentration, he began to make signs in the air, calling on the names of spirits. Suddenly a cloud issued from the censers, and from the midst of it swam forth a table laden with tempting foods, roast fowl, fresh vegetables, beakers of wine: the table floated to rest before the throne of the Proconsul.

Green and yellow with the effort, bar Yeshua turned first to the assembly, and then to the messengers:

"Can ye do the like?"

"No!" answered Saul, in a firm, clear voice.

"Show us, then, *your* magic!" commanded the Proconsul.

"We perform no magic," answered Saul, in the same high, clear voice. "We make no use of signs and portents, for our God is not a God of sorcery, and of sudden apparitions which amaze us today and tomorrow are no more. He is the God of eternal being. He is the God of the wholeness of creation. His magic and His signs are—you, I, and this sinner in Israel, who knows that his own heart is filled with evil and deception. The blade of grass in the field, the fruit of the tree, the tiniest blossom, the birds, the creeping worms—these are our magic, for they are the creations of our God. Not the bread and wine which are conjured down by deceptive sleight of hand and blinding of the eyes are the wonders of our God, but the bread which issues from the earth for our nourishment, the food which He sends to every crawling thing in the cracks of the rocks. God has seen your corruption and your degradation; He has seen that you are surrounded by falsehood and dissoluteness; He has taken note of your belief in the vile, which exploits the blindness of your eyes; He has seen you deliver yourselves to the lusts of your hearts and the lure of your sins; and He has taken pity on you and on us, and has sent to us from heaven the helper of Israel, the Messiah, son of Jacob, who took on the likeness of a man of flesh and blood. And he, the Messiah, suffered for us and with us, bled for us and with us. He died for us as an atonement for our sins, that we might be washed of our impurity and be brought into eternal life, into the glory of the rule of God's will, which shall be on earth as it is in heaven. In the name of the one God of Israel, and in the name of the lord Messiah, the anointed of Jacob, we stand before you here, O Sergius Paulus, and bring the tidings to thee and thine, that you may be saved from destruction. These are our wonders and our magic."

The Proconsul heard him out patiently and wrinkled his forehead in thought. His chin rested on his fist while he meditated on what this stranger, a citizen of Rome, put before him. No, he did not find his words convincing. A redeemer who came down from heaven to suffer with the poorest and most wretched? Why the suffering? Suffering was a sign of weakness and helplessness. To be persecuted and not to perse- cute, to be smitten and not to smite—how was this to be reconciled with salvation, majesty, and divinity? And yet—there was something in the man's words. The Proconsul was too much the philosopher not to per- ceive the justice of the observation that the greatest wonder was after all not the unnatural but the natural. How remarkable it was that this man Paul, the stranger, preached his God not in the name of the un- natural, as others did, but in the name, precisely, of the natural, which was the whole creation. Yes, this was something worth meditating.

"Tell me: when will he, whom you call the anointed, bring upon earth the Kingdom of Heaven, in which the will of God alone shall rule?"

"When he will come, O Sergius Paulus, with the clouds of heaven to judge all men, thee, and me, and even this one who deceives thee," answered Paul, pointing at the shrinking figure of the sorcerer.

He, the great sorcerer, who had just performed so notable a mira- cle, shrank from the accusing finger. His heart melted in him at the words of Saul; for he knew but too well that all this trickery of his was potent only for the gentiles, for the ignorant, who worshiped the work of their own hands. Within him he had never wholly abandoned his faith in the God of Israel, whose Name he could not but recall with pride. He had remained a Jew. Who then, better than he, knew the jus- tice of Paul's words, that all of his performances were both deceptions of human beings and sacrilege against the Jewish faith? Some day he would be called to an accounting. He knew that on the day of reckoning he would be pronounced a son of death, to be slain by stoning; he was as one of those who serve idols and unite their bodies with the bodies of animals. And while the messengers stood there speaking in the name of the God of Israel, he had opposed them with demonstrations of the art of Satan. Would he not do better, then, to fall at the feet of the Pro- consul, and confess that he was a swindler and liar, that all his tricks were childish ingenuities, sleight of hand, optical illusions, manipulation of mirrors, in which his assistants were his accomplices? Would he not do better to call on the Name of God, and sanctify Him in the presence of witnesses, even as the messengers were doing? But his livelihood? His security? His very skin? No! He could not follow the bidding of his heart, even though Saul reminded him of the day of judgment. And yet all the terror which comes over a Jew in the thought of the judgment day was spread upon his features. He held himself erect with the remnants of his strength, relying still on the success of his "miracle."

"What sayest thou to this, bar Yeshua?" asked the Proconsul, breaking in on his terror.

"What say I? What say I? Assuredly, great Proconsul, brother Saul is in the right. And if brother Saul is in the right, let him perform a miracle, let him produce a sign which shall support his words," stammered the sorcerer.

And at this point something happened. With slow, confident footsteps Saul approached the little bar Yeshua, to whom it seemed that the messenger grew in stature as he came nearer: the body expanded, it towered over him like a mountain, and he was like a worm at its foot. Saul looked down at him, looked a long time, and was silent. The seeing eye was fixed unwinkingly on the little sorcerer; and bar Yeshua felt the glance piercing him like a spear, touching the inmost secrets of his heart. And now it was as if this heart, hitherto concealed, had been haled out and, a swollen thing, oozing falsehood, impurity, terror, regret, lay visible to all—the heart of one who was as "an idol worshiper and slept with beasts." The eyes of the sorcerer were extinguished when Saul spoke to him:

"Thou who art full of all trickery and falseness, thou child of Satan!" And Saul lifted his hand. In that instant bar Yeshua saw the fingers curving before his eyes, the fingers of death. "Thou! The hand of the Lord is upon thee! Thou wilt be blind!"

("The hand of the Lord!" was the last thought of the sorcerer.)

A dark wall of night closed in upon him. He stretched out his hand toward it, seeking an opening, and sank on his knees like a smitten reed.

Sergius Paulus, Proconsul of Cyprus, did not accept the Jewish God and the faith of the Messiah. But the Name of God was sanctified, and the name of the Messiah was carried from end to end of the island.

Saul alone knew that in this sign which had been vouchsafed him was the fulfillment of the words he had heard on the floor of the

Temple court. From that time on he assumed the leadership of the group, and he no longer called himself Saul but Paul, in proof that his sins had been forgiven.

Chapter Eleven

ACROSS THE MOUNTAINS

IT was not an easy matter for young Jochanan-Marcus to accept Paul, upon whom still lay the shadow of the death of Reb Istephan, as the leader of the deputation. Bar Naba could accept all things from Paul, even the formal changing of the name; the shift of leadership found no obstacle in his love. But young Jochanan remembered too well that in Jerusalem the elders had not put their hands upon Saul and had not invested him with the authority. They had sent him to strengthen the hands of the faithful in Antioch, and here he was on a mission to the gentiles. It was true that Jochanan's own Rabbi, Simon bar Jonah, to whom he looked for guidance, had made certain concessions for the gentiles; still, Simon bar Jonah regarded his mission to the Jews as primary, his mission to the gentiles as secondary. But Saul—or Paul— was drawn always to the cities of the gentiles, where few Jews were to be found. What disturbed him more was that Paul, whose authority was now over him, tended to speak less and less of the God of Israel. But what, asked Jochanan, was the Messiah if not the servant of the God of Israel, who had come only to reveal the will of God to mankind? The chief thing was the belief in the one living God; only upon that followed the salvation of the redeemer. What would the salvation of the redeemer be without the faith in the God of Israel?

Now as long as the authority of the delegation had been vested in his uncle, bar Naba, upon whose piety and devotion to the Jewish faith there was no shadow of doubt, young Jochanan had received all the commands of his elders in humility and obedience. No sooner had Paul assumed the leadership than Jochanan began to manifest opposition. It was in Perga, where Paul decided not to go to the house of Israel in the great cities of Syria and Asia, but to venture, instead, to remote

306

places in the hills of Phrygia and Galatia, where only tiny settlements of Jews were to be found, that Jochanan first dared to speak out against his elders. "Why should we carry the cup of salvation so far afield, on the dangerous road which is of the gentiles, when the house of Israel is thirsty, and is, moreover, nearer at hand?"

"The easier road we leave for others," answered Paul. "I have chosen the harder one."

"The holy disciples of Jerusalem did not send us to the people of Galatia. They sent us to the congregation of Antioch in Syria, to instruct it in the right path. They gave us no authority for other work, beyond that boundary."

Bar Naba cried out, in deep perturbation:

"Jochanan! How canst thou speak thus in the presence of the messenger, after God himself conferred upon brother Paul the authority to carry the tidings throughout the world? Wert thou not thyself a witness of the miracle wrought through him? Didst thou not see with thine own eyes the sanctification of the Name which he brought about in Cyprus?"

"Where the cause of God is concerned, look for no miracles: so my Rabbis taught me. And I have nothing in my hand other than the authority given me by my Rabbis in Jerusalem," answered the young man, abruptly.

That same day he left them and returned to Jerusalem. But bar Naba, who had faith in Paul, clung to him with all his heart.

It was not enough, it seemed, that Jochanan should have abandoned them. As if God were now seeking to humble Paul, lest the pride of his heart be awakened by his triumph in Cyprus, He sent another trial upon him. The day of their arrival in Perga, Paul fell sick with malaria. A fiery circle was clamped about his head, while his bones were filled with ice, so that his blood was stabbed with alternating pangs of heat and cold. Bar Naba tended him lovingly, as a son tends his father. He sat day and night by his bed, applied oils to his body, and gave him warm wine to drink, until Paul's strength returned. No sooner was he able to stand up without his knees doubling under him than he insisted on taking up the journey into the hills, by the path leading to Antioch in Pisidia.

From the sea town of Perga to the city of Antioch in Pisidia was a journey of some five or six days—that is, if one survived the journey at all. For the road was dangerous in the extreme. Robber bands made

307

their homes in the mountain caves by the roadside, and all the efforts of the government to clear them out of their fastnesses had been of no avail. Merchants never traveled save in groups and with armed guards. But Paul and bar Naba undertook the journey alone. Moreover, faithful to Paul's resolution never to become a burden on the communities he visited, they borrowed no provisions in Perga and did not even take a donkey with them to carry their baggage. Not that there was much of it: their mantles, a change of linen, a few manuscripts, and a day's supply of food. This bar Naba loaded on to his own shoulders. Paul, still weak, could carry no burden but had to support his footsteps with a staff. Thus the two messengers began the ascent.

At the outset the journey had a good effect on Paul's health. The light, fresh wind blowing down from the forests of cypress and laurel slowly extinguished the fire still flickering in his bones. The time was early summer, between Passover and Pentecost. The upward road was set with countless oleanders which were kindling their delicate rose blossoms in the young sunlight. In the forests grew wild pomegranates, which peeped out from among the heavy foliage of the bushes. The earth, soft as a green divan, was covered with flowers and herbs, with jasmine and violet. The air was sleepy with the buzzing of bees and the murmuring of insects, and the branches of the cypresses and laurels housed innumerable birds. From hidden places in the forests came the sound of rushing spring water, a delight to the spirit. The familiar and unfamiliar blossoms sent out a sweet freshness. All this had a healing effect on the sick man.

Moreover, the district was thickly populated. Houses of dried clay, roofed over with branches, nestled among the trees, and about them loitered men and women and domestic animals. Cows grazed in tiny clearings, and herds of goats clambered wildly up impossible, green-covered crags. The tinkling of donkeys was a pleasant, homelike sound to the ear. Sometimes the travelers were refreshed by the sight of a flock of sheep feeding in a green hollow. Paul knew this district. He was walking on home soil, and the landscape was that of his father city, Tarshish. It was the hill country rolling from the shoulders of Mount Taurus.

But as they continued the ascent, a change came over the landscape. The blossoming oleanders ceased, and with them the delicious odor of blossoming pomegranate, the caressing green of the cypresses, and the heartening sound of hidden freshets. Now they beheld, on either side, crippled trees whose branches had been combed out by an iron wind. Here and there an iris clung with its last energies to the soil, opening its bluish lips among the harsh green growths. Here and there a lonely laurel dug its roots like nails into the ground, and held out in the struggle against the wind. No houses looked out cheerfully from among the trees. Instead, the travelers were aware more and more of the grim front of the mountain rocks. Here and there they beheld a water channel, but the water was gone, or almost gone, and in its place was the cascade of stones which it brought down from the heights.

On the fourth day they came to such a hollow, from which the water had almost disappeared. Evening fell suddenly; and as they were still a long way from the nearest settlement, they sat down by the inner edge of the water course, scraped up a little water from between the stones, and washed their hands and feet. Then they said the evening *Shema,* washed their hands again, and ate a few mouthfuls of dried figs and bread, washing it down with water. Within the shelter of the channel they found a softer place and lay down with their faces to the darkening sky. They talked awhile of the Messiah, and of his mission, which had brought them to this remote place; they talked earnestly, and with joyful hearts, until sleep overcame them. In the dead of night, when their eyes were heavily sealed with sleep, and the sky was spread peacefully over them, there arose an angry murmur. Bar Naba alone heard it. He sat up, listened, and did not know what to make of it. Unaccustomed to the hill country, he took the sound for that of a distant waterfall, which they had not noticed when they lay down. He therefore forebore to wake up Paul, who lay in a deep sleep of exhaustion. But the sound grew louder, and bar Naba was filled with uneasiness. Then suddenly, as if God had destroyed the boundaries of land and sea, a wave of water burst upon bar Naba and his companion, and the lower levels of the channel were filled with bursts of foam. In an instant bar Naba lifted Paul in his powerful arms, swung him on to his back and began to climb. Snatched out of deep slumber, Paul realized at once whence the danger came. As if he had been hurled across the years into his childhood, he saw once more the sudden waters breaking down from the mountain peaks at this time of the year, to flood the dried lake and river beds. "Faster, bar Naba!" he cried. Waist deep in water, bar Naba clambered desperately up the shifting slope, Paul clinging to his back. The stones under his feet rolled away, but he dug into the crevices and inch by inch lifted himself and his burden beyond the upper edge of the water course.

Escaping barely with their lives, their baggage carried off by the roaring water, the two messengers fell on their knees, put their faces to the ground, and gave praise to God.

"It must be that we are being tested, whether we are fit to carry the tidings of the Messiah to the world," said Paul.

Renewed in their faith, the messengers resumed the journey at daybreak.

On the fifth day they were surrounded by a robber band. The men who captured them took them before the leader in his cave, and he asked them who they were, whence they came and what they carried with them.

"We are Jews, we come from Jerusalem, and we carry with us a great treasure of the God of Israel."

"I have heard," answered the robber captain, "that Jews throughout the world gather money for the Temple in Jerusalem, and doubtless this is the treasure which you carry with you. Give us your silver and gold, your lives will be spared."

"Our treasure does not consist of silver and gold, but of something else; whoever possesses it has eternal life."

Then Paul told the robber captain of the treasure of the tidings which they, the messengers, carried with them. Of this treasure, he said, they could give him, for salvation was open to all. The robber captain, realizing that these were two empty-handed Jews on a mission of God, sent them away in peace with a store of bread and water.

So from Sunday to the afternoon before the Sabbath the messengers labored on, and on that afternoon they arrived at the gates of Antioch of Pisidia, where they asked for the synagogue of the Jews.

"Antioch of the hills" lay on a high plateau which was itself encircled by hills—the mountain ridge which stretched from the Taurus of Paul's boyhood to Mount Olympus. It was a city of commerce. The Jewish population, far from Jerusalem, the road to which was, moreover, difficult and dangerous for pilgrims, was sundered from the religious influence of the Temple. The Jews of Antioch in Pisidia had little learning, and scholars were few among them. A process of assimilation had set in, and there were cases of intermarriage between Jews and

Greeks. For all that, the community had its great synagogue and sundry institutions, with an appointed head, elders, cantors, and beadles, who kept guard over the life of the Jews, seeking to hold it, as far as they could, in the channels prepared by the Rabbis of Jerusalem. In this, as in many other cities of Asia Minor, there were many godfearing gentiles who had wearied of the worship of idols, and had been drawn by the decency and modesty of Jewish life into the Jewish faith. They frequented the synagogue on Sabbaths or on other occasions—which were far apart—when messengers came up to the city from Jerusalem. More than the men, whom the severe ritual of the Jewish law frightened off, it was the women among the godfearing gentiles who converted to the faith. In this, as in other cities, there were many women who made no secret of their conversion, and to some extent it was their influence which brought the men to the services.

The messengers, exhausted by the laborious and dangerous journey, dragged themselves through the streets to the synagogue. There they were received with the dignity and friendliness always accorded to wandering preachers, and given lodgment in the hospice near-by. The elders of the synagogue attended to their wants, and when a couple of days had passed, Paul and bar Naba had found their strength again. The Jews of Antioch in Pisidia were eager to hear them and waited impatiently for the rounding of the second week. The word had passed that messengers from Jerusalem would be present, and on the Sabbath the synagogue was packed with worshipers, Jewish and non-Jewish. After the reading of the Torah the head of the synagogue honored Paul with the reading of the Prophetic passage for the week. When this was completed he invited Paul to speak, with these words: "If thou hast a word of comfort for the people, let us hear it."

Then Paul mounted the pulpit and opened the scroll at the First Prophets, from which he had just read the week's passage, and lifted his hand for silence.

Something in the gesture, something in Paul's manner, struck them as different from the ways of other preachers. Paul did not address himself to the Jews only: "You men of Israel," he began, "and all you that fear God, hear me!"

He began the story from the point of the Exodus, leading through the Judges and the days of Samuel to the ascension of King David, who was mentioned in the Prophetic passage of that Sabbath. From

311

David he turned his discourse to the Messiah, who according to the words of the Prophet should be descended from the house of David; and he announced to the people that the Messiah had already come, in the person of one Yeshua, who had arisen as the help of Israel. Again he addressed himself to Jews and Greeks alike: "Children of the race of Abraham," he said, "and all those among you that fear God! It is to you that the Messiah has been sent!" He went on to tell them how the elders of the people in Jerusalem had not recognized the Messiah and had not heeded the words of the Prophets, which they read every Sabbath in the synagogue, and they had handed over the Messiah to the gentiles, and that had come to pass which the Prophets had foretold: he was tortured and done to death on the cross. But on the third day God raised him from the dead. And Paul continued to quote the sayings and hints of the Prophets and of King David's Book of Psalms, to the effect that all this had to be, and that this Yeshua was the true Messiah. And he closed with words which rang strange to the ears of Jews: "Everyone, be he Jew or Greek, who believes the tidings which I bring you, who believes in Yeshua the Messiah, shall be justified by him in all those things wherein they could not be justified through the Law of Moses."

Strange though these words were, the whole congregation took up the tidings in great joy. Many Jews and gentiles followed the messengers to the house to which Paul and bar Naba had been invited for the Sabbath meal. They wanted to hear more of these tremendous tidings which had been withheld from them till now. The Jews of this remote city were astonished that previous messengers, sent by the High Priest to collect the Temple dues, had made no mention of them; neither had other messengers, coming from the Pharisees. Thus the house of the host was filled that Sabbath afternoon with members of the congregation, and innumerable questions were asked of the messengers. Paul and bar Naba did not weary of repeating the details of their message; and when the afternoon was closing, the Jews and gentiles of the city asked them to remain another week and to preach again the following Sabbath on the same theme.

Paul and bar Naba did not need to be asked twice. Nor did they spend the week in idleness. When the Sabbath was over, Paul began to bind together the first of the new believers in the Messiah, whom he called Messianists, or Christians. He invited to the hospice all those whom he felt to be most taken by his speech and most inclined to accept the faith. He spoke to them separately, and formed them into a separate group, which should be a congregation apart within the congregation of Israel. He took into the new sect Jews and Greeks, making them equal in the brotherhood; and the Greeks showed themselves more eager to enter the faith of the Messiah than the Jews. For the first time a door was opened for them into the Holy of Holies of the Jewish God, without their having to pay for it through circumcision and observance of the laws of pure and impure food, conditions sternly enforced hitherto by the Jewish Rabbis. There were also Jews who were weary of the heavy burden of the laws, which were increased from day to day by the Rabbis—Jews who, lapsing from observance, always felt sinful and trembled at the thought of the Judgment Day. Here, suddenly, by their faith in the Messiah preached by the messengers, they were freed from the yoke; not only was their future free, but the sins which they had committed in the past in transgressing the laws of purity, in housing with gentiles—sins for which they were being constantly reproached by the Rabbis—were wiped out, and they were washed clean as by the High Priest on the day of *Yom Kippur*. Most assuredly this was something which imparted a special attraction to the words of the messengers. So all that week Paul labored, and bar Naba with him; and the hospice was like a beehive. All that week people came and went. Moreover, Paul went to them, too. And with the second Sabbath those that had received baptism were already of the congregation of the Christians.

But in the house of the elder of the synagogue the week was one of tumult and protest. When the city learned of the work of Paul and bar Naba, there were many who looked upon it as a breaking up of the community. And the head of the synagogue himself beheld how, without his permission, he suddenly had a second congregation, in which there were Greeks who had not been converted to Judaism. Some declared openly that this was a betrayal of the Jewish faith, an attack directed at the heart of the Jewish sanctities. Without any proof, without documents or attestations from the Priests or the Sages, this man came and preached the Messiah, and, worst of all, preached it without imposing any obligations on the gentiles, so that these entered the congregation of Israel uncircumcised, unpledged to the commandments and the good deeds which were holiest to Israel: and devoid of such fulfillment, they were promised that which was dearest to Israel—the Messiah. They argued in the house of the head of the synagogue: "If faith in the Messiah is higher, and brings greater redemption, than the Law of Moses, and if Greek and Jew are equally entitled to the faith, let them come to us, to the head of the synagogue, to admit the Greeks as equal brothers; let him not create a second congregation behind the back of the synagogue authorities."

Angriest were the women, the pious gentile women who had left their gods and the gods of their forefathers—the gods who had been the protection of their homes: they had locked themselves out from their own peoples in order to give themselves to the God of Israel. They were hated and scorned by their own families, they were avoided by their own people, for they took no part in the services of the gods, but sent their offerings to the unseen God in Jerusalem, and prayed in His synagogues. Many of them had wrought devotedly to persuade their husbands and children to follow their example. And now, suddenly, there appeared two men, giving themselves out as messengers from Jerusalem, who said that this painful acceptance of Judaism had been wasted, was meaningless. Every gentile, they said, who only believed in the Messiah, was more entitled to the promises of Israel than were they. "What means it," they asked, "but that all our devotion was a folly? They who until now worshiped idols and defiled themselves in their temples have a greater portion in the God of Israel than we, who kept ourselves pure. Assuredly the heads of the synagogue are right: these messengers are deceivers. If it were true that the Messiah has come and the Law of Moses is done away with, messengers would surely have been sent to us by the Priests and Sages of Jerusalem. These are false messengers! Let them be driven from the city!"

So the division deepened and grew more stormy throughout the week. The merchants spoke of it in the marketplace, the workers in their shops and in the vineyards, Jew and Greek everywhere, even in the temples. There were two views: one, that the messengers were true messengers and their message was true, and the opposite, they were false and their message was false.

On the second Sabbath Paul and bar Naba came to services, they and their followers in the new faith, among the other Jews. When the reading of the Scroll was ended, and Paul mounted the pulpit, a tumult broke out in the synagogue, and the shouting continued until Paul descended and left the synagogue.

314

On the next day, when the elders of the Jewish community assembled, a number of gentile women, converts, appeared before them, and complained most bitterly against the messengers. Then, in order to arrest the dissension in the city, the elders decided to ask the messengers to begone.

Before the two messengers left, Paul said:

"It was necessary that the word of God should be uttered to you first. But inasmuch as you have rejected it, and do not consider yourselves worthy of eternal life, we turn to the gentiles."

Chapter Twelve

"PERSECUTIONS AND AFFLICTIONS"

SO the messengers continued on their way, Paul leaning on his staff, bar Naba carrying the bundle of provisions. The road wound among the hills. Sometimes they spent the night in the clay hut of a poor villager, and in exchange for shelter and a cup of goat's milk they told him the tidings; sometimes they slept in the open, under the starry sky. Often it would happen that the fire they lit for their protection would attract shepherds; then the story of the redemption would be told by firelight in the field. The people of the hills were simple. They listened wonderingly to the recital, and they looked up at the great stars, as if they expected God to show himself straightway in the clouds. Robbers came to them, too, and they, together with Paul and bar Naba, warmed themselves at the fire, while Paul preached. The messengers feared no robbers. Their treasure was any man's for the asking. Sometimes Paul and bar Naba climbed to precipitous heights along narrow paths between cliff and abyss. Five days out of Antioch of Pisidia they came to the friendly shelter of Iconium.

And though the Jews of the former city had as it were flung the writ of divorcement in the face of the messengers, whereupon these had replied, "Now we will turn to the gentiles," who was there, after all, to listen to the story of the redemption? Who but Jews, who had been waiting so long for the Messiah, would understand them? Well, then, they had quarreled with the Jews of Antioch of Pisidia: but were the Jews of Iconium the less their brothers therefore? And so their footsteps turned of themselves to the Jewish synagogue. There only could they be certain of an open heart and a ready ear, whether among the Jews or among the godfearing gentiles who consorted with them in their services.

The messengers remained a longer time in Iconium. It was a pleasant spot in the heart of the Phrygian-Pisidian hills. The soil was fruitful and watered by many wells and rivers. The air came in cool waves from the heights. The people hereabouts were simple and hardworking, and altogether different from the inhabitants of a Roman colony like Antioch in Pisidia. Greeks and Jews dwelt together, peasants, artisans, small merchants. Among this simple folk Paul was happy and at peace for a time.

And he needed rest. The malarial fever which he had contracted at Perga suddenly broke out again, and his bones were eaten up by the reawakened fire. Also there was a recurrence of his falling sickness, of which he had believed himself permanently cured. As he stood one day in the pulpit and preached mightily, he tottered and fell, and the foam burst out on his lips. His eyes turned inward and a dreadful expression came into his face. The Jews covered him with a sheet and later carried him to his bed in the hospice. When Paul came to he felt himself humbled and rejected. He was greatly ashamed, not so much before the Jews, who were homely people, but before the gentiles, who had been present in considerable numbers in the synagogue. He felt that now his words were wasted because of what had happened and that no one would listen to him again. For what sort of tidings could he be bringing to others who was himself tormented by sickness and could find no cure? These were his thoughts. But he was filled with wonder to observe how the people passed over the incident with a marvelous greatness of heart, behaving toward him as though nothing had happened. They came to him in the hospice, bringing him little gifts: this one a bowl of milk, that one a cruse of oil, a third a vase of ointment. Nor was it thus only with the Jews, from whom it was to be expected; there came many pious gentiles, and Paul was deeply moved. They had heard him in the synagogue, and they came to visit him in his sickness. They brought wreaths of flowers to adorn his bed and sweet-smelling herbs and roots. There was one woman who tended him with especial care. She sewed shirts for him out of the cloth which others brought him as a gift and gathered the best oils for him. She also brought him wine of pressed figs to restore his strength, and every day she made his bed for him, speaking to him comfortingly and praying for his recovery. Paul was grateful for every little kindness. His eyes filled with tears and his heart was warm with faith and hope; he thanked God for having humbled him in his own eyes, so that he might not fall victim to pride of spirit and for having uplifted him in the eyes of others, especially strangers and gentiles.

In those days Paul spoke much about the gentiles to bar Naba and taught him to see the good in them:

"Go forth and behold the grace which God has wrought with them through the salvation sent through the lord Messiah. Even before they know him, he has already prepared their heart for understanding of him. If a Jew were to do what these folk have done for me, we should not hold it of special account. When the garden has been tended by a gardener, sown, planted, weeded, and sheltered with a strong fence from beasts, what is there to wonder at if it yield lovely fruit? Jews are children of Abraham, and they have inherited the virtue of compassion from their fathers; God renewed it for them in the Law which He revealed to Moses on Sinai. But when the gentiles do thus, whose garden has neither been tended, nor sown, nor weeded, nor fenced about, gentiles for whom there was neither an Abraham nor a Mount Sinai, great is the wonder and grace, for it is against their nature. Their nature says to them: Steal, rob, slay, torture, do according to the desire of the heart. And they do kindness, as they have done with me! They have learned the grace of compassion from their own hearts, and they have created the loveliness of God's fear with their own hands. Great is their merit! May my portion be with them! Now arise and see how the gentiles long for salvation, and we hold it back from them. Who are the sinners, we or they? God has opened a spring of help in Yeshua the Messiah; let it flow forth and make fruitful the whole desolate earth! If the gentiles will not become Jews, the Jews will become gentiles, and their soil will become as blasted and as barren as the soil around them. We cannot remain any longer closed in by our narrow limits and feel ourselves to be righteous, when the world is going under in a flood of whoredom and sin. We must carry salvation to the world. The well of waters which God has opened through the Messiah must pour into a thousand canals;

lakes and rivers must be filled in every land, and the whole earth must be made fruitful with the living waters of God's word, even as it is written concerning the lord Messiah: 'I have set thee as a light to nations, and thou shalt be a salvation to the uttermost ends of the earth.' "

A rush of energy returned to Paul and filled his limbs and nerves. Once more he threw himself into the work of winning souls for the faith of the Messiah. He preached on Sabbaths, on Mondays, and on Thursdays, after the reading of the Scroll. He spoke in the synagogue and in the marketplaces, he visited the workshops, went out into field and garden and the homes of the rich, as well as those of the poor. Wherever men assembled he was to be found. He spoke to the freedman and the slave; none was too high or too low for him. In the faith of the Messiah there was for him neither freedman nor bondman, neither master nor servant, neither men nor women: all were born equal. He bound Jew and gentile in a girdle of faith in the Messiah. A new congregation blossomed in Iconium, which had a great population of Jews and Greeks. The new believers began to spread their faith among their own, their kinsfolk and their fellow laborers, their friends and fellow members of the synagogue. And before long the city was divided: one half of it was with the messengers the other half against them. In either half there were both Jews and Greeks. Families, too, became divided. Dissension began with words and passed into deeds. There was quarreling in the homes, at table, in the marketplaces, the synagogues, and the temples. Whenever Paul appeared in public, he became the center of a crowd; and whenever he opened his lips it was the signal for a fierce dispute. The Jews and gentiles who were on the side of the messengers stood together. And those that were opposed to them also united, their purpose being to drive the messengers from the city; for they blamed the latter for the dissensions, but they laid the guilt mostly to Paul. And some of them planned to lay hands on him, lead him out of the city, and stone him. The followers of the messengers, hearing of the plot, warned Paul and bar Naba of the danger, whereupon they packed their belongings and set out from the city.

But in this place Paul left behind him a deep-planted congregation of Christians, consisting of Jews and Greeks. Before leaving he charged them to hold fast to the faith in God and His Messiah, and God would take them under His wing.

From Iconium the messengers set out across the mountains, and made for the region of Lykonia, and the cities of Lystra and Derbe.

In Lystra an unwonted incident occurred.

When Paul had finished preaching in the synagogue, he observed among his listeners a paralyzed man. The face of the man flamed with faith in Paul and in his power to perform miracles. He stretched out his hands to Paul and asked for help. Then Paul remembered how Simon bar Jonah had more than once performed miracles with the power of the Holy Ghost, which he possessed; therefore he did not turn from the sick man, but approached him and looked steadfastly at him. The half-closed, half-blinded eye of Paul bored deep into the eyes of the cripple and took his will captive, establishing complete authority over his thought. The cripple, interpenetrated with faith, believing that Paul could help him, destroyed his own will in the presence of Paul's. The longer Paul gazed on the cripple, the more he knew that he held him, as the potter holds a pot; and suddenly he lifted his voice and commanded:

"Arise, and stand on thy feet!"

And the miracle came to pass: the lame man stood up on his feet.

The Greeks of Lystra believed in Jupiter, to whom there was a temple in the city. The local priest had persuaded the people that Jupiter and his attendant and servant, Mercury, were about to appear in Lystra. When the Greeks saw or heard of the wonder which Paul had performed with the cripple in the synagogue, they ran through the streets of the city crying: "The gods have appeared to us in the likeness of men!"

So it came to pass that when Paul and bar Naba were standing soon after in the city gate, speaking of the Messiah to certain people, they saw a large crowd drawing nigh. Men and women were dressed in festival attire, and the women wore wreaths of flowers as for a visit to the Temple. The men had on multicolored tunics and girdles, and little boys ran naked by their side. The priest of Jupiter was in the midst of them, leading an ox with gilded horns, and with him were boys and girls carrying baskets of flour, and dancing and singing about the ox. And suddenly Paul and bar Naba beheld themselves encircled by this throng. The priest in his ceremonial robe came forward, threw himself at the feet of bar Naba, and cried out:

"Almighty Jupiter! I knew thou wert about to descend from Parnassus, and hadst taken thought for thy city. Always I assured thy people that thou wouldst reveal thyself to us. Now thou art here. The people know thee. Great Jupiter, in thy graciousness accept the sacrifice which we bring to thee at the gates of the city."

And the multitude, gazing at bar Naba, kept crying: "Jupiter! Jupiter!" And pointing to Paul they cried: "That is Mercury, who accompanies, for he is the chief speaker!"

An improvised altar was erected on the spot and covered with the branches which the people carried. A tripod was there, too, and from it ascended the smoke of incense.

The crowd was beside itself with joy and kept pointing at bar Naba and Paul, crying:

"Seest thou that black beard? Every hair of it can pull up a mountain from its base! Seest thou those eyes? The fire in them gives light to the sun and stars!" And of the nervous, restless Paul: "Seest thou! He cannot stand still an instant! That is Mercury. His hands and feet are wings! He flies like an arrow from the bow to fulfill the commands of Jupiter!"

And indeed it was thus with Paul: he could not stand still. All his wiry, bony body trembled, as if in a fit. And bar Naba, shamed, bewildered, looked on him helplessly. About them the people danced, and the priest, with many ritualistic gestures, made ready to sacrifice the ox.

Suddenly Paul tore his clothing, in sign of mourning, and bar Naba, seeing him, imitated the action.

Then Paul lifted his voice and shouted:

"O men and women, why do ye this?"

For an instant the people suspended the dancing and singing. A breath of fear passed over them. And Paul, taking advantage of the silence, addressed them. His voice quivered with pity and suppressed anger:

"Hear us! We are only mortals of flesh and blood, even as you are. Look at these bodies! They are like yours! We have come hither to preach to you, so that you may cease from folly and abandon your gods, which are but emptiness and delusion, and turn to the one living God, Who has created heaven and earth and the sea and all that is in them. And though formerly He allowed the nations to wander and err in their own ways, He did not relinquish His authority over them: they were ever in His hand. And He is the God of all of us, beneficent and loving;

320

He is the God who sends down rain from heaven and the season of fruits, and he fills our hearts with nourishment and peace."

The crowd listened, the priest of Jupiter gesticulated desperately over its head, seeking to silence Paul. What else could he do? He had so often told the people that Jupiter would appear one day in its midst, that their acclamation of Paul and bar Naba was for him providential. And here one of these men was denying it, in the very presence of the sacrifice; and as if that were not enough, he was actually urging the folk to abandon their old home gods and to turn instead to the God of the hated Jews. Grimacing, hopping from foot to foot, the priest made signs at Paul to hold his peace, to accept the sacrifice, to concur in the deception. He flourished the sacrificial knife, and in a final gesture of compulsion turned toward the ox. But Paul would not let the sacrifice be consummated. Rushing forward, he overtured the improvised altar, never ceasing to talk and to preach the tidings of the Messiah.

The priest understood at last that there was no coming to terms with this man. From the midst of his astounded dupes he began to yell:

"The Jews have fooled us! They came to us in the guise of our gods and they preach their own God! The Jews have fooled us!"

The astonished crowd heard the cry and began to withdraw from Paul and bar Naba. Like a slogan, the words sped through the streets and reached the temple of Jupiter. That day the city rang with: "The Jews have fooled us! They disguised themselves as our gods in order to preach their own."

The next day there arrived men from Antioch of Pisidia and from Iconium. They reported how the messengers had spread disaffection against the old gods in those cities and had introduced dissensions between Jews and Jews, Greeks and Greeks.

From then on the anger against Paul and bar Naba grew day by day in Lystra. But Paul affected to ignore it. He still went among the people, Jews and Greeks, and preached the Messiah. He spoke in the synagogue, appealing to Jew and non-Jew; he quoted the Prophets to prove that Yeshua was the Messiah, sent by God to aid mankind. To the Jews he preached the Messiah, to the gentiles the one living God. And in the face of opposition and danger he created here too a congregation of Christians, and strengthened it, and proved to it by his own example that in the spreading of the faith there should be no fear.

321

The hatred of Paul mounted in the city: of Paul rather than of bar Naba, because the former was accounted the spokesman and therefore the chief mischief-maker. Among Jews the hatred was as intense as among Greeks. But it was fiercest in the heart of the priest of Jupiter, who burned with the shame of Paul's exposure of him. And on a certain day, when Paul was preaching to a small group, an angry crowd of Jews and Greeks descended on him, scattered his listeners, and dragged him off outside the gates of the city. When they came to a hollow in the ground, they flung him into it, and began to pelt him with stones. They continued to throw stones until they thought he was dead, and then they returned to the city.

Covered with the blood which streamed from his wounds Paul lay in the field outside of Lystra. His body, his head, his face, were bruised and cut. His eyes were closed. Lying thus, half conscious, not knowing whether he lived or was dead, he was aware of a figure which emerged out of the night, and it was in the likeness of something he had seen in Jerusalem in the old days, when his name was still Saul and he was of the enemies of the Messiah. He saw an angel which had fallen from heaven to earth, and was imbedded in stones to the waist, so that only the upper half of the body was free; and the face and wings of the angel were lifted to heaven. Paul remembered that this was the image he had seen when he sat and guarded the clothes of the witnesses at the stoning of Reb Istephan.

A great joy flooded his heart, and he said to himself: Now I know that God has forgiven me for my share in the shedding of the blood of Istephan. Like him, I have been stoned for the sake of the Messiah.

Lying and meditating thus, his heart rejoicing for what had happened to him, he felt suddenly a light hand, like the hand of an angel, passing over his body, wiping away the blood and softening his sores. Love and devotion were in the touch of the hand; it was gentle, sweet, hardly to be felt, as though it were the impalpable hand of a spirit. It was a soul tending his soul. And he thought within himself: "God has surely sent an angel to comfort me." Opening his eyes he saw standing over him the likeness of a lad of fourteen or fifteen, and indeed the face was the face of an angel, and the eyes looked down on him with infinite love and compassion; and the love and compassion had a healing force in them. Paul said:

"Who art thou, my son?"

322

"My name is Timotheus. My father is a Greek, but my mother is a daughter of Israel. I have heard from my mother of the God of Israel, whom thou preachest, and from thee I have heard of the Messiah whom He has sent, and for whose sake they have stoned thee. And I wait for him, as do all the Jews of the city. I saw what these men did to thee, and I am here to help thee."

Then Paul embraced the boy and kissed him with his bloody mouth. With his blood-stained fingers he felt the boy's hair, his throat, his shoulders, and he said to him:

"Thou art a faithful son of Abraham, for thou hast his virtue of compassion. May thy like be increased in Israel."

By this time the believers whom Paul had won over in Lystra came out with bar Naba and found the place of the stoning. Paul was already standing up, leaning on the lad Timotheus, and he returned to the city in the company of his disciples. There he went into the house of Eunice, Timotheus's mother, with whom her mother lived. All in the house were Jews, though Eunice had married a Greek, and all awaited the coming of the Messiah. The women washed Paul, and wiped the blood off his body, and anointed it, and he stayed until the second day. And on the morning of the third day he baptized Timotheus in the name of the Messiah.

Then he made preparations for his departure. He strengthened the hearts of the new congregation, said farewell to the lad Timotheus, and together with bar Naba turned back by the road to Derbe.

They did not stay long in Derbe. It was the intention of Paul to visit briefly the towns from which he had been driven out, and to see that the work he had begun at the risk of his life should not perish. Bar Naba was shaken and astonished when he heard Paul say that they should go in turn to Lystra, and Iconium, and Antioch in Pisidia. But he obeyed without questioning, believing as he did that God was ever the guide of Paul.

They stole into the cities under cover of night and knocked softly on the doors of the believers. "Yes, we have returned!" In Lystra, Paul assembled the faithful in the house of Timotheus's mother, and there they fasted and prayed together. He strengthened them, saying: "We shall have to bear with much to be worthy of entering the Kingdom of Heaven. But for his sweet name's sake we shall endure it all!"

If for the Jews the belief in the Messiah was the continuity of their old religion, a fulfillment of Prophetic messages, and a miracle for which they had long waited, for the gentiles it was a completely new birth. God had breathed a new soul into them. The old life of impurity fell away, and a new life began for them. They felt that for the sake of their portion in the Messiah it was incumbent on them to guard their lives from uncleanliness, and to practice the virtues which the Messiah had taught. Love, devotion, and faith were the commandments and virtues; this was their law, as binding upon them as *their* law upon the Jews. And as the Jews were faithful to the law of Moses, and were ready to lay down their lives in the observance of it, so the new believers were called upon to lay down their lives, if necessary, for their fellowship in the Messiah.

Wherever Paul came, overtly or in secret, he called together the new congregation. He no longer preached openly, for he sought to avoid the tumults and dissensions which had attended his first visits. He was content now to preach only to the believers, to strengthen their bonds in the Messiah and their brother-spirit for each other. He made firmer their foundations; he picked out the ablest and most devoted among them and set them as elders over the others; he chose cantors and beadles, in the fashion of the synagogue, and they were the leaders of the congregations.

But on the road back he made a longer stay in Perga, where, because of his sickness and the dispute with Jochanan, he had not fulfilled his mission. He founded a congregation now in the busy port of Perga, according to the model of the other cities. From Perga he went to the port of Attalia, and founded a congregation there too. Then he took boat for Seleucia, avoiding his native town of Tarshish, for he desired now to render his report to the congregation which had invested him with the authority to spread the faith.

But in Antioch in Syria they had already heard what Paul and bar Naba had wrought in the communities of Galatia. For there had been travelers and messengers. The elders of the community of Antioch came out to receive the two apostles. In the doors of all the houses of the Messianites, or Christians, lamps and candles were lit in honor of the returning messengers. When the elders of Antioch heard from Paul and bar Naba the details of their work, the communities they had founded, the souls they had won to the Messiah among the gentiles, their joy and wonder were boundless. "Surely," they said, exulting, "this is the finger of God. God has opened the gates to the gentiles, and through the Messiah He fills them with faith. Now we must pray that the gates be flung open even wider, so that they may never be closed again."

Paul and bar Naba stayed a longer time in Antioch. They needed rest after their journey. But during those days Paul took up the task of training Titus as a helper in future missions.

But in Jerusalem not less than in Antioch there were reports of the work of Paul. The elders learned that Paul had admitted uncircumcised gentiles to the congregation and that he taught a strange doctrine which had not been taught by the Messiah. Without the laying on of hands, without the authority of the holy congregation, and only with the consent of the congregation of Antioch, he had set out on a mission to the cities of the gentiles. A storm broke out among the holy ones in Jerusalem. What was in the mind of Saul, they asked? Was he seeking to establish a new authority? Had not the lord Messiah vested the authority in his disciples? They alone, the first disciples, had the right to transmit this authority by the laying on of hands, and the Holy Ghost did not rest on any community until Simon bar Jonah, the rock, had first been there. Very dangerous was the precedent set by the community of Antioch in Syria in its compact with Saul, who had already occasioned so much suffering to the congregation of the Messiah.

Messengers were dispatched from Jerusalem to the community in Antioch, with the warning that all the work done till now by "the young man Saul"—thus they still called him in Jerusalem—was as a house built on shifting sand. There were no gentiles in the faith of the Messiah. Whosoever desired to enter the faith must first enter into the covenant of Abraham; without the yoke of heaven there could not be the Kingdom of Heaven. The achievements wrought in the name of the community of Antioch were delusions and falsities. Without circumcision there was no salvation.

Paul beheld himself confronted by the undoing of all his labor. There was nothing for it now but to take up the struggle in Jerusalem itself. He was no longer "the young man Saul, who once persecuted the faithful and now bears witness for the Messiah." He was Paul, who had traveled through the length and breadth of Galatia, planting a chain of gardens of salvation. He had testimony thereto. Had not his sins been wiped out by the work he had done? If the sacrifice of the gentiles had not been acceptable to God, He would not have turned their hearts toward goodness. And his foremost witness was Titus—the first of the fruits which he had won for the God of Israel: uncircumcised, Titus wrought exactly as if the Law of Moses were inscribed on his heart. Was he not filled with love, goodness, compassion, with sympathy, piety, and fear of God? Let Titus the uncircumcised appear in Jerusalem and testify for the work of the Messiah.

Titus would be his vindication! Paul had left the youth in Antioch, and now the whole congregation of that city bore witness to his choice. Titus had not rested a moment from his labors. He had brought his pagan nature, in which he had been bound as in chains, and had laid it at the feet of the Messiah, an offering. He had surrendered everything for his faith: his youth, his health, his pagan longing for joy, merriment, and Eros. He had gone into the house of the poor, visited the sick, comforted the weak. He had shared his food and his couch with the poor. No word of anger, pride, or self-esteem had ever passed his lips. He was a model of what could be wrought in a pagan by baptism in the Messiah. The water of baptism became blood in the veins of the gentiles. This was the virtue—to be circumcised not in the flesh, but in the heart.

So Paul took Titus with him as a witness for the gentiles, and the three of them, Paul, Titus, and bar Naba, went up to Jerusalem. They went by way of Phoenicia and Samaria, and in every city Paul stopped awhile to tell how God had opened a door to the faith for the gentiles.

Chapter Thirteen

THE OPENED DOOR

FOURTEEN years had passed since Paul had last seen Jerusalem; for the visit at the time of the beginning of his ministry with bar Naba had lasted only a day or two, and he had not even looked about him. Now the city was so changed that he scarcely knew it. The famine was not yet over. The streets of Jerusalem were filled with emaciated beggars who besieged the gates and colonnades of the upper city, sheltering themselves from the sun and stretching out their hands to passers-by. The Court of the Gentiles in the Temple was filled to overflowing with the poor, with women and children who came to the charitable institutions for a handful of dried figs, or a measure of barley, out of the supplies which had been purchased by Queen Helena in Egypt and Phoenicia, or for a copper coin, the gift of the Jews of the Diaspora. Judaea —and Jerusalem even more than Judaea—had suffered under a double plague: the famine and the burden of taxes imposed by Herod Agrippa. This King of the House of Herod, in whose blood there had been but a faint admixture of the Hasmoneans, had not been a raw Asiatic tyrant, like his great-grandfather. Neither had he been a true patriotic leader, like a Hasmonean. He had been primarily the Roman aristocrat and man of the world, an enthusiastic lover of sports and a passionate dice player. True, he had introduced a new note into his life since the experience in Alexandria, at the time of the pogrom. In Jerusalem he had given himself out as a patriot, the protector of the Jewish law and tradition; he so far hoodwinked some of the Rabbis of Jerusalem that they, influenced also by his pious wife, held him up as a model to the people. But he did not abandon his extravagant aristocratic habits. Like every other Herod he was the victim of a building mania; he showered the provincial cities with gifts, rows of columns, gymnasia, and statues of the Caesar. For these, and for other ambitious projects, he ground the face of his people. In his provincial residence, remote from the eyes of the Jerusalemites, he built himself sport arenas, theaters, and circuses, instituted gladiatorial combats, and did not hesitate to pollute the soil of Palestine with combats between men and wild beasts. But he was skillful in deceiving the Rabbis of Jerusalem; knowing that the reports of his behavior came to their ears, he assured them solemnly that he pursued those heathen practices not out of inclination, but as a matter of state. For he was not only King of Judaea, but likewise the ruler of pagan provinces. He ingratiated himself with the Priesthood by the prodigality of his sacrificial offerings of oxen and other cattle. He softened the hearts of the orthodox with the democratic gesture of the Day of First Fruits, when he went up to the Temple carrying his basket on his own royal shoulder. The patriots and the zealots were impressed by his building of the Third Wall about the city, extended to include the district of Bethseda and the foot of the Mount of Olives. And all the while he squeezed out of the masses their labor and their money; he exploited their patriotism, though it was certain that as a high-placed Roman and friend of the Caesar it would never occur to him to encourage a rebellion against Rome.

After the death of Agrippa the hope of independence was deceived. Jerusalem and Judaea again became Roman provinces. Alexander Tiberius, the apostate Jewish idolater, who ruled after Agrippa, treated his Jewish brothers exactly as any other Roman official would have done. Filled with the over-zealousness characteristic of every apostate, fearing, too, the universal resentment of his apostasy, he made the burden heavier. The High Priesthood was in the hands of Ishmael of Phabias, and these were the darkest days of the Priesthood. The partisans of the candidates quarreled and fought in the streets, each side eager for the spoils of office.

When Paul came up to Jerusalem the believers were again in the condition of terror in which they had lived under Agrippa; for, bad as was the lot of the population as a whole, that of the believers was worse. These were, however, sure that any day now Yeshua the Messiah would return and the reign of the Kingdom of Heaven on earth would begin. They were no longer concerned with the winning of new souls to the congregation, whether Jews or gentiles. To what end? they asked. Thus they fell back upon a self-contained communal life, such as they had had in the beginning. Most of them gathered in the large court of bar Naba's sister, Miriam, outside the city. Certain of the disciples were there, under the leadership of Simon. But others of them wandered about the streets, hungry, half naked. Jacob ben Joseph was more than ever sunk in prayer, fasting, and mortification of the flesh: he was exerting himself to hasten the redemption. He had joined, or had attracted to himself, a large group of Pharisees, among them his brother Judah, and all of them spent whole days lying in prayer on the marble steps of the Temple court. Or else he would kneel hour long on the stones, like Jeremiah of old, praying that the Temple might not be destroyed and that God hasten the advent of the righteous redeemer, Yeshua. His knees and those of his companions had become as hard as a carapace with constant kneeling on the stones; and his legs were stiff, like the hind legs of a camel, moving only all of a piece.

Now Simon bar Jonah was dissatisfied with the inactivity of the believers and strove to continue the old work. He was at the height of his strength, and though he looked like an old man he was only in the middle fifties. For the eighteen years since the death of the Messiah, Simon had carried the tidings of the resurrection to every corner of the Holy Land, to its Jews and gentiles. He had been in Joppa, in Caesarea, in Samaria; and he was always ready to lighten the burden of the Jewish law in order to draw in converts from among the gentiles.

In spite of his apparently complete withdrawal from sublunar matters, and his complete absorption in the things of the spirit, Jacob ben Joseph kept a watchful eye and a firm hand on the affairs of the new congregation. He was jealous for its purity; he trembled lest the believers in the Messiah diminish even by one iota their devotion to traditional Judaism. He knew of the dangers and temptations in the path of the various scattered communities of the faithful; and whenever it came to his ears that in this or the other locality there had developed a certain laxity in regard to the orthodox observances, he at once sent his messengers with stern instructions to take the situation in hand. This man, who had divested himself of all worldliness, knew how to maintain a systematic discipline among the believers and to anticipate or correct any deviation from the way of Jewishness. Moreover, he possessed authority, and the communities trembled at the thought of his displeasure. Even "the rock," Simon bar Jonah, looked up to Jacob ben Joseph, as though he were not a man but the graven tablets of the new law—this in spite of his, Simon's, belief in his own power of communion with the Holy Ghost.

It was to Jacob ben Joseph that Paul brought the gentile, Titus, as his demonstration of the perfection which the non-Israelite could achieve without conversion to traditional Judaism; it was from Jacob ben Joseph that he wanted to obtain the admission of Titus into the covenant of the Messiah.

The believers, under the rigorous spiritual rule of Jacob ben Joseph, would not even converse with the gentile, let alone admit him to the table of the common meals. How could they possibly break bread at their sacred ceremonial with one who was uncircumcised? They looked askance at Titus, and they looked askance at Paul too, for having introduced this temptation and stumbling block into the congregation of Jerusalem.

All of Paul's obstinacy was now concentrated on this achievement —to obtain the admission of Titus into the congregation with the blessing of Jacob ben Joseph himself, to spin between Titus and Jacob the thread which would later be drawn as a circle about all the uncircumcised who craved admission into the congregation.

And Titus himself wandered about the hot streets of Jerusalem like a confused and bewildered soul. He heard the piping of music, but he did not dance; he heard the sound of lamentation, but he did not weep. Everything was strange to him, above all the vast flood of pilgrims in their multicolored robes, with their exotic gestures, their queer, outlandish customs. Assuredly he was impressed by the grandeur of the Temple. As a gentile, one of the uncircumcised, he could not penetrate further into the sanctuary than the Court of the Gentiles. But he saw the pious multitudes, he felt the awe and devotion which came upon them and watched the privileged ones mounting with ecstatic countenance the steps of the inner court, whither they brought their sacrifices; he saw the innumerable worshipers lying with their faces pressed to the marble floor of the court, the whole tremendous picture of faith and surrender. It was indescribably impressive; yet it left him cold. The profound religious earnestness of the Jews, their severe discipline, their strict observance of all the minutiae of the laws, the division of the men and women, reminded him, by sheer contrast, of the dissoluteness, the uncleanness, the orgiastic abandon, the drunkenness and the lust which reigned in the temples he had known in his childhood. He was filled with deepest reverence for the mystic and exalted divinity which ruled here. Yet he stood without. He had abandoned his own temples, his own gods; but he was not admitted to this Temple and this God. For what Paul had given him had not been a redeemer for the Jewish people and the Jewish faith, but a God whom he, Titus, accepted naturally, as he had once accepted the gods of his fathers. With all this that went on about him he had no connection: Paul had taught him, specifically, that he was free from the laws and disciplines and obligations of the Jews: Yeshua the Messiah had freed him from them! Immeasurable was Titus's gratitude to the new God who had been so gracious to him. He felt like a beloved child to the Divinity which had liberated him from the yoke which the others had to carry.

This then was Paul's unshakable desire: to bring together the heavy-laden Jacob ben Joseph and this spoiled child of the gentile world, Titus, to whom everything had been forgiven by the grace of faith. It was to perform this miracle that he had come to Jerusalem with Titus.

Now Paul knew well that in Simon bar Jonah he would find a sympathetic listener to his plea, even though the latter stood under the influence of Jacob ben Joseph. Simon bar Jonah lived with his wife in the house of Miriam, at a considerable remove from the place where Jacob ben Joseph had gathered his Pharisees about him. It was to Simon bar Jonah that Paul first presented his Titus, this model of the redemption of the uncircumcised.

Simon bar Jonah sat in the garden of Miriam the widow and listened with the liveliest emotions to the account given him by Paul and bar Naba of their memorable journey through the cities of Galatia. In particular, Paul described in minutest detail the rebirth which was experienced by the uncircumcised gentiles when they entered into the faith of the Messiah. Their baptism in the name of Yeshua performed miracles in their lives even as did the Jewish law in the lives of the Jews: the water of the baptism, he said, passed into them, became blood of their blood, changing their natures and inspiring them with new principles of action. And Paul placed at Simon's feet the bags of money which the baptized gentiles had sent to the holy ones and the poor of Jerusalem. Yes, the gentiles had been taught by baptism to share their crust with the Jews of Jerusalem. Was not this a miracle performed by heaven? Was it not the desire of the lord Messiah that the gentiles should come to him?

"Take away the stones which the law has put before the feet of the gentiles, and then the whole world will stream to the Mount of Zion: there will arise our houses of prayer in all the cities, yes, in the remotest and most forlorn villages. Wherever God has planted the seed of man, there the Name of God and that of the Messiah of Jacob shall be uttered. Let us," said Paul, "divide our ministry; thou, Simon bar Jonah, the first of the disciples, to whom the lord himself entrusted the care of the congregation, shalt bring the tidings of the Messiah to the House of Israel. And I shall bring those tidings to the gentiles. And the Messiah will bring together in one bond Jew and Greek; he will bind them and lay them at the feet of God, and the Kingdom of Heaven will begin on earth."

Simon bar Jonah listened attentively, his heart flooding with the joy of the great expectation. Yet, in the midst of his joy there was the fear which haunted Jacob ben Joseph, the fear that the vast masses of gentiles, streaming into the congregation of the Messiah, and not taking

331

upon themselves the yoke of Jewishness, would in the end overwhelm the Jews themselves with the power of their heathen spirit: the gentiles would not become Jews, but the Jews would become gentiles. But when he uttered these fears, Paul hastened to reassure him.

"Wouldst thou see the miracle which is wrought in the gentile by faith in the Messiah? I have brought with me, hither to Jerusalem, a gentile uncircumcised in the flesh—and yet he is, in the spirit, a child of Abraham. Wouldst thou see him? Wouldst thou put him to the test, Simon bar Jonah?"

"Yes, I would see him. Bring him to me. I would see the miracle which God works in the gentiles through the faith of the Messiah."

Then Paul went out and secretly brought Titus and presented him to Simon bar Jonah, "the rock."

Titus knew well before whom he stood. This was the first and oldest of the disciples! This was he to whom it had been granted to minister to the Messiah in his lifetime. Titus knew that he was in the presence of him to whom the Messiah himself, none other, had entrusted the leadership of the congregation: Simon bar Jonah, the rock! Titus would have fallen at Simon's feet, he would have kissed the hands which had touched the sacred fire which had been the Messiah's body. But he did not dare. For he was a gentile! He stood like one petrified in the presence of the holy man. And Simon looked at the tall, beautiful young man and into the simple, crystalline blue eyes, which dared not respond to his look but were turned downward in modesty and awe. Titus scarcely dared to breathe, and when he drew breath a trembling passed through his body. The knees of the powerful youth shook; in another instant he would prostrate himself! And this, indeed, was what happened. Titus knelt down before the first of the disciples and buried his face in bar Jonah's robe, whispering:

"My lord! My lord!"

"Rise, my son," said Simon. He spoke Aramaic, which Paul translated into Greek. "Rise! We do not kneel before those of flesh and blood! We kneel but to the one living God of Israel. Neither do we call any man 'lord'—save the holy one in Israel, the Messiah, Yeshua the Nazarene." And Simon stooped and placed his hands on the shoulders of the kneeling youth.

Titus obeyed and rose to his feet.

"Tell me, my son," asked Simon bar Jonah. "What brought thee to the God of Israel? And what brought thee into the congregation of the believers in His Messiah?"

"It was my hunger for the truth, and for the meaning of our existence; and I found these in the one living God and Creator; it was my longing to be redeemed from my sins—those which I committed in my ignorance—and to enter into the grace of faith, which promises me a portion of the help which is Israel's through the Messiah, Yeshua the Nazarene, as my teacher and guide, Paul, has taught me."

Simon bar Jonah pondered the answer long. Assuredly this was a declaration of faith in the God of Israel. But he probed deeper.

"And to what art thou obligated by this faith in the one living God of Israel and thy acceptance into the congregation of the Messiah?"

"I am obligated to live my life out in the grace of the faith; to accept as my ever-present model the life of our lord, Yeshua the Messiah, as he was when he lived on earth; to love others as myself, to love those that hate me, to bless those that curse me, to drive all evil thoughts from my heart, to remember that the lord died for me and that he is in me, as I am in him, therefore to do in all things as he would do were he in my place—even as my teacher and guide, Paul, has taught me."

"And dost thou not know, my son, that in thy acknowledgment of the one living God of Israel, and thy belief in the Messiah, thou art a son of Abraham—and with the children of Abraham it is the law that they shall carry upon their bodies the sign of the covenant between Abraham and God?"

"My teacher and guide, Paul, taught me that we, the gentiles, are freed from the yoke of the law and that we are under the sign of the grace of faith, that by our faith alone we become children of Abraham."

"But suppose thy teachers and guides shall tell thee that in order to become truly a child of Abraham thou must have the sign of the covenant on thy body—what then, my son?" asked Simon bar Jonah.

Titus was silent for a space, and the blood withdrew from his features. Paul too became pale. Then Titus recovered his self-assurance and answered in a firm voice:

"Did not the lord Yeshua the Messiah die for me? Did he not suffer for me? Is he not in me and am I not in him? And though I live in my flesh and blood, in my spirit I live in him, therefore my flesh and my blood and my limbs are his. And if my teachers and guides in the faith should tell me that I must let my body be burned in the fire for the

333

sake of the lord Messiah, I would assuredly do it. The more then, if they tell me that I must bear the sign of the covenant on my flesh, in order to be truly in the grace of the faith, would I do so. Do with me what seems best in your eyes."

"Uncircumcised as thou art, thou art nevertheless a faithful son of our father Abraham. God grant that such as thou multiply among the gentiles," answered Simon bar Jonah. He kissed the young man on both cheeks with the kiss of peace, and he sat down at the common table with the uncircumcised convert.

Simon brought the full report of his conversation with Titus before Reb Jacob ben Joseph. Reb Jacob listened in silence and became thoughtful. Of late there had been an increasing uneasiness in his heart because of the great influx of gentiles into the ranks of the believers. On the one hand he could not but rejoice in the grace which God bestowed on the gentiles; on the other hand he trembled lest Israel should be carried away and lost in the tide of the gentiles.

It was high time, he reflected, to come to a definite decision on this question. It was not alone the traveling apostles, returning from successful journeys, who were posing the question; wherever congregations were founded, springing up of themselves, the problem arose, and inquiries were addressed to Jerusalem as to what should be done in regard to the uncircumcised converts. The deaf could hear the knocking of the gentiles at the door of the Temple, their supplication to be admitted to the sanctuary of the Messiah. It was impossible to keep the doors closed, for the multitude of gentile suppliants grew from day to day, and the pressure of their need was not to be withstood.

Simon bar Jonah, the oldest of the disciples and the formal head of the congregation of Jerusalem, Reb Jacob ben Joseph, the spiritual leader, and Jochanan of the Zebedees, the three pillars of the new faith, called together the Sanhedrin of the congregation in the old dwelling place in the David wall. In the first rank sat those disciples to whom it had been granted to serve their Rabbi when he was on earth and to whom their Rabbi had shown himself after his death: but not all the twelve were present. Some were missing, and their places had not been filled by others. Jochanan of the Zebedees had aged greatly since his brother's death; he had fallen into a mood of mysticism, was continuously seeing visions and speaking in tongues. His gestures and his general deportment had lost the crude strength and primitiveness which had characterized him during the life of his Rabbi. He was self-absorbed, meditative, deliberate in his motions. But it was also true that all of the disciples had aged beyond their years. Perhaps this was the result of their many fasts and self-mortifications, and perhaps it had to do with their longing for a death which should make them eternal witnesses of the faith, as had been the case with Reb Istephan and with Reb Jacob.

There were also present at the special assembly many new faces. There were old men with white beards, long earlocks, and large fringed garments thrown over their sackcloth garb. These were, for the most part, Pharisees who had joined the congregation. They were the counselors, interpreters, and scribes of the congregation. All of them sat on low stools, or else on the earth, at the feet of the first disciples. There were also present men with beards still black. Particularly prominent was the swarthy, clear-cut face of a young man who put the beholders strongly in mind of Reb Jacob ben Joseph. He was, in fact, the brother of Reb Jacob—Reb Judah, of the holy seed of the Messiah. A dark, lustrous beard framed his oval face, in the midst of which twinkled two lively, coal-black eyes. Though he was a comparatively young man, he was not seated in a lower rank than the older sages, but above them. His rank, as a member of the holy family, was next to that of his brother; and he permitted himself to speak more often than the older disciples.

Simon bar Jonah was the official head of the community; but the session of the Sanhedrin was conducted by Jacob ben Joseph.

The session opened with the repetition of the prayer which had been taught them by their Messiah, and this was followed by a brief prayer uttered by Jacob ben Joseph, who implored the intercession of the Holy Ghost, that it might rest with the assembled during their deliberations.

First on the agenda was the report of the apostles. But here, in this place, it was bar Naba who did the speaking, and not Paul; for bar Naba alone had gone forth with the authority of the holy congregation.

Bar Naba rehearsed the record of their travels through the cities of the gentiles. He pointed out that to whatever place they had come they had gone first, according to the original instruction of the Messiah, to the House of Israel. They had gone to the synagogues, and in Sabbath sermons they had delivered the message of the redemption, had cited the books of the Prophets and Psalms in evidence. Many Jews had converted and had accepted in their fullness the tenets of the new

335

faith. Others had refused. Therefore dissensions, leading sometimes to physical clashes, had arisen in the communities. But the apostles had borne everything. Bar Naba also told of the wonders and signs which it had been vouchsafed Paul to perform with the power of the word. Himself he placed in the background of the narrative, giving all credit to the powerful gift of speech of his companion. In still greater detail he recited the story of the mission to the gentiles: he would have the assembly understand beyond all doubt that God desired to bring the gentiles into the ranks of the faithful: the compassion of God had been awakened toward the gentiles, and He had prepared their hearts for salvation. They were beating with their foreheads on the thresholds of the synagogues, imploring admission. And as an instance of the power of conversion in the lives of the gentiles, bar Naba continued, they— Paul and he—had brought with them to Jerusalem an uncircumcised convert, with whom Simon bar Jonah had already had speech. Further, there were the gifts which the converted gentiles had sent with the apostles to the holy ones in Jerusalem, proving beyond all doubt that the virtue of compassion, the first of the attributes of Father Abraham, had been implanted in the gentiles.

The assembly listened attentively to the long report. Many of the faces showed open joy at the tidings, and tears of gratitude flowed down their cheeks. But there were also faces which darkened perceptibly during the course of the recital and some which even began to burn with suppressed indignation. Voices were raised, asking for permission to speak. The first utterance following bar Naba's report was addressed sharply against the admission of the uncircumcised.

"He who cannot summon up enough courage to submit to circumcision for the sake of the God of Israel, is not worthy of admission into the congregation of the Messiah. He is a coward who cannot fight the battle of the Lord. For the Messiah is the battle of the Lord. And only those shall be admitted to the ranks who have the strength to give their blood to the covenant: even as it is written: 'And in thy blood shalt thou live!'"

A few voices called out in protest. Figures rose dimly in the shadows which filled the corners of the room, and pearly starlight fell upon the obscure shapes, through the openings in the walls. A flood of excitement and exaltation passed invisibly but tangibly across the assembly.

One voice, louder and more insistent than the others, was raised—in Greek—to defend the uncircumcised converts.

"God created all men and all peoples according to their separate natures, and faith must follow the nature of the man and of the people: only then can faith be solid and enduring." The voice was that of Silo, a leader of the Greek-Jewish congregation, a man who knew well the ways of the gentiles.

And then a second of the Greek-speaking Jews, one bar Saba, came to the defense of the uncircumcised converts.

It was a custom from of old in the Jewish Sanhedrins that the younger members of the assembly should take the floor first: the purpose of this custom was to give the young members freedom of utterance and not to subject them to the influence of the sages of authority before their chance came to speak. However, before submitting the question to general discussion, the leader of that evening asked the second of the apostles whether he had anything to add to the report of his companion.

Paul was holding down the passions surging in him. He was capable of such discipline when the occasion demanded it. A flood of fury, of resentment and bitterness was at work in him, set loose by what he had heard this evening. He knew that on the results of this session depended the ultimate issue of "the gentiles." It was his intention, therefore, to keep himself in check and to reinforce bar Naba's recital with his own, concerning the miracle wrought by the faith among the gentiles. And yet, though he had planned to speak first regarding the gentiles, he began instead to speak of the law.

"What law is strong enough," he began, "to throw and maintain an iron circle about the tides of our desires, lusts, and passions? The serpents of sin are sure to find a crack in the wall, wide enough to afford them entrance, as long as they feel that a welcome awaits them within. What law is so wide, so all-embracing, that the shadows of its wings cover every little act, if the heart of man itself is a swamp in which unclean things breed? How many messengers will not the chiefs of the courts of Jerusalem have to send forth to the cities of the gentiles, to keep watch and ward over all the transgressions and to report that in every place all the fences which the Rabbis have drawn about our lives still stand, unpierced? And let this be asked: do we ourselves, who stand under the sign of the law, comply with the law? Who of us would be accounted blameless before the law? And what other law is capable of tearing out by its roots the nature of the gentiles, or of melting them and pouring them into the common mold of the children of Abraham, if not the law of the one living God, and His holy Messiah, whom He sent to us? Like a fiery broom that faith has passed across the hearts of the gentiles. It has taken the granite of the hearts of the gentiles, crushed it, and made it as soft as a sponge, to suck up the sorrows and torments of humanity and the balm of compassion which falls from the heights of heaven. I brought to them a faith in the one living God Whom they have never beheld, neither have they heard His voice nor received the report of His power; I brought to them the God of a people which is despised among the nations; I brought to them faith in a Messiah who suffered, who was scourged, tortured, crucified: and they, the gentiles, have cast away, for this God, this Messiah, their gods of power, of perfection and beauty and fruitfulness. And now they stand before us, they and Israel, prepared to let their bodies be consumed by fire for the God of Israel and the holy Messiah. Who awakened in the hearts of the gentiles this thirst for salvation, if not the God of Israel Himself? Who troubled them, and made them unhappy, in the midst of their sleep of drunkenness, so that they began to stretch out their hands for salvation, and to find it in the crucified Messiah of Israel? Was it not He who sent this desire into their spirit? And this being so, these blossoms being planted in the hearts of the gentiles, would you uproot them? Let the Messiah perform his wonders, let him gather up the peoples of the world as the reaper gathers up the sheaves; and all the nations will bow the knee to the Holy One of Israel, to the righteous Redeemer. Then all men will be brothers, held in a common bond of faith; the glory of God shall be poured out upon the whole world, and all will perceive that Israel was right; the world shall see the fulfillment of the words of the Prophet: 'The lowland shall be lifted up and the mountain shall be brought low; the crooked shall be straightened out and the rough places made smooth. And the glory of God shall be unveiled and all flesh shall behold it, for the mouth of the Lord has spoken.' "

This speech of Paul's, more passionate than he had intended it to be, was not without effect, as might be seen from the faces of the listeners. Even the faces of the oldest disciples, which had remained somber during the recital by bar Naba, now lightened somewhat. But the protest was correspondingly vigorous from the other side. Among those who were grouped about Reb Jacob ben Joseph there was a sharp unrest, a muttering and whispering, portents of an approaching storm. They chose as their spokesman the young brother of Reb Jacob, Reb Judah. He, with arms uplifted like swords, thrust his way through to the front and began to speak:

"With the permission of my Rabbis and guides, I will ask the apostle who has just reported on the wonders which God has wrought among the gentiles through the righteous Redeemer, this question: What shall henceforth be the guide of the gentiles if not the law which has been entrusted into our hands? Who is strong enough and great enough to place the responsibility for all human conduct on the frail and delicate framework of faith? What is faith without deeds? Love of God? Surely love of God is a most high attribute—for him that can accomplish it! We are but human, with good and wicked impulses. About us is the chaos and confusion of the world; and in this chaos and confusion God has planted the little island which is Israel; and he has buttressed this island with laws and commandments. Take away these laws and commandments and we are carried away by the chaos and confusion of the world. The laws and commandments are our guides: without them we wander eternally in the desert; without them there is no salvation."

"True! True!" cried the men grouped about him. But their cries of approval provoked a counter-demonstration among those opposed to them, and for a moment it seemed as though the assembly would lapse into utter disorder. But suddenly there was silence. Even the young Reb Judah, who had been speaking vehemently, unfolding his arguments against the admission of the uncircumcised, broke off. For now it was the oldest of the disciples, the lion of the congregation, who had risen to his feet. The crowded room seemed as it were to fall back from him; and for a time the passions unloosed by the question before the assembly were again in leash. With one hand Simon made a gesture of conciliation toward the Pharisees, drawn together about Reb Judah, the brother of Reb Jacob; with the other he pacified the group of representatives of the Greek-speaking communities, gathered about bar Saba, Silo, and the apostles. His mild look circled the divided throng, and then, in a simple voice, and in a simple manner, he began to speak:

339

"Men and brothers! You know that the lord long ago made his choice of me, that the gentiles might hear from my lips the tidings of the redemption. God knows the heart of man; and God pointed to the gentiles and decreed that the Holy Ghost shall rest upon them even as it does on us. He made no division in this respect between them and us, and He purified their hearts through faith. And now, why do you try God? Why would you put a yoke on the neck of the apostles to the gentiles, such as our forefathers and we ourselves have not been able to carry? We believe with perfect faith that by the grace of the lord Yeshua the Messiah they will be saved even as we are saved."

The silence in the room had been dense and palpable. Faces were turned dumbly and in fear upon each other. This was Khaifa who had spoken! He had said that which had been in the hearts of many of the believers for months and years, and they had not dared to utter it. But those who were on the side of the Pharisees were thunderstruck: *this* was the utterance of the man who, of all men, had been nearest to the Messiah and to whom the Messiah had transferred the responsibility for the welfare of the congregation!

Only Reb Jacob had been silent and motionless throughout the whole passionate debate. He had listened, but he had neither spoken nor given any evidence of his feelings. But his mind had been working fiercely. He too was preoccupied with this fateful question: what was to be done to make it easier for the gentiles to enter the congregation of believers? He too had been moved by the wonder of the many conversions; and he too had been seeking a method which would grant them admission without too many barriers, and yet leave them close-knit to the Jewish congregation. He had repeated to himself, time and again, the old saying of the sages: "He that desires to enter heaven shall be helped by heaven." Likewise he had learned that, according to the sages, it sufficed for gentiles to observe only the primal commandments of the sons of Noah: the recognition of the one living God, the rejection of idol worship, the abstention from whoredom and from eating the flesh of a living animal or of an animal which had been strangled. Now these commandments the uncircumcised gentiles observed when they entered the faith of the Messiah. If that was so, they were entitled to a portion in the Kingdom of Heaven. Why, then, should they be thrust back? As to the other commandments, faith would bring about their observance. The gentiles would come to the synagogues of the Jews, they would sit with them at the common ceremonial meals—and thus they would be drawn into the Jewish faith, as had happened in Jerusalem. Having weighed these considerations, Reb Jacob began to speak:

"Men and brothers, hear me! The Prophet has said: 'Then it will come to pass that I will return and I will rebuild the tabernacle of Jacob, which has been cast down, and I will rebuild the ruins thereof, and the remnant of mankind shall seek the Lord among all the peoples where My Name shall be spoken; thus speaks the Lord.' Therefore it is my opinion that we shall not trouble the hearts of the gentiles who have turned to God, but we shall write them that they shall refrain from the abomination of idolatry, from fornication, from blood, and from the eating of strangled animals: for from of old Moses has his people in every city, who preach his law, and it is read there in the synagogues every Sabbath."

Now that the two pillars of the congregation, Khaifa and Jacob ben Joseph, had delivered themselves of their views, the controversy was at an end.

It was resolved by the assembly to reconfirm bar Naba and Paul in their apostleships and to send with them bar Saba and Silo, who should carry letters with them from the oldest of the disciples to "the brothers of the gentiles" in Antioch of Syria and in Cilicia, bearing greetings, as well as the record of the resolution: "Whereas it has come to us that certain of our brethren have gone out among you and have troubled you with their speech, and have misled you with their utterances, namely, that you must be circumcised in the flesh and observe the law of Moses, and whereas we have not authorized such utterances, therefore be it known to you that, having sat in deliberation on this question, we have resolved to send to you our beloved Paul and bar Naba, together with certain other of our men."

At the first ceremonial meal following the session, Titus the uncircumcised gentile sat with all the others. True, Reb Judah ben Joseph chose a place somewhat removed from him and was afraid to touch him. But Simon bar Jonah and Reb Jacob ben Joseph gave him a special welcome. And it was granted to Paul to see his dream come true: Reb Jacob ben Joseph and the gentile Titus sat together, and broke bread together, and repeated in union the prayer of the lord.

This was the happiest day in Paul's life.

As for Titus, since he was admitted to the common meal, and since the city of Jerusalem had taken him in as a brother, it was as if a new soul had been breathed into him. There still remained a certain strangeness between him and the Jews; he was still afraid of them, and he was still overawed by the mystic power of this people, to which he was bound now forever, in destiny, in blood, and in faith. But he saw the strangeness with other eyes. They were his brothers: not only the holy ones, the disciples, and the "Messianists," but all the people, bound as it was to the Creator of the world—the people which had taken upon itself the yoke of the law, which had been blessed with the blessings of God and cursed with the curses of the nations. This was the people which had been chosen for the bringing forth, from its body, of the Messiah, and in Titus's eyes it was uplifted, acquiring an other-worldly greatness, part of the Kingdom of Heaven. And though their customs were strange, and he was, as it were, isolated in the midst of them, he looked upon the people, and upon the houses, and even upon the stones, with the eyes of faith, and his heart was moved by ineffable emotions. Through these streets the Messiah had walked; these were the stones his feet had touched. No ordinary streets and stones, these, but streets paved with stones fallen from heaven. Jerusalem itself was built up of the fragments of the clouds of heaven, and its covering was a celestial silver dust. Strange indeed were the Rabbis to him, with their hosts of pupils assembled about them in the Temple courts; but he saw them with loving eyes; out of their midst the Messiah had come; among them he had lived; he had studied in their study houses; he had preached and performed his wonders among them; he had looked like them; he had been garbed like them. And he, Titus, was now with them in a bond which would never be broken. He had exchanged his forefathers for theirs, his future for theirs. A stranger among them, he was already part of them, flesh of their flesh.

Chapter Fourteen

"IN THY BLOOD SHALT THOU LIVE"

ON the Sabbath the Messianists, or Christians, of Antioch assembled in the synagogue on the Singan street, among the warehouses and shops on the other side of the river. After the reading of the law, the two messengers from Jerusalem, Judah bar Saba and Silo, were presented to the congregation, and they read forth the letters entrusted to them by the holy ones of Jerusalem.

That day there was indescribable joy among the brother-gentiles in the faith. For now, in the end, they had been accepted as equal children of Abraham, and yet they did not have to pay the penalties which the Jews paid for it. There was the same joy in the heart of Paul, for he had thrown down the walls which divided Jew and gentile and the Messiah: now there was but one congregation in God and in the Messiah.

And it was high time for him to set forth on his apostleship. He therefore proposed to bar Naba that they first visit once more the cities where they had founded congregations and thereafter consider whither they were to go.

*   *   *

Bar Naba was of a mind to take along with him his nephew, Jochanan-Marcus, but Paul was unalterably opposed. This was in no way an act of revenge on Paul's part because of Jochanan's withdrawal from the journey to Pamphilia; nor was it the feeling that he could not be accompanied by one who had once shown himself a deserter. There was a deeper reason; and even the loss of the companionship of his dearest friend could not influence Paul. Paul had been wearied by Jerusalem. He did not want to have guardians and watchmen with him on his journey. He needed only such as would help him without afterthought or hesitation, who would see eye to eye with him, and whose sole desire would be, like his, the winning of as many souls as possible into the faith, such as would "give up everything for the Torah"—and he used this phrase because to him the Messiah was the Torah, being

343

the equivalent of all of it. One who did not feel as he did on this point would not serve for the purpose. It did not matter how intimate was the bond between his soul and that of bar Naba, and how deeply bar Naba was lodged in his heart. Was he, after all, living for himself? To himself Paul was dead. He lived only in the spirit and for the Messiah. For the cause of the Messiah he did whatever was needed—and he did no other thing besides. Therefore, when bar Naba, objecting at first to Paul's refusal to take Jochanan with them, hinted that without Jochanan he too would not set out on the journey, Paul answered:

"Joseph, my brother, we are both servants of the lord. Whithersoever the lord sends us, there we shall go, together, or separately. The ways of the lord have brought us together; and now the ways of the lord will part us. But they will surely bring us together again, for all the ways of God lead to God."

Thereupon the two friends fell on each other's necks, and after a long embrace they set out on their separate paths.

Instead of bar Naba, then, Paul had with him one of the messengers from Jerusalem, Silo. And Silo was welcome, for was he not one of the men who at the session in Jerusalem had defended the admission of the uncircumcised converts? And had he not been sent in person to advise the gentiles of the resolution passed by the assembly, to the effect that they were free of the law of Moses? Silo had been a participant in the debate, a witness of the resolution, and a messenger. Moreover, he carried with him the letters of the holy ones of Jerusalem.

Paul left the young man Titus behind him in Antioch, to keep watch over the affairs of the congregation and to report to him on its progress. He also advised Titus that on occasion he would send him out on special missions. Silo was his only companion, and they left the city of Antioch with a small bundle of provisions; for even though the city was a great one, and wealthy, Paul still clung to his principle of making himself no burden to any of the believers. In the places which he would visit he could always find work at his trade.

Paul and Silo took ship to Tarshish, Paul's birthplace. Without stopping there, they set out on foot across the landscape, so familiar to Paul, of the Taurus mountains. In his boyhood Paul had been a skillful mountain climber, and it was he who now helped his younger companion on the ascent.

So they advanced, footstep by footstep, across the crags and ra-

344

vines, as Saul had once advanced with bar Naba: through dangerous passes under overhanging ledges of ice and snow, into the regions where the last gaunt cedars battled with the cold and wind. Then, after a time, even these hardy growths ceased, and all they beheld was the gloomy, pitiless fronts of the rocks. All the storms that had ever passed across the Taurus heights were petrified in those crags. But were not these grim masses of granite stations and guides, as well as obstacles, on the path of their missions? The mightier they grew, the more forbidding, the more strongly they drew the messengers on. Once again Paul passed the nights in the dangerous hollows of the wadis. At last they reached the dangerous ledge which was known by the name of "the Cilician Gates." On either side the slopes fell away to dizzying depths; one false step and the traveler was flung down upon the countless spears of the upthrust needle rocks. Eternal winds raged about this narrow passage. They bit and clawed at the bodies of the two messengers, tugged at their clothes, and thrust them toward the dangerous edge. With infinite care and obstinacy Paul and Silo advanced, crawling most of the way. And now the way led downward into the frozen chaos of stone. They came finally upon green spaces, and their feet trod in little swamps of melted snow. When night fell they took shelter in an old, dilapidated camel stall—there were many such on the road which descended to the flatlands of Iconium. They passed the night on rotting sackcloth, among camels and donkeys and their drivers, and their bodies were eaten by vermin. Weeks passed without their having tasted a warm meal or cooked food. Their fare consisted of dried cakes, and as these began to give out they plucked edible leaves and herbs from the roadside. They showed the endurance of camels in sustaining their bodies from one place to the next. As they came down from the higher regions, they were plagued by swarms of insects and by scorpions, which became ever more numerous as the vegetation increased. Thick clouds of winged insects darkened the air, drifting out of the swamps. Their blood was poisoned, and their bodies broke out in boils. Paul's hands became like those of a leper, and from a hundred places the blood and pus oozed forth. His good eye was covered by a heavy blister, so that he was blinded, and it was in this condition that he arrived, led by Silo, on the level stretch before the city of Iconium.

Paul's heart was heavy with foreboding when he entered the familiar city. He made inquiry after the house which had sheltered him

345

before. This was the second time that he was returning to Iconium sick and broken in body, and on top of it he was practically blind. Knowing the spirit of the gentiles and their regard for the perfection of the body, he dreaded the effect which would be produced on them if they saw him in his present condition. But to his delight and astonishment, he found waiting for him, despite his sickness and his shocking appearance, a welcome full of love and tenderness. It was as though they had received a visit from an angel. It was their leader who had returned to them, he who had brought them the tidings of salvation and had given them a share in it. They lifted up Paul and put him to bed; the same loving feminine hands as had tended him before tended him now. They smeared his body with healing oils, and if looks of tenderness and affection could have healed him, he would have risen from his bed immediately. In the evening the believers assembled in the house; they crowded into Paul's room and about his bed, and they comforted him with the good news that the numbers of the faithful were, God be thanked, growing constantly: there were daily additions of converts, both from among the gentiles and the Jews. The old disputes among the Jews had been forgotten. That had happened which usually happens in a community: when a dispute is first introduced and the issue is in doubt, the quarrels grow fiercer from day to day: but when the group responsible for introducing the issue becomes the stronger, the others hasten to establish peace with it. The Jews in the synagogue had become accustomed to the gentiles. True, there were still occasional differences, but these no longer had the character of the early hostilities, for they were intramural, inasmuch as all the disputants belonged to the congregation of Israel.

The apostle, temporarily blinded, lay on his bed surrounded by the good people of Iconium. He felt the warmth of their affection enfolding him. He felt them sharing his physical pain with him, and he was moved by the endless flow of their gifts and attentions. And it was indeed as though their loving spirit was more potent to heal him than their medicaments, for he felt the hardened, burning flesh growing softer and the poisons draining out of him. His heart swelled with gratitude, and it was only the blisters on his eyes which held back the tears welling up to them. Who had ever so comforted him before in his life? What hand had touched him with as much love as the hands of these gentiles? Oh, if he could but bring the men of Jerusalem hither to Iconium and show

346

them the miracle of faith! The tears beat against the bars drawn over his eyes, as once they had beaten against his blindness when he lay in Damascus. And suddenly he beheld, with the eyes of memory, all the faces grouped about him.

They questioned him eagerly concerning the time that had passed since his last visit. What had become of the second apostle, the beloved bar Naba—he of the majestic figure and great black beard and black, sparkling eyes?

"Where is he," they asked, "who was like Jupiter in his bearing, and why did he not return with thee?"

"In my Father's house, so the Messiah taught us, there are many mansions," answered Paul. "And they who are in the Messiah are always united."

Two weeks had to pass before Paul recovered his strength and could resume the journey. But he more than recovered his strength; the loving reception had been like a rebirth for him. From Iconium he traveled to Derbe, and there again he encountered familiar faces. God be thanked, there too the congregation was growing in numbers. The opposition to the gentiles on the part of the Jewish congregation had died down, and the community of the faithful was at peace.

Wherever Paul came he heard references to the young man of Lystra, Timotheus. The faithful of Iconium and Derbe told him how Timotheus had visited them and had preached in their synagogues on Sabbath days; he had taught them the foundations of the faith, and the proofs and prophecies contained in Holy Writ. The young man was learned in the Hebrew lore, and by the power of his tongue and the faith in his heart he convinced many of the truth of the Messiah's tidings. Moreover, he was modest, and therefore beloved by all. Paul remembered the young man—no, the lad, as he had last seen him. How could he forget that likeness of an angel, which had laid healing hands on the wounds torn in his flesh by the stones? How could he forget the boyish ministrant, who had stolen out to him from the city, and found him where he lay, bathed in his blood, or the kindness of his mother Eunice? How gently and graciously she had received him into her house! Nor had he forgotten Timotheus's grandmother, an old, old Jewess, Lois by name, who sat, with trembling lips, her big-veined hands folded in her lap, listening intently to the words of the messenger. How happy she had been when Paul had received her grandson into the

347

congregation of believers! His heart yearned toward those people, and he hastened from Iconium to Lystra, to see the congregation he had founded there and the young man whose name was on everyone's lips.

* * *

Old grandmother Lois lay sick in bed, and her daughter tended her. Hearing of the coming of Paul, the grandmother took on new strength, rose from her bed, put on her Sabbath robes, and went forth to meet him. A frail, trembling old thing, she pressed her toothless mouth to the apostle's shoulder. It had been granted her to see him once again before God called her away. To her the aspect of Paul was like that of the High Priest of Jerusalem, whom she remembered from the one visit to the Holy City in her far-off childhood, when she had accompanied the family on a pilgrimage. Her heart was full of gratitude to the apostle for the grace he had wrought with her grandson. She had but one wish now—and that was to see her grandson accepted into the covenant of Abraham, like all other Jews; then she could close her eyes in peace, secure in the faith of her fathers.

"He is a *Jewish* child, after all," she murmured, indistinctly. Her furrowed, fleshless hands shook as she held on supplicatingly to the robe of the apostle, as though it were a rope thrown to her in the sea. "He is a *Jewish* child. He always wanted to know about Jewish things. When he was still almost a baby, he used to accompany the women to the Sabbath services. He stood with open mouth listening to the words of the Rabbis, when they preached the law of Moses."

"Yes, it is true," added the mother proudly. "My husband took him to the temple of Jupiter, but the child did not find it to his liking; his heart revolted even then against idol worship. Even then he preferred the divine prayers in the Jewish house of worship to the sacrifices of Jupiter. When he grew into boyhood, he went with the other lads to the gymnasium and prepared himself with them in the baths and rubbing rooms for the competitions; but within him there was a struggle between the god Jupiter and the God of Israel. Oh, I felt it! During the days he was like the other lads; he learned what they learned, he took part in their games. The priest of Jupiter was fond of him and would have made him a priest too. But in the evenings he would sit down near me and near his grandmother, and ask us to tell him about the God of the Jews, about Jerusalem and the Messiah. And we told him whatever we knew. My mother told him what she remembered of the Holy City

348

—I myself have never been there—and what she had been taught of the Jewish faith. The lad began to visit the synagogue by himself then, and my husband permitted it. In the end I moved my husband, too, to accompany us, to hear the words of the Prophets being read there in the Greek tongue. Before his death my husband became one of the pious gentiles and would not miss a Sabbath service: God be thanked for that. But my boy was still divided in soul. Sometimes he was drawn to the laughter and merry games and dances which were part of the service of Jupiter—he would not relinquish his youth. And sometimes he was drawn more strongly by the words of the Prophets and the stories of the Patriarchs, which he heard in the synagogue. Often I watched him sitting apart in the evenings, his spirit sad and confused, not knowing to which of the worlds he rightly belonged. And it was thus until you came, like an angel of the Lord, and brought him with your own lips the tidings of the Messiah. Since he heard you speak in the synagogue, indeed since he set eyes on you, but above all since you brought him into the faith, he has been heart-whole. Yes, he has preached in the synagogues, here and in neighboring cities, and he has studied the sacred Books, so that he might cite the evidence in them. Many listen to him; but there are others who say that he is a stranger, one of the uncircumcised, and is not of the congregation of Israel. And how comes one of the uncircumcised, they ask, to be talking to us of the Messiah?"

Paul looked steadfastly at the young man who stood before him with trembling heart and lowered eyes. The face of Timotheus was wholly that of a gentile. At first glance there was not in it a single softening touch, a single suggestion of weakness: a strong, bronze-like face, with clear, powerful lines. So it was with his body too, perfect and powerful. The shoulders were massive, the breast an arch of muscles, the hips strong, and the head rested on a straight, proud neck. It was as though a master sculptor of the old times had created the form, and life had been breathed into it. Every detail was perfect; the nose was straight, the lips were delicately outlined, and above his eyes were the two perfect arches of his brows. One would have said that never a shadow of reflection or care had passed across this brow, from which the locks were drawn back to fall on the shoulders. Only the eyes belied the pagan radiance; for they shone with a divine awe, with inquiry and devotion: the eyes were Jewish. They were eyes filled with supplication, eyes which flashed into the heart of the beholder and could never be forgotten. One more sign of the Jew was on him : the little tender beard, just beginning to sprout, which he wore like every other Jew. This alone, in his outer aspect, brought to mind the spirit of his mother's people. And as it was in his outward appearance, so within him there had been the contradiction between his two heritages. The heart that had once been proud, hard, self-confident, had yielded to the humility of the faith. In the place of that perfection and harmony which are born of ignorance, there was within him the perfection and security of knowledge. Knowledge of the faith had begun to inscribe its record on the empty page of his heart. So, if one looked more closely, one caught also the first external manifestation, a warmth which was inscribing itself in the flesh and adding a touch of tenderness and pain to the iron features ; and as time would pass, the seal of his faith would stand more strongly upon the flesh of his original paganism.

The apostle looked long at Timotheus. He saw him standing humbly before him, he heard the beating of his heart. And Paul's own heart was moved. He reflected that this young man, Timotheus, unlike his first gentile disciple, Titus, had been brought to him not by the search for the truth, but by the heritage of his forefathers, the heritage in the blood. His pagan nature had been thwarted by the Jewish strain; the lad was an authentic plant of the garden of Israel. His mother's milk had poured into his veins an ineluctable love for the God of the Jews. And Paul heard an inner voice: "Bethink thee! God has sent thee a helper, a staff for thy latter years!"

Paul drew the lad aside and signaled to him to enter the other room. Then he locked the door, and sitting down on the floor, drew the lad close to him, between his knees. He looked into his eyes and asked:

"Tell me, my son, how didst thou come to the faith in the one living God?"

"O my father and teacher, when I was a child my mother took me with her to the synagogue. There I heard of the miracles which had been performed for our forefathers; I learned how God had made an eternal covenant with them, in their name and in ours. There, in the synagogue, I also heard that the day would come for the fulfillment of the promise which He had given our forefathers and that he would send his anointed one to draw all the nations to the Mount of Zion, that they might know the Name of God. How I thought of him, and how I longed for him! My mother, and my pious grandmother, protected me

350

from all uncleanliness, and because of them I did not participate in the idol worship of my father. I was not touched by the abominations about us, and I waited like all Jews for the coming of the Messiah. And when you appeared in our city, O my father and teacher, and brought us the tidings of his advent, my heart was filled with dread and joy: it was as though I had seen the glory of God unfolded on all the earth. And when I stole out of the city that night and saw you lying, all bloodied and wounded, for the sake of the Messiah, I envied you, my father and teacher, because you had shed your blood for the tidings, and I longed to have my portion in you. For your blood that was shed was the witnessing of the Messiah."

Paul looked closely at him, thinking: "Thus a son of mine would have spoken, and this lad Timotheus could have been my son!" And for the first time Paul was shaken by the longing for a true son of his own, one bound to him in the body. How marvelous it would have been for him, the most forlorn of all men, to have had a son like Timotheus, a son who would bear for him this same boundless love, this unquestioning devotion. "But is he not my son in his heart?" asked Paul of himself. "Have I not begotten him into the faith of the Messiah? Could another hand than mine have wrought so much with him and had so great a part in his soul? And could a stranger, no son of mine, have brought me the love which he brought me on the night when I lay stoned in the pit? Could one who is not my son look out at me as he does? And is not my heart filled with yearning and compassion toward him, as it is written: 'As a father has compassion toward his son'?"

The heart of the apostle, which had seemed dead for ever to such things, struggled with an unconquerable yearning to have this young man as his son, to bind him to himself in a personal bond, in some great act of love and possession. Yes, the lad was his son, born a Jew, like himself. If his mother was Jewish, he was Jewish—such was the interpretation; the calf belongs to the mother. He had been brought up at least under the shadow of the Jewish faith, and his hunger for the redemption was a Jewish hunger. If he were to go out and speak among the Jews, they would listen to him; they would listen, and the gentiles would listen, too. For the young man stood between the two, and in his blood Greek and Jew were united. And even as Timotheus was, so he, Paul, longed to be: formed like a pagan, strong, manly and disciplined, with love of order, respect for nature and the world: but his heart eternally aflame on the altar of God, his spirit bound in the thongs of the Messiah, and in his blood the unquenchable stream of the blood of Abraham, full of compassion, of humility before God, of longing for peace and love. And issuing therefrom, a life made noble in purity, in endurance, in sympathy with others, with a heart circumcised and baptized in the fire of the Messiah. "This, my son, shall be the exemplar to the world. As Titus is the first exemplar of the gentile-Jew, so shall he, my son Timotheus, be the first exemplar of the Jew-gentile. And let the two come together, and join hands and affirm that all boundaries have been wiped out between them."

Paul said:

"Hear me, my son. Thou hast desired that my portion should be thine. My portion *shall* be thine, and thou shalt come with me in my apostleship."

"O my father, my teacher!" The young man flung himself with his face to the earth, and with his lips touched Paul's sandal.

Then Paul spoke further:

"Arise, my son, and hear me. Thy mother is a Jewess, and through her thou art a Jew. And thou shalt carry on thy flesh the sign of the covenant of Abraham, even as all of us do, so that none shall reproach thee that thou camest to us out of strange places; but thou shalt speak to the children of Abraham as a child of Abraham and bring them the tidings of the Messiah which God has planted in thy heart, and they shall hear thee and be redeemed."

The young man was silent. His face had paled, and a flash of momentary fear had passed across his eyes. He found himself, rose to his feet, stood before Paul, and was still silent.

"Hast thou understood me, my son? Is it in thy heart to do willingly that which it is proper for thee to do?"

Timotheus let another interval of silence pass. His heart thundered in him. He looked straight at the apostle and said:

"My father and teacher, rise, and for the God of Israel and the Messiah of Jacob, bring me into the covenant of Abraham."

"In thy blood shalt thou live!" responded Paul. Then he rose, and took a knife, and with his own hand placed upon his son the sign of the covenant of Abraham, for only a son of Israel may perform this act.

Timotheus stood motionless. Not a muscle quivered on this rock-like face. With fists clenched, with eyes upturned, he repeated: "For the God of Israel and the Messiah of Jacob—for the God of Israel and the Messiah of Jacob."

"Thou art my son. This day I have begotten thee!" And Paul embraced Timotheus, and it was with Paul as if in this act he had bound the young man to him in an eternal bond of blood.

Chapter Fifteen

IN BATTLE WITH GODS AND MEN

LIKE an eagle that seizes its prey in its talons and vanishes with it into the heavens, so Paul carried away Timotheus from the place of his birth. With a swift farewell to the household, to the mother, to the old grandmother, and to the congregation, he set out once again.

They were three now that fared on the way. In the place of his faithful bar Naba, Paul now had Silo and in place of Jochanan-Marcus his own son Timotheus. At first the journey was among the cities where Paul had founded congregations, beginning with Antioch in Pisidia. Everywhere it was the same; the congregations of believers were growing in peace. In every city Silo ascended the pulpit and read forth the letters of the holy ones of Jerusalem, in which the gentiles were declared liberated from the laws and commandments of Moses but enjoined to observe the primal commandments of the sons of Noah. Everywhere the apostle was received like an angel of the Lord—and everywhere they inquired after the mild and beautiful bar Naba. Paul continued the journey. Now he did not make long pauses in the cities, as he had done before; he passed through them as though borne by the wind. He avoided the larger cities of Mysia, cities which were filled with Jews and gentiles longing to hear the word of salvation. He did not even enter the chief city of Asia Minor, Ephesus, famous for its sorceries and for the worship of Diana. He asked himself, indeed, whether he should not go into Ephesus, and, as Abraham once shattered the idols of his father Terah, shatter with the sword of his word those of the Ephesians and sweep away their remnants with a fiery broom, to make a way for the holy one of Israel. But he said in his heart that he would do this some day; now he sped past the city as if on the wings of the spirit. He avoided, too, the paradiselike green valleys, the lakes, the refreshing woods. He avoided Bithynia, and did not pause until he came to the shores of the Aegean Sea and Troas, Alexandria Troas.

Troas was the gateway to the civilized world. The port of Troas lay opposite Achaia on the north-south route to Macedonia. On the streets of Troas one encountered men of the race of Macedonians, who had come by way of Neapolis and Philippi to carry on their commerce with the shore cities of Asia Minor. There were also many Greeks in the city, for Troas was the business center for Mysia, through which the grain of Asia Minor flowed to Macedonia; and since the latter was also a Roman colony, Troas was full of centurions, soldiers, and Roman officials. Here Paul did not have before him the racial mixtures of the interior cities of Asia Minor; he did not encounter Arabs, fresh from the desert, with sick, suppurating eyes, or the degenerate idlers of Antioch in Syria, with their unclean Asiatic idols, their sorcerers, their Chaldaean soothsayers, and their other lying spirits. In Troas he felt, for the first time, the breath of Rome. He saw before him the purer manifestation of Greek culture; and because it was purer in manifestation it filled him with a keener desire to conquer it with the word of God and to win it for the faith of the Messiah. He was deeply interested in the disciplined man of Rome, for whom there was a secret respect in his heart. The order-loving Roman, brought up in the framework of law and deeply rooted in the Roman tradition, the Roman centurion and the Roman legionary, ready to offer up their lives "for Caesar and Rome," provoked Paul to a new fervor of spiritual will. Who knew? Perhaps this was the type of man who ultimately was best fitted to receive the faith in the one living God who ruled the whole universe and to accept Him in place of the wretched little idols whose "powers" ended with boundaries of their cities. Paul had known the Roman officials in his home city. Unlike most of his fellow countrymen, he did not despise the soldier. On the contrary, he was moved to admiration by the spirit of devotion and sacrifice. He regarded himself as a soldier of the Messiah. It was his dream to win the soldierly devotion and discipline of the Roman official to the right faith, to direct it along the channel of the true life, lived, not in the name of a man of flesh and blood, a Caesar, and not in the name of an idol, but in the Name of the living God of Israel.

On the streets of Troas he also met Jewish merchants of Salonika. They told him of the great Jewish community of their city, which waited for a word of comfort.

*　　*　　*

The odorous, green-clad shores of the Aegean sea lie dreaming in the sunlight which sparkles on the light waves. Was it not hereabouts that the older Troas lay, the Troas of the Homeric epic? Through the translucent mist which hovers over the landscape shines the form of the sacred mountain, Ida. On its summit mighty Zeus sleeps in the jealous arms of Hera; and together with him, as if wrapped in one slumber, rest the dreamy stretches of the antique world.

To this fabulous place comes the Apostle, Paul the Jew, with the word of God in his mouth. He stands on the shore and looks across the quiet, faintly-misted waters toward the hidden hills of Achaia. Over there stands Olympus with its gods, and Athens, with her memories of her great men of old, the sages whose names had rung so often in his ears in the schools of Tarshish. These are not the idols of Asia Minor, these are not the abominable priests of Syria. They have their authority, and their roots go deep. Their dreams are lofty, enclosing great vistas. But they too must be turned and channeled to the truth, to the One who is God of all, the God of the universe, and the God of all men. This one living God of the Universe shall reign everywhere, even as it is written: "And the world shall be filled with the knowledge of God as the waters cover the sea."

That night Paul had a dream. He is again on the road to the Galatians. He climbs the mountain. Tired in all his limbs, he comes to a slender waterfall which pours down from a cleft in the heights. The waterfall is like a ribbon let down along the face of the cliff; it falls into a small basin the sides of which are overgrown with moss. Paul sits by the basin in the moonlight and meditates on his mission. Suddenly he hears the voice of a man calling: "Help me!" He starts from his meditation and runs in the direction of the voice. He speeds down the slope and comes suddenly on a wide, grass-covered plain bathed in moonlight. The plain is enclosed by rolling walls of mist, by thick borders of bushes and evergreens. And faces appear, multitudes of faces, peering at him

355

from the mist and from the involved branches of the trees; human faces, it would seem—and yet not human. They are the faces of demons, spirits, goblins, in semi-human guise; the faces laugh, the eyes glare like the eyes of animals—and yes, he sees it clearly now, there are foreheads with horns. But before Paul can quite understand what it is he is looking at, a whistling sound is borne toward him, and out of the heavy mist the figure of a woman comes floating toward him, her robes outspread like wings, her feet barely touching the ground. He recognizes her! He knows her for the goddess whom the Greeks worship: Diana! She is encircled by a bevy of nymphs, graces, fauns—all dancing about her in a wheel. They move through the air like detached fragments of cloud. They are hunting a naked man. Broad-built, muscular, with the figure of an athlete, but a man no longer in his first youth, with a close-cropped beard and a face of metallic hardness, he flees before them. "Help me!" Paul wants to throw himself between the goddess and the man. And suddenly he himself is surrounded by a hundred nymphs, graces and fauns, who dance about him in close-locked, rolling masses. But Paul can still see how the pursued man has fallen down on the grassy field, under a bush. And now the entire plain is populated with gods and goddesses. He sees proud Minerva, high-throated, drawing her golden veils after her, wisdom written on her face. She walks with a touch of hauteur. She sweeps on past naked Aphrodite, surrounded by her tiny cupids. Zeus, encircled by his sons, sits on a throne, grasping the thunderbolt in his right hand. Wherever Paul looks about him, there are gods, only gods, as though all the inhabitants of Olympus had gathered for the sake of this one hunted man. Apollo is there, in blazing scarlet, Vulcan and Hermes, and the gods of Achaia, gods that Paul himself knows not, gods of the underworld —Pluto with his tormenting demons—and all of them assembled because of this one man, who keeps calling: "Help me!" And now Paul understands: the naked man is the world, calling to the Messiah for help, and he, Paul, must come to his rescue. With the lightning flash of understanding, a wild energy awakens in him, and with the cry: "In the name of God!" he bursts through the bands of nymphs and fauns, he speeds across the field. And now the multitudes of demons, spirits, goblins are infuriated; they bare their teeth at him, they run at him with lowered horns. He hears the shrieking of sirens seated high up in a cleft of the rocks, and the sound echoes down to him, across the fields, and back from other heights. The gods have started up in alarm, and the host of them assemble to do battle with him. Zeus points the thunderbolt toward him, and the crash of it seems to split the world asunder. Flames of fire start up from the womb of the earth. A chaos of flames, smoke, sparks fills the air, as though the flames of the nether world were now mingling with the fragments of fallen stars. Helios passes on his chariot and fiery horses across the upper levels. But Paul, with God's word on his lips, hews his way through the press—he mows them down, he leaves them petrified on the grass—and he draws nearer and nearer to the naked man crying "Help me! Come over to Macedonia and help me!" And now Paul is within reach of the man, and the gods make one last desperate effort to keep them apart. They throw a new wall of flame between them, and the flame is composed of blazing bodies of nymphs and demons. Hands come out from the wall and snatch at Paul's garments. Wild winds blow in his face, to force him back. But Paul, with the word of God on his lips, still thrusts forward. He has broken through, he has taken the man's hand in his, he draws him along, saying:

"In the name of God! Come! Come!"

And he is lifted, together with the man, above the enchanted plateau. The gods, attended by multitudes of demons, sweep after them. They fill the air behind the fleeing men, as the locusts fill the skies with billowing clouds. But still Paul holds fast to the man's hand, and now they see before them the lucid morning star, and they know that the night of terror is behind them. From far away they can still hear an ululation and lamenting, the desperate cry of the baffled demons.

The next morning, when Paul awoke, he washed himself and said his morning *Shema*. The first man to come to him that day was the man of his dream, a broad-boned, muscular athletic man, with a bronze face, with cold clear eyes in which shone the self-confidence of the gentile; a man no longer in his first youth. The close-cropped beard gave his face the aspect of a philosopher.

"My name is Lukas," said the man, inclining himself before Paul. "I am one of the gentiles who heard thee preach in Antioch. I would not accept the faith of the Messiah until I had studied the holy books of the Jews. Now I know that the words of the Prophets have been fulfilled. I have come after thee, all the way from Antioch. Take me with thee on thy mission. I can be of use to thee in the places thou wilt

357

come to. I am strong in the speech of the Greeks, and I know well the ways of the Romans. I am skilled in the ways of the seafarer, too. I know the roads of many lands. I am a healer and have many recipes for wounds and boils and bruises. And thou wilt surely need a healer on the path which thou choosest."

Paul looked closely into the steely-cold eyes of the gentile Lukas: "How knowest thou the path which I choose?"

"Seest thou not that the people of Macedonia have need of thee?" And Lukas pointed seaward, toward the invisible shore of Macedonia.

So they took boat from Troas, and this time the uncircumcised Lukas was of their company. And they went by the direct sea route to Samothrace, thence to Neapolis, thence to Philippi, the chief city of Macedonia, which was a Roman colony.

The road from the port of Neapolis to Philippi led through rich fields, vineyards, and olive groves. Heavy willows, their locks hanging earthward, stood on either side of the road, which was marked with milestones. Philippi itself was a mighty city, sparkling with cleanliness; its narrow streets were paved with marble blocks. All that they encountered at first was Roman—the houses, the people, the speech. The men and women on the street were pleasing to the eye, tall, broad-built, draped in togas: Roman officials, Roman soldiers, Roman functionaries, even Roman merchants and Roman shopkeepers. The Asiatic type, with its small features, was to be met only among the slaves, the artisans, and the small stall keepers, who belonged, together with the Greek population, to the poor part of the city. The Roman women were tall and graceful, like cypresses. A new wind blew over the spirit of the apostle. This was his first encounter with the true Graeco-Roman man. But it was only an encounter. How was he to draw close to him?

The messengers asked in vain for the Jewish synagogue, which in all other cities had been Paul's first contact. No synagogue, no place of prayer for the God of Israel seemed to exist in Philippi. The city was filled with the temples of the Greek gods—and without a synagogue it was as if the place were locked for the messengers with seven seals. In vain did Lukas and Timotheus attempt to awaken interest in the Messiah among those whom they stopped: the Greek or Roman whom they addressed looked at them as if they were babbling in a foreign tongue. What was to be done? The synagogue of the Jews was the only open ear for the message of the Messiah, and without it there was no passage to the rest of the city.

Yet it could not be that there were no Jews in the city. So the messengers waited until the Sabbath. For the Sabbath was the touchstone of the Jews. It was the unmistakable sign. And if there were Jews in Philippi, then the messengers would assuredly see, here and there, a booth closed for the Sabbath, a work stall abandoned in the market-place, a chimney from which no smoke would be issuing. And in some place all those that belonged to the family of Israel would be assembled, and in song and praise, in the Psalms of David, they would worship the one living God and thereby unite themselves with the Jews of every part of the world.

And, indeed, it was thus that it fell out. Lukas, who knew the city, was the one who found the sign. Lydia, the rich dealer in dyed stuffs, whose shop swarmed with customers every other day in the week—men in ample togas, women in noble robes, all came to test and purchase her goods—was missing on the Sabbath from her accustomed place. The shop was locked. Nor was it only her place of business, prominent among the rich stores in the marketplace, which thus singled itself out: her factories, her dyeing-vats, her weaving rooms, were all closed. All the slave workers, those who trod out the sea insects for their colors and distilled the juice of plants, all her slave weavers, all her workers in the shop, were released for that day. For on the seventh day, not only the Jewish master rests, but his servants and his slaves and his beasts of burden. Soon the messengers observed other shops whose owners were observing the seventh day of rest for the God of Israel. There too the workers and slaves rested. Then Paul and his companions followed certain of these people—the majority of them were women—and they came outside the city. Through a green meadow, set with shadowing willow trees, flowed a modest rivulet. There, on the bank, in the shadow of white birches, women were seated. Their heavy coils were hidden by veils. They sat in small groups, apart from a group of men. And like the Jews on the river banks of Babylon, who hung their harps upon the willows, saying, "How can we sing the songs of Zion on an alien soil?" these men and women sat, in silence. They sat and remembered Jerusalem and the Temple. These women had no learning; nor was there much learning among the men. But after a while one of the men would recall a stray verse from a Psalm, in Greek, a fragment of a prayer, which everyone repeated three times, calling also: "Hear, O Israel, the Lord our God the Lord is One." And the women echoed: "Hear, O Israel, the Lord our God the Lord is One."

It was to be observed that not all the men and women were of Jewish stock. Here too gentiles had been attracted by the pure life of the Jewish family, by the sanctity of the Sabbath, and, above all, by the Jewish God; and they came with their Jewish friends to the bank of the river, whose waters were for them a symbol of the purity of the faith. So they sat, Jews and gentiles, and the land about them was soiled with desecration. Under every tree stood the altar of an idol, and therefore they had sought out the clean bank of the Gangites. Here a stream of warm water broke out from the earth, and they considered the place more fitting for their worship of the Eternal. They had no Scrolls of the Law, and they did not read from the Law on the Sabbath day. There were no synagogue officials among them, no leader, no cantor, no beadle; but there were two or three pious Jews who had, once or twice in their lives, made the pilgrimage to Jerusalem. They collected the Temple dues from their fellow Jews and sent them over to Salonika, where there was a great Jewish community, with an appointed leader, whose authority also extended to this forlorn place, Philippi. The pious Jews here, though they often bore Greek names, were thoroughly Jewish in appearance. They told the others of the Temple, of the High Priest, of the law of Moses, and of the Prophets, and of the promises which had been made to the Jewish people: a Messiah would appear and assemble the Jews from the four corners of the world, and even the gentiles with them, and lead them to the Mount of Zion.

And suddenly, into the mood of that Sabbath, there broke a tumult. Men and women started where they sat—they who were so remote from the camps of Israel. Messengers had appeared among them. Yes, messengers from the Holy City, sent to them by the sages, the elders, the holy Rabbis. And the seated Jews listened, open-mouthed, to what the messengers had to say.

The first of the speakers was he who looked most like a Rabbi, with his bald head, his handsome, forked beard, his great fiery eyes. He spoke, and speaking he drove the message home with gesticulations of his thin arms. And as his eyes burned, so his words burned, too.

"The Messiah who was foretold by the Prophets, and whom God

360

promised to our forefathers, has already come. Though a child of the heavens, higher than all the angels, he came in the form of a man of flesh and blood. He taught all men what manner of life they should lead, loving each other, forgiving each other their trespasses, so that all of them might be united in the congregation of God and the Messiah. And this Messiah, who took on the form of a man of flesh and blood, consented of his own free will, and in his love, to take upon himself the sins of mankind, in order that he might with his own blood expiate the sins of the world. And even as the Prophets foretold, he give his body to the smiters. He died the death of a slave, in order that all men might be free and the world liberated from sin. All those that believe in him have their sins forgiven, and they become free of the law. And this not only for the Jews, but also for the Greeks, for in their faith they are uplifted and become children of Abraham, cleansed from sin and bound to the God of Israel. And all this came to pass, according to the testimony which is given in the Holy Script, in the Prophets, and in the songs of King David."

Young Timotheus spoke, too, and he, with his boyish passion, poured forth his heart in quotations from the Prophets. But on that day it was Silo who produced the greatest effect. He took out the letters which he carried with him, letters written by the hands of the holy ones in Jerusalem, of the community of the city of the Temple, and he read forth the promise that all gentiles who accepted the Messiah were released from the discipline of the law of Moses.

The congregants rose to their feet. They were still bewildered by the suddenness and significance of the tidings. It was as though a message had pealed down from heaven. But the first to take it in were the gentile women and some of their husbands: it appealed strongly to them—without the heavy burden of the Jewish law they would be admitted to an equal share in the Messiah of Israel; their bodies would be purified of all the sins which they had committed in ignorance, and their souls would be linked with highest purity—that of the divinity of Israel. Their portion in the world to come was now assured them, and they had no more to fear from the day of judgment. More: their share in all the blessings which God had bestowed upon the Jewish patriarchs —the choice of Jewry, of whom they had heard so much from their Jewish friends—would be equal to that of the Jews themselves.

The first one to join the new faith preached by the messengers was the rich widow, Lydia, the dealer in dye-stuffs, who came from the city of Tiatira. She was not a Jewess, but a Judaizing gentile. On the morning following the sermons she and her household were baptized, in the name of Yeshua—she and her slaves, her workers, her shop managers, and all the immediate members of her family. She made but one condition: that the messengers should make her house their home. And her purpose was not empty honor, but the desire to prove that after she had accepted the faith in the Messiah she was the equal of all other Jews, and that none should reproach her house, and call it unworthy, because it was not the house of a Jewess.

But indeed it was high time that the messengers should find themselves in a proper place of shelter. Paul, who, wherever he went, would seek to obtain money for the holy ones and the poor of Jerusalem, sustained himself by the labor of his own hands. But in the latter years of his journeys he had not stayed long enough in any one place to be able to work properly. Moreover, this last journey of his had been begun with no attention to the question of costs. A little help he had accepted from the good women of Lystra, the mother and the grandmother of Timotheus. The messengers had arrived in Philippi with their sack almost empty of provisions. They had gone to an inn, not having been able to find a Jewish home. Therefore Lydia's urgent invitation to her home came at a welcome moment. But Paul read into it something more than the answer to their trivial problems of the flesh: he regarded it as the symbol of the open door, the ready ear, which they had sought at first in vain in the city of Philippi, and to which God had led them in His own good time.

The widow Lydia was too much the practical woman, the woman of affairs and of understanding, not to perceive at once the material condition in which the messengers found themselves. Herself the manager of a far-flung enterprise, superintending both the manufacture and the sales of her dyed stuffs, she saw the work of the apostle in its organizational aspect, and it was evident to her that skilled, practical help was badly needed. She made this offer to the messengers but made it so modestly, and seemed to regard it as such a self-understood thing that they should let her be responsible for the needs of their mission, that Paul, deeply touched, departed from his steadfast principle of accepting no help from his congregations. From the widow Lydia he would take what was needed for the carrying out of their mission. Paul had never

362

held—not even in his youth—a too high opinion of womenfolk, least of all of such as mixed in communal affairs. He had asserted more than once, in his sermons to the believers, that it was for women to be modest, quiet, and obedient to the voice of their husbands, who would carry the responsibility for public matters. Of the widow Lydia he made an exception. He was himself much too practical not to have perceived that in many cases the wife was more sensible, more realistic, and more reliable than the husband. Where he encountered such cases, he did not let himself be blinded by his general attitude. There were women who, with their love and insight, had contributed greatly to the success of his mission. He had not thrust them away, nor discouraged them. Nor could he fail to reckon with the fact that whatever his general attitude toward women, they were always the first to follow him. His influence over them was too striking a fact to be ignored. It lay in his temperament, in his reckless self-dedication to his cause: these were keys to the heart of woman. And more than once it had been the soft hand of a woman which had applied medicinal oils to his sick and wounded body, the speech of a woman which had strengthened him in time of great trial.

Soon, with the help of Lydia, the woman of affairs, there grew up on the bank of the rivulet, outside the city, a little synagogue, to which Jews and pious gentiles resorted for prayer. And Paul and the other messengers preached there the tidings of the Messiah and won many souls among the Jews and Greeks.

It chanced that once, as Paul was on his way with his companions to the synagogue, where he was to preach, there ran after him a half-crazed girl who was possessed of an evil spirit. She was led about like an ape at the end of a cord. Passing Paul that day, she caught some words of his, and when she had gone a little distance she tore loose and ran after him, crying, "These men are the servants of the High God, and they show us the path to salvation."

It was a common thing to find in the slave market a slave who was possessed of a demon—which is to say that the slave had convinced himself that a demon sat within; and at certain moments the slave would fall into convulsions and utter wild, disjointed words which bystanders would catch up as prophetic utterances. The markets sold slaves for every trade and occupation, from the heaviest physical labor to the highest type of intellectual work. Greeks supplied the markets

363

with women intended as concubines, boys trained in the satisfaction of unnatural lusts, musicians, philosophers, educators and trainers of the young, and skilled copyists of manuscripts. Syria, Chaldaea, and other Asiatic countries exported star-gazers, healers, snake-charmers, and all kinds of sorcerers. And occasionally there would be a slave who was considered a "prophet"; for as soon as it was discovered that a slave was afflicted with epilepsy and would babble when his fits came on him, he would also be trained in the art of prophecy. Such a slave brought a high price. He was kept on a leash and led around by his owner, sometimes to visit the sick, and especially the mentally deranged, and sometimes to perform for rich people who were believers in soothsaying. Sometimes the sick slave would bellow like a wild animal, sometimes he would assume the grave tones of a prophet, and sometimes even assert that he spoke for a god who had entered into him. The cost of one of these "prophets" was such that rarely could an individual permit himself the luxury of private possession of one. Thus it came about that associations were formed for the purchase of one of these wretched souls, who would then be exploited on a regular business basis. There was at that time in Philippi a famous slave girl who was led from customer to customer to forecast the future, and it was known that her owners were deriving an enormous income from their human property. It so happened that this girl was Jewish by origin. She knew of the Messiah for whom the Jews waited; she also knew of the one living God in whom the Jews believed. And thus, when she was led past Paul on that day and caught some stray words of his discourse, there awakened in her deeply imbedded memories of her childhood, a recollection of an ancient bond with the God of Israel and His Messiah, a bond which had been brutally broken by her captors. She turned back and began to scream: "These men are the servants of the High God!"

They dragged her away. But the incident repeated itself several times. Whenever she caught sight of the apostle or his companions at a distance, she would drag wildly at her leash and a lunatic frenzy would come over her. Her eyes would become injected, foam would break out at her lips, and she would repeat:

"Look! They are there! They are the ones who know the road to bliss!"

These incidents were a source of discomfort to the messengers. The curious would gather about the demented creature and look from her at the messengers; and her wild way of screaming about the Messiah and his sanctities threatened to turn the message of the apostle into a vulgar or ridiculous thing. When several encounters had taken place, the rumor spread that the messengers, too, were more or less possessed. For a time Paul ignored the girl, but concluding that the problem would have to be faced, he stopped short once, as she began to scream at him, and approached her. The girl stood still. Paul drew near, fixed his half-blind eye on her, gazed steadfastly awhile, and addressed the demon within her:

"In the name of Yeshua the Messiah, I command thee to leave her!"

The Messiah! She knew of him! The Messiah ben David, the righteous redeemer! In their name the demon within her was being abjured! And those who stood around and watched the transformation coming over her could almost see the struggle that was tearing her apart. They could almost see the demon lodged, tooth and fang, in her vitals and in the walls of her body. It seemed as though he too had heard the word of command and was digging deeper into the flesh and nerves of the girl, stemming himself against the power that was thrusting him forth. Now it was not the girl, but the demon within her, that was screaming—a dreadful, inhuman sound, a wailing, a snarling and gurgling and howling, in which there was a horrible note of supplication. It was as though the pitiful body of this girl had become a battleground between the oracle of Apollo, which her captors had conjured into her by suggestion, and the holy spirit invoked by the man who stood opposite her, gazing at her steadfastly. Then it was as though a knife had ripped her open, for one last desperate scream came out of her, and she fell to the ground, spitting out the demon.

Her guardians lifted her up, wet as she was with the agony of her trial. But she stood there looking at them with eyes to which they were not accustomed. She seemed to ask: "Where am I? What am I doing here?" They told her, she was being taken to the sick, to prophesy over them. But how was she to prophesy if the unclean spirit had left her, and she was now purified and healed? The guardians threatened her. They scourged her with her leash. "Prophesy!" they shouted. But how should she prophesy if her heart was empty? Apollo had left her, the demon was gone!

They led her away, but her owners knew now that something

had happened to their precious and costly slave. The Jews had spoiled her! They had used a magic of their own to kill the magic in her. She was a broken vessel, a shattered instrument.

The next day a mob assembled before the shop of Lydia, in the marketplace of Philippi. The Jews! They had slain the spirit of the slave prophetess! These were the same Jews who were preaching new gods, new customs, and new ways. The Jews were bringing discord into the city!

They broke into the shop and laid hands on the two chief messengers, the leaders of the guilty group. A gigantic Roman seized Paul, twisted his arms behind him, and led him out. A Greek had similarly taken Silo prisoner. Accompanied by the roaring multitude, which chanted, as in a chorus: "The Jews are leading a revolt in the city," the officers dragged the messengers across the marketplace to the council of the elders.

"These are the men who have brought tumult into our city! They go about preaching gods and customs which are hateful to us Romans!"

There was no investigation. No one asked what it was the Jews had preached. The words "Jews" and "tumult" were enough. On the spot, the two messengers were flung down and the clothes ripped from their bodies. Then Paul was taken up first, and his naked body, lean from years of fasts and privations, was tied to one of the marble pillars of the building, his flat breast against the stone. After him Silo was tied to the neighboring pillar. Two gladiatorial lictors, naked except for the aprons which covered their sex, came striding out of the inner chambers. In their hands were gigantic whips, the thongs of which, loaded with leaden riders, had been steeped in vinegar. The signal was given, and the scourging began. The thongs whistled through the air and fell on the shoulders, the backs, the necks, the cheeks of the messengers. Rivulets of blood, mingled with perspiration, streamed down the lacerated flesh. They could have uttered a single phrase: "We are Roman citizens!" and they would have thrown their tormentors into a panic. But they did not utter the phrase! Had they come to Philippi to preach the tidings of the Messiah under the aegis of their Roman citizenship? Their aegis was God: this alone was their protection when they set out to carry the tidings to the ends of the world. Silently they accepted the burning lashes, rejoicing in their hearts that they were privileged to

366

suffer for the sake of the Messiah. "How sweet, O Lord, are the sufferings thou makest us to bear for the holiness of Thy Name!" The gentiles pressing about them, Greeks and Romans, watched with delight the scourging administered by the lictors to the Jews; vulgar and obscene jests flew about, and fingers pointed at the sign of the covenant of Abraham on the flesh of the messengers. Not a word of complaint, not a whisper of resentment, issued from the lips of the scourged men. Finally they were unbound from the pillars; two officials were detailed to place them under arrest, and to be responsible for them with their lives. Paul and Silo were dragged through the corridors of the building and thrust into a cell. A chain was thrown about their legs and fastened to a heavy block. They were bound in such fashion that they could neither stand up nor lie down. It seemed to them that their limbs were no longer their own, but part of the dead block to which they were chained. The captors locked the door and departed. And then—what is that? Out of the black cell comes an incredible sound, a song of praise, a blissful utterance of gratitude to the Lord for the sufferings endured in the name of the Messiah. Within the cell the men are caught up in an indescribable ecstasy. The heavens are open, and they can see across them to their seventh level. Fire and light surround them. Yes, they are chained to the block, they cannot move; and yet they uplifted. And they sing: "Yea, though I walk in the shadow of death, I fear no evil, for Thou art with me." The prisoners in the other cells listen in a mixture of wonder and terror. They already know of the scourging of the Jews by the lictors; they know that the Jews are bound to the block. But they hear the singing, they catch the words—words of praise and gratitude and exaltation.

More than all the prisoners and warders, it was the chief jailor who was astounded by the bearing of these prisoners. No! Such men could not be tumultuaries, much less criminals. Their endurance during the scourging, the silence, the absence of complaint—and now, the singing, in which there was such pure, unaffected joy! Was it possible, he asked himself, that these were indeed the servants of the one living God, as the slave prophetess had said? Something he had heard, too, of the tormented savior who had come down from heaven, the savior which these men preached. Something he had heard of "the Son of God," who was soon to come with the clouds of heaven to sit in judgment on all men, according to their deeds. All men—all, without exception. And it was because they were so certain of the truth of their contention, that the prisoners sang with pure joy. But if this was so, woe to him, to their jailor, woe to him who had this part in their suffering!

And now something happens which sets the seal upon his fears. A thunderous sound is heard from the foundations of the prison: a flash of lightning illumines all the cells, and a furious wind passes through the corridors of the building. From all the cells a wild yelling issues. The gods are angry! The gods are angry because the messengers of God have been scourged. Zeus is filled with wrath. Peals of thunder and lightning flashes follow in close succession. The iron locks of the prison are burst asunder. Then darkness, and in the darkness tumult and panic. The doors of the prison are wide open. The jailor does not move. He is afraid of the anger of the gods—or of the anger of God, he knows not which. The prisoners are escaping, but still the jailor does not move. Of what worth is his life to him now? Has he not forfeited it? The jailor seizes his sword, there is a flash of steel in the darkness. Paul, the only one who has kept his head in the midst of the storm, the only one who has observed the struggle going on in the heart of the jailor, cries out: "Hold! Do thyself no harm! We are all here!" The jailor flings his sword away, falls at the feet of the apostle, and stammers: "My lords, my lords, what shall I do to be saved?"

A few moments later the messengers are unchained from the block. The jailor attends them in person, washing their wounds. Trembling, he offers them bread and wine. And he keeps on whispering: "Save me! Tell me what to do!"

The chief jailor of the prison of Philippi is received into the faith of the Messiah.

He was not the only one to bethink himself of the evil he had done. The elders of the city of Philippi, who, without investigation, without a pretense at trial, had condemned the messengers to the lash and had had them flung into the prison, learned of what had taken place in the night. They sent word to the jailor to set the prisoners free.

Now, when God's name had been sanctified and they had been saved without the protection of Rome, the messengers revealed who they were.

"They scourged us without trial, openly and in the presence of the

368

people, and we are Roman citizens," declared Paul to the elders of the city.

There was consternation in the hearts of the elders of Philippi. They had scourged Roman citizens! One by one they came forward, pleading with Paul and Silo to forgive them, but pleading also with them to begone from the city. And it was in Paul's mind to leave Philippi, not indeed because the elders entreated him to do so, but because he was called elsewhere. Paul and Silo hastened from the council to the house of Lydia, and there they said farewell to her and to such of the faithful as were present. They left behind them Lukas, skilled in the Roman tongue, to strengthen the foundations they had laid, and went out of Philippi toward Amphipolis, on the road to Salonika, where there was a Jewish community and a synagogue.

The moment he arrived in Salonika Paul looked for employment at his trade. He was anxious to return to his old principle of being a burden to no one; he was anxious, too, to set an example, to preach with his fingers the moral of labor. The work of the Messiah was not something at which a man should earn his bread. And so, the whole first week in Salonika Paul worked at the loom, and on the Sabbath he would go to the synagogue.

He had sought out in Salonika a Jew by the name of Jason, recommended to him in Philippi. In Jason's house he found lodging and his first convert in the city; on the Sabbath Paul preached in the synagogue. So it was, three Sabbaths in succession. He preached as he had always done, with citations from the Prophets and other Holy Writ: proving how, according to their words, the Messiah had been bound to suffer, and to die, in order that he might rise from death. A few of the Jews were convinced and many of the pious gentiles; there were also women among them, both Jewish and Greek. Paul founded a congregation of believers in Salonika, but here, more swiftly than elsewhere, he aroused the anger of the Jews who would not believe. To them, for one reason or another, his discourses on a Messiah who had already appeared and had been slain, were stranger than to all others. Moreover, they could not bear what he said against all that had been sanctified by the tradition and by the martyrs of many ages. And Paul was not skillful in utterance when faced with opposition; nor did he use sweet phrases and honeyed words. He said what he had to say, sharply, as though he were wielding a knife. Soon the word passed around that these were the men who had incurred the wrath of so many other Jewish communities. They had introduced discord and tumult everywhere else, and now they had come with this purpose in mind to Salonika.

Salonika was a city of gross market and harbor workers, men with little learning. The Jews of Salonika, like those of Alexandria, were employed about the port; some of them were pack-carriers, to whatever extent this work was not done by slaves, others were sailors, shipwrights, and exporters. They were of a type which was easily inflamed to riot, and the men who were opposed to the messengers went about the Jewish dock-workers inciting them, saying that Paul was taking away from them the Kingdom of the Messiah, for which they had always waited, and was giving it to a certain Yeshua, who had been killed.

The messengers took refuge in the house of Jason. Thither they called all those who had accepted the belief in the Messiah, and Paul and Silo taught them the ways of the new faith. But after a while Lydia heard of the danger which threatened the apostle in Salonika, for there was a lively commerce between the two cities; and unbidden, she sent certain of her men to help the messengers. Paul was deeply moved by her thoughtfulness, and he hid away in his heart the recollection of her help to him in his hour of need.

The opposition to the messengers grew apace, until one day a mob of dock workers and pack-carriers burst into Jason's house, intending to take fast the disturbers of the peace. But the young congregation which Paul had founded had been keeping an eye on the rabble, and the messengers were spirited out of the house before the arrival of the mob. Jason and certain others who were found in his house were haled before the magistrates, and only when Jason assured them that the messengers had left the city was he set free with his companions.

Paul's gift of attracting to himself individuals from among his opponents and making them faithful followers, ready to serve him with their lives if need be, had stood him in good stead in Salonika. One Sabbath, as he was preaching in the synagogue, he observed before him a little shrunken Jew, who listened to him open-mouthed, his round blue eyes shining with enthusiasm. Paul took note of the man, approached him later, and drew him to himself. This Jew's name was

Aristarchus, but in name alone was he Greek, for his heart was filled with the hope of Israel, and he placed himself at once in the service of the Messiah. It was this man who, some time later, accompanied Paul on his most dangerous journeys and shared his prison cell. He became in a sense the servant of Paul. It was Aristarchus, too, who brought the report of the mob's approach and guided Paul in the flight from Jason's house and on the road to Berea.

In Berea, by contrast, the messengers found an open ear and a receptive heart for the tidings of the Messiah. Here too they turned first to the Jews. They went to the synagogue and preached, according to their rule. But the Jews of Berea were not content with the Sabbath preaching alone. They gathered with him every evening, after the evening *Shema,* and read the Holy Script. Paul, surrounded by the old people of the synagogue, taught them where to find all the passages in which the Prophets and King David had foretold the coming of the Messiah. The Jews of Berea decided to found a congregation of believers and to draw into it all the pious gentiles, men and women, who frequented the synagogue. But Paul was ill at ease in Berea. His heart tugged him to return to Salonika. He had left there a sapling, just planted in the soil. The men of Berea would not hear of Paul leaving them. Meanwhile it came to the ears of the opposing faction in Salonika that Paul was in Berea and that he was winning many souls to the faith of the Messiah. A number of zealots, convinced that they were doing the work of God, set out for Berea and tried to stir up the city against the messengers.

The enmity of the zealots was, however, directed not so much against Paul's companions as against Paul himself, chiefly because of his sharp utterances against them. The congregation of Berea decided, therefore, to send Paul away, and to go "as far as the seashore." Silo and Timotheus remained in Berea, to complete the work which Paul had begun for the faith in Macedonia. Paul, accompanied by some of the faithful of Berea, went on to Athens, to await there the coming of Silo and Timotheus.

Chapter Sixteen

THE UNKNOWN GOD

LONG before the ship which was carrying Paul and his devoted Berean followers to Athens touched the port of Athens-Phalerum, they perceived, far off in the crystalline air, the mighty statue of Athena towering upon the Acropolis. Paul knew well what this gigantic symbol represented. This was the goddess whom the Greeks held in highest honor, the most beloved daughter of Zeus, who had sprung forth complete from his head, that is, from his wisdom. This was the child whom Zeus never refused a favor. And it was because she was always on the side of the strong, the triumphant, that she was accounted the goddess of wisdom.

For, like the goddess they adored, the Greeks recognized only the achieved, the known, the tangible, that which they could hold in their hands, as one holds a jewel. Only that which one had in possession could be said to have value. So they took the substance of human achievement, and they divided it into departments. Over every department they set a genius. Thus, the night belonged to Artemis, and through its darkness she moved in the company of her nymphs and fauns; through moonlit fields shimmering with dew, she glided in the robe of creation. And as Artemis ruled the night, so Apollo, the sun, ruled the day. Mounted on his fiery chariot he rolled through the heavens, and the spears of his radiance rained earthward. Darkness and death fled from before him. And Eros was the inmost secret of creation, the cosmos in emergence. The gods, with their attendants, were set separately over all that the intelligence had achieved, and they ruled, each in his domain. But only the known, only that which the intelligence had captured and framed, was given to the gods. Now among these gods, and among their worshipers, there appeared a sick man, bringing the discovery that the achieved, the demarcated and tangible and compartmentalized, was not the matrix of the truth; truth, he said, lay beyond the achieved and tangible; it lay in the great realm of the

372

inconceivable, the unachievable and unconscious, where the God of Israel had His domain.

In Phalerum Paul said farewell to the Jews who had accompanied him on the journey from Berea. He embraced them, and wept as he parted from them, and beseeched them to send to him, at the earliest possible moment, his beloved son Timotheus, whom he had left behind. Paul was ill at ease, and his heart heavy-laden. For all his unshakable faith in his mission, Paul had in him the touch of the artist, who always trembles with uncertainty when he approaches a new work. But outwardly he was heavy of heart for the fate of the Salonika community, from which he had fled while its foundations were still so insecure. What hopes he had built round his spiritual conquest of Macedonia! With what love and devotion he had sought to bring its gentiles into the fold of the new covenant which God had made with man through His holy servant, the Messiah!

"Pray with me," he said to his departing friends, "that God may see proper to bless the work of our hands. Pray with me that the seed we have planted shall not be carried away by the wind and lodged in barren sand. Guard the young shoot as you guard the apple of your eye, for with it grows the hope of Israel. And send me my son!"

His farewells said, Paul lifted up the bundle which contained his change of linen, his scholar's mantle, the tools of his trade, his phylacteries and prayer-shawl, his manuscripts of Isaiah, Jeremiah, and the Psalms, and took the road from the port to Athens.

On either side of the road from Phalerum and Piraeus to Athens, stretched two high walls, dating, it was said, from the days of the Trojan wars. The road was paved with blocks of stone for the passage of carriages. The month was Elul, the time of day early morning, when the apostle set out for the city of Athens. An east wind, the harbinger of the sirocco, blew across the landscape, leaving a fine film of dust on the lips and eyelids of wayfarers. Long caravans of donkeys and mules, driven by slaves whose short chitons barely reached their thighs, carried bales of goods from the port to the capital. Under the tread of countless hoofs, the clouds of dust went up from the road to mingle with the clouds of dust brought in by the pre-sirocco winds. But as Paul strode Athensward he could make out, on either side of the road, through the swirling, stinging dust, one temple after another, their

373

façades and pillars covered as with a fine snow. For the most part the temples were empty and deserted. Here and there, on the steps, or before an altar, stood a lonely priest swinging a bell. In one place the priest, despairing of attracting attention by simpler methods, had surrounded himself with flutists and girl dancers who clashed their cymbals to the rhythm of their steps. But there was such a superfluity of temples between Piraeus and Athens that with the best will in the world the travelers could not have given them a noticeable quota of worshipers. And so it seemed to the apostle that he was walking not between temples, but rather in a cemetery of forgotten divinities.

All of these deities were familiar to him, both from his native city and from the cities he had visited in his travels. One by one he passed them: a temple of Zeus, a temple of Athena, a temple of Vulcan, of Aphrodite, of Artemis, of Hermes. These were assuredly not the grotesque idols of the Asiatic peoples, those monstrous demons whom a wild priesthood served by bringing down, to the lowest, the most unimaginable levels of debasement, of drunkenness, whoredom, and sexual perversity, a population only too ready to make the descent. These gods were born of the intellectual exertions of men, they represented some sort of search and experience, an attempt to create order in the multitudinous ways of life. They were the expression of the desire for system in the chaos of human environment, and they had in them a measure of creativity, of purposiveness, or at least as much purposiveness as could be envisaged by the senses. The hierarchy of the gods indicated their functions and powers. But the attributes of the gods were no more than that which could be bestowed on them by men. "And how," the apostle asked himself, "can the sense of man enfold and comprehend both the known and the unknown senses? These gods are earthy, earthbound, insectlike, even as earthly man is. Man has endowed them with his own attributes, both good and evil; he has made them the outward bearers of his own desires and passions. That which he could not attain to with his own strength, he strove to attain by attributing it to his gods. So the gods are made by the hand of man, and in man's form. There are legitimate gods and illegitimate gods; gods begotten by Zeus on his spouse Hera, and bastard gods, which he has begotten on his light-of-loves, some even the wives of men. And the function of the god corresponds to his position in the hierarchy. To

374

those children which he begot on his legitimate spouse Hera, Zeus has relegated the government of the sun, of the night, of the creation and weaving of life, and the powers which slumber in the depths of the earth. One of his sons is Vulcan, whose temple stands idle and desolate here on the road. As to those bastard gods, he has, just like a man of flesh and blood who begets a horde of illegitimate children with a riff-raff of women, given them minor heritages—the smaller functions. Now is it not strange that this should come from the clever and experienced minds of the subtle Greeks, in search for the foundations of experience? Wonderful are Thy works, O Lord! Who can comprehend Thy deeds? Who can count them and give their record? Why is it that the clever Greeks cannot see that the Father in heaven, who has created all things, those which we see and those which we cannot see, is the one living God of Israel? Can we say that only the powers which are locked in the breast of the earth, and the murmuring powers of the night, are hidden from us? Are we not hidden even from ourselves? Man, dost thou know thyself? How foolish ye are, ye wise ones of Athens! Like mites who work on a tattered garment hung away in a cupboard, so ye crawl about and believe that you have put up a ladder whose summit ascends to heaven. Only the ladder of the dream of Jacob has its topmost rungs in heaven. It was put up for our father by the hands of faith."

Paul drew near to a well, built into a semicircular wall which also enclosed a pillar surmounted by the figure of Hermes-Mercury, who was always represented at a crossing or division of roads. By the well sat a group of veiled girls and women, with graceful vases. There also came up some donkey drivers, to draw water for their beasts. Paul wanted to dip his hands in water and wash the dust from his eyelids, and he asked one of the young women for the loan of her pitcher.

Was it far from the city, he asked her. No. After the first statue of Hera, which stood among some winged victories, he would reach the gates. He asked the women whether they knew of any Jewish houses of prayer in the city. No, they had not heard of any. But the apostle knew that every religion had its temple in Athens, and therefore the Jews assuredly had a house of prayer near the entrance to the Street of the Camel Drivers, by the temple of beloved Demeter. As to this street, the women told him he would easily recognize it, because

375

there he would see a high pillar with the statue of Mercury atop. Then the women resumed their own conversation, which Paul's approach had interrupted.

Paul, resting, listened. The conversation was about a certain Demetrius Aristophanus, a teacher of sword-fighting, with whom a young Roman nobleman of the house of Caesar had contracted a friendship. Demetrius had been taken to Rome, since when his wife, Aglaia—who was one of the women by the well—had not seen him. He had left her with her two children, and she longed for him. His contract had been for one year, and since he was a freedman, he could return at the end of that period. But now some two or three years had passed and still he had not returned. Every day Aglaia came out with her friends to draw water from the well, and every day she renewed her complaint. Her friends comforted her and advised her to seek out another man; but Aglaia would not be comforted. She had already done everything to conjure back her husband. Every day, when she came out to the well, she brought with her a wreath of flowers and laid it before the statue of Vesta, the goddess of the family hearth, begging her to send home her man. But it had been of no avail. Lately a man who had returned to Rome, where he had also been a teacher in the same house as Demetrius, told her that her husband, his contract with the nobleman ended, had hired himself out as a gladiator to a rich senator; and he did not know whether this Demetrius was still alive or not. But Aglaia herself did not know whether to believe the returned teacher, since he had made advances to her and sought her as his wife and was ready to take her together with her children. In any case, her heart yearned for Demetrius, and she would wait for him until the gods would vouchsafe his return.

"Why dost thou not offer a rich sacrifice to Hera? She is the guardian of the home and the protectress of the purity of the family. She herself is a sorely-tried wife, as we know, after everything she has had to endure from her husband, old Zeus, who has betrayed her a thousand times with others. She will hear the cry of thy ·heart, Aglaia," said one of her friends.

Aglaia answered that she had already invoked the help of the goddess Hera. She had, indeed, gone to her first, though others had counseled her to approach Aphrodite. She had offered much to Hera —almost all that was left to her after her husband's flight from her—

white meal, doves, and cruses of oil, and a fat suckling pig on top of all that. And last the priests had even taken her long braids of hair—that is to say, she had sold her braids to wig-makers. And now she was afraid that even if Demetrius returned he would leave her at once, for her hair had not yet grown back. Yes, indeed, she had tried the goddess Hera, but without avail.

"And what about Aphrodite?"

"Aphrodite? I served in her temple two months"—here Aglaia leaned over and whispered something in her friend's ear—"and that too helped me nothing. I will tell you what I have learned from my experience with the gods. The great ones have no time for us, the little folk, the poor; they are all taken up with the affairs of the world, with directing the lives of the rich and mighty, who demand all their time and strength. Yes, the rich keep the great gods busy, with their wars and loves, with their struggle for government and power. So the poor can go only to the little gods, who are not held in esteem by the great gods. So I am looking for one of the fauns or satyrs, and I will tell him what troubles my heart. I know that they, the little gods, mean well, and do not deceive us."

"Let me tell thee," said an elderly woman, whose eyes gleamed with a peculiar luster. "My best experience has been with a certain foreign goddess, Isis, whom the Egyptian priests have brought to our city. She has much to offer to married women in her ritual. Men dare not be present at the ritual. I come away from those services edified and cleansed, and all my wishes are granted. I tell thee, the worship of the goddess Isis is altogether different from the worship of our home gods. You become bound up with the goddess in the ritual, and those women who have lost their man, or one of their children, are much comforted by her." And with this the woman began to sing a prayer of the goddess Isis:

> "Even as Isis suckles the young Horus,
> So I will suckle thee at my breast.
> Thou art the young Ra,
> Who art returned to the world.
> I am thy mother, who bore thee,
> I am thy sister, whom the god Ra
> Hath appointed for thee."

"Of late," said another woman, "I have found much comfort in the services of the god Adonis. When I press his image to my heart, I become like Aphrodite herself, and my heart, like hers, is filled with yearning for my slain husband, and I wander to him in the underworld, and through my sorrow and lamentation I am united with him, and all my longings are satisfied. Oh, thou knowest not how sweet is the lament for the god Adonis." And, following the example of the elderly woman, she too began to sing:

"Oh, weep and mourn for Adonis,
  For the sweet god who lies among the hills,
  In his death and beauty.
  I am Aphrodite, who thirst after thee, Adonis,
  Come to my arms.
  My love will bring the breath of life into thee again.
  O Adonis, sweet Adonis!"

A woman who had just come by, and was busy drawing water for the many vessels she carried, called out: "All the gods are good as long as you bring them rich offerings."

The other women bethought themselves of their tasks, and rose.

"Dost thou hear," said Aglaia to the Isis worshiper. "Take me with thee to the worship of Isis. I have been longing for her of late."

The women scattered, and the apostle remained seated on a stone under the figure of the god Hermes-Mercury. He had listened with interest, for the ways of men, everywhere, were his concern. His heart was filled with sadness for the women whose conversation he had just overheard. He lifted his eyes to heaven, and all his being was filled with prayer: "Father in heaven, have compassion on thy poor creatures, let them see that there is but one God in heaven and but one intermediary between man and God, Thy Messiah, Yeshua."

He rose at last and resumed his way. But as he walked cityward he perceived among the statues of the gods and goddesses one altar which seemed abandoned and forlorn more than any other altar he had seen so far. It was thickly covered with the dust which rose from the feet of passing beasts of burden. Paul, who, like every pious Jew, avoided the sight of idols and kept his eyes lowered when he passed by them, could not avoid the sight of this altar. Its desolation seemed suddenly to speak

378

to him, and a power which he could not understand impelled him to turn aside from his path and approach the altar. No image, no likeness of god or goddess, adorned its sides or stood upon a pillar near by. And Paul was filled with wonder, and asked himself who had erected this stone altar, and for whom. He drew near. On the side of the altar there was a brief inscription. He bent down to read the half-obliterated words, and they were these:

"To an unknown god."

Paul stood astounded. What was this humble, anonymous altar in the midst of the vast and opulent temples of Ares and Zeus and Aphrodite? what was this forlorn and modest tribute to an unknown god? And suddenly it was as if a light had burst upon him from within, and as though a sign had been given, the answer to the prayer which he had just uttered in his heart.

"No!" he cried. "Not to an unknown god. But to *the* unknown God." So Paul corrected, in his mind, the faded lettering.

Then he saw what he had not seen before. On one corner of the altar lay a tiny wreath of fresh flowers, and somehow he was convinced that this was the wreath which he had seen in the hand of one of the women grouped about the well. And his heart blossomed in him, and he lifted his eyes again and cried out:

"See, O God, it is Thee, and Thee alone, that they seek in their blindness. Even when they worship the idols, it is to Thee that their hearts are turned."

Chapter Seventeen

THE FOOL OF THE MESSIAH

DUSTY fig leaves hung into the street over the white walls of the courtyards. On the flat and level roofs the women sat, mending clothes and household utensils. Two young men, wrapped up to the throat in their white himations, came springily out of one of the gates and turned

379

in the direction of the Agora. A slave in a short shirt, with naked arms and legs, was leading to school a lad who carried in his hands his writing tools, a stylus and a tablet. In front of one of the houses there was a crowd of women and old men: a woman, whose husband had come home altogether too late from some nocturnal banquet, had thrown him out of the house, and the idlers had assembled to enjoy the scene. A heavy odor of vinegar went up from the wine cellars, the doors of which were almost closed off by great amphorae. Men came out through the doors, carrying wine skins. Before a baker's shop a group of women was assembled. A tripod stood in the open street in front of a sausage shop, and the air was filled with a pleasant odor of frying meat. Hungry bystanders, slaves and idlers in short smocks, women in tattered mantles, stood about the sausage shop, their nostrils dilated, breathing in the smell of the frying meat, while the saliva dripped from their mouths.

Deeper down the alley, between the olive press and the cheesemaker, opposite restaurants and cheap inns, Paul found the synagogue of Athens, shut off from the street by a wall.

The synagogue was closed. It was not used during the day by the teacher of the little children, or by the Rabbinic court, as was the custom in other cities. There was no one about to extend a welcome to the visitor. The head of the synagogue, who, Paul learned, lived not far away, was absent. He was in the Agora, selling his purple-dyed linens to the rich young students who were so numerous in the city—not for them, but for their concubines and dancing girls. The scribe of the synagogue was also in the Agora, selling jars. If a visitor came from out of town to the synagogue, he could wait.

A Jewess living in a neighboring house took pity on the waiting stranger, obviously a Jew, and invited him in. She placed before Paul a wooden bowl containing warm water, with which to wash his hands and feet. Then she offered him a cup of goat's milk and a piece of bread. The stranger blessed her for her kindness, in the name of God.

"In the name of the God of Israel," added the woman, and wetted her fingers in the warm water, so that she might not be mentioning the sanctity with unwashed hands.

"In the name of the God of Israel and of his holy servant, the King-Messiah, Yeshua the Messiah!" said Paul.

380

"Yeshua the Messiah?" said the woman, her eyes filled with wonder.

"Yes. Hast thou never heard of him?" asked the messenger, as he ate his small portion of bread.

"No, never. We are far from Jerusalem. Has the Messiah come, then? And we have heard nothing concerning his coming?"

"Yes, the Messiah has come, and I have come here to tell you of his coming," answered the apostle.

"When was it? What was the manner of it? And why have they not advised us? The Rabbi who was here but a week ago, the messenger of the High Priest, mentioned no word of it."

"They did not recognize him," answered Paul.

"What? They did not recognize the Messiah? The mind cannot grasp it."

Then the stranger told her wondrous things—and the Jewess stared at him, her eyes filled with bewilderment and a touch of suspicion. She did not seem to understand what he was saying. But what she wanted to know first was whether the Jews were now ready to leave the scattered cities in which they dwelt and foregather in Jerusalem. It was a pity, she said, that her husband had only just been given employment by a silversmith in the Agora, where he was making ornaments for the Athenian women. It was a profitable business. There were many rich students in Athens, among them scions of the Roman nobility, and they had brought much money with them to the city. Because of his new and profitable employment, the husband had bought a number of new things for the house; a bronze couch, and some bowls of cedar wood. Besides, they were buying the house in which they lived, and had already paid nearly half the price. All this they would have to give up if the Messiah had come—their share in the house, the husband's employment in the silversmith's factory, which brought in such good money, the security which he had built up; and they would have to go to Jerusalem. And who knew, she asked, what would happen in Jerusalem, with so many Jews streaming in from the four corners of the world, all of them, no doubt, looking for employment, and snatching the bread out of each other's mouths. No, the woman was not at all delighted by the tidings of the coming of the Messiah. And she said as much as she placed before the messenger a little bowl of olives and a cruse of honey. She would much rather have things remain the way they were; she was glad to send her taxes to the Temple, as long as the High Priest would let her remain with her family where she was, especially since they had lately improved their dwelling. Other Jews could go to Jerusalem, to the Messiah; but she and her husband, and their two little children who were at school, would much rather remain in Athens, if things only went as they had been going till now.

Not more enthusiastic was the reception which awaited Paul from the head of the synagogue, when the latter returned from his cloth shop on the Agora and found the messenger waiting for him in the court of the synagogue.

"By Zeus!" said the head of the synagogue. He was a little man, with a short neck, a round belly, and an asthmatic wheeze; his panting voice barely forced its way through his throat. "By Zeus! By Jupiter!" He meant no harm by this exclamation. It was his way of talking with his customers in the Agora. "We really don't know what to do with all these messengers from Jerusalem. They don't give us time to catch our breath between one and the next. Why, only a week ago the messenger from the High Priest was here and took away with him seventy-seven drachmas, collected from our little community. And a little while before that there was a messenger from the Pharisees; fifty silver drachmas he got out of us. And apart from these, there are visitors, thou understandest, just so—Rabbis and preachers and all that. And now, of a sudden a new one. Tell me now, what desirest thou, and who sent thee to us?"

"He who sent me to you," answered Paul, "sent me not to take but to give. I shall be no burden to you. I am a weaver by trade, and I weave goat's hair cloth for tents and mantles. Is there not one among you who will give me employment during my stay in the city? I have brought my tools with me in my bundle. As for that which I will give you, I ask no payment for it. For he who sent me has said: 'Ye obtained me for nothing, and for nothing shall ye give me.'"

This was indeed something new! A Rabbi sent on a mission from Jerusalem, who asked no contribution from the community and who would earn his daily bread with his own hands! It had not been heard of before. True, even the Athenian Jews knew that there were learned Rabbis in Jerusalem who earned their livelihood with their own hands and taught the law without receiving any recompense; but they had never set eyes on such a Rabbi. Those that came to them from Jerusalem were sent for the purpose of collecting contributions. The head of the synagogue, quite deflated, said to Paul:

"There is a little hospice attached to our synagogue. A messenger may lodge there while he is with us. He may also be fed from the treasury of the community; such has always been our practice, and our pious women will see that thou lackest nothing. And on the Sabbath we will hear what thou hast to say to us."

Paul accepted this temporary hospitality, and for the moment he did not look for employment. He did not know yet how long his sojourn in Athens would last. He was waiting impatiently, too, for the arrival of Timotheus and Silo, to know what had happened in Berea and Salonika, for his heart was ill at ease concerning those places. Besides, he had with him a little money which he had earned in Salonika, or Thessalonika, as they called it, though he had spent most of his earnings in paying the fare of the Bereans who had accompanied him on the sea journey.

* * *

On the Sabbath, when the reading of the law had taken place in the synagogue, Paul received the permission of the head of the synagogue to mount the pulpit and address the worshipers. In giving him this permission, the head of the synagogue whispered: "See that thou makest the serman short. We work hard all week, the Sabbath is our day of rest, and we would be gone to our homes."

Paul began to speak of the Messiah who had already come, who had not been recognized, who had been tormented and put to death for the sins of all men. He proved, as was his wont, that all this had had to come to pass, according to the words of the Prophets. He quoted from Holy Script all the passages which concerned the coming and the manner of the life and death of the Messiah.

"And now, be it known to you all that the Messiah was the first to rise from the dead, and that he will come soon to judge the world. And the only salvation on the day of judgment will be faith in the Messiah, and if ye will recognize him, and acknowledge him, and say that he was raised from the dead by God, then ye shall be saved. And not alone for the Jews did the Messiah come, but also—"

Half way through his sermon Paul perceived that many of his

listeners were practically asleep, and others had simply left the synagogue. As to those who were listening, it was quite clear to him that their interest was confined to the effect which the coming of the Messiah would have on their personal condition.

"By Demeter!" exclaimed a tall Jew, "a fine thing it would be for all of us, if we had to return to Jerusalem. No, not I! Let who will go up to the Holy City. I have my wine business here. I can live like a Jew without the Messiah."

"By Hercules!" exclaimed a second Jew, one with a short, well-tended beard and eyes touched with black; he was dressed like a learned Athenian in a mantle falling over him in graceful folds. "By Hercules! I am of an old Athenian family!" He spoke with the accents of an educated Athenian. "My grandfather came hither as a messenger of the High Priest Hyrcanos, whose statue stands today in the Agora, and he elected to stay here, in this city which is the capital of the world, and to become an importer of wines. My father extended the business so that now it flourishes. We have our own vineyards now, and branches and offices in all the principal cities of Greece. I myself frequented the finest academies of Athens. I am of the school of the Stoics. I have many friends here in the city. My sister is married to a member of the High Council. And now this man appears and tells us that the Messiah has come. Does it signify that I must leave the city of my birth and pack off to Jerusalem, to become a subject of the Messiah? No, such doings are not for me!"

"No, by Zeus the just! Messengers come to us, many messengers. One asks for contributions to the Temple; that we understand easily. Another asks for contributions for the Pharisees. That too we understand. But what desires *this* messenger?"

Everyone who was not asleep in the synagogue was talking now. Voices were raised. Finally the head of the synagogue mounted the pulpit and tried to pacify the worshipers:

"Good people!" he cried. "Be calm. Do you not see that an important messenger is here from Jerusalem? The matter which brought him here is an important one, nothing less than that of the Messiah ben David, for which the House of Israel has been waiting so long. And this Messiah has already come! Moreover, the Romans slew him, but he rose from the dead, the first to rise from the dead. And this Messiah appeared to our messenger, who stands before us, and told him to

384

go to the House of Israel, in every corner of the world, and to bring it the tidings of the advent. Now if these things be so, surely we are duty bound, all of us here, to rise up, even as we are, to leave our houses and gardens, our workshops and stalls, our vineyards and farms, the yoked horse and the yoked mule, and to go up with song and music to Jerusalem, to throw ourselves at the feet of the Messiah and to say to him: 'We are come to claim our portion in the inheritance of Israel.' But thou tellest us"—and the head of the synagogue turned to Paul—"that it was not the Sanhedrin of Jerusalem that sent thee, and that the Sanhedrin has not ratified thy mission, and even knows nothing concerning it. Hast thou no letter from the High Priest to show us? Thou wert sent here by another congregation, one we have never heard of. No, thou sayest, it was the Messiah himself that sent thee, bidding thee carry the tidings to the end of the world. So let it be then: we accept that too, and we are ready to listen to thy words, and to hear thy commands and instructions in the name of the Messiah. But surely thou hast with thee evidence of the ratification of the Messiah, and the proof that it was he, and none other, that sent thee to us. Hast thou some sign with thee, something to corroborate thy words, that we may indeed know that the Messiah spoke with thee as thou didst tell me, man to man, as it were, when he showed himself to thee? Come then, produce the sign, and show it to us. Thou toldest me that thou didst not come to perform miracles. Thou saidst we must believe thee even as thou speakest, and thou wilt not open the roof of the synagogue that we may see the fiery chariots bringing down the Messiah. Therefore, for the sake of thy word alone, we must abandon the law of Moses, and abandon likewise our houses, our shops, our fields, and follow thee to Jerusalem. Is it thus that we must take thee?"

A voice cried from the synagogue: "But do you not all see that the man is a deceiver! What sense is there in this discourse with him?"

"A deceiver! A deceiver!"

"Nay, not a deceiver, but a rebel against the word of God, who would take us off the path of faith!"

"Out into the street with him!"

The head of the synagogue fell into a panic. "Good people!" he shouted above the tumult. "This man is not a deceiver. He is but slightly touched in his mind," and he pointed to his forehead.

A burst of laughter filled the synagogue, making its walls tremble. The laughter served the purpose intended by the head of the synagogue; the anger was forgotten, and the threat of physical violence was forgotten with it.

But Paul was not the man to shrink from discouragement or to be turned from his purpose by mockery. What had he not already sacrificed for his faith? What had he in the world, and what was he, without his faith in the Messiah and his service for him?

How much more respectfully even the ignorant and uncouth Jews of Salonika had listened to him than these sophisticated Jews of Athens! How much more of true faith there was even in those who had opposed him with all their strength. Indeed, the blows and curses of the simple and sincere folk of Iconium were far better than the laughter of these Jews of Athens. With those others, of Salonika and Iconium and Antioch, he felt himself more closely bound in the common bond of the hope of Israel. Here, in Athens, there was nothing but cynical indifference.

Therefore, after that Sabbath, he waited with more longing than ever for Timotheus and Silo, who would come from Berea and Salonika, perhaps with words of comfort. Salonika, after all, had been the touchstone of his work. If God had but willed that his labor in Salonika should bear fruit! If God would but grant it to him to have broken through the hard foreheads and the flinty bosoms of his brothers there! Meanwhile there was nothing he could achieve in Athens. He did not even look for employment. He needed so little for himself that the handful of coins left him sufficed. The hard bench in the hospice—they did not refuse him that—was good enough for a few hours of sleep he permitted himself. He avoided, as much as he could, even the hospitality of kindly people. For there were such, and among them some of those who had laughed so loudly at him in the synagogue. After all, he was a Rabbi of Jerusalem; and they did not forbid him to speak a second time in the synagogue, and they did not withhold their attention from him when he addressed them privately. So he came day after day to the synagogue, and now and again he found someone to preach to. They listened to him, but they could not refrain from smiling. "Ah, yes, yes! We hear thee! Thou art the man that tellest us that the Messiah has come, and has sent thee to us."

386

In the night Paul lies on his hard bench in the hospice. Ancient wounds, the wounds that had drained his life in his youth, open again, and he is bathed in torment. Doubt lays hold of him, seizes him as a wild beast seizes its prey. Would that his companions were with him, to comfort and strengthen him! For the hundredth time he asks himself the unanswerable question: "Why do the Jews reject my message? Why are those who belong to me, flesh of my flesh, blood of my blood, deaf to my message? The Messiah has sent me with the tidings of the highest import, and when I speak to them, I do not see the hidden hope come forth from the secret places of their hearts; no song awakens in their blood, which from of old carries the memories of the ancient prophecies and the words of our forefathers. Instead there is a tumult and mockery, and the highest Jewish blessing is transformed into a curse." He remembers all the cities in which he has preached the tidings to the Jews and remembers the riots which were his reward; he remembers the sullen faces, the rages, and the hostility. But the gentiles, who are remote from him, and who know not of the hope—it is in *their* blood that an echo of divinity responds, a survival of that which God had planted in them in the days of creation. And this echo mounts and becomes a glorious song, so that their faces are illumined. How they long for the Messiah! "God, why hast Thou closed as with an iron bolt the hearing of my own flesh and blood? Why can I not enter into them? Was I not forged in the same fire as they? Did I not wait, as they do, for the Messiah, and do I not know the remotest hiding places of their souls, where the seed of the Messiah waits? Why speaks not the heritage in my blood to the heritage in their blood? Surely it cannot be because I tell them that the Messiah has abrogated the little law that stands between them and the world. Can they not see that all the laws, all the benedictions, all the commandments are contained within the one great law of the Messiah? It is for the hope of Israel, for the Messiah, that I do away with the lesser law. Nay, it is something else. There is a mighty wall between me and my brothers, and all my words are flung back by the wall and fall into the sand. My love toward them, my desire, and my innermost longing are thrown back upon me. The hearts of my brothers are locked against my word, as they are locked against uncleanness and abomination. What is it then? Is there something unclean and forbidden in me? Aye, have not these hands shed innocent

387

blood? Have they not shared in the slaying of the righteous? Can I truly know that I have been forgiven and washed clean, that my sin is no more, so that my words, which should be the trumpet tones of salvation, shall not peal in the ears of my listeners like the challenge of an enemy? Or am I indeed an enemy appearing before the walls of the cities? Do I in fact bring with me the divine bliss to the inhabitants of the city?"

And suddenly he beheld in the darkness hundreds of faces, the faces of simple Jews, the Josephs and Simons and Judahs and Menachems—and their eyes shone with the light of faith. Their bodies were covered with stripes from the bloody scourgings they had endured. He saw them all lying on a field of stoning, and among them, imbedded in a heap of stones, was the angel with his arms and wings stretched toward heaven. An angel with flaming red hair and beard it was, in the image of Reb Istephan; the eyes were wide open, the lips parted as if a cry had just been torn out of them. But strangely, this was not only the face of Reb Istephan, it was his own face, too, Paul's. And yet he, Paul, was not the angel imbedded in the heap of stones, for he was seated near the edge of the pit on the field of stoning. His feet were folded under him, and before him lay a bundle of clothes. By his side stood the witnesses, his own men, Paul's, their arms, their legs, their hairy bosoms naked; they were flinging stones at the figure of the angel, the Paul-Istephan with flaming hair. But the Paul that was seated by the edge of the pit was white-faced. His eyes were narrowed, and they sparkled with a hateful joy, his lips were contorted in a grimace of delight at the flowing of blood. A shudder passed through Paul, lying on his hard bench, and he whispered:

"God! My God! I am a murderer! How shall they listen to me? God, wash me clean of my sin! Help me!"

He closed his eyes, as though in the darkness he could shut out the vision. It was not Reb Istephan that he could not bear to look on. He himself, the Paul at the mouth of the pit, filled him with horror. Through his tightened eyelids shot needles of flame, and all his flesh was wounded.

Those nights in Athens were for Paul a time of self-searching and of delving into the secrets of his soul. He was at once the witness and the judge. In the darkness he reviewed his life, and it was as if he were carding his soul as he carded a bundle of goat's hair, to cleanse it of impurities. The mornings were better, for as they succeeded each other, he felt his confidence returning; and like a donkey resuming the yoke, he returned to his labor, for labor was his only salvation. So, in that period, he sank and rose again, and the grace of his faith restored him to his mission as the bringer of tidings. And he applied to himself the verse from Holy Writ: "Were it not for Thy law, I should be utterly lost in my poverty."

Chapter Eighteen

HELLAS

IT was no longer the Athens of Pericles, of Socrates, and of Sophocles. Among the painted porticoes of the Agora the disciples of Zeno still debated the problems of life and death, using the Socratic method of question and answer; but the Stoics were not deeply rooted in the old faith, and the nourishment for their philosophy was drawn from the shallow spring of their own intelligence. Thus the lessons taught in the stoa, though they had to do with the highest impulses of man and theoretically achieved a supreme morality, linked to the immortality of the soul, carried with them no moral obligation for the individual. The Sophists, who in their dialectic ingenuity could create and demolish whole worlds effortlessly, had reduced the Greek genius to a condition of static impotence. Sophism had condemned the Greek spirit to fruitless repetitiveness; it was as though Apollo were compelled to drive his fiery chariot in a circus ring. By that time the gods had ceased to be beautiful and clever, strong and harmonious; but beauty and wisdom and strength and harmony, as pure abstractions, had become gods. On the Acropolis the masterpiece of Phidias evoked more admiration than the goddess which it represented.

Paul went into the marketplace of Athens to bring the tidings of the Messiah to the gentiles.

The great Agora, surrounded by hillocks and temples and citadels, started at the Piraic gate, ran the length of the Piraic street along the foot of the Acropolis, and was bounded on the other side by the Areopagus.

One part of the Agora flowed about the Areopagus, which was a steep rock surmounted by a plateau or platform. Narrow, winding stairs, hewn in the stone, led to the summit. About the platform were ranged the stone benches of the judges, for here, on this hill, which was called the field of Mars, assembled the elders and judges of Athens. Tradition had it that the first trial ever held here concerned the god of war, Mars, who had committed a frightful crime against his sister goddess Aphrodite. Ever since then the Athenians had chosen the hill for the sessions of their councils and courts. At the foot of the hill, around a gigantic statue of Mercury, was the chief market of Athens.

The market of Athens differed little from the other markets of the antique world: narrow bazaar-alleys, covered with sheets or with woven olive branches, little stone stalls, and booths to which one ascended by narrow steps, and everywhere a swarming of artisans and shopkeepers. The artisans had their stalls hard by the shops where they sold their goods. There were goldsmiths and silversmiths, weavers, sandal-makers, sellers of cloth and of completed garments, such as tunics and veils; perfume mixers worked side by side with garlic and onion dealers and with potters. Slave sellers chanted loudly the merits of their human merchandise. One might see a coal black Ethiopian mother standing on the block, and the dealer pointing to her heavy sack-breasts, crying out that this woman was a breeder of mighty sons: every one of her offspring a veritable Hercules: a whole generation of gladiators, he roared, had already sprung from her loins. Nor was her fruitfulness at an end, but those mighty breasts would yet nourish another generation of fighters. On another block stood a naked "Adonis," a youth of mighty proportions. The merchant had anointed him with oils, so that the flesh shone like metal. Slave girls, their heads adorned with wreaths of violets and white daisies, stood in a circle, themselves like a wreath of flowers. In the King's Row—so called in memory of an ancient king, Archon, a mythological being, half man and half fish— were displayed the wares of the sculptors and metal workers, whose chief product consisted of images of the gods and goddesses of Athens, in a variety of materials. Dominating all the others were the figures of Pallas Athene, protectress of Athens—wretched copies of the famous Phidias statue on the Acropolis. Second in popularity to her was

Demeter, and a close third was Hera, the goddess of fruitfulness. There were also many statues of Apollo and Hercules, for an image of these gods had to be placed in every school and gymnasium; the rich would have such images in the bedrooms of their youth, to serve as inspirations to beauty and strength, and there was a considerable business in copies of the Aphrodite, and of Bacchus, the god of wine and of theatrical spectacles.

This market of Athens, in the shadow of the Areopagus and under the gigantic statue of Mercury, resembled, then, all the marketplaces of the ancient East. Yet there was a difference. Eros had fashioned the world out of chaos, and love was the weaver of life. Athens was filled with youth and with love. Athens subsisted on her ancient glory; she received donations from the rich of all lands, for the sake of her past, and for the sake of her students. Athens was the Jerusalem of the gentile world. The aristocracy of Rome and of the provinces, those who planned great careers for their sons, whether in politics, or in the army, or in the imperial administration, sent them to the schools of the sages in Athens. Every lawyer who looked forward to a rich practice, every scholar and professor who dreamed of a position in a university, every actor even, whose ambition lay with the general public, knew that a first prerequisite was an Athenian reputation. Thus the city was filled with her own students and with students and professors who had already eaten their fill of learning in other lands.

Even in the marketplace the visitor caught at once the specific character of this university city. Young students clustered about the forges of the rapier smiths; with expert eye and hand they appraised the supple blades, tested the sound of the metal, and waxed enthusiastic over some exceptional piece of craftsmanship. Here and there a circle would be made and a fencing bout would take place. Other students were gathered about the dealers in robes, learning the difficult art of flinging a mantle over the body in such wise as to bring out the most graceful curves and folds. One shop of oils and ointments attracted a particularly large crowd of students. The dealer, an Asiatic Greek of Antioch, swore by all the gods of Olympus that his oils and perfumes had the mystic power of awakening the love of a woman, to rouse her to such a pitch of desire and jealousy that the mere emotion brought on pregnancy. In the shops of dyed stuffs young men sought presents for their latest loves, and from the cloth merchants went over to the gold- and silver-smiths. The prosaic mingled with the exalted; side by side with the purchasers of love gifts were the buyers of vegetables, dried fish, skins of wine. But these commodities, too, were often destined to serve the same purpose; they were preparations for a banquet. There was also a constant demand for flowers, fruits, herbs, spices, and plants of all kinds: sugarcane, mustard seed, myrtle, apricots, castor seeds for oil, and, for adornment, great masses of delicate cyclamens of all colors, with petals like the tongues of kittens, sensitive mimosa twigs with yellow boles, red oleander flowers, pink and white, and orchids—orchids in the forms of women's sandals, orchids like animal tongues, orchids like women's breasts, orchids like tiny amphorae with nectar for the gods. The flower-stalls were riots of color, from dark brown to a bloody purple, from cinnamon to flaming saffron—and all for the youth, which bought generously, in order to make wreaths to hang on the doors of the beloved.

The older folk, the more seriously inclined and the more learned, were to be found in the book and papyrus shops. Here, on grass mats, sheltered by awnings from the sunlight, sat learned slaves, dipping their sharpened metal pencils in colored inks and copying out manuscripts, word by word, as dictated to them from a reader on a pulpit. The shopkeeper would hang up single leaves of covered papyrus, samples of the work produced by his copyists. Prospective customers were grouped about the leaves of papyrus on display; old scholars with bald heads, young men with heads of bushy hair. This was their opportunity to examine the classic text of an ancient work for themselves, instead of having to hear it recited badly by poor actors and worse mimics. Before one of the bookshops the dealer had hung out several pages of one of Aristophanes' comedies, and a lively discussion was going on among the students and scholars on the everlasting theme of the attitude of that ancient writer toward the gods and heroes of Greek mythology. The discussion was lively but apparently pointless, for the scholars who took up the theme that Aristophanes was a blasphemer were themselves Sophists, and, having carried their point, turned round and declared that blasphemy was the highest form of praise for the gods. The only result of the discussion was that a bystander could no longer guess who of the disputants was for Aristophanes and who against him. For those who had begun by defending him now took up the view that inasmuch as he also mocked the great god Bacchus, the patron of the theater, and therefore the god of merriment, and held in disesteem the deeds of Hercules, his influence on the youth could not be but harmful.

Such was the marketplace in the Agora of Athens. But it was only part of the Agora. From the foot of the statue of Mercury an alley of pillars led across to the second half of the Agora, at the foot of the Acropolis. Entering this section, the visitor was lost in a confusion of temples, altars, and statues which rose along the slopes and steps toward the supreme temple on the summit.

There was competition among the gods, in the matter of the beauty of their temples and altars. This competition was echoed by the heroes, the poets, and the warriors. Every ruler wanted to see his statue erected among the divine images and altars of the Agora. The Roman generals who conquered Athens treated the city with a respect and consideration granted to no other province. They themselves were eager to contribute buildings to the city. Not only the mightiest of the Romans, a Julius or an Anthony, but even the lesser overlords, competed with each other in their gifts of temples, statues, colonnades, and porticoes. It was a mark of high culture for a ruler to squeeze taxes out of his groaning subjects in order that he might add something to the adornment of Athens. The Jewish tyrant, Herod the First, had sought feverishly the privilege of having one of his own buildings in Athens. He never achieved it. No statue of his was to be found in the Agora. But one of his predecessors, the High Priest Hyrcanos, had, strangely enough, risen to this apotheosis, and his image stood among those of Athenian rulers, heroes, poets, and legislators. Very little praying was done in the temples of Athens; one might almost have said that there were more temples than serious worshipers.

In this part of the Agora Paul wandered about, lonely and bewildered. He wandered among temples and altars which, like those he had seen on the road from the Piraeus, made him think of a cemetery of the gods. He read the inscriptions. The one at the foot of the statue of Mercury ran: "Go and do no evil." A second declared: "Never betray thy friend." He watched the unattended ceremonials which were carried out in the temples of Dionysus-Bacchus, of Apollo, and of Two-Faced Janus. His Jewish temperament turned passionately from the beauty of the architecture and the fine severity of line of the Doric columns which supported the temples. His heart was moved to anger, and he burned with zeal for God. He thought within himself: "They have a father-god and a mother-god, son-gods and bastard-gods, and gods who go whoring after the daughters of men. But not one of them can speak or hear."

The sacred path led up to the temple mount, the Acropolis. Here the temples seemed to be hewn out of the primal rock. The tall pillars soaring into the air broke at the top into a burst of leaves. From among the temples peered out fragments of the basic rock, and sometimes one could not tell what had been formed by God and what by the hand of man. Sometimes a ledge was thrust out like a frozen wave of stone, threatening to overwhelm the graceful terraces, the measured lines and walls and colonnades; and yet the temple walls were a harmonious continuation of the rock, as though they had sprung from it of themselves.

The apostle went by the temple of Aphrodite and the temple of Vulcan, both of them nestling in a cleft of the rock. Statues of poets, tyrants, heroes, rulers, men and gods, in all poses, looked down on him in throngs as he ascended the broad marble steps leading to the summit. There, above, only one goddess reigned, before her glorious Parthenon —Pallas-Athene, the protectress of Athens. Her mighty figure, fifty feet high, was reared on a broad platform supported by columns. She was surrounded by a host of gods whose figures reached barely to her knees. The golden three-pointed helm flashed on her head, flashed over the Acropolis, over the city, over the Aegean Sea, and over the spirit of Greek thought.

The features, cut in ivory by the master hand of Phidias, betrayed no touch of femininity. Not here the subtle and alluring smile of the goddess Aphrodite. Pallas-Athene was severe and just, dedicated to the useful and the necessary, the patroness of the known and experienced— the patroness of wisdom. Her rulership was not indicated by the rounded lines of a mother-body; nor did it rest in the proud lines of her throat. Her rulership was through wisdom alone, and that shone in the great and steadfast eyes. The master had clothed her in a long, massive, golden robe, the folds of which fell in a straight cascade over her bosom, her hips and her knees, down to her ivory ankles. (There were other robes which were drawn over her figure at times—but on this day she stood in the golden mantle of Phidias.) Her golden·shield, blazing in the sun, was adorned with scenes of battle. In one hand she held her long golden spear; in the other arm she held the image of Tyche, who stretched out to her the olive wreath of the conqueror. At a certain time

394

the goddess had conceived a great envy of Aesculapius, the son of Apollo, who had discovered many cures for sicknesses. Therefore she had ordered that a gigantic serpent, symbol of medicine, be wound about her feet. It lay there now, in golden coils, the cleft tongue protruding from the open jaws. Thus she stood, the goddess-protectress of Athens, clothed in her attributes, on the summit of the Acropolis, and the wild, rearing steeds on her golden helm were the symbols of the swiftness of thought, her domain.

Behind her stood the loveliest building in Athens, the most perfect and most harmonious human utterance ever expressed in architecture— the Parthenon. It was not the procession of the gods, hammered into its frieze, which wrought the perfection of the Parthenon, but the sheer simplicity of its form. Not a single superfluous line marred the integrity of the structure. Whatever had been put into it was there by virtue of need and rose from the hunger of the human eye for beauty. The calm severity of the building made one think of the quiet murmur of a spring; it was the song not of a mighty cascade, but of a still-flowing rivulet among the shadows of heavy cypresses. The power of the Doric columns which stood like guards about the building did not appall the eye of the beholder; rather, against the white background of the marble façade, they seemed to beckon him hospitably into the shadow of the robes on the graceful bodies of the feminine figures, there to become one with the harmony which streamed out of them.

Before the towering statue of Pallas-Athene stood a little Jew, Paul the apostle, known in Israel as Saul—a Pharisee and a son of Pharisees—and he gazed up at the goddess. For him it was no goddess; there was not even a demon in the figure. For he did not believe that there were gods and goddesses; there was only the one God of Israel, who filled all the worlds; His glory was in all places; no image, no statue, could enclose Him, and no word could express Him, who had said: "I am that I am." Everything but Himself was the work of His hands. The dead image of gold, erected by the clever Athenians as their goddess, was the creation of one of His creatures. The material of which the image was wrought and hammered was created by Him. The thought which begot the figure, the senses which endowed it with its lines, and inspired it with the manifestation of the lofty, the earnest, and the beautiful, were the gift of God to the craftsman. In this sense, and so understood, the image before him was not an abomination, as others thought: for of itself it was without force. It was not in itself a usurpation of divinity; and those that believed in its divinity were merely transferring to it their own concept of the divine, and that, limited as it was, related actually to the one living God, Whom they in their blindness could not perceive, so that they worshiped the creation, even at second remove, rather than the Creator. "Their gods are silver and gold, the work of their hands; They have mouths, but speak not, eyes, but see not, ears, but hear not, nostrils, but smell not; their limbs are without motion, their throat is without sound." And the apostle said to himself, addressing the image in thought: "Thy gold will be thy evil spirit and thy undoing, goddess of Athens. For it will provoke men to shatter thee and melt thee down, and with all thy glory and strength thou wilt be defenseless against them."

The sun rays grew stronger and the golden glow of Pallas-Athene's robe deeper and fiercer. The long, perpendicular folds were like runlets down which a fiery light streamed, emphasizing the loftiness of the image. The ivory whiteness of her towering throat took on the pallid glow of living skin. She stood there with spear and shield, a living giantess, a mighty demon, descended from Olympus. The gods behind her, on the temple frieze, took on life, too, as though they were starting out of the sleep which the master craftsman had thrown upon them. They awakened and from behind the goddess glared resentfully at the apostle who had come with this message of doom. Even almighty Zeus lifted his gigantic head, bearded and crowned with heavy locks— and on his face there was resentment; the calm detachment of Olympian all-knowledge had fled from his countenance. It seemed, too, that the Doric columns which guarded and supported the temple had lost their harmonious calm and their graceful simplicity of line; they seemed to be moving forward and closing ranks, as though to protect the majesty of Olympus from the assault of the alien Jew. But the Jew stood calmly before them, stared back, and continued in his thought:

"And your temples will become desolate; their pillars will be used to support the roofs of houses of God. And the name of the God of Israel, through His holy servant, the Messiah, will be sung gloriously from end to end of the world."

It was quiet upon the Acropolis. The dying rays of the sun lay on the pillars of the temples, on the façades and on the steps. The tattered sandals of the apostle clattered on the marble as he descended, between temples and gods, from the summit of the Acropolis. His shadow was thrown back upon the altars, and they seemed to shrink from the stern sound of those sandals descending cityward. The gods stared after the alien Jew, brooded on his footsteps, on his frail, bent form, on the huge head. Apart from the sound of his footsteps, there could be heard on the Acropolis, at that hour, only the tinkling of bells which priests sounded at the entrances of the temples, to remind the worshipers that the gods were still there. Then suddenly the messenger came to a halt. Before the image of one of the gods stood a young couple, hand in hand, addressing him in prayer. At the feet of the god lay a garland of flowers. The man was chanting aloud the hymn of Cleanthes to Jupiter. Its words were familiar to Paul, he had often heard them declaimed, and in many places.

"Thou, most praised among the gods, O thou, immortal Jove,
Highest on earth below and in the heavens above:
Thou, the first great cause—thy word is nature's law.
Before thy throne we mortals bow humbly,
For we are of thy seed, and to man alone is it granted,
Yea, to man alone, to lift his voice to heaven."

"God of Israel," said the apostle, inwardly, "how near are men to Thee. Through the darkness of the night they have groped their way to Thee. For Thee alone all men mean in their prayers, and for Thee alone their words of praise are fitting. Turn Thy countenance upon them, O God, and see how they hunger after Thee, turn Thou to them and renew Thy bond with them, through Thy holy servant, Yeshua the Messiah, whom Thou hast sent as a help to mankind."

And in that moment it became clear to him, clearer than ever before, that God had indeed turned His countenance upon man; in Athens, on the Acropolis, among the idols, it became thus clear to him. In the infinity of the world this spot had been chosen for a sign; out of the unknown He had sent a glimmer of the known. He had set a limit, an appointed hour of judgment, through the Messiah he had chosen.

* * *

It was evening when Paul re-entered the Agora. The images, the altars, and the pillars were shrouded in shadow. In the Agora itself there was a lively tumult. Crowds were streaming toward the eastern wall of the Acropolis. They came on, holding torches aloft to illumine the path. Here and there sober lanterns, raised on bamboo poles, twinkled like stars. Young men pressed forward, holding hands and keeping step to the sounds of flute players. Sometimes a litter, in which reclined one of the councilors of Athens, threaded its way through the crowds, preceded by heralds who called out the name of the important man who demanded passage. There were many women, too, heavily robed, veiled, surrounded by their suites of overseers and servants. All were streaming toward the Dionysus theater in the eastern wall of the Acropolis; for in that amphitheater a play was to be given that night, with one of the famous actors of Athens in the leading role. The play was the *Oedipus Rex* of Sophocles.

Paul turned and let himself be drawn along with the crowd. It seemed to him that the whole population of the city was making for the amphitheater. The rising tiers were packed with young and old, and vast though the amphitheater was, it could not accommodate all who wanted admission; and there were fierce struggles for places, mostly between the slaves who attended their masters. The ushers, priests of Dionysus, with handsome curled beards and white robes over their bodies, tried in vain to maintain order. At the gates of the theater mobs pressed forward, and the larger the numbers of those admitted, the larger were the crowds left outside.

Paul was carried into the theater in a sudden rush. He was anxious to see the play. He knew it, as he knew many other of the ancient masterpieces of the theater, from his student days in Tarshish. He also knew that of all the great Greek tragedies this one embodied most perfectly the world outlook of the man of Greece.

The stone benches closest to the arena were occupied by the leading citizens of Athens. Further down, about the empty throne which was reserved for Dionysus, "the bringer of joy and of play to man," stood a group of his priests. It was the popular belief that Dionysus attended every one of the plays and rendered judgment on the quality of the performance. The remoter tiers, reaching far up the slope, were packed with the ordinary citizenry. Jammed together, the occupants of the seats maintained a ceaseless clamor. Friends shouted to each other above the heads of others, and even threw each other their flower wreaths. In the open arena stood the players and the chorus of old men.

Some of them were clad in fantastically colored costumes and held in their hands the masks they would put on during the performance. The audience was mightily interested in the actors, and as it recognized one favorite after another, his name was cried out loudly. It was as if the spectators were encouraging gladiators to the fight. Other actors, who had disgraced themselves lately, were greeted with laughter, even before they had put their masks on for the performance.

The priests of Dionysus lifted the trumpets to their lips, and at the silver sounds the audience slowly grew quiet. From high gaiety the on-lookers passed into a mood of earnestness and concentration, for this was not merely a theatrical performance which they were attending; it was also a religious service.

Even before Oedipus was born to his parents, the King and Queen of Thebes, the gods had set his dreadful and unalterable destiny: that he should slay his father and wed his mother. Why was this done? Paul asked himself. Was this trial planned for the prince in order that his character might be perfected, his faith strengthened, his soul clarified— as was the case with Job—and that he might in the end issue triumphant in spirit over adversity? Not by any means. *That* was the planned purpose of the Jewish God. But the gods of Olympus had laid this ghastly future upon the noble King of Thebes and upon his unborn son for no reason at all related to them; they did it out of a sort of playfulness! The King and Queen of Thebes, learning from the oracle of the decree of destiny, or of the gods, did all in their power to evade its oncoming. They were prepared to sacrifice the child rather than let it live into the unspeakable fulfillment of the future. But they were impotent; and not they alone; even the gods were impotent to prevent the unfolding of the course of events which they had themselves decreed.

All the beholders knew the story; but once again, faced by the masterpiece of the great dramatist, they lived through it as though it were new. Breathlessly they followed the scenes. They saw first the calamitous results of the sin—the pestilence in the city of Thebes. For the decree had become reality. Without knowing why, without the co-operation of his will, Oedipus had fulfilled to the letter the words of the oracle—had slain his father, had wed his mother, and begotten two daughters on her. And now the gods demanded vengeance for the sin! They demanded it first through the pestilence of Thebes; and Oedipus, in darkest ignorance of the source of the calamity, dedicates himself to the discovery of the criminal act which has moved the gods to anger. His mother-wife, knowing to what a dénouement his discovery of the truth will lead, seeks in vain to discourage him from the search.

"The mother : 'I implore thee, do it not.'
Oedipus : 'I cannot cease. I must know the truth.'
The mother : 'For thy sake do it not. I mean it for thy good.'
Oedipus : 'I grow impatient of thy good counsel.'
The mother : 'Woe to thee, thou broken vessel !' "

The end draws on with the swiftness of a flying arrow. The mother cannot prevail on the son to remain in happy ignorance, "to live from hand to mouth." She takes her own life. Noble-spirited Oedipus, learning the truth, stabs out his own eyes and condemns himself, a blinded creature, to eternal exile.

Paul's heart was moved, as never before, by this evidence, in the gentiles, of a ceaseless aspiration toward the truth, even to their own undoing. For this was not Oedipus alone; this was the gentile world at its best. He was moved, too, by the awe with which the assembly followed the tremendous story of the Theban prince. All of them, seated on the stone tiers, were participants in the Oedipus tragedy; all of them were chained to blind destinies. Their gods knew only of destiny, but nothing of grace. No redeemer had been born to them; there was not in the heavens one to represent them, to be their Adam Kadmon, the primal man.

Oh, he learned much that evening, and his heart was full of it. He felt as though he was about to spring to his feet and to cry out, in the heart of the gentile world, in their theater : "No, no, this is not the truth that you have been shown. Man is not a beast among the other beasts, tied to the destiny of his own nature. Man is the chosen of creation. God has appointed a special grace for man. He formed man in His own image and endowed him with His own attributes. He has breathed into man a soul which is a part of Him. He prepared the blessing before the curse, salvation before calamity. Yes, even before He created the first man, God created the savior of man, the first heaven-man."

Fountains of bliss opened in immeasurable depths of his heart as he remembered the name of the savior in this place; the living waters came up and bathed him and refreshed him. When he went homeward in the night through the streets of Athens, there was a dancing in his footsteps. He was drunk, not with wine, but with joy. He saw before him, as in a crystal-clear vision, the power of the Messiah.

That night Paul, the apostle to the gentiles, experienced a heavenly ascension. First he saw the world spread out before him, like a linen cloth on a table. Over the spread-out world men walked, in cities, on hills and in valleys, through forests and wildernesses; man and woman, young and old, they went, some singing and dancing, some wrapped in their own shadows. There were heroes among them, and there were also weaklings, who leaned on the shoulders of their friends; there were also blind ones, who tapped on the road with their staves. There were some who were blind but who thought they could see, and they strode forward boldly, arrogance shining in their eyes. The rich were there, attended by their servants, preceded by their heralds and the poor, the robbed, in tatters. Some that were sick were carried in litters, and there were crowds that ran pursued by evil demons in the form of sicknesses. Paul heard the tinkling of the bells carried by lepers, and the whining cry: "Unclean! Unclean!" And he saw men that had been half eaten away by disease; they dragged themselves along on the ground, clutching at their sores with their scarred hands. He saw others who walked gaily, their heads covered with wreaths of flowers, and they were accompanied by flute players, harp players, and dancing girls. Sages paced along gravely, surrounded by their disciples. Jesters skipped through the crowds, showing their teeth in the grin of idiocy. All these, going for ever forward, began to converge; the paths ran closer till they ended in a single path on the brink of a volcanic pit which opened suddenly at their feet. All unknowing, they had been approaching this fiery mouth, and suddenly they were swallowed up, the young, the old, the strong, the weak, the hale, the sick, the sage, the foolish—all, all of them, were swallowed up by the pit, all of them shared the same destiny.

And suddenly Paul beheld *Him!* His likeness filled all space, from the topmost heavens to the nethermost deep. His likeness was that of a man. His feet covered half the earth, his head towered into unreachable heights. He bent down and thrust his mighty hand into the bowels of the pit; wave after wave of the lost returned, and the mouth of the pit was closed. Out of his body came wings, blue as the evening skies, and fringed with silver light. And now Paul beheld the heavens transformed into fields covered with dewy grass and set with young cypress woods. The throngs rescued from the bowels of the pit were scattered

401

upon the eternal green of the heavenly fields, in eternal youth, eternal spring.

Paul knew whom he beheld. This was the Adam Kadmon who from the bowels of the pit scooped up the lost, wave after wave, and brought them to himself, to the heavens of peace which he had prepared for them.

Then Paul fell to the earth and covered his eyes with his hands.

Chapter Nineteen

OF ONE BLOOD

IN that part of the Agora which lay beneath the Acropolis, near the beginning of the Sacred Way which led to the summit, stood "The Painted Portico," behind a statue of Solon, the founder of the Athenian constitution. It was a tradition since the days of Socrates that every wandering professor who visited Athens had the right to speak in the open air, opposite The Painted Portico, on any subject of his choosing, to any who would stop and listen. There was no lack of wandering professors in Athens, and no lack of listeners in the Agora, always ready to hear something new in the way of philosophy, science, or politics. The Athenians were noted for their insatiable curiosity and for their readiness to give a hearing to whatever theories were brought to them from the ends of the Roman Empire or beyond.

On the morning when Paul first issued into the Agora to deliver the tidings, there were several professors addressing their little groups of listeners. One of them was lecturing on the life and philosophy of Zeno, the founder of Stoicism, who had taught the theory of the one God, the beginning and the end of all things. God had delegated the management of the world—so the professor explained in his exposition of Zeno's views—to demons who were of a kindly inclination toward man, and these demons were the gods of the Greeks. The Stoics also believed in the immortality of the soul, but not for all human beings; that privilege was reserved only for such as were educated and followed

402

the path of justice in their lives. When such men died, their souls were translated to higher spheres. But the lore of the Stoics was aimed only at the perfection of the individual, that is, of the intelligent individual, who was in this view the highest achievement of creation. So the professor taught, and not far from him another professor was addressing his group on the subject of the Epicurean system, as founded by Epicurus.

"The gods," he declared, "can do nothing to change a man's destiny. The gods have no interest in the destiny of the individual. The body of man consists of a substance which ceases to exist with his death. Therefore man should not fear death. Death is that which does not exist, and that which does not exist cannot be felt."

A third professor, a fourth, a fifth, and a sixth were all addressing their groups upon their special subjects, and listeners wandered from group to group. In one place a professor had attracted a larger crowd because he had only just arrived from Alexandria, bringing with him, from the famous Museum of that city, a new interpretation of the theory of atoms as originally taught by Democritus. Thus they stood in the morning light, in the Agora, these multitudes of teachers who had brought to the metropolis of the Greek world every variety of thought which the ancient world afforded. And listening awhile to them, Paul was aware that in their confusion of views they were not seeking the ultimate truth; this much of the Sophists was in all of them, that their desire was to win a debate, to prove their sharpness of wit and their ingenuity in argument. And indeed, many of the listeners had come with that same purpose in mind, and the Agora of Athens was little more than an arena for mental acrobatics. The glory of the name of Athens had drawn hither many professors and many students. Their robes had trailed in the dust of a hundred roads before they had achieved the great intellectual privilege of teaching or learning in the Agora. And now Paul stood among them, ready to begin his mission: a man who did not know whether his labor here would be more successful than it had been in the synagogue where he had been greeted with laughter. His last money—the few drachmae he had brought with him from Salonika—was gone. Of late he had been very sparing of his food, in order to stretch his means; his bed had still been the bench in the hospice to which the head of the synagogue had admitted him out of pity. His sandals were worn through, his robe was tattered. He had nothing in the world except his faith in God the Creator and His Messiah. And this was enough for Paul, the Jew, with his unprepossessing appearance, his provincial Greek, his outlandish accent. When he had heard his fill of the verbal ingenuities of the professors, he sprang suddenly on to the pedestal of a pillar (he did not even notice that its summit was crowned with the image of a god!) and addressed himself to the all-wise Athenians, the students, philosophers, and scientists.

What was he going to say? Whatever God put into his mouth!

He began with the Alpha and Omega of the Stoics, the God of the beginning and the end of all things, the God of the universe. This at least was not a phrase and not a philosophic hypothesis—it was reality. That God existed. He was the God of Israel, who was implicit in every thought and could not be expressed by any word. The God of the universe had taken compassion on the crown of His creation, man, and first He had made a bond with His people, Israel. Now the time had come for God to extend His compassion to all mankind. No, the God of the universe was not indifferent to the destiny of man. God had not relinquished man to the evil beast of nature. He had lifted man to the summit of His creation. He had appointed a time when all men should come under the sign of His Messiah. Therefore, the time having come, he had sent a savior to mankind. He had sent him in the person of the Messiah, who had been promised to the forefathers of the Jews through the Prophets. The Messiah had come, he was here. He was living among them. Though he had died, like all other men, he had been the first to rise from the dead. He, in turn, would awaken all men from death, that they might face the judgment of the Messiah.

Paul had his listeners, like all the speakers in the Agora; some of them were Athenians, others foreigners. All were attracted by the vague hope: "Who knows? Perhaps this stranger brings hither the wisdom of the East, the philosopher's stone. Perhaps he has secrets to unveil such as we have never thought of before." Even Paul's strange appearance wrought somewhat in his favor: his high, bulging forehead, beetling over his fiery eyes, his flushed and radiant face, and the general air of exaltation and transfiguration which shone from him: this in spite of the long nose, the disproportionately large ears, the beard, the frail body which was gripped by a convulsion when he spoke of his mission. But this was true only of some of his listeners. For as he stood talking one of them exclaimed:

"Do not the gods love beauty? Do they not choose the handsomest of men to be their priests? And is not every handsome man himself a god? How comes this creature to be talking to us of divinity? With that face, and that body!"

"And that pronunciation," groaned another. "That Asiatic dialect of his pierces my ears as with thorns. Could not the God of Israel have sent us a messenger with a decenter accent?"

"The God of the Jews is fond of ugly things," declared a third. "No doubt He Himself is somewhat of a cripple. Did you not know that the God of the Jews has forbidden His followers to represent Him in images? That is why the Jews conceal Him from the world and from themselves."

"Not always does the wisdom of Athene inhabit the body of an Apollo," said a fourth. "I have heard good things from other gods, too."

But there were some in the crowd that listened attentively to the apostle. One addressed a serious question to Paul:

"Does the speaker imply that not only will our souls be transformed into heroes of legend, but that our bodies will be reassembled in life?"

Paul answered:

"Our bodies, in the form and substance of their lives, will rise from their graves when the lord will come to judge the world. And even as I saw him with my own eyes, even so I believe that we shall all rise."

"If I had a face and body like the speaker's," muttered one bystander, "I much doubt whether I should desire to be restored to them. Now if his God would only promise me the figure of Apollo—"

A scholar with a long, earnest face, who had been listening closely, said to those about him:

"The man speaks well, he speaks wisely, and he speaks like a philosopher. Not only the soul, but the body of man too shall rise with the resurrection. The man gives you full value for your money, mark that well. For when all is said and done, what has man apart from his body? And the body is that which measures and bears the worth of the man." The scholar turned to Paul and said, loudly: "Tell me, thou man of learning and philosophy, how shall the body, which corrupts away in the earth, be brought back again to life? Dost thou mean thereby

405

that, in accordance with the theory of Democritus and Leukippus, our bodies are composed of atoms, and that these atoms shall be reassembled, to reconstitute the body of the man, with all its functions? If that be so, perhaps the learned speaker will tell us what is to happen with those atoms which, having fallen away from one man's body, have been incorporated in another man's body? Will they be returned to the first owner, to enable him to become himself? And if that be so, what is to happen with the second body? And what experimental proofs has the learned speaker brought us concerning the veracity of his theories? If the learned speaker will be good enough to produce them, I am sure that the scholars here assembled will examine them with the profoundest interest. Nay, we will all of us be indescribably grateful for the privilege of witnessing the experiments which the learned speaker will no doubt perform in our presence." The speaker, now addressing Paul mockingly in the third person, looked around with a grin, and asked: "Does not one of you, O scholars and philosophers, happen to have a corpse in his possession, for the purpose of the experiment? Or perhaps one of you will permit himself to be temporarily killed in the name of wisdom."

In the simplicity of his soul Paul did not catch the mockery in the man's voice, did not even notice the laughter of the bystanders. He was so steeped in earnestness that to him it seemed that it was the mocking professor who was the simpleton; and he was filled with pity for him, as one is filled with pity for a half wit who suffers from the delusion that he is a sage.

"O ye wise one of Athens," he began his answer. "From what atoms are they that you are made? Who formed you and reared you into manhood? A stinking drop was sown in your mother's womb, and out of it was born a man. Know you the bread that you eat? A seed was placed in the earth, and a blade of wheat grew out of it. And what atoms are they with which God formed the world? Who gave Him the material therefor? Who gave Him the drops of water to fill the oceans? Who brought to His hand that wherewith He created the stars in heaven, the seen world and the unseen, the known and the unknown? Who formed you and caused you to grow? Who made the earth firm beneath your feet? Who spread the heavens over your heads? Will it be hard for Him that did this to gather together again the man whom

He has sown in the womb of earth? Will it be hard for Him to open the gates of the tombs, and wake the sleepers in the night? Can you put a boundary to the deeds of God, ye who are blind worms, ye sages of Athens?"

"The man's babbling! Why do we stand here?"

"Do you not see he is half-witted?"

"Nay, he does not babble. He preaches concerning a certain Yeshua, and the resurrection, matters which we hear now for the first time."

"What? He brings alien gods to Athens? He brings us still another cult from the barbarians?"

"Assuredly. He is an enemy of the gods."

"Methinks I smell mutiny. Down with him! Hale him before the city council."

Laughter had become anger. A dozen hands were stretched out to the apostle. He was dragged down from the pedestal and carried up the winding stairs to the platform that topped the Areopagus. The councilors were seated on the stone benches, discussing the affairs of the city. Suddenly Paul beheld himself surrounded by white heads and white beards. He was standing in the center of the council, and about him was the ring of the councilors, their grave faces turned upon him with a uniform expression of amusement and contempt. He heard the furious complaints of those who dragged him thither.

"He brings strange things to our ears!" shouted one.

"He preaches alien gods!"

"He preaches a certain Yeshua who created the resurrection."

"The resurrection?" asked a councilor. "What is that?"

"The dead climb out of their graves."

"And have you brought the Jew here because of such empty nonsense?"

But one of the councilors turned a puzzled gaze on Paul.

"Tell us," he said, "what is this new doctrine that thou preachest? We are curious to hear of it."

But a few moments ago Paul had not known what he was to say. He only knew that He who sent him with the tidings would put the right words into his mouth. And now he spoke to the councilors and sages of Athens:

"Ye men of Athens! I see that you are in all things superstitious.

For as I came this way past your sanctities I saw an altar on which was written: To an unknown god. For He whom ye worship unknowingly, him I preach.

"The God who created the world and all that is in it, being the Lord of Heaven and earth, inhabits no temple which you have made with your hands. Nor is He served by the hand of man, as though He were in need, for He gives life and breath to all things. He has fashioned of one blood all the peoples, so that they might inhabit all the earth. And He set the times, according to the dwelling places of men, in which they should seek Him, though He is close at hand, for we live and breathe in Him; even as several of your poets have sung: 'For we are descended from Him.'

"Now therefore, because we are descended from God, it is not becoming to us to believe that the divinity can be likened to gold, or silver, or stone, hewn into certain forms by the master craftsman. But the time of this ignorance has been brought to an end by Him, and He has commanded that now all men shall repent and turn to Him. He has set a day on which He will judge the world in justice, through the man whom He has chosen. And this was assured to all when he awakened this man from the dead."

The councilors had listened more or less patiently; but when Paul uttered the words "awakened from the dead" a storm of laughter rose from the benches of the councilors.

"See ye not, the man is out of his mind."

"Aye, true, something is lacking here," said one councilor, pointing to his head.

It was the mockery of the councilors which saved Paul from the charge of blasphemy against the gods. One councilor even clapped him on the shoulder, saying:

"Hearest thou, good man, some other day we shall hear thee out to the end. But now get thee gone home, and rest thee."

And with this he was dismissed.

Plodding homeward, Paul said in his heart: "I shall yet disturb the wisdom of the wise and shame the understanding of the sages!"

*   *   *

Finally Timotheus arrived from Thessalonika, and it was high time. He found the apostle in a grievous physical and moral condition.

Timotheus brought with him a little money, the gift of the good and wise Lydia, the dealer in purples in Philippi. Sending the gift to Thessalonika, she had also reported on the welfare of the community of believers in her city, and Paul was rejoiced in heart to hear of the firmness of the foundations he had laid there. Timotheus took Paul out of the gloomy little hospice by the synagogue and installed him in a regular hostel. He also bought new linen and an outer garment for the apostle, for what the latter was wearing was nothing better than rags. He took Paul to a steam bath. In all things, he served Paul as a devoted son serves a father. And while he washed the weary, almost fleshless feet of the apostle he gave him a detailed report of the progress of the group in Thessalonika. It had not crumbled and been washed away, as Paul had feared it would. His labors in Macedonia had taken permanent root, and already the first fruits were evident. But there were difficulties. Certain of the believers really believed that the coming of the Messiah was quite imminent, and that there was no sense in carrying on the business of this earthly life as heretofore, buying, selling, providing for the morrow, and the like. These had abandoned their regular occupations and were spending their days in idleness, living on the charity of the community. But there were some who, on the other hand, showed even less than faith, for they could not disaccustom themselves from their idolatrous habits and customs. Many had relapsed into a dissolute life of whoredom, and they deceived and fooled each other in their behavior. For the rest, God's measure of the worth of deeds was accepted among them; that which was good in the eyes of the lord Messiah was good, and that which was bad in his eyes was bad. They thought often of the apostle, and of his lessons. They longed for his return, spoke of him incessantly, and considered him an angel of the lord. They frightened the backsliders by speaking of the apostle's return.

Paul listened to the end and gave thanks to God for the sign which He had vouchsafed him. He knew now that he should not have let Timotheus come to him, seeing that he was so badly needed elsewhere, and he bade the young man return to Thessalonika. In vain did Timotheus plead to be permitted to stay and to tend his father and teacher, as he called Paul. Silo, he said, was in Salonika, and he was a great worker. But Paul was insistent, saying:

"God comfort thee, my son, as thou hast comforted thy father

409

Paul. The Lord calls thee elsewhere to His work, and thou must go."

He sent Timotheus back to Macedonia and himself made preparations to proceed to Corinth.

Chapter Twenty

THE BIRTH OF THE CHURCH

HE took boat at Piraeus and sailed for Cenchrea, the port of Corinth. All the way he reproached himself for his failure in Athens, laying the responsibility at his own door. He had not done well to try and overcome with worldly wisdom the worldly wisdom of the sages of Athens. He should never have gone to the philosophers of Athens, who were convinced that they had exhausted all the seas of knowledge, whereas they were but as moles wandering about in blind little alleys of earth. From now on, he promised himself, he would not bring to the world the wisdom with which he had sought to make himself great and acceptable to the Athenians. He would speak to men and women as one speaks to children, and not to corrupt adults. He would nourish them with the milk of faith, as he had done with his beloved Galatians and with the Macedonians. This resolution of his comforted and strengthened him. He said, moreover:

"As long as the cause of the Messiah shall not be confirmed in Corinth and Achaia by the Messiah himself, no shears shall touch my hair, and my lips shall not taste meat or wine, except the wine which is the blood of the lord. This is my sacrifice to God, and it shall not cease except when I have brought a sacrifice of redemption to the Temple in Jerusalem."

He did not know to whom he was going, and whom he would address. The moment he set foot in Cenchrea he felt the breath of a new wind. This was not the harbor city of dead gods, like Phalerum, the port of Athens. Cenchrea was a port of the living. Life rioted here among the innumerable masts of ships which came from every province in the Empire. The paved streets resounded with the footsteps of sailors, merchants, and travelers. He met here a number of Jews, brought thither by the commerce which took a great forward leap when Corinth was declared a Roman colony. This city had a great future, standing as it did between the Asiatic countries and the mother country of Italy. Even now there was such a concourse of ships here as could hardly be seen in any other port. They brought grain, wines, spices, ores, arms, and dyed stuffs from the Asiatic provinces, from Alexandria, Phoenicia, Cappadocia, Phrygia, and Pamphylia; and though their ultimate destination was farther west, all the boats called at the port of Corinth. The city was expanding visibly from year to year. Jews too came from every part of the Empire, from Asia, from Antioch, from Palestine, and from Rome. These Jews brought with them little centers of the faith in the Messiah, which, in spite of much internal opposition, could not be destroyed. Paul was astonished to find in Cenchrea a little community of believers in the Messiah, and from them he learned of the community which already existed in the city of Corinth.

Corinth was a young city, which was unfolding into greatness. The old and famous Corinth which had flourished under the rule of the Greek tyrants, the Corinth of ancient temples and ancient treasuries of art, had been completely destroyed by Pompey. Julius Caesar had begun the rebuilding of the city, intending to make of it a Roman commercial center. He settled it with freedmen and encouraged colonists from all parts of the Empire to settle in Corinth and to develop the commercial and industrial possibilities of Achaia, so that Corinth might take the place of Athens. But there was nothing whatsoever in the character of the city which entitled it to the proud title of the capital of Achaia. It was a city without tradition, without a dominant unifying language, without a uniform culture. It was a mixture of races and a Babel of tongues. Freedmen and slaves—the former predominating— worked in the foundries, the potteries, the weaving and dye factories, the oil presses, and the gardens. Phoenician, Egyptian, and Asiatic cults of all kinds took root in the city. Some fame had already been acquired by the temple of a Venus Pandemos who was in reality a Phoenician Ashtoreth. More than a thousand girls served there under the overseership of the priests, conducting a huge trade in prostitution under the cover of a sacred service. The temple was naturally much frequented by transient sailors, who spent there the money saved up on long journeys. The city was always full of drunken sailors, who rioted in the streets, crowded the hostelries and restaurants, and lost their hard-earned demeters and Roman dinarii at dice to the local sharps. From the narrow streets of Corinth there went up continuously the angry shouting of drunken and swindled sailors and the shrill laughter of whores. The visitors who passed through Corinth carried the repute of its wealth and dissoluteness to the ends of the ancient world, and a constant stream of peddlers, merchants, and artisans swelled the population of the city. It also happened, some time before Paul's arrival in Corinth, that riots broke out in the city of Rome because of popular resentment against a certain "Xrestos"; and the Emperor Claudius drove many Jews, both Messianists and non-Messianists, out of the capital. Among those that fled to Corinth were Aquila and Priscilla.

The pious couple brought with them, out of Rome, two gifts—their faith in the Messiah and their skill as tent makers; and soon after their arrival in Corinth they transplanted both gifts, so that they flourished in Corinth as they had flourished in Rome.

The sect of the believers was in no way to be distinguished from the other Jews who had settled in Corinth. All prayed together in the synagogue erected by the Jews of Corinth; and as was everywhere the custom, the Jews purchased for themselves a little plot of earth for a separate cemetery. The exiles from Rome were quickly absorbed into the older Jewish settlement. In their home city the Messianists among them had been at odds with their fellow Jews regarding the new faith; here, in exile, they forgot their differences, as Jews in exile are wont to do, and helped each other to settle into the new life. There would be time for the differences to emerge once more when the settlement had become stabilized. The brotherhood of the Corinthian synagogue came generously to the help of the newcomers; from it Aquila obtained a loan, without interest, with which to put up his weaver's stall in the marketplace.

On the evenings of Friday and the Sabbath Priscilla would illumine her little dwelling with many lamps, as had been her custom in Rome; and again her home became the meeting place for the believers and their families, each one bringing a contribution to the common meal. The believers crowded into the small room, seated themselves according to their ages, and services were resumed. Each one was free to speak. Some told stories and repeated sayings of the Messiah which they had heard from visitors to Jerusalem; others spoke as the faith moved them. There was singing of the sacred Psalms, and words of comfort were uttered concerning the imminent advent of the Messiah.

The Sabbath gatherings of the Messianists in Corinth were their greatest source of strength, enabling them to bear without rancor the mockery which their faith awakened in others. Their belief in the Messiah and in his approaching return became for them, profoundly and sacredly, part of their Jewishness, so that they could not understand how one could enter the ranks of the Messianists without having first been received into the congregation of Israel. Certainly they would have liked to see their own community increased by additions from among the Jews of Corinth, but their own numbers were as yet so small, and the memory of the quarrels in Rome so fresh, that they did not dare as yet to become proselytizers, and to risk disturbing the peace of their new-found home. They were therefore content, for the time being, with the privilege of pursuing their faith undisturbed, with the joy of their common meals, and with the practice of helping each other in need; and when they met in discreet seclusion, they greeted each other with the kiss of peace.

This was the condition of the community when Paul arrived in Corinth.

* * *

While he was yet in Cenchrea Paul heard that Priscilla and Aquila were in Corinth, that they had set up their business there as tent weavers, and that they were the center of the community of Messianists. His joy was the greater because he would be able to find work at his own trade while pursuing his mission. As to the latter, he felt that here, in Corinth, there was a ready field waiting to be worked. Corinth was not Athens, corrupt with intellectual pride, unapproachable and impenetrable. True, Corinth suffered instead from the opposite evils of ignorance and grossness, but the basic human material was not rotted through and through. These were still to be saved. His first decision, then, was to obtain employment with Aquila, his second to cast about for the best approach to the salvation of the Corinthians.

From the first moment of his encounter with Aquila and Priscilla Paul knew that he was again amongst his own. He was at home

413

in the workshop in the marketplace, and at home with the pious couple. It was enough for him to see the friendly open face of Priscilla. The warmth which breathed from her restored him after the bitter, frosty reception he had known in Athens. Priscilla took it for granted that the apostle would share their home with them, a little dwelling of four wooden walls, covered with a roof of goat's hair cloth, which her husband had put up. A corner was curtained off for Paul; a bamboo mattress was spread on the floor; from somewhere Priscilla obtained a wooden bench and a three-legged stool; and this was his home. Paul was able at last to unpack his bundle, to take out the scrolls of the Prophets, which he always carried with him, the tools of his trade, and his mantle. Here he ate his first home meal, which Priscilla prepared for him; vegetables, soup, flat cakes of bread, and olives. Offered meat, he put it back gently, for he was under the vows of a Nazirite.

When he returned in the evening, Priscilla had prepared for him a wooden bowl of hot water in which to rest his aching feet; and Paul was filled with gratitude for the manifold blessings vouchsafed him; this roof over his head, this friendly, motherly hand to care for him, and the wide field that lay before him to be sown in the faith. What more could he have asked for?

Among the stalls and booths of the artisans of Corinth, in the marketplace of the city, Aquila had put up his looms under awnings of goat's hair cloth. The goods he produced, material for tents and mantles, he sold on the spot. Women, black as pitch, carded and washed the goats' hair at the foot of the looms. To one such loom Paul himself was harnessed. His face, his eyes, his forehead, his pointed beard, his naked hands and feet, were covered with dust. His hands were busy on the threads before him, his feet worked the treadles below. Swiftly and skillfully he shot the mounted spools from right to left and left to right across the frame, using threads of many colors from dark-brown to deep purple. He worked faster and more neatly than the young men, and there was a sharper sound when he brought the wooden beam against the framework of the loom. A high degree of skill was needed to bring the board, with its teeth, exactly against the openings in the framework. But the limbs of the apostle seemed to work of themselves, like horses continuing on the right path when the driver has fallen asleep. And though this driver was not asleep, his thoughts were elsewhere. For even while he worked he was talking, passionately, to a circle of men and women gathered about the loom. His words sounded above the cries of drunken sailors, the singing of street-walkers, the chaffering of merchants and buyers, the tinkling of coins in bronze trays. His clear, metallic voice, laden with the power of faith, was something distinct and apart from the tumult about him, like the sound of a bell above the murmur of human voices. Those that were listening to him were his own people, and it was to them that he sought to give strength, knowing that they were afraid to spread the faith lest it lead to dissensions in their place of refuge.

"These eyes," rang the voice of Paul, "saw him on the road to Damascus, these ears have heard his voice. And when he appeared to me in the Temple court he bade me carry the tidings of his coming from end to end of the world. And ye of Corinth bid me be silent for the sake of peace in this place? What is this peace that ye seek? It is the peace of the cemetery. Will Satan make peace with you? He too has sent his son into the world, to corrupt and to lay waste, to make you into sinners before the day of judgment. What answer will you give to our lord the Messiah on the day of judgment? See, a black cloud hovers above us, to darken the path, to lead our footsteps to the sides of the pit—and you would make peace in order to be silent concerning the one salvation which is left to man? The lord Messiah has touched my lips with the fire of his hand and with the wounds of his body, and there is no power, neither in the heights of heaven nor in the depths of the earth, neither among the angels nor with Satan, which can close my lips and make them cease from the preaching of the Messiah."

A refugee from Rome took up the argument. "But we have only just saved ourselves from the flames! Our community in Rome was destroyed because of dissensions. We have only just set foot in this new place. We are a young plant which can easily be uprooted. And when the Jews here will learn of your arrival and will remember the disputes which were called forth by your words in so many congregations of Israel, the flames will break out here too. We shall be uprooted again—"

Another broke in, to plead: "Canst thou not wait with the tidings until we have ordered our lives here on a firmer foundation?"

"God's word is not patient," answered Paul. "It is not like a beggar standing at the door, waiting to be admitted. God's word is like a storm in the night; and though thou desirest it not, the lightning

415

finds thee out and strikes. Thou canst not swallow God's word, like a bite of food; for it will become like boiling lead in your vitals. There is no place where you can hide from God's word. Could Jonah hide himself, even in the belly of the great fish?"

"Hear, O apostle! Hast thou no word of comfort for thine own flesh and blood? Why must thy words ever be sharp as a sword, and stinging like thorns, when thou turnest to the House of Israel? The consolation and the hope of the Messiah which God grants to the gentiles thou bringest not to thine own brothers, but in their place dissension and war. With the word of the Messiah thou kindlest a fire in the house of God." Thus spoke, loudly enough for all to hear, Rabbi Andronicus, a man held in high esteem, for he had been one of the first to spread the tidings in Rome, and he had come with the other exiled Messianists to Corinth.

The apostle turned pale. Rabbi Andronicus had given expression to that which had long been lodged in Paul's mind, as a thorn might be lodged in the flesh. Had not the Rabbi touched upon the secret reason why he, Paul, could not obtain a hearing among his own brothers? He had a tongue for the gentiles, but not for his brothers. All knew that. "No, it is not my fault," said the apostle, inwardly. "No, I am not to blame."

Aloud he answered:

"I do not knead my dough with honey. That which God puts into my mouth, that I utter."

"For the gentiles thou dost indeed knead thy bread with honey!" cried one man, furiously. "For the Jews thou hast only a rod. Oh, it is widely known! The holy ones in Jerusalem are not ignorant of it."

"The gentiles are but children in the faith," responded Paul. "And even like children they must be nourished with milk. But the Jews were brought up by the Prophets, and they can digest the strong meat given to grown men."

"They are afraid of men, but they fear not God," came a woman's voice. It was Priscilla. She spoke from the door of her shop, where she had been busy selling the products of the little factory. She turned to those who were questioning and upbraiding Paul and raised her voice, which rang sternly: "The Lord God on high has issued His commands to the apostle. Do you think you will dissuade him from obedience? See to it that you sin not! And if it be our portion indeed to suffer once more for the Messiah, we shall know how to endure it."

With this the discussion ended, for the voice of Priscilla was the voice of authority in the little congregation. However, Rabbi Andronicus could not resist a last appeal to the apostle:

"Reb Paul," he said, in a tone of supplication, "heed thy words and be guarded in thy speech."

On the first Sabbath, immediately following the reading of the Scroll, Paul asked and received permission to preach. His listeners were Jews, and his sermon was addressed to them; and on this occasion he heeded his words and was guarded in his speech, saying nothing that might offend the worshipers, as he had done in other cities when he had, for instance, spoken of the abrogation of the Mosaic law. The entire sermon was devoted to the Messiah of the Jews, to him who had come to the Jews in the person of Yeshua the redeemer. However, he went on to explain that the Messiah was not, as many Jews thought, an earthly redeemer, a king of grace who would redeem the Jews from the yoke of Rome. The Messiah was the Adam Kadmon, of whom the Prophet Daniel had spoken, who would come with the clouds of heaven. The race of mankind derived from him and was bound up in him. He was a heavenly being, higher than the angels. God had sent this heavenly being down to earth in the semblance of a man of flesh and blood, to liberate man from the sins of Edom, which kept all mankind in chains and delivered it to the Devil, to Satan, to the Evil One. The liberation of mankind from the sins of Edom could be brought about only through the sorrows and pains which the Messiah had taken upon himself of his own free will. By his blood, which had been shed like water on the stones of Jerusalem, he had cleansed mankind of its sin and restored it to the condition it had known before the sin of Adam. The suffering and death of the Messiah were foreordained, according to the words of the Prophets and of the Psalmist, King David. He was, moreover, the first to have risen from the dead. His return was imminent and was to be expected at any moment. Therefore it behooved all that believed in him to gather into the fold of his salvation as many of the children of Adam as was possible, persuading them to accept baptism and to take upon themselves the rules of the holy life of brotherly love, of charity, of compassion, of care of widows and orphans, of purity of the body and of the eschewal of whoredom and every other manner of uncleanness.

417

These words, new for him, wrought warmly on the listeners, who heard in them the echo of the hope of Israel. The Messiah was of the Jews! Every Jewish sect knew baptism—it was everywhere a prerequisite for entry into the faith. Because he had spoken of the Messiah in terms of the ancient Jewish faith, and of ancient mystical longings familiar to the Jews, Paul awakened in his listeners a host of tender associations. Moreover, he quoted the Prophets and the Books of Moses and referred to the promises given the Patriarchs. Flames of hope shone from the eyes of the Jews, fountains of joy were opened in their hearts.

And still there were such as waited, and asked themselves what their Rabbis would say concerning this, the supreme hope of Jewry. Who, they asked, were the men who had sent the apostle to them on this mission?

"Surely he does not expect us to respond at once with the words: 'We will do and we will obey,' as our forefathers did at Sinai," argued one Jew. "For we are not like the gentiles, who one day sacrifice to Zeus and Aphrodite and the next day worship the gods of Egypt."

"What comparison is this thou makest?" asked another Jew. "God help thee! Make not unclean the name of the Messiah by uttering it with thy lips. For the Messiah himself preaches the one living God, who through him fulfills for us the promise made to our forefathers."

"But why have we not heard of this until now? Why have the Rabbis been silent?"

Another Jew said: "Methinks we would do well to wait and hear the opinion of those Jews who have gone to Jerusalem on a pilgrimage. They will return soon."

However, after this sermon the head of the synagogue, whose name was Crispus, invited Paul to accompany him to his home. This Crispus was a pious Jew, a simple man, with little learning; like many others, he had long been waiting for the redemption, and his heart was filled with the certainty of faith. The words of the apostle had moved him deeply. All that Sabbath day the apostle sat with Crispus, who was a little man, bowed with the burdens of life, and it seemed as though the words of Paul made him shrink and become even more bowed. On the following day, Sunday, he and all his family were baptized by Paul. He was the first to be won by the apostle in Corinth.

The winning of Crispus was a great triumph for Paul; and when

418

the Messianists who had come from Rome saw that the apostle had prevailed with the leading Jew of Corinth, who was held in esteem for his piety and good deeds, they were ashamed for having tried to dissuade Paul from doing the work of God and were completely won over to his opinion.

Paul's second triumph followed close on the first. Among the pious gentiles who frequented the synagogue on Sabbath days there was a rich man by the name of Stephanus. His name was respected throughout Corinth, for he was wealthy, and he had a great family, that is to say, he possessed many slaves, who worked in his bronze foundry. He and all his family were likewise baptized by the apostle.

About that time there arrived in Corinth Silo and Paul's beloved son, Timotheus. They brought good news from Salonika and Berea. They also brought greetings from Lukas, the healer, who had remained in Philippi, and from the good widow, Lydia, who had again forwarded a sum of money to enable the apostle to continue in the work in Corinth. These good tidings, together with his own renewed success, reawakened the spirit of the apostle, and he was filled with new hope. Was not all this a sign that God was with him in his labor for the Messiah? Yes, from now on he would speak otherwise. He would not plead and implore for the sake of the Messiah. Did the Messiah need to come begging? Had he not the power to compel? Was the Messiah a hungry wanderer at the door of the synagogue, waiting for a kindly soul to admit him? In the mouth of the Messiah was the word of God, in his hand the salvation of Israel. He could bring salvation whether his listeners desired or did not desire.

So, like a man whose authority had been confirmed, Paul ascended the pulpit on the second Sabbath, and pointing to the passage in the Torah which had just been read forth, thundered:

"The Messiah is the fulfillment of the Torah, in righteousness, for everyone who believes. And when thou wilt acknowledge with thy lips and believe in thy heart in the lord Messiah, thou wilt be saved!"

And then, speaking of the veil which hid the face of Moses, Paul became like one drunk with his own words, and proclaimed once more that the Messiah was not only the fulfillment of the promise, but the fulfillment of all the law. Without the Messiah, he declared, there was no Torah or law; and not only was there no Torah without the Messiah, .but without him there were no children of Abraham, even; for the children of God were not children of flesh and blood, and they of the true seed were those who were called the children of the promise. Thus it was that in his second sermon Paul seemed to take away from the Jews that which alone remained to them and to give it freely and without price to the gentiles. Not the Torah, but the Messiah was the core of the faith:

"No man can be justified before him through the work of the Torah, for it is through the Torah that the sins of man are known; nor shall a man be justified by circumcision, for he is not a Jew who is thus externally: he is a Jew who is thus within and who has been circumcised in his heart, in the truth, and not in the fleshly sign. And when Yeshua is within you, your bodies are dead to all sin, but your spirit lives in righteousness."

The worshipers were appalled by his words. For who was he, and who had sent him? The authorities in Jerusalem knew him not; he had no letter either from the Sanhedrin or from the High Priest. And was it not known that this man had brought dissension into countless Jewish communities?

Yet a power that he could not control forced the words out of Paul; they seemed to tear a passage through his flesh. Pain and regret haunted him later in the nights. He was utterly weary of the quarrels which he provoked among his people, whose blood he was so proud to own; they had reached such a pitch by now that their original cause and purpose had been forgotten; it was no longer a dispute in the name of God, but a sort of rivalry between the God of Israel and the Messiah, the God of the gentiles.

And now the apostle performed an act which he had never permitted himself before.

No matter how bitter the dissensions between himself and the Jews had been in the cities of his mission, he had never separated himself from his own people. Yes, he had threatened to do it, he had thrown the writ of divorcement at their feet, saying: "Now I will go to the gentiles." Nevertheless, no sooner had he arrived in a new city than he had inquired first for the synagogue; and thus the quarrels, such as they had been, had remained confined to the four walls of the Jewish house of prayer. Here, in Corinth, for the first time, Paul went away from the synagogue, and rented a house from a godfearing gentile by the name of Justus. The house stood close to the synagogue, and there, almost cheek by jowl with the Jewish house of prayer, Paul opened his own prayer house for the congregation of the Messiah, which consisted both of Jews and of Christians. And Crispus, the former head of the synagogue, now became the head of the new prayer house of the Messianists. It was only by creating the impression that his house of prayer was Jewish that Paul could hope to escape suppression by the authorities.

But in the nights the apostle could not sleep, because the lash of his conscience would not let him. He would review a hundred times over the words he had uttered in the day; he would weigh them again and again in the bloody balance of his heart. Had he done well? He had set out to conquer the world in the name of the Messiah of the God of Israel; and now he had thrust a wedge between Israel and the world; he had cut the thread which bound the Jewish hope to the Messiah. He saw only too clearly that he was winning the gentile world at the cost of his own people. Because he was a Jew, he knew, beyond any shadow of doubt, that no other path was open to the Jews. He knew, through and through, that the Jews could not abandon the law merely at his behest. But neither was he able to divide the Messiah into a Jewish Messiah and a gentile Messiah, even as he could not divide God. There could be but one Messiah, even as there was one God of Israel. Had he a right, then, to do as he had done? He needed a new sign, a corroboration, the direct approbation of the Messiah, to validate his act. And in the nights he lay on the floor of his room and wept for the sign. In a passion of belief and doubt, in an ecstasy of uncertainty, he prayed ceaselessly, and throughout the night he felt a crown of fire pressed upon his head. Foam issued from his lips, and a heavy weight was pressing on his eyes. Thus lying one night, thus suffering, it seemed to him that a form took shape in the darkness. He could not distinguish its outlines, but he knew it to be the form which had hovered before him on the road to Damascus. He heard a voice: "Fear not; but speak and be not silent, for I am with thee."

The vision put an end to his doubts. On the morrow he felt that there was no turning back, there was no ground for hesitancy; he had been called to his new task, he was a faithful servant of the Messiah.

All day long he sat at his loom in Aquila's workshop. His hair, which, because of his Nazirite vow, he had not cut since his arrival in Corinth, hung in knotted locks over his face, his shoulders, and his neck, mingling with the strands of his beard and of his earlocks. Hair and beard and earlocks were alike gray, and there was a big bald patch in the middle of his head. Priscilla and her pious simple husband, as well as the entire Christian congregation implored the apostle to be more heedful of his health, to give up his work at the loom, and to devote himself entirely to the mission to which the Messiah had called him. But they pleaded in vain. Paul continued to work, like a day laborer, at his loom. "My daily labor is part of my mission," he said. He still insisted that in all things he had to serve as a model, particularly in the matters of independence and industriousness. Moreover, he wanted to remain independent for his own sake. Least of all would he permit himself to be supported, in his work as an apostle, by the gentiles of Corinth, in whom he still found much to criticize and correct. On these same grounds, that is, in the desire to be free in act and word, he had founded the new synagogue in the house of Titus Justus, hard by the old synagogue; there, in the evenings, after a day of labor at the loom, and after a meager supper, he preached to his flock of Jews and gentiles.

Now the new synagogue was in fact independent of the old one, having its own head—the former head of the old synagogue, Crispus— its own cantors and officers, its own worshipers, among them Stephanus and his large "family"; nevertheless there was a connection between the two synagogues, for both of them observed the same Sabbath and the same festivals. On Friday evenings the synagogue of the Messianists or Christians was bright with Sabbath candles, just like the synagogue of the Jews; and on Sabbath mornings there was the reading of the Scroll, after which Paul preached on the Messiah. The common feasts, which for a time had been held in Priscilla's home, were now transferred, because of the increase of numbers, to the synagogue. There were already, among the Messianists of Corinth, some prominent citizens in addition to Crispus, Stephanus, Justus, the Jewish Messianists, and one Erastus, an official in the city administration. Likewise there had been added to the Messianists numbers of freedmen and slaves, baptized by Paul's assistants, Silo, Timotheus, Aquila, and Priscilla.

Though Paul preached that justification lay in faith, not works, he knew that works were the flesh and blood of faith. It was not enough to feel oneself united with the Messiah; it was needful to imitate him in the actions he had performed on earth. Therefore he began to teach his gentile converts the Ten Commandments and to educate them in the behavior of faith.

As part of this system of education for the gentiles he followed the plan begun in other cities; he enjoined them to contribute according to their means to the community fund for the care of widows and orphans, the sick and the needy. Until that time the collection of funds for charitable purposes had been known only to the Jews; but Paul made it the practice of the converted gentiles, too. This work could not be done on the Sabbath, for the handling of money was forbidden on that day; moreover, it would have been a desecration of the spirit of the common feasts to transact any business, even with charitable intent, on the night of the Sabbath. Therefore Paul instituted a new procedure and had the members of his congregation assemble on the day following the Sabbath, that is, the first day of the week, the day of the creation.

Thus it was that the congregation of Messianists gathered every Sunday in the synagogue of Justus, and every member brought with him, as his donation, whatever he was able to spare. Even the slaves were not exempt, and their contribution—perhaps not more than a single copper coin, and perhaps less than that, perhaps only a trifling object— was accepted with the rest. On that day Paul preached of sanctity in earthly things, of charity, of love, of decency in deportment, becoming to the congregation of the Messiah. In this wise, because of the collections for charity, the Messianists found themselves observing two Sabbaths, the Jewish Sabbath and the Sabbath of their congregation. To the second Sabbath they gave the name "the lord's day" because on that day the Messiah had risen from the dead.

It was in Corinth that Paul at last found time enough to attend to the complete organization of a congregation.

One of the first rules which he laid down for the members of the Messianic sect was, that everyone was obligated to earn his daily bread honestly with the labor of his hands. Following the tradition of the Jewish communities, Paul founded a number of charitable brotherhoods, charged with the care of the poor and the sick. But whosoever was in good health was not exempted from daily labor. Paul had by then formulated the phrase: "He that will not work shall not eat." For the faith in the Messiah which Paul preached sought not merely to save men after death and give them a portion in the Kingdom of Heaven; it sought likewise to change the world order of the gentiles and to uproot all evil. Faith as Paul preached it was to penetrate all rules and customs, to regulate the life of the individual in his relations to the state, to purify family life, and touch human conduct at all points. The gentiles who accepted the faith of the Messiah were forbidden to participate in the feasts and celebrations arranged by the city in honor of the local gods. But participation in such celebrations was the symbol of citizenship, and when gentiles, converting to the new faith, abstained from participation, they sundered themselves, even as the Jews were sundered, from the rest of the population, whereby they incurred the same hostility as was incurred by the Jews and were subject to the same suspicions and accusations. Now this self-isolation from their fellow citizens fell harder on the gentiles than on the Jews; they needed a special degree of faith to be able to withstand the pressure of their environment and their old associations. In order to buttress the gentiles in this act of sacrifice, the young Christian church adopted the organizational forms of the Jewish synagogue. The officials of the synagogue were duplicated in the officials of the church. Every group elected its overseers and submitted to their authority. Like the Jews, the Christians came to their officers and elders with their problems, whether these concerned the articles of the faith or the rules of life under the faith.

Paul was constantly concerned with the task of keeping the life of the congregation holy. He was on the alert against any infraction of the purity of family life. He strove to introduce a strictly monogamous conception of marriage, with love and respect on the part of the man, love and obedience on the part of the woman: this was his remedy against the dissoluteness of the surrounding world. In some respects he went further, in his prescriptions for the new community, than the Rabbis had done in the case of the Jews. Leaning on the doctrine taught by the Messiah, he forbade divorce. Moreover, members of the Christian congregation were forbidden to take any of their disputes before the city courts. They were compelled to submit to the adjudication of their own arbitrators, even as the Jews did, bringing their litigation to the court which sat in the synagogue. Very early in the history of the new church there was felt, therefore, the need for men learned in the law; and such men began to appear, as they had appeared from of old among the Jews, constituting councils of elders, heads of synagogues, after the Jewish fashion. The elder of the congregation was the highest authority, and his word was law. His functions embraced not only the religious needs of the congregation, but its entire life. He was charged with the education of the young and the appointment of teachers. He kept an eye on the conduct of all the members. When the congregation became too large for the personal supervision of a single elder, he was authorized to choose assistants, among whom he distributed various functions.

And before they quite knew what had happened, the gentiles suddenly perceived that Paul, who had liberated them from the yoke of the Mosaic law, had placed them under the yoke of the law of righteousness. And Silo and Timotheus were his helpers in this gigantic labor.

* * *

In this fierce concentration on the faithful of Corinth, Paul did not for a moment forget the congregations which he had founded in other cities and in other lands. Every congregation was like a beloved child. Very dear to him were the Galatians, the first fruits of his mission; but very dear too were the Philippians, the only ones from whom he had accepted monetary help. And not less dear were the faithful of Salonika, the much tried. The field which he had sown in haste, and had left to the storm, had become golden with the grain of the Messiah. He could not be with his congregations; therefore he would have to teach them from a distance. He remembered his teacher, Rabban Gamaliel; he remembered how he had accompanied the Prince of the Pharisees to his office in the Temple court. There the elders of Israel had been assembled and had received the delegates sent by the various Jewish communities throughout the world to the supreme authority of the Pharisees, bearing questions of all kinds. And Rabban Gamaliel had written letters to all the ends of the great Dispersion, containing the decisions of the sages of Jerusalem. Out of that office in the Temple court the threads had run to the ends of the world, binding the congregations to the center, to the root of Israel, the Torah. Why should not he, Paul, do likewise with the congregations of the Messiah which he had founded? Word came to Paul that there had been many deaths in Salonika, and the faithful of that city mourned because they who had died would not be privileged to see the second coming of the Messiah. Did they not understand, those poor, faithful ones of Salonika, that they who had died in the Messiah lived in the Messiah, and that they would behold the redemption sooner than the living, that they would hear the trumpet of the Messiah before the sounds of it could reach the ears of the living?

Paul called to his beloved son Timotheus and sent him out to buy a roll of papyrus; and he began to weave the network of epistles into which he worked not only the vision of the faith, as he saw it, but the strands of his own life. The letters became the record of his stormy wanderings, the echo of his soul's cry, the mirror of his inner struggles and doubts. They were filled with the dark sound of mourning, with the thunder of rage, with the moaning of his heart, the cry of his triumphs, the ringing of swords, and the kiss of peace. Like a skillful weaver he worked the pattern of his emotions, his desires, his longings, into the texture of his letters; and all was shot through with the fiery colors of this temperament and the somber shadows of his Jewish soul.

"Brothers, for your sake we are comforted in our sufferings and our needs, and because of your faith.

"For now we live, when you are firm in the lord.

"Not with cunning lust, like the heathen, who know not God, shall we be. None shall trespass upon his brother or deceive him in anything. God has not called us to impurity, but to holiness. Therefore he that shames another shames not a man, but shames God, Who has given us His holy spirit."

"And concerning brother love, you need not have me write you, for you are taught of God to love each other."

"And see that ye be modest, and that ye labor with your own hands, as we have instructed you."

"As for those that have fallen asleep, mourn not for them, as those do who have no hope."

"For if we believe that Yeshua died and rose again, so God will bring again those that are asleep in Yeshua."

"And concerning the times and seasons, brothers, you need not have me write you. For you know well of yourselves that the day of the lord comes like a thief in the night."

"Therefore comfort one another, and improve one another, even as you do."

"See also that you return not evil for evil, but pursue ever the good. For yourselves and for all people, rejoice ever."

"Sow and pray, without ceasing."

426

"Thank God in all things, for this is the will of God toward you, and the will of Yeshua the Messiah."

"Extinguish not the spirit."

"Brothers, pray for us, and greet all brothers for us with a holy kiss. I conjure you in the name of the lord that this letter shall be read to all our holy brothers. The grace of our lord, Yeshua the Messiah, be with you. Amen."

Afterwards Paul bade Timotheus take a second roll of papyrus, and he dictated once more:

"And I instruct you, brothers, in the name of our lord, Yeshua the Messiah: ye shall separate yourselves from every brother who does not conduct himself according to the ways which you have taught him. For you know how it is proper for you to obey us, and to act even as we acted among you. We have not eaten the bread of any man in idleness, but we always labored in order that we might not be a burden to any. And this not because we lacked the power, but because we desired to be an example to all of you, for all of you to follow. For when we were with you we instructed you thus: 'He that will not labor, he shall not eat, either.' For we have heard that there are some among you whose conduct is not becoming; they do not labor, but are forever concerned with the affairs of others. And such we command, in the name of our lord, Yeshua the Messiah, that they shall labor silently, in order that they may eat the bread of their own labor."

When Timotheus had ended writing, Paul took the letter and added a few lines with his own hand:

"Greetings from Paul, in my hand, which is a sign on each letter. I write you:

"The grace of our lord, Yeshua the Nazarene, be with all of you. Amen."

Paul took the letters which he had dictated, bound them in linen, and hung them on the breast of a messenger. The name of the messenger is unknown and matters not. Whosoever was a believer in the Messiah was a soldier of the Messiah, and he would surely deliver the message. Thus he sent his epistles to the congregation of Salonika. But Timotheus and Silo he retained with him in Corinth, "for he needed many helpers in the work which lay before him."

427

Chapter Twenty-one

UNTO THESE LAST

EAST and west met and kissed like brothers on the shores of the little peninsula of Corinth; or it might be said that, like husband and wife embracing between them a beloved child, so the Aegean Sea on the one side and the Adriatic on the other sustained Corinth the blessed. In ancient times the name given to the peninsula was, "The Bridge of the Seas," and this it was in very truth. The ships that brought the wealth of the East to Rome passed through Corinth. A canal had been cut in the narrow strip of land which connected Corinth with the motherland, Achaia, whereby the ships not only shortened the journey, but avoided stormy weather. The port of Cenchrea covered the eastern end of the canal, the port of Leucas the western, at the outlet to the Adriatic Sea.

Corinth was famous for her bronze foundries. The Corinthians possessed a secret formula for the mixing of copper, imported from Cyprus, with gold and silver. They had the secret of producing various alloys in perfect proportions; their slaves also had a special skill in imparting to bronze a patina suggesting great age, while at the same time the metal acquired a peculiar bell-like timber. Corinthian bronze was valued above all other metals in the ancient world—not excluding gold. Temples would boast that their gods and goddesses were fashioned of Corinthian bronze. Even the Jewish Temple had its famous gates of Corinthian bronze, which were reckoned among its greatest treasures. Roman patricians, opulent merchants, and provincial aristocrats took a special pride in serving their guests in vessels of hammered Corinthian bronze. The alloy, perfect in the proportions of its elements, reflecting a green shimmer from its surface, emitting a delicate tone when touched, was the work of countless slaves. Men and women smelted the various metals, poured them, mixed them, allowed them to cool, and hammered them. The products were sold in the markets of Rome and Alexandria and were transported even into the mountain cities of Galatia. The workers in Corinth were trained in

428

their special skill from earliest childhood, for only those who were long accustomed to it could endure the heat of the furnaces and could work the metal as it was poured into its molds.

The port of Cenchrea was a forest of masts; and the dominant color of the sails furled about them was cinnamon brown—the Cypriot color. The ships came in with heavy cargoes of copper ore from the interior of Cyprus. Lines of slaves loaded on their heads the baskets of yellow ore and ranged them on the quays. The sweat ran in rivers on their naked bodies shining in the sun. Other slaves were dragging down from the decks of ships huge tree trunks. These were cedars of Lebanon, imported as fuel for the Corinthian ovens, for it had long been established by the metal workers that only Lebanonian cedar would produce the right degree of heat for the smelting of the metals.

The heaviest labor, that of the pack-carriers, was the cheapest; they were the lowest form of human merchandise, supplied to Corinth and other cities by the merchants who accompanied the Roman legions. Unskilled in any trade, they had but their brute strength to offer. They were fed according to their physical production. When their strength failed them, or they fell sick, they were simply thrown out, to be eaten by the beasts of the field and the carrion birds.

The smelting ovens were in deep caverns hollowed out in the rocks, either by the hand of man or by nature. At the farthest end was the oven itself, and close to the oven was the section set aside as the dwelling place of the slaves. These never issued into the light of day; their food was let down to them at the end of a rope. When one of these slaves died, his body was cast into the flames. Not human beings but moles they were, leading from childhood a subterranean life: moles of a special kind, able to endure the eternal heat of the caverns, to move, labor, produce in the midst of a furnace, to pass from chamber to chamber, one hotter than the other, and to draw the fiery air into their lungs. The blood in their veins became a fiery liquid, their limbs the rods and pistons of a dead mechanism. A hot vapor forever clung to their bodies. Face, chest, shoulders, hands were pitted and marked with innumerable circular scars—the result of the ceaseless torrents of metallic sparks: moving about in the glow of the ovens, these slaves looked less like men than like wild, legendary demons.

The life of one of these cave-workers was a short one. The ovens kept their maws open, like some Moloch, swallowing generation after generation of the young. And like the hell of tradition, these caverns had their various limbos. Moving among the flames as if their own bodies were not subject to heat, the slaves dipped long-handled ladles into the boilers of molten copper and carried the fiery liquid to another set of boilers, where the skilled masters of the foundry mixed the various metals in the proper proportions. This part of the work, calling as it did for knowledge of the craft and nicety of judgment, was highly esteemed, and the craftsmen were not treated like the oven slaves. Their food was better, their quarters more comfortable. But precisely because of their value, they were more closely watched, for the loss of such a slave was a serious matter; and worse than the mere loss of such a one was the possibility that he might impart the secret of the craft to an outsider. For this reason the mixers were never permitted—any more than the stokers and carriers—to leave the caverns. Their beds were comfortable, but they were chained to them. For them as for the others, the cavern was a living tomb.

When the bronze had cooled in the molds in which it had been poured—molds in innumerable forms, vases, dishes, trays, beakers, or even gates and images of gods and goddesses—it was passed on to the cleaners and hammerers. These worked in the open air, by the seashore, or in the fields, under awnings or roofs of branches. Slaves armed with whips stood over them, to correct and punish mistakes, or to drive them to faster work.

Endless were the rows of hammerers. For this work women, and children of the tenderest years, were preferred to men. Seated on the ground, their feet encircling a wooden block, they hammered and filed at the raw edges left on the images and vessels by the molds. Objects made of Corinthian bronze were expected not only to present a certain appearance; the tone emitted by the metal was expected to be unique, too. Privileged slaves, with a fine eye for lines and a sensitive ear for musical sounds, supervised the hammering and cleaning of the metal. They examined the patina of the finished product and tested the note emitted by the metal. At regular intervals stood the overseers, their whips drooping at their sides, their sullen gaze passing up and down the line. Every now and again the gaze would come to a halt, the whip would be lifted, and the lash would fall on the withered breast of a mother or on the thin face of a sleepy child. Most of the children taken into this work

430

were such as had some physical defect, or some sickness, for which reason they could not be sold as house servants or prostitutes. These unfortunate discards of humanity were the dregs of the slave markets. Their purchasers regarded them as inferior animals; and the bronze works of Corinth were full of them. Their youthful, tender hands were best fitted for the delicate, ceaseless hammering which reduced the metal to the needed consistency. But besides hammering and filing, the children also cleaned the bronze, and polished it until it had acquired its specific patina. The polishing stalls were almost exclusively occupied by children. Where these wretched youngsters worked, they lived. When night came their bodies collapsed about the blocks and stalls at which they had worked all day. In the morning the overseers woke them with the lash. Barely given time to swallow the meager ration allowed them—flat cakes of oaten bread, and a measure of water—they resumed the ceaseless labor which was their life.

The mating of slaves was always encouraged by owners and dealers, and the birth rate among them was high. But the fruitfulness so encouraged or even compelled, did not yield good stock; and defective children were therefore the rule. They were bought and sold in lots, without differentiation; they perished and were easily replaced. It did not pay the bronze masters to treat their human cattle any better than they did; it was cheaper to squeeze their last energies out of them and buy a fresh stock. Blindness occurred very frequently among the child slaves of the bronze works; the dust flying up under their files entered their eyes. Blind children were quite useless. They could not even be yoked to millstones, for they lacked the strength. When a child slave in a bronze works became blind, it was simply flung aside, driven away. More than one mother who had come with a child of hers to the bronze works had to look on when the little one, sightless and useless, was unchained and pushed out of the line, to crawl away, like a beast, into the heaps of filth, slag, ashes, and garbage which lay about the works. And if she tried to rise from her seat, a lash from the metal-loaded whip reminded her where she was.

When the statues and images, the bowls and ewers, the beakers and vases of Corinthian bronze, finished at last, shining with the subtle color of their characteristic patina, ringing with the characteristic Corinthian tone, had been tested and passed, they were carried by lines of slaves to the other end of Corinth, to the port of exit, Leukas. There

431

the ships were waiting to carry the unique product of the city to every corner of the Empire.

Thus a chain of slaves connected the two seas, the eastern and the western, across the peninsula.

* * *

When Paul baptized the household of the wealthy Stephanus, there was among his servants a freed slave by the name of Portinaius. This man had originally been brought in a shipment of slaves from Galatia—men taken captive by the Romans in the suppression of a local rebellion. Portinaius was a Greek scholar. His purchaser, Stephanus, had early recognized his merits and abilities and had given him a post of responsibility in his business. Portinaius was especially skilled in rhetoric, had an excellent voice, and declaimed pleasingly. Stephanus had also used him as a reader. Not long afterwards the master gave Portinaius his freedom. Now a freed slave was not by any means a burgher or citizen. It was always within the power of the owner to revoke the manumission. True, the freedman had privileges denied the slaves, but he was still another's property. He had no will or opinion of his own. Thus, when Stephanus was baptized by Paul, Portinaius, whether he so desired or not, was baptized with his master. This Portinaius was, like many other Greeks, unfriendly toward the Jews. The Jewish way of life, the mystic adoration of an unseen God, repelled him. But he was a man given to careful meditation, and he listened with honest attention, with receptive readiness, to Paul's sermons in the synagogue of Justus, and to his discourses at the common meals. He pondered long and closely what he heard. He was astonished to learn that the Jewish God whom Paul preached was not, like the Greek gods, a product of the intelligence of man, a radiation of man's wisdom, able to help man only to the extent that man could help himself within the limits of his destiny. The Jewish God, Portinaius heard, for the first time, was beyond all wisdoms, powers, and weaknesses. He it was who broke the chains of destiny and liberated man from the animal bond with nature; and in this activity He was immanent, directing the course of man's life at every instant.

Slowly but steadfastly Portinaius grew into the Messianic faith. He saw in it not merely the salvation of the great and mighty, who

432

needed the protection of the gods for the maintenance of their power, but the salvation of the weak, of those whose hopes had been extinguished, those whom the gods had rejected and abandoned to the cruelty of human beasts. When Portinaius thought of "the weak" his mind reverted naturally to the slaves, among which he—like so many of his countrymen of Galatia—had been counted only recently. He thought of those forlorn human beings who were condemned to the fiery darkness of the bronze works: them the gods had utterly abandoned and rejected. Now there was One who was ready to accept them and take them under his wing—one who had been of their number, had suffered in his own flesh the torments which were their daily portion, one who had died the death of a slave: and yet he had been the Son of God, the chosen Messiah. He was ready to shepherd them into the Kingdom of God, where they would be seated about him and his heavenly throne.

Understanding these things, Portinaius read forth the chapters of the Psalms to his master in quite another spirit. Joyous and festive was his voice when he declaimed the words of King David: "Yea, though I walk in the shadow of death, I fear no evil, for Thou art with me." God was the only One Whose hand was stretched out to sustain the falling, to snatch them back from the pit of destruction. And God made no distinctions and was no respecter of persons: it mattered not if you were weak, of nameless origin, a slave, or a lord and master and owner of men. Faith in the Messiah was a new birth, wherethrough you became a child of God. And Portinaius was filled with longing to bring the tidings to those who dwelt in the valley of the shadow of death—the slaves in the bronze foundries.

A high and seemingly unbreachable wall separated the outside world from the world of the slaves of the furnaces. For all that, there were channels of communication between the slaves who labored in the sunlight and those that labored in the fiery heat of their subterranean prison. (A large percentage of the slaves of Corinth came from Galatia: inasmuch as the greater part of the soil of Galatia was in the possession of a powerful aristocracy, the province exported its surplus population in the form of slaves, who either became such for failure to pay debts or were condemned to that condition for some crime to which hunger had driven them.) There were secret exchanges of information and messages. And despite the vigilance of the guards Portinaius was able

433

to smuggle two slaves out of the caverns and to bring them to the synagogue of Justus, in order that they might hear the tidings from the lips of Paul.

It was on a Sabbath morning, after the reading of the law, that the slave Lucius stood in the synagogue of Justus and listened, among the worshipers, to Paul's sermon. Lucius was a native of Galatia. He had long ago forgotten the appearance of the green pastures of his homeland, the hillocks of cypresses surrounding his native city. Moreover, he was by now half blind, and his body was thickly covered with the scars and pits of the metal sparks which fell upon his skin. And though he was not yet in his fortieth year, his face was old and wrinkled, and the flesh was withered on his pointed bones. Bent in two, half naked, clutching his meager garment of sackcloth, he listened to Paul's words:

"When our earthly home shall be destroyed, we shall yet have the house of God, which was not made with human hands, and which is eternal in heaven."

Lucius saw the house of God waiting for the faithful in heaven. In the house of God all were equal; there were no lords, no slaves, no free, no forlorn. And he sighed, and longed for the house of God. He thought of the peace and rest he would find in it, for he was weary with labor, and he hungered for rest. He heard the apostle say that for everyone on earth there was a place and portion in the house of God; and the body of every man—even his own body, eaten by the heat, charred by the sparks—would rise from the grave in glory and beauty. He, even he, Lucius, who came from a far country and had lived in utter ignorance and blindness, in sin and in uncleanness, he, Lucius, would rise with the resurrection, and he would find a corner reserved for him in the house of God. And who had prepared it for him? He who had taken upon himself, out of his own free will, all the sufferings of Lucius. He had died the death of a slave in order that he, Lucius, a stranger, an alien, abandoned of the gods, trodden underfoot by man, might have his portion in the inheritance beyond the grave. Like one who struggles in a stormy sea, even so the prematurely aged slave caught at the rope of salvation which was thrown to him before the shadows of death closed on him.

Portinaius led Lucius up to Timotheus, and the latter baptized him in the name of Yeshua the Messiah.

434

That Sabbath evening Lucius the slave, half naked, was admitted to the common feast in the synagogue. The little lamps burned modestly about the circle of the faithful. Lucius shrank back against the wall, in order that he might not be observed: he was still afraid of being thrown out. For how had he, a slave, dared to venture here among the free? But Priscilla, marking him, and observing that he was afraid, went to him, and with her motherly hand drew him closer to the table, at the head of which sat the apostle, breaking the bread and distributing it.

"I am a slave," said Lucius, with trembling lips. "Will the lord Messiah inhabit this body?"

"We are all free in the lord. Through him we have all become children of God."

The apostle took the flat cakes of unleavened bread and broke them. He gave a piece to Stephanus and a piece to Lucius. Then he took up the beaker of wine, and he made each of them, master and slave, taste of it, and he said to both of them:

"Take, eat and drink. This is my body which I have broken for you."

And when Paul bestowed upon Lucius the kiss of peace, Lucius felt that he was part of the body of the Messiah.

*　　*　　*

In the mephitic underground world of the bronze foundries, among the red flicker of the caldrons, the word spread swiftly that there had arisen in the world an offer of redemption and reparation; and the story was told of a house of God the doors of which were open, beyond the grave, for all the righteous. On the threshold of the house of God stood the Man-God who had prepared the portion of the righteous. This Man-God had lived on earth, and he had suffered like themselves, he had died as they died: and now he stood on the threshold, beyond the grave. He would receive them, wipe away their tears, comfort them for their sufferings, and he would reward the good according to their goodness and the wicked according to their wickedness. And no matter how low they were sunk in slavery here, in the lord, the Man-God, they were free.

Above ground, among the polishers and hammerers, a woman slave sat with her children. On her knees she held a bronze vase, on which she was working. Part of the process intended to bring out the special luster of Corinthian vases demanded that the women polish the metal against their own skins; thus, it was believed, the oils of the human body would soften the color of the bronze. The vase which the woman was polishing with her flesh was a particularly precious work of art, destined for one of the richest customers of the bronze-master. It had the form of a young girl's body, supple and curved, with a long slender neck, and an opening that suggested soft, parted lips. Near the mother, who sat mechanically rubbing the vase against her hips, was a child, a girl, perhaps six years of age. But the face of the little one scarcely resembled the face of a human being. From head to foot the child was covered with sores. Her eyes were closed by heavy blisters so that she could hardly see. In her bony little hands she held a bronze cup, part of the set which belonged to the vase, and with the last remnants of her strength she, in imitation of her mother, was polishing the metal against her flesh. But there was neither warmth nor softness in the child's body; all that it exuded was a yellowish matter mixed with blood, which stained the surface of the cup. An overseer had marked this, and he passed the word to one of the half-naked slaves who carried whips. A brutal hand was laid on the child. The mother half rose, and was flung back by the flick of the lash. She turned, with a choked cry, to the woman at the next block.

"Tell me, quickly, what is his name—the one who waits on the other side—the one whose name was given us by Lucius—quick—his name!"

"Jesus Christ."

"Jesus Christ, take my child unto thee!"

Chapter Twenty-two

THE PORTENT

ON a certain Sabbath morning the worshipers in the Corinthian synagogue came pouring into the street after prayers and, instead of dispersing to their homes, stood about in little knots, talking excitedly. It had been reported to them that on this selfsame morning the apostle, preaching in *his* synagogue, had made some extraordinary statements. He had said—so ran the report—that not only was Yeshua the Messiah, but that God had relinquished into his hands the government of the world; he had said further that not only had the Law of Moses been abrogated, but that the Law, the Torah, made man sinful, and Yeshua the Messiah was releasing man from this bondage of sin; and not the Jews, who carried on their flesh the sign of the covenant, the circumcision, were the heirs of Abraham, Isaac, and Jacob, but the gentiles, who carried the sign in their spirit—*they* were the true heirs of Abraham, Isaac, and Jacob. The blessing of Abraham had been taken away from the Jews and bestowed upon the gentiles.

"To what may this be compared?" cried one of the Jews, lifting his voice for all the worshipers to hear. "It may be compared to a father of flesh and blood, whose years are coming upon him. His strength is giving out, he sees the end approaching, what shall he do? He calls in his son and speaks to him thus: 'My son, here are the keys of all my rooms and granaries and storehouses. Go now, and take over the management of my house, and my servants, and my cattle, for I am old and weak and I scarcely know what is happening around me.' Now this is the Jewish Messiah whom Paul has brought to the gentiles."

"I tell you, I would have cared little if he had gone out preaching to the gentiles their own idols, Apollo and Zeus, saying, Zeus has become old, it is the turn of Apollo to take over the government of the world. But why must he do it with our God and our Messiah, the Jewish God and the Jewish Messiah? Is the Lord short of gentiles?" shouted another.

"Bethink thee what would happen to this man if he were to appear in the temples of the gentiles and there preach that the gods have become senile and that the laws of their gods make men sinful! There would be left of him a handful of ashes! He would be torn apart like a fish!"

"But brothers, what are you saying? Have you not heard him speak on other occasions?" said one, in defense of Paul. "It is the God of Israel that he brings forth both to the gentiles and the Jews. He speaks of the Messiah ben Jacob. It is you who are putting up these walls between the Messiah and God. It is you who bring rivalry between them. There is but one God, and there is but one Messiah!"

"Snakes and scorpions fill thy mouth! Hast thou not heard what he said today, that the laws and commandments make men sinful, and that the gentiles have been chosen, and theirs is the election? Look! There they go! Behold the new children of Abraham!"

The services in the synagogue of Justus had come to an end, and the worshipers were streaming out—Paul's congregation. They were a mixed crowd: Jews who had accepted the Messianic faith, some of them of the old congregation nearby, Jews who had come from Rome, a number of slaves, a handful of prominent citizens. In addition to these there were many Greeks—the most suspicious element in Paul's congregation, for among them were to be found those who "desired to drink both of the cup of the lord and the cup of the devil." And indeed, as they came forth from the synagogue of Justus on this Sabbath morning, one would not have suspected them of being too heavily weighted with the obligations and responsibilities of the new faith. It had come too easily to them; they had been fed generously with the promise of inheritance of the Jews, and in their eyes was not the humility of the convert but the pride of the heir. The relations between the two synagogues were by this time distinctly tense. The Jews of the old synagogue could not but read into the satisfied smile of the gentiles the unuttered boast: "It is in vain, O Jews, that ye bear the yoke of the Mosaic law! The reward therefor belongs to us!" It was impossible for the Jews not to look upon the gentiles as strangers who had broken into their Father's house, to rob them of their inheritance, theirs by the merit of long faithfulness and patient suffering.

When Paul, in the company of some of the Roman Messianists, and of Crispus, the former head of the Jewish synagogue, appeared on the threshold, a clamor of voices was raised among the bystanders.

"Like Esau, thou sellest the birthright cheaply, for a pot of lentils!"

"Aye, the gentiles can buy everything from him, as long as he can sell it!"

"Hear, O Crispus! To this blasphemy hast thou been led by thy misleader! Art thou too of the same mind, and dost thou too say that from this day on the gentiles are the children of Israel?"

The gentiles among Paul's congregation began to shout back.

"Yes, yes, we are the Israelites, we are the children of Abraham— we are in the Messiah! You are the husks, the empty shells! Ha! Ha! Ha! You live in the darkness of law, we live in the light of faith!"

438

"Children of Abraham!" responded the Jews scornfully. "Aye, we know! Return to your homes, uncover the altars of your idols, sleep with your fathers' concubines! Look at them, the new children of Israel!"

The two crowds surged toward one another, and blows would have been exchanged, had not Sosthenes, the head of the Jewish synagogue, come out at this moment, and pacified his people. Sosthenes was a man of dignified appearance, old, white-bearded and slow; he was learned in the law and widely known for his charitable deeds. And while he held back his congregants, Paul did the same with the Christians and with the help of Crispus and Sosthenes averted the clash for the time being.

But only for the time being. Neither of the two groups would scatter. The air was charged with anger. The Jews of the old synagogue began to upbraid their own elder, Sosthenes, for doing nothing to prevent the continuation of this blasphemy against the God of Israel.

"There is a new Procurator in the city!" cried someone. "He is reputed to be wise and just. Let us take Paul before Gallio. Let Gallio judge whether it is permissible for a Jew to preach against the law of Moses, and dissuade his own people from serving the God of their fathers."

"To the Procurator with him!"

Sosthenes, the man of peace, did everything in his power to prevent the inevitable clash. He reminded his congregants that this was the Sabbath day; it was a great blasphemy to disturb the peace of the Sabbath. Let them put off the dispute to another day. But neither the Jews nor the Christians dispersed, and the former kept up their demand that Sosthenes do something in the matter.

"Why," shouted one, "must he have his house of prayer so close to ours? Why must he provoke us, and make our blood boil, by preaching his blasphemies within our hearing? Sosthenes, thou art our head, thine is the responsibility!"

And Sosthenes, unable to withstand the pressure, turned to Paul: "Art thou the apostle to the gentiles? Then why goest thou not to the gentiles, Paul? Why comest thou to disturb the peace of our household?"

"But did the Messiah come for the gentiles alone? Did he not come to the forlorn children of Israel? Yea, first to Israel, then to the

439

Greeks. And I have come to make one out of the two, to throw down the barrier between Greek and Jew in the faith of the Messiah."

"But is that part of the Torah? Hast thou the authority of the Sanhedrin therefor?"

"I have the authority of the Messiah," said Paul.

"An Israelite who rebels against the Torah of the God of Israel! To the Procurator with him!"

And suddenly the two groups mingled in conflict. Hands were lifted, blows were exchanged; Jewish faces, gentile faces confronted each other furiously, the crowd rocked and swayed this way and that. A few instants had passed, and Paul had already been lifted up and was being carried off. The heads of the two synagogues, wedged into the mob, were forced to accompany the wild procession as it burst through the streets until it came to the marketplace, opposite the house of the new Procurator, Gallio. And at that moment Gallio himself was holding public judgment before the great portico.

Junius Aeneus Gallio was a man of wide learning and of just spirit; he was the son of a learned father and a brother of the great philosopher, Seneca. Gallio was a statesman, a dramatist, and a rhetorician. Something of his high character and multiple achivements was evident in his appearance and his bearing, as he sat that morning before the portico. The might of Rome was personified in his massive head, his high forehead, his eagle's nose, and his cold blue eyes. No muscle quivered on his long, heavy face, no glimmer of interest lit up his eyes, as he listened to the cases brought before him. With the same impassive remoteness he heard to the end the complaint of the Jews who had haled Paul before the seat of justice. The head of the synagogue spoke, followed by various witnesses. The burden of their charge was: "He dissuades the people from serving God according to the law of the Torah." Gallio, the Roman, the man of logic, the man of might, was bored by the Jews. He was bored and wearied by their Asiatic superstitiousness which, to his regret, was spreading far and wide in Achaia. Paul watched the Proconsul. He admired the statesmen of Rome and could not think of them without a special longing to bring them within the fold. Here, he thought, was an exceptional opportunity to preach the tidings before one of the great. But when he opened his lips, Gallio silenced him with a gesture and, without looking either at the Jews or at the apostle, said:

"Were the matter before us one involving an injustice or a crime, I would listen to you. But inasmuch as it concerns only words, and those words of your law, look to it yourselves. We shall not judge of such matters."

Having thus delivered himself, with great dignity, Gallio gave the signal to his officers, who drove the Jews, the Christians, and Paul from before the seat of the Proconsul.

O wise Gallio, O just Gallio, was it wise and just of thee to have acted thus? For what is this that follows on thy words? What is the meaning of those cries of triumph, those shrieks of outrage and pain? Gallio the dignitary unbends just a little, and from the height of his raised throne casts a glance at the scene beyond the pillars of the portico. The Greek Christians, jubilant at the verdict issued by the just and noble Gallio, have laid hands on the old head of the synagogue, Sosthenes; they are tearing his clothes and beating him about the head and body—in the very presence of the seat of justice. And where is thy wisdom and honor, O Gallio? With one word thou canst still the tumult, and restore order—and the word is never spoken. . . . For the chronicler tells us: "Then all the Greeks took Sosthenes, the chief ruler of the synagogue, and beat him before the judgment seat. And Gallio cared for none of these things." And not only did he not care, but it might have been noted that the steely eyes under the heavy brows flickered for a moment, as in amusement. For it was amusing, indeed, that these Jews—and to Gallio such Greeks as had accepted the Messianic faith were also Jews—should be at daggers drawn concerning empty, foolish "words" and those only the words of their law, and for the sake of them should stain the gray head of Sosthenes with his own blood. Didst thou not, at that moment, O Gallio, bethink thyself of the noble utterance of thy brother, the great Seneca, which of a certainty thou hadst heard many times: "A holy spirit dwells in us, observes our good and evil deeds, and keeps watch over them. Even as we deal, so shall we be dealt with. No man is good without God."

And Paul? And the one-time head of the Jewish synagogue, Crispus? And the Jewish Christians who had come from Rome? And the other Jewish Christians? How was it with them? What did they feel, what did they do, when they saw Jewish blood being shed by the hands of those who had but lately been converted to the Messiah of the Jews? The chronicler has nothing to say concerning Paul's attitude in the matter. Only later, in his letter to the Corinthians, Paul writes: "Through the will of God and Sosthenes our brother." Sosthenes had become so important a figure in the eyes of the Messianists that Paul considered it necessary to mention his name when he wrote his severe strictures to the Corinthians.

The importance attributed to Sosthenes by the Christians of Corinth, and the love which he manifested toward them, assuredly did not have their origin in that brutal attack before the judgment seat of Gallio. Something intervened between that wretched episode and the writing of the first letter to the Corinthians, and to him who now reconstructs the record, it was this:

The Jews lifted up the bloodstained body of Sosthenes from the polished marble stones. His white beard, his face, his clothes, were stained crimson. They wrapped him in a white sheet and carried him home. Paul, stricken to the heart, had witnessed the scene, and he felt then as Moses felt when, descending from Sinai with the tablets of the Law, he beheld the Jews dancing about the golden calf: for he saw all his work undone, lost, destroyed. He did not join the procession of the triumphant gentiles; he felt that his place was by the side of the beaten Jew. And as he went with the others, and they reproached him with the crime, for they held him responsible, he kept his head sunk on his breast and did not answer. Nor was he alone. There went with him Crispus, white with shame because of what had been done to the man who had followed him in the headship of the synagogue; there went also Stephanus and the Jewish Messianists of Rome, Aquila and Priscilla among them, and they wept loudly and begged forgiveness for the gentiles "who know not what they do." They came into the house of Sosthenes, and they comforted his family. And Aquila helped to wash the wounds of the old man and to bind them up. Not that they were at once permitted to do these things. For when they reached the house of Sosthenes, the others tried to thrust them forth, and kept on shouting:

"See! See! Such are the deeds of those who believe in the Messiah!"

"To these shedders of Jewish blood you have transferred the promise once given to our fathers, the birthright of Jacob and the hope of Israel!"

Paul heard and did not answer. Who was he, when his Messiah was being blasphemed by the acts of his own followers?

That evening Paul sat on the floor in the house of Priscilla, as one sits in a house of mourning. His head was sunk on his breast and he would not be comforted; and after a while his companions became as dumb as he, and all sat in stony silence.

The apostle Paul sat on the floor, and his long, unshorn locks fell on his shoulders, and mingled with the locks of his unshorn beard. The world was a black shadow for him. In his flesh he felt the burning of the thorn which always returned to torment him when the road had been darkened for him, and he felt that Satan stood before him. It was as if his eyes and lips had become petrified in anguish, as though they were locked and would never open again. Timotheus, sitting near him, had given over his efforts to console his father; and he himself felt as though he could not be comforted. Stephanus—now a deacon in the church—and Crispus stood by, helpless and wordless. When the silence had lasted a long time, it was Priscilla, she who managed the new congregation of Corinth as a mother manages her household, who dared to break it. She would not see the congregation ruined for the sake of the folly and wickedness of some of the Greek Christians. And after a time, she spoke up, as it were half in anger, and said:

"But let us see, after all, what has happened here? They who wrought this act of folly are but human. Only yesterday they were idol worshipers. Only yesterday they were steeped in the lusts and passions of the gods. Can we expect them to overcome their nature so easily? Thou, apostle, hast thyself said that children must be fed with milk. And if thou wilt teach them, they will be ashamed of what they have done!"

But Paul did not answer; he had no word even for Priscilla, the mother of the congregation. His eyes were locked, as though their gaze were turned inward; and it was as though at this moment he was brooding on unborn worlds. Did the apostle then have a foreboding of times and generations to come, and of events which made his blood run cold? For when he finally opened his eyes, they wandered from face to face, as though they sought the answer to a dreadful question. When he came to Timotheus and read in his face the infinite love and devotion which his son bore him, it was as though he had found what he sought— a hold, a hope for the future. His countenance brightened suddenly, he rose to his feet and he said:

"Come, Timotheus, light the way for me."

They looked at Paul in astonishment. And before they could ask him "Whither?" Paul himself answered:

"That which has defiled the name of the Messiah shall be made to sanctify him. Come, lead me to the house of the head of the synagogue, Sosthenes."

"Sosthenes?"

"Is there a thing which is impossible to God?" said Paul, speaking not to those about him, but to himself.

He came into the house of Sosthenes and approached the bed where the old man lay, bandaged, and breathing hard; and Paul bowed down three times and said:

"I have come to ask thy forgiveness of the lord, inasmuch as the sins of the followers of the lord have made him responsible before thee. Therefore for him, and in his name, I ask thy forgiveness."

"Of what lord speakest thou? I know only one Lord, and he is the Lord of the world," answered Sosthenes.

"The Lord of the world is thy Lord and my Lord also, and the lord Messiah is His holy servant. And for the servant of God, who is the lord of all us that are human, I have come to ask forgiveness."

"What have I to do with thy lord?" asked Sosthenes.

"He is also thy lord. Because of the suffering thou hast endured in his name, thou hast been baptized with his baptism; not with water, but with blood. It has been granted thee to carry his sign upon thy flesh. The blows which were rained upon thy body are the nails which were driven into the living body of the lord. Thou art nearer to him than all of us. Thou art the first in Israel who hast suffered at the hands of gentiles uttering the name of the Messiah. In thee they have blasphemed his name. Through thee they have crucified him again, and through thee he must be sanctified again. In thee the baptism of the gentiles has been shamed and brought to naught. Through thee they have fallen back into sin. Because of what they did to thee, the blood of the lord has been shed in vain. And thou must help the gentiles to find their way back to the lord."

"I shall thus help the gentiles at whose hands I have suffered?" asked Sosthenes, astounded.

"Suffering is our portion, brother Sosthenes. Our forefathers sold us as slaves unto the high God, even before we were born. And for His Name's sake we suffer daily, and our flesh is wounded daily by the wild

444

thorns which grow in their wild gentile natures. And we must help them to free themselves from the abomination, to enter under the wings of the glory of God through faith in the Messiah. This is the grace which God has bestowed on us. We must return love for the blows they rain on us. It is our duty to lead the gentiles out of the darkness, for we are the light of the world. We cannot be saved alone. Salvation must come for all the world. God created all men of one blood. There is no salvation for a single people. The Messiah came for all men, and upon us, the nearest to him in the flesh, his brothers in the promise, lies the obligation to help him bring the world to the throne of the Lord of the world."

"But how?" asked Sosthenes. "By creating a division between God and His Messiah?"

"God forbid! There is no division between God and His Messiah. There is but one God of Israel and but one intermediary between God and man, and that is the man, Yeshua the Messiah!" answered Paul firmly.

"And what is the law which thou teachest? Are these the ways of the Jewish Messiah?"

"Know, my brother Sosthenes, that whatever I do I do for the sake of heaven. And in order to bring the gentiles into the grace of God, they must first be made obedient to the Messiah. And when all will be obedient to him, then the Son, who is obedient to the Father, will make them all obedient to Him."

"And what desirest thou of me?" asked Sosthenes. "What shall I do?"

"I ask thee to help strengthen the gentiles in the faith in the one living God of Israel through the Messiah."

Sosthenes did not answer Paul there and then. He wanted time for reflection.

*　　*　　*

On the Sabbath Paul stood before the congregation of Christians, Jews, and Greeks, and in a voice that trembled with pain spoke of the unhappy incident before the judgment seat of Gallio:

"Know ye not that ye are the tabernacle of God, and that the spirit of God rests among you? And if one tears down the tabernacle of God, God shall tear him down. And know ye not—" here Paul's voice be-

445

came strong—"that your limbs belong to God, and that they are the instruments of the Messiah? Did the Messiah make manifest the truth of his words by smiting those who opposed him, or did he make it manifest through love and patience and forgiveness?"

And as Paul continued to speak, the heads of his listeners sank lower and lower, and a weeping was heard among them. Hands were lifted up tremulously, imploring forgiveness—and then, suddenly, in the midst of the worshipers, appeared Sosthenes, the head of the synagogue, standing at the side of Paul. Breathless with astonishment, the worshipers gazed on the old man, whose head was covered with bandages, and they heard him say, in a weak uncertain voice:

"Be comforted, my brothers, be comforted. Come, let us pray to God our Father, that He forgive us our sins as we forgive them one another."

And when the short prayer had been repeated by each man in his heart, Sosthenes raised his hands, saying: "Peace be with you, my brothers." And with that he went out from the church and returned to finish his prayers in the synagogue.

From that time on no more was heard of dissension between the two congregations. Both belonged to the God of Israel, and they housed side by side in the city of Corinth.

Chapter Twenty-three

THE BREAKING POINT

ALTHOUGH Paul preached to the gentiles that there was no need for them to obey the law of Moses, he was in his own life a strictly observant Jew, submitting to the commandments as though the Torah had been given to him direct at Sinai, for his own use but not for the use of others. Thus, when the time came, and he saw that the conditions of his Nazirite vow had been fulfilled, and he had been privileged, in the face of many difficulties and set-backs, to found a congregation of the Messiah in Corinth, Paul prepared to leave for Jerusalem, to perform the final ceremony of the absolution in the Temple, according to

446

the law. He appointed elders of the Church, to be in charge after he had left, together with those whom he had appointed before. Then he took farewell of the congregation and, accompanied by Aquila, Priscilla, Timotheus, and Silo, descended to Cenchrea, the port of Corinth.

Obeying strictly the letter of the law, he had his hair cut in Cenchrea; for this much he could do before arriving in Jerusalem. At Cenchrea he took boat for a Syrian port, planning to re-embark there on a ship carrying pilgrims to the Holy Land.

His first boat set him down at the port of Ephesus, the city which he had always avoided on his previous journeys because of an inner voice which warned him then against attempting to carry his mission to the center of the idolatry of Asiatic Hellenism. But now, without having planned it, he was in Ephesus, and it was as though the hand of God had guided him to it.

On the very quay he encountered a group of Syrian star-gazers. Their uncovered bodies were tattooed with pictures of the constellations, of the Milky Way, and of astrological symbols, beasts harnessed to chariots and demons with wings. Because of the tattooed pictures the naked bodies seemed to be covered with a weave of cloth. The star-gazers held in their hands rolls of papyri, on which were drawn the mysteries of their craft, cycles of the planets and likenesses of gods. The magicians were surrounded by eager listeners, many of them strangers, who had arrived by ship, or overland on donkeys, mules, and wagons. There were also sick people, who had come to make inquiry of their destiny according to the dates of their birth and the constellations which had ruled at the time. When Paul and his companions left these crowds behind and approached the gates of the city, they were stopped by a star-gazer, tattooed like all the others, and like them carrying the scroll of his mysteries in his hand. The man fixed his eyes on Paul and cried out suddenly:

"Halt! Thou shalt not dare to pass under this gate, for thou goest to thy destruction."

Then he drew nearer, and still keeping his eyes on Paul, said:

"Stranger, in the lines of thy forehead I read that thou wert born in the month when the fiery chariot of Apollo ascends in the east. Thou art caught in the chariot wheels of Apollo. This day is a fatal one for thee. Therefore I counsel thee to turn aside and pass this night

447

in one of the nearby booths. In the early morning, when the morning star will show in the east and the evening star will have sunk in the west, thou canst cross the threshold of the city of great Diana. But remember, thou shalt set thy left foot forward when thou enterest the city. And for thee and thy companions, my charge is one drachma a head, Athenian weight," whereat the star-gazer thrust out his open palm.

"Accursed be the abomination," muttered Paul, in the formula of a pious Jew, and spat out three times.

"Stranger, thou goest to thy death! Great Diana will be wroth with thee."

"Dost thou not see," cried another star-gazer from a little distance, "that these are Jews, who believe not in our gods?"

To which the first answered, in disgust: "Strangers multiply from day to day in our sacred city. They spread disbelief wherever they come."

*   *   *

The city of Ephesus was filled with pilgrims from every part of the Asiatic and Roman world. They came from the frontiers of Babylonia and from the banks of the Tiber, men, women, and children, to bow down before the wooden image of Diana, the image which had fallen from heaven. The temple of Diana was one of the seven wonders of the world, for it was the greatest and most magnificent temple in heathendom. Like every shrine city, Ephesus was full of inns, hospices, and hostelries; and there was no end to the rows of stalls on which the goldsmiths, silversmiths, and coppersmiths displayed their copies of the idol.

The heathen pilgrims came with their sick, leading some by the hand, bearing others on their backs. The wealthier were carried in litters. Everywhere groups formed about the magicians, star-gazers, snake-charmers, Chaldaean doctors, and Arabian herb-sellers. One sold phials of water from a lake in which the goddess had been seen to bathe; it was good for all sicknesses. Another sold leaves for boils, a third spices which awakened love, a fourth roots which opened the womb of the barren. Paul and his companions pushed their way slowly through the dense crowds and managed at last to discover the Jewish synagogue. And as he sat in the cool shadows of the synagogue court, surrounded by the elders who had come to greet the strangers, Paul felt his heart swell with pride for his own flesh and blood, and he thought: "How goodly are thy tents, O Jacob, thy tabernacles, O Israel! In an ocean of heathendom thou hast remained pure as a new-born child. May my portion be with thee, O Israel!"

On the Sabbath which followed he preached in the synagogue. And this time he did not quarrel with the Jews and in no way provoked them. On the contrary, he quoted the law of Moses, and cited Moses himself as a witness that the tidings of the Messiah had to be brought to Ephesus, the fount and source of abomination. The Jews listened in astonishment to his words. They were filled with eagerness to know more of the Messiah, concerning whom Paul spoke and to whose wonders among the gentiles he testified. After the sermon, the elders accompanied Paul to the house of the head of the synagogue. There they implored him to sojourn a while in their city and to preach to them of the Messiah. But Paul would not be persuaded.

"Now I cannot stay longer with you. I must observe the approaching festival in Jerusalem. But God willing I shall return to you."

Such was his resolve. With God's help he would return soon to Ephesus, for though he had avoided the city till now, an inner voice told him that here a rich harvest for the Messiah awaited him. To this place the heathen, afflicted with all manner of sickness, came to seek help and hope for the future. They sought help from the goddess Diana, but their hearts were softened by suffering, and they were ready for the word of the true faith. But before he could take up this work, there was the fulfillment of his vow in the Temple at Jerusalem.

He left Aquila and Priscilla in Ephesus, to prepare the ground for the seed of the Messiah, even as they had prepared it before in Corinth. He said farewell to the Jews of Ephesus. Together with Silo and Timotheus he boarded a ship which was taking a group of Jewish pilgrims to the Holy Land. At Caesarea he disembarked and went up straight to Jerusalem.

* * *

The moment Paul set foot in the dwelling of Reb Jacob ben Joseph, intending to bring his greetings to the congregation of Jerusalem, he felt as if an icy wind had wrapped him round. It was as though he were still the young Saul of earlier years. The people in the dwelling shrank from him. He sought in vain someone to listen to the wonders which God had performed through him. He went out from the dwelling to seek Simon Khaifa, who, he was certain, would gladly hear his

449

tidings. But he learned that Simon was not in Jerusalem; he had gone to Antioch.

In the days that followed he caught scarcely a glimpse of Reb Jacob, the brother of the Messiah. As of old, Reb Jacob spent most of his time in the Temple court, fasting and praying. The younger brother, Judah, avoided Paul, not as though he were a stranger, but as though he were an enemy. And from this unanimity of unfriendliness, from these hostile eyes that glanced at him and then glanced away, Paul began to understand that something was being planned against him.

Nor was this coldness confined to the Jerusalemites. Within a short space Silo, his beloved companion, who had undergone the travail of so many journeys with him, Silo, who had taken the place of bar Naba when the latter had left him, Silo, too, fell away from him and began to avoid him.

Paul longed to see Simon Khaifa. Simon, he felt, would reward him for all the pains he had suffered, for the humiliations he had endured, at the hands of strangers and at the hands of his own, and for the humiliation which he was now enduring in Jerusalem. "The work is not yet ended," said Paul. Unable to wait longer, he set out with his beloved Timotheus for Antioch, to find Simon Khaifa, who was called Peter.

But many things had happened to Simon since their last meeting.

Paul's flaming words concerning the door which God had opened for the gentiles had filled Simon with a great restlessness, so that he could no longer remain in the Holy City. Simon longed for the gentiles. Ever since the day when Paul had brought the young man Titus to Jerusalem, and Simon had seen the face of the converted gentile shining with the faith of the Messiah, he, Simon Khaifa, whom they called Peter, had known no peace of mind. He said to himself: The world is full of such as Titus. And why should not he, Simon, the rock, bring the faith to them? Had not he, bar Jonah, been the first to go to the gentiles? And was it not to him that the Messiah had appeared in a vision and done away with the difference between the *kosher* and un-*kosher* foods? On a certain day, when the restlessness was too great to be borne, Peter had left Jerusalem, together with his wife, whom he did not call "wife," but "sister," for she was his sister in the faith, and with his pupil Jochanan-Marcus, who was to serve as his companion and interpreter. He had also taken with him, as befitted the head of

450

the community of believers, the robes of his dignity. Thus accompanied and equipped, he had set out for Caesarea and at Caesarea had taken boat for Antioch.

The fame of Simon went before him, and in Antioch the first of the disciples was received with infinite love and respect. The believers, hearing of his coming, came out to meet him, and their multitude was such that he could not proceed. They crowded about him to touch his hands, they lay down in his path that the dust of his feet might fall on them; for these hands and feet, which had been in the service of the Messiah while he yet lived were not only holy: the touch of them opened up the springs of benediction, of eternal salvation, and of freedom from sin. Those eyes, which had seen the Messiah, those lips which had spoken to him, nay, the very garments which clothed Simon, could perform miracles. The breath of his mouth could cure all sicknesses, could purify body and soul, and insure everlasting life. So they threw themselves at his feet, implored him to touch them in passing. They brought their little ones to him to be blessed, and they begged him to give them his garments, his robe, his girdle, anything that had touched his holy body.

Simon bar Jonah was deeply moved by the love and respect manifested toward him by the believers of Antioch. He became soft and was himself filled with love, and love made him blind and forgiving of all things. Here in Antioch, freed from the constant discipline and regulation of the Jewish faith, freed from the watchful gaze of those who had trembled over him in Jerusalem, Simon bar Jonah followed the instructions of the vision he had seen in Joppa. He came into the houses of the gentiles, he lived with them, ate at their tables, and paid no regard to the question of clean and unclean foods. The gentiles were filled with love and gratitude that he, the first of the disciples, did not consider himself purer than they. And this love of the gentiles was the sin offering which absolved them in all things.

The Christian congregation of Antioch now had its own house of prayer, hard by the synagogue after which it was patterned. There were rich men in the church of Antioch, Greeks as well as Jews, and the foremost of them was the wealthy merchant Menachem. Moreover, the congregation was strongly founded and well organized, with its own elders and deacons and leader. The church of Antioch regarded itself as the second after Jerusalem and even claimed a large degree of independence. It had early assumed the right to ordain its own apostles and to send them forth to preach the tidings. Moreover, the house of prayer of the Antioch Christians, though built and organized in the style of the synagogue, began to develop along its own lines, so that, both in the building and in the ceremonial of the worshipers, differences slowly appeared and multiplied. Thus, side by side with the picture of the sacrifice of Isaac, which appeared in mosaic on the wall, as it did in every synagogue, together with the *shofar,* which was the symbol of the resurrection, there now appeared, in the place of the candelabrum, other symbols, painted or worked in mosaic by Greek artists. Such was the cross, the symbol of the Messiah's sacrifice for the salvation of mankind; or the table, with twelve seats arranged about it, and bread and wine on the table. But as yet no human figures had been introduced into the pictures. The common meal was everywhere the highest ceremonial in the prayer houses of the Christians; but in Antioch this ritual had been desecrated.

Simon bar Jonah, who had come to be known in Antioch as Peter, with his wife—the "sister"—and his disciple, Marcus, were the guests of the wealthy Menachem. The Christian community of Antioch counted among its members certain wealthy Greeks, merchants and shipowners. Some of these had begun a special practice, ever since the large increase in converts, of celebrating the common meals of the lord among themselves, in their opulent homes. Thus the "breaking of bread" in the name of the Messiah became transformed into rich banquets. It was quite natural that they should invite Simon to their celebrations, and Simon did not withhold his presence, but his heart bled to see the holy table of the lord made the excuse for the indulgence of the flesh in riotous eating and drinking. The luxury of these gatherings sickened him, and his heart cried out in protest against the division introduced in Antioch between the rich and the poor in the community. But Simon bar Jonah was a man of peace, and he could not bring himself to disturb the harmony of the congregation. Yet, as time went on, the pricking of his conscience moved him to action, and he began to refuse these invitations of the wealthy. He did what he could to identify himself with the poor.

In the membership of the church of Antioch there were many poor Jewish workers who had been among the first to accept the faith of the Messiah when the tidings had been brought back to their city by pilgrims returning from Jerusalem. Living among them were also many poor Greeks who, accepting the Messianist faith in the early days, conducted themselves almost wholly as if they were Jews. It was to these Jews and Greeks that Simon now turned. He removed his lodgings from the house of Menachem the merchant and went to live in the poor quarter; and it was here, among the rejected, at the modest common meals of the believers, that he recovered the certainty of spirit and the calm which he had known among the disciples in Jerusalem. From now on his place at the synagogue celebrations, on the Sabbath eve, was among the poor who lined the walls; and it was here that he experienced the return of the Holy Ghost, which descended on him and which he communicated to the celebrants.

For all that, he did not break off his relations with the rich Jews and Greeks. He still attended some of their celebrations, ill at ease though he was among them. He could not bring himself to make the breach complete, for it seemed to him that, if he did so, he would only help to widen the gap which already existed between the Jewish Christians and gentile Christians. Indeed, the only force which held them together in some measure was Simon himself, the first of the disciples.

So it was until the break came.

Messengers arrived from Jerusalem with denunciatory letters from Reb Jacob ben Joseph, from his brother Judah, and from others among the holy ones. Innumerable complaints of the bitterest kind had reached them from all the provinces, brought in person by the pilgrims who went up to Jerusalem, and all the complaints were of one tenor: wherever Saul, or Paul as he was now called, had appeared in the Jewish communities, he had created dissension and strife. The Jewish Messianists were horrified by the doctrines which Paul preached among the gentiles. It was impossible to describe the unhappiness of the Jews over the sermons which the apostle to the gentiles directed against the law of Moses. They declared unanimously that Paul was seeking to erect a barrier between the one living God and the Messiah, inasmuch as he presented the latter in the light of a new authority.

The preaching of Saul, they said, went far beyond the liberation of the gentiles from the heavy discipline of the Jewish law; what he proposed was that the Jews themselves should abandon the law, and this was altogether against the spirit of the decision which had been taken at the meeting of the Messianist Sanhedrin in Jerusalem. It was therefore necessary, so they decided in Jerusalem, to strengthen the spirit of the Jews, in order that they might not fall away completely. This was the news which the messengers brought to Simon bar Jonah in Antioch. Moreover, similar letters had been sent to all the communities which had been visited by "Saul" (so the letters named him), warning them that the messenger had never been granted the authority of an apostle by the holy congregation of Jerusalem. Furthermore, it was specifically stated that the gentiles could not be saved unless they submitted to the laws and commandments of the Torah.

Shaken to the depths of his Jewish conscience, Khaifa now realized the full meaning of the division which the apostle to the gentiles was creating in the congregations of the Messiah. He realized also that in his hankering after peace, in his affection for the gentiles, he had permitted the believers to depart from the Jewish way. It was his duty to remind them that, together with their faith in the Messiah, they had accepted the obligation to lead a pure and holy life. From that time on, Simon bar Jonah refused to eat at the tables of the gentiles, however the refusal might pain him, until they had proven their readiness to lead a life in the faith of the Messiah and in the fear of God.

It was at this point that Paul arrived in Antioch.

When they stood face to face, Simon, called Peter, spoke boldly, remembering that it was to him that the Messiah had entrusted the care of the flock, bidding him guard it against all evil from without and from within.

"Brother Saul," he said, "what hast thou done? Our Messiah sent us forth to plant his good vine in the garden of God, but thou tearest out the tree of Israel, in which all of us are rooted. The Messiah sent us forth to be a light to the gentiles, but thou takest the light and with it settest fire to the House of Israel. Thou teachest things which it is hard to understand. We, to whom it was granted to minister to the lord, we who heard the doctrine from his own lips, can testify that never did he command us to do that which thou doest—to tear out the Messiah from among the Jews and plant him among the gentiles. Are we, God forbid, the rebels and backsliders? The Messiah is the fulfillment of the promises made to our forefathers, the fulfillment and the hope of Israel: without Israel there is no Messiah! Now see what thou hast done, Saul. We are like unto those who made the golden calf! Let us mourn, and let us pour ashes on our heads."

"Brother Simon," answered Paul, holding in his anger, "thou art the apostle to the Jews and art proud of thy work. I am the apostle to the gentiles, and I am proud of my work. And my mission I have received from none other than the Messiah himself. I say there cannot be one God for the Jews and another for the gentiles: there is but one God. Likewise there cannot be a Messiah for the Jews and a Messiah for the gentiles; there is but one Messiah. Thus there cannot be a congregation of Jews and a congregation of gentiles; there can be only one congregation."

The answer given by Paul came like a thunderclap to Simon; and the report of it was no less devastating among the other apostles and messengers. Paul was preaching the Messiah according to his own interpretation! The letters of Reb Jacob ben Joseph, of his brother, and of the other saints in Jerusalem, made a deep impression on the Jewish Messianists. Wherever Paul appeared among them, he was surrounded by a wall of silence. The Jewish Messianists withdrew from his presence. And once again the stories of his early years, when he had been the young man Saul in Jerusalem, were brought into the light, nor could the years of his labor expiate the memory. In the heart of Paul a fire of anger and scorn was kindled. Assuredly he had never sought any reward for his sufferings and labor; but it was intolerable that he should be challenged in the matter of the authority which he had received from the Messiah himself.

Few were those who remained at his side, but in them he found some measure of comfort. There was, first, his disciple Titus, the Greek, whom he had brought into the faith. It was a long time since he had seen Titus, but he had received frequent reports of the work which the young man had done in Antioch. There was also his beloved son, Timotheus, who met Titus now for the first time, in Antioch. And these two were the mainstay of Paul. They were with him, serving him and guarding him in Antioch.

Then the following came to pass.

There was a great assembly of rich believers in the house of Menachem, the merchant. They had come to observe the ceremonial meal, as their custom was, among themselves, because of the large number of the faithful in Antioch. Peter had broken with the rich believers, but he could not refuse an invitation to the house of so important a member of the community as Menachem. Of the apostles and messengers there were present Paul, with his faithful followers, Titus and Timotheus, Peter, bar Naba and bar Naba's nephew, Jochanan, called Marcus. When the time came for the seating of the celebrants, the head place was offered to Peter, the first of the disciples, but Peter refused. For on entering the room of the common meal he had perceived that this was not a breaking of bread in the Messiah which was toward, but a gross banquet. The table was laden with roasted pheasants, prepared by Syrian cooks to look as if they were still alive, with their feathers attached to their skins. Nor were there lacking unclean foods which a Jew was forbidden to taste. Simon Peter recalled the last meal he had celebrated with the lord, in the dwelling of Hillel the water-carrier, in the old David wall of Jerusalem. He recalled how the lord had lifted up the simple cup of wine and had blessed it, so that it seemed as though his soul passed into it, filling it with his holiness. And was he, Peter, now to sit down in the name of his lord at a table which the gentiles had prepared like the feast of idolaters? No, he would not sit at this table, either at the head or elsewhere. And soon bar Naba and Jochanan-Marcus ranged themselves with Peter. In vain did they plead with them.

"I beg you, do not dishonor our table. The most important members of the congregation are assembled here."

And Simon whose surname was Niger pleaded: "What will the gentiles say? They will say that thou art ashamed to sit with them at one table."

And Lukas of Cyrene added: "Thou sittest with Jews, they will say, but it is beneath thee to sit with us."

"Surely I sit with the Jews," answered Peter. "I sit with them when they break bread in the synagogue, for they do so humbly, in purity and holiness."

He thrust his sinewy fingers into his thick beard and looked with simple, obstinate eyes on the richly bedecked table:

"Take them off!" he exclaimed. "Remove those abominations. I will not sit with those who eat uncleanness and make of the breaking of bread a banquet of idolaters. I will not sit at table with gentiles."

The leaders of the community of Antioch stared at him; they were pale, affrighted, speechless. Paul, who was standing to one side, felt his blood growing hot in him with anger. He did not want to shame

456

the first of the disciples, but his anger overcame him, and he ran forward, and confronted Simon bar Jonah:

"The gentiles whom you shame, Simon bar Jonah, will let their bodies be burned for the faith of the Messiah!" he burst out.

"They eat the meat of strangled animals, they drink blood, even as the idolaters do at their feasts. I will not sit with them!"

"And thou, Simon bar Jonah," retorted Paul, fiercely, "before the men of Reb Jacob ben Joseph reached this city, didst eat with the gentiles. But when these men arrive, thou dost refuse. If thou art a Jew, and livest as a gentile, why shouldst thou force the gentiles to live as Jews?"

On the faces of many guests appeared an ironical smile, and a titter was heard in the corners of the room. But Simon Peter, the simple fisherman, listened to the reproach, and like the Messiah who had been his teacher, he was silent and forgave.

He left the banqueting hall and went back to the little room which the congregation had rented for him near the synagogue. There he wrestled with his shame, and covering his face with his hands he murmured:

"Thou knowest full well, my lord and redeemer, that it was not in order to shame thy young congregation of the gentiles that I did this thing, but only to fulfill the will of thy Father in heaven, and to strengthen the foundations of the House of Israel, which others would destroy. And if I have sinned against thee, break me, as a pot is broken, and cast me away. But if I have done according to thy will, and as thou hast taught me, comfort me, for my heart trembles in fear before thee, my lord."

Then his agony was resolved in tears, and as always when tears, welling from his eyes, washed away the torment of his heart, he felt as though the wings of the glory had been spread over him, and he was taken into the glory as a child is gathered to the bosom of its mother, and he was comforted.

Chapter Twenty-four

PAUL THE APOSTLE

BUT in the end it was not Peter who was thrust forth from the congregation; it was Paul.

There are certain souls which God has graced with such harmony, that no matter into what errors they fall the grace of their harmony restores their balance, and in the sum all is well with them. The warmth which radiated from Peter's heart, which flooded the world about him as a field is flooded with the song of a bird, won everyone to him. Not only did they forgive him for having shamed the gentiles; the Greeks were startled by the reproaches of the first disciple, of him who had been entrusted by the lord with the power to bind and loosen; they were startled—and they reformed. But as against this, the letters which arrived from Jerusalem, condemning the doctrines which Paul taught, made a deep impression on the community. Thus it was not only the Jewish believers, with their deference to the authority of Jerusalem, who drew back from Paul; even the Greek believers were frightened, and began to look upon him with unfriendly eyes.

Paul was suddenly cut off from his own congregation.

He wandered about the narrow streets of the Jewish quarter, a lonely figure. Once, when he had passed through these streets, the doors of the houses and shops had been crowded with his followers, who greeted him joyously from afar. The whole quarter had been illumined with lanterns when he returned from his mission to the Galatians. Now he was aware of lowering brows and angry eyes. And he heard, or seemed to hear, the bitter whisper of voices as he passed:

"There he goes, the traitor of Israel!"

"Yes, he who would tear out the Torah by its roots."

"Is it any wonder? How long is it since he openly persecuted the holy congregation of the lord? And how long is it since he went out to the cities, carrying with him chains to bind the faithful? My life upon it, but he still has some of those chains in his keeping!"

"No doubt! He was ever a man who desired to work himself into

458

the good graces of the High Priest. And knowest thou why? The High Priest had a daughter, and Saul sought her in marriage. And when the High Priest showed him the door, Saul turned against him, and before the day was over he had become one of the faithful."

"Now I see it! And as he once persecuted the faithful, so he now persecutes the congregation of Israel. He lights the flames of discord in every community which but admits him. He provokes the gentiles against the Jews."

"Traitor in Israel!"

"The High Priest's son-in-law!"

Such were the rumors concerning himself which came to Paul's ears.

On the Sabbath, when he came into the congregation, he felt upon his back the angry and ominous look of the believers. Nor was this all. Some of the zealots among the faithful, having seen with their own eyes the letters addressed to Antioch by the holy ones in Jerusalem, confronted him, and one exclaimed:

"What dost thou in the congregation of the Messiah, traitor in Israel!"

"Balam! Korah!" exclaimed another.

It seemed as if the sanctity of the church would be desecrated by scenes of violence; and were it not that Titus and Timotheus accompanied him, it might well have been that the apostle would have been flung into the street.

They did not know, either in Antioch or Jerusalem, how much the apostle had wrought, what virgin fields he had plowed and sown for the lord. All that they heard was the cry of the communities concerning the dissension which Paul created, making of the Messiah a stranger who could not house with Israel. In Jerusalem, the scene of the early persecutions of Saul, the bitterness against him was boundless. They did not or would not know of the chain of communities which he had founded across the mountains of Galatia down to the Aegean Sea; it did not move them that he had carried the name of God and of His Messiah to nations which had never heard of the one or the other and had planted the hope of redemption in hearts which had been sealed by uncleanness. A word became current in Jerusalem: "Has God need of many?" God, they said, needed the individuals, the chosen ones, who by the sanctity of their lives should testify to the Mes-

459

siah and by the purity of their deeds forge, as in a smithy, the living Torah which Moses had taught. These, the elect, the incorruptible, should stand as pillars of fire in the night, lighting the world.

Reb Jacob ben Joseph sent forth his letters. In these he wrote, among other things:

"What avails it, my brothers, if a man say he have faith, and he has not good works? Can his belief bring him salvation? And when a brother or sister is naked, and has not bread for the day, and one says, 'Go in peace, be clad and sated,' what shall it avail if neither clothing nor food be given?

"So faith is dead in itself, if it cannot show works.

"So one might say: Thou hast faith and I have works: show me thy faith without thy works, and I will show thee my faith through my works.

"For faith acts only through works.

"As the body without the soul is dead, so is faith without works."

The simple, straightforward words of Reb Jacob ben Joseph deeply moved the faithful, particularly the Jews among them. The rich, too, were taken aback and affrighted. They pondered in terror the words of Reb Jacob: "Come, ye rich, mourn and lament for the tribulations which shall come upon you."

Such were the letters of Reb Jacob.

Nothing was spared Paul. There were those who made it their business that he should know the dark and spiteful things being said of him, down to the last word. He heard and did not reply. His heart was hot with anger, but he was silent. Only in his tablets he wrote down the fiery sentences which were later to be entered into his letters. As long as the rumors and accusations concerned only his person, he strengthened himself and permitted himself no overt act or word against the men of Jerusalem, that he might not split the congregation which had been founded by the lord; for it was there, in Jerusalem, that the lord had ministered, and it was to those of Jerusalem that he had entrusted the care of his flock. Paul swallowed down his bitterness, and the taste of it was like poison.

So it was until that happened which he could not endure in silence.

Reports came to him in Antioch that the messengers of the elders in Jerusalem had reached the cities of Galatia. Paul saw the work of his hands tottering, like a house built on sand. Certain of the Galatians appeared in Antioch, and they told him of the confusion which had been created in those mountain communities by the letters of the elders. The poor, simple Galatians did not know whom to believe and what to do. Nor was it only the Jews who saw themselves shamed and misled by Paul, traitors through him to the faith of their fathers. The gentile Christians, too, were confused and bewildered. They learned from the letters that Paul, who had once persecuted the faithful in Jerusalem, had never seen the Messiah and had never heard his doctrines from his own lips. For the Messiah had said (the letters insisted) : "Sooner shall heaven and earth pass away, than one jot or tittle of the Torah." Therefore it was clear that they, the gentiles, could not be saved and could have no portion in Israel, if they did not fulfill the laws and commandments of Moses. Paul had indeed claimed that he had seen a vision; but he could not on such grounds abrogate the very words of the Messiah, which they, the elders had heard. In any case, Paul had no authority to spread the tidings of the Messiah according to his own interpretation. The only ones who had the authority to preach according to the instructions of the Messiah were they, the holy ones of Jerusalem, the direct disciples of the Messiah, of whom Reb Jacob ben Joseph, the brother of the lord, was the head. Paul's doctrine, then, inspired by his own interpretation, was a doctrine of "false gods," and the faithful dared not so much as listen to him.

Many of the gentile believers were so terrified by the message from Jerusalem that they came to the Jews and begged to be admitted into the covenant of Abraham, through circumcision. But others, the weaker ones, fell away completely from the faith. In between these two groups were the undecided ones, who knew not which way to turn. And all this, reaching the ears of Paul, filled him with dread and anger; for the building he had erected was now collapsing, as though it had been the work not of God but of the Devil.

It could not have been worse if Paul had seen the heavens open above him, and had beheld, descending on the fiery clouds, not the lord, the King Messiah, but—God forbid!—the son of the Devil. They came up before him like a visitation, those poor gentiles of Galatia who but yesterday had been idol worshipers; he saw their faces, on which was written utmost confusion, for now they did not know whether they were standing with God or with the Devil. The eyes of the Galatians were turned upon him, upon Paul, imploringly. What had he done with

461

them? And Paul suddenly beheld himself and all his work about to be swallowed up by the earth, as Korah had been swallowed up together with his congregation.

On the day when the visitors from Galatia gave him this report, Paul was like a stricken man. He crawled rather than walked back to his garret in the quarter on the farther side of the river. And when he crossed the threshold of his room he fell on the floor in convulsions.

In the vision which came to him in the fit, he saw himself standing on a narrow pathway. He began to climb upward, through the mountains which led to the Galatians, but suddenly the path came to an end. On either side of him were black abysses, out of which protruded upward immense needles of rock; and before him was space, gaping like the opened jaws of a crocodile. There was no turning back for him. Somewhere in front the path dipped and rose to the summit of a mountain. He could not see the summit, for it was swathed in mist; but he felt it towering over him. The path on which he stood was not bare; it was covered with a low, dense growth, with gnarled roots, with savage cactus plants, some of them with wild red tongues, others with pincers which fastened into his flesh. Hot claws snatched at him, and fierce eyes glared at him, from a thousand unfamiliar plants. And as he stood forlorn, these unspeakable creatures began to move, to close in on him. From under his feet other plants rose, silent and malevolent, pushing aside the green, mossy mold. Silently they wound themselves about his feet, while the other closed in on him steadily and remorselessly. He must get out of this place! He must begone! But there is no forward, there is no backward!

A cry tore its way out of the innermost heart of Paul:

"Lord, lord! I did not come alone upon this path. Thou didst take me and place me upon it. Help me now!"

Then he perceived, stretched out toward him through the confusion of fiery tongues and claws, a hand—a hand stretched down from the summit of the mountain, which was suddenly unveiled for him. With that, the fit passed, and his body relaxed. Paul, awake now and bathed in tears, cried:

"Father in heaven! Set me not at odds with my own flesh and blood!"

He saw Titus and Timotheus standing over him. They lifted him up and placed him on his bed. Paul felt on his face and forehead the

462

cool, soft hands of Timotheus, which were bathing him with vinegar.

"All will be well," said Paul, still speaking to the vision. "It was not I who chose the road to Damascus. Thou alone didst set my feet on it. Thou didst lift me out of the gutter of sin, where I lay, and with thy blood thou didst wash me clean. Thou hast forgiven me, and who shall now reproach me with it? Thou hast chosen me as thy vessel, and who shall break me? Thou didst send me on thy mission to the gentiles, and who shall take the mission from me? Even though they in Jerusalem close the gates of their synagogue for me, as all the Jews have done, I have built mine own church, with the authority which thou didst give me, out of thine own mouth, lord. The world is my church, and all men are worshipers therein. To them I will bring the tidings of thy advent, which I have learned not from other men, but through thy revelation of thyself unto me."

Now the path before him was clear. He asked Timotheus to bring him papyrus, pen, and ink. This time he did not dictate, but wrote with his own hand. He sat on the floor, his legs folded under him; his brows were drawn together, his face was tense. Trembling, he dipped the metal pen into the colored fluid, and began his letter to the Galatians, in which he declares his independence and authority:

"Paul, an apostle, not by men, and not by one man, but by Yeshua the Messiah, and God the Father, who raised him from the dead:

"I certify unto you, my brothers, that the gospel which I preached to you is not according to man, for I did not receive it from man, nor was I taught it by man, but by the revelation of Yeshua the Messiah.

"Know that a man is not justified by the works of the law, but by the faith of Yeshua the Messiah.

"For ye are all children in God, by faith in Yeshua the Messiah.

"And because ye are sons, God sent forth the spirit of His Son to your hearts, crying Abba, Father!

"Therefore thou art no more a servant, but a son, and an heir of God through the Messiah.

"Stand fast then in the freedom in which Yeshua has made you free . . . be not entangled again with the yoke of a servant, the yoke of the law, wherein you cease to be sons and fall again into servitude and heathendom, and fall away from grace.

"For in Yeshua the Messiah circumcision and uncircumcision are without meaning, only faith has meaning, which works through love.

"The whole law is fulfilled in this word: thou shalt love thy neighbor as thyself.

"See now how long a letter I have written you, and by my own hand."

*   *   *

Now it was time for him to set to work. Had he not left behind him, in Ephesus, a congregation of Jews who had implored him to return and sojourn among them? Was he not haunted by the vision of the sick and the possessed who came in hordes to the Temple of Diana, there to be consumed by human birds of prey, magicians, soothsayers, and false prophets? Had he not vowed in his heart that he would not rest until he had planted there the Name of the God of Israel, and of the Messiah, and brought the sick and blind of Ephesus into the light of salvation? And did not his heart also yearn toward the congregations of Galatia, the first fruits of his mission? He longed to see them in order that he might repeat with his lips what he had set down on papyrus, to uphold their hands, to hearten and encourage them, and to strengthen them in the faith. Moreover, did he belong to himself, that he should permit himself to be crushed by the burden of persecutions? Was it not God Who had loaded on to his shoulders all the weight of the salvation which was to be carried to the gentiles? Was he not as a Canaanitish slave unto God, sold for all the years of his life? Why then was he sitting here in idleness, and why did he not go out into the field to labor, as every hired laborer was bound to do?

But before Paul left Antioch there came to him bar Naba, the friend of his youth, to say farewell.

Bar Naba was torn in twain between the two lions who contended for his heart, between Paul and Jacob ben Joseph. Himself bound to the faith in the Messiah through the law of Moses, he nevertheless was powerfully drawn toward Paul.

The friends met and gazed long and silently at each other. The years since their last encounter had left upon their faces the folds and wrinkles of many labors, many sorrows. Bar Naba's immense black beard was streaked here and there with white. His handsome, clear countenance, with its great gray eyes and its lofty, luminous forehead —the countenance which had put the gentiles in mind of Jupiter—had been plowed by the plow of the lord; and therefore its creases shone with the light of grace.

Before him stood Saul, his boyhood friend, the bearer of his dreams, an old, broken man, with tear-sacs under his eyes, his forehead crowned with a wreath of gray. Like David and Jonathan, they held hands, and bar Naba said to Saul (for to him he had always remained Saul):

"My brother, wheresoever thou wilt be, I will be with thee, for I know that whatsoever thou dost, thou dost in the name of heaven. Saul, my brother, tear not thyself away and cut not thyself off from thine own flesh and blood. For the God of Israel and for His Torah, thy brothers are everywhere trodden under foot, by whosoever is stronger. They are lower than the dust, shamed and rejected, a prey to all the world. They belong to none but God, and it was for them that God sent His redeemer."

Paul looked steadfastly into bar Naba's face and answered:

"God forbid! I have not come to create discord with my brothers, but to make peace; not to break up, but to unite and to remove all barriers. Have I ever preached, God forbid, that the Jews shall cease from circumcision? Do I want them to be like the sons of the rich in Jerusalem, who do all manner of things to be able to come naked into the arena, and none shall see upon them the mark of circumcision? I say, those that are circumcised, let them remain circumcised. But if the external circumcision of the body become the only gate through which there is entry into the Kingdom of Heaven; if only through the circumcision of the flesh can one become a son of Abraham, Isaac, and Jacob; then, I say, all our labor is in vain; for if justification is only through the Torah, then the Messiah died in vain."

* * *

Across the wooded slopes of the Taurus range, the homeland of Paul, three travelers were faring again, afoot. One, tall and young, went before, laden with baggage; the second, also young, was supporting the footsteps of the third, an elderly, stooping man. They advanced slowly, disentangling their feet from the soft moss and the labyrinth of roots which covered the earth. Tenderly, with tremulous attention, the second young man guided and supported his companion past the mounds

465

of stones and across the rivulets which started out from the soil. So they fared from morning till night, pausing at noon for rest in the shadow of green cypresses and in the evenings kindling little fires against the coolness descending from the slopes. At night, if they could not find a dwelling, they slept in the abandoned booths of shepherds, or in the open air, in the scooped-out hollow of a dried stream.

For the third time the apostle was climbing toward the dread "Syrian Gate," to bring the tidings to the cities of Galatia. On the first occasion the mission had consisted solely of Jews—Saul and bar Naba. So it had been on the second occasion. Now, on the third occasion, only one member of the mission was a Jew, the apostle himself; his companions this time were Timotheus, half Jew, half Greek, and Titus, wholly Greek, and uncircumcised.

So, by the old, laborious route, they came to Galatia. Once again the apostle passed through the familiar cities and through his communities, the first fruits of his planting. Great was his joy to be among them again, and great was theirs to have him in their midst. Familiar faces, familiar figures, familiar greetings. He preached for them and strengthened them. He sought to allay the storm which had been raised by the messengers of Reb Jacob and which was threatening to spread far out to Derbe, Lystra, and Antioch in Pisidia.

The apostle Paul saw again the mother of Timotheus. There, in the house, he found a new disciple, Gaius, whom he took with him on his journeys to Antioch and to remoter cities. So they traveled, part of the way on foot, and part of the way in carriages, through Colossae and Leukida and Hieropolis, cities of the gentiles, but these were gentiles whose spirit was parched for a word of salvation. And Paul said to himself: "I will return this way, and stay longer with them," but he could not pause now. For he was in haste to reach Ephesus, the famous city of the goddess Diana. The memory of that source of abomination provoked in him the lust to conquest: and he longed, like a general with his emperor in mind, to conquer the city and to lay it at the feet of his lord, the Messiah.

Chapter Twenty-five

FOR LOVE OF THE GENTILES

THE more idolatrous and unclean a city was, the closer did its Jews huddle together and the more firmly they clung to their quarter, as if in fear of being washed away by a flood. Each found help for himself, and extended help by guarding his neighbor against infection. Only their constant vigilance saved them from dissolution.

In Ephesus, under the shadow of Mount Prion, there was a sandy stretch surrounded by olive and cypress. There the Jews had put up their dwellings, on the foundations of ancient ruins, or amid crumbling walls covered with creepers. This was the Jewish quarter, from of old. It consisted of a labyrinth of courts running into each other. As the number of Jews increased, the labyrinth widened and became more involved. Long before the coming of Paul, the Jews of Ephesus had been established in the right to observe their Sabbath and to practice their religion; the High Priest Hyrcanus had obtained the charter from Julius Caesar, and subsequent Emperors had ratified it. The Jews of Ephesus lived a life apart, sundered from the universal worship of Diana which was the spirit of the city. Among the goddesses of the Asiatic and Roman world Diana of Ephesus, whom Apollo himself had sent down from heaven, was one of the most prominent and mysterious. A sacred, demonic power, she had inspired a cult of intimate and esoteric rites, with adepts who guarded the formulas of her control in the "Books of Ephesus." Asiatic, Hellene, and Roman alike owned her sway. She had been worshiped from before the beginning of recorded time. She was ancient when Alexander the Great had bowed before her and offered sacrifice on her altar before he set out to attack Persia. The veil of mystery drawn about her by her adepts and magicians had an extraordinary appeal to Hellenic man and filled him with emotions associated with no other divinity. She was a competitor of many gods, and not only of the dark gods of Asia, but of the Olympians themselves. Those of the gentiles who felt obscurely an impulse toward faith

467

were attracted by Diana of Ephesus and by the mystic aura which surrounded her.

Against this tide of adoration the Jews in their separate quarter held out consistently, generation after generation. This miracle they achieved by their separation and by the continuity of their contact with Jerusalem, a miracle all the more noteworthy in that certain of the Jews were dealers in the magic which they themselves derided and despised. Ephesus was the metropolis of many provincial towns, a city of great commerce. Most of the Jews were dealers or hand-craftsmen. Some of them only made copies of the "mystery books," added cabalistic formulas of their own, sold amulets and sacred medicaments. The attraction of the tremendous market was too much for them.

They well knew that the Rabbis were bitterly opposed to the traffic in amulets and other objects of superstitious worship. The Rabbis were forever protesting, upbraiding, and warning that assistance to idolaters in their error was the equivalent of idolatry itself. More than one peddler of love philters and magic manuscripts had been scourged in the synagogue portals; some had even been excommunicated, a dread punishment in those days. Still they persisted in the traffic, hunger being stronger than fear. The recollection of the Rabbinic prohibition suddenly recurred to one of the men, for, without apparent reason, he began to defend himself.

"But what shall I do?" he asked his companion in sin. "I have a wife and children to feed, have I not? Let them find me another livelihood, I would gladly practice it. Do they think I like this abomination?" and he spat in vehement disgust.

It was in one of the Jewish courtyards, in the shadow of Mount Prion, that Aquila and Priscilla, whom Paul had left behind him in Ephesus, had made their new home. There they set up likewise their little factory of goat's hair cloth. When Paul, after wandering for months, together with his companions, in the mountain cities of Galatia, arrived at last in Ephesus, he asked his way to the Jewish quarter, knowing that Aquila and Priscilla had prepared a home for him there.

So it was—a home, though little to look at, externally: in a corner of a court they had put up four wooden walls, and made a covering of sheets of goat's hair cloth. But here in Ephesus, as before in Corinth and once in Rome, the spirit of Priscilla triumphed over the poverty of her surroundings. The frail booth, for it was hardly more than that, became a gathering place for those that Aquila and Priscilla sought to convert to the faith. Here too a wanderer could find rest and a spoonful of warm food. Together with ministration to the body went ministration to the spirit, and it was hard to tell which was accepted more gladly. For Priscilla had this gift of attracting and holding people; and in this wise she prepared the field for Paul.

The men and women Paul found in the company of Priscilla, in Ephesus, were not yet wholly convinced Messianists, for they did not yet believe that the Messiah, whose advent they expected momently, had already come. They were for ever preparing themselves for him. They were, in particular, deeply under the influence of the call which had been issued by Jochanan the baptist, whose voice had reached to every corner of the Jewish world. Not in Ephesus alone, but in many other cities, there had been founded "Brotherhoods of the Messiah," which had accepted baptism in the name of Jochanan and which lived in piety and in separation from the world, much like the Essenes, praying, fasting, and keeping their lives pure for the advent. The tidings of Jochanan had come to Ephesus, and their effect had been strengthened by the arrival of a certain Jew of Alexandria with the Greek name of Apollos. The Ephesian Jews, or such of them as were under the influence of Jochanan, regarded the latter as a sort of Elijah, the forerunner of the Messiah. Later, Aquila and Priscilla convinced Apollos that the Messiah of whom Jochanan was the forerunner had already come, and Apollos received baptism in the name of Yeshua the Nazarene. When Apollos set out for Achaia he carried with him letters from the devoted couple to the brothers on the Greek mainland. However, those whom Apollos had so strengthened in the faith of Jochanan held that the Messiah had not yet come, though his coming was imminent, and for the time being they contented themselves with the baptism of Jochanan.

Paul gathered these men—there were twelve of them in all—in Priscilla's little home, and addressed them:

"In vain do ye baptize yourselves, in vain do ye prepare, in vain do ye fast and purify yourselves. All these things are worthless and of no account if ye believe not in Yeshua and baptize not in his name."

In front of the synagogue of Ephesus, a building which like all structures of its kind in the city was surrounded by Ionian columns, a crowd of Jews was assembled on the Sabbath morning, after the prayers and the reading of the Torah. Instead of dispersing to their homes, they were discussing excitedly the contents of the sermon delivered by the messenger Paul, on the subject of the Messiah. On this morning they had heard for the first time the public declaration that the Messiah had already come and that the time of expectancy was gone for ever.

Now the congregation of Ephesus had been well prepared for the revelation of the advent by the work of Apollos of Alexandria, whom they remembered with affection. For even now, as they debated whether indeed the Messiah had already come in this same Yeshua the Nazarene, they adverted again and again to the unforgettable messages of Apollos.

"Yes, he speaks not at all badly," they said of Paul. "He has power, that cannot be denied, and clearly he is strong in the Holy Script. But can one mention him in the same breath with the Alexandrian? Do you remember, when he, Apollos, opened his lips, it was as though a stream of pearls issued from between them. Ah, do you remember with what a voice he uttered his verses, and how he interperted them? As for instance the one from Isaiah: 'The spirit of the Lord was upon me, for the Messiah was with me, and he sent me to bring the tidings of pain. . . .' Ah, brothers, the words! The tongue that uttered them! The voice that carried them! 'I am sent to bind up the broken of heart, to call the captive to freedom!' Why, he gave you the Messiah like a gift, as if it were a precious stone he put into your very hand."

One said: "Well, whether this Messiah be indeed the Messiah, or not—that we shall yet discuss. And if Jews decide that he is the Messiah, why then, I shall not stand up against them. Still, what a pity that this Paul has not the honeyed tongue of our Apollos. You know, friends, that I am a lover of fine speech and am not ignorant in the books, and I am by no means unfit to teach children the ways of Jewish learning, as you should long ago have perceived—and I know what fine speech is, and I say—"

He was interrupted by one Reb Joseph, a sandal maker, a man with many children, most of them sick, so that it was said of him that he, in his family, was the image of all the diseases that were to be found in Ephesus. He was a bald man, with a thin, scraggy beard, for every disaster that came on him plucked out a handful of hair, as a sign of its presence. Poverty and sickness had made Reb Joseph a great pietist and believer.

"Now what point is there," he asked, "in comparing the preacher of Alexandria with this man? Apollos was a great preacher, assuredly, but only a preacher. But this man is not a preacher. God save us, brothers, he is a messenger—what say I?—*the* messenger, and of the Messiah himself, who entrusted him with the tidings, placed his hands upon him, bidding him go forth to proclaim the truth. And on whomsoever the Messiah places his hands, in him dwells the Holy Ghost. You have heard of the twelve. They have the power. Whomsoever they touch, that man is healed. So it is with this man. With the glance of his eye he drives the evil spirit out of one possessed—for he is full of the Holy Ghost. You have heard, have you not, what he did for Abraham the dyer. For Abraham's wife lay sick—she had been lame for a twelvemonth. And this man went into the tent of Abraham the dyer, touched the woman with his hand, looked upon her and said, 'Arise!' And she arose. Ah, would that my wife would thus be healed, she and my children, who lie sick without a mother to tend them."

A silversmith indicated Reb Joseph with his thumb and said to the others, significantly: "Our friend Reb Joseph has no doubt been a visitor of late in the house of Aquila and Priscilla."

"Surely I have," cried Reb Joseph. "And what of it? More than one good Jew has been a visitor there. It is a good Jewish home, and those that need to hear a warm Jewish word may very well go there."

"What? And should one also receive baptism at the hands of the two gentiles whom Paul brings with him, those two saints of the heathens—what are their names, Titus and Timotheus?"

"Gentiles, you say! Would that many Jews were as saintly as these two gentiles! If they be gentiles, well, write me down as a gentile, too," said Reb Joseph, hotly. "They believe in the one living God of Israel, and in his Prophets—and thou callest them gentiles. May my portion be with such gentiles."

Half laughing, half reprovingly, another Jew said: "Thou art well tangled in the net, Reb Joseph."

"And why should he not be? A man with a sick wife, with sick children—and he believes that the apostle can cure his wife, so that she may cure the children. All that the apostle need do is but look at her and call on the name of Yeshua the Messiah, as he has often done before."

471

Still another put in, seriously: "Ah, but he has indeed done it, and he has healed many a one in the name of Yeshua."

And so it had been, indeed. For as soon as Paul had looked upon the Jews of Ephesus, he had understood that they were touched with the superstitions of their neighbors and that they were inclined to respect the deeds of the soothsayers and the healers. Therefore he had decided that, to wean them from this inclination, it would not suffice for him to preach and explain; philosophy and argument would not convince them. What they needed was a demonstration of power, the overwhelming evidence of deeds. Therefore he had determined to destroy the goddess of Ephesus with her own weapons. Of his power to do so, Paul was utterly certain. He needed but to call upon that power, for the cause of the Messiah, and it would manifest itself. He believed that nothing was impossible for him, no act beyond him, if it served the faith. It was as if his high intent had unlocked for him all the secrets of knowledge, unveiled all mysteries, and given him the means to triumph over all demons. Even as the apostle to the Jews, Peter, had been granted such powers, so the apostle to the gentiles had been equipped with the demonstrative strength of the Messiah.

Of this he had been given evidence long before his coming to Ephesus. The gift of command had been entrusted to his eyes, and he had power over the spirits and the bodies of men. The command was uttered in and by the name of the Messiah. Limbs which had long been paralyzed, which had long refused their office, failing to respond to the impulse of the mind, became responsive again when the flesh received the overwhelming call from the eyes of the apostle. The name "Yeshua the Messiah" was like a scourge, driving demons before it. The glance of Paul penetrated the flesh, making a path into the vitals of the sick, so that evil spirits fled, groaning, squealing, screaming. And here, in Ephesus, such demonstrations, similar on the surface to some of the performances of the priests and magicians, were peculiarly in place. Thus it was that, by degrees, the name of Paul, as a healer, became known among the Jews, and not among them alone.

What Joseph the sandal maker revealed as his belief that Sabbath morning, became the belief of countless others. Thousands, who had never seen Paul, heard of him and were carried away by a wave of trust. They said of him that the touch of his hand, the breath of his mouth, nay, even his garments, had in them the power to heal, to drive out evil spirits, and perform all manner of wonders in the name of Yeshua the Nazarene.

*   *   *

In the end Paul came face to face with Apollos of Alexandria. He had heard nothing but that name ever since his arrival in Ephesus. In the synagogue, in Priscilla's home, in the streets, they talked only of this wonderful man who had done so much to prepare the soil of Ephesus for the tidings of the Messiah. Paul was by no means jealous of the reputation which Apollos enjoyed even in those circles which were disinclined to accept Yeshua as the prophesied Messiah; for Paul was aware of his own limitations. God had not endowed him with that soft, winning goodness, that graciousness of speech, that warmth, which characterized his fellow apostle, Peter. But he said in his heart: "With that which God has given me, I will serve Him, with the mind which he has set in me, with the tongue to which He has given speech."

After an absence of some months in the Greek cities whither he had gone to preach the baptism of Jochanan, Apollos returned to Ephesus. Almost on the day of his arrival, the two men met in the home of Priscilla. Paul beheld before him a towering, handsome figure, with large, lustrous eyes, a high forehead, and a serene face. The impression which Apollos made was that of a man who had just been anointed. His hair and beard were carefully groomed, his lips, full but delicately chiseled, closed firmly, as if to conceal a secret. In his dress he was as careful as in the care of his body; the folds of his outer garment lay upon him as if they had been arranged for effect by a skillful slave. Obviously Apollos had that regard for appearance which was enjoined upon the learned of Israel. The colored shift under his outer garment was of fine Sidonian linen; so was his wide girdle, which proclaimed him the scion of a wealthy and distinguished family. His sandals were new and fitted closely over his feet. And as he was perfect in appearance, so he was gracious and correct in his speech. Every sentence was carefully formed; its words were like the folds of a rich garment. His quotations were faultless. And he spoke in the charming accent of the Alexandrians. And yet, as Paul perceived at once, all this grace and balance of external appearance and manner did not wholly conceal a certain want of harmony within. There was not in Apollos of Alexandria the through-and-through serenity which Paul remembered in his young friend bar Naba. (Would he ever forget that glorious

473

youth who had taken captive the hearts of the gentiles?) Yes, the young man of Alexandria was faultless—but the harmony of the spirit was not in him.

Opposite the elegant Alexandrian sat Paul, whose clothes were formless, and whose face and body, given for years to the storms of his mission, looked as tattered as his robe. Dangers, fasts, scourgings, had left their mark on Paul. His flesh was hardened, his bones edged. They were alone, for Priscilla had tactfully arranged that their first encounter should be witnessed by no one. They sat opposite each other, and between them was a little table, on which lay a number of parchment scrolls; and about them went up the smoke of incense, for Priscilla, knowing of the gracious custom of Judaea, had placed in the room a number of braziers with sweet-smelling spices, so that the two teachers might be sustained and heartened in their sacred converse.

There was in Paul a peculiar desire to penetrate to the secret of that goodness in Apollos which had carried him thus far in his preachment of Messianic tidings. But thus far Apollos had gone, and no farther: he had preached the baptism of Jochanan, and he had been so far convinced by Priscilla of the Messiahship of Yeshua that he had received baptism in the name of the latter. Nevertheless, it seemed to Paul that Apollos had received his second baptism but weakly, and that he was still steeped, heart and soul, in the baptism of Jochanan. He had not found, in the ultimate sense, the fulfillment of the promise of Jochanan but still waited, in uncertainty and expectation, for a true advent. Paul exerted himself to the utmost to listen patiently—no light task for him—while Apollos unfolded his doctrine of the Logos, which he had learned from Philo in the academy of Alexandria.

Paul was well acquainted with the philosophy of Philo, as, indeed, was every educated Jew of the time. Philo had many pupils and disciples. His influence on thoughtful individuals, especially among the Hellenized Jews, was profound, and the carriers of his ideas were to be found in every corner of the Diaspora. Many Jews who were surrounded by the Hellenistic world had found in Philo's doctrines a bulwark against paganism. In their view the Jerusalem Jews were bound by a narrow provincialism; for the latter there was a single law which might be summed up thus: whatever was good was to be found among the Jews and in the God of Israel, whatever was bad was gentile. This was their answer to the progress of the world. But the Jews scattered throughout the Diaspora saw that it was not sufficient to say that the gentiles worshiped idols and demons and that their lives were unclean and dissolute. There were among the gentiles men of gentle ways and pure lives, thinkers concerned perhaps not less than Jews with the problems of good and evil; there were such as believed in the soul and accepted the principle of its immortality. Their worship was expressed in the adoration of beauty, and they strove to unite themselves with God through the harmony of their gods. Jews too had sought a bulwark for their faith in the intellectual systems of the gentiles. Philo was studied among thinking Jews. His transformation of the miracles of the Bible into a series of symbols and ideas had been an enlightenment to educated young Jews. Paul, too, had at one time been interested in Philo's system. He had even been very close to certain groups which accepted it without reserve. But a long time had passed since he had resolved the Logos in the Messiah. It was to the Messiah that he now ascribed all the universal attributes which made up the universe as such. And when Apollos went on to expand on the idea of the Logos as the first Son of God, and of Wisdom as the second Son of God, Paul found it harder and harder to contain himself and finally burst out:

"God has no first and second sons. There is one, and one only, who may be called the Son of God, and of whom God said: 'This day I have begotten thee.' And that Son is not the Logos, and not the order of the world, and not wisdom, for these themselves are only attributes, such as the gentiles speak of. The will-emanation of God is justice, as our Prophets have taught, and justification is to be found only in the Messiah of righteousness, whom our Prophets foretold."

Apollos was stupefied by the vehemence of Paul's outburst. He was not accustomed to be spoken to thus. He had always believed in the ancient Jewish saying: "And the words of the wise are listened to with pleasure." But Paul was not concerned with conducting a philosophic discussion. He was a man with a mission, and his mission was himself. The Messiah was not a thesis and not a subject for intellectual discussions. The Messiah was the stark reality of the world, which it was Paul's mission to unveil. He did not even notice the astonishment on Apollos's face. He spoke as though he sat confronting not Apollos, but the whole world of learned and subtle philosophers, to whom he was now bringing the Messiah as their one hope and salvation. But Apollos, brought up in learning and right conduct, mastered himself and betrayed no impatience. Anger, he knew, was a thing of evil. The philosopher does not yield to passion. Therefore Apollos curbed his tongue, and listened attentively, while the words poured like a torrent from Paul's lips.

"Justice," said Paul, passionately, "righteousness, is the equivalent of all these things, of logic, of wisdom, of beauty, of goodness, and even of law. The Law of Moses is but a part of righteousness, for the law, with all its arms, still cannot embrace the whole of life, and part of life must therefore be omitted by the law. This being so, God concentrated every aspect and extension of righteousness in a single instrument—and that instrument is the Messiah of righteousness, Yeshua. Whatever befall you, in whatever circumstance you find yourself, you must accept the Messiah as the standard of righteousness. He is the sole renewer of righteousness. He is not the ordered system of the world. That ordered system is delusion and a snare and a deception; it is an emptied cistern; thou approachest, and behold it is without living water. The Messiah is the flood of living waters, the ever-renewed. Therefore, Apollos, if thou seekest to bring to the world the Logos, beauty, goodness, law, wisdom, thou hast but to bring to the world the Messiah, in his oneness. He is the all in one. And since the Messiah is righteousness itself, all those that believe in him are dedicated and obligated to righteousness; they are quit of the law, but they are bound to righteousness."

Apollos listened quietly, though his whole being was in revolt. And when Paul was done, he asked:

"If, indeed, the Messiah is righteousness, and that little thing called law has been abrogated in the presence of the great thing called righteousness, tell me, I pray thee, what has become of sin?"

Paul thought awhile. His face became bloodless with his effort to find words. His eyes closed tightly, and his body began to sway like a branch of willow at the ceremony of the water-pouring in the fall. He shook like a pious Jew in the ecstasy of devotion, then answered in all humility:

"Sin is heritage, a part of the blood. Every drop flowing in my veins is heavy with sin, which I inherited with the blood of the first man, who was Adam. Even as it is written: 'And the intent of the thought of his heart is sin, all his days.' Before Adam's sin the world

476

was whole with the wholeness of purity, even as God had conceived it in His thought. Righteousness was then spread upon the world like the dew of God upon the fields. An eternal festival it was then, of blossom and greenness. The blades and twigs did not then compete for the sunlight, and peace was poured out upon all creation. Even as it is written: 'And God saw that it was good.' Now for that word 'good' read 'in righteousness.' The seed in the soil did not yield to the impulse to bring forth evil growths. The rose blossomed without thorns. Every cloud carried as much water as the earth needed, and no more. And man was the chosen and elect of creation. His daily life was a song of praise to the Creator, and all creation was a ceaseless hallelujah to Him. Adam it was who brought sin, and we have taken from him the heritage of it. Sin became our second nature. It sleeps within us like a wild beast; it wakens suddenly to attack us, like a robber in the night. It binds us, as a calf is bound." Paul tightened his eyelids. He became silent, but the swaying of his body continued. He trembled, and drops of sweat burst out on his forehead. His garb became wet, the veins on his temples became bluish, and he seemed to be casting his inward glance backward, seeing the stones that had lain in his path. And suddenly he cried out: "A thorn sticks in my flesh. Oh, who will save me from myself, if not thou, lord?" He tried to contain himself, but the words came tumbling out: "God took pity on His creation. He saw men drowning, unable to save themselves. He remembered the promise He had made to our forefathers, and He took His only Son, him Whom He had kept at His side since before the creation, to be the salvation of mankind, and He sent him down to earth in the likeness of a man of flesh and blood. And He gave him the nature of one of flesh and blood, that he might wipe away the sins of mankind with his blood. Every drop of blood that flowed from his veins became like a stormy sea; every pang of agony became a fiery star. Flood and fire cleansed away the sin of the world. But God showed His love not to us alone, of the seed of Abraham, he showed His love to all flesh, to all who have the blood of man in them. He is the God of the whole world—and He showed his love to all of us, when we were still little ones, to all of us, Jew and gentile. Even as through one sin came upon all mankind, so through one justification and righteousness shall come upon all men. This is my faith in Yeshua the Messiah. I bring this faith, according

477

to my own knowledge of the tidings, to mankind. For if we are justified by faith, so we are at peace with God through our lord, Yeshua the Messiah."

Apollos, long accustomed to the ways of scholars, to quiet commerce of ideas, listened to the end, and in his manner sought a way to answer his passionate opponent. There was something in his mind, something he had to impart to the apostle, and for the sake of which, in fact, he had returned to Ephesus, where he would find Paul. Therefore he rose, bowed before Paul, and said:

"With the permission of the apostle, I would utter the following: green and fresh as the leaves of the cypress tree planted by flowing waters are thy words, brother Paul. Thou standest close to the spring of faith, and thy roots draw in its waters. But to me too, the poor thorn bush in the wilderness, some of the waters of faith have reached. Assuredly thy words are true, and who can deny them? Thou callest the Messiah 'Son of God.' Of Solomon too He said: 'I shall be unto him a father, and he shall be a son unto me.' And He said, moreover, 'This day I have begotten thee.' Hence we may truly deduce that the Messiah is the Son of God. Even as ben Sira says, 'The Lord shall call thee son.' And even as Moses said concerning all Jews: 'Sons ye are to the Lord your God.' Likewise our sages have used the phrase: 'Sons of the Eternal.' Now if all the children of Israel are called sons of God, how much the more shall the Messiah be so called? As it is written in the Wisdom of Solomon: 'The Son of God, he is righteous.' And the righteous man is the atonement for his generation. For who are we that are of flesh and blood? We are like a ship that rides through the spaces of the sea and leaves not a trace behind; we are like the birds that fly through the air, and when they have passed none can tell the place of their passing. So we pass and there is no trace of our passage on earth. The just man stands between us and the Eternal, he takes upon himself the sins of his generation. The Messiah died for our sins, even as it is written . . ."

But at this point Paul, wearied to the soul of the quotations, verse after verse, with which Apollos adorned his speech, as was the custom among the learned; nor could he endure any more the calm elegance of the other's speech and diction, which was more fitted for public display than for intimate converse, and he broke in violently:

"Thinkest thou, Apollos, that the Messiah has need of many verses

478

and quotation, such as thou pourest out now like peas from a sack? And are we concerned here with a king, or with a righteous man? I talk now of the Son, the one and only Son, who was with God in heaven; I talk of the Messiah who was sent down upon earth to help mankind; I talk of him who died in torment, on the cross and under the lash, that his blood might redeem the sin in the blood of all mankind and that man might be restored to the Paradise that was his before the sin of Adam. Now why seekest thou to confuse me with sweet speech?"

Apollos stared, and then answered, but in another voice, and with less elegance, and more humbly:

"I have learned, concerning the Messiah, that he came to wash away with his blood the sin of Adam and to bring back righteousness. Whence it follows that whosoever believes in the Messiah is purified of the sin of Adam, which is to say, he has been returned to the world which is the Paradise of old time. Yes, this would all be true, and I would believe it if the Messianists, the Christians, the believers in the Messiah, would live such a life as was in Paradise before the sin of Adam. But if they live again in sin, then surely the blood of the Messiah has been shed in vain. Now I ask thee, Paul, do the Messianists indeed live in the world which was before sin? Do they indeed create a world of pure goodness, such as was of old before the fall, brother Paul? I have even now returned from the cities of Achaia. I have been in Corinth and I have lived among the Messianists, among those whom thou, the apostle, didst wean away from idol worship. What saw I? My sight was darkened, my heart trembled, and I was shaken by fear: I saw anger and quarreling, boasting and lying. To the feasts of the lord the rich bring their own rich dishes and the poor their own dry bread. They shame the body of the lord with their hoggish eating and their swilling. And what of their whoredoms? Nay, I tell thee that the like has not been heard among the heathen. For one of them has married his father's wife, and he still lives in the congregation. And to whom do they listen? Whosoever has the last word with them, he is listened to and believed. And there are some among them who say that they belong to the apostle Peter. They made even me one of the apostles; for after my sermons to them they began to call upon my name. They do not settle their disputes among themselves, and in their own courts, but drag the guilty before the courts of the unbelievers, before the gentile judges. Where is the righteousness which God has planted in the

479

congregation of the believers through his Messiah? Open thy eyes, thou apostle, and look about thee! Sin has risen like a flood which overwhelms all. The Messiah must be crucified daily—nay, hourly—in order that his blood might cope with the floods of sin; his blood must flow ceaselessly, eternally, in a great torrent, for ceaseless and torrential is the sin of the world." For a moment Apollos was speechless, and then, after a helpless gesture, he continued: "Thou hast placed the greatest of all obligations on the Messianists, but if the Messianists do not honor the obligation, in a life of righteousness, the blood of the Messiah has been shed in vain; and then thy words are as the wind blown into a ventless ram's horn, from which no sound issues."

Paul sat bowed, as if a hammer were raining its blows on his head. He seemed to be shrinking, as if he wanted to disappear into the earth. His face was yellow, his mouth distorted with pain. The sins of the Corinthians were his sins! He had committed them, each of them, singly, and all of them in the mass. His was the responsibility. Nor was this report unexpected. He had heard from others of the conduct of the Corinthians. Certain of them had written to him through Stephanus, putting various questions to him. In that same letter they had also asked him to return to them. But he had put the journey off. Therefore he was the derelict shepherd, he had abandoned the lambs, the young ones —abandoned them in a storm, in the dark of night, left them among the stones of a wild field. The wolves waited for them in the caves, the shepherd was not there. His was the guilt! Was it not written: "As a father has compassion on his son even so the Messiah would be compassionate to them"? But he, Paul, had not been compassionate to them, he had abandoned them in their need. And now he answered, in a broken voice:

"Brother Apollos! Did not the Jews, too, sin before the giving of the law at Sinai? And even when Moses was on Sinai they made themselves the golden calf. How many times was not God of a mind to destroy and utterly wipe out the Jews—but Moses intervened for them, and prayed: 'Nay, forgive them.' He offered himself as an atonement for the sins of the people. Now there is in God one cure, one single attribute alone which brings forgiveness, and this was the attribute which was strong in Moses: Love! The love which was strong in Moses for the Jews must be poured out upon all the gentiles who are drawn into the faith of the Messiah. I have put all my trust in Yeshua

480

the Messiah: Yeshua the Messiah, I said, would with his love lead the hosts of the gentiles out of the wilderness of sin and uncleanness in which they have so long wandered, lost. And from Moses, brother Apollos, we must learn one more thing, the patience which is the soul of love. Therefore of thee, Apollos, I demand that thou help me in the love of the Messiah. Thou art learned, thy heart is filled with knowledge, and thy mouth pours forth sweet speech. Come, then, help me to spread the love of the Messiah, so that it may fall like dew upon the withered field of the gentiles."

Chapter Twenty-six

ONE DAY IN EPHESUS

PAUL'S doctrine of the Messiah, formed according to his own vision and conception of his mission, crystallized in its strangeness and in its incomprehensibility to the traditional Jews, so that it called forth ever greater dissension even among his own followers. Beginning as the tidings of hope and consolation, it was transformed into cause of dissension and hostility. For what Paul had to say was something alien to the nature and spirit of the Jews, and his utterances were like a trumpet call to false worship. It was a challenge to the ancient zeal which the Jews had always demonstrated in their faith. Paul had not been in Ephesus more than a few months when his preachments called forth a bitterness of spirit, a tenseness, which drove a great many Jews into a fury of hostility against the faith of the Messiah.

That happened in Ephesus which had happened in other cities. Many Jews refused to listen to that which Paul had to say. And once again Paul was driven to widen the breach between his followers and the other Jews by the opening of a new church. For those that followed him were numerous enough to make this possible; and Paul hired, for the Messianists, a schoolhouse, with the right to assemble his followers there at certain hours of the day, when the children's classes had been dismissed.

Where did Paul gather the strength to face this division in Jewry? He found it in the extremity of his faith. He became "the fool of the Messiah," and in the folly of his love, devotion, and surrender, he made of his life a continuous sacrifice. Daily before dawn, when the rest of the world was covered with the mantle of sleep, he rose to pray and gather strength. When the dawn came he washed his hands, as every pious Jew did, said the morning *Shema,* ate his frugal breakfast of a small piece of bread and a handful of olives, which he washed down with a cup of water which barely tasted of wine or honey, and proceeded to his place in the workshop of Aquila and Priscilla. And while his feet worked the treadles and the shuttle flew back and forth, his mind was given to the problems of his infant church. In particular he was concerned with the welfare of his flock in Corinth, and he composed at his work the phrases which were to be woven into his letter to the Corinthians. He was tormented, day and night, by the news which reached him from that city, by that which Apollos and others had reported to him. Sosthenes himself, the head of the synagogue of the Jews, came to visit Paul in Ephesus, and what he had to say bore out the mournful tidings of Apollos. "Is it righteousness that thou hast planted among the gentiles in the name of the Messiah?" asked Sosthenes. "I tell thee they have fallen back into uncleanness, they are drowned in whoredom, they shame the poor, they drag the fatherless before the judges of the gentiles." Everything that Apollos had said was confirmed by Sosthenes—and more. For Sosthenes told of a spirit of hatred and envy among the Christians, a spirit of rivalry and hostility. One would say: "I belong to Paul!" And the other would cry against him: "I belong to Apollos!" Who were Paul and Apollos, the apostle asked himself with a groan. "I have planted and Apollos has watered, but it is God who sent up the shoot." And thus, as he worked at the loom in anguish, his mind gave birth to phrases. "Know ye not," he muttered, "that your bodies are the temples of the Holy Ghost, which is within you and which you have from God?" "Ye have been bought for a price; therefore glorify God in your bodies and in your spirit, which are of God."

So, laboring mechanically, and sharpening the arrows of his phrases, he sat until the eleventh hour, when the sun, rising toward its highest point in the daily arc, poured down a torrent of light and heat. At this hour the Ephesians suspend work. Each one seeks out a hiding place, a shelter, a spot of shadow; the windows are covered with cloth, awnings are laid upon frameworks. Some lie in the shelter of the columns of temples or the walls of houses. All is then at peace. The merchant and the slave and the laborer, man and woman—all rest. The streets of Ephesus, empty of passersby, doze in the fiery sunlight. Only the apostle Paul and his followers are awake and at work. They are gathered in the synagogue of Tiranus.

For Paul there is no midday pause. He has eaten a frugal midday meal, prepared for him by Priscilla—a salad, a few olives, a spoonful of honey; and in the company of his most intimate followers he has made his way to the synagogue.

There, in the cool and shadowed interior, his congregation sits on the little stone benches. Timotheus and Titus and Priscilla have brought them hither. Most of the listeners are Jews, such as have not been frightened away by his strange doctrine, but have, on the contrary, found in it consolation and strength and hope. Some of them have already accepted baptism. There are Ephesians among the listeners, but there are also visitors from towns nearby, merchants who, having heard strange reports of a wonderful message, have come to hear for themselves. They come from Colossae, from Laodicea, and from Hieropolis. What they have heard they will carry forth from Ephesus, even as they carry their merchandise; and as they sell the latter they will distribute the former. They will found new congregations and churches of the believers, which will grow into one great organization with the church of Ephesus as its center. Meanwhile they sit and listen, Arichus of Colossae and Nimphos of Laodicea and the others: Jewish faces, great lively eyes, mouths wide open in a trance of attention. They are frightened and overjoyed: "The Messiah has come! The Messiah has risen from the dead, the first of all mankind to rise from the dead!" Their beards bristle with astonishment, and the hairs on their heads stand up. Their hearts melt with terror and hope. Waves of hot and cold pass over them as they listen to the words which issue from the mouth of the apostle; that mouth, which can utter such bitter things against his own flesh and blood, can also bring forth such tenderness, can utter such consolation for the sufferings of his people. Now the apostle speaks of the end of days, of the last day: the trumpet will sound, the dead will rise from their graves, the heavens will open. The Messiah will come suddenly, like a thief in the night. He will come with the clouds of heaven, as Daniel of old prophesied. "Ah, what times these are we live in! Why are you silent? Come, let us spread the tidings of the Messiah throughout the world!"

Side by side with the Jews, who sit trembling at this appeal to their inmost sanctities, are the gentiles—men and women with faces as of chiseled granite. Not a muscle moves, not a tremor passes over them; their lips are locked in silence. They give no outward sign, but within a fire has been kindled, a hope shines and spreads its light; a spring of joy has opened, and the waters of deliverance well up. Hearts which were dumb begin to speak inwardly. "God has had compassion on the gentiles. Before they knew of him, the Messiah died for their sins, in order to redeem them. Now they enter into the new covenant, they become co-inheritors of the promise of God with the Jews." Old pagans sit, their faces furrowed by the winds of time, and young pagans whose faces are simple and naïve; the waters of faith flow over them alike. There are men with mighty bodies and others with the aspect of philosophers. No trace of their inner response touches their countenance. From without they seem hard, impenetrable, inaccessible; but in their hearts a mighty struggle is toward. Their pulses beat, their brains are in a turmoil. The words pouring from Paul's lips take lodgment, burst into blossom, break open the rigid stone of their one-time life. Only on the faces of the women, lined with care, with motherly sorrows, the glimmer of a response shines outwardly. Their eyes drink in the tidings, their lips tremble. "All are equal in the faith!" cries the apostle. There are children, too, which the women have brought with them, even infants and sucklings, held close to the breast in swaddling clothes. For they have heard that the apostle has not only words of wonder, but deeds of wonder, too. The touch of his hands, the breath of his mouth, the flutter of his garb, can bring healing. The women wait; when the messenger will have delivered his tidings, they will crowd about him and ask for his benediction on them and theirs. They will touch his sandals, and they will be healed of sickness as well as of sin.

But on this occasion the apostle pours forth his wrath against the cult of the magicians, the soothsayers, and the idolatrous healers. His fiery words consign the misleaders forever to the deepest pit of hell. He does not speak openly against the goddess Diana herself; his assault is launched against the whole world of idolatry, against the unclean life of paganism, against the philosophers and the wise men of the gentiles.

"Because they held themselves to be wise, they are become fools. They have exchanged the glory of God the incorruptible for a likeness, a corruptible image, a bird, a beast, a crawling thing. Therefore has God delivered them to the impurity of their passions, so that they shall debase their bodies, inasmuch as they have taken it upon themselves to worship the creature in the place of the Creator Who is blessed for ever— Amen!" "Therefore He has delivered them to shameful lusts . . . and they have received the proper punishment for their deception." "God has delivered them to a treacherous understanding. They are filled with all manner of unrighteousness and evil, they are filled with envy, murder, quarrelsomeness, deceit, and evil thoughts—chatterers, slanderers, enemies of God. But God has manifested His love for us, for inasmuch as we have been sinners, the Messiah has died for us."

Every word is like an arrow sped to the heart of the listeners. They behold about them the ocean of sin and dissoluteness in which they have been sunk; they understand the perversity of the desires which they have indulged; they know that their lives have been abandoned of God until this moment. Now the light of hope shines above them; help is let down for them by the hand of God; the saving rope is the death of the Messiah, who has suffered for them. And there is not a single one among the listeners, however petrified in the old ways of sin, however reluctant to give an outward sign, who does not soften with longing and hope.

* * *

But the synagogue was not the only field of Paul's activity. In Ephesus the apostle made use of a new method for the winning of souls for the Messiah—the method of individual personal contact. He went, like a beggar, from house to house. When he heard of anyone who was inclined to listen, Paul visited him at home, to speak with him alone, face to face. And sometimes he was led to a sick man, who felt himself to be dying, and who had expressed the desire to speak with the apostle before his eyes were closed, so that in the last moment he might hear of the hope beyond the grave. So Paul would sit with the dying man, would hold his hand and comfort him, saying: "In the faith of the Messiah death becomes nothing; death is but the threshold into the eternal life of the Messiah. The believer in the Messiah lives, even in his death." Sometimes Paul was asked to visit a rich man, who had ex-

485

pressed the wish to enter the faith together with all his household. The sick and the hale, the poor and the rich, Paul visited them all, refusing no request, and thinking none too little or too unimportant for his ministrations. He comforted with words, he healed with the touch of his hand. And at the end of the day, when a cool wind blew across the city, he returns to the humble dwelling of Aquila and Priscilla. There is no more strength in his body; his feet are like stones, his face is ashen gray, his clothes are tattered and covered with dust, his sandals are falling apart, his undergarment clings to his flesh.

The dwelling of Aquila remains humble because here, in Ephesus, his prosperity is gone. But no want comes near the apostle. Somewhere Aquila and Priscilla find a cruse of oil for Paul. Titus washes his teacher and anoints him. He draws a new garment over his body. Refreshed and rested, the apostle repeats the evening *Shema* and sits down with the household to a frugal supper.

But the day's work is far from done. There are still delegations to be received. They come to him from the provinces, from the congregations he has founded. They have innumerable questions to put to him. Gaius and Aristarchus are here, newly arrived from Macedonia. They implore the apostle to return with them to their homeland. Paul is filled with longing for the community of Philippi, where he left so many dear friends. And his conscience still torments him because he left Salonika in the hour of its need. He is torn with conflicting longings. He promises the Macedonians that some day he will surely return to them. But it is Corinth that must have his first attention. He has already sent Timotheus forth to Corinth and to Macedonia, to confirm the reports which have come to Ephesus. And this day there is a delegation from Corinth itself: Stephanus, with a group of the faithful. They bring greetings—and a letter. Corinth cries out for Paul to return and restore order. The community is in confusion; there are no leaders to answer the questions which beset them. They inquire, for instance, what they are to do in regard to meat. The only meat obtainable is that which is left over from the sacrifices to the local gods. The Jews have their own butchers and therefore are not short of *kosher* meat; but the gentiles have no butchers of their own, and they must either abstain from meat or eat the sacrificial meat sold by the idolatrous priesthood. But is it permissible for Christians, though gentiles, to eat such meat? Moreover, they are at a loss concerning the disputes which arise among

486

themselves and which they submit to pagan judges. Their family life, too, stands in need of regulation. They would like to know whether it is permissible for a husband who is of the faithful to live with a wife who is not of the faith, or whether a woman who has received baptism may continue to live with her husband if he has refused it. There are problems of divorce. All these questions present themselves daily, and the congregation is falling to pieces for lack of authoritative direction. There are also problems of another order. Certain of the new Christians are so exalted by the Messianic idea that they refuse to wed at all; others, being already wedded, will no longer live with their wives after their conversion. Only one man, and he the apostle, can restore the community to a normal and ordered life. But Paul has other plans. He cannot leave for Corinth; for he must and will visit Macedonia first. Nor has he yet ended his mission to the Ephesians. The congregation he has founded here cannot stand on its own feet. Paul knows only too well that there are backsliders, seekers of both worlds, Christians who, accepting baptism, practice in secret the worship of the ancient gods, resort to soothsayers and consult the mystic books. All this he must burn out from the midst of the Ephesians before he leaves them. For Ephesus must become an example and center for the whole province. Do not the Jewish merchants of Colossae and Laodicea look to Ephesus for guidance in the faith? Is not Aristarchus here, ready to return to his native town and found a community there? Besides, Paul is haunted by a great dream, which returns to him nightly. He will do a great thing, concerning which he has not yet spoken to any man. When his work is ended in Ephesus and in Macedonia and Achaia, he will go to Jerusalem—yes, to Jerusalem, even though death may await him there. And if he should leave Jerusalem alive, there is still Rome—Rome, the city of the Caesars. "The road to Rome," he said to himself, "leads for me through Jerusalem."

No, no, no; let them plead as they will, he cannot leave Ephesus now and go to Corinth. All he can do is prepare a long letter to the Corinthians, a letter in which he will answer all their questions, and teach them the way of the life in the Messiah. It will be a long letter, and a final one, a cornerstone upon which all the other congregations of the Messiah shall be built. Not the Corinthians alone but all the Messianists in all the provinces shall receive copies of the letter, and they shall guide themselves accordingly. "By the grace of God, conferred upon me, I have laid the foundations like a cunning builder, and others shall build upon these foundations. But let him that builds be heedful of that which he builds, for he shall use no other foundation save that which is in Yeshua the Messiah." And on this foundation of Yeshua the Messiah Paul seeks to answer all the questions which the Corinthians have addressed to him.

Late in the night, when the delegations have withdrawn, before he lies down on his hard couch, he calls over his faithful Titus. The tiny candle burns almost till the morning hour while Paul, tense with the labor of his thoughts, dictates. His body is gathered into a heap, the veins pulse on his forehead, the words come slowly, painfully, from his lips. It is the letter to the Corinthians:

"And though I should speak to you with the tongue of men and of angels, and I have not love, I am but as a tinkling cymbal. And though I should have the gift of prophecy and know all the secrets of knowledge and have faith so that I can move mountains, and I have not love, then I am as nothing. And if I should distribute all my worldly goods to the poor and give up my body to destruction, and I have not love, then it avails me nothing.

"Love is patient and long-suffering. Love is not envious. Love is not proud and swollen-up.

"And only these three remain, faith, hope, and love, and the greatest of these is love."

He has dictated the last words of the long letter. Titus has withdrawn, and Paul falls back on his couch, exhausted, and sleeps at last.

And even at that hour Priscilla approaches lightly and takes the apostle's tattered mantle and spreads it upon his feet. Then she extinguishes the flickering lamp, and darkness spreads to the corner where Paul lies asleep.

Thus his day ended, and his night began.

Chapter Twenty-seven

DIANA OF THE EPHESIANS

"GREAT is Diana of the Ephesians !"

Who knows it not?

Like waves of the sea arrested in mid-motion and turned to red marble, the walls of the Temple of Diana rise from the midst of the double line of Ionic pillars which girdle it. Four hundred and twenty feet is the length of the temple, two hundred and twenty feet is its width, and a double row of Ionic pillars sixty feet in height runs along each side. The wealth of Asia has been poured out to make this the greatest of all temples. Two hundred years it was in the building, and it was one of the seven wonders of the world. Kings, nobles, princes, and merchants of Asia Minor and Achaia sent their gifts generation after generation, that they might be part of the immortal building. One sent a pillar, another a statue, a third a bas-relief, a fourth a priceless vessel. Here stands the mighty column upon which the great Scopas has hammered out the image of the eternal struggle between Aphrodite and Mars, the love struggle between birth and death, between creation and destruction. About another column the Graces dance in everlasting beauty, their light feet swimming on the weightless air. Like young does they pursue each other in a circle, the pursuer pursued but never catching and never caught. For this dance is the flight and pursuit of time, which flies but never escapes, pursues and never catches. On a third column Mercury is poised in the instant of his departure on a mission from Zeus. What a hymn of beauty sings in the marble which the master has fashioned into this likeness! Glory upon glory, song upon song, the pillars and sculptures of the Temple of Diana are but a tribute to her that reigns within.

The temple stands in a flat valley. In olden times a great swamp spread its treacherous surface here. Now the swamp has been drained, and in the place of the miasmal scum there is a vast garden, or rather a series of gardens and meadows. Because of the low level of the ground, the temple stands on a platform, toward which the worshiper mounts by wide stairs between rows of columns. The great inner hall of the temple, the abode of the goddess, has been adorned by groups of amazons, the work of the foremost sculptors of the Greek world. Scopas, Polikletes, the immortal Phidias, and his peer Praxiteles, poured their spirits into the forms of the gigantic maidens who fill the inner hall. Only those mortals whose eyes the gods have kissed could see the human form under the aspect of such gracious and yet stormy beauty. Daughters of men they are, but consorts of gods. With more than regal dignity the womanly heads are poised upon the mighty throats; wisdom and beauty pour down from the broad foreheads. This is the very ecstasy of human praise, the last intimacy of human longing for divinity and beauty. The master sang to the goddess the ultimate song of harmony and grace.

Here is the group hewn by the hand of Polikletes. These women are human, earthly, motherly. He has poured into these outlines all that man can give—man's love. Desire breathes from the rounded stone, blood flows in the marble veins, milk uplifts the marble breast, and a tender warmth informs the delicate tracery of the robes. But more mightily than these figures, the group of Praxiteles cries triumphantly the greatness of the goddess. On the predella itself, at the feet of the image of Diana, his women athletes in shimmering bronze proclaim the might which towers over them. Endowed with infinite power, these figures subdue their power in humility, for in the presence of the goddess their strength becomes uncertainty; without her even their tremendous mastery of the flesh fails. And opposite the altar of the goddess stands the image of the young Alexander, King of Macedonia. Flushed with triumph, he pauses at the feet of Diana, under the portent of the greater triumphs which await him.

Figures, innumerable, powerful living figures, crowd the corners of the inner hall. It is not as though the image of Diana had fallen down from heaven, as the legend told. Rather one would say that all these images of men and women had been sent by Apollo to accompany the goddess in her deliberate descent. No accident had brought about this concourse of immortal figures. No accident had adorned the walls with such paintings, such trophies of war, such spears and breastplates and swords.

And in the very center stands the goddess herself. A double row of pillars guards her, and her body is swathed in a veil of Persian silk.

Each pillar is a single fragment of jasper. Before the goddess is her altar, a block of marble, the sides of which were hammered out by Praxiteles. A gigantic cupola swims above the head of the goddess, and no one knows how this gigantic semisphere has been suspended in mid-air. A flight of wooden stairs, cut from a single tree, leads from the lower to the upper level of the hall; and four balconies protrude from the outer wall upon the square before the temple. Upon these balconies the eunuch priests take their stand and blow their silver trumpets above the assembled crowds. The blowing of the trumpets proclaims that the silken veil is about to be lifted, and Diana will become visible to her worshipers. But only the great, princes, rulers, nobles, are admitted to the vision; the people, the plebs, must wait without, prostrate in the dust.

Now the great gates of the temple, made of cypress, swing open. The masses assembled from every part of Asia, from Galatia, from Cappadocia, from Macedonia, from Achaia, the hale and the sick, the cripples on their crutches, the blind led by children, the paralyzed carried on their litters, press between the columns toward the façade. All wait for the moment when the unveiling of the goddess will be proclaimed.

A long blast on the trumpets, a quick rolling of the drums, and then an interval of silence. A cloud of incense blows across the square. In the open, and within the hall, the worshipers lie prostrate and breathless. The silken veil is slowly withdrawn. On her pedestal of black marble, encircled with mystic hieroglyphics which none can read, stands the goddess, Artemis of Ephesus, whom Apollo sent down from heaven. About her is grouped all the beauty that human genius can express in stone and color—and she herself is a gross unlovely image! Her body is of black ebony or of ugly vine-wood. Black as charcoal, repulsive as a reptile, she stands there, an Asiatic horror!

Diana of the Ephesians was not the original Artemis, the moon-goddess of night, of dew and of weaving life. Diana of the Ephesians was more primitive. Her upper body was covered with metal breasts, symbols of fruitfulness; her lower body was fitted into a metallic frame on which were hammered innumerable heads of lions. Her nose was flat, Asiatic; her eyes were dull; her mouth was contorted. Horrible and mystic, loathsome, secretive, powerful, she spread awe and stupefaction about her.

But when she was unveiled, a shuddering cry spread from the hall to the façade, from the façade to the open square, to the thousands upon thousands of prostrate worshipers:

"Great is Diana of the Ephesians!"

The cry is taken up, translated, repeated in a dozen languages, a score of dialects. The curt accents of the Greeks, the nasal, long-drawn utterance of the Asiatics, the babbling of the Phoenicians—all mingle in local accents. Eyes are tight-shut, lips are taut, foreheads are drawn close, an ecstasy of hope and fear grips the vast, motley assembly. Incomprehensible syllables are flung upon the air, esoteric cries of the Diana worship. Some know the sounds by heart, others look furtively at fragments of papyri on which the syllables are written. And each one believes that this cry brings intimate union with the goddess. There are some who carry the syllables on talismans hung about their necks. Others repeat what they hear from the lips of others. Through the vast, open doors pour the billows of incense and the smoke of the sacrifices. And when the sweet-acrid fumes reach the prostrate crowd, a cry of ecstasy ascends to the sky. The prostrate figures rise, there is a stampede toward the temple doors. The blind, the lame, the sick gather up their last energies, crawl or thrust their way toward the unseen goddess, clawing at each other, screaming their supplications. Here and there wild voices are uplifted:

"The wonder has happened! See, the lame man walks! See, the sick man has stepped down from his bed!"

Then a group of priests issues from the temple door. They pass among the crowd, gathering up the crutches which have been thrown away. These will be hung as trophies on the walls of the temple, tributes to the greatness of Diana.

The priests are followed by a horde of magicians, who thread their way among the worshipers, selling their philters, herbs, and talismans. The bodies of the magicians are tattooed from head to foot with mystic symbols. The soothsayers and star-gazers offer for sale horoscopes cast by the First Astrologer, Babylus. Tiny models of the temple and of the goddess image are also for sale; some are of costly metal, the product of the workshop of the First Silversmith, Demetrius. Models of the goddess are a protection against the evil eye. Thus the wave of deceit, greed, and corruption laves the assembled crowd, till it is inundated, carried away. Before long a change comes over the spirit of the scene. Flute players and mimes now have their turn; the

492

eunuch priests conduct through the crowd women possessed of spirits, to tell fortunes; peddlers offer little scrolls in which the secret names of the goddess are supposed to be written; and there are rhymesters who sell stories and ballads of their own composition.

*   *   *

Great gardens and blossoming meadows surround the Temple of Diana. When the hour of worship is over, the pilgrims scatter and lie down in the grass. The sun is setting toward the Great Sea, and an azure, dewy light, shot through with streaks of crimson cloud, spreads over the gardens and meadows. Here and there a group of pilgrims takes up the chorus of a song. Lines of dancing girls with flower wreaths on their heads pass among the resting worshipers, to the accompaniment of flutes and bells. Hand in hand, young boys and girls join the dance, lifting their robes in rhythm with the music. Here and there a crowd is gathered about a naked athlete who makes skillful play with his muscles as he sways his body right and left. Somewhere a shrill cry of laughter ascends from a group of women; in their midst stands a eunuch complaining that the magic of the priests has failed to restore his virility. The sellers of viands appear, setting up their tripods in the fields. Priests bring out of the temple cartloads of slaughtered oxen, swine, sheep, goats: these will be sold to the cooks, who in turn will prepare the meat and sell it to the worshipers. The air is filled with the fumes of roasting meat. The wine dealers have put up their booths. A thousand lanterns and torches star the gathering darkness, and a spirit of recklessness, gaiety, and lust takes hold of the vast throng. Couples wander away from their companions and seek out the shadowy places under the bushes. Against this abomination Paul lifted the ax which Abraham lifted against the idols of his father Terah.

*   *   *

Among the gentiles whom Paul had won to the faith in Ephesus there was a man by the name of Tryphimus. This man was a scion of one of the oldest and most celebrated families of Ephesus. He had inherited from remote forefathers a great collection of idols, the work of many masters. These demons and images had been, as long as the records of the family went back, the protectors of the house, and countless generations had worshiped them and sacrificed before them. Habit and tradition were strong with Tryphimus, and though he had accepted baptism, he could not divorce himself from his pagan heritage. Thus he and his household continued to pray to the ancient powers, for Tryphimus was afraid that if he abandoned them his house would collapse on him and his, and his forefathers would return from the other world to take vengeance on him. When Paul, having baptized him, demanded that he yield up the gods which he kept in the family grotto, and consign to the fire all the mystic books of the priests, Tryphimus held off, not only because of the strength of the tradition in him, but simply because he still believed in them. The faith which he had accepted from Paul had not given him a tangible and visible symbol, something for eyes and hands. What Paul had breathed into him was an ideal only, something which to Tryphimus seemed to dwell beyond the confines of human conception—the all-present, all-filling, universal and invisible God of Israel. Even the Messiah who had died for him was an abstraction, and Tryphimus had no image to gaze on, to address himself to, to possess. Steeped in the immemorial habit of material presences, Tryphimus could not put his trust in the invisible. But Paul taught him that the first article of the new faith was utter belief in God, Who, though invisible, was everywhere about the believer. Without seeing Him Whom he addresses, the believer must know that his prayer is heard, more, that it is known before it is uttered. God knows the secret thoughts and the needs of all men, and every hair on the head of a man is counted. "And God demands," said Paul, "that thou accept Him blindly, and place thy life in His hands. And even when the waters have come up to thy lips, and thou thinkest there can be no help for thee, still thou must believe that God will help thee, and then He surely will." Paul told Tryphimus of the splitting of the Red Sea: how Moses had led the children of Israel out of Egypt and brought them to the shore of the sea. And behind the children of Israel were the chariots of Pharaoh, before them the angry and stormy waters. Then Moses had cried to God, and God had answered him: "Wherefore criest thou to me? Tell the children of Israel to go forward!" Whereupon Moses issued the command, and it was only after the children of Israel had gathered up their faith, after they had plunged into the roaring waters, after they had gone on fearlessly, till the waves were up to their lips— it was only then that Moses lifted up his rod, so that the waters, which had roared upon them and threatened them with death, were suddenly quietened and were reared up in two walls. Between these frozen walls the children of Israel passed in safety to the further shore. "Thus it is with every believer," said Paul. "Every believer must pass through the Red Sea, knowing that God will be with him. Therefore, Tryphimus, cast out the idols and demons in whom thou hast reposed thy trust till now; cast them forth and destroy them. And when God will see that thou believest in Him, he will bring thee into the grace of the Messiah. Thou wilt find thyself under the protection of His outspread arms."

And the day came when faith triumphed over fear, and Tryphimus passed through the waters of the Red Sea. In pain, trembling with fear, but with a faith stronger than pain or fear, he took the gods of his fathers, and broke them into fragments, and brought them to Paul to consign to the flames.

And thus it was with many other worshipers of the goddess of Ephesus.

So it came to pass that, on the day when thousands of Diana-worshipers were assembled before the temple of the goddess, Paul had assembled the believers in one of the courtyards of the Jews; and as the flames went up in the inner temple of Diana, other flames were kindled here, not in worship of Diana, but to consume her images. Thus the newly-won believers perceived that what they had accepted hitherto, so naturally, as divinity, was but abysmal darkness. They brought to Paul their copies of the secret books, heirlooms which their families had guarded for many generations, their most precious possessions; books of the soothsayers and of the interpreters of dreams, books with special and mysterious invocations to the goddess; they brought also all manner of magic instruments, bones of heroes, pieces of horn of the holy cow of Egypt, locks of hair from famous witches, costly things with great powers to bring back fruitfulness to the barren, to confer invisibility, to drive off the evil eye. There were scrolls containing horoscopes by Babylus himself, phials containing philters put together by Mithridatus, roots and herbs and dried plants, recipes of Appolonius. These, together with the sacred images, the models of the temple and of Diana, in stone, in gold, silver, and other metals, were brought to Paul.

But there were other and even more intimate relics, which they sacrificed. There was in Ephesus a frightful cult of the corpses of parents and children. The pagans knew not what to do with their dead. Some burned the bodies, and kept the ashes in stone urns, which, ranged upon shelves in the house, looked down upon the wildest orgies. Others scraped clean the bones of their beloved children and hung them about their necks as amulets. These things too, they brought to Paul, and a great heap was gathered for destruction in the Jewish quarter in the shadow of Mount Prion. The flames ascended, the amulets caught fire, the scrolls crackled, the images melted, the phials broke open. And still believers came, carrying the abominations and flinging them into the fire: "Accursed be the uncleanness!" Fiery serpents leapt from the vast pyre; it was as though the demons, the evil spirits, all the terrors of the ancient world of sin, were escaping. A world was being destroyed, the world of paganism, going up in crimson sheets and a myriad sparks.

And as Paul stood there, illumined by the flames, and crying ecstatically, "Accursed be the abomination!" it seemed to him that he was suddenly aware of a presence. A man had drawn near, the man he had seen in a vision in Troas, the man of Macedonia, black-bearded, splendid of countenance. He stood before Paul, and his shining eyes were open, as if seeking an answer to a question.

"Paul! Thou destroyest the beauty of Hellas!"

"Nay, not the beauty of Hellas," answered Paul, "but the idolatry of Hellas. The beauty of Hellas has been inherited by the Messiah, who has inherited, too, something greater than the beauty of Hellas— the man of Hellas."

Thus answering, Paul looked about him, and the man had vanished. There were only the believers, the flames, the triumph of purification. He heard only the crackling of the fire, the lamentation of the dying gods. He had been speaking to himself. And yet—perhaps not.

Chapter Twenty-eight

A THREAT TO BUSINESS

IN one of the interior halls of the Temple of Diana a meeting of the religious purveyors of Ephesus, of the silversmiths, the magicians, and the star-gazers, was in progress. Demetrius, the First Silversmith of the goddess, had called the meeting, for it was he who believed himself to be in the greatest danger. Advanced in years—he was in his middle eighties—Demetrius of Ephesus was still a man of demonic energy. His life had been a hard one, his career stormy. For sixty years he had conducted the fight to achieve the unchallenged position of First Silversmith, to win recognition as the special representative, in his field, of Diana. Now it was universally acknowledged that his statuettes of the goddess and his models of the temple were the most potent, having the sanction of the divinity herself. In them were concentrated, as in no others, all the healing virtues of Diana. True, there were other silversmiths in Ephesus, carrying on the same trade. But they existed by the sufferance of Demetrius. The competition among the manufacturers of sacred objects was bitter and unrelenting, and even in his supremacy Demetrius did not dare to relax his vigilance. A childless man and a Nazirite of the goddess, he was driven not so much by the love of gain as by a savage ambition. The struggle of six decades had fixed his character beyond change; first in his field, he was as contentious and restless as ever, and his attitude was one of constant wariness and hostility. He was reluctant to die, not because he feared death but because in death he would be demoted from his position. The bitterness which was now his second nature was expressed in his features. His skin was yellow, and hardened like the back of a turtle; it was as if his veins were filled not with blood, but with some metallic liquid. His mouth was beak-shaped, the pointed lips curving over his chin. As he sat among his competitors and colleagues, he kept cracking his bony fingers and muttering to himself, so that the lump in his throat bobbed continuously, as if he had swallowed a toad which was for ever leaping up again. And he muttered the same words over and over again:

"Swindlers! Liars! Deceivers! The man's nothing but a deceiver! A liar!"

These words had accompanied him through all his life. They had been his armory. He had a way of uttering them with such fury, such conviction, that he overwhelmed opposition. By sheer vehemence and repetition, sustained for sixty years, he had indeed overwhelmed his competitors, so that the public had come to take it for granted that any silversmith who claimed that his religious products were as potent as those of Demetrius was a swindler, a liar, and a deceiver. And even when he had no occasion to use the words, Demetrius would still mutter them, in a paroxysm of contempt and anger, directing them against no one knew whom.

Opposite Demetrius sat Babylus, wearing the high headgear of the astrologer and the decorated mantle, covered with constellations and comets, which was the sign of his profession. He too was no longer a young man, but age had dealt kindly with him. The beauty which had made him famous in his youth had been transformed into a certain majesty of which Babylus was only too well aware, and which he exploited with every art. As the First Astrologer of the goddess, and the leader in a learned profession, Babylus should have comported himself with becoming dignity. But a touch of coquetry was patent in his bearing. He knew that the women worshipers of Diana had a special feeling for him. He awakened the passions of the young and stirred the memories of the old. Tall, well-built, he gave special care to his appearance; his beard was dyed a deep black, and its locks were curled daily by the most skillful hairdressers of Ephesus. His eyes, which had retained the luster of youth, were ringed with kohol.

Babylus had two ambitions; the first was to remain, as long as he lived, the First Astrologer of Diana. The second was to become the sole guardian of all the documents and traditions relating to the temple, as they had come down from the time of the great Belshazzar. In the care of his body Babylus strove to impart to his appearance a suggestion of the Syrian-Babylonian. His hairdressers were all Syrians; and by the cut of his beard, by its ebony color, he evoked in the mind of beholders the ancient kings and soothsayers of the East. In order to sustain his reputation, Babylus was compelled to make public forecasts of important events. Sometimes his forecasts were fulfilled; sometimes they were falsified. In the latter case he placed the blame on the times and upbraided the worshipers of Diana with laxity, backsliding, and indifference. Because of their declining attention to the goddess, her grace was being withdrawn from the world, and the revelation of the future was denied her First Astrologer. Babylus, too, had had a difficult uphill fight to establish himself in his present position, nor was he as secure in it as Demetrius in his field. There were swarms of younger astrologers in competition with him, each one ready to prove that the exalted role was his by every right. They spread slanderous rumors about him, whispered to the worshipers that the man was too old for his exacting task; he was senile, unable any longer to read the stars aright and interpret their messages. But Babylus still retained the supremacy in Ephesus, less by the keenness of his intellect than by his appeal to the women. They were the first to remember his accurate forecasts, to forget his failures; they denounced his young competitors as envious ignoramuses, not one of whom knew how to cast a true horoscope or read the fate of a man. Babylus alone, they said, had the true secret and the tradition, as it had come down from the great Belshazzar.

Appolonius and Mithridatus were the "young men" of the assembly, but their pointed, yellow beards were already streaked with gray, and their faces were wrinkled with much concentration on their difficult tasks as First Magicians of the goddess. Peers in their profession, they felt no respect for each other. As Babylus went back to Babylonian Belshazzar for his tradition, so every magician claimed to have inherited, exclusively, the secrets of ancient Egypt, handed down through mystic teachers and contained in documents to which none but he had access. True, in public Appolonius and Mithridatus treated each other with great courtesy and according to the complicated etiquette of the guild of magicians. But in private they expressed the greatest contempt for each other and invoked upon each other's heads all the maledictions contained in their favorite scrolls. Public meetings were a great strain for them, and therefore they did their best to avoid them. But this was an occasion which overrode their mutual hatred. For a common danger threatened them, as it threatened all those who were the servitors of Diana.

These were the four principal figures at the meeting; with them were gathered some hundreds of lesser artificers, astrologers, and magicians.

Demetrius opened the meeting.

"My friends and fellow servants of Diana," he began—an unusual beginning for him, who called no man his friend and admitted no man to be his fellow. "My friends and fellow servitors of Diana! You are doubtless aware of the occasion for this assembly. There has arrived in our sacred city a man, a swindler, a liar, a deceiver, an unclean little Jew, who has begun to dissuade our people from the worship of our goddess. Is there any one here who does not understand the meaning of his work? All of us are the servitors of the goddess; our lives and fortunes come to us from her. But know you not that this man Paul"—here a mutter of rage and contempt rose from his listeners—

"this man Paul spreads his pernicious doctrines not in Ephesus alone, but in all the cities of Asia? And what are these doctrines? He preaches, forsooth, that those are not gods which are fashioned by the hands of men." Here a burst of savage laughter interrupted old Demetrius. "Do you hear that, you priests, magicians, and star-gazers of the great goddess? She whom you worship and serve and who is your support is in mortal danger. Great Diana, the wonder of Asia and of all the world, is threatened by a foul little Jew—Paul, the deceiver, the blasphemer, the swindler, the liar!"

A hissing and whispering passed through the assembly; eyes flamed, teeth were bared.

"Bethink yourselves, moreover," cried Demetrius, "what threatens our thousands of workmen, our makers of images, our writers of scrolls, our sellers of magic potions—bethink yourselves and ask of *them* whether they will watch their livelihood being filched from them!" Cunning old Demetrius! He knew what tactics to use in order to reach the masses and inflame them.

He sat down, amid an ominous silence. After him rose Babylus, the First Astrologer. His tone was altogether different from that of Demetrius. What it lacked in vehemence it made up in solemnity. He took a lofty flight in his appeal.

"Princes of the night! Wanderers in the lonesome paths of the stars! It is an ancient tradition which teaches us that the Jews have been, from of old, the enemies of the gods. Yea, even in the days of the great Belshazzar of Babylon the Jews refused to bow down before the golden images of the king's making. They were led then by some unclean member of their people, one Daniel, the Paul of his day; and Daniel, by false magic—such as Paul now uses—was able to interpret the dreams of the king; and thus it came about that our sages, the true servants of star-lore, suffered martyrdom. The Jews are by their nature destroyers of gods, poisoners of the wells of faith, deniers of our immortal arts. Even Haman of old warned Ahasuerus against them; and before that, long before that, Pharaoh had reason to know the character of the Jews."

Very learned was the speech of Babylus, as became his official role; he reviewed the history of the Jews and of their contacts with other peoples, demonstrating that from their beginnings they had spread contempt for the gods and derision of their high servants, the star-gazers and magicians. Unfortunately for his purpose, the excessive erudition of the great Babylus undid the ardor of hatred which had been inspired in the gathering by the simpler and more direct Demetrius. A pious sleepiness came over his listeners, and Demetrius, less patient, more cunning, interrupted him:

"All that thou sayest, great and learned Babylus, is true beyond challenge. But let us remember that we are not concerned now with that which happened of old to the kings of Babylon and Egypt; we are concerned, hearest thou, with our own lives, yes, the bread of our workers, and of their wives and children. I ask, how many have already felt, in the emptiness of their purses, the evil influence of the deceiver Paul? Compare, I ask, the number of silver statues which have been sold this year, with the number sold last year. What other argument do you need?"

"At the great festival last year our artificers disposed of eighty thousand images and models, of gold, silver, bronze, and lead. This year the number has fallen by a third," cried one of the silversmiths.

"Why, then, there you have it!" screamed Demetrius, clapping his hands together.

Another voice came from the assembly:

"A year ago, at the great festival of the goddess, we sold ten thousand parcels of roots for barren women and fifty thousand phials of love potions. This year we have not sold one half of those quantities."

"Well, then, how much farther will ye let this go?" cried Demetrius. "Will you wait until we must come begging at the doors of the Jews? Our temple and goddess, the pride of Asia, totter on their foundations. The bread is being snatched from our mouths and from the mouths of our children. And all because of one unclean little Jew!"

"Nay!" roared several voices. "Because of the Jews! They are all guilty, for they have hired and suborned this Paul to undo us."

"They hide behind his skirts. Their plan is to destroy us!"

"Why are we silent? Why do we sit here, listening? Great is Diana of the Ephesians!"

This was the watchword, the slogan, that Demetrius had waited for. This was the torch which could kindle the fanaticism of the masses of Ephesus.

501

"Great is Diana of the Ephesians!" he shouted in response.

Like a rhythm of waves, the cry passed back and forth through the assembly.

"Great is Diana of the Ephesians!"

Now no more oratory was needed. The slogan intoxicated the meeting. A drunken ecstasy, compounded of superstition, greed, blood lust, seized upon the hundreds of servitors of the goddess. And soon, above the roar of the slogan, something else was heard:

"Down to the theater! Down to the theater! Great is Diana of the Ephesians!"

Suddenly there was a rush for the door. The assembly streamed out of the temple, out into the open gardens, into the main street of Ephesus.

The Ephesians beheld the tumultuary procession. What was this? What had happened. Why were they shouting "To the theater! Great is Diana of the Ephesians!"?

In another part of the city, not far from the temple, between the hills Prion and Coressus, lay the open amphitheater of Ephesus. On the circling tiers about the platform fifty thousand citizens could sit in comfort. On the festivals of the goddess sacred plays were enacted here and gladiatorial combats took place. There were fights between armed men and wild beasts, and sometimes unarmed men, criminals condemned to death, were flung into the arena. On this day, when the yelling throng of magicians, star-gazers, and religious artificers poured through the streets, the theater was filled with spectators. Two leopards, whose strength and ferocity had been widely proclaimed, were being held in reserve as the climax of the religious games. The crowds in the street, beholding the demonstration, thought the moment had come for the release of the leopards, and some of them followed, hoping still to find room in the amphitheater. But others bethought themselves of another sport and made for the Jewish quarter in the shadow of Mount Prion.

A tremor of rage, of destructive fury, spread through the city. Those of the Ephesians who had not issued for the services now poured out of the dark houses and narrow alleys. Workers flung down their tools, abandoned their looms, their dyeing vats, and their benches, and poured into the main street.

"What is it? What has happened?"

And as always in moments of mob panic various rumors sprang up and were carried from group to group with the speed of the wind.

"The Jews have set fire to the Temple of Diana!"

"The Jews have thrown filth on the image of the goddess!"

Restraining voices were heard, too:

"It is not the Jews! It is only a handful of them, newcomers, strangers."

But others replied:

"It is all of them! All the Jews! They are the supporters of the strangers! They have brought hither Paul, the magician, to destroy us. Ephesus is in danger! Our city will become a wilderness! No pilgrims will come hither, there will be no more Ephesus!"

"Throw them to the beasts!"

There were two centers of fury in the city. The theater was filled with a howling mob which lashed itself into a frenzy with the rhythmic cry: "Great is Diana of the Ephesians!" And another mob was gathering about the Jewish quarter, a mob beside itself with the lust of destruction. It was as if the demons which had issued from the burning of the images and talismans had entered into the hearts of the Ephesians.

There were present in Priscilla's home, at this moment, the apostle, the two visitors from Macedonia, Gaius and Aristarchus, Aquila, Priscilla herself, and a handful of the Messianists. They heard the mounting tumult and guessed its significance. When the first blows fell on the door Paul rose and went out to speak with the ringleaders. But no sooner did he show himself than a great yell went up:

"There he is! That is the man!"

A hundred clenched fists were stretched out toward him, and in an instant he was surrounded and lifted off his feet.

"To the beasts! To the beasts!"

Among Paul's companions Priscilla alone kept her head. While the others yielded weakly and permitted themselves to be pulled along, she, with but a single thought, and that the safety of the apostle, flung herself through the confusion of bodies, thrusting powerfully to right and left until she had reached his side. In the insane confusion which had taken hold of the mob, no one knowing rightly who was who and what plan was to be followed, her fury was mistaken for part of the general frenzy against the believers. Like a tigress leaping to the rescue of a cub, she scratched and tore her way toward Paul, and, pulling down the men who held him, lifted the apostle in her arms. Then, before anyone knew what had happened, she had fallen back with her precious burden, had slipped to a side, and was out of the mob. She did not carry him back toward her home—they would surely seek him again there. She sped with him to a hut under the city wall, where Aquila kept his stocks of goat's hair. She entered, closed the door, and laid the apostle down on a heap of skins.

Slowly Paul came to. He looked about him dumbly. What was this? Where was he, and where were his companions, Gaius and Aristarchus? Had they not been carried off to be flung to the beasts in the amphitheater? What, then, was he doing here? His place was with them! His place was before the assembled Ephesians. He started up, passed his hand over his face, put his robe in order. He would not stay here another instant. His disciples, his companions, would be looking for him, their teacher and guide. Perhaps he could prevail over the passions of the mob with words; and if he could not, it was for him to sanctify the Name by his death, side by side with his companions. But as he rose unsteadily to his feet he encountered the gaze of Priscilla, and in it he read not the obedience of the disciple in the presence of the teacher, but the unshakable will of the mother determined to shield her child from all danger.

What was this? Who was this woman who was determined to prevent him from confronting the death to which his mission called him? And was it indeed death that he confronted? Had he not known danger before, for the sake of the Messiah, and had he not been saved again and again? Was not this but another offer of divine grace, waiting for him in the amphitheater of Ephesus?

Silently, coldly the two stared at each other, and a wordless struggle ensued. In Paul the sense of his destiny, his divine obligation, was uppermost now; but in Priscilla a primitive protective passion had swept aside all other considerations. It was as if, in snatching the apostle from the mob, she had realized the meaning of her childlessness. It was for this occasion that God had preserved all her powerful mother instincts; nay, more, it was as if she was called upon to protect the apostle against God not less than against man. And in her strange, hard look Paul read her purpose. She would not let him depart; she would retain him here, even if she had to resort to physical force. The apostle was dumbstruck.

Why did he make no protest? Why did he not struggle against her un-uttered command? And he asked himself whether it was not a higher will than her own which shone so steadfastly, so imperiously, from Priscilla's eyes. Quietly he permitted Priscilla to take him by the hand, to lead him back to the heap of skins from which he had risen, and to await the issue.

*   *   *

Not Gaius and Aristarchus alone were carried off to the amphi-theater. On the way the mob picked up stray Jews and added them to the procession. And meanwhile the exultant shouting increased:

"We have them! We are bringing them!"

But while this was happening, certain of the Jews, the elders of the community, were speeding toward the theater by another route. They were hoping that something could still be done to prevent the shedding of blood. For no one knew rightly what had happened and what was the cause and purpose of the disturbance. Hastily the leading Jews ap-pointed a certain Alexander, one skilled in the Greek tongue, to address the Ephesians for them. But Alexander would not go alone. He de-manded that a deputation accompany him. When they reached the the-ater and thrust Alexander to the front, that he might speak for them, it was too late. The crowd was in such a frenzy that no voice could dominate it. Moreover, Alexander, though he was Greek in his ways, had a Jewish face, and no sooner did the mob look on him than the tumult rose to a new pitch, and nothing could be heard except the rhythmic roar:

"Great is Diana of the Ephesians!"

No man could have foretold how the disturbance would end, with what bloodshed, with what general destruction of the Jewish quarter, if word of the agitation had not reached the Chancellor of the city, the chief municipal authority appointed by Rome. Knowing the Ephesian mob, he did not wait for a second report, but issued orders for the mus-tering of a cohort of legionaries, and descended on the theater; and no sooner was his majestic figure perceived in the arena than the mad shouting suddenly ceased.

The Roman official lifted up his hand.

"Men of Ephesus! Who knows not the greatness of your city, and the devotion of the Ephesians to the goddess Diana?" The crafty open-

505

ing sent a wave of pleasure through the throng. "Who can deny these things? And therefore to what purpose do you proclaim them? Is it not more becoming that you be silent, and do nothing in haste? And as to these men that have been brought here"—he pointed to Gaius and Aristarchus and the other prisoners—"they have neither robbed your temple nor blasphemed against your goddess. And if Demetrius and the artificers of the goddess have aught against these men, let the case be brought before the courts, and justice will be done. Or, if there be other matters toward, let them be discussed peaceably in a lawful assembly. For know that such tumults place us all in danger." And having thus associated himself with the citizens of Ephesus, he suddenly changed his tone, and issued the command: "Now begone to your homes."

The subtle mixture of flattery, cajolery, and firmness produced an immediate effect. But the strongest argument was the cohort of legionaries. Demetrius perceived that the Jews of Ephesus still enjoyed the guardianship of Rome. Gaius and Aristarchus and their companions were released, and the mob began to disperse.

Chapter Twenty-nine

WITH ROD AND LOVE

AFTER that day Paul felt that he could no longer remain in Ephesus, and he made preparations for his departure.

But his departure was not planless. Like a general who has a long and complicated campaign before him, who anticipates events and helps to shape them, so Paul peered into the future and laid his plans for triumphs of the congregation of the Messiah. In Rome the Emperor Claudius was no more; he had been put out of the way by his adopted son, Nero, and by Nero's mother; and these two became the rulers of the Empire. But even before the change of government the Jews had begun to return to the capital. Actually they had never withdrawn completely from the city; some had indeed been driven forth, others had merely gone into hiding. Now they showed themselves openly again in their old quarter; the refugees streamed in again from the provinces,

506

and among them were Jewish Christians as well as Jews of the old faith. Paul's eyes were fixed on Rome. He saw there the field of his next conquests, and he was haunted nightly by dreams of great achievements in the capital of the world. His first act was to persuade Aquila and Priscilla to return with the other refugees and to prepare the city for his coming. They had, indeed, already been anticipated by some of the companions who had come with them from Rome by way of Corinth. Paul considered that whatever could be done for the time being in Ephesus he had already done. The community had been founded, elders had been set over it, and it was now capable of maintaining itself without his assistance. Paul promised Priscilla that he would despatch a strong letter to the community in Rome, setting forth the articles of the Messianic faith according to his interpretation, as he had already done for the Corinthians. If he did not himself set out for Rome with them, it was because another commitment lay before him. He had to visit Jerusalem and call upon the saints of the Holy City. However, he was not going alone. He began to assemble a deputation of the finest representatives of the congregations he had founded in Macedonia and Achaia, a deputation consisting mostly of gentile Christians. He remembered how, by bringing the lad Titus to Jerusalem, and presenting him to the holy ones as the fruit of his work among the Greeks, he had won the approval of the Jewish Messianists. He hoped to win it again by displaying before them the evidences of new conquests for the Messiah.

For all that, there lurked behind his hopes the vision of the chains which awaited him in Jerusalem. He knew only too well of the reports which had been carried to the Holy City, from countless Jewish communities, of the strife and dissension which had followed upon his preaching. He could not doubt that the High Priest would invoke the law against him. Yet the voyage to Jerusalem was unavoidable. No matter how independent he felt of the authority of the saints of Jerusalem, no matter how convinced he was that his doctrine came to him direct from the Messiah himself, he would leave no stone unturned to prevent the splitting of the community into two hostile camps, one belonging to Jerusalem and one belonging to him. Though he should pay for the attempt with his life, he must seek reconciliation and unification. For though he had indeed contravened the law as it was interpreted by the Jerusalemites, though he had revolted against the authority of the saints, he was still a true son of his people, filled with pride

507

in his origin, and conscious of the discipline which this implied. Nor did he in any wise see himself as a rebel against the true tradition. What he sought to do was for the fulfillment of the vision of the Prophets; he would bring the nations of the world to the Mount of Zion. The Greek believers in his deputation were the symbol of this fulfillment. Let them come with him to the Holy Hill, let them learn to know their true mother, the congregation of the saints, and let them find in Jerusalem their spiritual home.

Therefore, while he assembled the deputation, he also set on foot an agitation in the communities of Macedonia and Achaia for the collection of funds to be offered to the poor of Jerusalem. Let the converted gentiles feel that, as they were part and parcel of the spiritual life of Jerusalem, so they were obligated to take thought for its worldly needs. For he had received reports that conditions had hardly improved in Jerusalem since the years of the great famine. Agrippa the Second, who had finally attained to the status of a king, had continued the public works of his father, so as not to increase the unemployment in his city; but in the end he had been compelled to abandon his plans, for lack of means. The condition of the countryside was no better than that of Jerusalem. The small landowner was rapidly disappearing. The estates of the rich grew from year to year, and the independent farmer class was being transformed into day laborers—that is, to whatever extent the capital was not drawing the landless and discontented to swell the ranks of its rebellious population. Throughout the Diaspora the Jewish communities were collecting funds for the unemployed of Jerusalem, and Paul would not have it said that his own communities, the believers he had won among the Jews and gentiles, were behind the others in their response to the cry of Jerusalem's poor.

However, before he set out to visit his communities, he sat down to complete his letter to the Corinthians.

What the utterances of the ancient Prophets, made in the midst of the people, had been to the Jews of old, the letters of Paul, sent from a distance, were to the gentiles of the communities he had founded. Like the Prophets of old, Paul could punish and upbraid with flaming words; but again like those, he could comfort and inspire with hope. He taught them like a father and ministered to them like a son. He rejoiced and sorrowed with them. Anger, consolation, reproach, tenderness, all the moods of the spirit, were in his letters to the churches.

"What desire ye?" he asked them. "Shall I come to you with a rod, or shall I come with love and a gentle spirit?"

"I write not these things in order to shame you, but to punish you as my beloved children."

But he that did the punishing wept with the punished:

"Until this hour we have suffered hunger and thirst, we are naked and homeless."

Paul used every means at his disposal, every method of approach. When he learned of the sins of the Corinthians, he sought to awaken their pity toward himself.

"It is reported on every hand that there is whoredom among you, such whoredom as has not been heard of even among the gentiles. But you cannot drink of the cup of the lord and of the cup of the Devil. You cannot have a portion at the table of the lord, and a portion at the table of Satan."

He threatened them. Let him that loves not the lord Messiah be thrust out from the congregation. And at the same time he humbled himself. He who had received his authority direct from the Messiah, he who demanded righteousness in others, confessed his weaknesses:

"We are the fools of the Messiah, but ye have been wise in the Messiah. We have been weak, but ye have been strong. Ye have been honored, and we have been shamed."

His letters were the mirror of the soul, and as the mirror knows no shame, but reflects what shines upon it, so his letters reflected his weaknesses in the sight of those whom he had just won from an alien world to the Messiah. But side by side with confessed weakness was prophetic anger.

"For now I hear that there is dissension among you, when ye come together in the congregation. And in part I do believe it. . . .

"I hear that when ye assemble it is not in order to eat as at the table of the lord. For each one takes his own portion first, so some are sated and some are left hungry. Have ye not houses in which to eat and drink? Or do ye seek to shame the congregation of God, and to shame the poor?"

Then, remembering their sorrow for the dead, he comforted them in another strain:

"I assure you by our glory that I have in Yeshua the Messiah, our lord, that I die daily. And if I fought with the wild beasts of Ephesus in human form, of what avail were it if the dead do not rise? For then we should say, let us eat and drink, for tomorrow we die. . . . Then suddenly the trumpet of the resurrection will sound, and the dead will rise uncorrupted."

The letter to the Corinthians was a personal confession as well as a declaration of faith. All that he said in his letters to the other congregations he wove into his letter to the Corinthians. He showed himself not only the bearer of the great principle, but the pitiful and loving human being; and thereby he left to his congregations, for all ages to come, a moving document of eternal beauty.

Paul sealed the letter and sent it to the Corinthians by the hand of some of their own people, Stephanus, Porthenatus, and Achaiacus; he also added to the company of the returning Corinthians one that was very dear to him, Titus. Timotheus had already been sent forward to Corinth by way of Macedonia. Very great indeed was Paul's trust in Titus. Titus had character, rocklike faith, and, above all, exquisite natural tact in the management of people. It was in Titus that Paul had scored his first great victory in Jerusalem. Greek by origin, and therefore natural in his approach to the gentiles, Titus had been transfigured by his faith. But Paul placed his greatest trust in the letters which he addressed to the faithful.

Yet an interval elapsed in Ephesus while Paul waited to know what he had wrought with his letters, for he hoped that the echo would reach him shortly. Perhaps one of his beloved assistants would return with greetings. While he waited he wrought on Apollos to go out into the field and to throw himself into the work among the Corinthians, for he could not deny to himself that Apollos had great power of speech. But Apollos could not be persuaded, for he was not altogether of one mind with Paul in the special doctrine which Paul taught. Thus it was that Apollos, like bar Naba long before him, took leave of the apostle and went, not into the field but toward Jerusalem.

No answer came to Paul from the congregations to which he had addressed his letters. His stay in Ephesus became irksome, and finally he took farewell of the believers, and above all commended himself to the love of Aquila and Priscilla. Priscilla was deeply moved by Paul's departure, as if in the mother-heart to which Paul appealed so strongly, she trembled for his welfare. But Paul comforted her, saying:

"God, who has been with me in all danger in the past, and has

510

brought me through to safety, will be with me also in Jerusalem, to rescue me from my own flesh and blood. I know of a certainty, Priscilla, that it will be ours yet to labor together for the Messiah in the city of Edom, which is Rome."

Aquila and Priscilla boarded a ship bound for Italy, Paul one sailing for Macedonia.

Troas, the port of Macedonia, was his first point of call. Here it was that, years before, he had seen in a vision the man that called him to Macedonia. Here, as elsewhere, Paul found his little band of believers, a congregation founded by Jewish merchants, with a certain Corpus at its head. Paul's stay was brief, for he yearned in his heart to be in Philippi. He therefore promised the believers to visit them again on his return journey, toward Jerusalem, and meanwhile enjoined them earnestly to gather whatever funds they could to send with him to the poor of the Holy City. But when the moment came for Paul to board the ship for Philippi, he was suddenly assailed by dread.

The journey from Troas to Philippi was one long torment for Paul. He lay on the deck, wrapped in his mantle, and cowering as though he were beset by wolves. For doubt had risen in him, and he was afraid. In the night he called on the lord, and it seemed to him that he heard a voice crying: "Jesus Christ!" But it was not as the voice of a dream or vision. His ears rang with the sound of it. He opened his eyes and beheld before him, in the wan moonlight, a vast, gaunt figure of a man, clothed in tattered raiment. The man was standing over the apostle and repeating the name: "Jesus Christ!"

"Whence knowest thou that name?" asked Paul.

"Art thou not the messenger whom the Messiah has sent to us? I heard the name for the first time in the cavern ovens of the bronze foundries of Corinth. Then I heard thee speak, and from that time on the name Jesus Christ has been my last resort and help. Look down, messenger, and behold!"

The man pointed downward, and Paul peered from his place on the upper deck into the bowels of the ship. There below, in their long rows, the galley slaves were chained to their oars and, to the sound of the hortator's hammer, were swinging back and forth rhythmically.

"In the night which has no morrow," the man said to Paul, "that name which thou hast brought among us is refuge and salvation."

But when Paul turned his shocked gaze back to the man, he was

511

gone, and again Paul did not know whether he had indeed spoke with someone, or whether he had been visited by a vision.

Setting foot in Philippi, Paul recovered his trust in himself. The strange depression he had experienced on the ship vanished. For much of this he had the Philippians themselves to thank, the good, simple, deeply-believing Philippians. They had remained untouched by the destructive forces which had manifested themselves in the other communities, and they still believed as firmly in the apostle as they had done on the day of his departure. Lukas, the healer, was now part of the congregation of Philippi, Lukas, whom he had left there many years before. The congregation of Philippi was strongly organized, and it was in intimate contact with the congregation of Salonika, which had developed well of late. Other congregations had been founded in various cities of Macedonia. Among the loving Philippians, and in the company of the pious and clever Lydia, Paul gathered much strength. He needed but to mention to his Philippians that funds were to be sent to the poor of Jerusalem, and they came forward at once with their offerings. The very poorest in the community, and those that had yesterday been idolaters, alien to the concept of charity, brought their pitiful contributions and begged the apostle to accept them for the saints of Jerusalem. But what made Paul happiest in Philippi was a visit from Timotheus, who came to him with a report from Corinth. And the news was good.

"My father," said Timotheus, "they read thy letter forth on the Sabbath after the reading of the Scrolls; and they read it again at the common evening meal. They read it constantly whenever they assemble, as if it were part of the Holy Script. Thy words have broken their hearts. Many of them, when they heard the letter for the first time, wept and confessed and repented. Many of them were filled with dread by the anger of thy words. They tremble in the fear of thy curse. They believe that thou hast the power to consign them to the deep pits of hell, where their souls will be lost in eternal night. They have sent me to thee, begging me to intervene with thee, and to soften thy anger with them. However, my father"—here Timotheus paused—"there are such as have risen against thee, and whom thy letter has roused to fury. They say that thou hast not the authority of the saints of Jerusalem, and that thy reproaches against the Corinthians are without meaning, inasmuch as thou art not the head of the communities. They say further thou boastest of thy labors and diminishest the work of the other apostles, that thou bringest dissension into the Jewish communities, that thou dividest the Jewish people, and settest one half against the other, creating a deep abyss between the Messiah and the flesh and blood of the Messiah. Now these speakers of evil are not without influence, my father, and thou must surely do something against them. If I may counsel thee, I would say that thou shouldst take boat straightway to Corinth, for only thy presence can repress the rebels and bring back peace to the congregation."

All in all these were happy tidings, for the one evil that remained was the division, whereas in other matters, such as Stephanus and others had reported to him, the Corinthians had repented and amended their ways. Paul bethought himself whether his words to the Corinthians had not been too harsh. Perhaps, if he had been softer, they who denied his authority and his right to preach might not have been moved against him. It seemed to him that before he proceeded to Corinth, it would be well for him to write them a second time, and in his second letter, while comforting the penitents and raising their fallen spirits, he would again reprove the rebels, but in another spirit, a softer and kindlier one.

"Concerning the love of which thou writest to them," said Timotheus, faithful in transmitting all the truth, "they say that he who wrote such words must be the first to set an example in his life in the spirit of his words."

Titus was somewhere in the field, wandering among the cities of Macedonia. Paul kept Timotheus with him, and in the nights that followed he dictated to him the second letter to the Corinthians.

"You are our letter, engraved in our heart, known and read of all men," he wrote to them. "You are revealed, as the epistle of the Messiah, written not in ink, but in the spirit of the living God." And again he told them of his sufferings. "We suffer on all sides, but we are not in fear; we are in need, but we do not despair; we are pursued, but we are not abandoned; we are beaten, but not lost. We carry ever with us in our body the death of the lord Yeshua, in order that the life of Yeshua might be revealed in our lives. . . ."

As to those who considered themselves his superiors because they had known Yeshua the Messiah in the life, and had been in his company, Paul wrote the Corinthians:

"He died for all, in order that those who live shall no longer live

513

for themselves, but for him who died for them and rose again. Therefore from now on we know no one in the flesh; and though we knew the Messiah in the flesh, we know him in the flesh no more. Therefore, when any one is in the Messiah, he is a new being; the old has perished, and all has become new."

Nor was Paul ashamed to defend himself before the Corinthians, in matters which had called forth their resentment:

"We have given offense in no thing, that the service of the Messiah might not be shamed. In all things we have been ministers of God, in patience, in affliction, in need and in distress . . . by pureness, by knowledge, by much suffering . . . by honor and dishonor, by good report and by evil report . . . sorrowful yet always causing joy, poor but always enriching others."

And in the midst of the letter came the cry of his heart:

"O Corinthians, my mouth is open unto you, my heart is wide!"

He told them also of the coming of Timotheus:

"We were comforted when he told us of your desires and sorrows, and of your longing for me. . . . For though I have caused you sorrow with my letter, I regret it not; but I rejoice that you sorrowed and repented. . . ."

And this much said, he confessed himself, too:

"Would that you might endure my foolishness. For I was jealous for you in the zeal of God." And he reminded them: "I robbed other congregations, and took wages of them, to serve you. But when I was with you I was a burden to none. Our brothers of Macedonia came to my support, that I might not be a charge on you."

Concerning those who denied the authority of his mission, he answered thus, pointing to his Jewish origin:

"Many boast according to the flesh, therefore I too will boast according to the flesh. . . . Are they Hebrews? So am I. Are they Israelites? So am I. Are they ministers of the Messiah? Let me answer as a fool, that I am more minister than they, I have labored more, been scourged more, suffered more in prison. I have known danger and shipwreck, I have been scourged five times with thirty-nine stripes, I have been in peril of robbers, in peril of the sea, in peril of my own countrymen. In pain and hunger, in weariness, in thirst, in daily anguish for the churches."

So it was indeed. He had paid full measure for his mission, among his own no less than among strangers. But his reward was the highest vision. He had been received into Paradise and had heard secret tones which come to no living ear, and he said of himself:

"Lest I should become too proud in the number of the revelations given me, there was given me a thorn in the flesh, the messenger of Satan, to buffet me and keep me humble of spirit. And I prayed three times unto God and he answered me: 'My grace is sufficient for thee, for My strength is made perfect in weakness.'"

Again he accused himself: "I have become a fool in boasting—but ye compelled me to it." Then he added openly: "I will gladly come to you, and spend and be spent for you, though the more I love you the less I am loved of you." He betrayed his fear of the reception which awaited him. "I fear that when I come I shall not find you as my heart would find you and you will not find me as you would have me; and there will be dispute and quarreling, envy and backbiting and tumult. Yet I will come to you for the third time."

"Finally, farewell. Be perfect, be comforted, be of one mind, be at peace, and the God of love and peace shall be with you. Greet one another with a holy kiss."

So he ended the letter with the words, "The grace of the lord Yeshua the Messiah be with you." And it was like the letter of a bridegroom to an offended but loving bride. He sent the letter by the hand of Lukas, whom he bade prepare the Corinthians for his coming.

Chapter Thirty

"I ALSO AM AN ISRAELITE"

BUT it was enough for Paul to appear in Corinth, and at once he was forgiven, and all that had been held against him was forgotten, and the community was uplifted by a great wave of love. Whatever harshnesses he had uttered were accepted as the sign of his devotion. Some there were in Corinth who feared Paul. It seemed to them that the power of the authority had grown in him and that he could annihilate with his

515

look. Others remembered only the sweeter and more tender words he had uttered, and they remembered that this man had rescued them from the abyss of pagan uncleanliness, had come to them with salvation when they did not know him, nor he them. As to those who, under the influence of the apostles of Jerusalem, denied authority to Paul, they too were carried away by the enthusiasm of the church of Corinth. They trembled at the new strength radiating from Paul, and their opposition melted and ran out of them. So it was too with those who only the day before his arrival had still breathed fury against him. Paul knew, too, whom to approach with gentleness, whom with stern authority; he knew what arguments were needed for various groups. To the Jews he pointed out that he lived under the discipline of the Mosaic law—perhaps more perfectly than they! But to the gentiles, who had been won by the messengers of Reb Jacob ben Joseph and were trying to live under the same law, he said flatly that all in vain had they taken upon themselves the huge burden of the Jewish disciplines. Among Jews a Jew, among Greeks a Greek, he labored to maintain the unity of the congregation of the Messiah. And all the Messianists of Corinth, Jews and gentiles, gathered about him, like sheep about their shepherd.

The beloved couple, Aquila and Priscilla, who had made his earlier visit to Corinth almost a homecoming, were no longer there. But as against this the love of the Corinthians for him had greatly increased. Paul made his home with Gaius, and it was from there that he dispatched his letter to the congregation of Rome.

The letter to the Romans came harder to him than even his letters to the Corinthians. Weeks and months passed during which he dictated and redictated to a certain Tertius. It was true that he had Lukas with him, and Lukas was a better stylist in Greek; but in this letter to the Romans it was not a matter of style. Before he left for Jerusalem, without knowing what was to be his fate there, he wanted to re-state and expand his doctrine of the Messiah, that doctrine which was his own, as he had received it, as he had unfolded it in many cities and expounded it to Apollos. In a hard exact style, with fine, hairsplitting distinctions and definitions, he set down his thesis, or rather, his interpretation of his mission. He repudiated sharply the pretended wisdom of the Ionians, the thoughts of the Greeks. "Professing themselves to be wise," he said, bluntly, "they were fools. They changed the truth of God into a lie and worshiped the creature rather than the Creator. And God gave them up unto vile perversions of lust . . . they became filled with unrighteousness, whoredom, greed, malice, with unnatural lusts and unmercifulness." But he went on to make it clear that the Jews who had the law, but did not live according to the law, were no better than the degenerate pagans. "Tribulation and anguish shall come upon every soul that does evil, the Jewish *first,* and then the Greek. But glory, honor, and peace to every man that works goodness, to the Jew *first,* and also to the gentile, for God has no favorites among persons. For such as have sinned without the law (the gentile) shall perish without the law, while those that have sinned within the law (the Jews) shall be judged by the law."

Here Paul took his stand almost upon the thesis of his opponent, Reb Jacob ben Joseph, and it is almost in the spirit of Reb Jacob that he exclaims: "For not those that listen to the law are justified before God, but those that do according to the law." But: "Behold thou callest thyself Jew, and makest thyself secure in the law, and boastest of God. . . . For he is not a Jew who is such outwardly, but he is a Jew that is one inwardly, circumcised in the heart and the spirit, not in the letter."

Paul did not stop here. He went further and abrogated the law in precise terms, and that for the Jews: "By the deeds of the law no man shall be justified in the sight of God, for by the law there is knowledge of sin. But now the righteousness of God without the law is manifested, the righteousness of God which is by the faith of the Messiah."

The Messiah is the personification of righteousness; it follows, then, that faith in the Messiah is the essence of the law, that is, of justification, which is the opposite of sin. And the Messiah is the only one who can bring salvation from sin, for it is through the law that we become sinful. "The law wrought in man to awaken in him all manner of lusts, for without the law sin is dead. . . . For though we know that the law is of the spirit, I, the man, am sold in my body to sin. . . . For I know that in me, that is, in my body, dwells that which is not good. . . . I have the will, but have not found my way to goodness. . . . I see another law in my limbs, warring against the law of my mind, and making me captive to the sin which is in my limbs."

In these sentences the apostle unfolded the tragedy of the inner struggle of man about his own destiny; for he saw man as the arbiter of his own destiny. Therefore he looked into the depths of his own heart, and he wept for the fate of man:

"Oh, wretched man that I am, who shall deliver me from the body of this death?"

He looked about him, like a swimmer in a dark sea, who beholds a single ray of light to guide him. That ray of light was the Messiah, sent of God: "Therefore as by the offense of one man condemnation came upon all men, so by the righteousness of one came justification for all. . . . And we all that were baptized in Yeshua, were baptized unto his death. For he that is dead is quit of sin. . . . We are no more in the flesh, but in the spirit." Only by the power of faith can man break the chains of his own destiny, hammered and laid upon his limbs by his own lusts. That which is impossible for the law, which was weak in the flesh, becomes possible through the spirit. "When Yeshua the Messiah is within you, your body is dead to sin and alive for righteousness. . . . And they that are led in the spirit of God are the children of God. Ye have received the spirit of children, whereby we cry *Abba*, Father!"

Then Paul proceeded, with true Pharisaic logic, to demonstrate that the law had lost its validity not only for the gentiles, but for the Jews too. "The law has dominion over a man as long as he lives, even as a women is bound to her husband as long as he lives. Therefore, my brothers, ye have become dead to the law by the body of Christ, and you should be wedded to another (to the living Messiah in the spirit) who arose from the dead."

In the long writing of this letter Paul lived again through all the torments of his own life. Seeing clearly now in what manner he was isolating himself from the Jewish traditional way, and condemning himself to loneliness, he struggled bitterly between his longing for the Messiah and the Messiah's salvation for all mankind on the one hand, and his natural affection for his people on the other. He could not but understand that the knife which he laid at the root of the Jewish law was also laid at the roots of his relationship to his people. But his love for the Messiah was the stronger. "Who shall separate us from the love of the Messiah?" he cried out. . . . "Neither the heights nor the deeps, nor any creature, shall be able to separate us from the love of God, which is in our lord, Yeshua the Messiah."

On the other hand, had the Messiah come for the gentiles alone? In the streams of blood which had flowed from the body of the

Messiah, that mankind might be saved, that man might be liberated from law and brought into the grace of faith, the apostle sought one drop that had been shed for his own people, from which he had sprung in the flesh—that people which had suffered the torment of the Messiah and had conjured him down from heaven by its longing. . . .

Who, Paul asked himself in agony, could fathom the depths of the Messiah's heart? Was there not within it a corner for his people? This was the thought that gave the apostle no rest. In the sea of love which the Messiah poured out upon mankind, there must be water enough for Israel too. So he labored, in pain, in frustration, longing to bring the whole world into the grace of the Messiah—in order that the prophecies might be fulfilled—and finding himself confronted by the obstinate will of the Jews to cling to their own faith.

In this labor he developed a fiery impatience which blinded him to the sense of justice, which moved him to a sharp intolerance and poisoned his understanding of those that opposed him. In his letter to the Romans he expressed all his love, but also all his scorn, toward his own people. He wounded them, so that the blood flowed, and with his mouth kissed away the blood. He alternated between benediction and malediction. One instant he rejected Israel, as if it were a broken pot, and flung the fragments at the feet of the gentiles; and in the next instant he exalted Israel as the precious vessel which alone was worthy of containing the oil of anointment for the Messiah. For Israel's sake Paul is prepared to make the highest sacrifice of himself; he will destroy not only his body, but his portion in the Messiah, only if Israel will accept that portion for itself. "I have great heaviness and continual sorrow in my heart. *For I could wish that myself were accursed from the Messiah for my brethren, my kinsmen in the flesh, who are Israelites*: theirs is the adoption and the glory and the giving of the law, and the service of God and the promises; theirs are the fathers from whom the Messiah came according to the flesh." Surely he could not have said anything higher of his people. And though he had just deprived them of the inheritance, saying, "Not all that are of Israel are Israelites, not the children of the flesh are the children of God, but only the children of the promise shall be reckoned as of the seed," though he had just said this, he now cried: "Brothers, it is the wish of my heart, it is my prayer to the God of Israel, that they shall be helped." But there was something standing in the way: "Israel, who followed after righteousness, did not attain to righteousness, because he sought it not by faith but by the works of the law. . . . For the Messiah is the end of the law for righteousness to all that believe." And again he starts back: "Do I say, then, that God has cast away His people? God forbid. For I also am an Israelite, of the seed of Abraham, of the tribe of Benjamin. God has not cast away His people which He knew from of old." And, "If their fall has meant the raising up of the world, and their harm the enrichment of the gentiles, how much more should the world profit by their fulfillment? . . . For I speak to you gentiles as the apostle of the gentiles, and I will magnify my office. Perhaps I will move those that are of my flesh to emulation, and some of them may be saved. For if the casting away of them be the reconciling of the world, what shall the receiving of them be but life from the dead? For if the root be holy, so shall the branches be holy." And to the gentiles he says: "Boast not against the branches (the Jews). And if thou boast, know that thou bearest not the root, but the root thee. But thou wilt say: 'The branches (the Jews) are broken off, so that I (the stranger) might be grafted in. True, they have been broken off by unbelief . . . but if they do not cling to their unbelief they shall be grafted in again. . . . For if thou wert cut off from a wild olive tree (that is, heathendom), and wert grafted, contrary to thy (pagan) nature into a good olive tree, how much the more shall not these, the natural branches, be grafted again into the good olive tree (the Messiah)? For I would not conceal from you, my brothers, this mystery, that blindness in part has happened to Israel until the fullness of the gentiles be come in." God had of set purpose withheld Israel from acceptance of the Messiah until the gentiles had caught up with the Jews in the election of God! "But Israel shall be saved, as it is written: 'There shall come out of Zion the deliverer, and shall take away the ungodliness from Jacob.' "

Deep and bitter was the inner struggle of the apostle. It was as if he were tearing at his own flesh, and the blood streamed from him, not from his people. Faithfulness to the gentiles, passion of the Messiah, love of his own people—these were at war in him, and the strongest was the passion of the Messiah. In the last torment of his separation from Israel he cried out to the gentiles: "According to the gospel, they are enemies for your sakes, but concerning the election, they are beloved for the father's sakes, for the gifts and appointments of God are without recall."

520

"And though you are free from the law, you are under the sign of righteousness." It is a new law that Paul proclaims for the congregations of the Messiah, a law rooted and blossoming in the fields of Jacob. The law of the Prophets grows where he has uprooted the law of Moses. Boundless is the law, for its source is love, which is in the Messiah; without bounds are its deeds, for the law is not judgment, but grace. And what judgment is there which can uphold the canopy of grace? It is as the sun in heaven, and as the dew in the night; and it has been given freely, through the grace of God.

In the spirit of the Messiah, in harmony with what he had taught in the byways of Galilee, on the shores of Kineret and in the narrow streets of Jerusalem, Paul the Jew addressed himself to the Romans: "I beseech you therefore, brothers, by the mercies of God, that you present your bodies a living, holy, acceptable sacrifice unto God. . . . For as we have many members in one body, and all members have not the same office, so we, being many, are one body in Christ, and are all members of one another. . . . Be kindly disposed to one another, with brotherly love, each honoring the other before himself. Rejoice in hope, be patient in tribulation, be constant in prayer . . . relieve the necessity of the saints, and practice the virtue of hospitality. Bless them that persecute you, bless and curse not. Recompense not evil with evil." And, in the spirit of the Messiah, he said: "In so far as possible, and as much as in you lies, live at peace with all men. Take no vengeance, and leave no room in you for anger. . . . If thine enemy is hungry, feed him; if he be thirsty, give him drink; so shalt thou heap coals of fire on his head. Let not evil overcome you, but do you overcome evil."

And he continued with words that he had undoubtedly heard in his far-off youth in the classes of his teacher Rabban Gamaliel, for they were of the essence of the tradition and of the school of Hillel:

"It is briefly comprehended in this saying, Thou shalt love thy neighbor as thyself."

Toward the end he advised them of his plans:

"Now I go to Jerusalem to minister to the saints. . . . I beseech you that you strive for me in your prayers to God that I may be delivered from them that do not believe, in Judaea, and that I may come unto you with joy by the will of God, and may be with you refreshed."

Then he added certain commendations and salutations. "I commend unto you our sister Phebe, a servant of the church at Cenchrea

. . . receive her in the lord and assist her in whatsoever business she asks of you. Greet Priscilla and Aquila, my helpers in the work of Yeshua the Messiah, who have laid down their necks for my life."

*　　*　　*

Phebe was a servant of the congregation of Cenchrea. She longed greatly to go to Rome, for she had children there. One was a slave, and the other, once a slave, had been set free by his master for his performances as a gladiator.

It was forbidden for slaves to send communications to each other. Thus, when a family of slaves was broken up on the slave market, its members lost track of each other. They were, moreover, taken and absorbed into the "family" of their new owners. But the slaves who had entered the congregations of the Messiah—and such congregations were to be found by now in almost every city—were enabled through the churches to re-establish contact with their own. The members of the Christian communities, even like those of the Jewish, maintained a close relationship with each other. When a member fell sick, or was imprisoned, or carried away into captivity, believers everywhere came to his help. And when one of the believers left his home town to settle in another, he was always provided with letters of introduction from the leaders of his community. Thus he was received easily into the new congregation and, if a free artisan, helped to find work. Through this constant flow of greetings and commendations brothers and sisters, parents and children, long separated, were enabled to communicate with each other.

Phebe, desirous of going to Rome, not only to see her children, but to bring them into the faith, turned to the apostle for a letter of introduction. Paul had a special place in his heart for slaves; he was interested in their welfare, even though he preached "obedience to the master." Whenever a "master" entered the faith of the Messiah Paul stressed to the newcomer the principle of equality and brotherhood in the Messiah. When Phebe came to him for a letter, it suddenly occurred to him that he might do well to forward the epistle to the Romans through her. Nor was there anything unusual in this idea. Paul regarded every member of the church as a soldier of the faith. Phebe was an elderly woman, of heavy build, with thick, stumpy feet. Paul took the roll of papyrus which contained his tidings of the Messiah, according to his vision and interpretation, and wrapped it, after the fashion of the Jews, in a linen cover. Then, with his own girdle, he bound the cover to the body of the servant woman, bidding her not to be separated from the scroll either by day or by night.

Many days were consumed in the journey from Corinth to Athens. The servant woman Phebe lay on many decks, and slept in dangerous places, but she never undid the girdle with the scroll from about her body. She went from ship to ship, from port to port, until she reached Puteoli. From Puteoli she went on foot to Rome, and arriving in the great city asked her way to the Synagogue of the Hebrews, on the right bank of the Tiber. There she met a Christian who led her to the house of Aquila and Priscilla. Only then did she unroll from her body the girdle of the apostle, and deliver into the hands of elders of the congregation the letter of the Apostle to the Romans.

*　　*　　*

And now Paul was ready for the journey which he had so long contemplated. He would go up to Jerusalem, to speak with the saints and perhaps stand trial in the court of the High Priest. It was not hard for him to foresee that the long, stretched cord which reached from the *Ebionim* in Jerusalem to the gentile Lukas was now so taut that it was bound to snap; and when it snapped it would be to let him fall. But he saw no other path before him.

He assembled the delegations which had been collecting funds in the congregations for the saints of Jerusalem: Supatros of Berea, Aristarchus and Secundus of Salonika, Gaius of Derbe, and Timotheus; from Asia, that is, from Ephesus, there were Tychicus and Tryphimus. All these Paul sent before him to the port of Troas.

When he arrived after them in Troas, he sent them on by boat to Assos, but he himself made the brief journey by land, and on foot, in response to a desire to rehearse the journey he had made long ago when he had first brought the tidings of the Messiah to these parts.

It was the post-Passover season of the year, and the spring was pouring out its benediction on the countryside. There was a need in Paul to sate himself with the sight of the land which was so dear to him and which he might be leaving forever. Lukas and the deputation were already on board, waiting for the apostle. From Assos they sailed to Mitylene, and thence to Chios, not far from Ephesus. Paul did not intend to visit Ephesus, or to spend any time in Asia, for he was anxious to arrive in Jerusalem for the Pentecost. At Myletus he sent messengers to Ephesus asking the elders of the congregation to come to him, that he might say farewell to them, as he had said farewell to the communities of Troas and Philippi. Very moving were his last words to the elders of Ephesus, to whom he opened his heart:

"I am going up to Jerusalem, bound in the spirit, without knowing what awaits me there—save that the Holy Ghost has been with me in every city, foretelling suffering and chains. But I care not, and my life would not be dear to me were it not that I still hope to end in joy the work which I have taken on me at the bidding of the lord Messiah, Yeshua. I have no regard to myself, but I have regard to the sheep whose shepherd I have been made by the Holy Ghost. . . . I fear that after me wolves will steal into the flock. . . . I commend you to the grace of God. . . . You know what these hands of mine have done for my needs and for the needs of those that go with me. I have taught you that we must so work as to support the weak among us with the labor of our hands, and you must bear ever in mind the saying of Yeshua the Messiah that it is more blessed to give than to receive."

(It was Lukas, the physician, who wrote down the words which Paul uttered on that occasion to the elders of Ephesus.)

They fell upon his neck and kissed him, and wept because of the intimation that they would never look on his face again. And on the day of his departure they accompanied him to the ship.

There were many sailings in those days from Upper Asia Minor to the coasts of Phoenicia. A great stream of supplies flowed southward into Tyre and Sidon, and northward came the colored stuffs of the two cities. Paul and his company boarded a ship heavily laden with freight. They sailed direct for the Phoenician coast, passing by the island of Cyprus. At Syria, where the ship unloaded, Paul and his companions went on shore. A company of the Christians of Tyre came out to meet them, and Paul stayed in their midst seven days. The faithful of Tyre, who lived in constant communication with the not distant city of Jerusalem, knew more exactly than Paul, and that not merely in forebodings, what he might expect, and they exerted themselves to dissuade him from the dangerous journey. But Paul would not be moved.

On the eighth day he took boat again, and on the shore the congregation of Christians knelt and prayed for him as his ship moved southward toward the port of Akko. In Akko Paul and his companions remained but a day and then made the short journey to Caesarea, in order to visit Philippus in his home. Philippus, who had been the first to carry the tidings to the gentiles, lived there with his four daughters, all virgins and gifted with prophecy, the oldest of them being Zipporah.

Paul and Zipporah had not set eyes on each other since that memorable day when he, in the service of the High Priest, had come to her house in Jerusalem, accompanied by the armed guards of the Temple, in order to take her father prisoner. She had flung a reproach at him that day: "Paul, thou art a respecter of persons, and hast favorites." But it was not true, and he had proved the untruth of the accusation throughout these years. He had been a respecter of none—including even himself. But she too had disproved the words that he had uttered in the long ago. He had said, bitterly: "Thou, Zipporah, wilt cast away thy prophecy, in order to take a husband." But she had dedicated her virginity to prophecy. In those days they had both been young. Now they were both old. They stood and looked at each other. The convulsive visitations of prophecy at the common meals of the faithful had withered the body of Zipporah, and it was as though her youth had not faded from her, but had been sucked out by leeches and burned up by flames. Tall, lean—scarcely more than skin and bones—she flashed her dark eyes in their sunken sockets at the apostle. Gray-haired she was, and her body was covered with sackcloth. Was this Zipporah, the tender, the soft, the adorned? Was this she whose ornaments had tinkled as she had walked in the cloud of incense which had always enveloped her, she who had left the air laden with the sweetness and radiance of her passage? Yes, it was she; and a smile of transfiguration passed across her lips as she reassured the apostle that this was Zipporah, the daughter of Philippus.

That evening Paul and his companions sat at the evening meal with Philippus and the elders of Caesarea. Paul recounted at length the story of the founding of the Christian congregations which were now sown in the lands and cities of the gentiles.

Suddenly Zipporah appeared in the doorway, and all eyes were turned to her. Her eyes glittered, her gray hair fell wildly over her shoulders. She was carrying, in her frail hand, a little phial of Syrian

525

glass, with a long thin neck. Wordlessly she approached the apostle, and slowly she turned the delicate phial, mouth downward, over the apostle's hands. The drops of clear oil came out one by one, like tears glistering in the quiet lamplight. And Zipporah said:

"I anoint thy hands for the chains which await them."

Paul grew pale, but then a smile passed unevenly across his lips. He did not answer.

*　　*　　*

Paul did not have so thorough a knowledge of Lukas, the physician, as he had of his two other co-workers, Titus and Timotheus. Lukas had come to him a grown man, a completed soul, one trained in the wisdom of the gentiles, a knower of the lands and seas, and likewise deeply versed, though in translation only, in the Holy Script. Powerful and harmonious as he was in his body—he was broadshouldered, and his tranquil face was as of poured bronze—he was not less harmonious of bearing. No break was visible in him, no scar of the passage from his Greek gods to the one living God of Israel and His Messiah. When Lukas had appeared before Paul in Troas—the fulfillment of the vision of the "man of Macedonia"—Paul had accepted him as a sign from heaven. Paul had likewise perceived at once the excellent qualities of Lukas: his gentile calmness, his consistency, his endurance, his tactful management of people; and besides these, his training, his mastery of medicine and his knowledge of languages. All of these gifts proclaimed him a valuable helper in the work. Thus, even at the beginning, the apostle had left Lukas to direct the affairs of the congregation in Philippi. But he did not know the man well at that time. He learned to know him somewhat better in Corinth, when, after his second letter to the Corinthians, he visited them to restore order among the faithful. But it was only on the journey to Jerusalem that Paul found the opportunity to gain an intimate insight into his companion, and the intimacy was established in the manner peculiar to Paul.

Lukas knew well Paul's opinion of the gentiles, an opinion frequently expressed and in unmistakable language. Lukas remembered the passage which Paul had dictated in his letter to the Romans: "And because they held themselves to be wise, they became fools. They have exchanged the truth of God for a lie, and have worshiped the creature instead of the Creator; therefore God has abandoned them to shameful lusts." With all his devotion, with all his love for the Messiah, who had come as of the flesh among the Jews, Lukas could not reject, as one rejects an old and unclean garment, his great heritage of Greek culture; and he sought to rescue from that old world of his those glories which could be rescued and transplanted to the new faith. And he was deeply wounded by Paul's bitter gibes at the gentiles. Nor was Lukas's feeling for the Jews at all commensurate with his love for the Messiah. He had accepted their heritage, because it was indissolubly bound up with the faith. But he could not warm to this people, and in his heart there was an uncontrollable longing for the harmony of the pagan world. Therefore he was for ever seeking a synthesis of the old world with the new.

These matters came up for discussion between him and Paul.

"The gentiles," he said once, to Paul, "do not worship stone and wood, O my teacher and guide in the faith. The gentiles worship perfection and harmony, symbolized in the gods. Therefore it is not the creature, but the Creator, that they bow down to. For in their adoration of beauty they pay tribute to the eternally-enduring, eternally true, which is incorporated in beauty. Now the gods are only the demons who have taken possession of the images and mar the beauty and perfection which the great masters, under the inspiration of their thought, have uttered in imagery."

Paul understood well what it was that troubled Lukas, the gentile. He knew the tenor of his ideas, which was familiar to him from observation of other gentiles. He recalled, as Lukas spoke, the vision which had come to him at the burning of the magic books and talismans in Ephesus; and he remembered that Lukas was the personification in the flesh of the vision of "the man of Macedonia." It had often happened to Paul that men and women whom he met in the flesh were the realization of men and women seen in visions. Therefore he now answered Lukas as he had answered the visionary figure which had come to him at the burning of the instruments of idolatry in Ephesus:

"The Messiah has inherited the gods of the gentiles. In him is realized the highest perfection, which is love. He, the Messiah, is the fulfillment of all harmony, for in love there is everything."

That evening in Caesarea, when Paul and his companions broke bread with the believers in the house of Philippus, Lukas returned to the subject. Lukas could not understand why Paul insisted on going to Jerusalem; and in this he was but as the other gentile Christians, who were equally bewildered by the obstinacy of the apostle. The deputation which Paul was leading with him to Jerusalem consisted of men who had been well-established citizens. Some of them had even held positions of responsibility in their respective provinces. They had sacrificed everything to their faith in the Messiah; they had abandoned the gods which had been dear to their fathers, they had changed their habits and their way of life, they had exposed themselves to the contempt of their neighbors, they had divided themselves from their families. And now the apostle was leading them to Jerusalem, where they knew not what awaited them, while the apostle himself was for ever filled with dark forebodings. They would have asked, if they could have clarified their thoughts, whether the Messiah could be found only among the Jews and in the Temple of Jerusalem, that Paul was now compelling them—and himself in the face of the danger which threatened him—to proceed to the Jewish capital.

Now later that evening, in Caesarea, a strange incident came to pass. As they sat together at table, the door was flung open, and there entered a man of wild aspect, with stormy locks and fiery eyes. This was the prophet Agabus, who wandered from community to community. One day he would be encountered in Jerusalem, another day in Antioch. His appearance in a community had come to be interpreted as a promise of evil things to come. He would foretell disaster, and then vanish; and on his footsteps followed sickness, famine, evil decrees, and death. He entered the assembly like a demon of the storms, rushed up to the apostle, took off his girdle, and bound his own hands with it.

From another door Zipporah entered, bearing again a phial of oil. Those that sat at the table were thrown into terror. And again voices were directed at Paul:

"Go not to Jerusalem!"

Then Lukas said to Paul:

"Was it not thyself, apostle, who hast said that though thou didst know the Messiah in the flesh, now thou knowest him no more in the flesh, but in the spirit? Is not the spirit everywhere, poured out upon all the earth, wherever the name of the Messiah is mentioned? If this be indeed so, wherefore must thou journey to Jerusalem? Why canst thou not make of Antioch, or Corinth, or Ephesus, or perhaps Rome itself, the new Jerusalem?"

528

"What is the Messiah?" asked Paul, hotly. "Is he the husk of a grain, which the wind lifts and carries away? What is the Messiah, I ask? Is he a broken branch, is he a seed carried into the wilderness? God forbid! Is he not the fruit borne by the tree of Israel, rooted in the earth of Zion? The Messiah is the fulfillment of the promises of God, given to our forefathers; he is the vindication of the Prophets; he is the son of David, who came to judge the world upon the Mount of Zion. Help came, first to Jews, then to the Greeks."

"But, apostle, seest thou not the chains which wait for thee in Jerusalem?" they cried. "Seest thou not that thou goest to thy death?" And they burst into tears.

"What do ye? Why weep ye?" said Paul, summoning anger to his aid. "Why do ye break my heart? Surely I am prepared not only to be thrown in chains in Jerusalem, but to die there, also, in the name of the lord, Yeshua the Messiah."

He said this so abruptly, with such firmness of conviction, that the others desisted from persuading him. They only said:

"Let the will of God be done."

And the next day they packed their belongings and set out, in the company of other believers, for Jerusalem.

Chapter Thirty-one

GRANITE BETWEEN THE MILLSTONES

ONCE again Israel was re-assembled in the House of God, and his children came from the cities of the Diaspora, from Syria, from Galatia, from Macedonia, from Asia, and from Achaia. They came also from Babylon, and from Damascus, and from all the cities of Palestine. The streets of Jerusalem were thronged with men and women, old and young. They poured up the inclines to the area through which the processions of the Palestinian Jews passed, with their baskets of vegetables, fruit, grain. For this was the eve of the Pentecost, when Israel brought the first fruits of garden, field, and vineyard to the Temple of the Lord.

Now in those days, when the Jews were bringing their offerings to God, another offering was being brought from the gentiles to the Jews, and the place of its delivery was the upper chamber in the wall of David, there where the Messiah had eaten his last meal: an offering, this was, from the gentiles, to testify to their faith in the Messiah.

There, in the upper chamber which was the holiest of all places to the Messianists of Jerusalem, Paul presented the messengers of the gentiles to the saints of Jerusalem.

Reb Jacob had risen from his place to greet the gentiles, had come forward with outstretched arms and shining eyes. His mantle, though of poor material, was white; his face was pale, his beard silvery, his hair long and snow-white; and his feet were bare. For all the poverty of his garb, it was as though he was robed in the raiment of the High Priest. He had said to the gentiles: "Blessed be ye, that come in the name of the Lord," and he had commended them to the love and grace of the Messiah.

Khaifa, or Peter, was absent from Jerusalem; therefore the seat next to Reb Jacob was occupied by Jochanan, "the son of the storm," one of the closest disciples of the lord, whose name was widely known among the gentiles. But now he was no longer the son of the storm. His flesh was withered, his skin furrowed by the plow of time, his body frail, almost transparent. His face, which shone with a mystic light, was wrinkled from brow to chin. A sad longing radiated from him, a longing to be where his brother was—with the Messiah.

Among the leaders also sat Reb Matthew, of whom the messengers knew that he had once been a publican, and the lord had called him and he had followed. And there were others, whose names rang mystically in the ears of these believers from afar, like Judah ben Jacob and Simon the zealot. And some there were, younger than these, and unknown, but near to the first disciples, and already the leaders of the Messianists.

Before the assembled saints Paul led forth his deputation: Supatros of Berea, Aristarchus and Secundus of Berea, Gaius of Derbe, Tychicus and Timotheus and Tryphimus and Lukas. And each member of the delegation came before the elders, and bowed low, and placed at their feet the bags of coins which the believers, the gentiles not less than the Jews, had donated for the poor among the saints of Jerusalem. And among the copper coins and the silver drachmas there was more than one piece which represented the sacrifice of some slave, the bread he had taken from his own mouth, an offering to a strange people which had once been hated and despised, but had now become part of the Messiah. This was the first fruit of the gentiles, sent to Jerusalem.

Reb Jacob lifted his hands to heaven and praised God for the miracle which He had wrought among the gentiles. And the disciple Reb Matthew acted as interpreter and translated the prayer from Aramaic to Greek, though it was hardly needed, for the words passed from heart to heart across the barrier of language.

After the presentation and the benediction in the upper chamber, Reb Jacob led the delegation down into the courtyard, to meet the simple brethren in the faith. The whole space before the David wall was covered with tents and booths, ramshackle structures of branches, rags, and leaves. In these improvised shelters were housed the poor and the sick, skeletonlike men and women, half-naked, and surrounded by skeletonlike half-naked children. The dregs of Jerusalem's misery were gathered in the courtyard of the Messianists before the David wall; for the rumor had gone round that the *Ebionim,* the Jerusalem Messianists, were distributing bread and figs for the starving, and perhaps clothing for the naked. So there assembled in this place not only the poor who had known, in better times, how to earn their livelihood by labor, but the professional beggars, the idlers, the perpetual takers of alms. Reb Jacob ben Joseph had never set up the distinction so rigorously accepted by Paul. He did not even try to separate the willing from the professional idlers, and he had never said: "He that will not work, neither shall he eat." In this respect Reb Jacob followed the Rabbinic tradition, which had it that a hungry man is not to be questioned, and if a man is in need of food he must get it, whether or not he be willing to work. It was this that drew masses of the starving to the courtyard of the Messianists. Many of them had settled there and constituted a sort of commune; the booths stood there, the women of the congregation cooked, and the idlers ate. The men of the congregation brought the provisions from the city and spread out sackcloth rugs on the stones. So the poor sat at table and partook of common meals. The saints, with Reb Jacob at their head, sat down among the poor; nor did they pick and choose, so that they might as often as not be sitting next to someone with an infectious disease. No one was so low, unhappy, broken, that Reb Jacob would think of discriminating against him. The younger of the *Ebionim,* or Messianists, served the older ones. All dipped their hands in the common dish, and no one shrank from contact with another. Before eating they repeated the lord's prayer; during the meal they sang chapters of the Psalms, while between chapter and chapter one of the disciples would recall the life of the lord and his deeds and sayings and parables. And then all the assembly, the sick and the hale, the poor and wealthy—for there were wealthy ones who came, not for earthly sustenance, but to render service—was fused into one joyous spirit of hope in the Messiah.

But the deputations that had come with Paul, the gentiles of the Greek world, did not find it easy to sit down indiscriminately with the dregs of the populace of Jerusalem and dip their hands into the common bowl. All that had gone into the making of their lives protested and revolted.

In the evening the visitors met with the Jerusalemites to break bread in the upper chamber. All, Greeks and Jews alike, sat on the floor, at a bare, simple table, and their food was a little piece of bread, a handful of olives, and a sip of wine from a clay pitcher. Very quiet and earnest was the assembly, as if the lord had but just left them and the impress of his shadow were still on the wall. It was not a meal, but a religious service. After the eating the disciples again recalled the actions and utterances of the Messiah. They spoke Aramaic, and from time to time someone translated their words into Greek. But there was one disciple who related the words and deeds of the lord in Greek, and he had many memories of him. This was Matthew.

And Matthew told again what the Messiah had said to them on the Mount of Olives:

"Before he came down to eat his last meal with us he said to us: 'In the day when the son of man will come back in glory, amid the angels, he will sit upon his throne. And all the nations of the world shall flow to him, and he will make fences about them, even as the shepherd separates the sheep from the goats. He will place the sheep on his right hand, and the goats on his left. The king will say to those that are on his right hand: "Come, receive the benediction of my father and inherit the kingdom which has been prepared for you since before the beginning of the world. For I was hungry, and ye fed me; I was thirsty, and ye gave me drink; I was a stranger, and ye took me into your midst; I was naked, and ye clothed me; I was sick, and ye visited me; I was thrown into prison, and ye came to me there." ' " And Matthew continued: "In that day the ones on his right hand will reply: 'Lord, when wert thou hungry, and when did we feed thee? When wert thou thirsty and when did we give thee to drink? When wert thou a stranger to us and we took thee into our midst? Or naked, and we clothed thee? And when did we see thee sick or imprisoned?' Then the lord will answer them, saying: 'Of a truth, that which ye do unto the least of my brothers ye have done unto me.' Then he will turn to those that are on his left hand and say: 'Begone from me into everlasting fire, and let Satan and his angels have dominion over you, for I was hungry, and ye gave me not to eat, I was thirsty, and ye gave me not to drink.' "

And Reb Jacob ben Joseph, gathering the purport of Matthew's words, nodded piously and added, in his own tongue:

"Every gift and every donation is from above and comes from the Lord of light, in whom there is no change and no shadow of turning."

Then he taught them:

"When ye fulfill the law of the king according to the words: 'And thou shalt love thy neighbor as thyself,' ye do right. But if you are respecters of persons, you do evil, and will be punished even as the evil are punished. For he that keeps the whole law, and yet fails in one matter, shall be as one that failed in all."

Paul, seated among his companions, knew whom Reb Jacob meant with those last words.

*   *   *

The next morning, when Paul came to visit Reb Jacob, he found him seated in a corner, his form rigid, his face bloodless, his eyes stony. The hollows in his cheeks had deepened overnight. And when Reb Jacob perceived Paul he became even more rigid, and he began to speak in a thin, lamenting voice:

"Saul, Saul, the cry of the Jews goes up against thee, God have mercy on thee. How didst thou dare to lift up the ax against the roots of Israel? Dost thou not know as well as I that Israel has been chosen to be His witness eternally, until the end of the world? Knowest thou not as well as I that Israel is holy, eternally to be untouched? Has not God said of Israel: 'The rivers shall not wash thee away, fire will not swallow thee, flames will not touch thee'? And it is thy desire to destroy Israel in the name of the lord!"

"Destroy Israel?" echoed Paul, astounded. "It is because I spread the tidings among the gentiles that I am hunted even as a beast of the field. It is because of the love of the Messiah, which I bring to a suffering world, that I am persecuted. Wherever I came, I tell thee, I brought the tidings *first* to the Jews. But they have stopped up their hearts, and have become more stiff-necked than ever, even as the Prophet said of them of old: A stiff-necked people!"

"I thank thee, O God, for the obstinacy which thou hast put into our hearts in the matter of our faith!" cried Reb Jacob, ecstatically. "Holy is the obstinacy of Israel—and let us pray to God that He be gracious to the congregation of the Messiah and plant in them the obstinacy of faith which is in the heart of Israel. Thy zeal for the lord makes thee blind, Saul, if thou seest not the holiness of the obstinacy of Israel. For in the place of the promise, in the place of the hope of Israel, in the place of the highest consolation, the Messiah of Israel, thou bringest a sword. For thou hast broken with Israel, thou hast abrogated the laws and commandments, thou hast uprooted the tree of Israel and seekest to replant it in the soil of the gentiles. It is the path of temptation and failure that thou hast chosen, Saul. See, there are in Jerusalem thousands of Jews who believe but they are also zealous in the Torah, in the law. They have heard concerning thee that thou teachest those Jews who dwell among the gentiles that they shall abandon the law of Moses, and that they shall give up the circumcision of their children. And now, what shall we do? The people will surely assemble against thee, for they know that thou art here."

"What is your desire?" asked Paul. "Would ye take the Lord of all the worlds and enclose him within the four narrow walls of the Jewish law? His spirit is fire and will burn down all barriers erected by the little thoughts of men. For what is man, that he, a worm, shall dare to claim the wholeness of God as contained in his own spirit? Would ye make of God an appendage of Israel? He is the Lord of the whole world. He sent His Messiah as His deliverer, the Messiah of all mankind, of all men that have common blood with him. Faith has created a new brotherhood among men; the lord binds them into a single family. They become children of God in the faith, not in the laws and commandments!"

"Woe to the ears which must listen to these words," wailed Reb Jacob, shuddering from head to foot. "Who dares to say that we seek

534

to confine the Lord of the world in the four narrow walls of the law? The Lord of the world is 'He That Is.' Thou canst add nothing to that word, nor canst thou take away from it. All else is idolatry. But it is we that are concerned. What are we? Gods—perish the thought!—or angels? We are naught but wretched things of the earth, filled with temptations and failings. Our hearts are filled with lusts, and chaos surrounds us. And in the midst of this chaos God was gracious to Israel and set guides and markers for him. This is his law, his Torah, given to us through Moses. That alone made of us the elect people; that alone sustained in us the longing for the Messiah of righteousness, which is the hope of Israel for the sake of the whole world. And only Israel has paid the full price—only Israel, none other beside him. And thou wouldst take away from Israel the rights conferred upon him by God, through the fathers, and give them away to others?"

Who better than the apostle to the gentiles knew that the heart of man is filled with evil desires, and that in the chaos God had set guides and markers, which he, Paul himself, had sought to bring to the gentiles? And was it just to say of him that he sought to take away the rights of Israel? In pain and anger he retorted:

"If it be true that I would take away the rights of Israel, what am I doing here, in Jerusalem? Do I not know well that tears and chains await me here in Jerusalem? Is this what thou callest uprooting the hope of Israel? And as to the Torah, the laws and commandments, am I not an observant Jew, even as you are? Do I not observe the laws and commandments?"

Reb Jacob paused. He was moved by Paul's cry. He rose stiffly from his place, came over to the apostle, and took his hand.

"If what thou sayest is true, brother, hear my counsel, and do as I bid thee. There are here, among us, four men who have taken a vow. Take these four men and purify thyself with them. Pay the fee for the cutting of their hair, so that all may know that what has been said concerning thee is false, and that thou keepest the laws and commandments of the Torah. And concerning the gentiles, we ourselves have written that they need not observe all our commandments, but that they must only refrain from bringing sacrifices to the idols, from practicing whoredom, from shedding blood, and from eating the meat of strangled beasts."

(Now concerning the four men who had taken the vow. It often

535

happened that Nazirites took up their quarters in the courtyard of Reb Jacob. A man under a vow, having reached the term of the vow, had to pass through a purification of seven days. During that period he withdrew with other Nazirites into a special chamber reserved for this purpose in the Temple. Here he avoided all impurities. When the period of purification was over, he was free to bring the expiatory sacrifice of the Nazirite to the Temple. This was called "the cutting of the hair." And it was a custom in Israel that when a man of standing came to the Temple to mark the term of his vow, he would pay the "fee" for the cutting of the hair of poor Nazirites, that is, the cost of their purification and their sacrifice.

Paul did as Reb Jacob bade him. He took four Nazirites from the courtyard and locked himself with them in the special chamber of the Temple, to prepare himself for the offering of the sacrifice. And he did all this because he would not separate himself from the body and community of Israel, though the forces he had set in motion threatened to do it for him. He was bound, inwardly, with all the strands of his being, to the continuity of Israel, and therefore he observed all the details and minutiae of the law. He was striving to fuse into one person —and this was a gigantic task—the two Pauls, Paul the Jew and Paul the Greek. He had brought the one externalization of himself, the Greek converts of the far-off cities, to encounter and confront the other externalization, the saints of Jerusalem. But what was taking place within him was not a fusion; it was rather as if he were being ground between an upper and a nether millstone. Nor was it a handful of seed that was being ground; it was a rock, as hard as the millstones themselves. Only an equal love for Greek and Jew could have produced this phenomenon, Paul.

And though he was a Greek with the Greeks, Paul had remained in his inner structure the complete Jew, with the feverish restlessness of the Jew. He was burning to cleanse himself of the sin he had committed in bringing division into the fold, to unload from his shoulders the curses he had called down upon himself; he wanted to win pardon for the bitter words he had uttered in sorrow and torment: words often torn from him by sheer contrariness and born of the impulse to provoke, words for which he had wept later, in the night. And in isolating himself for seven days in the chamber of the Temple, reserved for the Nazirites, he was hoping to make a final accounting with his soul.

536

Meanwhile the delegations which Paul had brought with him to Jerusalem were lodged with a certain believer, Munason by name, a native of Cyprus who had settled in Jerusalem and who had a commodious house. During the day the gentile visitors wandered about the streets, went up to the Temple, and visited the Court of the Gentiles. But they could not help feeling the barrier which lay between them and the Jews. Beyond the Court of the Gentiles they could not pass, in the Temple. Beside the magnificent gates of Corinthian bronze which shut off the Court of the Women, they read these words: "No stranger shall cross this meta. And if one should be caught beyond this meta, he shall himself be responsible for the death he has earned." They knew, the visitors, that their acceptance of the Messiah did not make them Jews as long as they were uncircumcised. They saw the joy which shone on the faces of the Jews as they brought their first fruit offerings to the Courts. In the streets they sometimes encountered Jews of their acquaintance from their native towns, and the Jews were astonished to see them here, and wondered what had brought them. But among the Jewish pilgrims to the Temple there were also thousands of Messianists, who were faithful as of old to the Torah of Moses. Among such Jews the presence of the gentiles in Jerusalem was not a matter for astonishment. They understood what it was that drew Christians to the homeland of the Messiah.

Tryphimus, who, out of love for the Messiah and on Paul's persuasion, had thrown over the gods of his fathers and had brought the fragments of his idols and the instruments of their worship, precious for countless generations to his forefathers, as a sacrifice to the pyre— Tryphimus had an inner need for service in a Temple, for such had been his upbringing. He had believed that through his faith in the Messiah he had become a co-inheritor of all the sanctities of the Jews, had, in fact, become a son of Israel. The Temple of the Jews, which the Messiah himself had worshiped in, became in the eyes of Tryphimus his own temple. He felt that he had a right to pass beyond the bronze gates with their stern inscription. Had not Paul told him that he, Tryphimus, was circumcised in heart and spirit? Were not the forefathers of the Jews therefore his forefathers? In his simplicity he would have ignored the inscription on the gates, would have tried to set foot in the exclusive Courts. But Jews who were in his company at the time forbade him and warned him he would be risking his life.

537

"Why?" he asked, in astonishment. "Why? I am a son of Israel! The Messiah was here, and this was his Temple."

And so certain was he that they were in error that he would have persisted, and no doubt a riot would have ensued, had it not been that just then certain other Jews, fellow countrymen of his, with whom he was acquainted, appeared on the scene, and being told what Tryphimus purposed, dragged him away, meanwhile persuading the other Jews that the gentile had merely been mistaken, and had intended no desecration.

But the incident, though it passed off peacefully, had unfortunate repercussions. For the story got abroad that Paul, the man who was dissuading the Jews from the loyalty to the Torah of Moses, had brought gentiles to the Temple and had encouraged them to penetrate to the forbidden sanctities. The name of Tryphimus was mentioned everywhere, and there were those who remembered they had indeed seen Paul in the company of Tryphimus, and this was proof enough that the accusation was well founded.

But meanwhile Paul remained in the Nazirite chamber of the Temple. He and the other Nazirites lay on the marble, each man in his own corner, and they confessed all the sins they had committed before the time of their Nazirite vows. In the early hours of the morning they plunged their bodies into the water of the ritual bath. Afterward they issued into the Court, speaking to no man, but kneeling down and concentrating their thoughts on prayer. No word passed their lips, for they addressed neither the other Nazirites nor any of the Temple visitors. Their food consisted of green vegetables and water. They drank no wine; nor was any oil permitted to come upon their skins. Thus it had to be for seven days. And four days had passed. On the fifth day Paul came out of the chamber with the other Nazirites. He kept his place in the file, a bent and humbled figure, his heart filled with contrite thoughts, and his spirit bowed before God.

Chapter Thirty-two

PHARISEE AND SON OF A PHARISEE

JERUSALEM had sucked up the spirit of revolt as a sponge sucks up water. Foreign and domestic tyrants had driven the people into a state of desperation. It was about this time that there began to appear in the Temple courts the "Sicarii"—as they were afterwards to be called in a foreign tongue—assassins who carried daggers concealed under their cloaks, sidled up to their victims, and assassinated them in the midst of the crowd. The Temple Priests were scrupulous in their attention to the purity of the courts. No stain was permitted to appear on the marble floors, or on the garb of the Priests themselves. Unspeakably horrible was it to find the courts not only spattered with blood: but often a dead body, a victim of the Sicarii, would be found in the courts when the crowds had withdrawn. The chief guilt for the condition which produced this form of revolution in the people lay with the oppressive government of the Roman Procurators, of the Herodian dynasty, and of the bought-and-sold High Priesthood. Between the Jewish and the foreign tyrants the masses were squeezed like olives between the stones of a mill; taxes, levies, decrees combined to starve the body and humiliate the spirit of the Jews. A last, desperate, and impossible hope was left to the people—revolt against the armed and constituted authority. All manner of "seers" and "Messiah-bringers" circulated among the masses, provoking them to futile, disorganized outbursts of violence. And as these increased, the brutality of the repressive measures taken by the Procurators became more general and indiscriminatory. To break the spirit of the people was their conscious purpose; and the legionaries stationed in Jerusalem were ordered to strike right and left without distinction of age and sex. But instead of reducing the people to terrified apathy, these retaliatory pogroms only stung it to more frantic determination.

While on the one hand the masses were sinking to a level of indescribable poverty, individuals of the High Priesthood were accumulating enormous fortunes as tax farmers and speculators, on top of which they had their perpetual income from the tithes, and this they increased beyond any measure contemplated by the Mosaic law, which their hired "interpreters of the law" distorted to the advantage of their masters. The desperation of the people took the form of a wild, unattainable longing for political independence. Wherever the voice of reason was raised, not in treachery but in sober appeal to the cruel realities of the situation, it was drowned out by the wild cries of the "Zealots." Among the latter there were incensed and unbalanced but honest patriots; they, unfortunately, were the cover to assassins whose instincts of murder found expression in the call to rebellion against Rome and the Herodean dynasty, whatever the practical consequences might be.

In the nights there was whispering and weeping on the flat roofs of the house of Jerusalem. The prayers of the Jews ascended to the heavens in a bitter appeal for the salvation of the Holy City.

In those days the High Priest was one Chananyah ben Nadabai, of the hated house of Chanan. By intrigue, by bribery, and by collusion with the Procurator Felix—a man who did not hesitate to make his own use of the Sicarii—Chananyah remained longer in office than any of his predecessors. But long before him the High Priesthood had fallen into an abyss of corruption. The "Sons of Chanan" had changed that office from the pride and glory of the people to its greatest shame, and the present incumbent of the house had made himself one of the richest men in the country. The Priesthood had sunk so low that even the High Priests themselves no longer called upon "the Holy One of Israel" by that title; and instead of the simple word "God" there came into use, among them, the indirect allusion—*Ribon,* Lord.

The only group which understood the condition of the country, and understood the profound danger which confronted it, was that of the Rabbis, the Pharisees. But they were without power. The masses were under the influence of the Zealots, and beyond the control of the Rabbis. The great Rabban Gamaliel was now dead. The one spiritual leader among the Pharisees who enjoyed some measure of standing with the folk was Rabbi Jochanan ben Zachai. He saw what was happening, he did what he could to arrest the process of demoralization in the people. So sunken were the masses as the result of the Priestly misrule, that Rabbi Jochanan ben Zachai abrogated the old practice of administering "the bitter waters" to a woman as the test of her faithfulness. . . . He saw more clearly than anyone else the catastrophe that was drawing close; and as far back as those days, in anticipation of calamity, he was attempting to shift the center of spiritual gravity of Jewish life from the Temple to the Prophets, from Priestly regulation to moral principles of grace and love, on values which were not bound to physical instruments subject to destruction by the enemy—principles and values which the people could, when it came to the worst, carry away with them into exile. He gathered about him groups of young scholars, brought up in the tradition of the Venerable Hillel, that tradition which had concentrated the meaning of the Jewish law in the one ancient phrase: "And thou shalt love thy neighbor as thyself."

A deep and passionate God-longing grew in Israel in those days. The humiliated soul of the people turned to the eternal Source, and it was as though a Job-mood of faithfulness in disaster had descended on Judaea. The days of the Temple were numbered; and the earth of Palestine seemed to open, while from the cracks were heard the voices of the Prophets; in language that was not of this earth they warned the people that the fiery sword which God had held over the head of Jacob was about to descend. The flame of the Eternal Light in the Golden Candelabrum, guarded by the Priesthood, flickered out. There were other portents. Blood-red stains appeared suddenly on the "lashon," the cloth of the scapegoat which hung in the Temple. Men and women had visions—they beheld fiery wheels revolving in the sky. All this, passed on by word of mouth, produced a universal feeling that the earth was about to dissolve. What was there left to the children of Israel but to fasten, with their last energies, to the God who had saved his people so often of old? A religious fervor took hold of Jerusalem and Judaea, and a renewed piety and faithfulness to the tradition, the ancient ritual. They were ready, in those days, to suffer death for the minutest details of the prescribed forms of their religion. All national passions, all the moral values, the heritage of the fathers, transmitted across countless generations, were intermingled in a fierce jealousy of faithfulness. Nor was this upsurge of emotion confined to Palestine; it set in like a tide among the Jews of the Diaspora, and the number of pilgrims from foreign lands grew to immense proportions. It was as though they feared that if they did not go up now to look upon the Temple, they would never have the opportunity again. The Jews of the remotest provinces and the tiniest townlets of Asia came to Jerusalem for the festivals. They brought with them, to swell the flood of longing, hope, and revolt in the Holy City, the love and promise of the Jews scattered throughout the world. But they also brought with them a deep bitterness against any attempt to uproot the last of their hopes. It was not the Messianists or Christians whom they regarded as the destroyers from within; their rage was directed against him who was preaching that the law and tradition of Moses, their rock, the content of their lives, the heritage of the fathers, had been abrogated. What wonder that the Jews of Asia were interpenetrated with hatred of him who openly preached this destructive doctrine in the synagogues—with hatred of Paul?

From Ephesus came to Jerusalem Chananyah the silversmith. His wife had borne him a son—his first—whom he was bringing to Jerusalem to redeem him for five silver shekels. Shortly after his arrival Chananyah met in the Court of the Gentiles Tryphimus, the shipbuilder of Ephesus, who, with a group of gentile Christians, was standing in awe before the gates of Corinthian bronze. The Ephesians who were with Chananyah recognized in Tryphimus one of the gentiles whom Paul had persuaded that though they were uncircumcised, they were true sons of Israel. A few moments later Chananyah and his companions beheld a number of Nazirites issuing from their ritual chamber. And who was that one, third in the line, who walked with bowed head, sunk in thought? Look there! By the robes of the High Priest, is not that Paul?

"Jews! Hither to me! See who goes there!"

"Paul!"

"He who dissuades the Jews from faithfulness to the law of Moses!"

"He who provokes the gentiles against the Jews!"

"He who brings the gentiles into the Temple! But a moment ago I saw Tryphimus of Ephesus, who declares that he and his like are the true sons of Israel!"

"And in our city, in Corinth, the gentiles who have taken baptism likewise declare that they are the true sons of Israel. We, they say, are the sons of Ishmael, while they are sons of Isaac!"

"That is the work of Paul!"

"And he dares, even he, to show himself in the court of God's House?"

"He among Nazirites, in the Holy Place?"

542

"Men of Israel, help! Here is the man who preaches everywhere against our people!"

Jews of Macedonia, of Galatia, of Achaia, many of whom knew Paul by sight, and who had accounts of their own to settle with him because of the dissensions he had introduced into their local synagogues, were gathered about Chananyah the silversmith, as the latter continued to shout:

"He has brought the uncircumcised into the Temple! He has desecrated the Holy Place!"

As if driven from other parts of the court by flames, men came running toward the group; and no one knew what had happened.

"Gentiles have desecrated the Temple!"

"Who? Where?"

"They have brought bones of the dead into the court!"

"Who? Samaritans?"

"No! A Jew! One named Paul!"

"He disguised some gentiles as Nazirites and introduced them into the chamber of the Nazirites!"

"Death! Slay him!"

And in an instant Paul was lifted up and was being carried out of the court. The bronze gates behind him clashed to. Heads, beards, glaring eyes, clenched fists poured along with the procession. Wild voices were raised.

"To the field of stoning!"

Like a flicker of lightning passed through Paul's mind the picture of Reb Istephan being carried off amid the same wild cries: "To the field of stoning!" He saw again the pit, the angel sunk half way in the heap of stones. He was being carried toward the same pit! Was this a sign from above? And in the midst of the tumult he recalled also the solemn voice of Rabban Gamaliel, quoting the words of the Venerable Hillel: "Because thou didst drown another, thou shalt thyself be drowned." But if this was going to happen, what of the mission to Rome?

Meanwhile, on the balcony of the Antonia fortress, a Roman sentinel beheld the riot. He smote his sword on his bronze shield. Outside the court, not far from the gates, was stationed a guard of Roman legionaries, under the command of a centurion. The sound of the sword on the shield was relayed from sentinel to sentinel till it reached the

Tribune Claudius Lysias, who was set that day over the city in festival to maintain order.

The command was passed to the centurion outside the court. In an instant the guard was in motion; it passed into the court and confronted the mob which was carrying Paul to the field of stoning; Paul was seized, and the chains which he had seen in his vision descended now on his hands.

The legionaries lifted Paul on their shields, out of reach of the howling mob, and carried him in the direction of the Antonia fortress.

But Paul's mind was working clearly. This people which was ready to tear him limb from limb was his people; it was the people to which he had been sent, the people which was waiting for salvation. Paul's one desire now was to be allowed to address the Jews, to declare his tidings in the Temple court to his own flesh and blood. On the steps of the Antonia fortress Paul addressed himself to the Tribune—in Greek!

"May I have word with thee?"

The Tribune stared at him, amazed. This wretched, bedraggled, wounded Jew, was speaking to him in Greek! He had taken him for one of the rabble, one of the barbarian, rebellious Jews.

"Art thou not," asked the Tribune, "the Egyptian who lately led a band of rebels in the wilderness?"

"No! I am a Jew of Tarshish in Cilicia, a citizen of a famous city!"

In his bewilderment, the Tribune gave Paul permission to address the Jews, and Paul, whose tongue had saved him in many a perilous situation, lifted his hands to the raging mob. There was that in his gesture and in his eyes which impressed the furious onlookers. Silence fell upon them, and Paul addressed them in Hebrew:

"My brothers and my fathers!"

"Hebrew! He speaks our tongue! Silence!"

"Let us hear what he has to say!"

"I am a Jewish man," cried Paul, "born in Tarshish. But I was brought up in this city, and I sat at the feet of Gamaliel. . . ."

Gamaliel! A disciple of Gamaliel! The words are like magic. He is a disciple of Gamaliel, the Prince of the Pharisees. . . .

"I am learned in the Torah, the law of our forefathers."

Now there was utter silence. It was as though the mob had suddenly become a class at the feet of a Rabbi. For he whom they deemed a traitor was about to open his heart to them. And Paul spoke. He spoke at length, telling them of his life, confessing that in years past he had been a persecutor of the Messianists. Then he told them of his vision on the road to Damascus, and how he had been changed from Saul to Paul. But as he reached this part of the narrative the listeners again became restless. The speaker was again the traitor—he who had wandered among the cities of the gentiles taking away the election from the Jews and conferring it upon the gentiles. He had brought the Messiah not to the Jews, but to the gentiles. And when they heard Paul say: "He, the Messiah, declared unto me: 'Go, for I will send thee to the gentiles,'" the tumult broke out again.

"It is a lie!" they screamed. "The Messiah of Jacob never told thee to go to the gentiles!"

"He has sold the election of Israel to the gentiles!"

"Death! Stop his mouth with sand!"

And some in the front rank threw off their upper garments—so it was that the witnesses who stoned Stephanus had thrown off their upper garments to make ready for the work.

"Nay, if the people is thus against him," thought the Tribune, "the man must be a robber."

He bade his men carry Paul into the fortress. Two heavy blocks were fastened to his chains—the blocks to which criminals were bound, for execution. They were stained with blood, and human hair clung to the clots. The hands of the apostle were thrust through the rings of the blocks. Over him stood two half-naked soldiers, the heavy whips, soaked in vinegar, uplifted in their hands. Paul, from whom the garment had been ripped, struggled, lifted his face upward, and for the first time appealed to the rights which had been conferred upon him by Edom.

"Darest thou scourge a Roman citizen without a trial?" he cried.

The Tribune started back as if a thunderbolt had fallen at his feet. What? This wretched, naked, battered little Jew was a Roman citizen?

"A Roman citizen?" he asked, stupefied. Was it possible? "I paid a great sum for my citizenship," he said.

"I did not purchase my Roman citizenship. I was born a Roman citizen," answered Paul.

"Unbind him!" said the Tribune. And to Paul: "If this be so, thou shalt be examined by thine own Sanhedrin, that they may discover what the people has against thee."

And he ordered that Paul be turned over to the Sanhedrin for examination.

* * *

The Sanhedrin no longer sat, as of old, in the great Chamber of the Hewn Stones, in the Temple. Its place of assembly had been shifted to a room in one of the "shops" of the Sons of Chanan on the Mount of Olives. Indeed, many of the old institutions had disappeared by this time.

The struggle between the Pharisees and the Sadducees, between the Rabbis and the High Priesthood, had reached an indescribable degree of bitterness. There was a continuous dispute between the two groups concerning the minutest details of the Temple ceremonial. But the Temple service was controlled by the Priests, and they did everything they could think of to flout and discredit the Pharisaic tradition. Thus it was in the more important matter of the Sanhedrin, on which the Pharisees were entitled to representation. The transference of its sessions to the shops of the Chanans on the Mount of Olives had been planned in order to discourage the attendance of the Pharisees.

The head of the Sanhedrin was the High Priest himself, but he did not always exercise this office and permitted himself to be represented by a lower official. On this occasion Chananyah ben Nadabai was determined to preside in person. He had special reasons for wanting to confront the apostle.

When Paul looked around him in the chamber of the Sanhedrin, he beheld before him an assembly predominantly Sadducean and Priestly. But the Pharisees were still represented. Some of them he knew well; they had been fellow students of his under Rabban Gamaliel. They sat now clustered about their leader, the gray Rabbi Jochanan ben Zachai. A flood of memories rose in Paul's heart. For a moment it seemed to him that he was still one of these, a disciple of Gamaliel. Therefore, when he was called upon to open his self-defense, he did not use the prescribed formula: "My lord High Priest," but addressed himself instead to his "companions," the Pharisees: "Men and brothers! With a pure heart I walked before God. . . ."

The heavy, sagging face of the High Priest flushed, his eyes became injected. He cast a glance at the guards. This traitor, this misleader of Israel, had dared to ignore him, the High Priest of Israel! One of the guards strode forward and smote Paul across the mouth.

546

Paul, who was ready to bear all things at the hands of his people, would not bear this affront from the one who sat before him. His half-closed eye glared at the Priest, and he said:

"God shall smite thee, thou painted wall! Thou sittest in judgment over me according to the law, and thou biddest thy servants smite me against the law."

And indeed, he who was enthroned in the judgment seat of the Sanhedrin was "a painted wall." This High Priest had not even the distinguished bearing of Chanan the elder, or the earnestness of appearance which had belonged to a Joseph Khaifa. This was a blown-up mass of flesh. Chananyah was widely known as a gross liver, a heavy eater and drinker, a type far more common among the Romans than the Jews. Bitter, unclean anecdotes were current in Jerusalem and Judaea concerning his appetites. He looked everything that he was; his belly was bloated, his cheeks hung down, his eyes were encased in flesh. His servants did their best to cover his repulsive body with clothes that would hide its shapelessness; they adorned him with costly silks and fine linens of Sidon. His Syrian hairdresser worked hard to impart some kind of seemliness to his beard and features. But it was in vain. The oil applied to his skin would not sink in, but glistened on the surface. So he sat there—"a painted wall."

But Paul's savage phrase had shocked his one-time "companions," and they cried out:

"Thou insultest the High Priest of God!"

Paul knew that well, and on the instant he regretted his outburst. He had gone too far, even under provocation. He was standing here as a stern disciple and observer of the law, and he had permitted himself to be provoked into the breaking of the law. For whosoever might be occupying the throne of the Priesthood, he was still "the Elder of Israel," the representative of the unbroken line of Aaron, called to speak for his people in the Holy of Holies. He therefore mastered himself, made obeisance to the High Priest ("For my people I will endure all," he thought, inwardly) and made the only excuse he could:

"I did not know, brothers"—and he turned to the Pharisees, "that this was the High Priest. It is indeed written in Holy Writ: 'Thou shalt not curse an elder of thy people.' "

The assembly quietened. And having thus mollified the Pharisees, Paul turned to them a third time:

547

"Men and brothers, I am a Pharisee and the son of a Pharisee. And I am accused of having preached the hope of the resurrection."

When the Sadducees and Pharisees on the bench heard the word "resurrection" they started as if Paul had repeated his insult against the High Priest.

"Thou hearest it from his own mouth," screamed one of them. "The man has gone from synagogue to synagogue preaching a new Torah, a new law, of the resurrection, of angels and spirits. He preaches that one man rose from the dead—and we permit our people to listen to him."

But a Pharisee cried in response:

"We find no evil in this man. And if a spirit or an angel held converse with him, we shall not fight against God. Did not God speak to the Prophets through visions and angels and spirits?"

"But if these be your words you are all deniers of the faith and blasphemers in Israel," answered one. "You are believers in alien gods."

Who had dared to speak thus to the Pharisees? It was the High Priest himself, he who had brought the supreme office in Israel to the lowest level of contempt.

Now old Reb Jochanan ben Zachai rose to his feet, and the assembly relapsed into silence.

"My lord High Priest," he began, calmly. "The doctrine of the resurrection is not alien, but is of the transmitted tradition. For again it is written: 'The God of Abraham, Isaac, and Jacob.' But elsewhere have we not the words: 'The dead shall not praise God'? Whence it follows that Abraham, Isaac, and Jacob are not dead. All our Rabbis believed in the resurrection. We therefore see no evil in what this man has done. Therefore, with the permission of the High Priest, let this man be set free, without any accusation, and let us not deliver a just man into the hands of the gentiles."

Tumult broke out once more in the assembly. The High Priest saw himself about to be robbed of his prey. He turned to the Sadducean scribes in the room, to answer with equally authoritative texts the powerful arguments of Rabbi Jochanan ben Zachai. But his hirelings had nothing to say that approached in weight the texts and interpretations of the Pharisaic leader. Voices on either side grew louder, and the session became chaotic.

The Tribune, trembling for the security of Paul—he was respon-

sible with his own life for that of a Roman citizen—stood at the head
of a detachment of legionaries outside the room. Hearing the tumult
he issued orders to his men to break in. On the instant Paul was seized
and led back to the Antonia fortress.

So the incident came to a close. But the High Priest would not let
it rest there. The opposition of the Pharisees at the session of the Sanhedrin had balked him for the moment. But there were other ways of
achieving his purpose. He knew well that there were not lacking in Jerusalem men from the cities of Asia whose hearts were aflame with hatred
of Paul. And if these were not enough, were there not Sicarikoi in Jerusalem, the men who walked about with daggers concealed under their
robes? It would not be the first time that the High Priest had made use
of them.

So, within a few days after his failure at the trial, the High Priest
had instigated a conspiracy against Paul. But in order that it might be
carried out, it was necessary for Paul to be brought out from the
fortress where he was held in safe keeping. Therefore the High Priest
asked the authorities for a second trial, stating that he was not satisfied
with the first investigation. Once Paul was being led through the
streets, it was his hope that a "people's judgment" would be executed
upon him, as it had once been executed, with the help of Paul himself
—Saul in those days—against Reb Istephan.

The conspiracy, brought about unskillfully and in haste, came to
the ears of Paul's nephew, his sister's son, and the latter brought wind
of it to his uncle in the fortress. Paul sent him to repeat the tidings to
the Tribune, who wearied of the whole affair, and unwilling to bear
the responsibility any longer, decided to send Paul away. He ordered a
detachment of two hundred foot soldiers, accompanied by horsemen
and other auxiliary troops, to transfer the apostle in all haste to the
Procurator of Judaea, Felix, who was in Caesarea, and to deliver his
official report on the incident.

Chapter Thirty-three

THE SONG OF LUKAS

DURING the days of Paul's confinement in the fortress, the gentile delegates he had brought with him from the provinces wandered about the city like lost souls: all, that is, except Lukas, who alone remained calm, for he was withdrawn from the tumult, being concerned with matters of his own. He had made up his mind, in advance of his coming to Jerusalem, to utilize his stay in the Holy City in order to gather and note down all that he could learn from first-hand witnesses of the life, the deeds, and the sayings of the Messiah during his sojourn on earth. He permitted nothing to deflect him from his purpose, but continued, in his quiet, gentile way, on the program he had set forth for himself. He spent much time with the *Ebionim*, the Messianists of the group of Reb Jacob, who, during the tumult about Paul, were left unmolested. The High Priests were chary of adding tumult to tumult, and they did not dare to take action against Reb Jacob, who was regarded in the city as an authentic saint.

Lukas took over from Matthew all the material that the latter had gathered, either in notes or in his memory. Matthew had been privileged to hear the Messiah himself, and had the authority of the Messiah for his apostleship. Matthew had exercised great care in setting down all the doctrines and parables he had heard the Messiah utter. Lukas was also fortunate enough to find a "family letter," or genealogical table, which had been preserved and continued in the family of the Messiah for many generations. These "family letters," or "letters of status," were the most precious possessions among Jews. In the arranging of a marriage the family letter was of more importance than the economic or social standing of the contracting parties. The records of the Messiah's family went back to King David. Now it was universally known that David had been the descendant of Boaz and of Ruth. Boaz had been a descendant of Judah, the son of Jacob, the patriarch. Both Lukas and Matthew set down the descent of the Messiah. But Lukas was not content with this. He was anxious to collect as many details as possible concerning the circumstances of the Messiah's birth.

Matthew had recorded the birth of the Messiah on the basis of reports and rumors which were already in wide circulation among those who had been close to the Messiah. Such rumors bore the character common to the beginnings of all great prophets, such as Moses and Samuel, which the folk adorned with many evidences of election and predestination: the great one had always been dedicated to God "from his mother's womb." But Matthew, like Jochanan-Marcus, was less concerned with these details than with the words and deeds of the Messiah in his lifetime. Following the custom of the Jews, they emphasized the doctrines and the acts of their teacher, setting down with the utmost accuracy his fables and parables.

Lukas the Greek had brought to his faith in the Messiah that longing for beauty which he had drunk in from his worship of the gods. He could not think of the Messiah's birth in other than terms of beauty. What he longed for was the *myth* of the lord and of his birth. Who had been the extraordinary woman to whom, as Matthew recounted, the Holy Ghost had appeared, announcing to her that she would bear a son in a supernatural fashion such as no other woman had ever experienced? It was the longing of Lukas to penetrate the mystery of this creation, the creation of the Messiah. He obtained all the information he could from Matthew, but he felt it to be inadequate. For Lukas, the Hellenist, this was not enough. He resolved to carry the investigations further.

In the great house of Miriam, the sister of bar Naba, there lived the remnants of the Nazarene's family, which had come to join him in Jerusalem. The mother of the Messiah was no longer among the living, nor was Miriam of Migdal. There still remained a close relative of the lord, a sister of his mother. Susannah was her name, and she was old, very old, and white as a dove. Her body seemed no longer of flesh, but rather of the delicate fiber of a plant, transparent and spiritual. She no longer moved about, but lay on a couch swathed in white linen, waiting for the fulfillment of her heart's desire—to be called to the side of the lord in heaven. And she longed not only for him, but for all her own who were with him. She saw them all in visions and was more with them than with those about her. Often she conversed with the dead, and when she spoke to the living, it was always of the others. The women of the house looked upon her as a saint, connected as she was, and so closely, with the seed of the Messiah. They tended her in awe and listened breathlessly to her converse, much of which had to do with her sister and with her bringing forth of the Messiah. Some of her utterances had been set down by Matthew, but not all, for he considered many details as having no importance. Not so with Lukas. When he was introduced into the presence of the white-swathed spirit-woman he had with him an interpreter. Nothing that she had to tell concerning the circumstances surrounding the birth of the lord was without importance to Lukas.

He sat, the Greek grammarian, his soul filled with the longing for the beauty of the gods he had abandoned, at the foot of Susannah's couch, and put down on a scroll of papyrus every word she uttered. She herself, the strange, last representative of the line, had for him, for the Greek, the aspect of a mythological figure, a living symbol of the Jewish "Hellas" which he had made his own, a symbol of the Olympus of the Jews. Susannah spoke, or rather whispered, in the Aramaic tongue; the interpreter translated into Greek, and Lukas wrote diligently:

". . . I remember all clearly, as if it were today. We lived together, all the family, in a single courtyard. My sister Miriam was still at home, with her mother. My father was dead, and my mother the widow sustained the family with the little herd of goats and sheep which her husband had left her. Miriam helped in the vegetable garden and with the flock. She was already betrothed to Joseph, the wainwright. My husband worked daily in his vineyard, our family inheritance. And on that day he was in the field, and my mother was at the brook, washing our clothes. It was noon, and the sun was bright and hot. There was a great silence about us then, as though the last days were drawing near. And suddenly I, who was outside, saw my sister coming out of the house; and her face was white and filled with fear. She came toward me like a frightened hind, and fell to the ground, trembling, 'What is it, my sister Miriam?' I asked her. And she answered, in a voice that shook: 'A wondrous thing has happened to me, Susannah, my sister. I sat in the house at the loom, weaving my bridal dress. There was no sound, save that of the loom, and I was thinking of the first child I would bear, and saying in my heart that if it were a son, I would dedicate him to the Lord, as Hannah had done with hers. And lifting my eyes from the loom I saw before me an angel. His wings were of flaming amber, and he spoke to me: "Greetings, thou that art full of grace, the Lord is with thee. Thou art blessed among women." And I said not one word, out of fear. And I knew not whence the greeting came. Then he said to me something which I cannot confide to any living person.' She put her hands on her mouth, and was silent. But later, when the thing happened, we knew what the angel had told her: that she would conceive in her virginity and bear a son, and that the Lord would give him the throne of David.

"Then the time came for Joseph to report to Bethlehem, which had been his family's home since the days of David; for all those that were of David's house were bidden to inscribe themselves in Bethlehem, such being the decree of the government. But the time had also come for the bringing forth of the child: my sister told it to me later, and Joseph too. It was a bright night, and snow had fallen—the time was winter—and the fallen snow was like the dust of stars. My sister and her husband were in the street, for there was no room for them in the inns, which were filled with strangers from all cities who had come to inscribe themselves in Bethlehem. And indeed, if there had been room for them Joseph could not have paid the inn-keeper, for he was a poor man. That night my sister began to feel her first pains, and it was time to bring her to the stool. Then her husband ran about and found a group of shepherds not far from the town, and they bade him bring his bride and put her in the stall where they kept the lambs which had just been brought forth. There my sister bore her first child, and wrapped it in swaddling clothes, and laid it in a trough, and her husband helped her. They had been abandoned of all, but God had helped them, and He sent an angel, who stood before them and said: 'Fear not, for I bring thee tidings which will be tidings of joy to all the peoples.' And soon it was as if the heavens had opened above the stable where my sister lay with her little one, and legions of angels came down from heaven. There was a great singing for the child: 'Glory to God in the highest, and on earth peace and goodwill to men.' And soon . . .'"

Lukas, at the foot of the couch, was caught up in the vision of the opened heavens; he saw the angels, a golden stream, pouring earthward. They held harps in their hands, they stood in a circle about the new-born child. And Lukas heard the old woman murmuring, again and again: "Glory to God in the highest, and on earth peace and goodwill to men."

Lukas could write no more. He sat motionless, his writing imple-

553

ments at his feet, and his eyes were fixed on the distance. Something was happening in his soul; something was dying and something was being born. He heard, ringing in his ears, the words of Paul:

"The Messiah has become the inheritor of the gods; the myth of Hellas is dead, and the myth of the lord has begun."

Chapter Thirty-four

FOR THE HOPE OF ISRAEL

HAVING convinced himself that Paul was a Roman citizen by reason of his birth in Cilicia, the Procurator Felix placed the apostle under guard in the courtyard of the palace of justice which Herod had built in Caesarea, and awaited the arrival of the accusers from Jerusalem.

In a few days Chananyah the High Priest arrived in Caesarea. It was no small thing for the highest Priestly official to take such a role upon himself; but it had now become a personal ambition of his to obtain the condemnation of Paul after the case had been taken out of his hands. He brought with him a Sadducean interpreter of the law to prepare the indictment.

Felix was one of the worst rulers that had ever been set by Rome over Judaea. A freed slave, his soul had remained for ever slavish. "He was a man of unrestrained lusts, and extraordinarily cruel," runs the report of one of the greatest Jews of that time. Another contemporary, a non-Jew, says of Felix: "He was a freed slave of the Emperor Claudius, who carried out his master's orders with slavish baseness." This was the man, loathed by the Jews for his persecutions, whom the High Priest cringed upon. "Under thy power," said Chananyah to Felix, "we have lived in peace, and many are the benefits thou hast conferred upon us. And each of us in his place renders thanks to thee, mighty Felix." And through his lawyer the High Priest requested that the Procurator release to him "the man who has introduced dissension and tumult among the Jews of all the world, the man who sought to desecrate the Temple, so that we may judge him according to our laws after Lysias the Tribune snatched him from among us."

554

During one of the nights which he spent in the Antonia fortress, before his transference to Caesarea, Paul had a vision. He beheld the Messiah, who declared to. him: "Inasmuch as thou hast witnessed for me in Jerusalem, thou shalt also witness for me in Rome." Thence Paul knew that nothing could happen to him now in Jerusalem or Judaea before he had been in Rome. Standing before the Procurator with this assurance in mind, he answered boldly:

"In the ways of what they call the heresy, or sect, of the Nazarenes, whereof they accuse me of being the leader, I serve the God of my fathers, *and my faith is in everything that is written in the Torah and the Prophets.* And I cherish the hope that they cherish, that the dead will rise again in the resurrection, the just as well as the unjust. And when I stood before the Sanhedrin I said likewise: I am being persecuted now for the resurrection."

Felix, well informed on the case, knew that Paul had come to Jerusalem at the head of a delegation, bringing with him a great donation of funds for the poor of Jerusalem. Obviously, then, this man was of high importance in his sect; possibly he was a man of wealth, or perhaps he had access to the wealth of others: a prisoner to be valued then, according to the means he could command for his ransom. It was not in the nature of Felix to release such a prisoner without a handsome return. He told the High Priest that the trial would be put off for some days, until he could obtain further details from the Tribune, for this was a Roman citizen, and it behooved the Procurator to be circumspect. Thus Paul was turned over to a centurion, with instructions to accord the·prisoner as wide a liberty as possible, and to permit his friends to have access to him at all times.

The centurion was answerable with his head for the security of the apostle. Inasmuch as Paul was free to come and go, within certain limits, the officer had himself chained by his left hand to the right hand of his prisoner, so that he accompanied him everywhere, to his couch and to his meals. But the centurion was free, if he thought that his prisoner would attempt flight, to chain him to the wall. When Paul saw himself chained to his guard, he resolved at once to win the man over, and perhaps even convert him to the faith. There was in Paul a special power in attracting and holding the affections of men.

Lying at night in his prison, side by side with his keeper, Paul suddenly started and, tugging at the chain, awakened his companion.

"What is it?" asked the centurion.

"I desire to pray to my God."

"Now, in the middle of the night?" asked the centurion, astonished. "The temple of Augustus in the city is closed, and here, in the prison, we have no image of god or goddess for thee to kneel before or bring an offering to."

"The temple of my God is never closed," answered Paul. "He dwells in no house erected by human hands; His dwelling-place is the heart of man. We do not see Him with the eyes of our flesh, but we see and feel Him at every instant in our hearts, for He alone guides our actions."

"Ah, yes, that is the God of the Jews, for the Jews worship an invisible God."

"Nay, he is not only the God of the Jews. He is thy God, and my God, and the God of all men. For all of us come from Him and we are all created in His image."

"What? I too, who do not belong to Him and have never brought Him an offering?"

"Thou too. Before thou knewest Him, He had already chosen thee. He chose and won thee by His love of thee."

"What love can He have for me, a stranger, who know Him not, and have never brought Him an offering."

"No man is a stranger to my God. And God bestows not His love in return for offerings. God bestows His love freely on us because we are His children."

And Paul sat in the darkness, chained to his keeper, and told him of the God of Israel, and of Yeshua the Messiah, of his death, which he had taken upon himself of his own free will so that all men—including this "stranger"—might be redeemed from sin, and brought into the eternal life of the Kingdom of Heaven.

Something the centurion had heard concerning Yeshua the Messiah. He knew that many in Caesarea, Greeks as well as Jews, believed in "the Son of God." But now for the first time he heard the doctrine explained, and the manner of Paul's explanation went straight to the heart of the Roman. They talked through the night, and before the dawn came Paul's keeper was filled with longing to win through to the faith which promised rest for his soul.

556

Paul also continued his work within the walls of his prison. The delegates from the provinces followed him to Caesarea, and whereas they had been prepared to comfort him, it was he who strengthened and comforted them. He bade them return to their native cities and to make firmer the foundations of the faith. Thus they kissed and parted. He retained only Lukas, who was altogether absorbed now in his transcription of the record, and of the account of "things as they happened in truth." Still another insisted on staying—Aristarchus of Salonika. He, the simple man with the great, dreamy eyes, asked that he be allowed to minister to the apostle.

There are souls which have no light of their own, but which can be flooded with light from without, and of such was Aristarchus. From the first moment of his meeting with Paul he was bound captive, and a sacred awe filled him for the work of the apostle. He made naught of his own life, or, rather, made naught of it for himself, but offered it up in unreflecting sacrifice to the teacher. Aristarchus was a man of subtle intuitions, sensitive to the unspoken needs of Paul. He stood day long at the gate of the prison, begging the soldiers to admit him. Later, being admitted, he stayed there, to serve the apostle. He was not only Paul's servant, but his messenger to the community of Caesarea, and more than once Paul found himself deriving new strength from the presence of this simple man whose shining eyes reflected the light of an unquenchable faith. It was as though his work shone more steadily in the eyes of his servant than in his own heart, making a constant light in the cell.

There was a great spirit of love and devotion among the believers, a nearness between man and man such as had often been found in Jewish sects. The Messianists of Caesarea, who were especially numerous among the Jews of the locality, did all they could to lighten the burden of Paul's imprisonment. The daughters of Philippus prepared *kosher* meals for him, and Aristarchus brought the food daily into the prison; Paul's friends visited him, according to the permission granted by Felix. They came, indeed, not only as a service to him, but to seek his counsel on the affairs of the congregation. From his place of imprisonment Paul sent out messengers to various communities, in response to their requests for guidance on questions of the faith. Thus he spread the faith, according to his own vision of it, in imprisonment,

557

just as he had done in freedom. The centurion whom he had won over even permitted him on occasion to leave the precincts of the court and, in the company of a guard, to attend the common meals in the house of Philippus. But Paul took advantage of this privilege only on rare occasions, for fear of imperiling the life of the centurion.

More than this, the Procurator Felix often had Paul brought to his own palace—the luxurious building of white marble which Herod had constructed. Drusilla, the Jewish wife of the Procurator, had been brought up strictly in the faith, her mother having been greatly under the influence of Rabban Gamaliel, and more than once Drusilla herself had seen the Prince of the Pharisees in the palace of her father, King Agrippa the First. She had heard the white-bearded old man speak of Israel's hope in the Messiah of Jacob. Drusilla's conscience weighed heavily upon her. Her beauty had won the hearts of many gentiles, and her father had betrothed her to an obscure Asiatic princeling, from whom the Procurator had taken her away. Now she was living with this gentile, when she was in truth the wife of another, whose faith she had accepted. The touch of Hasmonean blood in her veins, of which she was inordinately proud, gave her mind no rest. She too was of a dynasty which had once enjoyed Messianic standing among the Jews—the Hasmoneans. She loved to hear the apostle speak of the hope of her people and of the dream which had become reality. Yet, whenever the apostle confronted her, she felt his glance piercing to the secret place of her heart, uncovering her regret and shame. And as if to sting her deeper, the apostle spoke in her presence of the righteousness which faith in the Messiah imposed on all men and women, the righteousness, the purity, and the modesty against which she had transgressed. Nor she alone. How much righteousness was there in her husband's conduct of state affairs? How much purity and modesty was there in their common life? She listened to the apostle, and her face became pale, her eyelids fell; and within her her heart hammered. Like a prophet the apostle sat before her, unveiling her hidden thoughts. She was seized with dread when Paul spoke of the last day, when the Messiah himself would ascend the throne of judgment, and every soul would be called to an accounting. And the dread in Drusilla's heart touched an answering chord in the heart of her husband. But it was not of the Messiah that Felix was thinking; he dreaded the day when he

558

would be called to an accounting for his misdeeds before the Caesar in Rome. Sometimes, in the night, Drusilla would wake, screaming: she had seen the Judgment Day in a dream. Then her husband trembled too, thinking of the complaints which streamed into Rome from the Jews, from the Samaritans and from other peoples. So it would often happen that, in the midst of a conversation with Paul, Felix would break off, without permitting the apostle to finish.

"I have no more time now," he would say, hastily. "I will send for thee another day."

Yet, so struggling with his conscience, he could not relinquish his habits. He would long ago have released Paul to the High Priest if he could have forgotten the bag of gold which he might yet squeeze out of his prisoner. Behind the reproachful words of the apostle he heard always the ringing of gold dinars. He was tired of the man's presence, but he would not hand him over to the High Priest. So days passed, and months, until two years had been fulfilled, and the Procurator was called to Rome to give an accounting of his stewardship.

A new Procurator, Festus by name, replaced Felix. A very different man this was: a typical representative of Roman legalism. For him only the law existed. No feelings, no opinions of his own, ever intruded on his literal understanding of the law. His body was as inflexible as his spirit; a bronze image, polished and adorned: a bronze image in a silver breastplate, and a row of glass medals. His first act as Procurator was to visit Jerusalem, the capital, and to receive a deputation of the representatives of the Jews, with the High Priest at their head. The High Priest did not fail to present a petition demanding that Paul be finally released to him for judgment according to the Jewish law. During the two years of Paul's imprisonment the servants of the High Priest had accumulated a vast quantity of material on the case. This man had indeed preached in the synagogues that the law of Moses had been abrogated, and there were the statements of several hundred witnesses. Also he had cursed the Temple. But Festus, a true Roman official, could not deliver up a man, and that a Roman citizen, without having heard both sides of the story. Therefore he bade the High Priest attend him in Caesarea, where he would hear out accusers and accused. Thus it was; in Caesarea Festus called for an open trial. He took his place on the judgment seat, and had the apostle brought in. The representatives of the High Priest, attended by many witnesses, made their charge.

Paul answered:

"I have transgressed neither against the law of the Jews, nor against the Temple, nor against the Caesar."

It became evident to Festus that the affair was specifically Jewish, falling exclusively within the competence of a Jewish court. The duty of the Procurator, the representative of Rome, was to follow the law of the land, guaranteed as it was by Roman decree. It was the business of the High Priest to judge all cases of transgression against the Jewish faith. Moreover, Festus was obligated to assist in carrying out the judgment of the Jewish court. He was told that Paul, too, had at one time carried out the instructions of the High Priest and had brought men, women, and children to be judged. There was only one course open to Festus. He addressed himself to Paul:

"Wilt thou go up to Jerusalem and be judged there before me?"

Paul was silent. A thousand thoughts came into his mind. He knew now that nothing could happen to him in Jerusalem before he had been in Rome; he had for this the promise of the Messiah. He knew further that under no circumstances would the Pharisees agree to his being sentenced. They had saved him at the first trial, they would try to save him again at the second. He had always been reluctant to make use of his rights as a Roman. He had reproved the Corinthians for submitting their disputes to other than the courts of the Messianists. But on this occasion Paul decided to avoid the Jewish court and deliver himself into the hands of Edom. . . . He knew well the situation in Jerusalem. He knew the hot mood of the populace. What would be the effect of an adverse sentence, even though he knew by the word of the Messiah that it would not be carried out? What riots would follow? No, he would not go up to Jerusalem. Rather would he put his head into the lion's mouth, having no assurance from the Messiah as to what would happen to him in Rome. After a pause he answered clearly:

"I have done no wrong to the Jews. If I have done anything worthy of death I am ready to die. I appeal to Caesar!"

There was silence in the judgment hall. The prisoner had decided his own fate. Then followed a whispering. Festus took counsel with his legal expert. A citizen of Rome had called on the Caesar's name, and no one could try him now save the Caesar himself. Festus answered: "Thou hast appealed unto Caesar, to Caesar shalt thou go."

*   *   *

The trumpets sound a fanfare. The legionaries are drawn up on parade, with their shields and broadswords. The unfolded banners of Agrippa, King of Galilee and Cherea, of Caesarea of Philippi and of other provinces, float in the air. Dressed in his white robe of royalty, silver-threaded, his tiara on his head, the King, accompanied by his sister Bernice and attended by a great suite, approaches the audience chamber of the palace. Bernice, who walks with her arm on Agrippa's, is not less famous than her brother. Formerly Queen of Chalcis, and still the Queen of Cilicia, she is equally famous for her beauty and her wealth. The dazzling whiteness of her skin shines through the thin veils of black which she wears because of her Nazirite vows. Over the black veils pours the cascade of her flaming, golden hair, of which the poets have sung in Jerusalem and Alexandria and Rome. Her throat is straight and slender like a column of alabaster, and she walks with swaying, rhythmic steps which bring out the suppleness of her young body. Between two lines of legionaries and officials, she approaches, on her brother's arm, the judgment throne, and takes her place by the side of the judge. It is as if a pagan goddess had come down from a pedestal in an Athenian temple, to mingle with men of flesh and blood. The princess Bernice is in the flower of her womanhood, being barely thirty years old. Already she had buried two husbands, one of whom was her uncle, Herod, King of Chalcis. It is whispered in many places—and among them the highest in Rome—that between this brother and sister there is something more than a natural affection. . . . It was to silence these rumors, they said, that the King had given her in marriage to King Palema of Cilicia, and the unhappy gentile, in order to win her, had had himself circumcised. But barely had he carried out the painful operation than Bernice left him and returned to her brother, reckless of the occasion this would give for the repetition and strengthening of the slanderous rumors concerning her relations with her brother.

Brought up in the highest Roman society and endowed with a deep understanding of beauty in literature and art (her reputation as a patroness was firmly established in Athens, where she supported many artists, and a statue of her stood in the Agora), Bernice could not exchange the company of her brother, the cultured aristocrat, even for the crown of the rich province of Cilicia. She lived in her brother's palace, sharing his royal functions with him. Thus it was now, when she came with Agrippa to the palace in Caesarea.

Before Paul had spoken a word, the heart of the King was on his side. It was enough for Agrippa that the High Priest and his representatives were the accusers to render Paul innocent in his eyes. A bitter struggle had developed between King and Priest, who were jealous of each other's powers. It was for this reason that Agrippa, learning of the case, had expressed the wish to hear Paul in person.

On either side of the Procurator and the royal pair sat the highest officials and military commanders of the province. Paul, still wearing his chains, was brought before the throne.

This was an opportunity of which Paul had long dreamed. He loved to speak to the poor and enslaved; but he desired not less to be brought into the presence of the mighty. He had never failed to take advantage of the presence of officials or military men in the cities of the Diaspora to preach his tidings, for, brought up outside of Palestine, he was a stranger to the hatred which Roman oppression had inspired in his fellow Jews of the homeland for the representatives of Rome. But here it was not a question of winning over a gentile. Paul had in mind none other than Agrippa—it was to Agrippa the Jew that he addressed himself, and in the language of the Jews, the language of promise and hope, of the resurrection, the Messiah, the Torah, and the Prophets:

"And especially because thou art expert in the problems and customs of the Jews, I ask for thy patient hearing. . . ."

Then Paul began the story of his life, from its first days in Jerusalem. He told how he had persecuted the Messianists in Jerusalem, how he had gone with the same purpose in mind to Damascus, and how he had been intercepted by the vision. He told of the voice which had spoken to him in Hebrew: "Saul, Saul, wherefore persecutest thou me?" Then followed the story of his conversion—how he who had been a persecutor became a protagonist of the hope of Israel.

"And there I stand until this day, and testify before great and small, and I say nothing save that which was said by Moses and the Prophets: that the Messiah will suffer and he will be the first to rise from the dead, and he shall be a light to Israel and to the gentiles."

Utterly fantastic this speech sounded in the ears of Festus: a savior of Israel who should be a light to Jew and gentile. Who had ever heard of such a thing? And the Procurator, forgetting his dignity, burst into a shout of laughter and cried:

"Paul! Thou art mad! Much learning hath made thee mad."

"Nay, noble Festus, I am not mad.... The King knows whereof I speak.... King Agrippa, believest thou in the Prophets? Nay, I know thou believest."

Agrippa was listening attentively. He was much too much the Roman aristocrat, the son of his father—brought up, like him, in the court of the Caesar—to entertain any aspirations for the independence of his people. His Herodian heritage, not less than his upbringing, had placed him on too high a level to sympathize with the nationalist longings of the Jews. The best he could do for his people was occasionally to risk the displeasure of the Caesar by pleading their cause against the decree of some high Roman official. But Agrippa the courtier would have regarded encouragement of the national dream of independence as outright rebellion. For all that he was not indifferent to those Messianic hopes and traditions on which Paul now touched. Something awakened in him, something was touched to life, and he had to call upon his courtly training in order not to betray his emotions in his answer to Paul. With a good-natured smile he said—ranging himself on Festus' side rather than on Paul's:

"Paul, almost thou persuadest me to become a Christian."

And someone else on the daïs was touched deeply by Paul's words. Bernice, the daughter of a pious mother, felt them even more than Agrippa. Very often, in the remorse which followed a sin, she had taken some Nazirite vow or other, to diminish the luxuriousness of her mode of life. She was seen more than once entering the Temple to bring her offering. She loved her people more than did her brother, and she had a deeper insight into its spiritual being and its moral values. Of these she often spoke with her learned protégés. Paul stirred her uncomfortably now. Her lovely blue eyes were flooded with a strange light, her breath came and went restlessly, and the perfumes with which her robes were touched spread warmly and beguilingly through the audience hall.

Paul perceived at once the effect he had produced on the royal pair.

To Agrippa's words, uttered half kindly, half ironically, he answered in a similar tone:

"I would to God that not only thou, but all those that hear me, might be even as I am—excepting for these chains," and he lifted up his bound hands.

A little later the royal pair stood with Festus in a corner of the hall, consulting as to what they could do for the prisoner. Agrippa would gladly have taken Paul under his protection and rescued him from the High Priest. What a blow that would be for the House of Chanan!

"The man has done nothing, nothing whatsoever, that calls for death or even the chains," he said with a sigh. "He should even now be set free, if he had not appealed to Caesar."

But the appeal to Caesar had been made, and there was nothing for it but to send Paul whither he himself desired to go—to Rome!

Chapter Thirty-five

SHIPWRECK

AT last there was collected in Caesarea a large enough number of prisoners from the provinces to make a regular shipment. Among the captives were many Jews taken by Felix in his sortie against the Egyptian "Messiah" on the Mount of Olives. The weaker among the rebels had been killed off, the stronger were to be sent to Rome to fight the wild beasts in the arena. Besides these rebels there were leaders of the robber bands which infested the highways of Judaea and others who, like Paul, were to be tried by a Roman court. Those that had already been sentenced to death were heavily chained and guarded by legionaries who had to answer for them with their lives. The entire contingent was under the command of an Italian centurion by the name of Julius, of the First Augustan legion, with headquarters at Caesarea. To Julius in person was entrusted the prisoner Paul.

Paul said farewell to the representatives of the congregation of

Caesarea, to Philippus, to his daughters, and to the other believers who had served him so devotedly during the two years of his imprisonment. Lukas, who had gone up to Jerusalem, returned, bringing with him the greetings of the saints, as well as a small sum of money which the congregations had collected for the apostle. Tychicus and Tryphimus had been sent by Paul to Ephesus. With the special permission of the Procurator, who had shown himself favorably disposed to the apostle ever since the visit of Agrippa and Bernice, Paul was permitted to take with him, on his journey, Lukas, Aristarchus, and his beloved son Timotheus, the last of whom he sent on to Ephesus, later during the journey. Titus was already in Corinth.

The centurion Julius had been duly informed that the prisoner thus entrusted to him was a Roman citizen who was going to the capital to stand trial before Caesar. He knew likewise that the prisoner was a man of some importance, who had appeared at an open hearing before the royal couple. From the Procurator he had received intimations that it would be well to treat the prisoner considerately. In addition to all this, Paul put himself out to win the friendship of his new guard. Julius was an honest and faithful soldier, a typical Roman legionary, ready to lay down his life in the execution of his duty; and Paul, who had always respected the discipline and devotion of the Roman soldier, knew how to ingratiate himself with the man. He showed him, from the beginning, that he was himself a great respecter of order. He spoke much to him of the faith, and though he did not succeed in converting him, Julius was softened toward his prisoner and became interested in his fate. Paul was granted privileges which no other prisoner enjoyed. In the hot July nights he was allowed to sleep, together with his companions, on the upper deck of the wretched, foul-smelling little ship which made the first stage of the journey, from Caesarea to a port in Syria. And when the ship touched at Sidon Paul was permitted to go ashore into the city, under guard, to visit his friends. The little congregation of Sidon had been informed in advance that Paul would pass this way on the journey to Rome. A delegation awaited the apostle, with useful gifts—a mattress, a warm cloak, which could also be used as a cover in the nights, and a supply of *kosher* food. Lukas was given a quantity of medicinal oils and wines.

It was only in the harbor of Myra, in Lycia, that the centurion found waiting for him a strong, roomy ship, which was carrying a cargo of Egyptian wheat, linens, flax, and pottery to Italy, and with these a group of merchants. Julius transferred his prisoners and his detachment of soldiers to the new ship, for the remainder of the journey.

Paul had no sooner set foot on the Alexandrian ship than he began to acquaint himself with the merchant travelers and the sailors. Among them were some who already belonged to the sect of the believers, and many more had already heard of Paul. An old and experienced traveler by sea as well as by land, Paul was able to speak more like a sailor than a traveler with the crew of the ship, with the chief helmsman, the anchorers, the men in charge of the sails and even the overseer of the ship's slaves.

During the first few days out of Myra the ship traveled slowly through a level, shining blue sea. The air was still, and the ship hugged the coast, to take advantage of the land winds. Paul, free to move about, circulated everywhere. He went down to the lowest holds where, in noisome, tiny cells, the prisoners condemned to death were chained to the side of the ship. Near them, in other cells, were tigers and lions which were being shipped to the arena of Rome. The prisoners could hear, daily and nightly, the roaring of the beasts which they, clad in the skins of beasts, would have to fight in the presence of the Roman mob. Paul spoke to the condemned criminals of the divine help which had been sent down for all men through the Messiah redeemer. Some of the prisoners had heard the faith preached before. Indeed, there were among them some Jews whose crimes had consisted in trying to hasten the coming of the Messiah; and if they had been the victims of false Messiahs, their faith had been pure and their intentions holy. Many heard of the Messiah for the first time, and they took with them, from this journey, a name to call upon when they would feel their lives ebbing out between the jaws of the wild beasts.

Paul spoke likewise with the sailors, and with the slaves who sat chained to the oars; to them, to the officers, to the helmsman, to the passengers, and even to the soldiers, he preached ceaselessly the salvation of Yeshua the Messiah.

In the evenings, when Paul sat down with his companions to their common meal, there gathered about them a group of soldiers, sailors, passengers, and resting slaves, and listened in thoughtful silence to the prayers and hymns which the strange man and his friends sent up into the heavens toward their invisible God.

So the ship moved forward at a leisurely pace, hungry for the wind, until it reached the island of Crete. There, at a port called Fair Haven, not far from the city of Lasea, they dropped anchor, and stayed awhile.

Meanwhile the High Festivals, or Days of Awe, the New Year and the Day of Atonement, had come upon them. Paul and the other Jewish Messianists on the boat observed the fast rigorously; they prayed as a congregation, and in their thoughts transferred themselves to the services in the Temple.

Now the Day of Atonement was considered among Jews the end of the sailing season. From that day on sea travel was dangerous, and no Jew would set foot on a boat after the Day of Atonement if he could possibly avoid it. But the captain had made up his mind to proceed with the journey and to turn the ship's prow toward the Adriatic. Thereupon Paul sent word to him through the centurion Julius, warning him that his decision was fraught with danger not only to the valuable cargo on board, but to the prisoners, sailors, and passengers.

However, Julius, who was eager to end the journey and to be rid of his responsibility, let himself be persuaded by the captain, who considered Fair Haven too small and uncomfortable to pass the winter in. He wanted at least to reach the livelier harbor of Phenice, on the other side of the island. There were two hundred and seventy-six souls on board—slaves, sailors, prisoners, and passengers—to be fed and provided with water, as well as the wild beasts in the hold; and the captain argued that he would run short of supplies in Fair Haven.

At first, when the ship turned westward, a moderate south wind sprang up and filled the brown sails; but before they were within sight of Phenice the sky suddenly darkened, and the sea began to heave. Soon the darkness became so dense that it was impossible to see a fathom's length in any direction, and at the same time a storm wind, the Euroclydon, burst suddenly upon them, and flung the ship about as if it were an oyster shell. The sails flapped violently and threatened to tear apart. The sailors clambered up the masts and furled the sails, and meanwhile sailors and passengers alike—Paul among them—labored to pull the small rescue boat aboard lest it be carried away in the storm. All hands likewise helped in passing strong ropes about the frame of the ship, for the fury of the waves threatened to crack it asunder. Now, without sails, without a helmsman, without rowers, the ship drove before the wind, rising on the dizzy crests of the waves and plunging into the troughs. At any moment it might smash into a thousand fragments against a hidden rock, for they were not far from the shore of Crete. Sky and sea were invisible; it was as though the ship were rolling over in the vast, dark jaws of a wild sea beast.

Two days passed in this fashion. Staggering from the holds to the deck, the sailors and passengers had already thrown a good part of the cargo overboard—precious sacks of grain intended for the citizens of Rome. Now they began to throw overboard even the tackle, and the costliest part of the cargo, the delicate pottery, the bronze vases, the phials containing Egyptian balsams. But the storm held on, and thus day after day passed, till the count was lost; for in effect it was one long black night, and one long, furious struggle with the wild sea beast. Ashen blue mists swirled about the ship, as if to contain it within the circle of death and despair. The waters, ice-cold, flung themselves with a metallic ringing against the walls, hammered at the deck, lifted the whole ship, thrust it down again into the depths. The sailors clung with teeth and nails to the sides of the ship, to the masts. Passengers and beasts were hurled from side to side of the hold; they rolled about among pails, bundles of rope, sacks, vessels. From below came up the roaring of the imprisoned beasts, mingled with the yells of the condemned criminals.

Then, for a moment, the ship found herself in the midst of a treacherous and suspended calm. It was as though the waves, defeated in their purpose, were in sinister consultation. The sea was flat, but it seemed to be sinking to a lower level, the ship with it. Then the prow began to rise, higher and still higher, and the ship began to spin. Suddenly the thick mist broke apart, and a vast wall, green like jade, frozen, suspended, appeared on one side. To the unspeakable horror of the passengers, the ship seemed to be driving straight for the green wall. The prow rose one or two degrees further, it cut into the wall, but near the summit, and a thousand torrents descended on the deck. The ship's timbers groaned from end to end; but they held. And scarcely had the first wall been pierced than a second appeared behind it.

Thus day succeeded day. The air in the cabins was heavy with a thick, salty odor. The travelers, unceasingly seasick, were choked with their own vomit, and could not touch food. Here, in the belly of the wild seabeast, all were alike, captives and captors, slaves and freedmen. Their bodies were flung together from wall to wall of the ship, intermingled with vessels and ropes. And they were united in one frantic desire—to escape from this interminable horror, either through rescue or through death. Their own bodies had become repulsive to them, and they were filled with revulsion at the sight of each other, at the smell of each other's unwashed and befouled flesh, and the contact with each other's limbs. They were exhausted, too exhausted to care about living. They no longer called on their gods. The captain was without authority, and the sailors were on the lookout for land; the moment they saw it they intended to fling themselves into the water. The soldiers clung together in corners, conferring, even in that condition, whether, if the ship threatened to break apart, they should not first plunge their broadswords into the prisoners, so as to be freed from the responsibility for them. But the prisoners knew what was afoot. They too were consulting with each other, more by steely glances than by words. One thought was in all of them: they were weary of the long waiting for death; if it had to come, it were well that it came swiftly. And in the midst of this spirit of despair, hatred, and murder, one man alone had retained his self-control —the apostle.

No. He had not been saved from the judgment of the High Priest in order to be swallowed by the sea. Moreover, he had been shipwrecked three times, and three times he had been saved. Not only would he be saved this fourth time, but all his fellow passengers would be saved, for his sake. This he had seen in a vision, which had again assured him that he would reach Rome and be judged before the Caesar.

In the condition which had descended on sailors, slaves, passengers, and soldiers, the one who had remained calm became the natural leader. He was set apart—they could observe it, even in their lethargy and despair—by his bearing, his self-assurance, and his faith. And when the moment came, he passed through the ship, saying to one group after another:

"Fear not, not one of you shall be lost."

And to Julius and the ship's captain he said: "Had you but hearkened to me when I warned you against leaving Crete, this would not have come upon you. But I have been assured that only the ship shall be harmed, but no man's life shall be lost!"

Who was it that spoke thus, the captain or one of the prisoners? It was one who was being led to Rome for trial! The centurion Julius and the captain stared at Paul in a daze. Down below, in the bowels of the ship, among the chained prisoners, the word passed that the man of wonders, who had spoken to them of salvation, had received word from God that no life should be lost on the ship. An angel had brought him the word. And there were some that believed, there were others too far gone in despair to believe—yet all waited for a miracle.

For fourteen days the ship had ridden the storm; and when the fifteenth was beginning, shortly before dawn, they felt the ship riding more evenly. The swell did not seem to come from the lowest depths of the sea, but was rather a surface agitation. Were they drawing near to land? The helmsman dropped the lead, and by the light of a lantern read the marks on the rope: twenty fathoms. Yes, they were not far from the shore. A little later—the dawn was still delaying—they dropped the lead again: fifteen fathoms. Now they knew not only that they were in the vicinity of the land, but that they were moving toward it. But what part of the island were they approaching? There were beaches, there were cliffs, there were savage rocks scattered under the surface of the water at certain points on the Cretan shore. The sea was still heavy enough to dash the ship against a submerged or half-submerged needle of rock, and crack it like an eggshell. Would it not be better to drop the anchors and wait till daylight? But when the captain gave the order, the sailors mutinied and ignored him. Instead of lifting the anchors, they made secretly for the rescue boat, and began to launch it. Paul, who was standing by, knew that the sailors had long ago made up their minds to abandon the ship at the first sign of land. He found the centurion Julius and advised him of what was afoot.

"They would leave the sinking ship! Do not let them!"

The soldiers rushed over and cut the davit ropes, so that the boat could not be lowered into the sea. They also surrounded the sailors.

Now the dawn began to break—a gray light stealing through the same mists as had engulfed them for two whole weeks. But Paul was not dismayed:

"We shall surely be saved," he announced, with infectious faith. "Be of good heart, take some food, and strengthen yourselves for the last effort."

He himself set the example. He took a piece of bread, made the benediction, and praised God loudly, "for that Thou hast saved us from the rage of the sea." And as the people assembled round him, amazed, he assured them again that not a hair of their heads would be touched.

"And now," he said, "let us throw overboard whatever superfluous weight we carry!"

The order was obeyed. Sailors and passengers spread through the ship and brought up on deck whatever of cargo, tackle, and vessels there was still aboard. The ship was stripped.

But the mist still hung like a heavy curtain on every side, veiling sky and sea. Very slowly it dissolved, but only in part. They beheld themselves not far from the entrance to a natural basin. The captain issued a command to unfurl the mainsails. Perhaps the ship would be driven by the wind into the harbor. The anchor ropes were cut, the ship was abandoned to the wind—for it was impossible to steer.

And the wind did begin to carry the groaning vessel toward the harbor entrance. Bursts of water washed over the deck, but the ship seemed to hold her course naturally for a time. Then an underswell turned her prow, and suddenly they felt the keel scraping on a sandy bottom. The stern swung right and left, battered by waves, while the forecastle gyrated in the grip of the sands. At last that which they had feared happened. With a fierce cracking of timber the ship began to break in the middle. From the upper deck sailors and passengers began to leap into the shallow water under the prow. What was to be done with the prisoners? A dreadful yelling came up from the holds, and the word passed rapidly among the soldiers that it would be necessary to kill every prisoner, lest any escape and remain at large. And what about Paul—Paul, who was behaving like an officer rather than a prisoner? Were they not responsible for him too? What if he sprang into the sea and escaped with the others? For an instant the centurion Julius hesitated. But it was unthinkable to him that any harm should be done to Paul. Julius had not been converted to the faith, and yet he believed that everything foretold by the apostle would come to pass.

"Open the cabins!" he ordered. "Let the men out! Let them take to the water, and those that cannot swim shall hold on to planks."

There was a wild scrambling up from the hold, and down the rope ladders hanging over the ship's sides. Some carried planks; others, trusting to their strength as swimmers, went down naked into the sea. In a few moments the waters were filled with bobbing figures. The swell lifted them, let them down, and carried them gradually shoreward. One by one the men were thrown on the sandy beach of the island of Melita.

They lay there, exhausted, and in the minds of all of them there was a bewilderment with regard to this fantastic man, Paul. Who was he, what was he? A good spirit or an evil spirit? Some thought of him as a prophet of good things, others beheld in him a sinister magician, to be dreaded. And later in the morning, when the islanders were attracted to the shipwreck, the bewilderment of the rescued passed to the natives. Like all primitive peoples they were suspicious of strangers, superstitious, equally ready to slay or to rescue. But Paul paid no attention to the curious and glowering looks which were cast at him. He ordered a fire to be lit, so that the sailors and passengers might dry themselves. He gathered fallen twigs and branches of the cypress trees rooted near the shore. And suddenly there rose a cry: on the apostle's hand hung a viper! There was the sign! The man was a murderer! No doubt of it! For it was accepted from of old among the islanders that when a murderer fled from justice, he was pursued by a snake, which never failed to catch up with him:

"A murderer!"

"An evil spirit!"

"Beware of him!"

Paul remained calm. He watched the snake as it wrapped itself on his arm. With his free hand he seized the viper by the head, holding it clear from his flesh. The thick coils tautened, then began to unwind, and with a swift gesture Paul flung the reptile into the fire.

A shout went up.

"No! Not an evil spirit! A good spirit! One sent to us from heaven!"

And the islanders crowded about him, open-mouthed with admiration. They implored him to come to their huts, to heal the sick. Before long word of him spread inland and came to the ears of the authorities. It was told of him that he had rescued a ship-load of men. The story of the snake was repeated everywhere. The governor of the island, having a sick father, sent for Paul, and Paul healed the old man. So for three months Paul remained on the island, treated more like a divinity than a human being.

*   *   *

The winter passed, and a mild and early spring began to breathe over land and sea. Ships sailed by the island of Melita, and one of them

572

dropped anchor in the port. On its prow were carved the two twin figures of Castor and Pollux, and it was on the way from Salonika to
Rome. The centurion put his prisoners on board, among them the apostle. Now the passage was smooth. They sailed over the short distance
between Melita and Sicily. In Syracuse they rested for three days, then
made their way through the narrow straits between Rhegium and Mes-
sina, into the southern end of the Tyrrhenean sea, and the steady wind
carried them to Puteoli, the port of Rome, by Naples.

In Puteoli there was a large Jewish community. The representatives of the Alexandrian grain dealers had their offices and warehouses
there; and in the midst of the community there was a little congregation
of Messianists. It was they who had helped Phebe to carry the apostle's
letter to the Romans. Soon the word spread among them that the apostle
himself was in their midst, in chains, on his way to be tried before the
Caesar; and a delegation came down to the boat, to greet him. The
centurion Julius was by now so accustomed to the unexpected where
Paul was concerned, that he was not surprised at this incident. A seven-
day sojourn in Puteoli was necessary, so that both soldiers and prisoners
might rest and arrive in good condition in Rome. Julius permitted Paul
to go down into the city, in the company of a legionary and to spend the
seven days among his friends. When the week was over, Paul said farewell to them, promising to return, a free man.

Julius assembled his prisoners, and the long convoy set out on foot
for Rome, a distance of three days. On the third day they came to the
Via Appia, which ran from Brundisium all the way to the capital. Long
before they set foot in Rome they felt the breath of its greatness upon
them. The road broadened, villas sprang up on either side. A mile out
of Rome's boundaries they paused at a way-station. There the prisoners
were fed and were given water to wash their hands and feet. They
passed the night in the way-station, and when morning broke they resumed the march. Paul, chained to Julius, marched with him at the head
of the procession. Lukas and Aristarchus, who were free, walked behind
Paul, carrying his baggage. The Via Appia, at this point, was set with
monuments and mausoleums. Carriages passed in both directions. Finally they came to the Appian Forum, and here a small delegation
awaited Paul. In the midst of it he recognized Priscilla, who stood with
arms outstretched to him.

He had come at last into the Eternal City! At the Inn of the

Three Taverns the elders of the community, under the leadership of Junius and Andronicus, were waiting for him.

*   *   *

It was early spring when the centurion Julius delivered the apostle at his destination. At that time of the year a damp mist rose from the swampy fields on either side of the Appian Way, south of Rome; and the mists of the marshlands mingled with the mists which rose from the Tiber.

Through the milky whiteness which lay on the city shone the palaces and columns crowning the hills of Rome. Paul, in the company of his friends, went with the procession of prisoners and soldiers as far as the Porta Capena. A curious sight he was in the midst of his loving and enthusiastic followers. Beards and tongues wagged, eyes shone, hands gesticulated. From moment to moment Paul's suite grew larger as men and women came out to join it. More than one Roman patrician, reclining in the litter which his slaves carried down the Appian Way, looked out at the spectacle of a Jewish prisoner accorded this strange reception at the gates of the city of the Caesars. They could not have helped thinking: "It seems that the conquered Jews have come hither to conquer their conquerors!" And they were not wrong.

574

PART THREE

Chapter One

OUT OF STRENGTH COMETH
FORTH SWEETNESS

WHEN the centurion Julius had relinquished his prisoners to the local guards, he strode off to the thermal baths of his barracks.

There was nothing to which a Roman soldier, returning from a long journey, or from a distant frontier, looked forward to more eagerly than to scalding and steaming his body in the splendidly appointed baths which Agrippa had constructed on the Campus Martius, near the Pantheon. There were other baths of course; emperors and nobles had strewn such institutions about the city, for next to bread and circuses the Roman populace loved most its steam baths. The rich had their private thermal chambers; the poor received a regular distribution of the metal checks or tickets which admitted them to the public baths. There were similar institutions even for slaves. The Praetorium had its own great building for the guards and overseers and soldiers about the Caesar. A visit to the baths meant, for the Roman, spending the best part of the day there. These were not simply bath houses. There were hot and cold basins, there were steam rooms, there were rubbing rooms —a bronze currycomb was used by the attendant, to set the blood in circulation—and there were also games rooms and dining rooms where the bathers assembled to eat, drink, play, and gossip.

After Julius had had his body thoroughly steamed, rubbed, and anointed, he went to lie down on a couch. Nearby lay a number of legionaries, members of the Praetorian guard. They were talking, when Julius came in, of the strange lot of prisoners which Felix had collected in Judaea and which had just been delivered to the city.

"By Jupiter!" said one. "I have heard that these men will touch no food save the nuts and figs which they have brought with them from Judaea. They will taste neither our bread, nor our wine, nor our meat. They spend all their time singing or muttering prayers to their gods. I have heard also that they are nearly all priests from the Temple of Jerusalem."

The speaker was Eubulus, a broad-boned, mighty figure of a man, a Macedonian, and a member of the Palace Guard.

"But the Jews are a queer people," interjected a Galatian legionary. "It is said they worship a god which no man has ever seen. I've had something to do with such prisoners. They've kept me awake whole nights. They do nothing but bawl hymns, and even the lash does not stop them. One would think they weren't prisoners of the Caesar, here in Rome, but free worshipers in their own Temple, at home in Jerusalem. They don't seem to be aware of our presence."

"I have heard that they built their God a Temple of pure gold in Jerusalem, and that he forbade them to put his image into it."

"Aye, and not that alone. They will not even let anyone carry the image of the Caesar across the threshold. I was in a detachment detailed to bring the statue of the Caesar to them. They threw themselves down in our path and would have let themselves be slaughtered to a man rather than let us pass. Many of them were, in fact, slaughtered. And when Petronius saw that he would have to kill off the entire people, he gave it up." This came from old Gabelus, who had served in Judaea under Petronius.

"And what reward do they get from their God for their fidelity? Are they rich? Are they powerful?" asked someone of Gabelus.

"They're the poorest of the poor. They're the slaves of their God, and He treats them like slaves. They're the weakest of the weak, trodden underfoot by everyone. I have never known a more feeble, a more helpless people," answered Gabelus. "Everyone spits upon them. Hast thou never seen the burlesques of them by our actors in the circus?"

"Why, then, do they cling to this God of theirs?" asked someone.

"It appears," said Julius, "that the full reward for their devotion will be given them in another world. This world is nothing to them. Their passage through it is only a trial of long suffering, hunger, and humiliation, even unto death, so that they may be with their God in heaven in a second life."

"Ha, who art thou, brother, that thou knowest so well the mysteries of the Jews?" asked Gabelus.

"I was stationed in Judaea. I have just returned thence with a batch of prisoners. My name is Julius."

"What? Of the Augustan Legion?" cried Gabelus, enthusiastically. "I knew thee not, brother. And thou art just returned?"

"This very day. And among my prisoners was a man of great importance, Paul by name."

"Paul? Paul?" asked Eubulus. "Methinks I have heard of him. In my native town of Philippi many people have converted to the faith of the Jews. And it is true; they sacrifice the life of this world for the sake of the life which awaits them when they have been ferried over to the other world."

"If thou wouldst know more about it," said Julius, "speak to the man I delivered to Caesar today. He is a most marvelous man, for he has filled my mind with thoughts of his God."

"Is he too a Priest in the Temple of Jerusalem?"

"That I know not. But he is of the Jewish people, even as their Priests are," answered Julius.

"Is it true that he saved your men from shipwreck?" asked someone, curiously. "I have spoken with one of thy soldiers, and that is his report."

"It is true. Yet I know not who the man is. There is a demon or spirit in him, that's sure, so that he is in communion with the gods. He foretold: 'Only the ship shall be lost, but not a hair of your heads shall be touched.' And thus the thing fell out, too. We had all given up hope in the storm; he alone remained calm. I know not what would have happened to us but for him. And it was his God, as he himself says—or it may have been the gods—that saved us all through him. Of that much I am certain."

"But that is nothing!" added Julius. "You should hear him talk of his God. Nay, more, you should see him perform miracles with the power of his God. I myself saw him heal a mortally sick man with nothing more than a look. But did I not tell you, there is a demon in him? Beware of him, if your turn should come to be his guard. I saw him do something more. I saw him take in one hand a viper that had wound itself round the other arm, tear it loose and throw it into the fire."

"Ho-ho, a magician, then!"

"I know not what he is, I tell thee. I have heard it said that he draws his strength from his God, or from gods. They have let their power flow into him."

"And wherefore is he here? What crimes has he committed?"

"It is a matter of the interpretation of their faith. The King of

579

the Jews, Agrippa, who is himself a Jew, heard the man plead his cause, and declared that the man had committed no crime. And he would have set him free but that he had appealed to Caesar. For the man is a Roman citizen."

"A Roman citizen!" exclaimed several of the legionaries, in astonishment."

"A Roman citizen, by inheritance from his fathers. His confinement in Caesarea was honorable. Festus gave him many liberties, and before we sailed I was ordered to be considerate of the man. Let me say, moreover, that he was an honest prisoner. He behaved loyally. In all the time that I have guarded him he has given me no trouble," said Julius.

* * *

That evening Paul returned with his escort to the prison precincts. There he was turned over to young, tall, broad-shouldered Eubulus of the Ninth Legion. Eubulus had just returned with Suetonius from the expedition which had been sent to repress the uprising in Britain. The cohort to which Eubulus was attached had distinguished itself in the campaign, and as a reward had been transferred by Burrus to the Praetorian Guard, which was stationed not far from the Caesar's palace.

Paul was exhausted after the long and perilous journey. The years were telling on him; long homelessness had sapped his strength; and even his endurance was no longer proof against the excitements of his mission. Eubulus did not insist on chaining himself to Paul; he had been impressed by the report of Paul's former guard, the centurion Julius. Paul was now alone in his cell; here, in Rome, his companions of the journey were not admitted to him; but they did not go far. They walked back and forth outside the walls of the Praetorium.

For the first day of his imprisonment Paul ate nothing, since the food offered him was unclean. He was also too exhausted to pay much attention to his new guard. He slept through the first and second nights, and when he awoke on the second morning he observed with astonishment that his hand was not chained to the hand of a keeper. He was not even chained to the wall. A legionary sat in another corner of the cell, his massive head sunk in meditation.

"Friend," asked Paul, "art thou my guard?"

"Yes, prisoner."

"What is thy name, legionary?"

"Eubulus."

"Eubulus. It is a fine name. Dost thou speak the Greek tongue?"

"I have brought the Greek tongue with me from the city of my birth. It is a Roman colony, but Greek in origin."

"Which is the city of thy birth, my friend?"

"Philippi, in Macedonia."

"Philippi, in Macedonia!" exclaimed Paul, pleased. "It is a fine city, and a famous one. Knowest thou Lydia, the dealer in purples?"

"Who knows her not? Though I have been long absent from Philippi—I have fought in Gaul, and I have also fought in Britain under Suetonius—I still remember Lydia. She had a good name among us when I was a boy in Philippi."

"She is my sister," said Paul.

"Thy sister!" cried the legionary, astounded. "Wert thou born in Philippi?"

"Nay, I am a Jew of Tarshish, in Cilicia. Yet Lydia is my sister. For we who believe in the one living God are bound, brother-and-sister fashion, in the faith, through the savior whom God sent for all of us—the savior, Yeshua the Messiah, from whom all of us have our life."

"What meanest thou, then?" asked Eubulus. "Thou hast thy life from thy father and mother, as I have my life from mine."

"Thou speakest of our earthly life. In our heavenly life we have neither father nor mother, nor sister nor brother; but all those that believe in the Messiah are of one family—brothers and sisters. For he has given us the heavenly life and has begotten us in the faith. And each one of us lives in the blood which he offered for us."

"Who was he of whom thou speakest?"

"He *was* not, he *is*. He is here with us. Though thou seest him not, he is within thee. Thou art not of my faith, yet thou art already no stranger to me. Thy goodness makes thee my brother."

"Thou wilt tell me more of this later. Meanwhile, I see that thou hast left there thy food untouched. I know that, since thou art of the Jews, thou eatest not the bread prepared by those of another faith. We have here, in the Praetorium, three priests of thy faith. I will have a portion of their fruit sent to thee."

"I eat not the bread of strangers," admitted Paul, "but I share the bread I have with my brother. And that which is pure for my brother

581

is pure for me, too. For all is pure that comes from the pure. Come, brother Eubulus, we will break our fast together."

Paul sat down next to his keeper, and they divided between them the bread and olives and water mixed with sour wine. While they were eating Eubulus said:

"There is a friend of mine here among the legionaries, an old soldier, Gabelus by name. He was stationed in the land of the Jews from the days of Caligula on. He told me that the Jews would not admit the image of the Caesar into their Temple and would not worship him as a god."

"To Caesar we render the things that are Caesar's, and to God the things that are God's. God alone is divine, and Him alone we worship. Caesar we serve."

Eubulus was silent, meditating on the distinction. After a while he said:

"Hear me, stranger. I have been told that thou art an intimate of the gods, and I would have thee do something for me. I had a friend, Aurusus Sevantus by name, an old soldier. He was as a father to me. We were together in Britain, in the time of Claudius. There was a battle, and the Britons surrounded us and rained spears on us. Sevantus and I took refuge in a thicket. I was wounded by a spear. Sevantus drew the iron out of my flesh, and bound up my wound. There came a second attack, and Sevantus and I stood back to back, holding our shields before us. Then, as the foe gathered to one side, Sevantus placed himself in front of me, and a spear passed through his breast, and he fell, crying out the name of Caesar. I would have given my life for him; but when the retreat sounded he was dead, and I left him there, in his blood. Canst thou not pray to thy God that he take Aurusus Sevantus to him in heaven, together with the believers? I have heard that thou art a pious man, and held in great regard by thy God. I am told that He appears to thee in person, and commands thee, as an officer commands a soldier. Pray to him for my friend Aurusus Sevantus."

"O, thou good Eubulus! Thou hast already prayed to my God the best of all prayers, the prayer of devotion and friendship. I know that my God, who sees the secret thoughts of all men, has heard thy prayer, even before thou didst utter it."

"What? He listened to me, a stranger?"

"Because of thy love thou art not a stranger to my God. Thou art as close to Him as I am. For all of us are of one blood in His sight."

Eubulus was confused. The words of the apostle conveyed nothing to him. He could not understand a faith which extended to strangers and made them brothers of the believers. He asked:

"And those that know not each other are also brothers and sisters?"

"Whoever a man be, of my flesh and blood or not, known to me or not, and wherever he be, if he believe in Yeshua the Messiah he is bound to me in God by the bond of brotherhood."

"Even though thou be a free man and he a slave?" persisted Eubulus.

"Among us that believe in our lord, there are no free men and no slaves, for we are all free in God. We belong to one another."

"No, no, these things are not to be understood," said Eubulus, bewildered. "I hear for the first time in my life that slave and free man are together as brothers. Wouldst thou have me believe that I, a soldier of the Ninth Legion, am the brother of the wild, barbarous, fiery-haired Britons who rebelled against Rome, and whom we have brought captive here, to Rome, to become beasts of burden? Such a man is my brother? Or the German, or the black African slave? Among us only Romans are brothers—for they worship the same Caesar and the same gods."

"But is not the wild, barbarous red-haired Briton kneaded of the same flesh as thou? When thy spear was plunged into his flesh, did he not bleed even as thou dost? When thou didst take away from him his wife and children, didst thou not see pain written on his face? The wild Briton, the German, the African, are as thou art now, ignorant in the knowledge of God. But bring them this knowledge, that one God made all of us and that God sent His savior on earth to redeem us all through his suffering—and in that instant they become our brothers in the faith."

Eubulus shook his head.

"Thou sayest, then, that all who believe in God become members of one family, brothers and sisters, though they are not of one father and mother, yes, even though they be of different races, born in different lands?"

"It is so, my son."

"Hear me then. I have friends here, old Gabelus, of whom I spoke, and Lucius and Sadonius. I would bring them to thee, and have thee

583

speak with them as thou hast spoken with me, so that we may all become brothers in thy God. Wilt thou do this?"

"Bring them to me this evening, bring them and bring others of thy comrades."

Eubulus was strangely moved. He did not know what to answer now. After a while he said.

"What wouldst thou have me do for thee?"

"Thou hast already done for me the greatest thing that one brother can do for another. The Lord has comforted me in thee. But if thou desirest to do me a service, hear me. Outside the gates of the Praetorium there are friends of mine, walking back and forth. Thou wilt know them easily. One of them is a short man, with a yellow beard, and big eyes. They await word from me. Say to them: 'Out of strength cometh forth sweetness, and out of the mouth of the lion the voice of God.'"

That night Eubulus brought his friends into Paul's cell. These were comrades stationed like him in the Praetorium. The cohorts which had been assigned to the Imperial Guard were stationed in the fortified Praetorian Camp, by the city wall, and they took turns in serving as Palace guards. Gabelus, Lucius, and Sadonius had long records as soldiers; they had campaigned in many lands, and borne themselves valiantly. Service in the Praetorian Guard was their reward. By the weak light of the oil lamp in his cell Paul was able to read the faces of the men. That of Gabelus was earnest; his cropped hair stood up like bristles; his beard was gray; his back and neck and shoulders were scarred. His eyes were brown. Lucius, much younger than he, was not less earnest, but his blue eyes were fresh and lively, and his lips were sensitive. Sadonius, who held himself more in the shadow, seemed to be a silent, thoughtful man.

Paul first asked each man where he came from. He knew all the provinces and cities they mentioned. "Ah—the hill country of Phrygia!" he exclaimed. "How often I have climbed over it! And the dark, cool waters of Galatia! I know them well!" Thus he praised the places of their birth. And he praised, too, their military records. He praised their faithfulness, their courage, and their devotion to the Caesar. "Our lord, too, when he was in the flesh, said: 'Render unto Caesar the things that are Caesar's.'" And he assured them that there was a reward for faithfulness. "But the Caesar is not a god. He is a man, even as we are men. There is but one God in heaven, and first He made a covenant with the

584

Jewish people. Then He had compassion on all men, and he sent His son down in the likeness of a man and through him made a covenant with all men." Then he told them of Yeshua the Messiah, how he had lived on earth and taught men to live in truth and honesty, to love one another, and to help each other in the hour of need. All men, said the apostle, were soldiers of the Messiah. "We are comrades, and we must share our bread with each other. We must not bear hatred against each other. We must forgive even our enemies that have sinned against us, for they know not what they do, and we must pray to God to turn their hearts to goodness. And the Messiah, in his earthly life, set an example for all of us. For though he, the Messiah, was the Son of God and had the power in his hands, he let himself be bound like a sheep, and he died in torment on the cross in order that we might be purified through his suffering. And Yeshua arose from the dead. He showed himself to his disciples. Hundreds saw him and heard him. He showed himself to me, too, and he sent me to the world to bring his tidings to it. This Yeshua, who is the redeemer, will come down from heaven in the near future, and he will sit on the throne to judge all men. The dead too will awaken, for they that believe in him are not dead in truth, but live in Yeshua and are with him in heaven. And then will begin the life of righteousness on earth. Until then our life is as nothing. It is as a struggle between wild beasts. The stronger devours the weaker, and men are sunk in sin. But those that believe in Yeshua, and live as he lived, have already begun the reign of righteousness on earth. To them nothing can happen, since for them death is but as a birth into the eternal life which the Messiah will bring upon all the earth when he returns. Meanwhile they are with him in the Kingdom of Heaven, and this is their reward for their faithfulness to him. Therefore it matters not what is done to them. They are prepared daily to die for the Messiah, for their life in the Messiah begins with their death."

The soldiers listened in silence. Gabelus was not wholly a stranger to these thoughts. For a long time something had been at work in him, undermining the foundations on which his whole life had been built—Caesar and the gods. Since the day when he had taken his oath to the Emperor-god, he had been a faithful servant. There was no stain on his record as a soldier. He had submitted proudly and readily to the disciplines and hardships of his calling—the endless marches, the climbing of mountains, the wading through swamps, the struggles with men and beasts. The history of his faithfulness was inscribed in scars on every part of his body. And how many campaigns he had known! He had helped to put down rebellions among the Gauls, among the tribes of Germany. He had fought near the mouths of the Rhine; he had crossed the narrow waters to Britain and had faced death among the mists and forests of that island. Yes, Caesar was divine, and he had worshiped him always, in piety and awe. To whatever land he had come, he had not failed to bring offering. Caesar was god, Rome the government, and to these he had given his life. When his time would come, Charon would find in his mouth the coin placed there to pay his fare across the Styx to the cypress-covered Elysian fields; and there the old soldier would meet his Emperor, Claudius, and would enter his service once more. But now—now—the question troubled him—was Claudius indeed a god, and was he really in the Elysian fields? What if Claudius were a man, and an evil man, and was in Tartarus, the abode of the accursed? He had been troubled before. In the days of his service in Judaea, when he had witnessed the obstinate devotion of the Jews, their refusal to admit the image of the Caesar to their temple, his faith had been tinged with doubt. For, was it possible that Gaius Caligula had been a god? Had he not been a man, and a disgrace to mankind? The Jews alone had declined to accept the mad Caligula as a divinity. Thus it was now, too, with regard to the new Emperor, Nero. Nero, too, would be proclaimed a god after his death, as Claudius and Augustus had been proclaimed before him. With what joy and hope he, Gabelus, had helped raise Nero to the purple after the death of Claudius. But now it was known that Nero had had Claudius poisoned; and afterwards he had killed his own mother, the daughter of the beloved general, Germanicus. The whole Praetorium had shuddered when they heard of this last incredible crime. But that was only a beginning! One faithful general after another had been executed. The gentle Octavia, of the noble line of Augustus, had been rejected by Nero, who took to his side a slave woman, and after her a vicious harlot. With what horror Gabelus had learned of the death of Octavia, whom all Rome had worshiped. And now there was not a Roman citizen who could be certain that he was not on the black list. A Caesar whose pastime it was to disguise himself nights like a robber captain, and lead out a band of ruffians to attack his own citizens! A Caesar who was not ashamed to wrestle with gladiators in the arena! A Caesar who surrounded himself with flutists and guitarists, and himself declaimed poetry—his own!—in the palaces and the circuses, like a cheap actor! What had become of the reign of law and order which had been the pride of Rome? Where was the justice and honesty for which he, Gabelus, had been at all times ready to give up his life? And how much of divinity was there in a Caesar who was known as a criminal, a beast, a murderer, a matricide? Suppose this Jew in the cell was speaking the simple truth? Suppose God alone was divine and of the Kingdom of Heaven which the new Caesar, the Messiah, the Son of God, would institute was the real kingdom? For such a Caesar, immortal and divine, for such a kingdom, eternal and just, a man could give his life. Only such a Caesar could reward the soldier for his faithful service with a second life beyond the Styx. Were it not better to die for him than for the Roman Caesar? Ah, what a pity that he had come to this notion so late in life, when he had spent his best for the old Caesar, and so little was left for the new. And as he murmured this thought aloud, he heard the apostle answer: "It is never too late to come to him. He was with thee before thou knewest him. And before thou knewest his name he had shed his blood for thee, and had borne the cross for thee, that thou mightest be saved."

Glory to the new Caesar, thought the old soldier, to Yeshua the Messiah! I swear by my honor as a soldier that from this day on I will be faithful to him, live for him and die for him! For he alone is worthy of the inheritance of the Caesars on earth.

And as old Gabelus was moved to these thoughts, he had, unknown to him, the company of his friends. So, when morning came to Paul's dark cell, the apostle had with him four of the Caesar's soldiers who had sworn eternal faith to the Caesar of heaven and earth, Yeshua the Messiah.

Chapter Two

I

ROME

IT IS easier for a man to die for his principles than to live according to them. In this respect Seneca, the great Stoic philosopher, was not better than every other man. His philosophic doctrines, which he taught in his many letters to his friends, were doctrines of discipline, modesty, continence, and contentment; but his life was one of unrestrained luxury.

But, living in Rome under Nero, the great Seneca, reclining in his ivory bed with the gilded corners, by the side of his young and lovely wife Paulina, knew no rest; and when he awoke in the morning out of his fitful sleep, it was invariably with a headache. Twice a day he submitted his aging, swollen body to the ministrations of masseurs, under the direction of his physician. The strong and skillful fingers of the masseurs, rubbing the costly Oriental oils into the philosopher's flesh, awoke in it a fleeting sensation of youth. It was not the fear of death which robbed him of his sleep—not even after Nero had fallen completely under the influence of the cruel and cunning Tigellinus and of the dissolute Sabina Poppea. According to his own Stoic philosophy death was, for Seneca, but the beginning of a new and purified life. But this life of his, which he was prepared to yield up calmly at any moment, and which was filled with abstract principles, was utterly devoid of personal values. He was indeed certain that the spiritual part of him, his doctrine of the moral life, which he taught so feverishly in his letters, was assured of a great future, like the spiritual part of any other philosopher; but his personal life was bounded by the confines of this world. It could not be said of Seneca that in his glorification of the abstract he had given no thought to his personal life. On the contrary, while he consistently denied the significance of this wretched, earthly episode which is the life of man, he had devoted himself with much skill and success to the accumulation of wealth, almost as if he expected to live forever. Only now, when he stood on the brink of the grave, did Seneca experience in the emotions what he had hitherto proclaimed in principle, namely, how foolish and idle it was to accumulate a fortune —like this of his which was scattered through the length and breadth of the Empire, estates, vast farms, palaces, costly furniture, art masterpieces, and gold which he had frivolously accepted from the hand of his pupil, Nero. But he had had to wait until he expected momently the visit of the centurion who should bring him the Imperial decree of death; he had had to wait until his life was as insecure as that of other Roman nobles and citizens, before he could respond in his heart to what had been dictated by his head when he wrote to a friend: "Not the count

588

of the days builds a long life, but their use in making a man his own master." In his bed of ivory and gold he was the slave of a tyrant whom he himself had been charged with educating. What, then, was the whole sense of his life? Death was liberation from every form of slavery. And he was not afraid of death: it was not the thought of death that took the sleep from his eyelids. It was the uncertainty of life which kept his soul in constant turmoil.

The granaries on his domain were full to bursting, his cellars were stocked with the choicest wines. Daily his slaves brought him from the estates in the vicinity of Rome fresh greens, ripe fruits, plump hens and pheasants, well-fed suckling pigs and tender lambs; they brought him exotic fish bred in his private nurseries. But all that Seneca ate was— fruit and vegetables; and he drank nothing but water, which he had drawn from the well. He knew that his doom was sealed. But he could not tell what the manner of his death would be. It might very well be that he would receive the message through one of the slaves of his own household—as many another had done before him. But who could foretell the time and the method which the tyrant would choose?

There came a certain night when Seneca had special reason to await the messenger of death. He had attended a banquet in the Imperial palace that day, and in the course of the meal he had offered Nero all his estates and palaces. He had also implored Caesar to liberate him from his responsibilities as Consul, to cease showering him with presents which awakened universal envy, and to permit him to retire to the country, where he might devote his remaining years to contemplation and study. Nero had turned the occasion into a theatrical performance. His smooth round face had taken on a tinge of deeper red. His watery blue eyes had overflowed. His thick, swollen neck had trembled, and his bosom had heaved in the stress of his emotions.

"Thou, Seneca," he had said, in a sickly, gentle voice, "thou didst guide my infant steps in the path of moral law and natural wisdom; thou didst induct my manhood into the ways of rulership. I ask thee, what would the world say if I sent thee away from my side? Will they not add this to the list of my cruelties? How canst thou be so unheedful of the good name of thy friend?"

Then Nero had leaned over, and had embraced the philosopher, and kissed him, and promised him many other estates. But Seneca had noted on the lips of Tigellinus the familiar, twitching grin of anticipation, and the cynical smile characteristic of him had flitted across the face of Petronius. Poppea had simply giggled, had tried to stop herself, and had failed. They knew, then, the three of them, that the decision had been taken. And it seemed to Seneca that in Nero's own fishy eyes there was a deadly glitter not unfamiliar to the philosopher. Thus the Emperor had smiled, thus he had spoken, in a voice broken by affection, thus his fleshy neck had trembled when he had taken his last farewell of his mother in the Baiae villa. And did not Seneca remember how Nero had uncovered his mother's bosom, and said, chokingly: "These are the breasts which suckled me"? Then, in all love, he had conducted his mother to the foot of the villa and handed her into the boat which was to be her hearse. It was an infallible sign with Nero; whenever he became sentimental, whenever his eyes filled with tears, he was contemplating some frightful deed, so that every exhibition of tender emotion on the part of his pupil affected Seneca by now like the stench of a dead rat.

This night, then, it would happen. Hour after hour he waited for the knock of the centurion on his door. But the night passed, and no message came. And with the morning, awakening from a fitful doze, he saw before him the hideous day. He would have to dress, he would have to put on his clothes, wrap himself becomingly in his toga, so that the folds of it should fall just so and not otherwise—just so, not too perfectly, even as the phrases he used in Nero's presence had to be skillful, but not too skillful; they had to serve as a worthy foil to the phrases of his master, but not seem to compete with them. In everything, in his bearing, in the appointments of his house, in the elegance of his banquets, he had always to lag behind the Imperial comedian. Now he would have to proceed to the palace, and become part of the hysterically flattering mob of courtiers who crowded about Nero, each seeking to outdo the other in outrageous eulogy of Nero's verses and Nero's performances on the lyre. If at least those verses of Nero's were frankly bad, and reflected some of the versifier's character! But that was the trouble. Nero's poetry, like his voice, was neither good nor bad. It was commonplace. All the gray commonplaceness of the mediocre man was concentrated in Caesar the artist. There was no foundation on which the slightest structure of individuality could be reared; his poems were like stagnant pools, the accumulation of used waters in which countless bodies had bathed. And, again like his singing, the poetry of Nero served to lull into slumber whatever remained to him of intelligence and emotion. It was an inspiration into decay.

The slaves were finished with their massaging of the philosopher's body, and as its owner looked down at it for a moment it seemed to him that it was a vessel about to be trodden under foot. A strange, unwonted protest arose in him, and he summoned to his aid, without any effect, the rules and principles of the Stoic life. But at this moment his body, the object of his solicitude, was being wrapped in soft Sidonian linens, through which the slaves stroked and caressed the tender skin. And after them slave girls entered, and anointed and perfumed the flesh. With delicate fingers they spread the Oriental balsam on his skin and worked it into the pores, so that the skin blossomed and sang. It was at such moments that he had dictated to his slave secretary his moralistic epistles to his friends. He wrote to his friend Lucius "On the Welfare of the Body and the Neglect of the Soul," warning him against preoccupation with his bodily needs, and advising him to pay more attention to the needs of his soul: "Hasten to return from the body to the soul, and discipline thyself in her day and night. . . ." And still he could not rid himself of the recurrent thought that now this body, which had received so much caressing attention, and on which he had bestowed, in spite of his philosophy, such loving care, was to have its functions suspended prematurely. It might happen this day, or the next. He had written: "The longest life is but a short moment in time; the shortest life is a perfect whole." What irked his soul was, that neither his life nor his death was in his own hands, so that he could open the door and step across the threshold at the moment of his choosing. Instead it was, like the life or death of the basest slave, at the mercy of a miserable tyrant. And all contrary to his doctrine, he reflected sharply: "What assurance have I, after all, that there is a soul which survives the body? Like any slave without will, I am but a vessel in the hands of my lord. Those privileges which we accord the intellect can be found only in the freedman; the slave, not being his own master, is not in possession of a soul of his own. That which does not exist cannot boast of a possession. There is no such thing as death for at the moment of its arrival no one is there to receive it. If this be so, then the kingdom of the soul is only the kingdom of the living—and in the midst of physical life the life of the soul ceases for the slave."

There were other heavy thoughts that came into Seneca's mind

591

when the masseurs and slave girls passed his body on to the hairdresser. The art of the hairdresser was highly respected at Caesar's court. Nero was particularly fastidious about his hair; the heavy, copper-yellow locks had to fall in certain designs on his fat neck and low forehead. And if the Caesar was fastidious about his hair, his courtiers could not be less so. In this respect Seneca was no exception. The Syrian hairdresser and his assistants did what they could to soften on Seneca's face the lines and pouches which the restless night had accentuated. And while the features were being fondled and smoothed out, while little beauty spots were being placed on them, he listened to the reports of the managers of his estates. Seneca had meditated much and thought much and written much on the virtues of poverty and the dangers of wealth—almost as much, indeed, as he had concentrated on the direction of his enormous business affairs. He lay and listened to the long reports on his granaries, his slave shepherds, his farms, his loans at interest; here and there he interjected a question: Would it not be better to sell this or that harvest, of grain or of grapes, immediately? Had they not too large a stock of produce in the granaries? And when he had completed the session with the directors, other slaves, under the eye of his majordomo, dressed him, drew the tunic of Persian silk over his body and threw over that the heavy woolen toga.

To "throw" a toga in the right manner over the body was a highly specialized task, undertaken only by experienced and skillful slaves. Properly "thrown," the toga retained its straight up and down folds throughout the day. Special slaves, "folders," were trained in this art. And it was only when the majordomo, reviewing the total effect of the hairdressing and the folding of the toga, had expressed satisfaction with the appearance of his lord, that the doorkeeper, who was chained like a dog to the corridor wall, threw open the heavy cedar doors.

* * *

Seneca's "domus" was surrounded by gardens which roused the jealousy of Nero, for they were larger, more beautiful, and better kept than even those of the Emperor. The most exotic plants had been brought from the four corners of the Empire to adorn the gardens of the philosopher's city residence. Long rows of pillars, wrought from Italian and African marble, ran parallel with the alleys of fantastic trees. There were basins set like jewels under overhanging trellises and surrounded by many-colored jasmine. Parrots, peacocks, and doves were kept in the gardens, and the grounds were adorned with innumerable statues by Greek masters—gods, goddesses, fauns, athletes, dancers, flute players, peeping out of ingeniously planted thickets. Long lines of blossoming oleander bounded by thick bushes sheltered the philosopher's residence from the noises and unpleasant odors of the streets.

At the foot of the broad flight of marble stairs before the house, the slaves already waited with the litter. Seneca disliked the ordinary litter, which he deemed fit only for women. He preferred the *sella,* a portable double seat. One place was for the mighty lord himself, the other, opposite, for his secretary, who took down his dictation or read to him. But this morning Seneca traveled alone.

No sooner had Seneca appeared before his house than there began to emerge, from between the pillars, from within the garden, men of every age, men in woolen togas, men who crawled rather than walked toward the *sella* of the mighty lord. Each sought to come as near as he could, pushing the others out of his way. With outstretched hands, with fawning smiles, with bodies bent double, they called out:

"Hail to thee, patron!"

"Hail to thee, lord!"

"My lord! Thy appearance is like that of the Capitoline Jupiter!" cried one little "client," who, cowering in the front of the throng, seemed to be crushed under the weight of his own stained and shapeless toga.

"Nay, not like Jupiter! Like Apollo!"

"Like neither, I say! Like Mars!"

And still another, who was by way of being a philosopher, cried out: "What commonplace, oft-repeated words are these that you address to our lord in stupid flattery! Is it thus that you would praise him? Leave such flatteries for those as ignorant as you. For the appearance of our lord is as that of a Plato, and none other."

Seneca turned with a sad smile to the last speaker. "And who flatters thee, Atonis? Is there anyone left to cringe on thee?"

"Aye, my lord, Atonisa, my wife, flatters me," answered the philosopher.

Seneca laughed. "True, in Rome everyone flatters and is flattered."

However the better nature in Seneca revolted from the corruption in which he saw the beginning of the end of Rome, however sharply he expressed himself in his letters against the "clients," he could not, as a Consul, dispense with the services of his claque. They were his propagandists, and he kept a large staff of them, like every other Roman politician. However, he did pay them a few sesterces more than the other patrons and was a little more generous in providing them with wool for togas—the robe of the freedman, in which alone they dared to appear before the master. But he did this more for his own honor than for any inner reason. He also was distinguished from other patrons in that he tried to pick his men among the more intelligent sort, professors without posts, obscure authors, unsuccessful dramatists and poets. With these he was compelled to mix "clients" of a more ordinary kind, so that he might be certain of reaching every level of the populace. His attitude was not without compassion, especially toward the "philosophers," for Seneca saw himself as nothing more than a "philosopher-client" of the Emperor. Carried in his chair, he thought "Clients, nothing but clients, that is what the Romans have become. As these are the clients of the 'mighty,' so we, the 'mighty,' are the clients of the one patron of Rome—the Caesar."

The procession was formed. In front were the African negro slaves, naked save for loin cloths. They carried long, silver-tipped staves, to break a path through the crowds. Behind them came the younger clients in their togas; it was their task to shout loudly: "Make way for the lord Seneca, the Consul." Between them and the older clients, who followed behind, rode Seneca. Crowding about the *sella* were Seneca's favorites and more intimate servants, his secretaries, majordomos, managers, and freedmen. The function of the older clients, who closed the procession, was to talk loudly among themselves, for all bystanders to hear, of the great merits of their patron, his services to Rome and the Empire, and his devotion to the Caesar. Some of the writers also declaimed their own verses, dedicated to the achievements of Seneca in the field of education and literature; others chanted of Seneca's great plans for the welfare of the Romans; how he would bring down the price of bread and arrange gigantic spectacles in the arena at his own expense. The whole procession was surrounded by a double row of slaves with pointed sticks and oxhide whips to keep the plebs at a respectful distance.

The wide gates of the private forum swung open, and the procession poured into the street.

Seneca's domus was situated in the fifth precinct, the quarter of the palaces called the Vicus Patricius, between the Viminale and Esquiline hills. Like all the other palaces of the patricians, this one was surrounded by narrow, dirty streets and alleys, in which every foot of ground was needed for the swarming populace. The stone houses rose five and six stories on either side, so that the lower apartments were in perpetual darkness. The inhabitants of the houses were of various levels. Patricians and plebeians were thrown together like herrings in a barrel. On the ground floors were the shops, booths, and work stalls; and since these were too small for the business transacted, the goods were displayed on the street, and fenced off, so that even the narrow passage between the houses was only partially open. Some of the ground floors were used as warehouses for grain, food, leather, and dried skins. Because of the crowding, a decree had been promulgated by Julius Caesar, and had been rigidly enforced by his successors, forbidding any wheeled vehicle from entering the streets of Rome during the day. But as against this, carts rumbled all night on the cobblestones, bringing in the daily needs of the city. From the shops came an odor of decaying meat, overlaying the odor which escaped from the openings to the Cloaca Maxima.

Immediately above the shops were the apartments of the patricians, the owners of the houses, or their most important tenants. In these apartments the rooms were fairly large, and the "windows" were covered with cloth curtains. On the window ledges, as well as on the balconies, stood vases and garlands of flowers, a perpetual danger to passersby below. With every ascent to another floor, the rooms grew smaller. The topmost floors, reached by narrow, twisted lightless stairs, were inhabited by the poorest citizens, who paid rent to the owner or chief tenant. In order to earn part of the rent, they subleased rooms, or parts of them, to lodgers. On the topmost floors large families were crowded into rooms that were nothing better than open holes. The sole furniture was the bed, on which the family slept at night and ate its meals by day. The plebs of Rome, freedmen drawn from every quarter of the Empire, were crowded into the upper floors of Rome's apartment houses. From the "windows" poured continuously the smoke of the three-legged braziers and the sour smell of unwashed linen, or of garbage and filth which the residents were too lazy to carry down and throw into the cloacae regularly. A perpetual tumult, shouting, quarreling, screaming, laughing, a confusion of voices of men and women and children, mingled here with the ringing of hammers, the grinding of millstones, the whistling of steam, the pouring of water. But for the most part the rooms were used only at night, for sleeping. During the day the inhabitants were to be found on the streets.

The naked negroes with the silver-tipped staves thrust a way through the dense crowd for the lord Seneca, towering on his *sella* above the procession. The clients, sweating in their woolen togas, shouted in rhythm:

"Make room for the lord Seneca! Room for the friend of Caesar!"

Soon the procession entered the gutter of Rome, the Suburra. This, the marketplace of the poor, was not very far from the rich homes of the Roman nobles. Here a babel of tongues, a yelling and chaffering of slaves and freedmen, went up about the movable wooden booths stocked with every imaginable variety of merchandise, dried meat, salted fish, phials of perfume, sackcloth coverings for slaves, silken Persian shawls, silver buckles—most of these articles of luxury being stolen goods— sausages which sent out a sharp tang of onion and garlic, and delicate spices. The booths of the smiths, the sandal makers, the shirt makers, the net weavers, were pushed into the street. The huge tuns of wine which the dealers had to keep in the open, for lack of space, would assuredly have been broken or emptied by the rabble, were it not for the guards who, with whips in their hands, were stationed at close intervals in the market. A strange mixture of all the races of the world, the prisoners brought to Rome by her legions from every frontier of the Empire, filled the Suburra. A red-haired Briton manacled to a black-haired Gaul dragged a load of planks across the market; blond Germans, bent double like beasts, carried a block of marble on a wooden frame. The slaves, all of whom wore about their necks the metal disc which bore the name of their owners, were in charge of freedmen. In one corner, somewhat withdrawn from the wild rush of feet, a woman of Judaea sat, her face covered with a veil of black sackcloth. Before her, in a basket, was her stock of goods—balsams and cosmetics. Not far from her a Chaldaean star-gazer offered passersby to read their horoscopes, next to him a snake-charmer blew into his flute while the heads of the snakes swayed before him in the basket. In a tiny alley a Syrian had arranged a cock-fight, and the crowd was betting. In the doorway of a restaurant a dice game was in progress, and voices were raised in

596

dispute. A drunken legionary, newly returned from the wars, was dragging a whore by the hair out of the door of an inn. And high above this sea of labor, sweat, drunkenness, and dirt floated the *sella* of the mighty Seneca.

Now the procession turned off from the gutter of the Suburra, and swung through an alley into the opulent and resplendent Via Sacra.

Here, a few steps from the Suburra, the richest shops and business houses of Rome displayed their wares for the aristocracy; gigantic pearls of the size of hazelnuts, shimmering, opalescent, and transparent as the skin of Poppea; precious stones flashing in all the colors of the rainbow; vessels of ivory, cunningly wrought, and overlaid with Corinthian bronze; shirts and tunics of Sidonian linen and Persian silk, drinking cups of the rare and costly Phoenician glass. On the Via Sacra, too, there were marketplaces for the sale of beautiful slaves, young athletes and Egyptian flute players with lithe bodies; not less expensive than these were the caged birds brought from Africa, among them parrots trained to repeat whole lines of Virgil. Very different indeed were the purchasers here. The aristocracy of Rome, and chiefly its gilded youth, strolled through the Via Sacra, accompanied always by its suites of freedmen and slaves. Here the purchases were made of rare, exotic fruits, and of flower wreaths, wines and honeys, for the nightly banquets. Fewer women were seen here than in the poor quarter. Men did most of the buying for the households. And where a woman was seen it was usually a matron carried in her litter: her face and lips painted, her hair built into a towering coif, her fingers and headdress adorned with jewels, her dress drenched with perfume; she too had her attendant suite of slaves, who brought for the outing her favorite pets, her ornamented parrots, apes, and trained wild animals.

How could Seneca fail to observe the frightful contrast between the human swamp of the Suburra and the boundless luxury of the Via Sacra lying cheek by jowl? Abysmal slavery and immeasurable self-indulgence almost in contact! But was not this physical condition symbolic of Rome's spiritual condition? Here was a government whose exact legal system was based on a supreme concept of justice, a government which had given the Pax Romana to the world; and at its head was a Caesar whose nightly pleasure it was to seek the entertainment of lust and cruelty in assaults on his own citizens! This, then, was the face of Rome: a Caesar who was a tyrant, whose chief minister was a robber, whose consort was a whore, and whose nearest kindred spirit, the "arbiter of elegance," was a pornographer.

And who was to blame? It was impossible for the philosopher to deny his own share in the moral degradation of Rome. Why had not his lofty principles enabled him at least to set an example in his own life? Was it possible that his philosophy was nothing more than a form of private intellectual entertainment, entailing no duties and obligations? But if this was true for him, the individual, was it not also true of the whole people, in respect of such a philosophy? Justice and law, the foundations of the government, were not enough to sustain a moral system. The government was, after all, only an aggregation of human efforts—and a Nero-Caesar had become the government. The justice preached by a moral system, too, was impotent to set a man's feet on the path of the moral life. Whatever the moral convictions issuing from the philosophic system, they lacked the power to impose themselves and be transformed into action—they lacked the voice of ultimate authority. "I, Seneca, am the living example thereof," he confessed. "My moral system has led to no obligation in my personal conduct. If righteousness is to be the ruling factor in men's lives, it must be grounded in the direct command of the divinity. The gods of Rome have everything, they can bestow everything upon mankind—everything save righteousness. And if the gods are to impose righteousness on mankind, they must themselves be righteous first. But the gods of Rome are not righteous. And who can give Rome a God of righteousness?"

Sunk in these meditations, the mighty Seneca was carried through the wide gates of the Praetorium, between the ranks of the German guards.

On the tablet which hung on the wall, and on which was inscribed the day's business, Seneca found, among other matters, the case of one "Paul, also known as Saul, born in Tarsus, a Roman citizen: appeal to the Caesar in connection with alleged transgression of the law of his faith, which is the faith of the Jews of Jerusalem, said law being under the protection of Rome." Appeals to the Caesar by Roman citizens were considered matters of honor by the Emperors and were taken very seriously. The Caesars Augustus, Tiberius, and Claudius had devoted much time to such cases, had attended the trials in person and had often examined the individual who had made the appeal. But Nero was not like his predecessors. Not for him the tedium of trials for the honor of

Rome. He had more important matters claiming his attention. Even at this moment, as Seneca was visiting the Praetorium, Nero was closeted in one of the chambers of his palace with a group of actors before whom he was declaiming at the top of his voice one of his thunderous poetical compositions. That night, at the banquet, he would inflict the same torment on his guests, who would compete with each other in groveling praise of the Imperial buffoon. All this Seneca knew. He therefore asked Burrus, the Commandant of the Praetorium, who was in charge of the office of the appeals, what had been done in the case of the man Paul.

Not long before, old Burrus had taken a heavy bribe from the Jews in connection with their appeal against infringement of their rights in Caesarea, but when the matter had come up before the court Burrus had used his influence for the Greeks. When Paul's case was brought to his attention Burrus had no inclination to look into it. He ordered the man retained; it was enough for him that the appellant was a Jew.

"It is only a Jew," he told Seneca. "I have much trouble with the Jews. Of late there was a delegation of the Jews of Caesarea in Rome. Doubtless this man is one of the rebels."

"But he is a Roman citizen, and has appealed to the Caesar. The man has committed no crime against the state. Festus, I see, commends him in a letter. He writes that King Agrippa, who is likewise a Jew, has looked into the case and found the man innocent. Had he not appealed to the Caesar, he would have been set at liberty. As a Roman citizen he is entitled to trial before the Caesar, and he must be treated with every consideration," said Seneca to the old general.

"Then the man must be judged by Caesar himself."

"True, Burrus, but thou knowest that if we wait until he will be brought before Caesar he may rot his life away in prison. Caesar has other matters to attend to. We, meanwhile, can make an investigation, and at least find out the nature of the accusation. And if he is not dangerous to the peace of the state, I see no reason why he should not be permitted to take up his quarters elsewhere, under guard, of course, until the case is brought up."

"I know nothing about these distinctions in crime, Seneca. Wouldst thou speak with the man?"

"I am interested in the man because he is a Roman citizen," answered Seneca. "Let him be brought to me."

PAUL BEFORE SENECA

PAUL, chained to a legionary, was led before Seneca who, having taken his place on his judgment seat, inquired briefly into the nature of the crime on which the apostle had been arrested.

"It is for the sake of the hope of Israel, which I preach, that I have been thrown in chains," answered Paul.

"The hope of Israel?" asked the Consul, frowning. "The hope of Israel? Revolt against Rome, then, and conquest of the world? Is it for this that thy countrymen have imprisoned thee?"

"Yes, conquest of the world," answered Paul, "but not through revolt against Rome. Rather through the savior and redeemer whom God has raised through the loins of Israel, to bring the world under the rule of the one living God of Israel."

"And what sort of savior and redeemer is it that God has raised? I have indeed heard that the people of Israel is persuaded that it alone worships the one living God, and that their Temple is the one spot on the earth in which the God of the universe dwells," said Seneca, with a faint smile. "But concerning this savior and redeemer whom He has sent for the benefit of the whole world I hear now for the first time. A people of fantastic conceits! Could the God of the universe find no more fitting a people from which to raise a redeemer for mankind than this barbarous Asiatic-Syrian-Palestinian horde? If at least He had chosen us Romans, or let us say the wise Greeks. . . ."

"God chose the people of Israel because the Jews alone, whose forefathers recognized the one living God, have worshiped him from of old," answered Paul.

"This too is the impudent conceit of an impudent people," said Seneca, contemptuously. "Not the Jews alone, but all of us, recognize and pray to the one living God of the universe. The gods are but agents, intermediaries between ourselves and the one God of the universe.

Paul was astounded not so much by Seneca's views as by his daring in expressing them. He cried out:

"O Seneca! How near thou hast come to salvation! But not the gods are the intermediaries between us men and the living God. Only he, the chosen Messiah, the man-God and God-man, Yeshua the Nazarene, whom God sent down upon earth in the likeness of man, is the intermediary. He alone acts between us and the one living God, his Father."

Seneca was suddenly interested, and the philosopher in him awakened. Not the gods, then, but a man-God had been appointed as the sole intermediary between man and divinity. He made a sign to the apostle to continue.

Paul knew well the name and reputation of the man before whom he was now standing; all his old longing to win over to the faith the high representatives of the Greek-thinking world started to life.

"Who and what are we, O Seneca, we, with all our wisdom and achievements? How far have these carried us? Can we, with them, break the iron ring of our earthly destiny? And for all our winged thoughts, which carry us into the highest heavens, do we not remain crawling things, subject, like every other earthly creature, to the laws of nature? How can we, with our intelligence and emotions, which are created, attain to that which we are not, the Creator? But God our Father has compassion on man. He has desired to lift him out of the chain of all other created things and to bring him nearer to Himself. Therefore He has breathed into man a soul, which is a part of man, and which awakens in him the longing for the divinity. But the soul can give us only the longing, the hunger, for divinity, even as it has given it to thee, O Seneca. The drink, the divinity, it cannot give. Therefore God took a part of himself, of the divinity, and confined it within a man. And He sent this man down upon earth, giving him all the nature of a man; and He made him pass through all the physical sufferings of a man, in order that, with his blood and tears, with his sorrow and suffering, he might bind himself to us and purify us of our earthy, beastly nature, and lift us with him. God is a portion within the Messiah. Thus we are a portion within the Messiah, too. For the Messiah partakes of both natures, and we that believe in him are thereby bound through him to the divinity; the Messiah is the cord which ties man to God; he is the channel through which the soul of God and the divinity flow to each other and mingle. The Messiah alone is the bond between man and God, and there are no gods besides."

Seneca listened attentively. He had little inclination toward the countless mystical religions which poured into Rome from the Orient—whether it were that of Egyptian Isis or Phoenician Adonis. For him they were of the same character as the star-gazing of the Chaldaeans, their snake-charming, soothsaying, magic, and the rest of those Asiatic superstitions which flowed from the Orontes into the Tiber. The enthusiasm of the Roman matrons for alien gods was for him but part of the general Roman degeneration. But this that he heard now, from the lips of the apostle, struck him as something other than Oriental mysticism; there seemed to be in it elements of clear philosophic perception. He could not deny that faith acquired a universal appeal through a medium which shared both natures, the human and divine. In his thoughts, and perhaps in these alone, Seneca was courageous and consistent. He did not shrink from the truth, whatever its source and philosophic consequences. And still he, the Roman, could not understand why God should have chosen, for the dwelling place of His spirit, the lowest of men, and that among the lowest of people, the Jews. Not even a King of the Jews—a Herod who had been brought up in the Roman court of Caesar Augustus! Instead, one who had died the death of a slave. He addressed himself to Paul:

"It is well: the God of the universe is filled with love toward man, His creature, and He would see man happy, joyous, and above all free in Him. Why then did God choose to incorporate His nature in a man who suffered and was slain? Why did He not rather choose one of the great of the earth, but made His instrument one of the lowest in the people of Israel?"

"O Seneca!" cried Paul. "Who are the great of the earth? With what measure measurest thou their greatness? Is it with the measure of man or the measure of God? Are they the great of the earth who debase the human species by the exercise of powers which chance has placed in their hands? Or are they great who by their heroic deeds, in which they pour out their blood, lift up the human species? Not in his heavenly nature alone is Yeshua the Nazarene divine; he is divine also in his human nature. The Messiah could have put away the bitter cup that was offered to his lips. He did not have to drink it for his own sake. But for all of us, and for all that will come after us, he took upon himself the death of a slave, for which thou showest such contempt. He went down to the lowest ring of hell, in order that he might be able to lift out the last of us who have been thrown into it. Not in his heavenly garb alone does the Messiah shine for us; he shines in the royal raiment which he won on earth, and stands before us as an example, bidding each of us bear his cross in love and humility and gratitude toward our Father in heaven."

But still the great philosopher could not understand. For him, as for the Greek sages, the divinity was that wisdom which he could measure and hold in his hand, a tangible possession. Wisdom was the path in the midst of chaos, the thread in the lightless labyrinth; let man but relinquish his hold on it, and he would fall into primeval confusion. Intellectual perception was the perfection of man, whether it led to the earthly or to the non-earthly. But that concerning which the apostle spoke stood higher than the intellect; it burst the bonds of the intelligence to unite with another category which claimed superiority over the intelligence. And this Seneca dreaded. Were the divine united with the intellectual perfection and harmony of a Socrates, he could accept it. It terrified him to think that the divinity united itself not with the perfection of the intellect but with the perfection of goodness. Goodness was the God of the weak, the oppressed, who had need of it; it was not the God of the man of mind, who sought the truth. And truth was accessible only to the intelligence. After a pause he answered, with a serenity which imparted to his face a suggestion of alabaster:

"Thy God has settled in the man of pain, not in the man of mind. He attained to divinity not of his own free will, which is the way of the man of mind, but under the compulsion of a destiny which had been prescribed for him in advance. And as the God of suffering, he is the God of those that suffer. He is a God for slaves. They will find in Him consolation and comfort to help them bear their fate, and inspiration to obedience to their lords. From the point of view of the state I see no objection to the spreading of such a faith among the slaves of Rome. But beware of spreading this faith among the Romans. Thou canst go."

With that Seneca rose from his seat and walked out to the *sella* which waited for him. He ordered the carriers to make haste, for the Jewish prisoner had broken in on his routine, that is, on his discipline and intelligence, and he had spent more time with him than he had intended.

On the way to the Palatine Seneca was busy with thoughts of another order. He was casting about for new words of adulation with which to greet the compositions which the Caesar would undoubtedly declaim before him. But involuntarily his mind reverted to the conversation with the man who would sooner or later appear before the Caesar. "Spiritual barrenness paralyzes the intellect, fruitful thoughts make it pregnant," he meditated. A dreadful boredom spread over his features. "I know not which death is easier, Nero's poison or his mediocre verses." He decided in favor of poison.

Later, encountering Burrus, he remembered Paul again:

"Concerning the prisoner whom thou sentest to me, Burrus—the faith he preaches is a good one for slaves. It will make them more obedient. From that point of view, it is an excellent thing for the state. But his doctrines are not such as a freedman will accept. By the way—he also distributes a second life in a world to come—it might interest thee when thy time comes." And Seneca smiled into the face of the old soldier, upon which already lay the shadow of Caesar's disfavor. "And mark this, Burrus, that second life is not for sages and philosophers; it is reserved for old soldiers like thee."

"If there is a Nero in Pluto's world, too, let the man keep his second life," muttered Burrus into Seneca's ear.

"Nay, he is not there. But thou wilt find there a certain slain slave, who is the lord of the other world. His name—wait now—I had it but a moment ago—his name is, methinks, Jesus the Christ."

"I have heard the name," answered Burrus. "I have heard soldiers in the Praetorium call upon it."

"Methinks this Jew has already been active here, and spreads his faith in bondage," said Seneca. "I fear that I was mistaken in him. It may be that he is a danger to the state." Then he added, "No, no. It is a faith that only the wretched and enslaved will accept. Never will the free Roman bow to it."

And with these words he decided Paul's fate for some time to come.

Chapter Three

DISPUTATION

THUS Paul was granted the privilege of living in private quarters, under the watch of a soldier, until such time as he would be brought to trial. These had to be in the vicinity of the barracks on the Palatine hill, since his guard was changed daily. His friends therefore rented rooms for him in an "insula," or lodging house, on the Aventine hill, on the other side of the Circus Maximus, not far from the home of Priscilla and Aquila, who, as in the past, charged themselves with the care of the apostle.

Paul's first thought, on his provisional release, was to put himself in contact with the heads of the Jewish community of Rome; he was perturbed by the thought that rumors might be circulated against him, chiefly to the effect that he intended to lodge a complaint with the Caesar against the Jews of the Holy Land. He sent Aristarchus and Timotheus to the elders of the synagogue, explaining that he could not come to them himself as long as he was a prisoner in his own home.

The elders had, indeed, heard of his arrival, and of the circumstances attending it; but most of them were unaware of his identity, and knew only that a Jew who was a Roman citizen was a prisoner in Rome. They, for their part, were anxious to discover with what the prisoner was charged and whether they could be of service to him. Many a Jewish prisoner had been brought to Rome, and it was a specially meritorious act to rescue a fellow Jew, wherever it was possible, from the hands of the Edomites—the Romans. A number of the elders therefore accepted the invitation and appeared one evening in Paul's apartment on the *coenaculum* or upper floor of the thickly tenanted lodging house.

During the time of his imprisonment Paul had aged greatly. For more than two years he had been deprived of liberty of movement, and for a man of his restless spirit this was even more exhausting than the wild journeys he had undertaken on his mission. He was tired, and his nerves were worn out. He who had been accustomed to answering

605

the call of far-off cities and provinces in need of the tidings, had been compelled to conduct his enterprise as best he could from within the four walls of a prison; he who drew people to him like a magnet was for long periods chained to a single individual and passed countless days and nights under the intimate observation of a guard, who accompanied him wherever he went. Sometimes, indeed, his guard had been sensitive of spirit, responsive to his message and to the warmth of his personality; sometimes Paul had broken down the wall between Jew and gentile and turned suspicion and hostility into friendship. Such had been the case in his relationship with the good Julius, who had accompanied him on the last journey. And he had made the Messiah, more than once, the common bond between himself and his keeper. But there were also times when even his faith and personal magnetism evoked no response in the dull, hardened soul of a brutalized soldier. There were times when the groaning of the apostle in the nights, his murmured meditations and his agonized prayers to his Father in heaven, awoke only the anger or derision of the creature he was chained to. And the harder the chains bore on Paul, the more closely he clung to him who was the occasion of his bondage, Yeshua the Messiah—he who had crossed the path of his youth and taken him prisoner forever. The Messiah became for him not only the center of his being, the source of life; he became likewise both the tormenter and the bringer of liberation. In the Messiah he had sinned, in the Messiah he had been redeemed. In him he had sunk to the level of a murderer, in him he had been raised to the level of spreader of the tidings for all men. The more he suffered for the Messiah, the dearer his sufferings became to him. He found in his sufferings an ecstatic exaltation, the torment of thirst, the assuagement of the drink. Yeshua was no longer for him the intermediary between man and God, the "holy servant" who was to bring all mankind under the authority of God, so that "when all had become obedient to him he would make them obedient to God." Paul now went a step farther; he began to weave a new robe for the Messiah. "Every knee that is in heaven and on the earth and under the earth shall bend to the name of Yeshua." Yeshua became a part of the First Principle; every tongue should acknowledge that "Yeshua the Messiah is lord of the Glory of God the Father." Thus he began to relinquish to his ideal that peculiar place which his tradition and inheritance had reserved for the Only One,

606

Who may be thought of, but Whose Name may not be uttered—the God of Israel. Only in the double likeness of Yeshua could man unite with God, become part of Him through His human aspect and nature. God was close, intimate. "Thou canst love Him with thy human nature. Thou canst quench thy thirst in Him. Thou canst become filled with the love of God, for through thy faith in the Messiah thou becomest part of him who is himself divine."

These meditations on the divinity in man, achieved through Yeshua the Messiah, were the sources from which Paul derived strength in his loneliness. Love for the Messiah consumed his flesh as if it were a burning fever. In the bleakness of his cell he would pass whole nights in ecstatic visions; and his days would be filled with exaltation. His body had been worn down to its framework, and his bones protruded through the withered skin on which the poisonous air of his prisons had cast a yellow sheen. His throat became stringy, so that every bite of food he swallowed could be followed in its passage to his vitals. The pear shape of his face became more accentuated, his hair thinner, his cheekbones more prominent in their slant toward his beard and earlocks. His thin, bony hands were restless; they seemed forever to be vibrating, like stringed instruments plucked by a passing finger.

Opposite Paul sat some of the elders of the Jewish community of Rome—Reb Sabbatai Zadoc, Rabbi of the Synagogue of the Hebrews, at their head. Reb Sabbatai, who had the official title of interpreter of the law, was the spiritual leader of the Jerusalemite Jews of Rome. He was himself a Jew of Jerusalem, a disciple of Reb Jochanan ben Zachai, and he was in touch at all times with the head of the Pharisees. Reb Sabbatai, not being of the Messianists, did not know who the Jewish prisoner was and what his dispute with the Jews signified. He saw only a Jew in bondage, a Jew chained by his right hand to the left hand of a Roman soldier—and the "captive child amid the gentiles" was addressing the small group softly and intimately:

"Men and brothers, I have naught against the customs of our fathers. I was delivered a prisoner into the hands of the Romans. They heard my case and would have liberated me, for they found nothing in me worthy of death. But when the Jews, the messengers of the High Priest, brought charges against me, I was compelled to appeal to Caesar. It is not that, God forbid, I have aught of which to accuse my people.

607

Therefore I have sent for you, that I might see you and speak to you, because it is for the sake of the hope of the Jews that I have been bound with this chain."

The eyes of Reb Sabbatai became moist as he listened to "the captive child." Reb Sabbatai's beard, like Paul's, was pointed and gray; like Paul's, Reb Sabbatai's earlocks trembled when he spoke.

"We have received no letter from Judaea concerning thee, and none of our brothers who have arrived of late has spoken of thee; and surely no one has brought any evil report concerning thee."

A member of the delegation threw in a word: "Indeed, we were desirous of hearing from thee concerning the sect against which so much is being said in every place."

"Aye, but they speak against all Israel in every place, and not alone against the sect," interjected another.

"It is true; the House of Jacob is shamed and humiliated," sighed the Rabbi.

"But it is precisely concerning this sect, against which they speak everywhere, that I would speak with you," said Paul.

"Then we shall appoint a day, and assemble again, and thou shalt speak."

So a day was set. And as the Rabbi was about to rise, he added: "If thou hast need of aught, we shall help thee."

"No, God be thanked," answered Paul. "Until this day I have fed myself with the labor of my own hands. But now that my hands are bound, God has been gracious and sent to my aid a pious couple, who are of the sect. They live not far from here, and their names are Aquila and Priscilla. She prepares *kosher* food for me and brings it to my lodgings. And my faithful companion"—he pointed to Aristarchus, withdrawn modestly in a corner—"attends to my needs. Thus it is with all the other members of the sect, who are with me. And for the rest, I trust in the Lord of the World."

On the appointed day the Rabbi of the Synagogue of the Hebrews came with the sages of the community of Rome to Paul in his lodgings. With these were representatives of other synagogues, like Reb Chaya-Emeth, of the new synagogue on the Via Appia. A whole day Paul sat in discussion with them, declaring to them his doctrine of the Messiah of righteousness, which the Messianists had accepted and which he was preaching not only to Jews, but to gentiles too, for the Messiah, he

608

said, had come to throw down the wall between Jew and Greek, and to make them as one.

As every one of the sages present knew, the Torah was divided into parts, the regulative and the discursive, the first being concerned with rules, the second with principles and edification. Now the *Halachah,* or regulative doctrine, which Paul taught, though in some respects it digressed from the traditional *Halachah,* was founded on the Ten Commandments, so that the listeners found little to dispute in it. It was derived from the Jewish body of law which Paul had studied in Jerusalem under Rabban Gamaliel.

He enjoined on women obedience to their husbands, on men love toward their wives, forbidding them to deal harshly with them. He enjoined upon children the duty of honoring their parents, and upon parents compassion toward their children. He even bade servants to be obedient to their masters, and against this, bade the masters deal justly with their servants, "for all of us have one and the same Lord in heaven." He warned them against idolatry and fornication. "Ye shall be pure, the children of God without stain."

The doctrine which Paul preached to the gentiles made a favorable impression on the listeners. Indeed, they saw in his preachment the hand of God, who had sent a messenger to save the gentiles from the depths of their uncleanliness or, as Paul said, "to put off the old man, who is corrupted by lust, and to put on the new man, who is created in the image of the God of righteousness and in true sanctity." Nor was it possible for them to see his preachment in any other light, and in regard to this part of his discourse they praised him and prayed for his success. Indeed, if the Messiah of whom Paul spoke had come only to lift the gentiles out of their life of abomination, it was a cause of great rejoicing to Israel, for now the knowledge of God would fill the earth as the waters cover the sea.

Thus they listened, approvingly, with only occasional interruptions, as long as Paul spoke of the regulative doctrine which he spread among the gentiles. But when he reached the second part of his discourse and spoke of the principles of the faith behind the regulations, when he placed at the center of the doctrine not the God of Israel, but the Messiah, they started from him. And how could it be otherwise? What new authority had come to replace the authority of Moses? And there broke out between Paul and his listeners a passionate dispute such as Jews, and Jews only, who had poured out their blood for their faith, could have conducted. The air became hot and charged, and the ceiling seemed ready to take fire. Bodies trembled, beards quivered, bony fingers were thrust out, as if to point at invisible texts. They quoted the Pentateuch at each other, they called on the Prophets, and they fought over the interpretation of texts. They would not listen to Paul, but stopped their ears with their fingers and shook their heads violently. But Paul was not the man to be put off. The hotter the debate grew, the more insistent he became on being heard out. And in the end he forced them to listen to the ultimate conclusions of his faith:

"Until the advent of the Messiah," cried Paul, "there was none to come in direct contact with God. God was God, man was man. God appeared only in a likeness, and men spoke to him through a cloud. Even Moses conversed with God across a veil. For a veil was upon the presence of God, Moses being but flesh and blood, begotten by man and born of woman. God spoke to Moses through the laws and commandments which He handed down to the children of Israel. For how shall a man of flesh and blood become one with God? Only with the advent of the Messiah, who is in his nature both a part of the heavenly divinity and a being of flesh and blood, did man and God become united in soul—and thus we are drawn into intimate union with God, directly, and not as through a veil, as it was with Moses, our teacher. The man that believes in the Messiah becomes thereby a part of the spirit of God. He is no longer guided by laws and commandments, which are issued for strangers, for those that stand without, for men bounded by flesh and blood; he is guided by a higher power, by the spirit of God, which is in him through his faith in the Messiah. Faith in the Messiah becomes man's share in the spirit of the divinity. It is his guide; it is the law and the commandments for him. It makes of him, though uncircumcised, a son of Abraham. It imparts to him supreme rights in the promise to our forefathers; and he becomes thus, circumcised or not, a ben Israel, a son of Israel. Circumcised or uncircumcised, Jew or gentile, man or woman, freedman or slave—all, all are uplifted to the divinity through faith in the Messiah."

But what Jews could hear such utterances issuing from the mouth of a Jew? The assembled scholars were astounded, even as others had been astounded before, among traditional Jews, and even among Jewish Messianists.

"The God of Israel is single and alone!" cried one. "The 'echad,'

610

the Oneness of God, is the fiery ring which encloses Him, and no one, no one, no one, can approach Him, not the fathers, not Moses, and not another!"

"Not the fathers, and not Moses," agreed Paul, "but the Messiah, yes, for he is part of the heavenly divinity."

Until this point in the debate Reb Sabbatai, the Rabbi, had been as fiercely active in the debate as any other. But when he heard Paul repeat these words, it was as if the strength had gone out of him. His eyes flooded and his face took on an expression of deep sorrow. And when he spoke now it was with a voice that trembled.

" 'What is man, that Thou art mindful of him,' " he began. "What are we? Dust and ashes. Who can be uplifted to God? Only the gentiles believe that a king of theirs can become a god, and that they can sacrifice to him. We, the Jews, know but of one God, He Who appeared to our fathers, He Who said to Moses: 'I am that I am.' All the rest is—emptiness and nothing! And we have no other human nature than the human nature of our Psalms, which cries out to God: 'Whither shall I go from Thy spirit, and whither shall I fly from Thy presence?' For this faith we have endured torture, and for this we are slain. For this we are despised and are trampled like the grass. Here, in the Babylon city, we are mocked in the theaters and circuses. In all the cities of the gentiles we are as the dust in their streets. And everywhere the flood threatens to carry us away. We have but One to hold on to: God. We have but one word from Him: the Torah, which He gave us as our salvation. With King David we say: 'I trust in God, and I shall not fear the deeds of man.' And if thou spreadest the Torah among gentiles, if thou teachest them the Ten Commandments, which are the law of Moses, if thou plantest in them the fear of God and love of good deeds, we say to thee: 'Blessed be thy hands and the work of thy hands.' Then we should pray to God that He crown thy labor with success. But thou comest to us and sayest that we shall, God forbid, relinquish the Torah of God for another authority. Then we say unto thee: 'Too much hast thou said. Sufficient is thy work with the gentiles! Leave unto the Jews their law of Moses!' "

Paul trembled with impatience while the Rabbi spoke but held himself in. Then he could listen no more. The debate had until now, despite its fieriness, retained some of the spirit of the Jewish academies. Now Paul burst out:

"Oh, how just were the words of Isaiah the Prophet, when he

spoke these words to our forefathers: 'They will hear, but they will not understand; they will see, but they will not know !'

"Now be it known to you, that the salvation of God is sent unto the gentiles, and they *will* hear !"

"Let the gentiles accept thy salvation, for they have no other. But we have the salvation which was given to our fathers, and was preached by our Prophets. Would that the gentiles accept thy salvation as we accept ours! Then it will be said of them, too: 'O stiff-necked people! They hear but they do not understand, they see but they do not know !' And when that comes to pass, thou wilt know that thy salvation for them is a true one, and will endure, even as ours is true and will endure. And if the salvation thou preachest is a true one, then God will bring us together with them. There is no true salvation without God."

And with these words most of the delegation left; and they left with that with which they had come. But a few remained behind with Paul.

Chapter Four

THE RINGING OF THE CHAINS

FROM the Porta Capena of Rome the Via Appia continued through the countryside, set on both sides with the monuments and the mausoleums of the mighty dead. In the swampy fields, and in the caverns formed in the volcanic stone, the nymphs and fauns had their homes. The Romans heard, coming from those parts, the singing of sprites, the murmur of gods; and they saw the shadows of demons stealing across the wastes. In this part of Rome, beyond the gates, a new Jewish settlement had sprung up.

A specific and important reason had brought about the creation of this new Jewish quarter on the Via Appia. The Jews did not burn their dead, as the Romans did, dedicating certain fields to that purpose. Believing as they did in the resurrection, the Jews placed their dead in caskets and deposited these on natural or hewn-out shelves in caverns; they therefore settled in districts where the soil lent itself to this purpose. The land about the Via Appia was well adapted to the forming of catacombs. The volcanic stone was soft, and it was not difficult to honeycomb it with twisting passages in the walls of which the shelves were cut out; at the same time it was not so soft as to threaten to collapse and bury the tombs.

The settlement on the Via Appia developed rapidly. The Jewish quarter in the Trans-Tiber was already so overcrowded that many Jews had moved away and had made their home among the gentiles on the lower slopes of the Viminal hill, in the vicinity of the filthy Suburra. But now that the new quarter had formed, and had acquired ground for a cemetery, on the Via Appia, the Jews moved out from the city, though the suburb was at some distance from the heart of Rome. A burial place was a fundamental consideration with every Jewish community, not less than a synagogue and a ritual bath. The Jews came from every quarter of Rome to swell the new district, and to these were added Jews arrived newly in Rome.

Soon, from the Via Appia district, as from the old Jewish quarters in Rome, there issued every morning toward the marketplaces a procession of black-veiled Jewish women carrying their baskets of cosmetic stuffs, manufactured according to ancient family recipes. They filed through the Porta Capena; and some of them, before proceeding to the markets, visited the homes of their aristocratic clientele, high-placed Roman matrons. With them walked men, young and old, with other commodities of their own manufacture, chiefly woven stuff and wrought silver; their booths were mostly in the marketplace on the Caelian hill. Patriarchal Jews sat among the pillars of patrician homes, waiting to be called in by the lord or the matron to interpret a dream, in the course of which service they would also tell of the God of Israel and of the Temple in Jerusalem. (These interpreters of dreams, these women peddlers of cosmetics, were an inexhaustible source of material for the Roman rhymesters, mimes, and actors.)

When Paul arrived in Rome he became aware that two parties were beginning to form within the sect. He discovered, also, that in spite of the large group which had come out to greet him when Julius brought him as a prisoner to the city, he was as isolated from his own flesh and blood as he had been in Antioch.

Nor was it the non-Messianist Jews alone who fought the spread of his tidings. There was division regarding his doctrines among the Jewish Christians too, many of them being under the influence of Reb Jacob ben Joseph of Jerusalem, whose word carried weight in the Roman community, as among all other Jewish Messianist communities of the Diaspora.

He had known, even before his arrival in the capital, that the first of the disciples, Khaifa—also known as Peter, and originally by his Jewish name of Simon bar Jonah—was in Rome. But the "apostle to the Jews" had not come out to greet him, "the apostle to the gentiles," when he entered Rome in chains.

Even now, a prisoner in his own home, under constant guard, Paul set to work on the creation of his own congregation of Christians, who should see and accept the Messiah in the light of the apostle's special doctrine. He had about him the men who had accompanied him on the journey; and within Rome there were those who had remained faithful to him from the days in Corinth. These he sent throughout the city to win new believers. He spread his interpretation of the faith, converting first those who came in contact with him and using them as the instruments of his mission. Nor did he neglect the guards who came in rotation from the barracks—some of them insisting on the letter of the law, and chaining themselves to him—in his ministrations.

Among his followers Priscilla stood out as his greatest help. In Rome, as in Corinth and Ephesus, she kept watch over the apostle like a mother keeping watch over her child. She prepared his meals for him and sent them daily through little Aristarchus. She comforted and strengthened him; she assured him frequently that he would soon be brought before the Caesar and set at liberty. And she organized the visits of groups of Jews to his home. Side by side with her labored the beloved Timotheus and the physician, Lukas.

Lukas was a help to him as a healer of the body, too. The sedentary life to which he was condemned had an adverse effect on Paul's health, and Lukas did what he could to strengthen him by means of medicinal herbs and roots. But better than these, in sustaining Paul's spirit and body, were the conversions he wrought among the members of the "Emperor's household," the soldiers of the Praetorian Guard. Old Gabelus brought to the new God whom he had found through Paul all the military discipline, the obedience and devotion which he had once lavished on the Caesar. In Priscilla's household he found that intimacy, that brotherly spirit in the faith, which Paul had promised him, and in his boundless gratitude he did his best to widen the circle of the "family." He sought out among his comrades in the cohort the men whom he judged to be most susceptible to the new faith, and he brought them in secret to Paul's house, at such times as the guard happened to be one of his own soldiers. Moreover, he did what he could to assign to this special duty men of the right spirit and such as Paul had already influenced. When the matter was not in his hands, he recommended for the duty men of mild character; and often he would slip a word to the soldier, reminding him that the prisoner was a Roman citizen, and adding that he was, moreover, a man of influence, well thought of in high circles. So it came about that before long Gabelus and Eubulus had about them, in their cohort, soldiers who were either of the faith or strongly inclined toward it. But these two soldiers were not content to use their offices only in the barracks. They were constantly in and out of the palace, and there they spoke of the new faith to the cooks, the bakers, the butlers—the slaves as well as the freedmen. At night servants of Caesar's household stole through the Porta Capena and were led to Priscilla's house, the lower floor of which was used by Aquila as his workshop. There, among heaps of goatskins and goat's hair, the common feasts were held, and "the kiss of peace" was exchanged by soldiers and slaves.

But the cohorts stationed at the Praetorian barracks were changed regularly. Every day, through the Porta Collina, another of the ten cohorts stationed in the Castra Praetoria, or Praetorian Camp, marched to the barracks near the palace, to relieve the cohort of the previous day. With banners flying and insignia held high the marching soldiers drove through the swarming streets, thrust passersby out of the way, upset and trampled upon the stalls and cruses which a merchant was not swift enough to carry out of their path. When the guard was changed, and Gabelus had not had the opportunity to do his work, Paul would, as often as not, be placed in the care of a rough, unmanageable soldier of the Alexandrian or another legion. Then Paul was chained again to his keeper and had to bear his company for twenty-four hours, and be accompanied by him even when he went to answer the call of nature. Worse than that, the soldier would drag Paul with him when he left the house, would force him to stay by when he entered the foul public comfort stations, where men and women sat side by side, indulging in the grossest and most revolting jests. As often as not, the soldier would take special delight in mocking Paul's Jewishness, imitating his gestures, interfering with his prayers and defiling his food by throwing into it a piece of pork. Sometimes it would happen that a soldier of the basest sort would compel the chained prisoner to be the witness of frightful obscenities, and when Paul, closing his eyes, whispered to God a prayer to release him from this torment, the soldier burst into brutal laughter. In the night, when Paul's devotions disturbed the soldier, the latter would thrust his elbow into the apostle's side, and bid him sleep. Then Paul lay silent, and meditated on the cause and meaning of his sufferings. He knew that it was the Messiah who had ordained that he, Paul, should thus be chained to a soldier. For what reason? The answer came to Paul in the midst of his prayers: in order to remind him again and again that he was an apostle to the gentiles. It was for this that, day and night, Paul was bound to another—to learn well the lesson that he did not belong to himself. He was no longer his own master, and he had forfeited his privacy, but had been chained to another, for good and evil, in order that he might bring salvation to that other.

And herein Paul discovered a new demonstration of grace and was strengthened. He therefore did not withhold his message from any man. No matter how cruel and base his keeper, no matter how revolting his conduct, Paul strove with all his might to forget his claims to his own individuality. He gave himself up to understanding the other, seeking the divine spark in him in the midst of all baseness, so that he might kindle it into the flame of the faith. He ceased to think of men as good and bad, believers and unbelievers. He thought of them only as ignorant or enlightened, and the most ignorant could be enlightened if only the way could be found to bring to bear upon him the knowledge of the faith. There was not a single guard whom Paul did not seek to win over to the faith.

There were others, besides soldiers of the Praetorium, for him to work on. Lukas, in his capacity as physician, soon made for himself a wide circle of acquaintances among freedmen and slaves. Some of them were scholars, readers, and secretaries, and he persuaded many of them to visit Paul. Timotheus, too, wandered through the streets of Rome and spoke with strangers in inns, restaurants, and barber shops. There were also women of Priscilla's circle, cosmetics dealers, who found among Roman matrons many who were susceptible of conversion, for the Roman matrons of that time were greatly interested in any kind of Oriental mystery.

So, as the days passed, the two Christian communities grew side by side. One consisted of the former community, which was preponderantly Jewish, with an admixture of gentiles who had either converted to the Jewish faith or else, not having gone so far as to submit to circumcision, had accepted "the commandments of the sons of Noah," according to the ruling of Reb Jacob ben Joseph, and who were taught that "not the faith, but the good deed, is important." The leader of that community was Peter, and his assistant and secretary or, as he called him, his "son," Marcus. The second community was new, save for Aquila and Priscilla; its members were chiefly servants of the household of Caesar, soldiers of the Praetorium, slaves, and freedmen. They gathered about Priscilla's house on the Aventine hill. The river Tiber divided the two communities.

* * *

It was the early morning hour in the hired house of Paul. The loud noises of the street floated through the "windows," which, because of the chill, were hung over and stopped up with sackcloth and other rags. Childish voices in a school on an upper floor were heard chanting the alphabet; and the sound mingled with the ringing of a hammer in a neighboring smithy. The smoke from the stove of a sausage maker in the next apartment was carried by the wind into Paul's room. The house was badly built, of poor materials; the walls were full of cracks, the ceilings faulty. Voices and odors penetrated everywhere, so that the denizens of the house felt that they lived partly in the street. The screams of a quarreling couple on an upper floor compelled others to talk at the top of their voices. From the shops below, from the cobblestones, from the "windows," a continuous tumult poured into Paul's room. Paul lay on the bed which was his only piece of furniture. A long chain passed from his wrist to that of the hairy, bearded soldier who sat at the window and shouted down to passersby of his acquaintance. This particular guard was a Corsican, whom Paul had met that morning for the first time. He was not of the cohort of Gabelus, and he had never heard of Paul before. But he was a kindly fellow; and he had been surprised and softened when, on his entrance, Aristarchus had encountered him with a pitcher of new wine. He sat now with the pitcher between his naked knees. Every time he lifted his arms to greet someone in the street, or to carry the pitcher to his lips, he tugged at Paul. Except for this thoughtless gesture, he did not disturb the old man. He did not drag Paul off his bed but sat patiently at the window, amusing himself with the lively scene below and injecting himself into it as often as he could.

Paul was weak and weary. His hands were blue and swollen, like spleens. There was not a drop of blood in his face. His cheeks were pendulous, the tear-sacs below his eyes unnaturally large, as if water had been injected under his skin. Only his thick eyebrows bristled with a strange liveliness above the pale shimmer of his eyes. Near him stood Lukas, the physician, ever calm, ever at peace. His black, well-kept beard and hair were streaked with gray; his mantle fell in careful folds on his body. With strong, skillful hands he massaged the flabby skin of his teacher, the face, the throat, and the chest. He had also prepared for his patient a special drink of fig juice mixed with herbs. After the massage and the drink Paul felt better. His eyes livened, and even the fringe of hair round his bald head seemed fresher and sleeker. Half lying, half sitting on the bed, he conducted a lively discussion with Lukas on the subject of the gospel which the latter was writing concerning the life and deeds of the Messiah. Paul was helping him with comment and interpretation. Almost every morning Lukas would come and read him a few paragraphs which he had written the day before; and Paul corrected them, to make the contents of the gospel correspond to his own preachment of the tidings. This morning, too, Lukas read forth from his papyrus scroll:

"And the lord commanded his disciples, saying: 'Ye shall not go to the gentiles, and to the cities of the Samaritans, but to the lost sheep of the House of Israel.'"

Paul, hearing this passage, started so violently, that he tugged at the chain, and caused the soldier to send a splash of wine to the floor. The soldier looked round angrily, but said nothing. But Paul did not notice the angry look. Those frightful words attributed to the lord contradicted everything that was sacred in his own doctrine:

"Who put those words into the mouth of the lord?" he asked.

"I found them in the record of Matthew, in Jerusalem. Matthew

618

reports them as a direct command which he heard from the Messiah himself."

Paul would not let him continue:

"To me the lord said, in the court of the Temple: 'I will send thee to the gentiles.' The lord is the master and possessor of all men, and he came to bring redemption to Jew and gentile alike."

But Lukas pointed to another passage which he had received from Matthew: "If ye greet only your brothers, wherein are ye better than the others? Do not the gentiles so?"

"It was not the gentiles that the lord meant with those words," said Paul, imperiously. "The gentiles are not sinners. They are but the unborn children of the faith; and he that is not yet born cannot be a sinner."

Thus Paul revised all those passages in the gospel of Lukas which bore on the relation of Israel to the gentiles. And in order to emphasize that Yeshua was not only of Jewish extraction, but belonged to all mankind, he had Lukas carry back the book of the generation of Yeshua beyond Abraham—where Matthew had ended—to Adam, the first of men.

But while Paul was thus busy with the revision of the record of Lukas, his eyes and ears were open to everything about him. He noted that his beloved son Timotheus was walking in restless absorption up and down the room. The years which the young man had spent with his father and teacher in voluntary imprisonment had aged him greatly. His tall, slender figure had acquired a stoop. His face, too, had become yellow in the framework of the lustrous, black beard, and a multitude of wrinkles had gathered on his forehead. Paul knew what was consuming Timotheus inwardly, the fate of the congregations of Asia Minor, of Macedonia, and of Achaia. In his wanderings through the streets of Rome Timotheus was always on the lookout for someone who could give him news of the churches which (as he felt) the shepherds had abandoned in the open field. Timotheus was always thinking of writing to them, or even of taking leave of Paul to visit them, perhaps taking Lukas with him. He did not discuss the matter with his teacher. He knew that on Paul, too, the fate of the churches weighed as heavily as the chain which bound him to his guard.

In the nights Paul was haunted by the thought of the infant churches. He had sent Titus to them, but what was one man? Paul too was contemplating a second delegation, consisting of Timotheus and Lukas. He composed letters in his mind to the leaders of the churches; but in order to forward the letters he would need a messenger. A messenger would have to be provided with money for the journey, and Paul knew that the funds of his congregation were low, though no one had ever told him about it.

In the doorway Aristarchus and Priscilla stood close to each other, talking in low voices. Paul knew why they kept their voices low. He knew that Priscilla had carried out of her house the last bundle of goat's hair and had sold it in the Suburra in order to pay his rent. In Priscilla's house there was nothing left that could be sold. Her husband's looms were idle because he had not the money for the purchase of raw material. Priscilla had spent the last of her money on food for the apostle —the pot of boiled grits and honey which she had brought him that day; and only the day before she had given money to Lukas for medicaments. What was to be now? Paul asked himself. His congregation consisted of soldiers and slaves and the poorest freedmen. He suffered in the thought that he was a burden to his congregation; always and everywhere he had sought to provide for his own needs with his own labor. His independence, his authority over his followers, had been bound up, for him, with his extreme scrupulousness in the matter of money. He did not want to be a debtor, however much he might consider that he was entitled to this form of help. If only his hands were free! Old as he was he would seat himself again at the loom and earn his own bread, as he had done in other cities. But his hands were bound, literally. Whence would help come?

But no sooner had he recognized this thought than he turned from it in shame. Did he not believe in the lord Messiah? Had not the lord himself reduced him to this condition? But had the lord meant to turn his life to nothingness? Had he not rather brought him hither, to Rome, a prisoner in chains, because he intended great things with him?

He called suddenly to Timotheus, who had some reports, gathered at random, of the welfare of the churches in Asia Minor and Achaia. The deputations which had gone up to Jerusalem had long since returned home, but there was no direct word from them. Tychicus alone had come over from Ephesus to Jerusalem.

"Titus should be sent to Crete," said Paul to Timotheus. "It is a gross and ignorant people, but there is a ready field for the Messiah. A strong hand is needed, and Titus is the man for it. It would be well to send Tychicus back to Ephesus, for Ephesus too is important. Many congregations have been founded in the cities round about. Thou too wilt go there. And thou—" he turned to Priscilla, who was standing in the doorway—"thou and thy husband must give up the house here in Rome and return to Ephesus. Out of Ephesus we must strengthen the hands of the new churches. No one has visited them, and no one has spoken to them—neither to Laodicea nor to Nympha nor the others."

"And what of the congregation here? What of Priscilla's house?" asked Timotheus.

"There is but one congregation and one Messiah. The new believers among the gentiles will have to turn to the other side of the Tiber; they will have to become part of the congregation of Christians which is with the first of the disciples, Peter, so that the two congregations may mingle and be united. Let the barriers between Jew and gentile be broken down. Let all belong to the single congregation of the Messiah!"

Priscilla nodded and said: "Yesterday the new believers met for the first time with the Jewish Christians at the *agape* and exchanged the kiss of peace and became as brothers."

"How many of them were of the household of the Caesar?"

"Thirty-six legionaries, brought by Gabelus and Eubulus, and upward of a score of the servants of the household of the Caesar, freedmen and slaves."

"I bend my knee before the Father of my lord, Yeshua the Messiah, upon whom all the hosts of heaven call."

"But what is to be—"

Paul did not let her finish.

"Priscilla, my sister. God had spread the seed from Rome to Ephesus. In every city there are congregations—and they will help in the completion of God's work."

"And who will look after thee in thy chains?"

"He who has looked after me all the years. The churches are more important than I."

While all this talk was going on between Paul and Priscilla and Timotheus, little Aristarchus stood by Paul's bed, holding in his hands the earthen pot with the grits and honey, and muttering continuously:

"Would it not be better, after all, for the apostle to eat something?"

621

Paul turned to him at last, and with his free hand took a few spoonfuls of food, sighing:

"Will it be granted to me ever to see again the children I have begotten in the Messiah? Ah, if these hands were not chained! I would fly to them. . . ."

"They will be free, they will surely be free. How often has not the apostle been encompassed by danger, and how often has not the Lord rescued him! For the Lord needed him for His work, and needs him still." So Aristarchus babbled eagerly, as he held the pot of grits.

"I must give up this hired house, and return to my cell until I am called before Caesar," said Paul.

"God forbid!" almost screamed Aristarchus. "What means the apostle by such words?"

"But where shall we take money to pay for these lodgings? We know well how matters stand with Aquila."

"We shall find it, we shall find it!" answered Aristarchus. "Has not the apostle more important matters to concern himself with? The Lord knows of our need. Today, tomorrow, a messenger will arrive from one of the congregations. And if none arrives, we shall talk with the Messianists. I say that if they are nourished in the spirit by the labor of the apostle, they must remember the verse: 'Thou shalt not muzzle the ox that treadeth the corn.'"

"Nay! Not from the gentile believers will I have it. They are children of the faith, and children must receive, not give," said Paul. "Cross to the other bank of the Tiber. Speak rather with the believers who are our brothers in Israel. They are grown in the faith, and they carry the burden lovingly."

"Whichever way it be," answered Aristarchus, "it is not for the apostle to worry. We shall do what must be done, and God will be with us."

There were footsteps at the door, and a stranger appeared, dressed in a Macedonian mantle and with a sack over his shoulder. The man's face and robe were covered with dust.

"Is this the house of Paul, the apostle to the gentiles? And is he to be seen?"

And looking toward the bed, the man, waiting for no answer, advanced and bowed deeply, saying:

"Peace be to thee, my rabbi and my lord! I have just arrived from

622

Philippi, in Macedonia, and I bring thee the greetings of the holy congregation in Yeshua the Messiah. They have heard that thou art in bonds, and they have hastened to send help to thee through me. They have heard that thou art in need, and this is an offering, made in love, from the congregation of Philippi." And the man placed at Paul's feet a small sack of money. It was the gift of the Philippians.

Paul's first thought was one of gratitude to the Almighty, and his first need was for prayer. With the help of Aristarchus he rose from his bed. Timotheus begged the soldier to come nearer, so that the old man might have more freedom of motion. Aristarchus brought a pitcher of water and washed Paul's hands and feet; then he drew over him his tunic and black mantle. Washed and dressed, Paul sank on his knees and murmured:

"Father of all living things, I am not worthy of the grace which Thou has manifested toward me. It is known to Thee that all that I have done was done for the glory of Thy Name; for Thy sake alone I have been alienated from my flesh and blood. May Thy Name, therefore, become known to all the peoples of the world through the redeemer whom Thou hast chosen. May Thy Name be sanctified in all the worlds, and may Thy spirit come upon all peoples. May all peoples make a covenant in Thee and be bound in Thee through the grace of the redemption which thou hast sent to the world through Thy holy servant, Thy chosen son. For all comes from Thee and all returns to Thee, the Holy One of Israel."

Then Paul rose with shining face, seated himself on the bed, and listened at length to the report brought him by Epaphroditus. When that was ended, he set about his new plans with the energy of his former years.

He had a role for everyone, not excluding the messenger from Philippi. He bade Epaphroditus go out into the city and discover what Philippians there were in Rome, in the streets, the shops, the inns, and to preach the tidings to them. Before their departure, Aquila and Priscilla, relieved now of their monetary anxiety, should give themselves wholly to renewed efforts for the faith. And hardly had Paul distributed these tasks than it was made manifest to him that God had indeed intended him to be reborn in labor. For that same day there arrived from Macedonia Tychicus and Onesimus, mighty workers. Demos came from Salonika. Paul's house was transformed again into a lively center for the uncircumcised Christians of Rome. Day after day the word went out to slaves and freedmen. Before long Paul had a little cathedra put into his room, and sitting there, bound to a soldier, or with hands free, he taught from morning to night, winning souls to the Messiah.

But he did not forget the churches which he had founded. At odd moments, chiefly in the evenings, he dictated letters to his beloved son, Timotheus. First he wrote to the Philippians, to whom he thought to send the letter by Epaphroditus. But Epaphroditus was not strong of body. Soon after his arrival in Rome he fell sick, and Lukas attended him. The Philippians were greatly concerned for Epaphroditus, and therefore Paul waited until he had recovered before he sent him back. In the letters which he dictated Paul, as ever, opened his heart, speaking without reserve. To the Philippians, who had always come to his aid when he was in need, like a mother attentive to the cry of her child, he wrote with special feeling and unashamedly told of the heaviness of heart which he had suffered because of his bondage, and of the faith which had triumphed over it.

"I would have you know, my brothers, that that which has happened to me has only served to help in the spreading of the gospel. Even my chains in the Messiah have been revealed in the household of the Caesar and in all other places."

"For me the Messiah is life, and death is a gain. . . . For I am in narrow straits between two paths. I long to go away and to be in the Messiah, which is the better way. But for your sake it is necessary that I remain in the flesh."

After having declared to them what "thought in the Messiah" meant, and that "every tongue should acknowledge that the Messiah was lord of the Glory of God the Father," he went on:

"Ye shall be pure and spotless, children of God without stain. . . . And let me have pride with you in the day of the Messiah, that not in vain did I run about, and not in vain did I labor. And if I should offer myself as a sacrifice for your faith and service in God, so shall I rejoice in his hope with you."

He wrote them further that he was about to send Timotheus to them, "for there is no one after my heart who shall care for you in complete devotion." "Others have sought to serve themselves, but he served with me in the spreading of the gospel as a son serves his father. . . ." Nor did he relinquish the hope of seeing the Philippians

624

with his own eyes. But he remembered also those who were exerting themselves to hinder him in his labors, and in a burst of anger he called them "dogs." "Beware of the dogs!" he cried.

In this, as in other letters to the churches, he dwelt on his Jewish origins. "I am a Jew of the Jews, of the Jewish tribe of Benjamin, a Pharisee, according to the law." But he was ready now to give up everything for the Messiah "in order that I may no longer have my own righteousness which is of the law, but that which is in the faith, the righteousness which is of God through faith." In his eagerness to emphasize faith, he even accounted that a loss which he had once accounted a gain. "Yea, I count everything a loss which I held before the great knowledge of the Messiah my lord, for whom I have given up everything." In his bitterness he spoke of his former belief as utterly worthless. Certain tones in the letter betrayed the discomfort of his chains —a human discomfort which his spiritual liberation could not wholly overcome.

For Paul was too human to rise completely out of his earthly circumstances. His highest spiritual achievements were flecked with complaint and betrayed the bitterness which had not wholly been cleansed from his heart. But these were nothing more than flecks. He was aware of them and regretted them passionately. Yet he could not help revealing them in his letters, though he rose, again and again, to heights of which he alone was capable:

"And now, brothers, whatsoever is true and honest and just and pure, whatever is of good report, and whatever is praised—on these things set your hearts."

In a surge of love and gratitude he said: "I do not speak to you out of want, for I have learned to be content with what I have, I know how to suffer want and how to deport myself in plenty. I can do everything with the help of the Messiah. But you have shared with me my affliction."

It chanced that a young Tuscan was Paul's guard on the day when he finished his letter to the Philippians—a new man, whom Paul had never seen before. Now when he had taken over the prisoner from the previous guard, the young soldier kneeled down and cried:

"I know that thou art a holy man, and art sent of God. I know that it is for Jesus Christ that thou art in chains."

625

"How knowest thou the name of the Messiah?" asked Paul. "Did Gabelus or Eubulus send thee?"

"Nay, but it is known on all the Palatine hill, and everywhere in the household of the Caesar they call upon it," said the soldier. "Take me, I pray thee, into thy faith."

Paul knelt down on the floor, by the side of the soldier who was his keeper, and lifted up to heaven the hand that was chained to the soldier's, calling out:

"See, O Lord! These chains which Thou hast placed upon my hands ring out Thy praise and Thy glory among men. I thank Thee for them!"

Chapter Five

PETER IN ROME

ROME, the city of "Edom," was looked upon by the Jews as the rod which the Lord had appointed to punish Jacob for his sins. In the legends of the Jews there were many that had to do with the origin of the city. One told that on the day when King Solomon took to wife the daughter of a Pharaoh, the angel Gabriel came down from heaven, lifted a mass of ooze from the bottom of the sea, and set it down where Rome was to be founded. On the day Jeroboam, son of Nebat, set up the two golden calves, in order to dissuade the Jews from going to Jerusalem, the twin founders of Rome, Romulus and Remus, were born, said another legend. But Rome was connected in the mind of the Jews with salvation as well as punishment. The city of sin, the new Babylon, was the fiery furnace of trial; it was also to become the gate of redemption. The Messiah sat, according to still another legend, at the gate of Rome, among beggars, waiting for the sound of the trumpet of the liberation. On the day of liberation Moses would come out of the desert, and the Messiah would come to meet him from Rome.

Rome and Jerusalem: each was built on the ruin of the other. Out of the heart of destruction would blossom the fruit of salvation: the Messiah would set forth from Rome, as Moses would set forth from the desert.

Peter, the first of the disciples, went to Rome to wait, in the lion's den, for the Messiah.

He too had made many voyages through far-off cities and provinces. He left Antioch after Paul, accompanied by his beloved disciple, or "son," Jochanan-Marcus. Like Paul he had climbed the hills of Galatia and had come to Cappadocia. Then he had gone across the mountain country of Pontus to Bithynia, where Paul had never been, and there he had founded congregations. Traversing Asia Minor, together with Marcus, he had reached the seashore and had taken ship for Rome. There, in the Jewish quarter in the Trans-Tiber, he had found a large congregation of Messianists. Among these the first of the disciples settled.

On the farther bank the ships from Astra unloaded their cargoes of vegetables, wood, straw, grain, and olives. Hundreds of Jews, Roman and foreign, had their booths and shops here, selling clothing, provisions, fish, spices, second-hand furniture, rags. Round every shop a horde of children played, tangling under the feet of the parents, who dragged the bundles and crates of merchandise from the ships to the booths. A constant noise of chaffering filled the air. Merchants competed and quarreled, swearing by the Temple in Jerusalem that their goods were the best and the cheapest. Names sounded in the air which were strange to Roman ears but familiar in this part of the city. It was a city within a city, Jerusalem in the heart of Edom.

But when the Sabbath came this stretch of the bank was silent, the shops were closed, the booths empty. Wisps of straw, vegetable leaves, lay scattered about. The Jews were assembled in their homes. Every window was adorned with a garland of flowers and leaves in honor of the Sabbath. The air was fragrant with the odor of cooked fish and of the spiced foods which were, then too, an endless source of merriment for the gentiles. For that matter, everything Jewish was matter for satire and burlesque among the mimes and actors of the circuses—but the Jewish Sabbath above all. The pamphleteers made a great point of the imbecilic Jewish habit of losing one day in seven, which was given up to utter idleness. The Jews, moreover, were incomprehensible in their treatment of children. Infanticide was quite unknown among them, and every child, *every* single one, was brought up. The Jews paid little attention to this endless mockery. "Let the gentiles laugh to their heart's content." On the Sabbath morning they assembled in the synagogues, prayed, listened to the reading of the Torah, and drank up thirstily the words of their Prophets, which were read to them first in Hebrew and then in Greek translation.

In one of the houses about the courtyard of the synagogue which had been named in honor of the just Emperor, Augustus, the first of the disciples, Simon bar Jonah, made his home.

The congregation of the Messianists was now so numerous in Rome that it had acquired a separate place of worship within every synagogue. After they had performed the services and repeated the prayers with all their fellow Jews, omitting no detail, they gathered for the special service of their own faith. They had their common meals, held meetings of their own, and collected money for the widows and orphans of the sect. Officially they belonged, of course, to the Jewish community of Rome, from which they made no attempt to separate themselves. They simply had their own modes and customs, their own smaller prayer and meeting houses. They invited to their gatherings the pious gentiles, the uncircumcised, only on condition that they took baptism. There had, indeed, been dissension on this score. Later, when the sect of the Messianists became numerous enough, it acquired an acknowledged position in the Jewish congregation of Rome. The Messianists increased greatly after the arrival of the first of the disciples. It was the simple fisherman, unlearned in the finer points of the law, who, with his warm speech, his winning manner, his charming parables, drew the folk to him. Throngs of poor workers, oil mixers, pack-carriers, peddlers, and vegetable stall owners came on the Sabbath to hear Simon bar Jonah's sermons.

On a certain Sabbath morning, following the reading of the Scrolls, Simon was seated in his special place in the section of the Messianists. The small prayer house was packed with Jews and gentiles. The apostle preached in the language of the Jews, Aramaic mixed with Hebrew words, and when he had ended, the sermon was translated into Greek by Marcus. Among the listeners were many women, who occupied places near the door. Children were present, too, and their fathers had conducted them to the front of the synagogue, where they made an awed

628

ring about the gray old man in the white robe. When the time came for him to speak, Simon bar Jonah, called Peter, rose and in a humble, low voice addressed the worshipers.

What was the substance of his sermon? He had not come to Rome to mend and re-interpret the faith. His God was perfect and completed, as He was for all Jews. His God was the God of the Psalmist, King David: "The Lord is my shepherd, I shall not want." Who and what was he that he should, God forbid, seek to penetrate into the mystery of God? He was an unlearned fisherman, a villager, and not the scholarly "brother Paul," who was so hard to understand. His God was the God of faith, to whom man in his loneliness clings with all hope:

"We serve and adore but one God, the Creator of all the worlds, and we observe his laws, the first of which is: 'Thou shalt love the Lord thy God with all thy heart and with all thy might.' Man is created in the image of God; therefore we must glorify God by sharing our bread with the hungry and our clothes with the naked; we must visit the sick, extend hospitality to the stranger, ransom him that is in captivity. For each one of us is created in God's likeness and belongs to God. As He that has called you is holy, so shall ye be holy. Even as it is written: 'Ye shall be holy, for I am holy.'"

And to the gentiles he said:

"Be as children that are obedient, and be not as before, when ye lived in your lusts. For ye know that ye were not ransomed with corruptible gold and silver, but with the dear blood of the Messiah, who is as a lamb without blemish. You are born anew, not through the corruptible seed, but through the word of God, which lives and is ever lasting. For all flesh is as grass, and all the glory of man is but as the flower of the field; the grass withers, and the flower fades, but the word of God abides forever. Therefore do off from yourselves all evil and falsity, all flattery and envy and evil speech—and desire the pure milk of the Word, like new-born children, in order that ye may grow."

The speaker was filled with the joy and adoration of God as a grape is filled with wine. And he sang his magnificat in simple, heartfelt prayers of his own composition. One of the impromptu prayers which he had uttered before another congregation than this had been remembered word for word, had passed from worshiper to worshiper, and was now being repeated everywhere on Sabbaths and Festivals; it was repeated here, too, both by the Jews and the gentiles of the faith, exactly as if it were a part of the Psalms. It was a prayer which came from the broken and humbled heart and glorified the one living God of Israel. It began with these words:

> "The breath of all that lives shall praise Thy Name,
> O Lord, our God. . . ."

and it ended:

> "All hearts shall fear Thee, all the inward parts
> Of man shall sing Thy Name, as it is said:
> 'My bones shall cry, Who is like Thee, O Lord?'
> Thou rescuest the helpless from the strong,
> The weak and poor from the oppressor-robber.
> The supplication of the wretched Thou dost hear,
> And answerest the weeping of the lowly.
> As it is said: 'The righteous sing of God,
> The just shall take delight in prayer. . . .' "

It was the cry of Israel which sounded in this prayer; it was the helpless bleating of a lamb clinging to a rocky ledge in the midst of a storm. What wonder that in spite of all divisions of opinion in the congregation, this psalmist-heart united all in a common speech before God? So the Jews received the prayer of the fisherman, and guarded it as a precious thing, and conserved it across the stormy ages, to repeat in our own day in the synagogues and at the ceremonial table of the Passover. For the words of Peter were those of a poor man among the poor. The apostle to the Jews uttered, for Jew and gentile alike, a prayer that was utterly Jewish: a prayer of faith and trust in the common Father in heaven.

And when Peter had ended preaching and praying, the women and children awaited him at the exit of the synagogue, so that the little ones might receive his blessing. After that the men conducted him to a Jewish home, where the Sabbath repast was spread on the table, and they sat together and ate in the joy of God. Then they thanked God Who had entrusted them with this special privilege of the holy Sabbath, on which they dedicated their bodies and souls to Him.

When he left the house, to return to his own dwelling, the children ran after the old man in the white mantle, crying:

"See, this is the messenger to the Jews!"

"Messenger, messenger, when will the Messiah come?"

And Peter answered them:

"In your days, and in my days, and in the days of all Israel, speedily and soon!"

Thus the first of the apostles lived among the Jews of Rome. He did not like to leave the Jewish quarter. Mostly he sat in his house, praying, repeating psalms, or recounting again and again to his helper, Marcus, the doctrine and the deeds of the righteous Messiah when he was still among the living. Marcus wrote down carefully all that he heard concerning the Messiah from the lips of Peter. Or else Peter would sit in his chair in the little prayer house, receiving all that came to him, Jew or gentile, and speaking to them in all kindness and gentleness. Once they brought to him a rich matron, who wanted to hear of the Messiah only from the lips of the first disciple. Peter shrank from the luxury and power of the houses of Rome; he feared these as he feared Rome itself. He had little faith in the Roman matrons, whose belief in their gods had always been a coquetry and a self-indulgence. They were willing to hear of any new Oriental god, and they included the Messiah in the list. Simon bar Jonah did not feel at home in the giant city, which he regarded as the source of all abomination: a drunken harlot it was, a painted Babylon, full of witchcraft, whoredoms, murder, and idolatry, raised up by God as the staff to smite Jacob. But from this place the Messiah would come a second time, "suddenly, and as a thief in the night," and he would ascend the throne to judge the mighty of the world.

The first disciple spoke much among the believers of "the great judgment day." Concerning Rome, he felt her power, without seeing it: Rome with her palaces and temples, her vast throngs, her slaves and legionaries, her nobles and rulers, filled him with dread. This power of Satan, of Asmodeus, who held nations and lands in a brutal grip, could be destroyed only by the Messiah. The Messiah would sweep away this blot with a fiery broom; the Messiah would cause a fiery sea to level Rome with the dust. In the evenings, at the common meals, the first disciple prophesied the dark end of the imperial city. He had visions of a rain of fire descending from glowing clouds. It was at such gatherings, after he had spoken of the torments which the Messiah had taken upon himself for the sins of the world, that he would rise to ecstatic, prophetic denunciations:

631

"In that day the heavens will disappear in storm and the foundations shall be burned. ... Hasten to come before the day of the Lord, when the heavens will dissolve and the foundations will melt, for we shall yet have the promise of a new heaven and a new earth, where ye shall dwell in righteousness."

Fear and trembling came upon his listeners, who beheld the earth open at their feet. The dark tidings of destruction were carried about by word of mouth. Jew and gentile learned that the messenger who had come from Jerusalem was foretelling the end of the world, the destruction from which only the believers, they who had taken baptism in the name of the Messiah, should be saved.

From the depths of the Trans-Tiber area the voice of fear, the tidings of the great judgment day, spread throughout the city, and there were many who came to seek salvation in baptism. So the congregation grew from day to day, among Jews and gentiles, and everywhere among the poor, the slaves, the oppressed, they spoke of the doom which was approaching.

* * *

Simon bar Jonah had heard that the apostle to the gentiles had been brought to Rome in chains, and that, a prisoner in his home, he was spreading the tidings among the gentiles on the other side of the Tiber. After a while Peter sent his beloved son, Marcus, to help Paul, even though he was not in accord with many of the things which Paul preached. For he also knew of the good which Paul was doing, how he was winning to the faith many of Caesar's household, teaching them to walk in the ways of God, planting good deeds in their hearts and making known the name of God and of His Messiah. But the special doctrine that Paul preached Simon could not understand, nor did he seek to understand it. Who was he, he asked himself, to scrutinize the intentions of God? God was to be feared, not scrutinized. This was all that he desired to know. He clung to the lord Messiah, who had lifted him out of the dust. And though he knew that the Messiah had had to suffer, that the suffering was part of his mission on earth, part of the redemption of mankind, the thought of that suffering was a physical torment to him. Before Simon bar Jonah's eyes the lord always appeared as his beloved Rabbi, the just man, the chosen one, whom he had known and served. He could not speak of the sufferings of the Messiah without a flood of tears; his limbs trembled, and the pity that welled

632

up in him was transmitted to his listeners. When he described in detail the torments which had been visited upon his Rabbi, the Messiah, "the just man, who had committed no sin, and in whose mouth there was no evil," the hearts of those that heard him were dissolved, and they were united with him and with each other in love of the Messiah.

Very often the Jewish fisherman was seized with an unbearable longing for the presence of his Rabbi. He hungered to be with him in heaven, as he had been with him on earth. He longed to see his white, shimmering robe, and to hear his sweet voice. He longed to bow down before him and to kiss the dust on his feet. But he knew that before he could be with the Messiah he would have to drain the same bitter cup as the Messiah had drained, for this was what the Messiah had said to his disciples while he yet lived. But Simon bar Jonah was a weak man, and his flesh quivered whenever he thought of the dark drink of agony. He wanted the day to be far off; and sometimes he whispered to himself that perhaps the day would never come for him. Then again, when the longing for the presence of his Rabbi overcame him, he felt himself ready to pass through the fiery circle. Sometimes he even prayed for the cup to be brought to him, soon, without delay. That would happen in the nights; in the day his flesh was stronger, and he thrust away the thought of the drink which he knew was being prepared for him, and which he would not be able to put away from his lips.

One day there came into his presence a man, a Jew of Jerusalem, a messenger from the holy congregation. His name was Yeshua, but he was also called Justus, because he was of the Greek Jews. He had dreadful tidings for Simon bar Jonah.

"After many years of waiting and planning, the youngest son of old Chanan, whose name, thou knowest, is also Chanan, became the High Priest, having purchased the office with a great bribe. The first of his official acts was to do away with the traditional form of the service on the Day of Atonement, the service which came down to us from of old and was acknowledged and sanctified by the Pharisees. For the Day of Atonement fell soon after the ascension of Chanan to the High Priesthood. The new form of service is that of the Sadducees. Moreover, Chanan boasted that as long as he was High Priest the form of the service should be purely Sadducean, without thought of the Pharisees. Thou knowest well, thou first disciple, what this meant and what bitterness there would be in the hearts of the Rabbis and the scholars.

633

The old enmities were reawakened, and were fiercer than ever. More-over, the new High Priest waited for an occasion to humble the Phari-sees, and this soon came. The Procurator, Festus, had departed for Rome, and the new Procurator had not yet come. So the High Priest was the sole ruler in the land. He took advantage of this opportunity to lay hands on the purest of the pure, on Rabbi Jacob ben Joseph. Him, and some of his followers, the High Priest caused to be seized, when they were at prayer in the Temple court. Without investigation or trial Reb Jacob was condemned, led out to the field of stoning, and there put to death. Before his soul left his body, Reb Jacob lifted up his hands and cried: 'Father, forgive them, for they know not what they do.' Now when the Rabbis and Pharisees learned of this murder, they rose as one man, and with Reb Jochanan ben Zachai at their head, they went to King Agrippa, saying that they would bring a charge against the abom-inable Chanan, even before the Caesar. And they chose a deputation to go first to the new Procurator, who was expected from Rome. King Agrippa at once deposed the High Priest. Three months Chanan was the High Priest, but on the day before he was deposed the leaders of the Pharisees broke into the chamber of the High Priest, and the old Reb Jochanan ben Zachai tore the lobe of Chanan's ear, so that he might thereby become a man with a defect, and therefore forever unfit for the Priestly office."

The apostle spoke no word, and Justus continued:

"He died as a saint, for the sanctification of the Name. The holy congregation of Jerusalem is orphaned."

The first emotion that was roused in Simon bar Jonah by the dreadful tidings was one of envy. He envied Reb Jacob ben Joseph, who had been gathered to the Messiah. And he himself, Simon bar Jonah, was like one who is left outside when a companion enters the house. But the second emotion of which he was aware was that of dread—dread of the responsibility which had now fallen on him. Simon bar Jonah had always needed someone to lean on. This was not because he had no faith in himself; he believed in himself and in his communion with the Holy Ghost. But he needed a support, someone who should be to him what Joshua ben Nun had been to Moses. He had relied greatly on Reb Jacob ben Joseph. In matters of doctrine, in all that had to do with the law, Jacob ben Joseph had been his right hand. Now he felt that

634

he alone, the simple fisherman, would have to bear the burden of the holy congregation.

But when the horror of the tidings broke through to his heart, he needed, besides someone to share his responsibility, someone with whom to weep; and suddenly he felt his heart being drawn to the great apostle to the gentiles—he who had founded so many congregations in the faith, and who, in chains, was still spreading the tidings of the Messiah. Who was nearer to him than Paul? All at once the divisions which kept them apart disappeared. What did this or that interpretation of the faith signify by comparison with the responsibility which now lay on him? Simon bar Jonah forgot the quarrel which he had had with Paul in Antioch. Indeed, it was not in his nature to harbor bitterness; and whatever was left of the memory of that incident dissolved suddenly in a flood of love.

He called to Jochanan-Marcus.

"Lead me, I pray thee, to the chained apostle to the gentiles, to Paul."

The three set out, Simon bar Jonah, Jochanan, and Justus. They passed over the bridge into the center of the city and made their way to the Aventine hill, near the Porta Capena, and having found the house, climbed up the narrow stairs to Paul's lodgings.

The two apostles, the apostle to the Jews and the apostle to the gentiles, fell on each other's necks, and for a long time they uttered no word.

In silence Paul listened to the recital of the fearful incident in Jerusalem, and when Justus had ended, Paul bowed before the first disciple and said:

"From this day on thou art the leader of the congregations, the shepherd to whom the Messiah has entrusted his flock. I am thy faithful servant."

"Not my servant, but my beloved brother Paul, whom the lord Messiah appointed to carry the tidings to the gentiles," answered Peter. "And as the seal of our brotherhood I give thee my beloved son, Jochanan-Marcus, to be thy help in all thy labors."

Chapter Six

ONE FAMILY IN GOD

THE death of Reb Jacob moved Paul to a great renewal of his labors for the church. The little rented apartment on the Aventine hill was now the center of the Christian congregations of Asia Minor, Macedonia, and Achaia. Messengers arrived and streamed forth again; and Paul, who could not be with the far-flung congregations in the flesh, which was chained, came to them in the spirit through his letters. His staff of assistants received an important addition in Jochanan-Marcus, the nephew of bar Naba, who became for Paul something more than a fellow worker. How much there was in Marcus that reminded him of the friend of his youth, for whom he had never ceased to long! And what precious memories came to life again in the presence of the "son" of Peter! Justus, too, who had lately arrived from Jerusalem, became part of the organization. Paul was now preparing to send a letter to the congregation of Ephesus, by the hand of Tychicus, newly arrived from Asia Minor, and to the Colossians by the hand of Onesimus.

In these letters the spirit of Paul is seen to be calmer and more clarified than in the preceding letters. They lack the bitterness, the bursts of anger, which marked the letters to the Philippians. Paul is no longer thinking of his personal enemies. His thoughts, in so far as they are concerned with enmity, are directed against the general enemies of the faith, the "philosophers" and misleaders, the Gnostics, the aesthetes, and "choice spirits," who would make even of the Messiah a privilege for the "inner circle," the initiated and educated, who teach that the Messiah cannot have died, since the Messiah was not a man, but was composed of pure spirit, his whole life consisting only of a series of symbols, intelligible to the trained mind and to that alone. The apostle to the gentiles sensed in this approach to the faith the attempt to transform the Messiah into a philosophized concept, such as Stoicism was among the Greeks and Romans. But the Messiah was not a symbol or a series of symbols; he was not a "philosophy," or wisdom, or the "Logos" for the cognoscenti. The Messiah was and is the flesh and blood of faith for all, the universal redemption. Every man is buried with the Messiah and every man is resurrected with him through faith in the work of God. In the faith every man shares the triumph of the Messiah over death, not symbolically, but in the flesh. By the death and resurrection of the Messiah, every man who accepts the faith is released from the laws of nature which govern the world, because he is no longer of the world; he is part of the order of heaven; he has died in the Messiah to the order of the world. "Why think ye of the laws, as if ye were of the world? If ye have arisen with the Messiah seek the things that are above, where the Messiah sits at the right hand of God. Think of that which is above, for ye are dead, and ye are hidden with the Messiah in God. When the Messiah, who is our life, shall be revealed, ye shall be revealed with him in glory. Therefore ye shall put to death your limbs, which are of the earth, and which are whoredom, uncleanliness, lust, base desire, idol-worship. . . ."

The conquest of death, the linking of the self with the Messiah, came to Paul in clarification after the death of Reb Jacob; on him, not less than on Peter, the martyrdom of Reb Jacob had had a decisive influence. Paul too envied Reb Jacob's ascension, and he longed like Peter to be united with the Messiah in heaven. Still he regarded the present part of his sojourn on earth as more important than any other part. An inner voice spoke to him, as to Peter, saying that his task was to prepare the church for a great event and a great trial. The trial would be such as to make a call on every resource of faith. Every believer had to be made to feel that he was one with the body and soul of Yeshua and therefore ready to abandon all earthly possession and being. He had to act as though there were nothing more to expect from this world, as though all hope and expectation were bound up with the world beyond the grave.

These are critical days for Paul. He feels that now, if ever, he must bring the church to unity in the Messiah. No inherited privilege, no reference to blood or law, must stand between believer and believer; all privileges are washed away by the one great privilege of life in the Messiah. And he writes to the Ephesians: "It is our peace that has made one out of two and has thrown down the dividing wall. Through his flesh the Messiah has destroyed the enmity of the Torah, which consisted of laws and commandments, in order that out of two men he might make one new one in himself, and to bring peace. For through him both of us, Jew and gentile, have access to the Father in one spirit. Therefore ye are no longer strangers and converts, but sons of the house in the family of God." The apostle Paul begins to find his way back to God, Whom he had for a time lost, because of his love for the Messiah, his zeal in his mission, and his bitterness against his enemies. After he asks the Ephesians not to be oppressed "because of my sufferings for you, which are a glory," he tells them: "Therefore I bend the knee to the Father of Yeshua the Messiah, in Whom all the families in heaven and on earth are named. . . ." "And it is one God and Father for all, One Who is over all and in all."

In no other letters does Paul labor so insistently to inscribe in the hearts of the believers the Ten Commandments which God gave to Moses, as in the letters to the Ephesians and Colossians. And though he absolves them of the laws and commandments, inasmuch as they have the fulfillment of these in faith, yet they must live on earth, and life on earth is sinful; so they must have guidance and rules. Purity of family life is one of the principles which he would plant forever in the lives of the gentiles; he speaks again and again of the bodily union of man and wife in a holy bond. "Be obedient to one another in the fear of God." "Wives be obedient to your husbands as to the lord, for the husband is the head of the wife. . . ." He, the apostle, who has known none of the happiness of family life, who, for the sake of his mission, has vowed himself to lifelong celibacy, recognizes with trembling awe the mysterious bond which holds man and wife in a sacred bond of body and soul. The celibate who has avoided knowledge of all earthly love for the sake of his love of the Messiah, penetrates to the heart of the mystery of earthly love, which he sees as a religious service. The sacred purity of the Jewish woman, which the tradition had transmitted from of old from mother to daughter, is for him the guide in the rule of family life for the congregations of the Messiah. And as he writes thus, he is surely not unaware of what he learned in his youth from the Pharisaic Rabbis: "The husband who loves his wife more than his own body, and honors her more than he does himself—in his tent peace shall dwell." "The *Shechina,* the Presence, dwells between husband and wife." "When a man divorces his wife, the altar of God sheds tears. . . ." The purity of family life which he observed in the home of his parents, the tenderness he saw in countless Jewish homes, is what he desires to transplant into the life of the gentiles. He exalts family life to the level

638

of high worship of God. "Husbands, love your wives! As the Messiah loved his congregation, and sacrificed himself for it, so shall ye husbands love your wives even as your own bodies." And in the spirit of the Pharisees, who said: "He that honors his wife honors himself," Paul wrote: "He that loves his wife loves himself." "As the Messiah is to the church, so is the husband to the wife, the limbs of his body, his flesh, his bone, even as it is written: 'Therefore shall a man leave his father and mother and cleave to his wife, and they shall be one body.' " ... All his longing for pure love is in the words: "Children, hear your parents in the lord." "Honor your father and your mother, which is according to the commandment, that it may be well with you and that ye may live long in the land." Indeed, for all his abrogation of the law and the commandments, the directives which he addresses to Jews and gentiles are taken almost word for word from the commandments of Moses; and they have been hammered out again in the school of Paul's Rabbi, Rabban Gamaliel. From the gates of Rome Paul sends them forth again. He nourishes his congregations with milk, as if they were children; and as if they were children he supports them in the first steps they take into the new life. "Put aside deceit and lying, let brother speak truth to his brother, for we are all members of one another. . . . He that has been wont to steal, let him steal no more, but let him work and do good with his hands, so that he may have that which to give to the needy. . . . Let no evil talk issue from your lips, but only that which is good and an aid to improvement." He bids servants obey their masters in fear and trembling: "Ye know that the good which ye do shall be returned you by our lord, whether ye be servants or masters. . . . And you that are masters, deal thus also with your servants, be not harsh with them, for ye know that your lord is in heaven and he is no respecter of persons."

Thus he enjoins the Colossians too, and those that are in Laodicea.

And toward the end of his letter to the Ephesians the new spirit of Paul, born in his latter years, after much suffering and want, sings with the tone of the Psalmist himself. Gone is the bitterness and resentment. Something toward this change had been contributed by Gabelus, the faithful soldier, and the men he brought with him to be taught. The legionaries of Caesar, in their adorned helmets, their shining bronze breastplates, had thrown themselves at his feet, imploring to be taken into the faith. Paul saw in them the host of the Messiah. He wanted

639

to transform all of them into legionaries of the faith, armed and armored against trial, but with arms and armor that would never rust. Before him rose the image of the believer whose weapons are in his hand to repulse the assault on his faith. "Put on the whole armor of God," he writes, "that you may be able to stand firm in the evil day. Gird yourselves with truth, and put on the breastplate of righteousness. Above all grasp the shield of faith, and on your head set the helmet of salvation, holding in your hand the sword of the Spirit, which is the word of God."

He labored hard and long with himself, the apostle to the gentiles, in order to create the image of the armed believer. In a sense all his life had been a preparation for this creation. He had made many detours; he had erred and blundered. But in the end his feet were on the true path, and he had found his brothers, whom he thought he had lost forever. Many others, both Jew and gentile, had found the true path, led to it by the simple fisherman, Simon bar Jonah, and by the martyr, Reb Jacob; they had found it long before Paul himself. It had been easier for them; they had not had to labor like Paul. Bitter and painful had been the path of the apostle to the gentiles; every discovery, every forward move, had been paid for in the sufferings of the flesh and spirit. He had learned by experiment upon his own person. But now: "The man that was is dead, and the new man has been born." It was thus that he saw the armed and armored believer. And suddenly he perceived, that with all the dissensions and quarrels which he had provoked and been a part of, he was one with all his brothers, on the same path as they. It was the path which the Jewish Prophets had made for the man of faith; it was the path of faith, of trust, and of charity. There was no other path; upon it were set the feet of all the righteous, and their steps moved to the sound of the music of the harpist and singer of Israel, the Psalmist. . . .

Paul sent out his messengers with these letters to the four corners of the world. Epaphroditus, having at last recovered his health, went back to the Philippians; Tychicus returned to Ephesus and Onesimus to the Colossians. And in the end there remained at Paul's side his faithful Aristarchus, Jochanan-Marcus, the nephew of bar Naba and "son" of Peter, Yeshua, called Justus, and his "son" Timotheus.

Thus he sat in his hired house on the Aventine, and the hand which was chained to the hand of the guard was uplifted in a proclamation of

freedom and redemption for the world. It was uplifted for the liberation
not only of the slave, but of the freedman too. This was the universal
freedom of God, beyond the law of man; no Caesar on his throne, no
evil in the hearts of men, should ever abrogate it. From his prison house
Paul conferred upon all men a new and irrevocable citizenship in the
name of the Messiah.

Chapter Seven

ANTONIUS THE STABLE BOY

TIGELLINUS, the criminal condemned and pardoned, and now the
favorite of Nero, owed his good fortune to his skill as a trainer of
horses. Nero, a passionate lover of horseflesh and of chariot races—he
himself had often participated as a charioteer—had made Tigellinus the
master of the stables, which were a very important part of the Imperial
household. But Tigellinus had ambitions. He was not content with the
relatively modest position of master of the stables. His eye was fixed
on the highest position under Caesar—commandant of the Praetorian
Guard. When old Burrus was put out of the way, Tigellinus, with the
help of Poppea, realized his dream.

Among the stable boys under Tigellinus there was a certain Antonius—a simple lad, one of the hundreds of unskilled servants and
slaves who performed the menial work—who had accepted the universal
citizenship of the Messiah. Antonius was not one of the privileged experts in the training of horses. His food was poor, his clothing shabby.
In the winter he went about in a thin tunic, with arms and legs exposed.
Barefoot he went through the slushy or muddy streets of Rome on his
errands. It happened that once some comrades of his persuaded him to
visit Paul, and the chained hand of Paul conferred on him the brotherhood in the faith. Enslaved in the flesh, he became free in the spirit of
God; a servant of Tigellinus, he became an equal brother in the new
family of the Christians. When, after his baptism, Antonius came for
the first time to the common meal in the house of Priscilla, and sat with

641

slaves and freedmen as an equal, he became aware of a will and a way of thought of his own, which no external circumstance could destroy in him. The human beast of burden of Tigellinus acquired a human dignity which none of the more privileged slaves of Tigellinus possessed.

It chanced that on a certain morning, when Tigellinus was having his wiry body, his muscular arms and his legs, bent by much riding, massaged by his slaves, and while one of his servants was repeating for him—that he might learn it by heart—a poem in which Nero was being likened to Orpheus, the overseer of the house entered and announced that Tigellinus's beloved Egyptian slave-concubine had given birth to a son.

It was a custom of the time that when a son was born to a Roman freedman, whether by his wife or by a slave, the new-born child would be laid at the feet of the father. If the father adopted the child, it was brought up with the other children of the household. If he refused to adopt it, the child was done away with.

After the massaging, Tigellinus sat in his library, and before him, on a sheet, lay the tiny infant, its red hands and legs lifted in the air, its face puckered, its mouth open in a long wail, its eyes closed. But even before the child had been brought in Tigellinus had made up his mind. Now that he had risen to the first position in the Empire under Caesar, he wanted no more of his bastards to clutter up the place. He was planning to take a new wife, and he did not care to burden her with the upbringing of still another offspring from one of his slaves. He therefore turned away his face from the infant, looked angrily at the overseer of the house, and muttered through his thin lips:

"Expose it!"

This meant, in effect: "Throw it into the Cloaca Maxima."

There was nothing extraordinary in Tigellinus's command. Countless new-born infants, failing of adoption, were thrown like new-born puppies or kittens into the Cloaca.

The infant was carried away from Tigellinus's presence, and the order to have it drowned was transmitted not to one of the educated slaves of the household, but to the stable boy Antonius.

And thus Antonius walked through the streets of Rome, bearing in his arms the tiny bundle of life, wrapped in a sheet. Through his thin tunic he felt the warmth of the quivering, wailing infant. Antonius went toward the opening of the Cloaca Maxima at the foot of the Capitoline, where the great sewer emptied into the Tiber. When he had received the order, it had never occurred to Antonius to disregard or challenge it. What was there unusual in it? What crime had he been asked to commit? On the contrary, his long training as a slave had taught him to feel that the only crime he could commit would be that of disobedience to the orders of his master: and for such a crime he could be thrown to the wild beasts.

Human life was of such little value in Rome that when, during the races, some valuable horse was thrown and trampled by the other horses, there was no thought for the rider, but only for the irreplaceable racer. The Romans had been long accustomed to the shedding of human blood in the arena, and whether it was a gladiator who was slain by his opponent, or a slave who was given to the beasts, the sight of the death agony of a human being awakened no feelings of pity. This was the city, this was the world, in which Antonius had been brought up. And threading his way through the streets toward the Capitoline hill, he was barely conscious of his mission. But as he drew nearer to the opening of the Cloaca Maxima he bethought himself suddenly of something that Paul had taught him. "God has compassion on all men. He sent his Son down, to suffer torment and death, so that he might with his blood redeem the sins of all mankind. And they who believe in the Messiah must be as the Messiah, ready to sacrifice themselves, even unto death, for their fellow men. They must love their fellow men, even as the Messiah did. Else they cannot be one with the Messiah, cannot approach his throne after death, cannot be received into the Kingdom, which will begin soon, when the Messiah will return to earth." Antonius stopped dead, bethinking himself of what he was about to do. Had he not, but a few days ago, been received into the brotherhood and the promise? Had not Paul just made him the equal of all believers, slaves and freedmen? Yes, Antonius believed in Christ, and believed that he must from this time on act in all things as Christ would have acted. He remembered again certain words he had heard from Paul: "Every man is born in the image of God, and all men are kneaded of the same flesh." "*Born* in the image of God!" "This is a child of God, an image of God," thought Antonius, in sudden horror. "It belongs to Christ and it is my brother. Nay! it shall be my child, for all those that believe in Christ are of one family."

Then Antonius resolved to disobey the order of his master. He would not throw the infant into the waters of the Cloaca Maxima. He would carry it to the other side of the Tiber; and he would leave it in an orphanage which the believers maintained in the vicinity of the synagogue. The women there would receive it and care for it. He would say to them: "This is my child, a Christian child! Take care of it for me."

But no sooner had he come to this resolve than he was seized by a great fear. What was this? *He* had decided? But a slave cannot make decisions, a slave has neither will nor soul. He was not his own man, he was the instrument of his master. His soul revolted from the deed, but what could he do? There rose before the eyes of Antonius the lash of the overseer, the iron collar, the chain, the arena. He saw the great fishes which swam about in the basin in his master's garden, and he saw the huge, slimy jaws, with their double rows of teeth, opening for him. On the banks of the basin, behind the bars, crocodiles basked. Had not he, Antonius, seen the slave who was Tigellinus's favorite, before he took the Egyptian flute player, thrown to the crocodiles? No, he had no will of his own. He dared not have a will. He was a dumb slave, the instrument of the will of another.

Covered with the sweat of his inner conflict, Antonius reached the opening of the sewer. From the most ancient times the marvelous Cloaca Maxima, one of the greatest engineering feats of the Roman world, had emptied the filth and refuse of the capital into the Tiber. The Tiber received, together with the city's garbage, countless human bodies, gladiators, criminals, rebels, prisoners who had been taken in battle, brought to Rome to grace a triumph, then beheaded or strangled in the temple of Jupiter and thrown into the sewer, to feed the countless tuna fish breeding in the waters of the river. Very often the waves washed up the remnants of carcasses. No one paid any attention to these fragments of human bodies—no one but the street cleaners, who shoved them back into the river. The banks of the Tiber were also places of refuge for the poorest of Rome's populace as well as for its sick and its criminals. When Antonius came down to the entrance of the sewer, with his wailing burden, he saw, lying on the stones, innumerable vagabonds, ragged, hungry, and verminous.

"If Caesar were only as generous with his bread for poor citizens as the nobles are with their bastards for the fishes!" one vagabond was saying.

644

Antonius stood paralyzed at the wide, black entrance of the Cloaca. The waves beat outwards from the dark interior, bringing with them a sickening odor. Filth, rags, carcasses of dogs and cats, floated on the surface. Antonius made an effort to detach the warm bundle of human life from his own body, but he could not. A violent agitation was in his heart, and his limbs trembled. Suddenly he sprang back from the entrance of the sewer: it seemed to him that he had seen, floating on the miasmal waters, not the body of the infant, but his own body. He himself was about to be thrown in.

Then, in his own tongue, he cried, "Jesus, Jesus, thou Messiah Christ, help me," and sank to his knees, clutching his burden. And while the sweat poured over his face he whispered:

"What was I about to do? I almost threw myself into the black hole of the Cloaca! But it was thou, Yeshua, Jesus, Christ, who didst rescue me. I would have thrown both my lives into the water! But thou, Messiah, didst save me, to take me to thee, to make me part of thee." He pressed the infant close to him, bent down to the earth, and murmured: "I thank thee, Jesus Christ, that thou hast saved me and this little one from the mouth of the pit."

By comparison with this horror which had been averted for him, all the other horrors, the lead-loaded lash, the iron collar, the beasts of the arena, the crocodiles on the basin edge, melted into nothingness. Assurance came back into the heart of Antonius. Whatever happened to him, Christ the Messiah was waiting for him on the other side, waiting with outstretched arms to receive him, waiting on the shining hill in the company of the saints. He, Antonius the stable boy, would be one with the Messiah, because of the torments he would endure for his sake. Now he knew beyond any shadow of doubt that what he was doing was good and right and proper; he knew that he could not do anything else. He was no longer a slave without a soul, a dead implement for the fulfillment of another's will. Yes, his body was at the mercy of his master, Tigellinus; but his soul was with Christ; his soul was free in the lord. Therefore he was following the command of his soul. Like any free man, he could now do that which was good in his eyes.

Antonius walked now with swift and certain footsteps. He turned back from the Tiber and made for the Aventine hill. There was a house on the hill which he had visited more than once. He had come there of nights, stealing out from the slave dormitory. There they lived who had taught him the meaning of brotherhood in the Messiah. There he had broken bread with freedmen, slaves, soldiers, Greeks, Jews, Romans. All had sat together, like brothers, and they had exchanged the brother kiss. It was there that, for the first time in his life, he had understood that he, the slave, had a soul and belonged to God. In that house lived Priscilla and Aquila. Priscilla had welcomed him into the companionship. She had led him forward to the table, where the gray old man from Jerusalem was seated—the messenger of Christ, who had known Christ in the life and had been sent by him to spread the tidings through the world: the apostle who had served Christ, shared his bread with Christ, had been kissed by Christ. Toward this house Antonius hastened, knowing that there his tiny charge would be received.

Priscilla herself received Antonius at the door, with a look of astonishment which deepened when she learned on what mission he had come. She had known many strange things to happen; many strange people had sought out the shelter of her faith, and many strange stories had been unfolded to her. But this was the first time that a slave had come, bearing in his arms the offspring of his lord which he had saved from death at the peril of his life. But when her first astonishment was past, she bethought herself that nothing could have been more natural. For Antonius was bringing a soul to her, a little one to be baptized instead of drowned, to be raised up in the faith of the Messiah instead of being given to the waters of the Tiber.

Priscilla could not take the little one to herself. She was overburdened with the tasks of the congregation. Moreover, she and Aquila were preparing to transfer their home once again to the city of Ephesus. Thither the apostle was sending them, intending, in God's good time, when he should have been set free, to follow. What would they do with a new-born infant on the perilous journey before them and the strenuous days that lay beyond? Priscilla resolved to give the child to some godfearing woman of the congregation. Which one she did not yet know; but until she had made her choice there were the two orphanages on the other side of the Tiber. One of these had been founded by the Jews many generations before; the other had been opened but lately by the Messianists, next to the home of the apostle. Priscilla snatched up a scarf, veiled herself, and, with the impetuosity that was characteristic of her, hastened forth, guiding Antonius across the Sub-

646

licius bridge. Among the narrow, tortuous alleys of the Jewish quarter, among the houses which were packed with Jews and poverty, stood the synagogue. About the synagogue court were the institutions of the community. One was the school house, another the ritual baths, a third a hospice. A building had been acquired by the sect of the Messianists; here Simon bar Jonah, the apostle to the Jews, had his home. And close by there was a hall, an annex, which had been turned into an orphanage. It consisted of a single large room with an earthen floor and rows of benches about the walls. Here the good and pious Miriam, aided by the sisters of the church, had installed the orphanage. And here the son of Tigellinus, the mightiest man in Rome after Caesar, was left, to be cared for with other orphans and to be given to some Christian woman for a Christian upbringing.

Chapter Eight

"AS A BELOVED BROTHER"

WHEN he had finally delivered the child into safe-keeping, Antonius found himself incapable of returning to the domus of his master. The exaltation which had sustained him till this moment seemed to ebb away, and he was again seized with terror at the thought of what he had done. He was terrified by this first exercise of his own free will, by this demonstration of power over himself. He had dared to defy, to destroy, to render as nothing, the gigantic discipline which had surrounded him since the day of his birth; and his faith was too young and inexperienced to provide him at a moment's notice with a counter discipline in which he could be confident. He had broken with ancient custom and deep-seated habit—but he had not a new custom and a new habit to replace them. Like one lost he wandered through the streets of Rome, and when evening came he found himself in the Suburra.

Like the banks of the Tiber, this low-lying section of Rome between the Quirinal and Viminal hills was the refuge of Rome's human débris, her poor and sick, her criminals, thieves and escaped slaves.

Lying cheek by jowl with the Forum and the elegant Via Sacra, the Suburra was in a sense the human Cloaca Maxima, the drainage of Rome's misery, crimes, and disease. The streets were narrower there than in any other part of Rome; the tall houses shut out the sky; passages led from house to house, creating a vast, impenetrable labyrinth, with caves, niches, and secret places. The lowest dregs of the plebs swarmed, like moles, in the underground of the Suburra. The diseases they brought with them flourished in the dirt and fetor of their refuge. Very rarely did a ray of sunlight penetrate to the narrow streets of the Suburra; the earth underfoot was damp, for when rain fell it did not drain away from this valley but soaked into the soil and accumulated in the cellars. The air was sour with exhalations of human sweat. At night the district was perilous in the extreme. Murder and robbery lurked in the darkness. The houses, built of cheap material, were dilapidated, and fragments of roofs and walls tumbled into the street. The lower floors were supported by flying buttresses, under which the "merchants" of the Suburra kept their stores. Often the top floors were nothing but gaping ruins, where, in the midst of exposed rafters, heaps of rubble and brick, families lived like wild animals. The police of Rome did not dare to venture by night into the lower labyrinths of the Suburra; and there an escaped slave might hide himself indefinitely, if he found the means of sustenance. And a Roman slave had learned to subsist on little: on decaying vegetables and occasional crusts. Sometimes the escaped slaves formed themselves into little bands. They would send out scouts who signaled the approach of the carts rolling in from the countryside before the dawn; then a regular assault would take place and masses of provisions would be taken away: sacks of grain, baskets of fruit, filled wine skins, pots of olives, sides of beef.

Like every other slave in Rome, Antonius knew of the Suburra and of its hiding places; and when that night came he had already found a niche for himself in a cellar. Six other escaped slaves had made their home there. When Antonius entered he was neither welcomed nor rejected. The slaves did not even interrupt their conversation, which consisted mostly of gross jests and insults.

After a while they turned their attention to the newcomer. They greeted him first as "Mercury's messenger," bringer of good tidings and of liberation; then as the messenger of Fortuna, and the carrier of the horn of plenty. Finally they addressed him with the title of Nero's cup-bearer. After all of which they approached him and began to search his clothes. Had he brought any money with him? Had he managed to steal something before he left his master? But they found nothing on him but his robe of sackcloth, whereupon they turned from him and resumed their conversation.

Said one: "If the guards should catch me, I shall give myself out as a murderer; then I will be thrown to the beasts, which is better than being a slave."

"I too! I know what awaits me if I return to my master. I shall be killed and quartered and my flesh given to the fish in the pool. Why shouldn't I amuse the people in the arena, instead? At least I'll sell my life dear."

"What carest thou who eats thee, fool, the fish in the basin or the beasts in the arena?"

"Maybe so. But I'll tell thee what. Those that catch me will have no easy task. A dozen lives for mine, I say."

" 'T will be the same with all of us. I keep my sesterce tied here round my neck, for Charon."

"Thou wouldst do better to spend it on wine as long as thou canst drink. Knowest thou not that the old boatman takes no slaves on his ferry? Slaves must stay on this side of the Styx, so that they may be reborn as animals."

From a corner came a voice. "Slaves have no gods."

"True again! In our domus they drove the slaves out before they did sacrifice to the gods. They said Apollo was offended when a slave was admitted to his temple."

"I know a god who came down on earth and suffered the death of a slave, in order that he might thereby redeem all men from sin," called out Antonius.

"A god who suffered the death of a slave? What kind of god is that?" answered a couple of voices, amid laughter.

"He is the god of all men and knows not the difference between slave and freedman. All that believe in him are brothers."

"Slaves too?"

"Aye, slaves too. We that are of his faith sit at one table in a common bond of love. . . . Because all of us become one body in him."

"Slaves too, sayest thou?"

"Slave and freedman become brothers in him."

649

"Then what dost thou here, among us? Why goest thou not to thy brothers?" asked a mocking voice.

Antonius thought awhile. Yes, why did he not go to his brothers, and hide himself among them?

"Well said," he answered, at last. "Tomorrow I shall go to my brothers. I know one who will receive me."

"Tell us, who are these thy brothers, who will conceal slaves who have fled from their masters?"

"My brothers are Christians. Each one who believes in this god calls himself a Christian."

"Christian!" someone repeated. "Christian! What is the name of the god who makes all men brothers?"

"Jesus the Christ."

"Jesus the Christ? Is it thus thou callest him?" And one of the men in the cellar came closer to Antonius. In the darkness Antonius could still make out a wild, hairy face and two swollen red eyes. A hand which was heavy and shapeless, like the paw of some primitive beast, fell on Antonius's shoulder. "Didst thou say Jesus Christ? But I have heard that name."

"Where hast thou heard it?"

"In the house of my master, Philemon, in Colossae."

"Was thy master a Christian?"

"Aye! There was a man came to our city and told my master of the new god; and my master was baptized."

"And yet thou didst run away from thy master! Was he harsh with thee?"

"Nay! I stole money from him and ran away to Rome. I had always dreamed of being a freedman. Now I tremble to leave this hole. They will catch me—and then thou knowest what will be with me."

"Thy master will forgive thee."

"What? A master forgive a slave the crime of theft? Never. A slave that steals has his hands cut off, then he is thrown into the water."

"But if thy master is a Christian he will forgive thee, I say. The God of the Christians bids us forgive each other our sins as He forgives us our sins."

"Not my sin!" said the other, obstinately. "A thieving slave is not forgiven."

650

"The Messiah forgives all that pray to him. And thy master will forgive thee and take thee back."

"I am not a Christian."

"Thou wilt become one."

"I cannot become a Christian. I am a runaway slave and a thief."

"Everyone can become a Christian. The Messiah accepts all that come to him."

The voice of the man changed. "I had heard of it," he said, "and I wanted to hear thee say it. I would have gone into the street before now and sought out the Christians but that I fear to be recognized as a runaway slave. And thou art the first to have spoken to me in his name."

"It is Christ himself who sent me to thee. Tomorrow I shall lead thee to the messenger of Christ."

* * *

Early the next morning, while the sky was still gray, two slaves ap peared before Paul's house on the Aventine hill. One of them, ragged and filthy, his feet caked with mud, his hair falling wildly over his face, stared about him timidly. The other, younger, cleaner, his sackcloth garb still whole, was surer of himself. Timotheus came to the door of the lodging and heard them explain that they wanted to see the apostle. He asked them who they were, and they answered simply that they were slaves who had fled from their masters. For what reason had they fled? asked Timotheus. Antonius, whom Timotheus did not recognize, revealed that he was a Christian, and told in what manner he had fled from the household of Tigellinus. Onesimus, hearing the confession of Antonius, told the story of his crime and his flight from Colossae. Before he admitted the two men, Timotheus went in to his master and made certain that the soldier on guard that morning was a brother Christian, of the cohort of Gabelus. Then Antonius and Onesimus came in. Paul recognized the stable boy whom he had brought into the faith. But what was most marvelous in the eyes of Onesimus, he remembered and described Philemon of Colossae, the master from whom Onesimus had fled. He knew the wife of Philemon, too; she had come to visit him in Ephesus. The apostle bade Timotheus wash Onesimus, bring him food, put a clean robe on him, and then lead him to Priscilla.

When that had been done, Antonius told Paul of his "crime;" of the infant he had refused to fling into the Cloaca Maxima, of his flight

651

from his master, his meeting with Onesimus in the Suburra, and his decision to seek the counsel and aid of the apostle. Paul listened to the end, then kissed the young slave, and said:

"My beloved son, Antonius; thou has found favor in the eyes of Christ. It was the Messiah who guided thee from the beginning, that thou mightest save the infant and thereby be led to save another soul, that of Onesimus. Great is thy portion in Christ, and Christ has set aside a great reward for thee."

"What is my reward?"

"That thou shalt suffer for the Christ Messiah."

Antonius became pale. But Paul, holding the lad's hand, went on talking:

"Thou wilt return to thy master's house, and thou shalt go to him that is in command over thee, and thou shalt fall at his feet and beg forgiveness from him for having absented thyself from the house this night. . . ."

"And concerning the child?" asked Antonius, trembling. "What shall I say concerning the life I would not take?"

"That is thy secret in the Messiah. Thy master would have slain the child—therefore it is no longer of his flesh. Thou hast begotten the child to thyself, in Christ. He is therefore thy child, and he is the child of the Messiah in the spirit."

"They will cut my body to pieces with the whip," pleaded Antonius, and he shook with fear.

"The lord will be with thee, and he will save thee from their hands. And as for the lashes thou wilt receive, is it naught to thee that thou wilt suffer for the service thou hast rendered unto Christ? When they scourge thee, bethink thee of that which the Messiah suffered for thee, and say to thyself: 'These are the lashes which I share with my beloved Messiah,' and feel thyself bound to him for ever. Go, my son, and endure thy suffering as becomes a freedman in the Messiah, a Christian such as thou art."

His heart strengthened, but his flesh still shrinking, Antonius returned to the domus of Tigellinus. He did as the apostle had bidden him; he appeared before his overseer, threw himself on his knees, and begged forgiveness for his absence of that night.

Antonius, though only a stable lad, was a willing and useful slave. He was therefore condemned to the lash, but not the heavy lash called the *flagrum*, the thongs of which were so loaded that they broke the bones. The lighter lash, called the *flagellum*, which only cut the flesh without any permanent crippling effects, was used on him. Thirty strokes was all he received; and as the blood streamed from his naked back, Antonius thought on the sufferings of the Messiah, and it seemed to him that Paul's words had come true: in the anguish of his flesh he felt the union of his spirit with Christ's, and not a moan or whimper escaped his lips. That day Antonius the stable lad was the only free man in the princely establishment of Tigellinus.

When two weeks had passed, Onesimus appeared again before Paul, a new man inwardly and outwardly. His hair was cut and combed, his chin shaven, his body decently covered. In the two weeks of his stay with Aquila and Priscilla he had given himself to the Messiah and had been received into the brotherhood of the Christians.

Paul called for papyrus and writing implements, and with his free right hand—the other being chained to his guard—he wrote a letter to the master of Onesimus, Philemon of Colossae:

"I beseech thee for my son Onesimus, whom I have begotten in my bonds. He who in the past was unprofitable to thee shall be profitable both to thee and me. I send him back to thee; receive him, for he is my own heart. I would have kept him with me, so that he might serve me, who am in bonds, instead of thee, in the spreading of the gospel. But I would not do this without consultation with thee, so that thy beneficence might not be enforced but might come of thy own free will. And perhaps it was necessary that he should leave thee for a while in order that thou mightest receive him for ever, no longer as a servant, but as a beloved brother, especially unto me, but how much more unto thee, in the flesh and in the Messiah. Therefore, if thou count me as a partner, receive him as myself, and if he has wronged thee, and owes thee aught, let that be written against my account. I, Paul, have written this with my own hand: I will repay it. Prepare also a lodging for me, for I trust that through your prayers I shall be given to you."

A slave had fled from Philemon; Paul returned him, a brother.

Chapter Nine

SABINA POPPEA

SABINA POPPEA was the granddaughter of Sabinus Poppeus, a Roman who had been a governor of many provinces and the recipient of many honors at the hands of the Caesar. Poppea's mother had been a famous beauty to whom the poets of her time dedicated countless odes. From her mother Poppea inherited her stately figure, her rosy, luminous, delicately-veined skin, and her magnificent crown of copper-colored hair, which her slave hairdressers had a special way of disposing, in cunningly wrought waves and hollows which caught and hid the sunlight in a strange translucent play. Two features of Poppea's were magically beautiful, driving the gilded youth of Rome to despair and its matrons into paroxysms of jealousy: her slender, towering throat and her dazzling skin. She heightened the effect of the latter by constant bathing in asses' milk and by the use of exotic oils and balsams prepared and applied by a large staff of experts.

While still in her teens Poppea had twice married and twice got rid of her husband, inheriting in each case a huge fortune. Her wealth, added to her beauty, made her the most famous and most desired woman in the Imperial court.

Poppea's ambition was not less magnificent than her beauty: she aspired to be the wife of Caesar. But not that in name alone; she desired power as well as rank. Therefore, though she knew that at the first moment of her meeting with the Caesar she had overwhelmed him with her beauty, she showed that she was not easily to be won. She played, she encouraged, she retreated, she coquetted. She flirted in the presence of Caesar with the handsome young prince, Otto. And she let Caesar understand that, if he desired her for his wife, he would have to throw off the tutelage under which he ruled. It was Poppea who persuaded Nero to rid himself of his mother, the ambitious and scheming Agrippina. She used every weapon in her armory to compel him to the act. She ridiculed him, who was a man, for remaining tied to his mother's apron strings, like a child; she wept for him, because he compromised his dignity; she threatened to leave Rome, and go to some distant province, in order that she might not be the witness of his humiliation. In the end she had her way: Nero put his mother to death. But Poppea's marriage to Caesar did not follow at once.

Seneca was ready to give his consent. No sooner had Nero declared to him, in tears, his love of Poppea, than Seneca consented to the suggestion that the Emperor divorce his wife, to whom he owed his throne. It was old Burrus, the commander of the Praetorian Guard, who stood in the way. With all his soldierly faithfulness to the throne, he could not permit Nero to cast off Octavia, the daughter of Claudius, the granddaughter of the mighty Augustus. Poppea turned to Tigellinus, and intrigued with him for the removal of Burrus. Here again Poppea had her way: Burrus was poisoned.

After this event, Seneca withdrew to his country estate to dedicate whatever remained to him of his life to his studies and to the famous moralistic letters which he indited to his friends. The reins of government were taken over by Faenius Rufus and by the infamous Tigellinus. Nero at last obtained permission to divorce Octavia, and he did this in the face of a storm of resentment among the Romans, who respected Octavia as the representative of the glorious Julian line. Octavia was banished; but this was not enough for Poppea, who did not rest until her rival was sent into the banishment from which there was no return. Twelve days after the divorce Poppea, accompanied by her five hundred asses—the providers of her baths—came to the palace as Nero's wife.

This beautiful and brilliant woman, "who had every virtue save virtue," had a queer inclination toward monotheism, and even coquetted with the Jewish God of Jerusalem. The matrons of Rome were jaded with the succession of religions which they tasted. Many of them were under the influence of the priests of Isis, who were as numerous in the aristocratic homes of the Roman capital as in their native Egypt. The rite of Isis was popular. It was a commonplace for a senatorial wife to put on black veils and lock herself in her chambers to perform the mysteries of the Nile goddess. Precisely because Isis was by now an ordinary cult, Poppea determined to attach herself to the Palestinian deity. It was for her a mark of distinction, like her baths of asses' milk and her exotic perfumes and salves, and she derived a perverse pleasure from her cautious attachment to the universally derided and despised monotheism of the Jews.

There was of course no thought in her mind, when she became acquainted with the Jewish God, of making Him the dominant principle of her life, to accept any moral responsibility, or to look into that distinction between good and evil which was His message. Poppea had one worship—her own beauty; one morality—her dominion over Caesar. Her body was her temple, and she the high priestess. She prayed to her white skin, her blue veins, her large, almond-shaped eyes, her copper-colored hair. She desired to die before these objects of adoration had lost their magic. Her flirtation with the God of the Jews was only an expression of her boredom. But there was enough of it to enable certain Jews to exploit it for the benefit of some of the prisoners who rotted in Caesar's prisons. The Jewish scholars and the Jewish masses, either of Jerusalem or of the Diaspora, did not know her. Those individuals who did know her hated her as they hated the whole of the Roman court.

On one occasion a young aristocrat of Jerusalem, a member of the Priesthood, was brought before Sabina Poppea by a Jewish actor of Rome. The young man had received a thorough and worldly education. He spoke excellent Greek, was acquainted with Greek literature, and had taken to the writing of history. From this young Jerusalemite Poppea wanted to learn everything concerning the mysteries of the Jewish God and of the services in His famous Temple in Jerusalem. The Jerusalemite spoke with much elegance, sprinkling his conversation with many quotations, and the impression on Poppea was an excellent one. He had sought the introduction to Poppea, it transpired, in order to plead for three Priests who had been sent as prisoners to Rome by the Proconsul Felix. This business disposed of, Poppea asked the visitor to tell her something concerning the life after death which was a feature of the Jewish religion. Yes; the young man confirmed the rumor; the Jews believed that each man would rise from death, in the same form as he had possessed in life, for the physical part of a man was interwoven with his spiritual being. Poppea was deeply interested; the possibility that she could arrange to be resurrected in all the beauty and charm which she alone possessed was something to be looked into. She would, of course, do her best to please the Jewish God. Had she not made a start with her promise to intervene on behalf of His three Priests? She did more. She saw to it that the young aristocrat, whose name was Josephus, should not leave the palace empty-handed. At the same time she made a note in her mind that before she died she would issue instructions that her body should not be burned. One could not be sure. The elegant young Jerusalemite and the Jews might have hit on the right path. She decided, further, to obtain a couple of Jewish Priests to form part of her suite, and to accompany her, with her other attendants, when she passed in state through the streets of Rome. This was as far as she went. Any hint that worship of the Jewish God was bound up with duties, penalties, obligations, self-denials, discipline of any sort, she rejected. This was not in her style. Sabina had dreams of becoming the "Helen of Rome," with a temple of her own, in which worshipers would offer sacrifice after her death. Certainly she was not going to ally herself openly with a people which was ridiculed in the theaters and circuses of the capital, which was the butt of every satirist and pamphleteer, a people which was said to worship an ass's head and to waste one day out of seven in sheer, meaningless idleness, a people which refused to touch pork and kindled many, many lamps on the seventh day; a people, moreover, accounted an enemy of the gods, which was tantamount to being an enemy of mankind. But that part of its religion which had to do with the resurrection was not, after all, to be ignored; and such service as she could render the God of this religion, without too much effort, she would not withhold from Him. There was the freeing of the three Priests, the presents to the visitor, the purchases of cosmetics and balsams from the Jewish women, and occasional favors to Jews. What more was expected of her?

Thus, on a certain day, two Jewish women, dealers in balsams, stood before her, pleading for some Jewish Rabbi who, they said, had been kept a chained prisoner in Rome for the last two years. The great lady sat back luxuriously on her couch. Her white skin filled the room with a subdued luster, overlaid by the glow of her hair. About her were ranged innumerable vases and phials, of bronze, silver, and glass, filled with the essences of Oriental plants. On a table lay the instruments of her toilet, scissors, tweezers, and files of every shape, while in a brazier glowed a row of hair curlers. A staff of naked slaves attended Poppea, under the direction of her chief masseuse. The utmost care had to be exercised, in tending to her beauty, to cause her no physical pain. The

657

slightest twinge brought immediate retribution, which usually took the form of a glowing tweezer applied to the skin of the clumsy slave. And if Poppea happened to be in a less gracious humor, she was capable of condemning the sinner to be thrown to the crocodiles. Some of the slaves worked on her hair, weaving it strand by strand into cunning folds. Others applied layer after layer of salve on the white skin, then, removing these, poured on precious oil. One specialist was occupied with Poppea's eyebrows, another with her breasts, a third with the tiny growths of hair on her neck, a fourth with her finger-nails, a fifth with her toe nails. Egyptian slaves, hidden by curtains, discoursed soft music. The Vestiplicae, the slaves charged with the care of the robes, laid out the tunics, veils, corsets, and sandals which Poppea would wear that night to the banquet.

Suddenly, for some unaccountable reason, Poppea's face clouded over. The delicate rose-white of her face turned to crimson. She reached out and thrust the prongs of a pair of tweezers into the breast of the slave who was manipulating her eyebrows. Without uttering a word, she closed the tweezers with all her strength. The slave turned white, but uttered no sound. Her knees gave way, and she fell to the floor. Two African slaves came forward and carried her away. Poppea did not even look round. She only signaled to the two Jewish women standing before her to speak.

"Great lady!" said one of them. "This oil which I bring you today is one pressed from the secret plant *Mor* and *Dror*, which grows but in one part of the world—the wilderness of our native Judaea; and only our Priests know the secret of extracting its essence. One drop of this oil, mixed with salve, imparts a sunlike brightness to the skin. There is not a queen anywhere in the world to whom this oil has been offered before. Today we received, for the first time, a few drops of this oil, direct from Jerusalem. I have mixed it with salve, and I bring it as a gift to our great lady."

The speaker, Dark Hannah, who was known to many Roman matrons, bowed low before Poppea. Then her companion spoke:

"And I have brought you, O Empress, a balsam pressed out of a cactus plant which grows in our land. The cactus is as hard as granite, yet it cannot be ground, for in the grinding it loses its virtue. It must therefore be beaten softly for three months, until the oil issues of itself. This oil is called Helbonah, and it is treasured more than precious stones. Only Queen Bernice has had the use of it till now, and that only in tiny measure. We had the cactus sent to us from the Holy City, and we beat it for three months."

Poppea signaled to her slaves, who took the phials from the women.

"Try them out," she commanded.

A drop from each phial was poured into the hand of a slave. Then the hand was rubbed and warmed, to bring out the aroma of the salves. When all this was done, the hand of each slave in turn was brought under Poppea's nostrils.

Poppea seemed pleased. She ordered the Helbonah to be applied at once to her skin, and while she was thus being ministered to, the Jewish women took courage and bowed again—not in the manner of the slaves, who stretched themselves out in obeisance before their mistress, for this was forbidden by their religion as befitting only before God—they merely inclined their heads, and bowed from the waist down.

Dark Hannah spoke: "Everywhere in Rome and throughout the world they speak of the great lady's graciousness and goodness, as of her beauty which has won the heart of Caesar. And everyone knows that, because of that beauty, the lady has the key to Caesar's heart. Loveliest of women, we have come before you to implore your clemency on behalf of a holy man, a messenger of God, who has been held prisoner in Rome these two years. The man is innocent of any crime and has committed nothing against the laws of the Caesar or against the laws of our God."

"Why, then, was he brought to Rome?" asked Poppea.

"Great lady! The man was placed under arrest by the High Priest for believing that the dead rise again to life. The Priests do not hold this faith, but it is held by all our Rabbis."

"Why was the man not judged in Judaea, according to the laws of the land?" asked Poppea. "Why was he sent to Rome?"

"The man, whose name is Paul, and who is an apostle of Jesus the Christ, is a Roman citizen, and he appealed to Caesar."

Poppea paused. This was interesting: a Roman citizen who had appealed to Caesar and who had been kept in chains for two years without a hearing. . . . Here was a Roman citizen who had waited two years because the Caesar was too busy singing his own poems to the accompaniment of his own music.

659

Later, when Poppea was with Nero, she mentioned the case to him. She was not afraid—she had already accustomed him to her reproaches. She was the only person in Rome who dared to speak the truth to Nero.

"Augustus, Tiberius, and Claudius," she said, "considered it a point of honor to try in person those who had appealed to the Caesar, for the Caesar is the fount of justice for all Romans. But this man has waited two years for justice, and my Caesar has done nothing for him!"

Thus in the end Paul's appeal to Caesar was answered. Not by Nero himself, for despite Poppea's reproach he could not tear himself away long enough from his more important occupations. A deputy of Caesar heard the case in the palace of justice on the Forum.

Whatever element of justice had gone originally into the drawing up of the Roman code of law had been corrupted in practice by the "clients" which every lawyer brought with him to a trial to applaud his utterances and influence the judges. The claques, consisting either of a regular body of clients or of men hired for the occasion, usually filled the hall. But on this occasion the hall was empty. Paul had no lawyer to defend him. Even the general public was absent, for those who had heard that a Jew was to be tried on some obscure and involved point of religious procedure did not think it worth while to attend. There were present, besides Paul and the deputy of the Caesar, two advisers and secretaries.

Not only had the High Priest failed to send a formal accuser to the trial; he had not even advised any of the Jews of Rome concerning Paul's crime. For the incumbent in Jerusalem at the time of the trial in Rome was no longer Chananyah, he whom Paul had roused to such fury by his defiance. It was, indeed, doubtful whether any of the Priests of the Temple even remembered the case. When Paul arrived in Rome, after his two years of imprisonment in Caesarea and his long and perilous journey by sea, he was told, by certain Roman Jews: "We have received no letter from Judaea concerning thee. And we have not heard, from any of our brothers, anything good or evil concerning thee." Standing before the deputy of the Caesar, whose only source of information on the case was the report drawn up by the one-time Procurator, Festus, Paul defended himself exactly as he had done before Felix, Festus, and Agrippa.

660

He was a Jew, a believer in the Jewish faith, which was sanctioned and protected by the Roman Empire; he had never offended against the laws of Rome or those of the Jewish faith; "they did not find me in the Temple conducting a dispute or moving the people to disaffection— neither there nor in the synagogues nor in the city. But this I confess; I serve the God of my fathers according to the ways of my sect; and I believe all that is written in the Torah and in the Prophets." Then he added: "The sole difference between them and us concerns the Messiah, of whom they say that he is yet to come, while we say that he has already come. Regarding the resurrection, that is, the awakening of the dead, my sect is at one with the learned men and lawgivers of Israel: they too believe that the dead will rise from their graves, and there is no difference between them and us on this score. I say nothing save that which Moses and the Prophets foretold: which was that the Messiah would suffer, that he would be the first to rise from the dead, and that he would be as a light unto his people and unto the nations. It is only the sect of the Sadducees which has persecuted me. The Sanhedrin of the Pharisees found no fault with me, neither did King Agrippa, before whom I defended myself in Caesarea. King Agrippa declared me innocent, and he said to Festus: 'This man might have gone free if he had not appealed to Caesar.' "

The Tribune who was Caesar's deputy that day was a man well versed in law; and it was his honest intention to apply in this case the letter of the Roman law, which he held to be the highest achievement of human justice and wisdom. For all that, he was unable to repress the queer feeling of contempt and disgust which was always evoked in him by mention of the barbaric cult of the Jews. It was an unpleasant and wearisome case that he had before him; and the best he could do was to divest himself of any feeling of relationship to it and to be done with it as soon as possible. Just like Festus, he regarded Paul as a maniac, seized with the typical religious disease of the Asiatics. As to whether a certain Christ had or had not risen from the dead, what concern was that of the Caesar and of the law of Rome? Besides, the Jews themselves, the plaintiffs in the case, had not even appeared to support their charges. If the man before him deserved to be cast into prison, it was not because he had done anything against the laws of the Jewish faith but on the contrary because he supported them! And the Tribune reflected that it was a great defect in the Romans to have extended the

661

tolerance of their laws to the Jewish faith and to have encouraged the follies of a cult which preached a resurrection, a Messiah called Christ, and destructive practices which were slowly penetrating, as he knew, into the homes of the Romans via the matrons of the city.

But the law was the law; it was for him only to administer it. And that same morning Paul was set at liberty.

Nearly five years he had been a prisoner and in chains. Now his dispute with the Jews was at an end.

Chapter Ten

"WITH JEWS A JEW"

IT WAS as if his liberation was but the beginning of his new dedication. He felt, on that morning, like an eagle released from a cage: there was not a moment to lose—he would open his wings and fly! Were not the churches of Ephesus and of the cities about Ephesus waiting for him? Had he not yet to make his first visits to Laodicea and Colossae? Had he not written to Philemon to prepare lodgings for him? And what of his beloved Galatians and Philippians, who were so faithful to to his memory? Hundreds of soldiers of the faith were waiting for him. But he had not rested during the years of his imprisonment, either. Here too, in Rome, freedmen and slaves in every part of the city had been won to the Messiah. He, the apostle in chains, had given freedom to the unchained. Now he could transfer his gentile converts to the care and keeping of the apostle to the Jews; let the two congregations mingle and become one.

That same day Paul assembled all his workers—Timotheus, Marcus, Lukas, Priscilla and Aquila. A great new enterprise was to be launched. The churches of Asia Minor were in danger. There had arisen among them a sect of false and narrow pietists, who were seeking to convert the faith in the Messiah into a rigid Nazirite and ascetic discipline, a variety of Hassidism. They rejected the world altogether, denied themselves to their wives, or refrained from marriage, did nothing but fast and pray in solitude. What was this but the narrowing down of the faith into a particularistic sect, the transformation of the universal appeal into the spiritual privilege of the handful of adepts? The tidings of Christ were for all men, for all humanity, and not for a sect with peculiar and extreme rituals of its own. This new tendency in the church was for Paul even more dangerous than the assault of the Gnostics. He felt that only his intervention among the churches could check the inroads of the wild pietists; and he needed all the help that he could muster.

Titus was already in Crete; Aquila and Priscilla were about to leave for Ephesus, there to set up their home once more like a nest of the faith. Timotheus would follow them before long, and he together with them would strengthen the congregation, choose leaders, purify the spirit. Meanwhile Timotheus had another task to perform. Paul was planning to send him with a letter to the congregation of Jerusalem. Now that he had thrown off the chains which Chananyah the High Priest had put on his hands; now that the congregation of Jerusalem was orphaned by the martyrdom of Reb Jacob ben Joseph, all the bitterness and hostility that had once existed between Paul and the believers in Jerusalem had dissolved.

And so, ready to leave Italy from the port of Puteoli, he indites his letters to the Hebrews.

It is an offer of peace which he sends them, an attempt to make whole that which had been split, to reassert the common bond of blood. Paul harks back to that which he learned at the feet of Gamaliel; he reviews the whole Torah, from Genesis on. He weaves into the letter quotations from the Torah and the Prophets, making use of the methods he had learned in the school of his youth, interpreting the verses according to the Pharisaic tradition. The tone of the letter is Jewish; it might have been written by a pious Jew who had in no way ever departed from the tenets of the traditional faith—it is written by one who is "with Jews a Jew." He does not use the second person, but the plural first: not "you," but "we." He is no longer at variance with his brothers, he does not cover the face of Moses with a veil, he does not abrogate the Torah. On the contrary, it is through the power of the Torah of Moses that he would win them to the Messiah. He addresses himself to their imagination and fantasy. He knows what sanctity attaches in the mind of Jews to the High Priesthood, and he would make of the

663

Messiah an eternal High Priest. The Messiah is descended in the flesh from Abraham himself. "He did not take upon himself the nature of the angels, but the nature of Abraham. Therefore it was fitting for him to be the equal of his brother in all things, that he might be a compassionate and faithful High Priest before God, who forgives the sins of the people." "For as he alone suffered so he is able to help others who are tried in him."

He speaks tenderly of the fathers, of Abraham, Isaac, and Jacob, also of Moses and the Prophets, and even of the Torah. He adorns the letter throughout with quotations from the Torah. "For this is the covenant which I will make with the house of Israel. . . . I will give my Torah in their midst, and I will write it upon their hearts, and they shall be my people and I shall be their God." He sees the embodiment of the sacrifice in Yeshua the Messiah. He compares him to the Temple, to the Holy of Holies—but it is one into which all enter, all the Jews, not the High Priest alone. Thus he speaks, "a Jew to Jews." And like a prophet of consolation he evokes the great and glowing hope beyond the night of trial, terror, and anguish. He would bring the Jews to the Messiah not by threats and gloomy forebodings as he has done hitherto, but by putting the glory of the High Priest's robes on the Messiah—the robes which the High Priest wears on the Day of Atonement when he enters into the Holy of Holies to win forgiveness and reconciliation for the Jews. "The Messiah Yeshua had come in order to be a High Priest in good things which are to come, by a greater and more perfect tabernacle, not made by human hands, not of this building; neither by the blood of goats and calves, but by his own blood he entered into the holy place, having obtained eternal redemption for us. For if the blood of bulls and of goats, and the ashes of a heifer sprinkling the unclean, sanctifies us for the purity of the flesh, how much more shall we be sanctified by the blood of Yeshua the Messiah, who through the Spirit offers himself without spot to God? How much more shall we be sanctified, and purged from dead works, to serve the living God?"

"Whomsoever he loves he chastens," Paul adds toward the close of the letter, and he reminds his fellow Jews of the saying of the house of Hillel: "Follow peace! Follow peace with all men, peace and holiness, without which no man shall see the Lord." Throughout, he appeals to them for the new covenant in the spirit of the old, making parallels, reverting to traditional commandments and events. He reminds them of the giving of the Torah at Sinai, and of the terror which came on Moses. He exhorts them to renewed observance of the Abrahamitic practice of hospitality. "Be not forgetful to entertain strangers; for thereby some have entertained angels unaware"—an allusion, striking deep into Jewish memory, of the encounter between Abraham and the angels of God.

He tells the Jerusalemites of his longing to see them again and implores them to pray to God that he might be "given to them" speedily. He ends the letter with the news of his liberation. This he does not do in open language, lest he should awaken old enmities in Jerusalem and provoke them to make fresh attempts on his liberty. He speaks indirectly, knowing he will be understood. "Know that our brother Timotheus has been set at liberty," he writes. But they to whom he wrote were well aware of the Pharisaic dictum : "That which the Rabbi is, the pupil is also." If Paul, the teacher, was imprisoned, so was his pupil; and when Paul was set free, so was his pupil.

Having completed the letter, Paul entrusted it to Timotheus, who had learned the holy language in his childhood days, and Timotheus set out for Jerusalem. Then, having consigned his congregation in Rome to the care of Simon bar Jonah, Paul gathered his companions about him and took ship for Asia Minor.

Chapter Eleven

BABYLON

THE words which Paul had spoken to the slave Antonius, of the household of Tigellinus—that the Messiah Jesus would reward him because he had saved a soul, and that therefore the Messiah would confer upon him the privilege of sharing his own suffering—these words sank deep into the heart of the new believer. From that day on he lost all fear of physical pain. He did not go out of his way to incur punishment, but neither did he seek to escape it by dereliction to his faith. And since he was determined to make no secret of his faith, he soon began to be singled out, by the oddity of his behavior, among the slaves of Tigellinus.

It chanced one day that a fellow slave of Antonius, much older than he, a worker in the same stable, incurred the displeasure of his master. An overseer observed that Gloria, one of Tigellinus's favorite horses, had been tied too closely by the tail, so that it had become restive and unmanageable. The offender, Colon, the Corinthian slave, was led out to be punished. There was a certain system in the punishment of slaves. Those that were younger, and therefore capable of many years of service, were handled with care; they were made to suffer, but not in such a way as to affect their usefulness. With old slaves this consideration did not exist; and the older the slave, the less it mattered if his bones were broken and he was crippled for the few remaining years of his life. Colon the Corinthian was stripped of his sackcloth shirt, the iron collar was closed about his neck, and the powerful slave with the *flagrum,* the massive, bone-breaking whip, was summoned.

It was when Colon had already been carried into the punishment chamber that Antonius, trembling and covered with sweat, came running, and threw himself at the feet of the overseer, who was a freed slave. *He* was the guilty one, he declared; it was he who had tied the knot too tightly and too high upon Gloria's tail; he was the one who ought to be punished.

It was an unheard-of thing, either in the household of Tigellinus, or in any other, that one slave should exculpate another and offer to be punished in his place. The overseer was puzzled. He decided finally that both slaves should be punished; Colon's bones were broken that day and Antonius's flesh cut with the light lash.

It was thus that Antonius attracted attention by his queer behavior; but before long it became evident that a general spirit of unrest and revolt had appeared among certain of the slaves. Antonius was not only young, and a willing worker; he was also well-built, with a powerful chest, narrow hips and powerful thighs. From the time of his adolescence on, it had been the practice to couple him with healthy slave women, for the begetting of a strong, new generation of slaves. Antonius had obeyed without questioning, forgetting on the morrow who had been his companion in the night. Nor did he ever feel the slightest interest in the result of the coupling, or in the children he had begotten. (Slaves were not allowed to have "families." It often happened that

666

brother and sister were coupled in one household.) But now it began to be observed that Antonius was failing in his duty as a breeder and that he would not couple when admitted to a slave woman. The slave women themselves lodged complaint against him. But this was not the worst. After he had been punished several times for his dereliction, Antonius did attach himself to a certain slave woman, but to her alone, expressing his determination to know who his offspring were and acting as though he had the right to create a family of his own. When the woman gave birth to a child, Antonius asserted that he was the father, and on several occasions he was caught in secret meetings with his mate, who brought out the child for him to see.

It had happened before that slaves had shown this tendency to exclusive preference and had made the attempt to build up a family relationship. But hitherto it had sufficed to apply the whip, or even to make a threat with it, and the incipient relationship had dissolved. The child would also be taken away from the offending slave woman and given to another to be suckled. Thus mothers forgot who their offspring were and did not know whom they were suckling in the general confusion of the slave quarters.

But the case of Antonius and his mate was different from previous cases of the kind. It was discovered that the mother had made a tiny mark on the infant, by which she could recognize it. It was discovered also that the obstinacy of this pair had infected other slaves and their breeding partners. This was a direct and dangerous threat to the whole system; for the privilege of family life belonged only to freedmen, and the attempt of slaves to arrogate this system to themselves was nothing more nor less than revolt.

It became evident after a time that the slaves who were taking part in this conspiracy had other practices in common. They seemed to have created a sort of brotherhood. They had a system of secret signs by which they revealed themselves to each other. They would make certain gestures in the air, they would draw on the ground a rough symbol of a fish, or of an anchor. This, then, was no accidental outbreak; it was the manifestation of a cult. It was seen, further, that many of the suspected slaves would come together in the evenings, either in the courtyard or in the slave quarters and would sing strange songs and utter strange names. Most amazing of all, they were caught sometimes exchanging a kiss of greeting. Along with these bewildering and irritating manifestations of a secret understanding, there came a perceptible diminution in the production of infant slaves; and sometimes a couple that had been thrown together for breeding purposes would be caught kneeling side by side and murmuring the name of a secret god by the name of Christ.

Soon the mass manifestations were connected with the Jews. It was widely known in Rome that every seventh day the Jews observed what they called a Sabbath. They closed their shops, they withdrew their peddlers from the streets, they assembled in the synagogues or in their homes, they lighted candles and they ate peculiar dishes of their own. The Sabbath was a popular jest among all Romans, slaves and freedmen alike. It was known as "the day of the Jews." But now "the day of the Jews" seemed to have crept in some incomprehensible manner into the household of Tigellinus. Regularly, when this day came around, certain of the slaves would be missing; and many of those that were in quarters evaded their tasks and went about murmuring under their breath the name of "Christ."

The attempt to put down this altogether incomprehensible form of revolt, which was without precedent, as far as its form went, in the experience of the overseers, began with a series of scourgings administered to Antonius and several of his fellow slaves. They were without effect. The punishment was received without complaint, the slaves went on working faithfully at their daily tasks—but on the seventh day the same laziness manifested itself, the same disappearances took place, and throughout the week there was the same avoidance of the indiscriminate couplings.

Soon it became known that the infection was not peculiar to the slaves of Tigellinus's household and not even peculiar to the slave class. Rome was suddenly aware that "the day of the Jews" had taken hold of great numbers of slaves and soldiers. On that day there was a general movement toward the Jewish quarter in the Trans-Tiber, where slaves and soldiers were to be seen loitering about the synagogues. In smaller measure this had been observed before, but only among freedmen and women—particularly the latter, who had picked up the habits of the despised Jews and were even introducing them into their own homes. Now, however, whole groups of slaves slipped away from their work on "the day of the Jews" and mingled with soldiers on the bridges leading to the Jewish quarter.

668

A new, more earnest, and more malevolent interest was now awakened in the phenomenon. Hitherto it had been considered enough to make the Jews objects of universal ridicule. But neither this nor the savage punishments visited on the slaves arrested the spread of the new Oriental fanaticism. That it was of Jewish origin was known from the beginning; later it was established that a particular sect was at work, a sect of "Christians," who derived their name from a certain Jew criminal, Christus, who had been put to death by Pontius Pilate in Jerusalem. This Christus, according to the superstitions of the sect, had risen, or was shortly to rise, from the dead, to become the liberator of the Jews. Those who, whether Jewish or non-Jewish by birth, joined the sect, at once accepted and made their own the unclean practices and base beliefs of the Jews.

The religion of the Jews had never enjoyed the respect of the Roman world. The aristocrats and philosophers despised it; the masses, perhaps not worse informed regarding it than the upper classes, made it the butt of a special type of humor; the "clients" of the Roman politicians, who spent their days gossiping in the baths or in the porticoes of the Campus Martius, when no gladiatorial shows were on, aped their employers and toadied to the plebs by their attacks on the Jews. The pamphleteers, taking their cue from the Egyptian careerist and slanderer, Apion, invented the most fantastic stories regarding the nature and appearance of the Jewish God. Whatever was repulsive and degrading in the superstitions of the idolaters they attributed, in intenser form, to the religion of the Jews. Of the ethical contents of Judaism they were incapable of forming the faintest conception. And now that they heard of a sect among the Jews, "Christians," responsible for the inroads on the religion of Rome, they transferred to these all the ignorant spitefulness and obscene inventiveness which they had devoted to the Jews in general. But in the new attack there was a tone of practical malevolence which had been absent hitherto. As long as the religion of the Jews had been confined to the Jewish quarter, it had been derided as a grotesque curiosity. But as soon as it stepped across the threshold of the synagogue, and in its new "Christian" form began to manifest itself in the "households," it ceased to be merely grotesque and became sinister. If an occasional freedman chose to make himself absurd by sneaking into a synagogue to hear a Jewish preacher, or by imitating the observance of the seventh day, it mattered little in Rome. After all, the Jewish religion was sanctioned and protected by Roman law, as were scores of others. But it was intolerable that the indulgence of the law should be exploited by the Jews to spread, in the name of this Christus, a theory of equality and liberation among the slaves. What was this but revolt? The fact was that the Christian agitation had penetrated to innumerable households, disturbing the relationship between slave and lord, encouraging a fantastic conceit among the former and limiting the authority of the latter. The very speed with which the agitation was spreading indicated, moreover, that in the case of Christus the Romans were confronted with a demonic manifestation of power which they interpreted in the spirit of their own hideous immorality. As the number of Christians grew, the scurrilities which were spread concerning them by the pamphleteers and clients became correspondingly more horrible.

* * *

Vestian Suberus was a typical "client." Born a slave in one of the provinces, he had in his youth won the favor of his master by a mixture of flattery and unnatural vice. He had been set free, adopted, and then made the heir of his owner, who shortly thereafter died of poisoning. Suberus sold his legacy and moved to Rome. Driven by his ambition for a political career, he concealed his servile origin with a set of false documents and sought to bribe his way into an official appointment. He maintained a rich home, bought handsome slaves, entertained lavishly, and bought frequent gifts for the Caesar's favorites. He also hired a claque of clients and in every other way conducted himself like a patrician. But he had reckoned without the ferocious competition of the capital. He not only spent his fortune in the hunt for office but went into debt and almost became a slave again. He managed, somehow, to extricate himself from this last dread extremity and was left with two lean slaves, who ran about the streets of Rome hungry and half naked. These too he lost finally at dice. He moved with his wife, whom he treated like a slave, into the coenaculum or top floor of a foul half-ruined apartment house in the Suburra. He was unburdened by children; those that his wife had borne him he exposed, afterwards throwing their bodies into the gutter or into one of the openings of the Cloaca Maxima.

However, he had managed to save his "toga," the emblem of his status as a freedman, and by virtue of it he found employment as a client with a rich patrician to whom he was recommended. Early every morning he would put on his toga, which his wife kept carefully in repair, and hasten to the house of his lord, to wait, together with the other clients, and to form part of the procession which accompanied him through the streets. In exchange he received from six to ten sesterces a day—according to the mood of his employer—and an occasional length of cloth for a toga. As a freedman he was also entitled to admission to the baths and spectacles and to the daily quota of bread and wine distributed occasionally by the Caesar or by some patrician currying favor with the mob.

Much of his time Suberus spent in the amphitheater, where the fights between gladiators or between condemned criminals and wild beasts, often went on for days at a stretch. What drew him to the amphitheater was not the sight of disemboweled men; he was surfeited with bloodshed. His eyes were fixed on the elderly women, matrons and widows, who found in the gladiatorial combats a last thrill for their jaded nerves and shriveled flesh. Nor was he alone in this interest. A host of idlers, charlatans, and ruffians frequented the arenas in the hope of attaching themselves to one of the wealthy female spectators. Here too Suberus was unable to sustain the competition. In vain did he keep his languishing gaze fixed on a prospective victim; in vain did he whisper passionate words into unresponsive and sometimes literally deaf ears. Vestian Suberus was no longer young. His eyes were rimmed with red, his cheeks puffed up, his limbs flaccid. He moved slowly, his belly sagging visibly under his toga. All day long he would see younger men approach the matron he was stalking, and he knew that he did not stand a chance. Late in the afternoon, wearied with the fruitless vigil, he would go to a free bath. Then he would remember that at home there waited for him his hungry wife, who had occasional moments of rebellion and was quite capable of emptying the chamber pot on his head if he returned too late. He would turn toward the Suburra, spend a few sesterces on a piece of putrefying meat, and bring it home for supper.

One day Suberus sat before the great façade of the Baths of Agrippa in the Campus Martius, in the company of a handful of "freedmen" like himself, the scourings of the city. The conversation turned, as it often did about that time, on the barbarous Oriental cult of the Christians which was making such inroads among the slaves of Rome.

"And do you know what they do at their mysterious meetings in the synagogues?" Suberus was saying. "They bring in an infant, cover it with flour, make a gash in its body, and let the blood run out into a beaker. Everyone present takes a sip of the blood, then they smear their privates with it. This is their way of unifying themselves with their deity." Suberus was repeating what he had heard in the domus of his employer the day before.

"Nay," said another idler. "That is not done by the Christians, but by the Jews. They have a Temple in Jerusalem, and in it a certain place which only their High Priest can enter, and that only once a year. They call it their Holy of Holies. A Greek is confined in that room for a whole year, and food is pushed in for him to eat. At the end of the year the High Priest enters and kills the Greek, then the flesh is distributed and eaten. I heard this from Apion when he was here in Rome." The speaker was a learned freedman who wrote pamphlets for his employer and painted posters which were put up at night on the walls of the Forum buildings.

"The Jews worship an ass's head, which they keep in their Temple," added a third.

"The Christians do that too."

"What mean you, the Jews, the Christians! The Christians are also Jews. They have all the superstitions of the synagogue, and some new ones besides, worse than the old," said Suberus, not to be outdone. "Do you know what they do when they assemble, men and women together, at their secret meetings? They strip themselves of their clothes and--" here Suberus leaned over toward his neighbor and said something in a low voice, not because he was ashamed to repeat it aloud, but because he thought it would titillate the curiosity of the others.

His neighbor burst into laughter.

"But what say you to this?" cried one, laughing. "I have heard that neither the Christians nor the Jews ever reject a child, even a cripple! They bring them all up—which is one of the reasons why they're crowding us out of the city."

"Nay, that is not to be believed," said one, and it was not clear which of the imputations he was denying. "I know certain Jews who have great businesses, here on the Campus. You will see them often together with Romans, in the amphitheaters and circuses. They dress like Romans and speak like Romans. They would not do such things."

"The rich Jews would not, perhaps. They are in some measure

civilized. They have learned some of our manners, at least. I have Jews among my friends, and they are decent people, not to be distinguished from us Romans. But the poor Jews over there—" the speaker jerked his thumb toward the Trans-Tiber region—"what *they* do in their secret synagogues and in their homes, in their courtyards!... Wert thou ever in the Jewish quarter when they observe their seventh day, their Sabbath, methinks they call it? Then thou wouldst smell something—their dishes, man, with nothing but onion and garlic and sour wine, are enough to poison you. And who knows what goes on behind those curtains, by the light of their lamps and candles? For my part, I can believe anything of them."

"And mark this: the Christians, as they call them, are always the poorest among the Jews, the fanatical foreigners who have never assimilated but maintain their Asiatic ritual over there, in the Trans-Tiber, as if they were at home in Judaea."

"It is a matter for wonder that the Caesar has tolerated this evil so long," said the pamphleteer, earnestly. "The danger spreads apace, and nothing is done. Know you what? I will write a new pamphlet on this very subject, and read it out in the Forum and in the baths, for all to hear who will but listen. I tell you Rome must be saved from the Jews —and that soon, or it will be too late."

* * *

Spring was approaching Rome on light, fresh wings. First a mild wind blew from the south, dissolving the veil of gray from the face of heaven; then the earth became young with a green blossoming. The willows shook their hanging locks in the little garden of the house of Hermas, out on the Via Appia, among the mausoleums of the great, not far from the new Jewish quarter. It was there that the congregation which Paul had founded in Rome assembled now that the apostle to the gentiles was gone. Once their place of assembly had been the house of Aquila and Priscilla, but these too were gone from Rome, at the bidding of the apostle. Before she left, Priscilla charged Hermas, one of the earliest of the converts, with the care of her group. Old Simon bar Jonah would also come to the assemblies or, rather, would be brought there by younger men.

On a certain day, when the spring winds were shaking the willows around the pool, the first of the apostles stood in a ring of the faithful, some of whom were seated on the grass, and told to them, as he always

673

did, of the time when he had served the Messiah. Bar Jonah spoke, and his heart was heavy in him; for whenever the spring came he remembered the sufferings of the lord. But this spring he was sadder even than his wont, for he was troubled with deep forebodings, as if his spirit were warning him of the dread trials which were about to be visited on the congregation of Rome. As he stood in the garden, the poppy buds, the lilies and the violets, the messengers of the spring, blossomed at his feet; and he told them of his first meeting with his Rabbi and savior. Such a day it was, when he sat in his fishing boat by the bright shore of Kineret in his homeland, and by his side sat his brother, Andrew. They had thrown their net into the water, and they were waiting for the evening to fall. When it was dark they drew in their net and rowed to the shore. It was there that they first set eyes on the savior; and from the first moment they knew who he was. Out of the darkness of the oncoming night he shone in his white robe. He looked at them and beckoned with his hand, saying: "Come, follow me, I will make you fisher of men." From that moment on they had followed him. Here he was, old Simon bar Jonah, in their midst, still a fisherman, and they, his listeners, were the fish of God. He told them also of that spring day when he had seen the lord among the blossoming trees in the narrow little street; he had seen him from behind a wall; and the robe still shone white, but it was blood-bespattered and streaked with the sweat of the the lord's anguish; and on his shoulder he bore the cross on which he was to die. "And from that time on, seeing that he did not put away the cup from his lips, every believer must be prepared to drain it again and must be prepared to bear his cross and to let his blood be shed."

Then the first apostle began to speak of the frightful time that was approaching and of the Messiah-pangs which would herald the second advent:

"The day of the lord will come like a thief in the night. On that day the heavens will dissolve in storm, and the foundations of the earth will be loosened. And the earth, and all that has been done thereon, shall be destroyed. And ye must hasten to come, before the day of God, when fire will sweep away the heavens and the foundation will melt! Beloved brothers! Prepare for that day, and be diligent to be found faultless, that peace may be with you. Be ready for the time of the great witnessing, when ye shall testify for the lord!"

Evening came on, and the shadows fell upon the breathless group of men and women and children clustered under the hanging willow branches. When the voice of Simon bar Jonah ceased from speaking, his listeners were afraid to move; it was as though the dread day was about to dawn and that even a whispered word would hasten its coming.

Chapter Twelve

NERO

NERO CLAUDIUS CAESAR AUGUSTUS GERMANICUS became—a bride. He—that is, *she*—put on the rose-bedecked veil of a virgin and went through the long and complicated ceremonial of marriage, according to the laws and traditions of Rome—the blessings of Apollo's and Aphrodite's priests, the sacrifice of a suckling pig—with one of his liberated slaves. Nor was it the first time that Nero was a participant in such a marriage, in the full presence of the Court, the council of ministers, the commandant of the Praetorian Guard, and the highest military figures of Rome. And the place of honor among the guests was reserved for Sabina Poppea, the wife of the Caesar.

Some time before Nero had had himself married to a certain Sporus, but on that occasion Sporus had been the bride, Nero the bridegroom. The wits of Rome launched a jest which it might mean death to repeat, but which was nevertheless heard everywhere: "How excellent it would have been for Rome and the world if Nero's father had taken such a bride." There were some who observed, at the second wedding, that Nero had done well to change his role; for with his great fleshy bosom he looked, at the age of twenty-six, more like a heavy widow than an Augustus. Nor had his famous hairdresser, Talamus, found it particularly difficult to dispose the Caesar's hair in girlish ringlets. Indeed, it was when Nero was in his manly mood that Talamus suffered; the smooth, oily skin, the rounded flesh, the full lips, the dimples, could not be manipulated into a suggestion of masculinity; while the feminine effect was heightened whenever Caesar opened his mouth,

675

for his voice, which his flatterers assured him was the noblest ever heard by human ears, was that of a capricious and affected woman.

Rome was not astonished by the curious ceremonials which were observed that day in the presence of the Senators and chief soldiers of the Empire. The Court poets were ready with a collection of odes which represented Aphrodite herself as smitten with envy of the beauties of the "bride." Lucan, the poet laureate, outdid himself on this occasion, though he was careful to introduce a number of blemishes into his poem, lest the meter and metaphors should pretend to compete with those of Caesar, who came to the wedding with a song addressed to himself. Petronius, arbiter of taste and master of obscenity, put everyone, including Tigellinus, in the shade with the fulsomeness of his flattery. Not that Tigellinus had ever distinguished himself in anything but vice and horseflesh; but it was not wise to offend him by outdistancing him publicly in the race for Caesar's favor. All in all the spectacle was thoroughly in the spirit of the time, and Rome was not astonished; for Rome was worthy of Nero, and Nero of Rome.

If Tigellinus could not compete with Petronius in flattery, he had other ways of commending himself to Caesar. On the day of the marriage the commandant of the Praetorian Guard arranged a great banquet in honor of the "bride."

The place where the banquet was held was the artificial lake in the gardens of Aprippa. Tigellinus had long since discovered that a certain degree of resourcefulness and inventiveness was needed in order to keep Nero in good humor. Chariot races were all very well in their way, and Tigellinus knew how to arrange a race—with the Greens, Nero's favorite color, as winners—better than any other man in Rome. But Nero was easily bored. He had had his fill of gladiatorial shows; he was, of course, always winning at the chariot races. He needed triumphs of a more difficult kind—in the field of poetry and song. The Muses began to push out the gladiators, the ringing of the harp drowned out the drumming of horses' hoofs. Every member of Nero's entourage was suddenly expected to become an expert in the arts. Patricians and senators, who had thought it beneath the dignity of a Roman to have an opinion on a statue or a poem, suddenly found it a matter of life and death to be able to speak like professors. They sent to Athens for the most intelligent slaves and the most admired works of art. Rome became the repository of the treasures of the Greek temples, and the culture of Greece was elevated to the status of a fashionable craze. To be able to quote the Odyssey and the Iliad in the original was almost indispensable for anyone seeking social distinction. On every corner of the Forum, in the baths, the restaurants and the barber shops, wherever Romans assembled, one might hear the verses of the classics declaimed. It was the same in the Campus Martius and in the gardens surrounding the Pantheon. A plague of poetasters and reciters broke out in the imperial city. And it all stemmed from the master of Rome. Nero would be a poet, therefore every Roman had to be at least a critic of poetry.

Tigellinus was as willing as the graceful, elegant, and cultured courtier Petronius to play the toady to Nero; but he lacked the first rudiments of literary taste. His learned slaves perspired to equip him with a few ready phrases to offer his master, but Tigellinus could not remember them at the right moment. He was compelled to fall back on baser forms of service. Petronius, the arbiter elegantarium, might supply Nero with the subtlest compliments; Tigellinus made up for it by the volume of applause which he organized. Petronius tickled Nero's vanity with choice comparisons; Tigellinus competed by bringing him the cheers of the masses and provoking the plebs to amazement and worship. The banquets which Tigellinus arranged in honor of the Emperor put every other form of entertainment in the shade. Exotic foods from the farthest corners of the world, game fish and fruit out of season, dishes which no one had ever tasted before, were Tigellinus's substitute for literary appreciation; and always the banquets were prepared so lavishly that the remains could be distributed to thousands of citizens in the name of the imperial master. In Nero's name, too, Tigellinus subsidized the corn imports, distributed vast quantities of oil and wine, provided magnificent spectacles, sought out the most skillful gladiators and the largest herds of wild animals, so that Rome might make merry and applaud Caesar. The games by day, the torchlight processions by night, were put on whenever Nero appeared in Rome, so that the populace implored the Emperor never to leave it. Nero, with his sickly hankering for the poet's laurels, was forever threatening to withdraw from the capital of the Empire and to settle in the capital of culture—Athens. He complained that the Romans were incapable of appreciating his immortal works; their enthusiasm, when he appeared in the arena, seemed to him to be lacking in the proper warmth. Only the Greeks, he cried, would understand what his spirit had brought into the world. And the Caesar, Nero Augustus, actually toured the provinces like a strolling player, to win the plaudits of his subjects. It was in Naples, which was predominantly Greek, that he was given such a thunderous reception when he recited in the arena that he complained at the comparative coolness and doltishness of the Romans and began to talk of a great triumphal round of performances, the climax of which would be reserved for Athens.

As he passed in procession through the streets of Rome to the banquet arranged for him in the Agrippa gardens, Nero was stopped by a huge delegation of "clients" hired by Tigellinus for the occasion. The "free" Roman citizens threw themselves before his *sella,* stretched out their hands to him and babbled hysterically:

"Apollo, Apollo, leave us not! What will we do without thy music?"

"August Caesar! Rome languishes for the sound of thy voice!"

"The gods have given thee to us, Apollo! Sing for us!"

Nero was touched by the demonstration. A smile settled on his thick lips as he looked out over the prostrate mass of suppliants. Poppea and his other wives—of both sexes—looked at him imploringly. It seemed that Apollo was conquered.

But the smile of satisfaction did not last long.

In spite of the immense and repeated ovations which awaited him along the route from the Esquiline hill to the Agrippa gardens: in spite of the groups of petitioners who threw themselves before his *sella,* Nero felt the old boredom and sadness returning. The smile vanished, the thick lower lip began to droop, and his fleshy lower jaw dropped to his chest. The time of year was summer, at the beginning of the month of July. The day was hot, the air heavy. The path of the procession lay in part through the foul, narrow alleys of the Suburra, which were jammed with an immense concourse of all ages and both sexes. The naked African slaves who headed the cortege swung their silver-tipped staves about them, to clear a way. The windows of the high apartment houses were black with spectators, who waved veils and kerchiefs at the Caesar. But neither roses nor other flowers fell from the windows of the Suburra; there was nothing to counteract the stale, fetid air, which often was carried by the winds as far as Caesar's palaces and gardens. On this day there was no wind; the foul, standing air enveloped the parade, and Caesar's face became contorted with disgust. The smell of

678

putrescent meats and fish rose thickly from the cellar depots, mingled with rancid exhalations from oil, vegetables, vinegar, and tallow. The hot sun had done its work on these, on the human bodies, on the damp mattresses in the apartments and the heaps of garbage outside. The multiple filth of poverty and indifference sent its noisome steam into the air, and Nero was thinking of the "Golden House" which he had long been planning, a huge edifice to link his palace on the Esquiline with that on the Palatine. In this house he would assemble the costliest of the art treasures of Greece, many of which were now scattered in his various gardens; here, too, he would build a gigantic amphitheater for the performance of his musical and poetical works. It was to be something that no Caesar before him had ever conceived, let alone attempted. But where was he to erect his "Golden House"? Over a garbage dump? For the Suburra was this and nothing more. It had to be uprooted. All the narrow, filthy streets of Rome had to be leveled with the ground. A new city had to rise from their ashes, eternalizing his name and filling the unborn generations with stupefaction at his achievements. None but he should be the architect; let the centuries know the multiplicity and inexhaustibility of his talents. It should be the city of divinity, for whatever he, Nero, did was divine. Apollo in music, Apollo in poetry, Apollo in stone—it was his duty to transmit his inspiration to the world: Nero's city—Neropolis!

But the stink of the Suburra broke in on his lofty theme. In vain did his freedmen attendants sprinkle him with perfume; in vain did precious oils drip on his skin; the Suburra was stronger than all perfumes and oils; and Nero felt an inclination to retch. Nor did this quivering in his vitals stop until he had been carried into the Agrippa gardens. The sour, sick look on the imperial features warned his courtiers that Nero was in an evil humor, and dread fell upon them. Each one trembled for himself and cast about for ways of making himself scarce lest the divine displeasure fall upon him.

Caesar was, however, given to rapid changes of mood. A few minutes after he had been carried into the riot of colors and voices, of laughter and joy, which filled every corner of the gardens, and particularly after he had learned of the new entertainment which Tigellinus had arranged for him, the smile reappeared on his heavy lips, the fleshy jaw was lifted from the womanish bosom.

Incapable of literary or intellectual perception, Tigellinus had a subtle understanding of his master's grosser egotisms. He was forever thinking up ingenious amusements such as no previous Caesar had ever enjoyed. On the artificial lake of the Agrippa gardens drifted a flotilla of barges covered with thick tapestries, decorated with garlands, and linked to each other with silken ropes. On the shores of the lake were erected rows of booths, woven of branches and flowers, and in them the matrons of Rome's highest society, the wives and daughters of the Emperor's suite, sat or lay in attitudes suggestive of the vilest houses of assignation of the Suburra—a combination of imperial splendor and gross vulgarity particularly suited to the imperial taste. Crocodiles floated on the surface of the lake, ready to pounce on anyone who should make a false step and fall into the water. For another element in Nero's favorite amusements was that of danger—to others. All this Tigellinus knew; he knew that Nero would be waiting for someone to tumble off a barge into the open jaws of a crocodile; and in any case he would enjoy the spectacle of the terrified slaves who, from their small boats, had to bring the dishes to the barges. The reptiles, their appetites awakened by the odor of food, swam after the boats and set them rocking. The girl dancers who had to perform on narrow ledges running round the barges were pale with terror; and the guests, reclining on couches at their tables, laughed drunkenly at the antics of slaves and dancers. The laughter rose into a shout of excited merriment when an unhappy youth or girl, unable to endure the test, fell with a scream into the water. A huge pair of reptilian jaws closed on the white body, and the water was stained red.

The food was rich and greasy. Boat after boat unloaded cargoes of roast white pheasant from remote provinces, huge boiled lobsters holding in their claws smaller marine animals, like shrimps, crays, and starfish. Finally a whole table was transported to Nero's barge; on it reposed a pig still in its skin, amid green leaves and miniature bushes. Tiny pigs were laid about the larger animal, as it were, sucking its dugs.

Sabina Poppea half lay and half sat at Nero's side. She was in an advanced stage of pregnancy, but she made no effort to conceal her condition. On the contrary, by dress, posture, and gesture she did everything to accentuate it. Like the animal brought on the table to Caesar, she had her breasts uncovered—long, heavy breasts, the nipples painted red to bring out the pallor of the skin. Her brown eyes, cold and motionless, were fixed contemptuously on the distance. Her amber-colored hair was woven into thick plaits coiled like a crown upon her head. The heavy golden ornaments on her throat, her ears, her naked arms, the great uplifted curve of her body, suggested the white marble statue, the "Helen of Rome," with which she identified herself. No muscle quivered on her face. It was as if she, and not Nero, were in control of her destiny.

A slave in the costume of a hunter approached the table, lifting up a huge carving knife. Nero snatched it out of his hand and slit open the belly of the pig, out of which tumbled a mass of tiny sausages. The guests reached out and grabbed for the delicacies. Nero Augustus Germanicus too snatched up handfuls of sausage and stuffed them into his mouth. A sudden flicker passed across Poppea's eyes; the whites were covered with a film of water, the pupils contracted. She cast a sideways glance at Nero, and in her glance was terror. A frightful thought had occurred to her; some day Nero would do with her what he had just done with the pig—plunge a knife into her and scatter her vitals on a table. She shuddered from head to foot.

Later, when the clusters of torches were lighted on the barges and the guests repaired to the booths on the edge of the lake, Nero remained in the company of his favorites. Then Tigellinus approached him on bended knee and implored him to sing for the entertainment of the company. Nero refused, abruptly and categorically. His face was clouded again, just as when he had passed through the frightful stench of the Suburra.

"No one in Rome loves me," exclaimed Nero in a melancholy, womanish voice.

"No one loves thee?" cried Tigellinus in horror. "No one loves thee? Command me, my Caesar, and at a word I will throw myself to the crocodiles."

Tigellinus had hardly uttered the words than all the blood withdrew from his face. It seemed to him that he just uttered his own death-sentence.

But Nero paid no attention to Tigellinus's offer, much to the disappointment of Petronius and the other courtiers. Nero only grimaced sourly with his thick lips, drew down his eyebrows, and let his eyes sink into the surrounding folds of fat. He said:

"If you Romans loved me, you would know of yourselves what I desire and I would not have to utter it."

The courtiers looked at each other in bewilderment. They opened and closed their mouths, without saying anything, until finally, wrinkling up his eyes even more than before, Nero exclaimed:

"Rome stinks!"

The courtiers started back, consternation settling on their faces. They hesitated blankly on this explosion. Nero evidently disliked Rome. They knew what happened to a man whom Nero disliked. Nero had but to indicate dislike, had but to lift his little finger, and a soldier would appear. No instructions would be needed. It was enough for Nero to have expressed displeasure. But what in the name of Pluto was to be done if it was Rome that Nero disliked? The courtiers were tongue-tied. Even the quick-witted Petronius was at a loss for words.

Tigellinus was the first to come to.

"Rome would rejoice to go up in flames for thy sake, O Caesar. Rome longs to burn for thee! Rome will burn for thee!"

The fleshy folds retreated from Nero's face. A spark of triumph lit their watery depths. Nero put his hand heavily on Tigellinus's shoulder:

"See! This is the only friend I have in Rome!"

This was clearly Tigellinus's day. He had scored a great victory over his enemies.

Petronius, the craftiest and most gifted of the sycophants, stood on one side, observing the triumph of Tigellinus. The vicious smile died on his lips. He put on an earnest look, struck a pose, and stretched out his hand to Nero:

"Now I see it! Now I understand! What is Homer's description of the burning of Troy? For thee, O king of poets, the gods have reserved the greatest of all songs of flame: thou shalt be the singer, and Rome, the queen of cities, shall be thy model!"

Nero rose from his couch, approached Petronius, and kissed him on the mouth.

Petronius shot a triumphant, crooked smile at Tigellinus.

Chapter Thirteen

DAY OF WRATH

ALL Rome witnessed Caesar's withdrawal from Rome, when he set out for his summer palace at Antium. Tigellinus had seen to it. The cortege which accompanied Caesar on that day was such as no living Roman had ever beheld before. The masses of Rome, and especially the poorest of the plebs, beheld the grandeur and wealth of the Emperor streaming out into the country.

Who could count them all, the senators and generals, the patricians and the matrons, carried high in their litters and palanquins, as they followed the glittering chairs of Nero and Poppea? Who could count the freedmen, the secretaries and overseers and chamberlains, each with his own staff of servants, the masters of the bath, the hairdressers, the perfume mixers, the masseurs, the masters of the robes, the cooks, the waiters, the butlers, and the wine tasters? There went along, also, hordes of slave musicians, flute players, harpists, cymbal players, psaltery players, lutists, each with his or her instrument. There went along Egyptian dancing girls, with lotus flowers in their jet black hair. There were actors, comedians, clowns, mimes, many of them famous throughout the Empire. The mob perceived its favorites among them, and so far forgot itself as to cheer them instead of Caesar. For the actors and mimes were not idle in the procession. They danced, they tumbled, they caricatured the great of Rome, not excluding those that were actually in the cortege. They sang, they made obscene jests, they uttered their scurrilities against the aristocracy. They were some who even dared to hint at the Caesar himself, alluding to one who had sent his own mother and his stepfather into the nether world. They did not have to mention names; they did not have to speak; they imitated a woman floundering in the water—that was Caesar's attempt to drown Agrippina; they lifted an invisible drink to the lips, and contorted themselves in mimic agony—that was the death potion which Claudius had finally been made to drink. The mob howled with glee, and repeated the couplet so popular in Rome:

Behind the mimes came the freaks, cripples, cretins, and jesters, some of them half animal, and some more animal than human. They hopped on one leg or they crawled on all fours. The mob stood on its toes to see them; the more grotesque the creature, the wilder the applause. From roofs and niches ragged spectators shouted down encouragement, and spasms of merriment passed like waves across thousands of brutal faces. After the freaks came the *bestiarii* or animal fighters, the men reserved for battle with wild beasts in the arenas: they led chained lions and tigers. What wonder that the mob applauded these as loudly as the Caesar?

The procession lasted several hours. The head of it was already entering the Via Sacra when the tail was at the Esquiline hill. It poured through the Forum and into the Via Nova, past the Circus Maximus. Hour after hour it drew through the poverty-stricken streets and alleys around the Circus Maximus, winding about like a huge serpent. Nero was anxious that Rome, and particularly the poorest sections near the Circus Maximus, should see him and hail him on that day. He kept on greeting the mob, blowing kisses to it with his stumpy fingers, and the mob answered in a delirium of joy. The mob was happy with childish wonder at the endless files of naked gladiators, magnificent figures with rolling muscles; at the herd of richly draped elephants, led by African slaves, at the cages containing birds of paradise, cockatoos, flamingoes, fighting cocks, peacocks, and all kinds of feathered wonders of brilliant colors. It applauded even the long procession of asses, some of them shod with gold, which provided the milk for Poppea's daily baths.

Before the litters of Nero and Poppea slaves walked, strewing flowers. Again the hired clients threw themselves on their faces before him, stretched out their hands to him and cried imploringly: "Augustus! Abandon us not!" The Augustus smiled benevolently at them; he even blew a few kisses at them. The Augustus was inundated by a feeling of tenderness for the Romans. The slaves clearing a path for him had been instructed not to be brutal with the mob that day and to let a handful here and there approach to get a closer glimpse of the divinity and his spouse. There were also more substantial expressions of the divine favor. Coins were flung to the masses, copper and silver and even gold, and the citizens of Rome groveled and fought in the dust for their share of Caesar's bounty.

All this took place a few days after the magnificent banquet arranged by Tigellinus in the gardens of Agrippa.

A few more days passed and on the night of July eighteenth, in the year sixty-four, according to our chronology, fire broke out in the oil and flour depots among the houses of the thickly populated area about the Circus Maximus.

There was nothing very remarkable about a fire in Rome. The labyrinths of streets were filled with inflammable material, and from time immemorial there had existed a city fire brigade. Also the police, the soldiers who were on guard in every precinct, and the citizens themselves, were called upon to help in localizing a conflagration by razing the adjoining buildings to the ground. But on this night of July eighteenth not a hand was lifted to extinguish the flames or to prevent them from spreading. On the contrary, numerous witnesses reported later that they had seen certain individuals—no one could tell whether they were slaves or freedmen—running through the alleys with lighted torches, and throwing them into the houses. The fire spread with lightning speed, feeding on stores of oil, wax, grain, leather, and rope. A dense, choking cloud of smoke burst from the flaming houses, covering the flames with a black envelope, so that it was impossible to penetrate to the center of the fire. Then, from various corners in the vicinity, new tongues of flame rose into the night. The men with the torches were seen to be speeding from street to street. No one made an effort to oppose them, for they acted like men who had received instructions from the authorities. So heavy were the billows of smoke which accompanied the flames that it was impossible even to approach the adjoining houses in order to demolish them and to create a space about the conflagration. The population of the district simply fled from the asphyxiating fumes, with no thought but of escape.

In an incredibly short space of time the fire had leapt across into the Circus Maximus. The immense structure was empty at that hour. There was nothing to prevent the flames from taking hold. Moreover, the vaults were filled with inflammable material, wooden beams, benches, cages, and stables, as well as hay and straw and other provender. There were special rooms in which were stored enormous quantities of

685

clothing—the masks and costumes of the actors. Sacks, awnings, saddles, chairs—everything fed the fire, and the flames, increasing from beneath, sprang higher and higher, so that within an hour or two the whole vast building was a roaring inferno, from which waves of intense heat spread out in all directions.

One wave rolled toward the twelfth and thirteenth precincts on the lower slopes of the Aventine hill, where a number of granaries immediately flamed up, the fire leaping thence through alley after alley of flimsy and dilapidated houses, the homes of some of Rome's poorest inhabitants. A second wave threw itself mightily on the Coelian hill of the second precinct. Here too the houses and shops were the prey of the fire; the marketplace in particular added fresh fuel! A third wave flung itself up the slopes of the Palatine hill in the tenth precinct.

Here the fire met with some resistance in the vast and massive buildings which had been erected by several generations of Caesars. There were temples which had been standing on the Palatine slopes for centuries. On the northern side, opposite the Circus Maximus, stretched the long row of structures which had belonged to the domus of Caligula. But the resistance was only temporary. Continuously renewed from below by inexhaustible stores of fuel, the fire grew in volume and intensity. Metal gates and railings melted in its path. With a triumphant roar it hurled itself across to the military barracks and to the stables of the Germanic mounted auxiliaries. Like a wild beast lifting its cubs in its angry paws, it seized building after building. So, through the first night, through the day that followed, through the second night, the second day, the third night, the immense fire raged, until, by the third day, the whole vast area of three precincts, among the most populous in Rome, had been converted into a fiery sea. It was only at the bank of the Tiber that the flames halted, and by then the city of Rome was covered with a dense cloud of smoke by day and illumined by lurid flames by night.

The belated efforts of the fire brigade and the police were of no avail. They pulled down row after row of buildings, but they could no more stop the advance of the flames than they could have held back the inrush of the tide at Ostia. Millions of sparks were blown across the hastily improvised spaces; tongues of flames spanned them. The buildings behind the fire fighters began to burn, and no sooner had they leveled these than the buildings on the farther side were already beginning to glow. Moreover, with the heat on every side, with the smoke that blinded them, the fire fighters lost their sense of direction. Exhausted, bewildered, choking, begrimed, they fell at their posts, like insects sucked in by a candle flame.

On the third day the fire suddenly changed its line of march. Instead of moving from the Palatine hill into the Forum, where it would again have encountered some resistance from a group of massive stone buildings, it mounted the sirocco wind which had set in and turned to the third precinct, on the Esquiline hill, and like a beast tonguing its prey, began to lick the houses on the lower slope.

One might almost have said that the fire had set itself a program, like a conscious destructive force. On the various hills the flames had to work hard at the various stone buildings and to overcome them one by one. In the valleys between Rome's hills there was no resistance; here it could spread effortlessly and joyously, covering the dense labyrinths of Rome's poverty with a pall of flame and smoke. The valley which meandered between the irregular slopes of the Aventine and Coelian hills was a particularly choice titbit. The foundations of the houses were rotten; the walls were supported by innumerable wooden buttresses, dry as kindling. The twisted stairways, the niches, the narrow alleys, set up a series of draughts. The cellars and the lower floors of the lofty apartment houses were filled with moldering refuse, pieces of wood, rags, and smashed furniture. Moreover, every cellar had its store of house fuel; and above the cellars were the workshops of the poorest artisans. The valley was transformed into a flaming canal. Many of the inhabitants, having waited until the last moment, were caught in the fiery trap. Mothers snatched their little ones to their bosoms and sought to escape over the roof tops. But most of them never emerged, for somewhere on the third or fourth floors the wooden stairways gave way under them. Some sprang through the windows into the street, to be dashed to death against the glowing pavement or to be buried under collapsing walls. The men snatched up some of their possessions, the tools of their trade or the most valuable pieces of merchandise, and fought their way from the ground floors into the street. Before the fire had reached its highest intensity, the pavements were cluttered with accumulations of tools and merchandise, bales of cloth, rolls of leather, bundles of sandals, furniture, pots and pans. These not only burst into flame under the showers of sparks; they also prevented the inhabitants of the precinct from escaping, so that those who managed to get into the open found themselves running like insane things in a circle of flame from which there was no escape. The young, the old, the sick, some running, some crawling, some being carried, collapsed in the midst of their flight. There was no way of knowing where the flames had caught, whence the next sheet of fire would burst out. The people on the upper slopes ran blindly toward the valley; those below tried to make their way to the upper slopes. Whichever way they turned, they were confronted by the implacable beast. And perhaps the greatest horror was produced by the unexpectedness of the eruptions of fire. At one moment the visible length of the street seemed to be secure; at the next moment a dozen tongues of flame shot simultaneously from the cellars and lower windows, setting fire to the heaps of merchandise on the pavements. Fire seemed to rain down from heaven and to burst upward from the earth.

Not that any street in the poor district was anywhere visible for a considerable length. The streets were narrow and tortuous. A mother, insane with fear for herself, with pity for the child she was carrying, would reach a turning, only to find that further progress was barred by a house that had collapsed. Speeding back to the last turning, she would find that the fire had made a circuit to confront her again. So locked in, there was nothing for her to do but throw herself screaming to the ground and wait for death. Men and women went mad, either with the madness of screaming panic, or with that of dumb paralysis.

In many instances the fire seemed to have become a living thing, with strange hypnotic power to draw people into its blazing heart. There were some men and women who might have escaped, before the district was completely inundated; but they became the victims of a self-destructive panic or of a horror which robbed them of the will to act. If they did not scurry about insanely and planlessly, they seated themselves on the bundles of their household goods and, with faces from which all intelligence and feeling were withdrawn, waited for the destruction to reach them. Some actually threw themselves into the flames. Mothers who had abandoned children in the houses, thought they heard above the crackling and bellowing of the flames the screams of their little ones. They screamed back, "I'm coming, I'm coming," tore themselves out of the hands of the men who sought to hold them back and dashed into the blazing houses. There were merchants and artisans who, seeing their possessions, their life's accumulations, or the means of their livelihood, given to the fire, ran into the roaring ovens to perish. Some who had become insane stood about laughing wildly; others cried out to the gods or against the Caesar, before they gave themselves up to a fiery death.

On the sixth day those that survived of the Roman population were camping in the streets, for even in the sections which had not been reached by the fire, no one dared to remain indoors overnight. It seemed to everyone that Rome had been condemned by the gods to destruction by fire; they could not know, then, at what moment the doom would come upon their homes. Strange rumors had begun to circulate. The Caesar had given order to burn Rome so that not one stone would be left on another. The districts so far untouched by the fire were crowded as never before; for to the freedmen, the citizens, and artisans who had escaped from the destroyed areas, there were added tens of thousands of slaves who were left without homes and without masters, without a place to report to, without someone to give them commands, so that they wandered aimlessly through the jammed streets of the spared precincts.

The population of Rome had never achieved any degree of unity or even of uniformity. Races, tribes, and nations, civilized and barbaric, from every part of the Empire, had their contingents in Rome. Slaves had been brought in from beyond the confines of the Empire. Arabs from the hot wildernesses of the East mingled with Britons from the fog-enshrouded north; swarthy Asiatics rubbed shoulders with blond Germans. Among these multitudinous elements there was no feeling for the character or welfare of the city. In particular, the slaves, whose lives had been one long alternation of labor and punishment, were filled only with hatred for their masters, and all the bitterness and resentment of their years of brute suffering found expression in this time of calamity. But there was also in Rome a vast criminal class, an underworld population for whom the hour of chaos was the hour of harvest. Its members swarmed out freely now from the dark cellars and niches of the Suburra, and from the tunnels of the sewers. The police, the military, the slave-hunters, had lost their authority. A wave of criminality followed on the wave of fire. The wretched victims who had escaped from the destroyed precincts with little bundles of food or household goods were not safe in the streets. Countless murders took place, often for the sake of a handful of food. Even the houses of the rich were without defense. Bands of masterless slaves combined with groups of criminals and attacked the residences of the rich, so that pitched battles took place in the wealthy sections which the fire had left untouched. The "Pax Romana" which kept a world in order collapsed at the heart of the Empire.

On this sixth day the fire, still unexhausted, had surrounded the entire Esquiline hill. The Via Sacra, a sea of flame, had carried destruction to one side of the hill, while the Via Triumphalis had kindled it from the other side, where the palaces of the aristocracy were grouped. The summit of the Esquiline was inhabited by patricians. Nero had one of his palaces here, in the midst of theaters, temples, and monuments of immemorial antiquity.

Tigellinus took fright. He sent word to Caesar to return to Rome at once. He called out the Praetorian Guard, including the squads which manned the "ox-heads" or battering rams used for the reduction of fortresses. These siege implements were now turned against a ring of buildings on the Esquiline. Walls, pillars, and porticoes were thrown down, countless trees were uprooted in the gardens, and a space was cleared about the heart of the Esquiline. Thus the fire was held back, though not before it had destroyed many famous national monuments, such as the Temple of the Moon, which Servius Tullius had erected many, many centuries before, the Temple of the Vestal Virgins, and even Caesar's palace with the masterpieces which he had brought to Rome from Greece. The works of Praxiteles, statues of Venus, of athletes and Amazons, lay in fragments among the fallen and shattered columns, among the heaps of rubble. Precious vessels of Corinthian bronze, ancient Greek vases whose sides had been adorned with bas-reliefs by the old masters, were now either shapeless masses of metal or heaps of shard. Among the blackened remnants of ivory stools and couches were scattered the ashes of rare manuscripts and of silken carpets and hangings, imported from Persia and India. And in the midst of this smoking chaos there hung the faint odor of Oriental unguents and perfumes—the immense collection of toilet articles which had been the pride of Sabina Poppea. The belly of Caesar's house had been ripped open, like the belly of the pig on that festive night in the Agrippa gardens, and its contents scattered abroad.

Caesar finally returned to Rome, though Tigellinus's last and greatest service to him had been only partially successful in one respect, and somewhat too successful in another. The fire had indeed dried up the swamp of poverty and ugliness at the foot of the Palatine, but it had left in all its foulness the swamp on the farther side of the Esquiline—the Suburra. Moreover, the fire had wrought destruction among the palaces of the rich. But at the end of the sixth day, when it seemed that the flames had been brought under control, they suddenly broke out anew, and this time the place of origin was in the gardens of Tigellinus, which bordered Caesar's gardens on the side leading toward the Suburra.

Again there were seen those mysterious men who, six days before, had run naked through the streets of the slums bordering on the Circus Maximus, flinging blazing torches, soaked in oil and wax, into the houses of the poor. This time the conflagration was not so sudden and so furious; as against that, however, it was better prepared and more solidly founded. It proceeded, step by step, down the slopes of the hill until it reached the cramped homes of the Suburra, where it found an immense accumulation of fuel. Here it spread swiftly again, roaring from street to street, until it joined hands with the fire on the Via Sacra, where the great shops and magazines of the rich merchants were still blazing. Thus the Esquiline hill was surrounded at last on three sides by an immense sea of fire.

Standing on the summit of a watch tower which had remained unscathed in the central area of the Esquiline, Nero looked down and beheld the capital of his Empire transformed into a blazing pit. He could catch from afar the desperate screaming which went up from the trapped population of the Suburra. He could even make out, by the lurid sheen of the flames, tiny individual figures scampering about like poisoned mice. In whichever direction he looked there was fire, only fire. Rome was roasting like a sacrificial beast on an altar. At that moment Caesar drew on an actor's robe, covered his face with an actor's mask, and, harp in hand, broke into ecstatic song for the benefit of his suite, improvising his "Destruction of Troy."

"Thy song is worthy of the model, O Caesar! The world will for ever remember both," said Petronius, indicating with a wide gesture the burning city.

Chapter Fourteen

IN SEARCH OF A SCAPEGOAT

NERO was content. For once the bestial nature in him was sated. Rome had served as the model for his great ode. Now Rome lay, like a ravaged, brutalized woman, at his feet. Out of his satiety he set about the saving of what was left, or, rather, he set about the task of deflecting suspicion from himself. Now the Caesar was to be seen everywhere. He took personal command of the legionaries who demolished with battering rams the rows of houses in the immediate path of the fire. Only now was the order given to open the sluices of the aqueducts, which for some mysterious reason had remained shut during the conflagration. The destruction was halted.

Nine days the fire had raged, and a vast part of Rome had been converted into a glowing midden. Only those quarters which made an outer ring were completely unscathed; such were the first precinct about the Via Appia, and the fourteenth, in the Trans-Tiber area, where most of the Jews lived. The Tiber had acted as a barrier and not a single house had been touched. Similarly, the ninth precinct, which contained the great empty palaces of the Campus Martius, and the eighth precinct, which enclosed the Forum, were untouched. Of the remaining precincts, four, the most densely populated, in the heart of the city, were completely gutted, while six were partly demolished, but less by the fire itself than by the fire brigades and troops who, under Caesar's direction, destroyed entire streets in order to clear a wide space about the flames.

The heart of the city was a vast, glowing oven, covered with the ruins of fallen walls and roofs, which had buried whatever and whoever had remained behind. That part of the population which had managed to escape crowded the streets of the other precincts, making passage and communication almost impossible. Nero suddenly emerged in the role of the tender-hearted father of his people. He had the great Campus Martius, with its baths and gardens and temples, thrown open to the homeless populace. He even placed his own gardens, palace, and circus, on the Vatican heights across the Tiber, at the service of the city. He ordered all available ships to be mobilized to bring stores of grain and olives up the river from the port of Ostia. Tens of thousands of slaves were set to work clearing the ruins as soon as they could be entered, and to carry the ashes and rubbish in sacks, baskets and carts to the banks of the Tiber. The ships which brought in cargoes of food were then used to remove the huge heaps of refuse and to dump them into the sea outside of Ostia. Further, Nero reduced the price of grain by one-half. He showed himself daily to the people, who wandered among the ruins of their former homes, hoping to save some remnant of their possessions, or to identify the charred bones of their beloved. Nero's little eyes were always covered by a film of tears. He had the trick of weeping on order, and it suited him now to weep copiously and continuously over the misfortunes of his people. He went so far as to lift homeless and parentless children in his arms, so that Rome might see to what depths the Caesar had been moved by the universal calamity.

And in the midst of his activities and of his demonstrations of sympathy, Nero did not cease to comfort the citizens of Rome and to promise them a new city the like of which no ruler in the world had ever bestowed upon his subjects. It would be a city of glorious, wide streets, of great, regular houses of a certain, limited height, with wide façades, and in every house there would be a supply of fire-fighting apparatus. As the first token of his benevolent intentions, Caesar ordered his treasury to extend credit to every citizen who was prepared to start rebuilding his home. A tax was laid on every province of the Empire in order to finance the reconstruction of the capital. Engineers and architects were called in. Great quantities of fire-resisting stone were brought from the quarries of Gabii and even from as far as the Albanian mountains. Nero promised to build a vast ring of colonnades, baths, theaters, circuses: and then there was, of course, his "Golden House," which would stretch all the way from the Palatine to the Esquiline, combining his palaces on the two hills.

A fever of activity took hold of Nero. He seemed suddenly to have forgotten all his other artistic talents in the passion of his architectural dreams. For days on end he did nothing but suggest plans for the new Rome; and no sooner were the plans drawn than he began to put them into effect. Hundreds of thousands of slaves worked under the direction of the architects and engineers whom he had brought to the capital. Their first task was to clear the ruins and to set aside the materials which could be used in the new constructions. Order was gradually restored. The slaves who had fled from their burning homes were rounded up and set to work. The criminal element disappeared from the streets, and the police was once again in full control of the city. Several cohorts were called in to Rome in case of emergency. Rome was itself again—and Caesar too was himself again.

But somehow the Roman populace was not itself again. It was no longer the cynical mob which had watched with gross good humor the antics of its ruler. It was no longer to be contented with "bread and circuses," confining its protests—if such they could be called—against Caesar's bestialities to applauding the mimes and rhymesters who mocked the imperial criminal. Rome was no longer what it had been. Rome had become earnest, silent, mournful, and unresponsive, sunk in a dark, implacable mood. The Romans listened to the words of comfort which Nero offered them, they accepted the gifts he brought to them— and they were silent. Caesar appeared everywhere, and everywhere faces were averted. In vain did Caesar shed tears, in vain did he express, by word and gesture, his immeasurable sorrow, his sympathy with the sufferers, his readiness to help. The people remained cold. It reacted neither to his tears nor to his theatrical generosities. It even failed to manifest interest in his promise to arrange a performance of that mighty poem "The Destruction of Troy," in which he had immortalized the catastrophe. Nor did it avail that Tigellinus organized greater and ever greater bands of clients to mingle with the populace wherever Caesar showed himself. The people of Rome refused to be whipped into a mood of enthusiasm. Instead, there welled up in the masses a flood of suspicion, soon transformed into a certainty, that it was the Caesar, and only the Caesar, who was responsible for the destruction of Rome. Daring voices proclaimed openly that the conflagration had been started on the orders of the Caesar. Hundreds of individuals declared that they had seen the naked men speeding through the streets on the eve of the outbreak of the fire, flinging lighted torches into the stores of the Circus Maximus district. Moreover, it was soon bruited abroad that while the fire was still raging Nero had posted himself on the summit of a tower on the Esquiline and there had chanted his ode. Nor had it ever been a secret that Caesar had been dreaming of a new Rome, and of a "Golden House," to immortalize his name.

The Romans turned to their gods. The corrupt and cynical masses

694

underwent a religious revival, and the temples were suddenly filled with worshipers. The Sybilline books were consulted for the significance of the disaster. The temples of Vulcan, in particular, were haunted by great crowds. The matrons of Rome, in renewal of the ancient worship, brought offerings to the Capitoline Jupiter and to the other gods. It became clear that Rome had averted its face from the Caesar in order to turn it toward the gods.

Therefore it also became clear to the Emperor and his advisers that it was high time to look for a scapegoat upon which to deflect the suspicions and passions of the masses. A sacrifice was needed. Someone would have to suffer in order that the tacit rage of the Roman masses might be stilled. Words and gifts alone would never calm that subterranean storm of bitterness and take away the memory of the nine days of horror. In the ears of the Romans still rang the screaming of their children who had perished in the flames; their nights were haunted by recurrent pictures of themselves and their dear ones running back and forth in panic between the blazing ends of narrow streets. They saw also, by the power of suggestion, the naked men with the flaming torches. Who had they been? Who had cunningly prepared the ground for them by pouring oil and wax on the stores to which they applied the torches?

Nero could not hide the truth from himself. Something had happened to the soul of the Roman people. A wound had been opened in its depths, and it was not to be healed by the old, superficial methods. Something as terrible, as horrifying as the conflagration itself, some cruelty proportionate to the crime would be needed in order to obliterate from the soul of Rome the agony inflicted upon it, to exorcise the memory of the apocalypse. The blood of the new sacrifice would have to be copious enough to wash away the stains of the old and to wash away at the same time the accusations directed at the Caesar.

Where was such a scapegoat to be found if not in that element of Rome's population which was at once the weakest, the most alien, and the most despised—the Jews?

"The Jews! The Jews, who blaspheme our gods, and who disdain to take part in our religious festivals! They have even refused to recognize the Caesars as gods. They despise our gods, they despise us, they are the enemies of mankind. . . . They have brought with them, out of their barbarous country, a horrible and mysterious religion, a god whom nobody sees, a god who demands of them that they sacrifice to him their joy and happiness, and even their lives. For the sake of their god they let themselves be sacrificed like sheep. Would it be any wonder if their god commanded them to destroy the city of their enemies? Have you not noticed how many candles they light for him on the eve of their seventh day? Does it not prove that their god is a lover of fire? The oil drips from the lamps which they kindle in the window of their houses, it falls on the heads of the passersby. And what does it mean that the fire which destroyed Rome did not touch a single house in the Jews' quarter, but stopped dead on the banks of the Tiber. Nay, more than that: the fire did not even spread in the other direction, along the Via Appia, where the Jews have settled recently. The people of Rome will easily understand that these Jews, who live in our midst and are not of us, but cling obstinately to their fanatic faith and their wild ritual, were the only ones capable of committing such a crime. Have not these same Jews been talking lately of a certain 'Christ,' who has appeared as their liberator? Who is this 'Christ'? What does he portend?"

Such were the sentiments expressed by the poet Lucan, who had long been known as an enemy of the Jews. He pointed now to the number of Roman temples destroyed in the fire as additional proof that only the godless Jews could have perpetrated the crime.

* * *

When Nero called together the council of his intimates to discuss the question of finding a scapegoat, he also invited old Seneca.

Ever since Nero had freed him from the consular office, Seneca had clung to his private life, spending his days either in his city domus or at his country estate. He had given himself completely to his studies. He was engaged, in his latter days, in a final, desperate search for the essence of the divinity which he had not found among the gods but which he believed could be found in the laws of nature, as they expressed themselves in her multiple phenomena. He was working on the theses in which he compares the laws of nature with the laws of ethics. His discovery that there is in natural law not only an imperative logic of cause and effect, but a higher logic which provdes a counterpoise to evil, brought him to the threshold of that faith which he never entered. "We believe," he wrote, "that we are in the temple of nature; but the truth is that we still linger in her corridors." Though he did not cross the threshold, his new perceptions were not without influence on his character. In his latter days he actually began to live in closer accord with the principles which he had so long proclaimed in his letters. He overcame his lust for worldly possession; he abandoned the pursuit of wealth, and he lived the life of a Nazirite. His food consisted of bread and water. His one wish was to be forgotten by Nero and by the shameful world of Nero, so that he might dedicate himself without interruption to his studies. In this he was disappointed, for on important occasions Nero demanded his presence in the council. It was known that the old philosopher, for all his world-weariness, still had an open ear for the intrigues of the court. His protestations were received with skepticism, and it was suspected that he was associated with a conspiracy directed at the Emperor. This, too, made Nero reluctant to abandon his hold on Seneca. He had released him from his public duties—but he needed his counsel, and he wanted to keep an eye on him.

At the secret council which discussed the question of the scapegoat, Nero asked Seneca for his opinion.

"I consider," said Seneca, "that the faith of the Jews in an invisible god, and their blind devotion to him, is something fit for slaves, but unworthy of freedmen. Nevertheless, their faith has been legalized, and the sanction has been renewed by the greatest Caesars, by Julius, Augustus, Tiberius, and Claudius. The Jews had lived in Rome from time immemorial, and they are to be found in every part of the Empire. The people of Rome, like that of all the provinces, is in daily contact with the Jews in a hundred different fashions; and though it is true that the plebs have always derided the Sabbath of the Jews, many Romans have begun to imitate it, and to visit the synagogues of the Jews, both in Rome and in the cities of the provinces. It will not be easy to convince the Romans that people who have their shops and stores in the rich streets of the Campus Martius, and on the Via Sacra, and who are spread in all the precincts of the city, set fire to Rome in an act of self-destruction. Moreover, the persecution of the Jews here may call forth a rebellion in Judaea, and riots in other parts of the Empire. Nor would it be amiss for me to say that one cannot wipe out the evil deeds of others by committing evil deeds oneself." The old philosopher looked calmly at Nero as he uttered these words. "Nor, Caesar, is it by accusing the innocent that one can cleanse oneself of guilt. It is only by goodness that one can overcome evil; only by our good deeds, in assuaging the grief and suffering of Rome, can we cleanse ourselves of our own guilt. As far as this concerns me, I relinquish the greater part of my possessions for the rebuilding of Rome; and it is my advice that all who are present do likewise. Thus we shall convince the Romans that each of us feels himself untouched by the suspicions which attach to the great ones of Rome."

The assembly heard these words in silent consternation. Caesar himself was dumbstruck. He began to say something, but his mouth remained open, and all that issued from it was the tip of his tongue. His short, fleshy neck expanded, till it resembled a huge goiter. The locks which surrounded his face became damp and sticky with perspiration. Seneca alone was at ease. A patient smile settled on his hard, granitelike features. His eyes were filled with a fresh, steady light. At last he had conquered his cowardice and his passions; at last he had overcome the fear of death and had uttered that which was in his heart rather than that which Nero wanted to hear from him.

"Tigellinus!" exclaimed Nero, and his voice was hoarse with rage. But since it was not in Nero's nature to give open expression to his anger, the courtiers knew that Seneca's end had not yet come; had it come, Nero would have smiled softly instead of showing anger.

Tigellinus began in a pious, restrained voice: "The calamity which has fallen upon the city of our gods and Caesars is so great that only thou, O Caesar, wert able to lament it fittingly in thy immortal ode. The gods are aghast at the destruction of their temples, and they are not to be placated, O Caesar, by prayer and sacrifice alone. Who knows what greater calamity awaits us if we do not placate them with that act of vengeance which they await from us? And as the gods are, so is the Roman people. Rome is sick and angry, Rome is thirsty for the blood of those who have reduced her city to ashes. The act of horror can be atoned for only by another act, of greater horror. There is but one way for thee to win again the favor of the gods: to find the guilty and to visit upon them such punishment as will satisfy the gods. Thus it is, too, with thy people. The Romans long to be sated with the torments of those who have so tormented them; they must behold flesh torn, bleeding, burning in an act of retribution. Thou, O Caesar, canst still the thirst which tortures thy honest Romans. Thou must show them that thou wilt not stand by indifferently when they clamor for revenge. Thou must appease Rome and the gods by a judgment which no Caesar before thee has ever rendered and carried out. There must be great spectacles, at which all the punishments which were rained by Pluto on the daughters of Danaus shall be rained upon those who are guilty of the destruction of Rome. And who are the guilty? No, not all the Jews; assuredly not all the Jews. I agree with Seneca. We cannot take an entire people and throw it to the beasts. We cannot ascribe the guilt to a religion which has been sanctioned and legalized by a line of Caesars. It can, indeed, call forth rebellions and riots. But who said that all the Jews are guilty of the burning of Rome? Assuredly the rich merchant of the Campus Martius or the Via Sacra would not consign his own shops to the flames. Assuredly there are decent Jews, who have acquired our manners and our civilization. But there are masses of poor Jews swarming in their quarters on the farther bank of the Tiber. They call themselves 'Christians,' after a certain criminal, Christ, whom Pontius Pilate put to death in Jerusalem. Now what is the meaning of his name, 'Christ'? I have found it out. 'Christ' means 'the anointed one,' a king, a Caesar; and the fanatical Jews indeed believe that this Christ is a king and Caesar. They believe that their Christ was slain and rose from the dead, and that one day, soon, he will return and ascend a throne of judgment. And knowest thou whom he will judge? Thee, Nero. He will judge thee, and me, and all of us. He will judge the Romans, he will judge those who do not believe in him!" A burst of laughter, partly derision, partly relief, broke out in the assembly at this point. Tigellinus waited, then continued: "This same Christ is their Caesar, O Nero—not thou. And as if it were not enough that they should be sunk in this criminal fanaticism, they seek to drag others down to their level. The slaves of Rome are infected with the disease of the Christians. I have found Christian slaves in my own home. They comport themselves as slaves have never done before. They insist on knowing their own children and creating their own families; they avoid work on the Sabbath, the seventh day of the Jews, and they disobey all commands which are contrary to their ritual. They have but one Dominus, and that is their Christ. Search well, all you that are assembled here, in your own households, you will find the pestilence among your slaves. Nay, more; I have heard that there are noble Roman matrons, wives of patricians, who are tainted with the criminal superstition. I have reason to believe that the wife of a certain senator, who shall remain nameless, has accepted their faith. And that is not all! The legionaries themselves have been corrupted. In thy own house, Nero, there are slaves, freedmen, and legionaries who worship, not thee, but Christ. They assemble secretly in the nights and celebrate mystic rites, commit frightful crimes. I have this on the authority of my own spies. They prostrate themselves before an ass's head, they eat human flesh, they drink the blood of slaughtered infants. It is they who set fire to Rome. They did it at the command of their god, their Caesar. Theirs is the guilt if our gods have withdrawn their favor from us. And I have already ordered that my Christian slaves be put to the torture, so that they may reveal the names of their fellow conspirators. The courts will do the rest. Rome demands revenge, O Caesar. The gods demand revenge! The whole world demands revenge against the enemies of mankind! And thy hand, O Caesar, shall be uplifted to give the gods, and Rome, and the world, that which they demand!"

Nero rose from his chair, went over to Tigellinus, and kissed him resoundingly on the mouth.

Chapter Fifteen

THE GREAT TRIAL

ANTONIUS, the stable boy slave in the household of Tigellinus, had been made to endure every form of torture which the ingenuity of the Romans had devised. The bones of his hands and arms and legs had been cracked one by one between the claws of iron pincers. The skin had been torn, strip by strip, from his quivering flesh. One by one the nails of his fingers had been pulled out by the roots. His flayed feet had been held over a slow fire. He lost his human aspect and was reduced to a bundle of raw, blistered flesh. Still he would not reveal what he had done with his master's child. For the secret of his contumacious refusal to obey his master's instructions had been betrayed, under similar tortures, by a fellow slave. Tigellinus himself witnessed and directed the torturing of Antonius. Two physicians were in attendance, to see to it that Antonius remained alive, and sensitive to pain. When he fainted, the torture was relaxed, and he was nursed back with drinks and unguents into consciousness. He was promised his freedom and a reward if he would confess that he had turned the infant over to the Christians, so that they might use its blood for their mystic rituals. But Antonius kept his eyes and his lips closed, and in the fiery ring which rotated about his head he beheld a great flight of steps mounting from earth to heaven. Above the wide platform at the summit of the steps the figure of the Messiah swam in the midst of luminous blue clouds; and the arms of the Messiah were stretched out to him, the slave, who, agonizing step by step, was mounting heavenward. Everything that had been foretold for Antonius was happening to him: "The Messiah awaits all those who have suffered for him." Every pang of pain was dear to him; the deeper the claws of iron crushed into his flesh and bone, the hotter the flames under his crippled feet, the nearer he knew himself to be to the glory swimming out toward him from the blue clouds. Already he felt on his flesh the cool touch of the marble steps. And then the steps themselves yielded and softened and became blue clouds on which he was being wafted toward the outstretched arms. He floated higher and higher, and the radiant figure drew nearer and nearer. The clouds passed him on, as from cradle to cradle. Now he was in the very midst of the inmost blue which surrounded his savior, a bright, fiery blue which did not burn but soothed and healed and filled him with bliss. Antonius lifted responsive arms, and all his being was filled with one desire, one thirst, one cry:

"Take me, lord, take me to thee!"

Tigellinus looked down in stupefaction at the ripped carcass of the slave. His attendants were equally amazed. This they could not understand, this they had never seen before: that a slave should endure such tortures and not betray his kind. The boon of death was not granted Antonius on this day. He was saved for the arena.

Not all the Christian slaves of Tigellinus's household had shown the same fortitude. There were some who had only looked on the *flagrum,* the pincers, the iron collar, and they had recanted in terror, had confessed their association with the Christians, had confessed anything that their tormentors wanted to hear. They had told of a day of judgment which was momently awaited by the believers in Christ. Before the coming of that day, they had told, a rain of fire would pour down from heaven, to sweep away, as with a besom, the sins of mankind. . . . It was enough! There could not be any doubt now that the believers in Christ had set fire to Rome, in order to fulfill the prophecies of their judgment day. Some among the slaves also told of secret assemblies of Christians, where unity with the godhead was achieved by "eating his flesh and drinking his blood." What did this mean but that the Christians ate human flesh and drank human blood?

The same scenes were enacted in other households. The torture was applied to every slave suspected of association with the Christians; the same proofs were everywhere obtained of the guilt of the Christians in the burning of Rome.

The preparations for the mass accusation were made slowly and carefully. The masters of Rome were anxious that the suspicion should be planted widely, nourished skillfully, so that the cry for the condemnation of the Christians should come from the people rather than from the rulers. The blood-libel was spread assiduously among the masses. Agitators were sent out daily among the homeless citizens camping in the open places, among the porticoes, the baths, the gardens, and the palace of Nero on the Vatican hill. Slowly the agitators spread the widening ring of accusation. They themselves had heard the confessions. They themselves had witnessed the torturing of the Christian fiends. Then, shifting their ground from the blood-libel to the fire-libel, they told that at last the torch carriers who had been seen on the first night of the fire had been identified. Some came forward and proclaimed that they had with their own eyes seen black-bearded Jews applying torches to the holy Temple of Luna on the Coelian hill. No, it was not the worshipers of Isis who had done it; that goddess of a thousand names, "the one who is all," was the goddess of the rich matrons of Rome, and her temple too had gone up in flames. No, it was not the Egyptian priests who had done it; it was the Jews of the Trans-Tiber and of the new Jewish quarter, those Jews who belonged to the new sect of the Christians, those Jews who had spread their criminal faith among the slaves of Rome.

"See you not how the fire began at the Porta Capena, where the Jews have lately settled, and ended at the Tiber, where they have their old settlement? The Jewish quarters alone were untouched by the fire!"

Thus, day after day, the dark suspicion grew; day after day the tide of popular resentment set in toward the Jews. The plebs cried out for vengeance. Blood, only blood, could wipe out the unspeakable guilt of the Christians; only the wild beasts of the arena could carry out the punishment.

Then, when the temper of the masses had been roused to the right pitch and turned in the right direction, the first public measures were taken.

The Jews of Rome saw the heavens darkening above them. The good fortune by which their quarters had escaped the fire now turned out to be a measureless calamity; and as they watched the day of wrath approaching inexorably, they did what Jews have always done in times of trial: they assembled in their synagogues, they fasted, they recited the Psalms. The lights shone on the swaying masses, and a dolorous prayer went up to their God:

> "For Thee we are given to the slayer all day long.
> My tears have become my bread, day and night.
> All day long they ask me: Where is thy God?
> The waters have come up to my lips."

*　　*　　*

Even though assembly increased the danger of detection, the Christians gathered in their accustomed places of prayer, in the synagogue courts and in homes. They chanted the same prayers as the Jews, the same chapters from the Psalms:

> "For Thee we are given to the slayer all day long.
> My tears have become my bread, day and night.
> All day long they ask me: Where is thy God?
> The waters have come up to my lips."

Now, more than ever, they felt the imminence of the judgment day. The first signs had appeared. The first section of the prophecies uttered by Peter and Paul had been fulfilled: the heavens had rained down fire, Rome-Babylon, the city of sin, was leveled with the dust, and above its ruins the figure of the Messiah would shortly appear. Many of the Christians also saw special signs in the heavens: new stars blazed up in the night, great comets appeared, pointing toward Rome. Some reported that they had seen a fiery sword suspended above the city, others that at a certain hour the clouds had opened, revealing the heavenly sanctuary and the hosts of the angels gathered about the Messiah. A clenched fist had appeared above Rome. Fingers had traversed the heavens, leaving behind an incomprehensible fiery script. The day was at hand! The lord was coming, the long awaited was about to happen!

Among Jews and Christians two extremes of mood emerged in confusion—panic and hope, terror of death and expectation of salvation, utter despair and indescribable exaltation, the judgment of Nero and the judgment of the lord. The boundaries between reality and fantasy wavered and disappeared. Men knew not what they saw: was it the ravening beast issuing from its cage in the arena, or was it the form of the savior descending from heaven? Were they sinking as the ground yielded under their feet, or were they being lifted to the glory of the heavens? But in this confusion and alternation they were aware of a single desire: "Let happen what will, but let it happen soon!" They were also aware that the two extremes met at one point: the terror of death was the portal to eternal life; the last evil on earth heralded the beginning of the reign of eternal justice. As in a dream, they stretched out their hands to the fire of God, though they knew they must perish in it. Therefore they did not hide themselves but assembled to confront together the danger and the hope.

In their chapel which adjoined the synagogue court in the Trans-Tiber, the Christians gathered in the evening and lit their lamps. The women brought cakes of bread, and Peter sat down among the believers and broke bread with them. Then the cup was filled and passed round, and when all had touched it with their lips, Peter lifted his hands above the bowed heads, and spoke.

This time he did not tell them of the life and death of the lord, as was his wont. Instead he recited, in the Hebrew, a chapter of the Psalms, and after every verse a member of the congregation translated the words into Greek:

"As the hart panteth after the living streams, so panteth my soul after Thee, O God!"

And the congregation repeated in Greek:

"As the hart panteth after the living streams, so panteth my soul after Thee, O God!"

"My soul thirsteth for the living God. . . . How long before I shall see the face of my God?"

And they repeated:

"My soul thirsteth for the living God. . . . How long before I shall see the face of my God?"

As the antiphonal murmur rose from the chapel, a band of soldiers, led by a centurion, made its appearance in the streets of the Trans-Tiber. The men were armed. Their shields and helmets shone in the night, their swords swung at their sides. When they opened the door of the chapel none turned to greet them; the murmur of prayer continued without interruption.

The centurion strode forward, and the worshipers, lifting their eyes, beheld old Gabelus, of the Praetorian Guard.

"Come," said Gabelus to Peter. "Come with us. It is time."

Peter rose and looked about him, not knowing what to do.

"This night," said Gabelus, "they will come for all of you. The command has been issued to arrest the Christians."

Andronicus, the first elder after Peter, addressed the apostle:

"Thou must be the last, Simon bar Jonah. The congregation needs thee. Go with them."

Peter accepted the decision.

"In thy hands, Andronicus, I leave the congregation of the Messiah. Thou shalt lead them to the cross, where he waits for them. It is his desire that we shall have our portion in his pain and that our blood shall be mingled with his, in order that we may be one with him."

"For his sake we will endure everything," answered the congregation, and the prayers were resumed under the leadership of Andronicus, until such time as the soldiers should appear.

Gabelus and his men took Peter and led him across the bridge and through the city to the district on the Via Appia. There they hid him in the house of Hermas, near the catacombs.

*   *   *

The command had been issued to the police and the Praetorians to arrest all Jews who belonged to the Christian sect, and with them all converts among the non-Jews, in whatever household they might be found. But the line of demarcation between Jew and Christian was so faint that no one could discover where the one ended and the other began. The task was, in one sense, simpler among the non-Jews. If a slave, asked who he was, answered: "I am a Christian. I am a slave of Caesar, but a Christian. I have received my freedom from Christ himself," he was immediately taken. But the Christian Jews could not so easily be identified. They looked like the other Jews, lived like and with them, spoke the same language, prayed in the same synagogues, worked side by side with them, observed the same Sabbath ritual. The same books were to be found in the homes of all Jews. On the other hand, a non-Jewish Christian could much more easily clear himself of the charge. He had but to call on the names of Jupiter and Apollo and to throw a pinch of incense on their altars or on those of the deified Caesars. But all Jews, Christians or non-Christian, refused to call on the names of the gods, or to offer incense on their altars. The police and the military therefore arrested them indiscriminately, on the assumption that anyone who denied the gods of Rome was of the hated sect.

*　　*　　*

The courts of Rome had always been heavily overloaded, and even in normal times the judges had been unable to cope with the long lists of deferred cases. With the mass arrest of "Christians" anything like an orderly judicial procedure became utterly impossible. The judges had neither the time nor the background of information to question each individual intelligently; nor was the public mood one which encouraged care and discrimination. All day long the judges sat in the basilicas on the Forum, and hour after hour new batches of prisoners were brought in. There were men and women, Jews and non-Jews, young and old, dragged from the homes of the patricians or from the Trans-Tiber and Via Appia quarters.

The procedure became automatic.

"Who art thou?"

"I am a Christian," was the answer in most cases.

This was equivalent to a confession of complicity in setting fire to the city.

Here and there the case lasted a few minutes.

A young man of noble appearance was brought before the tribunal. He had been taken in a raid on a Christian chapel. The judge looked into the delicate face, with its short beard and dreamy eyes. He noticed the toga which the young man wore. He was a freeman, then, and probably a scion of a patrician family.

706

"Who art thou?" asked the judge.

"I am a Christian."

"Who are thy parents?"

"I have no parents. My father is the Lord of the world, my faith is my mother."

"What is thy occupation?"

"I am a slave of the Messiah."

"From what land comest thou?"

"I am a stranger on this earth, a wanderer, until I shall come to my heavenly homeland, which is the Jerusalem of the heavens."

A mother and child were brought before the judge.

"Who art thou?"

"I am a Christian."

"And thy child?"

"Born in the Messiah."

An elderly Jew who had been dragged out of his home appeared before the judge.

"Believest thou in Christ?"

"I believe in a Messiah whom God will send to free us and all the world."

"A Christian, like the rest," said the judge, curtly.

"I am a Hebrew, and my faith is sanctioned by the law," protested the Jew.

"Throw incense on the altar of the divine Augustus!" commanded the judge.

"I do not recognize the Caesar as a god. My God is the one and only God of Israel, and Him alone I worship."

"A Christian, a Christian like the others!" repeated the judge, impatiently.

So much of legal procedure was allowed in the cases of freedmen. Slaves were not even brought to court. The "trials" took place in the slaves' quarters, and their purpose was to obtain not a confession—since suspicion was tantamount to guilt—but the names of other Christians; and whether the torture yielded the desired result or not, the trial ended in one of two ways. Either the slave died under the torture, or else he was carried off and flung into the cellars of Nero's private circus on the Vatican hill.

In this fashion Nero prepared for the Roman masses a spectacle such as Rome had never beheld before—a gigantic blood bath which, he hoped, would be remembered through the ages.

Chapter Sixteen

IN GREEN PASTURES

THERE was not a Jewish home in the Trans-Tiber from which somebody was not missing. Happy were those families from which only one member, the father, the mother, a son or daughter, had been dragged before the tribunals. A single cry of mourning and desolation went up from the area; and while the tortures went on in Nero's circus on the Vatican, the remainder of the congregation gathered in the synagogue under the guidance of Reb Sabattai Zadoc, and from early morning till late in the night there was praying and chanting of Psalms for the martyrs agonizing in the cellars and crypts and the arena for the sanctification of the Name.

All day long the women wandered in despair about the walls of the circus which Caligula had built on the Vatican and which Nero had appropriated as his own. Their faces covered with black veils, they streamed back and forth across the Janiculum hill, greeted everywhere by the mocking laughter of the Roman mob which was drawn, for very different reasons, to the same area. A cordon of Jewish wives, daughters, mothers, sisters lingered about the circus and the walls of the gardens. Their grief was not silent; it broke out in passionate gesticulations and in a high wailing which tore its way through constricted throats and quivering lips. Hands were lifted frantically to heaven, imploring the compassion of the Almighty. There were some women who had torn their clothing in sign of mourning and strewn ashes on their heads; others beat their heads, their faces, and their bosoms with their clenched fists. In a wider ring about this cordon of despair the Roman masses, men and women in festive attire, with garlands on their heads, moved gaily, enjoying these preliminaries of the great slaughter to come.

"Ho there, look at that Jew-woman tearing the hair out of her head!"

"Oi, oi, Eili, Eili, oi, oi," cried another, mocking a Jewish wife who had been thrust out of the cordon by a soldier and now stood at a distance from the wall, wringing her hands frantically and crying to the God of Israel.

"Ho, where's that God of yours who promised to come down with the clouds of heaven to judge the Romans? Where is he? Why doesn't he show himself? Why doesn't he save you now from the jaws of the Roman wolf?" cried a client joyously, his face shining with sweat, his toga clinging to his body in the heat of the summer sun.

"Where is he who ordered you to burn Rome? Why doesn't he appear to protect you, now that you've been caught?" howled another, pushing his way through to a group of weeping women.

"Why don't you go home and light the Sabbath candles?" shouted a third, as he thrust toward the entrance of the circus, afraid of finding the best places taken.

A fourth, equally eager to get to the entrance, found time however to pause sportively before the group of women, make a pig's ear of the corner of his toga, and shake it gaily:

"Won't you try a piece of swine's meat, Jewesses? It's excellent food—very strengthening, too!"

Meanwhile the populace was assembling in the circus. There came not only the plebs, but the aristocracy of Rome, patricians in their litters accompanied by their hordes of clients. It was to be a long and thrilling spectacle, and the spectators brought provisions with them, bundles of food and jars of wine. The August sun blazed on the city out of a cloudless sky; but long before its rising the excited Romans had been afoot, streaming across the bridges toward the Vatican. Hundreds had camped through the night outside the circus. Ten thousand unwashed bodies, melting in the heat, sent out a foul odor. The Vatican hill was covered with the booths of food and wine merchants, and those who had failed to bring their own provisions now laid in a stock to last them through the whole day and into the night. For the day would not suffice. It would take much blood, much excitement, many victims, to compensate the Roman people for its calamity. Nero had been as good as his word. Never before had anything like an equal number of human victims been prepared for a single spectacle. The mob knew that the

709

crypts were jammed with "Christians" and that there would be a happy variety of victims and of sights; one would see tender children who would yield their little bodies to the beasts without a struggle, one would see strong men making frantic and futile efforts to escape or to defend themselves, one would see graybeards and tottering old women shrinking from the jaws and fangs of the animals. The Roman mob licked its chops in anticipation, as if it were itself a composite beast waiting for the banquet of human flesh. Those who came late, and who would have to sit on the outer ring, lamented loudly that they would not be able to hear the crunching of the bones. The Roman women were in the grip of the same bloodthirsty fever as the men. They pushed as furiously through the crowd, to be as near as possible to the spectacle; they thrust with their elbows; they threatened to scratch out the eyes of the men and women who jammed the entrances. The ushers could not maintain order. Within the circus late-comers crawled over the heads of the seated spectators to find ringside places. The struggle carried the mob to the very walls of Caesar's loge. Here and there actual battles took place as the massed slaves of patricians cracked skulls right and left to clear a path for the litters.

At last the gigantic circus was so filled that the gates had to be closed. Without remained only the disappointed late-comers and the cordon of wailing Jewish women.

When the movement ceased, some sort of order was restored, and the spectators settled as best they could into their places. Now a sea of white togas, garlanded heads, and half-naked bodies rose about the arena. In the midst of his people, surrounded by his intimates, Caesar lolled on his throne, while Poppea, swollen with pregnancy and shamelessly uncovered, sat at his side. A squad of Praetorians, resplendent in silver breastplates and horned helmets, guarded the imperial loge, under the command of Tigellinus.

Because of the heat Nero had dropped the citizen's toga and sat comfortably in his light tunic. In the tradition of Rome, this was an act of disrespect toward the people, but Nero, though he might be wooing the Romans on this day, had not the discipline to submit to physical discomfort. It was an old habit of his to throw off the symbol of his Roman citizenship, the outlived emblem of Roman equality, even at sessions of the Senate, and to show himself in his tunic—an act which, in public, was offensive and contemptuous. However, since the old traditions were almost dead, there were many who regarded this gross impropriety as a demonstration of democracy and familiarity. The wreath which his slaves had arranged with such care, with such ingenuity of coquetry, on his locks, had slipped to one side, as though he were already drunk. The smell of sweaty flesh that rose from the imperial loge was as heavy and sickening as that which rose from the masses jammed into the tiers.

The preliminaries to the spactacle lacked the festive pomp which the plebs had expected. Nero's behavior did not lend itself to formal demonstrations. He sat slumped on his throne like a resting butcher. Now and again he leaned over familiarly to a member of his suite to whisper in his ear. He threw smacking kisses to familiars of his, men and women, in other loges. Only Poppea, half-naked though she was, seemed to be disturbed by this utter want of dignity in her consort.

The procession of the victims, which always preceded a spectacle of this kind and which was always intended as a foretaste, to whet the appetites of the spectators, fell equally short of expectation. The men and women and children who were driven at the point of the lash into the arena came out wailing and lamenting. Only Jew-Christians, enemies of mankind, would permit themselves to spoil, by their wretched behavior, a great festival arranged for the benefit of Rome by the Caesar himself. Even the men made no effort to display the courage, the sense of privilege, proper to those who were about to die in the presence of the Caesar. The highly disgusted Romans saw a pitiful mob, consisting largely of miserable Jew-peddlers or artisans and their wives and children—the silversmiths, sandal makers, oil mixers who in normal times swarmed, basket in hand, about the Porta Capena. The non-Jews in the arena were for the most part slaves. But even the non-Jewish freedmen and matrons who had been taken in the roundup made a wretched spectacle; they had become Judaized in appearance; the men had beards, the women walked with a stoop—there was nothing at all of the Roman about them. They refused to play up to the occasion. A number of them had been prepared for the spectacle in a manner long familiar to the Roman mob; they had been dressed in skins of lions, leopards, bears, foxes, and sheep. Even little ones had been thus covered. But they simply would not respond with the expected behavior. The sacrificial procession was, in short, a miserable failure, due to the lack of public spirit of the Jews. The only contribution which the

711

criminals made to the festivities came from the women; these, having been stripped naked and thrust into the arena, struck the most amusing poses as they tried to cover, with their hair or their hands, their private parts.

And when these half-crippled tatterdemalions were driven past the imperial loge, they did not so much as bestow a glance on Caesar, or on the mob. Instead, they muttered to themselves, and if the circus had not been in such an uproar, one might have heard strange words mounting heavenward: "The Lord is my shepherd, I shall not want. He maketh me to lie down in green pastures, He leadeth me beside the still waters." But in a little while the voices became firmer. "Yea, though I walk in the valley of the shadow of death, I fear no evil, for Thou art with me." Mothers and fathers intoned the verses, children repeated them. This was the armor which Simon bar Jonah had supplied them, to take into the arena; and as they advanced into the place of death they put it on, and it wrought wonders for them. They saw the tranquil meadows beyond the abyss of death; and on the meadows waited one with open arms, saying:

"Come to me, all ye that suffer and are heavy-laden."

The murmur grew stronger, it swelled into a chant which became audible above the obscene uproar of the circus.

"For Thee I hope, O God. Into Thy hands I commend my spirit."

"What's that they're singing? What are they saying?" the spectators began to ask.

"They are saluting their god, before they die."

"What? Saluting their god? Not Caesar? To the beasts with them! To the beasts!"

Tigellinus, seated in Nero's loge, bit his lips. The filthy Christians had spoiled the parade. He gave the signal to the overseers in the arena, and these drove the victims back into the vaults. Tigellinus felt that the Christians had done this deliberately to disgrace him before the Caesar.

"If Tigellinus had only paraded a flock of sheep through the arena, they would have shown more courage, O Caesar," whispered Lucan.

But on the other side Petronius whispered: "Nay, the trouble is that they show too much courage. They have the courage to ignore even thee, O Caesar."

In any case, it was high time to get down to the business of the

712

day, for the mob was weary with the waiting and fumbling. Caesar gave the sign and the trumpets blew a fanfare. The doors of the cages holding the wild beasts were drawn back.

A herd of wild oxen were the first to be released. They stood bewildered at the doors, blinded by the sudden light, confused and irritated by the tumult. Only when they moved out of the shadow of the circus wall did the audience notice that a woman had been bound to the horns of each ox. The white bodies flashed as the sunlight struck them. Even in this extremity of danger, the women were still contorting themselves in shame, trying to cover their nakedness with their hands. Womanly hair, falling across the eyes of the beasts, roused them from their stupor. A wild rearing and stamping ensued. The beasts flung themselves about, trying to rid themselves of their human burdens. One by one the white bodies were flung into the air. A scream, an unintelligible outcry—and the body was lifted into the air again, but this time on, and not between, the horns of the ox. The body quivered, the blood streamed out of the gored flesh. The smell of fresh blood sent the beasts into a frenzy, so that they pranced and circled with their impaled victims, snuffing the hot steaming air. Again the bodies were flung down on the sand, again they were lifted up; and what had been, but a few moments ago, a human being was now a mass of ripped and trampled flesh, covered with splashes of red.

This was something new. The audience rose to its feet, applauding. The men clapped their hands, the women flapped their veils, and a great roar of salute to the Caesar rolled across the arena.

A few moments later the attendants charged in and herded the oxen back to their cages. Half a dozen carts were trundled in, and the bodies were flung into them pell-mell. Fresh sand was strewn over the red patches, and the second spectacle began.

The entrances to the prison vaults were opened. A gang of slaves drove out thence a company of men, women, and children covered with the skins of animals. The skins were fastened about the shoulders, so that they could not be thrown off. The horrible, motley group shrank back. Some of the men and women were standing. Others had been so fastened in their coverings that they had to crawl; or perhaps it was the tortures they had already undergone which left them incapable of walking. Here and there a woman was holding an infant to her breast. As the whips fell on them, they moved forward in a confused mass; and again no face was lifted to the Caesar or to the mob. Again the strange chant, so infuriating to the spectators, rose from the ghastly assembly: "Yea, though I walk in the valley of the shadow of death, I fear no evil, for Thou art with me." In vain did the slave attendants lash them on their faces, to drive them apart. They would not scatter, they would not approach the imperial loge. They clung together, a compact mass, chanting the Psalms.

Who can fathom the secret of those souls? Who can penetrate to the mystery wrought by God, in that moment, with His elect? Only one who has been touched by His grace who has rested in the shadow of His love—only he knows how God lifted His chosen ones to Himself and in that moment transformed their earthly anguish into heavenly glory. For they no longer saw with the eyes of the flesh, they no longer knew what was taking place about them; translated into spheres inaccessible to us, they were beyond the reach of mortal evil.

Even before they were driven into the arena, they were intoxicated by floods of light from above. Before the lash fell on them, they were already like sleep-walkers. All night long they had kneeled in the crypts, hearing about them the roaring of lions, the baying of hounds. In each of the crypts there had been, among the prisoners, one of the older converts, long adept in the faith. Here it was Andronicus, there Junius, in a third crypt another—founders of the Roman congregation. Some of these elders were Jews, some non-Jews. Andronicus and Junius were not only Jews, they were from the Holy Land, and from the Holy City; more—they had been, many years before, eyewitnesses of the agony of the Messiah. All night long they had strengthened the faithful with stories of his life and death, reminding them of his last words:

"Father, forgive them, for they know not what they do!"

And the faithful obeyed their elders, and in the hour of trial remembered the example of the Messiah: they were told to repeat his words, they were told not to take with them across the threshold of life a single bitter thought, a single pang of hatred, but to appear before him who awaited them as pure as himself. And if they were successful in this last test, they would assuredly see, even before their eyes were closed in death, the Messiah, the lord. He would assuredly come to them in the arena and stand before them with open arms; he would draw them up to him on the cross, so that their sufferings might mingle with his and they might become one with him. And the elders, that night,

714

also taught every one of the believers, to repeat the "Hear, O Israel" at the moment when they felt their souls leaving them. They were to be happy when that moment came and accept death with love and joy, that their sanctification of the Name should be perfect and without blemish.

So, when these were driven into the arena, though their bodies shrank from death, their souls were not mournful, but filled with bliss, and they did not lament. The admonitions of the night remained with them. For Reb Andronicus had also rehearsed a special prayer with them:

"A song of the Temple steps, for David. I rejoiced when they said to me, Come let us go to the house of the Lord."

When they had repeated this verse, some in Hebrew, others in Greek, they went on:

"Hallelujah! Praise ye the Lord, praise Him all ye servants of the Lord!"

At this point the gates of the cages were pulled back, and a pack of wild bloodhounds emerged on the rim of the arena. Trained from birth to hunt and attack wild animals, they had been kept these last few days in cages adjacent to the crypts and had been starved into a condition of extreme ferocity. They bounded forward toward the human group huddling at the center of the arena and then paused for an instant, a few steps from their victims. They lifted their muzzles, sniffed, and emitted a long howl.

That brief instant sufficed for the men and women who clung together to perceive the Messiah.

The mothers were the first to see him—the mothers who were waiting to offer themselves and their children for the sanctification of the Name. They saw him, distinctly, unmistakably, in front of them; the vast cross was lifted over him and he had stretched out his arms to them.

A woman threw herself to the ground with a cry:

"The Messiah is with us! I see him! I see him!"

At once a dozen voices rose about her:

"I see him! I see him!"

"Lord, lord, take us to thee!"

The burst of excitement seemed to have startled the bloodhounds. They moaned in their throats and paused. The spectators rose in one mass, astounded by the picture: men, women, and children singing as they knelt in the shadow of death and the beasts hesitant before their prey. Then one of the bloodhounds crept forward, sniffed, and closed its jaws suddenly on a piece of goatskin covering a child. The nostrils of the bloodhound quivered at the smell of the uncovered human flesh; and as if stung by an arrow, it reared and flung itself with fangs and claws on the little one. This was the signal: in an instant the strange spell was snapped, the howling, baying pack dashed forward, the skins on the forms of the men and women were ripped down, and wild canine jaws closed on human flesh. Here and there a brute managed to disentangle its prey from the head, and the body of a child, or of an old man, was dragged aside toward the arena walls. The victims did not struggle. The flesh was ripped, the blood burst forth, and only a cry, strange and terrible in the ears of the Romans, went up:

"Hear, O Israel, the Lord our God, the Lord is one."

"O Lord, take us unto thee."

The howling of the dogs had subsided into a hot, throaty growling and panting. The blood made runlets in the fresh-strewn sand. Then something happened which made the vast assembly on the tiers draw breath. As the dying victims were dragged apart by the bloodhounds, a fantastic picture was revealed at the center. A man was putting up a fight! But he was not fighting for himself. Kneeling on all fours, he was shielding with his ripped flesh a little child wrapped in a lambskin. With some strange idea of escape in his mind, the man held the child close to his belly with one hand. With the other hand, and occasionally with a foot, he was attempting to beat off the attack of the bloodhound, while edging his way toward the side of the arena. But it seemed also as though the bloodhound was set on the child rather than on the protecting adult. It kept thrusting its red muzzle under the man's belly, to get at the white flesh of the little one; and the man somehow managed to twist and squirm and push so as to interpose himself between the beast and the victim. The astounding spectacle roused in the Romans a mixture of emotions: suspense as to the outcome, and a strange feeling of sheer pity, utterly out of keeping with the place. Twice already the man had made the circle of the arena, escaping with his precious, tiny charge from the bloodhound. But now the beast fastened its jaws on the man's leg and began to drag him backwards. In front of Caesar's loge the dog came to a halt, and the eyes of the tens of thousands of spectators were focused on this picture. The man was ripped from head to

716

foot. The blood was streaming from a hundred wounds. But with a last conscious effort he was still shielding the infant. Had it been a mother who was offering this mad and hopeless resistance to the inevitable, the brutal Roman mob would probably have let the incident pass unnoticed. But this was a father; and that a father should display this desperate love, this tenderness at the gates of death, this self-forgetfulness, was strange and somehow moving. And now the spectators flapped their veils, lifted up their thumbs, and shouted to Caesar:

"Mitte! Let him be!"

But Caesar did not give the signal of the upturned thumb. No attendants rushed forward to drive off the bloodhound. And now the man in the arena was at the end of his strength. With bloody claws and dripping fangs the dog thrust and snapped at the infant, ripping the man's interposed limbs. One last snap of the jaws overturned the man, and the child rolled into the sand, dead. The bloodhound dragged it off.

The man lay in the sand, motionless. The watchers took him for dead. But suddenly he stirred, and stemmed his gashed elbows against the ground. He could not struggle to his knees. He only managed to lift his head, and to make a signal toward Caesar's loge with one hand. Then, in a loud, clear voice, he called out, in Latin:

"Tigellinus! Tigellinus! The child thou hast rejected is now with the lord!"

Tigellinus recognized his slave, Antonius.

In the same loud, clear voice Antonius called out the words which the Messiah had uttered when he breathed his last on the cross:

"Father, forgive them, for they know not what they do."

He dropped into the sand again, murmuring:

"Lord, take me to thee!"

Attendants in Charon-masks cleared the arena of the hounds, carried out the remnants of the dead bodies, sprinkled sand anew on the ground, and made ready for the third spectacle.

So it went on throughout the day. Group after group of human beings, pack after pack of wild beasts. The mob began to be bored: always the same things—men, women, children, blood, prayers, roaring, claws, fangs. The hot sun beat down; the stink of dead meat and of living, perspiring flesh hung into the air. There was too much, too much of everything. It was always so with Nero's enterprises; they lacked proportion; they ended up by producing the contrary of the effect sought.

717

Besides, the Christians did not fight; they only prayed and let themselves be eaten. The arena was not an arena but a vast abattoir; the spectators might just as well have been watching a group of butchers at their daily work. On the tiers children and elderly people were already nodding. Many of the spectators, thoroughly wearied, would have been glad to slip away; but they were afraid of the countless spies scattered throughout the circus. It was not safe to be lacking in the proper enthusiasm at a great spectacle generously arranged for the Roman masses by the Caesar. But the applause dwindled from spectacle to spectacle; no roars of salutation rolled toward the imperial loge. And Nero himself was bored. But he did not move; he lay inert and perspiring, his thick flesh oozing out of his tunic, in the midst of his suite. And while the Caesar was still in his loge the parched, thirsty masses on the tiers did not dare to move. Petronius had used up all his prepared jests, trying to keep up the interest of the Caesar; and, wearied as he too was with the dreary spectacle, he racked his brains vainly for something to say. The "arbiter of elegance" was in danger of showing his boredom openly. In his soul he cursed Nero for this interminable, monotonous, unimaginative slaughtering of groups of Jews. Nor was he the only one to feel thus in the imperial loge. Poppea, for all her cold, insolent bearing, was weary to the soul. Her attendants kept pouring out perfumes on her flesh to drive away the stink of blood and perspiration from her nostrils. Most disgusting to her was the proximity of the imperial carcass. And Nero himself would have been glad to call a halt, to enter the arena himself, and to entertain his people with a performance of his "Destruction of Troy." But he felt obscurely that the longer he sat there, the more he suffered the dreary and bloody spectacle, the more completely would he efface from the minds of the Romans their original suspicion of his guilt. And once again his gross and stupid strategy miscarried. For as the masses became sated and oversated with the slaughter, as their restiveness increased with the lengthening of the day, their attention and resentment swung from the arena to the Emperor. There was nothing left to hate in the miserable Christians; the popular fury faded; here and there even the dulled, brutish hearts of the Romans were touched by the spectacle of so many women and children fed to the wild beasts. The singing of the victims, their tenderness toward each other, their appeal to their faith, began to produce an effect. Among the spectators there were some who dared to

718

whisper to their neighbors: "But is this how criminals perish? Is it thus that men and women who set fire to a city face death?" Had it not been for the presence of the spies, such remarks would have been made loudly, would have risen in many places and grown into a demonstration. But Tigellinus's men were everywhere. And so, from time to time, the Romans called out, wearisomely, "*Habet! Hoc habet!*" and in their hearts they wished that Nero, and Tigellinus, too, were in the arena instead of the Christians.

At last the signal came for the suspension of the spectacle. The mob dashed as furiously from the circus as it had dashed into it in the morning. The booths, fountains, and drinking stations in the campus were surrounded by panting and hungry men and women, who snatched up the reeking sausages and stuffed them into their mouths, washing them down with gulps of sour wine. And through this swarming, masticating, guzzling crowd moved Nero himself, with his suite. He was determined to show the Romans that he was with them on this day. Petronius, who had been cursing him in his soul for the hideous and revolting show in the arena, cursed him even more heartily for being compelled to take part in this demonstration of democratic sentiment.

And still the great punishment of the criminals was not at an end. New forms of torture were to follow.

Along the middle of the campus on the Vatican hill stretched a double row of crosses, on each of which was nailed a human form. The nails driven through the hands and feet of the men and women were reinforced with ropes. The bloody limbs of the victims were steeped in oil, and the crosses heavily overlaid with wax. Throughout the day the crucified had suffered, but death was to be withheld from them until the coming of night.

When dusk fell the signal was given, and the human torches were kindled. Then, at one end of the alley of blazing bodies, Nero appeared in his chariot. He was wearing a red tunic, the symbol of Jupiter, and at his side the attendant held aloft the imperial eagle of Rome. Tigellinus, dressed in green, Nero's color in the races, flashed a white cloth.

Nero tugged at the reins, the white horses started forward, and the imperial chariot sped down the alley between the blazing crosses. A wail of pain accompanied him down the flickering alley. An old Jew, hanging on one of the first crosses, cried out:

"Father in heaven, forgive them, for they know not what they do."

719

And down the long course of the fiery crosses the cry was taken up:

"Father in heaven, forgive them, for they know not what they do!"

The old Jew on the burning cross raised his voice again:

"Hear, O Israel, the Lord our God, the Lord is One!"

And again down the double line of torches the cry rang out:

"Hear, O Israel, the Lord our God, the Lord is One!"

*　　*　　*

Even that last thrilling and ingenious performance of Nero's—his running of the fiery gauntlet between the double line of crosses—failed to cleanse him, in the popular mind, from the recurrent suspicion that he had set fire to Rome. When the "day of retribution" ended, the final impression retained by the Roman masses had nothing to do with the guilt of the Christians; it centered, instead, on a picture: the man crawling on all fours round the arena, interposing his flesh between the fangs of the bloodhound and the infant he protected. On the way home the exhausted Romans discussed that incident, and the question was raised:

"What? Did infants also set fire to Rome?"

Among Nero's intimates the same words were uttered.

"What thinkest thou, Petronius," asked Lucan, "did infants too set fire to Rome?"

"The children suffer for the sins of the fathers," answered Petronius.

"I understand thee not."

"Didst thou not hear what the slave called out to Tigellinus? And dost thou not grasp the meaning of it? Tigellinus set fire to Rome, and the child of Tigellinus was therefore thrown to the beasts."

The bitter witticism was repeated and became very fashionable in Rome.

"What? Infants too set fire to Rome?"

"The children suffer for the sins of the fathers."

And everyone knew what and who was meant.

Chapter Seventeen

KADDISH

LATE in the evening there came messengers to the Jews assembled in the great synagogue, with the account of the slaughter in the arena and of the fiery sacrifice at nightfall. The worshipers had fasted and prayed all day, under the leadership of Reb Sabbatai Zadoc. Now they learned that the souls for which they had been praying had departed in all purity, with forgiveness on their lips. Then Reb Sabbatai rose and said:

"My brothers in Israel: not by that which is unclean can the hearts of men be brought near to the spirit of God; not by abomination can they be persuaded to take upon themselves, in love and forgiveness, all the tortures which were visited upon these saints by the Edomites. Therefore, I say, blessed be he that has drawn so many souls into the shelter of the divine wings, brought them to the spirit of God, and made them into a people as stiffnecked as Israel. And if he did not come into the world for us, for the children of Israel, assuredly he came into the world for them. This is a great day in Israel. Many are the souls that have been born this day unto our father, Abraham: our faith has given birth to a daughter worthy of her. God's Name has been sanctified throughout the world, and it will be sanctified whithersoever the name of the martyrs will be carried, from now on and for evermore. A great day of the sanctification of God is this! Sanctified be all those that have perished in Him; and whether they be Jews or gentiles who served God with their souls, from this day forth they are our brothers. Therefore let us rise and bless their memory, let us utter a great *Kaddish* for their souls to the one, living God of Israel."

Then the Rabbi stood before the Scrolls and cried out:

"Judge of the world, Father of all living, God of Abraham, Isaac, and Jacob, accept the blood of thy servants which has been poured out before Thee like water. Gather up their bones, which were scattered before the beasts of the field. For Thee alone, Thou one and only living God, was the sacrifice made. Let it therefore be acceptable in Thy sight. Assemble the martyred souls under the wings of Thy glory and bind

721

them in the bond of eternal life. Let not the blood of Thy servants have been shed in vain, but let it be like the pillar of fire which Thou didst send as a guide unto Thy people in the wilderness; and let Thy Name be spread in all the corners of the earth, so that every knee may come and bow before Thee, for Thine alone is the glory and the praise. Let all peoples make a bond to serve Thee in utter trust. Let Thy justice be unfolded over the earth, so that evil may cease. Let the reign of evil end and the reign of the just Messiah, whom Thou hast promised us through Thy Prophets, and for whom Thy faithful ones wait with trembling knees, begin, for we can wait no longer. The waters have come up to our lips. Look upon our pain and our wretchedness, have mercy on Thy creatures, Thou eternal God of Israel!"

The Rabbi could no longer hold back his tears. His voice shook as he began to intone the *Kaddish* for the martyrs:

"Magnified and sanctified be the Name of God."

The whole congregation, the widows, the orphans, the brothers and sisters of the martyrs, repeated, weeping, the *Kaddish*:

"Magnified and sanctified be the Name of God."

*   *   *

Late in the night groups of Jews, the widows and orphans, the brothers and sisters of the martyrs, stole out of the pent alleys of the Trans-Tiber. They carried little oil lamps. Quietly they wound their way through the streets and open places and crossed the Janiculum to the Vaticanum. There, on the campus, a few of the crosses were still smoldering, but most of them had fallen into ashes, and amid the ashes lay the bones of the martyrs. The silent group from the Trans-Tiber went from cross to cross, gathering up the bones and wrapping them in cloth. The sleepy soldiers on the campus did not interfere, for the Jews were within their rights. There was, besides the crosses, a great heap of garbage which had been carried out from the circus, and the Jews searched it for human remains. Carefully and lovingly they gathered up bodies, limbs, bloody fragments, and wrapped them in cloth; and when they had collected all that which seemed to them to have belonged to a human body, they went in procession to the Jewish burial place, which was a cave far out in the Trans-Tiber. There a great weeping broke out, of widows and orphans. But the leaders of the Jewish community and the leaders of the new faith, who accompanied them in the task of giving Jewish burial to the remains of the martyrs, said that it was not fitting at this moment to weep for the martyrs. It was fitting, rather, to sanctify the Name of God, even as the martyrs had done. Thereupon the orphan sons were led forward and ranged about the large common grave, and the whole people accompanied them in the saying of the *Kaddish*:

"*Yisgadal ve-yiskadash sh'mei raboh.* . . . Magnified and sanctified be the Name of God. . . ."

Chapter Eighteen

IN THE CATACOMBS

CRIVES FASTANUS was a gladiator who had been pardoned and set at liberty by Caesar Claudius. Some time afterwards he was given a position as an attendant in Nero's circus on the Vaticanum. A man in the middle fifties, he looked back on a life which had for the most part consisted of mortal struggles with four-footed and two-footed beasts and which he had preserved only because his astounding physique had endured far beyond the age at which gladiators were still expected to make a good showing in the arena. But for every combat from which he had emerged victorious, there was a sign on his body, a memento which he would carry to the grave. Indeed, his body was a sort of record, for it was covered as with a network of scars, old sword wounds and the marks of teeth and claws. His nose was flattened, his eyes were slit—one of them was missing—and there was a hole on one cheek, constantly suppurating. In the preservation of his own life he had taken the lives of so many others, he had slashed so many bodies—the number was beyond his computation—that he had lost all feeling with regard to the death of a human being, and the sight of a man in his last agonies moved him as little as the sight of a dying insect. Yet, here was Crives Fastanus walking anxiously through the alleys of the Trans-Tiber district, inquiring of every coppersmith and sewer of sandals, in a low, gentle voice:

"Canst thou tell me where I shall find Miriam the perfume mixer?"

The men to whom he addressed the question invariably started back from him. His vast, naked breast was like a ruined battlefield, his mighty arms were like battering rams. They started back also from the dull, heavy light in his one remaining eye. By his helmet it could be seen that he was an old gladiator; the bronze tablet on his bosom proclaimed that he was a servant in the imperial household, an attendant in Nero's circus. And every Jew of the Trans-Tiber quarter knew that in the house of Miriam the perfume mixer there occurred regular meetings of the Jewish Christians. Therefore whoever answered the gladiator— there were some that actually fled from him—answered him in the negative. How was it that Miriam had escaped arrest? Surely her name had been known. Was not this, then, a belated attempt to take her? But then, if new arrests were toward, where were the police, and the military? A man would not set out alone to make new arrests. Besides, there was something strange in the bearing of this gigantic, elderly gladiator; his voice was rough, but low and beseeching. He stretched out his arms to a Jewess selling home-baked cakes at her stall to the workers on the barges, and said:

"In the name of Pluto, to whom I have consecrated so many lives, tell me, thou, where lives the woman whom they call Miriam the perfume mixer. I have important business with her."

The stall-keeper looked at him dumbly. For all his humble bearing, there was about this gigantic man too much of the arena. She would not answer, and the gladiator passed on. Finally he found one who would converse with him, a seller of pots who had his stall on the Tiber bank: Mordecai-Sabbatai, who was of the sect of the believers.

"Whence hast thou the name?" asked Mordecai-Sabbatai, cautiously.

"It was given me by one of the Christians, before he was driven into the arena."

"Given thee by one of the Christians? Nay. Why should a Christian betray one of his kind to thee?"

"I begged it from him, hearest thou? I would become one of them."

"*Thou* wouldst become a Christian?" And Mordecai-Sabbatai shrank away from the old gladiator.

"Thou hast heard me."

724

"But seest thou not," asked Mordecai-Sabbatai, lowering his voice, "what they do to them?"

"I would rather die with you than live as I have lived till now."

The pottery merchant remained silent, revolving the case in his mind. Was this the trick of a spy? It could not be. Brutal the man's face might be, but utterly devoid of cunning. And even the brutality was softened by something shining from within.

"A Christian gave thee the name, thou sayest."

"Yes. Hear me. I was among those who drove him with the whip into the arena, and I envied him. For more than twenty years I served the Caesars in the arena. I have seen many men perish in pain; but I tell thee I have never seen men perish as these men and women perished, with song on their lips and joy in their eyes. I would be one of them, hearest thou? I asked this Christian to give me the name of one to whom I could turn, who would receive me into the company of the Christians."

Mordecai-Sabbatai made up his mind swiftly. He turned over his stall to the care of a neighbor and led Crives Fastanus to the house of Miriam the perfume mixer.

On this day, as on many others, there was a gathering of the faithful in the little apartment on the uppermost floor of the old house. There were fewer in attendance; and the clothes of the faithful were torn in sign of mourning for those who would never break bread with them again in this place. Miriam and her visitors were seated on the floor, according to the ritual, for it was less than a week since her two sons and their wives had been done to death in the arena. It was a matter for great wonder that they had let her be, for her house was as well known among the Christians of Rome as that of Priscilla and Aquila had been in the past. Most of the leaders of the congregation, indeed, had been taken. The few that remained were with Miriam even now. There was Rufus, one of the founders of the congregation, and his mother, an old woman with sorrowful eyes. She came from Jerusalem, and all her life she had longed to return to the Holy City. There was Linus, a man in middle age, with a stern, strong face set in a black beard. On the very day following the dread slaughter in the circus and on the Vatican campus he had begun to reorganize the remnants of the church. He was helped by Eubulus and Pudens. There were others,

725

too, and they sat barefoot on the ground with Miriam. In the corners of the room stood the cruses in which the oils were filtered for the perfumes. Fragments of dried plants, roots, and herbs were mingled on the floor with parchment manuscripts. The voices of the assembled were low. They did not speak of the martyrs and of the past, but of the church and the future. Now, after the great slaughter, they feared there would be a complete falling off in converts. The congregation would remain a tiny group; perhaps it would even be scattered abroad, as in the days of Claudius. They discussed plans for bringing together those that remained alive and conducting them to Simon bar Jonah, who was in hiding in the Via Appia quarter. Simon bar Jonah alone could comfort and strengthen them. . . . And as they sat thus talking in low tones, there was a knock at the door. Mordecai-Sabbatai the Jew, who was one of them, entered, leading Crives Fastanus, the attendant in Nero's circus, who but a few days before had been whipping the Christian prisoners into the arena.

The assembled were not all as easily convinced as Mordecai-Sabbatai that the old gladiator had come to them with pure intentions. How many lives had the congregation not lost because of the spies who had stolen into its midst! But Crives Fastanus lay at their feet, his face turned to the floor, and begged them in a broken voice to believe him.

"I come," he wept, "from the lovely land of Galatia. It is a green land, and the moss on the stones always makes you think of spring. I was a child when they snatched me from my mother's side; and from that day on I have lived in the midst of blood. They taught me to fight and to preserve my life by taking the lives of others. Nay, I lived only to take the lives of others. I learned and believed that to be alive was the greatest happiness and that naught mattered save that which helped me to remain alive. I believed it until I saw your men and women dying with song on their lips and joy in their hearts. And then I knew that my belief had been a false one, and there is a greater happiness than life, there is an eternal happiness, which is, to die in your faith. I implore you, return me to the springtime of my childhood, to the heavenly home of which I heard your men and women speak, the heavenly fields where their good shepherd, Christ the Messiah, feeds his flock. I would be one of his sheep!"

"When didst thou hear them speak thus?"

"In the hours of their imprisonment and in the hour of their

726

death. I heard them sing of green pastures by still waters, and of the shepherd. All the years of my manhood I have sent men to their death, but never have I heard one go hence with song on his lips. And before the last of them were driven out into the arena, I implored them to take compassion on me and tell me who would make me one of them. And there was a man who believed me, and he gave me the name of the woman to whom I might address myself. Turn not your faces from me, but lead me to the good shepherd, Yeshua the Christ, whose name I have learned to call on."

The believers looked at each other, and one said:

"Surely it is God Himself who sends the tormentors to take the places of the martyrs in the ranks of the congregation. Blessed be the Name of God!"

They received the gladiator that day into the faith and taught him all the signs of the faithful.

*   *   *

As it was with Crives Fastanus, so was it with many another who had witnessed the deaths in the arena by day and on the campus at night. For the first time masses of Romans had heard the song of hope and triumph on the lips of those who were entering the shadows of the underworld, and there were many who forgot the shadows and remembered the hope and triumph. They were seized with an irresistible desire to learn the secret of the faith which transformed the darkness of the underworld into the light of everlasting life.

When Rome slept, figures came stealing through its streets; they came out of rich homes which had been spared from the flames and out of the crowded shelters where the homeless were congregated. There were Jews and gentiles, freedmen and slaves. They exchanged the signs of the faith, and they whispered instructions to each other: the gathering was to take place near the house on the Via Appia. There they would break bread, eat the common meal, and hear words of comfort from the first of the disciples, Simon bar Jonah.

Thus the fears of the leaders of the congregation were proved to be vain. For the greater the torment visited upon the believers, the stronger grew the faith. It was as if a competition had set in tacitly between the two powers, the cruelty of Nero and the love of the Messiah, as to which would prevail in the heart of man; and it turned out that the greater the danger of fellowship in the Christian congregation, the larger were the numbers that were drawn to it.

Among those Jews whom love of a precious and painfully sustained tradition forbade the acceptance of Christ as the Messiah, a profound impression had been created by the martyrdom of the Christians. Was not such martyrdom itself of the tradition? Were not the newcomers, who had learned to die as Jewish martyrs had died from time immemorial, to be regarded as brothers? The traditional synagogue, which was allowed by Roman law, became the cover to the Christian faith. It was to a Jewish synagogue in the catacombs that the Christians, exchanging in the night their secret signs, drawing upon the air the symbol of a fish, or an anchor, were now hastening. Across the Sublicius bridge, down from the Aventine hill, and even from the slopes of the Palatine, they slipped through the darkness toward the Porta Capena and the Via Appia.

As the Jews were allowed their own synagogues, so they were allowed their own burial place; and after the synagogue the Jewish cemetery, in this instance a catacomb or series of catacombs, was the dearest and most sacred place of assembly for the Jews, who came thither to share their joys and sorrows with the dead. Now the catacombs on the Via Appia, being new, were as yet unknown to the spies of Tigellinus and were well suited to the secret meetings of the believers. At the center of the catacombs there was a large subterranean hall, from which extended the labyrinthine corridors. The hall was put to a variety of uses; here funeral orations were delivered, assemblies of the congregation held, and anniversary services for the dead conducted. In certain of the corridors were the vaults of the elders of the synagogues and the most important members. The walls of the hall were adorned with sacred designs, candelabra, the citron, grapes, palm branches. Here and there appeared the image of the *shofar,* or ram's horn, symbol of the resurrection which would come with the Messiah, and of the Ark of Noah. There were drawings of Abraham and Isaac, representing the sacrifice, and of Jonah in the belly of the fish—motifs full of tender associations for the Jews. Here, seated on benches, under the light of oil lamps, the Christians found refuge and a place of worship.

On this first re-assembly of the Christians after the great calamity, there were strange and moving encounters. Servants and masters who had not suspected each other of fellowship in the faith came face to face as brothers. Men and women who had hidden their inner lives from each other and had been circumspect for fear of betrayal embraced and wept in joy. The blood which Nero had shed, the sword which he still held suspended over the community, drew the Christians together in a bond which was stronger than ever. They were not brothers and sisters of one family, they were as members of one body. No one here knew when he would be called upon to testify for the Messiah, but all knew that sooner or later death would also be their common portion; and beyond death, which was but a gate, rebirth and everlasting life in each other would also be their common portion.

When the believers had taken their places, Simon bar Jonah was brought in from his hiding place. They crowded about him, and bar Jonah lifted up his voice and spoke. He used the Aramaic tongue, and though there was no interpreter, they understood him, for his heart spoke to theirs. When he had uttered a brief prayer, he kneeled and buried his face in the ground and remained silent in ecstasy, and his followers did likewise. After a long pause he prepared to celebrate their holiest ritual. Bread was broken and distributed; the cup of wine was passed from hand to hand. Then all felt that they were sanctified and united in the Messiah and in his sufferings. Mothers lifted up their children, whom they had brought with them at the peril of their lives, and, pointing to the white-haired old man, whispered:

"Remember, that is the first of the disciples, Peter, who leads us to the lord. If thou remainest among the living, tell thy children that thine eyes have seen Peter."

*　　*　　*

At one of these assemblies, not long after, Peter knelt on the floor of the catacomb hall, and his followers were seated about him. He lifted his arms to heaven and said:

"Secret are Thy ways, O Lord of the world. We know not why Thou hast planted the path of redemption with the sharp stones of suffering and pain. But see, Father in heaven, naked feet tread the stony path, and naked bodies pass through the forest of fire. With bloodied feet and burned bodies Thy hosts draw near to Thee. Take them, O holy One of Israel, for they are Thy flock. We are Thy portion and

Thy inheritance, those that have died for Thee and those that live for Thee. Make us one with the martyrs who have given up their lives for Thy Name. Take us into Thy host, for we are Thine!"

They listened, and in their hearts they felt themselves united with the Messiah and with the martyrs who had died for him.

That night the hall of the catacombs was surrounded by a band of legionaries. Tigellinus's spies had at last discovered the secret meeting place of the Christians. There was no cry of terror, no sign of panic, when the soldiers broke into the service. The worshipers remained where they were, their faces pressed against the cold stone, their thoughts obstinately given to the Messiah. And even when they were chained and dragged out into the night, they uttered not a word, but meditated on their faith.

Among the prisoners were the first of the disciples, Simon bar Jonah and the one-time gladiator, Crives Fastanus.

Chapter Nineteen

"I HAVE KEPT THE FAITH"

ACROSS the ruined streets of Rome, where thousands of slaves were at work, a heavy guard conducted, in chains, the apostle to the gentiles, Paul. This time no deputation had come to greet him on the Via Appia, and no one had awaited him in the city. He had come with one companion—the physician Lukas, who walked at a distance behind him, in order that he might not be observed by the guard.

Where had the apostle been throughout the days which had led up to the frightful slaughters in Rome! It were easier to ask, where had he not been! He had passed, as on a storm wind, across the world. From Rome he had hastened to Ephesus, and to the cities round about, where new congregations, never visited by him before, had been founded. He had been in Colossae, thence he had passed to Nikopolis and to Berea. He had been in his beloved Philippi, of Macedonia, and he had gone with Titus to Crete, where, since the time of the shipwreck he had been considered a holy man; and there in Crete he had founded new congregations. He had been for a time in Naples, and from Naples he had gone to Troas, where he had lodged in the house of a certain Carpus. It was there, in Troas, in the house of Carpus, that he was arrested on the charge that he was a Christian and was spreading the pernicious and forbidden doctrine among Romans and slaves. He had been thrown in chains and carried aboard ship. Now he was being led to the Praetorian Guard house until such time as he would be brought to trial in one of the basilicas on the Forum Romanum.

So hastily had he been taken that most of his belongings—a mantle and a few parchment documents—had remained behind, with Carpus. In the damp prison of the Praetorium he greatly needed his mantle, but he missed more sorely the parchment rolls with their sacred messages. On this return to Rome, Paul felt like a man forlorn and abandoned. The companions with whom he had set out on the last of these travels, or had picked up on the way, were gone from him. Some he had himself sent forth on missions or left behind him to complete his work: Crispus was in Galatea; Titus had gone to Crete and Macedonia; and his beloved son Timotheus was in Ephesus. And when the persecutions of the Christians began in the provinces, spreading thence from the capital, some of his companions abandoned him. Demas, who had served him throughout his first imprisonment in Rome, had left him, "because he loved this world," and had returned to Salonika; Tryphimus had fallen sick in Mylitte, and had remained there. A certain Alexander, a coppersmith, did him "much evil." Aristarchus, his faithful servant, was taken with many other Christians at Troas, to be tried before the local courts. Lukas had neither fallen away from him nor had he been taken prisoner. The completely Greek appearance and bearing of this believer had stood him in good stead; he was able to accompany Paul when, as a Roman citizen, the latter was called to be tried in Rome a second time.

Sensitive to the end, Paul felt himself bowed under the burden of his loneliness. And yet the persecutions had not destroyed all his communications with the world of the believers. Closely guarded though he was in the Praetorian prison—and it did not matter now that he was a Roman citizen; the crime of Christianity obliterated almost all distinctions—he managed after a little while to exchange messages with friends. Among the soldiers taking turns outside his cell there were

731

members of Gabelus's cohort. Gabelus himself had been arrested in the Jewish catacomb, together with Peter, and in prison he was a great help to the aged apostle. But in the cohort, too, the Christian thread was not broken. The place of Gabelus was taken by the gentle and noble-spirited Eubulus. When these men were on guard, they carried messages to and from Paul and his friends; they also enabled Lukas to attend the apostle; and, what was of the utmost importance to the latter, they obtained writing materials for him, and enabled him to send forth letters to the communities.

Who can penetrate to the inmost mysteries of faith? Only the utter devotion which is born of faith could have moved Paul to demand of his companions that they confront the threat of death with the same calmness as himself. In the darkness where he sat, his head resting on his hand, Paul was more aware than ever of the eternal light which is kindled in us when we conquer death. "In faith there is no death, there is only eternal life," he had taught. He was quite incapable, therefore, of understanding—let alone of sympathizing with—any manifestation of panic. He expected everyone, without exception, to continue with the work as diligently as heretofore, and not to withhold, out of fear of death, a single act of service from the lord. He was filled with contempt for those of the believers who fled before the persecutions or who refused to renew contact with him for fear of discovery. He understood weakness, he understood timidity, but he could not associate them with faith. Yet his contempt was mingled with compassion, for he could not but interpret defection as a loss of the greatest of treasures, faith. To those who had avoided him on the occasion of his first trial in Rome, he said:

"Be not ashamed of risking danger for the lord, and be not ashamed of me, his prisoner, but share his suffering."

The cell in which he was now confined was dim at noon-tide, pitch black in the morning and afternoon. But Paul sat steeped in light, as though the walls about him had dissolved and the heavens were shining freely on him. He might have been wholly at peace, were it not that he feared the fear of others, was in a panic lest panic should seize the believers. Concerning his own life, he knew the time had come for an accounting with himself; he looked back steadfastly on the course of the years, and it seemed to him that everything was as it should be. He could leave the world now no man's debtor; even himself he owed nothing.

732

Faith had come as a peace-maker between him and the world. For there was no death; there was only one great life which passed from this world to the next, and wherever God wanted him, why, there God would find him! Those who were afraid of death were the ones who were bringing death into life. Ah, how he longed to plant this truth—the ultimate truth of the faith—in the hearts of the congregations! If they could only see this truth as deeply as he saw it! Then there would be no timidities and no defections; then they would reach, even on this side of death, to the high perception of the Messiah, and the passage through death would be for them like the stepping across a narrow threshold.

The door of the cell swings open. Daylight is diffused toward the dim corner where the apostle, seated in chains, is steeped in his own inward light. It is good Eubulus who has opened the door. He leads in a man. Paul looks up, and beholds the stranger, tall, stately, black-bearded. Eubulus pulls the door to, and the cell is dark again. The stranger speaks in the darkness.

"I am Onesiphorus of Ephesus. I have come to pay my respects to the apostle to the gentiles."

Joyously Paul asks:

"Thou hast come to greet me here, in Rome? Wert thou not afraid? Wert thou not ashamed of my chains?"

"Afraid to come to thee? Ashamed of the chains which the Messiah has loaded on thy limbs for the salvation of men?" The tall stranger falls on his knees before Paul, and kisses the chains. "These," he says, "are the ornaments of the faithful."

"Are there many of thy like among the faithful?" asks Paul, eagerly.

"Everywhere the faithful go with song on their lips to encounter death."

"Say not death, say not death," cries Paul. "Say rather, eternal life." He struggles to his knees. "Oh, praise unto the Messiah, who has destroyed death and unveiled eternal life!"

It was under the inspiration of this visit that he wrote his farewell letter to his beloved son, Timotheus. Eubulus smuggled in, that day, pen, ink, papyrus, and a lamp. By the dim flame Paul wrote laboriously, adjusting himself to the heavy manacles.

Very different is Paul's condition now from that in which he lived

733

during his first imprisonment. Then he was in his own house. Now he is in the dread Praetorium prison. In those days the daily guard chained to him could—if he were not already a Christian—be more easily moved to friendliness. The horror of the Christian accusation had not yet seized the city. Now only a Christian legionary permits himself to be friendly with the apostle—and that only when another Christian is stationed outside the cell. For even the inclination to pity the "enemies of mankind" may be regarded as a sign of that infection for which the only cure is the arena. The longest record of faithfulness in service to the Caesar then avails nothing—witness old Gabelus, awaiting his trial along with the rest. Paul's Roman citizenship performs one service for him; he does not have to wear the frightful collar or neck manacles, chained to the hands and feet, which are put on the arrested slaves. But one hand is chained to his jailor and one foot to the wall of the cell.

When it chances that both guards—the one within the cell, and the one without—are both Christians, a letter can be written. But it must be written at one sitting. Neither the papyrus nor any of the other writing materials may be left in the cell overnight. In the morning both guards will be changed. Neither of the new men may be Christians. If the letter is discovered it is death for the guards, and death for the men and women whose names are mentioned in it. Yet Paul mentions names—he sends greetings from Eubulus and Pudens and Linus, and to Aquila and Priscilla. He must write fast. He cannot utter all that is in his heart; he must indicate his thoughts. He knows that the end is near—and yet, he does not seem to give up hope. He remembers that no one came forward to defend him at his first trial: "notwithstanding, the Lord stood with me and strengthened me, that by me the preaching might be fully known, and I was delivered out of the lion's mouth. And the Lord will deliver me from every evil work and preserve me unto His heavenly kingdom."

With incredible obstinacy the apostle excludes from the last letter to his beloved son all mention of the bloody calamities which have befallen the Christians and of the persecutions which they suffer. Is it hope, or only the same obstinacy, which forbids him to mention his impending death? He calls on Timotheus to proceed at once to Rome, though he knows that he bids him thereby put his head in the "lion's mouth." "Hasten to be here before the winter!" he writes. Concerning those who did not stand by him at his first trial, he says: "I pray God

734

that it be not charged against them." And as if to deny his own pre-monitions, he bids Timotheus bring with him the mantle and the manu-scripts which were left behind, in the house of Carpus. And yet the let-ter breathes expectancy of earthly death. "I am now ready to be offered, and the time of my departure is near at hand." And "if we die with the Messiah, so shall we live with him; if we suffer with him, so shall we rule with him; and if we deny him, so shall he deny us."

Life and death are mingled in the letter, as though the two have become indistinguishable in his eyes, as though the two are one, and their oneness is linked with the Messiah. No matter what happens, Paul will accept it, not with stoical indifference, but with love—that love which is the faith. It is a letter both of life and of death. One instant he is laying down plans for the future, the next he takes a father's lov-ing farewell of his son. It is Paul's last letter, and it pulses with the sensitiveness of his soul.

Only the inexhaustible driving force of his faith, as strong toward the close as at the beginning of his mission, could blind him at moments to the certainty of the issue of his trial. There is no trace of fear in him, no echo of the approaching footstep of the dark angel, or of the thunder of persecution about him.

But it is to his son, to his beloved Timotheus that he is writing, to the one personal joy that he has permitted himself in life; and he cannot repress, in this half-conscious cry of farewell, a tenderness, a sentimen-tality almost, which we seek in vain in his other letters: "Greatly I de-sire to see thee, remembering thy tears, remembering the unfeigned faith that is in thee, which dwelt first in thy grandmother Lois and in thy mother, Eunice."

Timotheus alone had awakened in Paul's heart the slumbering in-stincts of family and fatherhood. Hence the peculiar touch of tender-ness, of pathos; hence the intimate recollection of his sufferings, which are not so much a plaint as an expression of closeness, a loving father-to-son revelation: "Persecutions and afflictions which came to me at Antioch, at Iconium, at Lystra—but out of them all the Lord delivered me." He cannot help these allusions. But he does not close the letter with them. He knows, from that which he learned in his youth under Rabban Gamaliel, that "the words of parting between Rabbi and dis-ciple shall be words of the Torah. The father parting from the son shall leave with him words of wisdom to take along on the path of

735

life." He therefore turns from the tenderly personal to the admonitory:

"God has not given us the spirit of fear, but of power ... hold fast the form of sound words, which thou hast heard from me, in faith and love which is in Yeshua the Messiah." In feverish haste he sets down the leading principles of the mission of his son: "Preach the word; be instant in season and out of season ... watch in all things, endure afflictions, do the work of an evangelist, make full proof of thy ministry. . . ." And here the words slip from him: "For I am now ready to be offered."

And then, it is as though he had paused a moment for reflection, casting a backward glance over his life. "I have fought a good fight, I have finished my course." He looks down the long years of his wandering, those of his body and those of his spirit; he sees the devious routes, the detours, the returns, and he knows that in the end his feet are on the straight path. He sees that the sum of it all is just, and he adds, in complete assurance:

"I have kept the faith."

And he sees, too, his reward. It is not, he knows, the crown of grace, the reward of one better than himself; it is the crown of righteousness, hard-won, by a life of labor. For all his life was given to bringing men under the sign of righteousness. "That has been my life," he thinks, "the hard way of righteousness." He has not been tender with himself; he has not shrunk from suffering, he does not shrink from death. And the same discipline he would impose on others, even on his beloved son. Just a few moments ago he wrote him with infinite gentleness; now he bids him come to Rome! Bids him, too, bring Marcus with him, "for he is useful to me in the ministry." It is an invitation to share his fate and the fate of the believers of Rome, extended to his beloved son, and to Marcus, the nephew of his beloved boyhood friend, bar Naba. For when the moment of personal tenderness, almost of weakness, has passed, he is back in the spirit of his service, and faith reminds him that there is no break, no death, for those that serve the Messiah.

The light trembles on the papyrus as he hastens through the last lines of his missive. Paul is motionless. His yellow, wrinkled face, his lofty forehead, shine in the half darkness. His eyes are fixed on the distance, beyond the heavy walls that imprison him. His heart is at peace, with the peace of fulfillment. He has reached the point where joy and sorrow are one. Everything that was to be done has been done, everything has been said. He is ready now to abandon the earthly instrument which has served him so long and so painfully.

*   *   *

The end came soon. Two days after his letter to Timotheus had been smuggled out of the Praetorian prison, Paul was brought before the Tribunal. The investigation was short. He identified himself with the words, "I am a Christian"; he refused to offer incense before the image of Caesar; he made no appeal to his Roman citizenship. He was led out and conducted to the prison reserved for those already condemned to death. There he found Simon bar Jonah, the first of the disciples, Gabelus, once of the Praetorian Guard, and many another whom he had won to the faith of the Messiah.

Chapter Twenty

"THE GRACE OF THE LORD BE WITH YOU"

FROM of old the word "Tullianum," the name of the dungeon prison, was uttered with dread by every Roman. Hewn out in the solid rock of the Capitoline hill, on the steep side overlooking the Forum Romanum, the Tullianum was one fastness from which there was no escape. Prisoners were lowered by ropes into its lightless depths, and high above them, about the "entrance" which they could not have reached without external aid, a strong guard was kept day and night.

As a rule the prisoners who were lowered into the Tullianum never saw the light of day again. They were not starved to death so much as eaten to death. Food of some kind was given them, but they in turn, while still alive, were eaten by monstrous rats and crawling things which bred in countless numbers in the foulness of the cells and corridors. The prisoners were chained, either to rings in the walls or to great, immovable blocks of wood. The floors of the prison were littered

737

with human offal, with moldering bodies and bones gnawed clean, and the poisonous air ate into the lungs and skin. A thick ooze dripped from the walls, and dampness caused the bones and flesh of the prisoners to swell painfully. Their limbs, often immovable in their chains, rotted, became gangrenous masses. The diet of bread and water undermined swiftly whatever health they brought with them into the prison. When a prisoner died, the warders would unchain the carcass and roll it over toward the nearest heap of offal, so that the chains might be ready for the next one.

Simon bar Jonah, the old fisher-Jew of Galilee, endured through nine months of imprisonment in the Tullianum.

He had been thrown into the underground dungeon together with the other Christians taken at the last service in the Jewish catacombs. His name was not unknown to high Roman officials. Caesar himself had issued a special order that he, the apostle to the Jews, should be taken, and with him the apostle to the gentiles. But at the time of Peter's arrest Nero was not in Rome. He had gone to Athens to find a sympathetic audience for his poetical and musical compositions; and the officials were waiting for his return before carrying out the execution of the important prisoner. Moreover, it was expected that there would be a repetition of the spectacle offered by Nero in the Vatican circus.

In those nine months of imprisonment the aged apostle passed, in the flesh, through the seven limbos of hell. He was chained by both legs to a ring in the wall, and often he would awaken out of a fitful sleep to feel the rats gnawing at his feet. Out of the black corners the frightful odor of decaying flesh, living and dead, assailed his nostrils. No light ever broke into the prison. Yet he endured. He endured in the knowledge that, when the Messiah saw fit, he would come for him. About him he heard the moaning of his brothers in the faith, but he could not see them. Day long and night long—though there was only night in those depths—they called on the name of Christ, imploring him to hasten. But the Messiah did not hasten, and there were some among the Christians who in the horror of the Tullianum began to fall away from the faith. From his plot of darkness the apostle uttered his words of comfort to the dying, assuring them that beyond the portals of death the Messiah waited for them; he was calling them to his cross, that they might share his sufferings and his eternal life. But often, between these moments of ministration, Peter himself pressed his face against the damp stone,

738

whispering, "My God, why hast Thou forsaken me?" At other times he chanted Psalms. Warders who came down into the cells would stumble on him in the darkness and beat him with their fists for his interminable praying. Criminals, murderers, and thieves who were flung together with the Christians into the Tullianum would howl him down; and sometimes, if they were stationed near him, they would reach over and strike him in the darkness. His hair and beard were sticky with blood; and if his skull had not been so powerful it might more than once have been split when a wild hand flung it at random against the rock wall. In particular there were two highway robbers, Proseus and Martinus, admitted some time after Peter and chained hard by him, whom his prayers infuriated and who thrust at him with hand or foot to close his mouth.

Gabelus, the old soldier, was among those whose faith began to fail them when the salvation which they expected delayed beyond their strength; and the apostle, whose faith was mightier than the surrounding rocks, wept when he heard Gabelus, like the others, yielding to despair.

"Come, lord," prayed Peter in his heart, "come, help me, for the waters have come up to my lips."

Then, on a certain day, the trap door above the prison was opened and a prisoner was let down. Two warders entered from a side door and fastened the newcomer to a ring in the wall opposite Peter's place. When they had withdrawn the prisoner called out:

"The grace of Christ the Messiah be with your spirit, Amen!"

Peter, who had not been able to distinguish the face of the new prisoner, recognized the voice. In sudden joy he cried out:

"Is it thou, Paul, my brother?"

The Christians, languishing in their corners, feeling the last embers of their faith dying out in them, started up when they heard that name. Feebly they cried out:

"Paul the apostle is with us!"

"Yes, I am your brother Paul, a servant of God. I have come to bring you the hope of Israel in Yeshua the Messiah! The Messiah calls you to share his suffering. The grace of our lord be with you all, amen!"

"It is Paul! That is his greeting!" whispered several voices.

"I know him! It is the greeting which he sent us in his letters!"

"Paul, my beloved brother, Paul," was all that Peter could say.

"Yes, thou first of the disciples, thou rock of the Messiah, it is I, Paul, thy young brother. I have come to share thy chains in the Messiah!"

"My beloved brother!" wept Peter, and the tears coursing down his cheeks seemed to him to soften the pains in his body. "Where art thou?"

From opposite walls in the narrow cell they reached across to each other with their free hands and intertwined their fingers; and it was as if they could feel their whole bodies through the contact; they embraced, they kissed each other, in the touch of their fingers. And as if at an inner signal, they began to chant aloud the Psalm:

"Yes, though I walk through the valley of the shadow of death, I fear no evil, for Thou art with me!"

In an instant the black chamber resounded with the song of hope:

"Though I walk through the valley of the shadow of death, I fear no evil, for Thou art with me!"

Paul felt someone crawling at his feet; he reached out, and his hand touched a face, a beard, warm flesh.

"Paul, thou bringer of salvation!"

"Gabelus, art thou with us? Praised be God who has given thee a share in the sufferings of the Messiah," cried Paul.

"Praised be God who has found me worthy to be one of His soldiers," answered Gabelus.

"Brothers in the faith!" said Paul into the darkness. "May God, our eternal help, accept our suffering as a sacrifice! Rejoice in your sufferings, for they bring you nearer to the Messiah. Oh, who shall take away from you his grace, and who shall rob you now of the gift of his love? Come, brothers, let us give utterance to our joy, let us sing a great song. God has chosen us to suffer with the Messiah. Let the Name of God be praised from now on and for evermore."

From the cells along the invisible corridors, across the heaps of refuse, of decaying flesh, of skeletons, through halls of death and darkness, there came a sound of voices. It was as though the wind were stirring in the valley of withered bones, in the vision of Ezekiel, when he beheld the flesh blossom again on the remains of the long dead. The voices rose, they took on power and self-assurance, they shook off the weakness of the flesh.

"God has chosen us to suffer with the Messiah! Let the Name of God be praised from now on and for evermore!"

"Brothers in the sufferings of the Messiah," cried Paul again, "let us rejoice with a great rejoicing! All you, who are united in pain for the faith, shall be united in the resurrection and grace of salvation. His faith enfolds us, for your sufferings have brought him nigh. From the darkness which is about us, let us send up a mighty song of praise to God! Out of the narrow prison house let our voices go up like a trumpet of rejoicing, because He has granted it to us to suffer for the faith! God has chosen us, to bestow upon us a portion and inheritance in the Messiah! Let the Name of God be praised from now on and for evermore!"

"God has chosen us, to bestow on us a portion and inheritance in the Messiah! Let the Name of God be praised from now on and for evermore!"

Louder and louder rang the voices, repeating after Paul, in the Greek tongue, the verses of the Psalms. The Jews among the prisoners recalled the original Hebrew version, as it was sung on the Temple steps in Jerusalem; and they took up the chorus in Hebrew, with the melody of the Levites:

"Hallelujah hallelu . . . Praise ye the Lord, praise Him all ye servants of the Lord. . . . Praise ye the Lord, for He is good, for His mercy endureth forever. . . ."

They repeated the *Hallel,* as on the day of a great festival observed amid the glory of the Temple courts. The Greek mingled with the Hebrew, the two melodies rose side by side, like double fountains of joy. The flood of strength and renewal filled the whole underground prison —health, liberation, hope were found again. It was as though a flood of sunlight had shattered the rock of the prison and the glory of the heavens had burst upon the prisoners.

"I see the lord sitting on his throne!" sang one man from his corner. "Oh, he is calling me, he is signaling to me!"

"Even as a father comforts his son, so he brings us into the Holy of Holies," cried Peter, ecstatically.

"Who can divide us from the love of the Messiah? Come terror, come pain, come even death—his love shall be with us! *Hallelujah, Hallelujah!"* responded Paul, triumphantly.

The criminals in the prison, and after them the warders outside, listened in stupefaction to the song of exultation issuing from the half-dead Christian prisoners. It was utterly incomprehensible to them. And the wonder grew from day to day. Ever since the new prisoner was lowered into the deeps, it was as if a wind of life passed through the decaying bodies and withered bones chained to the walls and blocks. It was clear to the criminals and warders that in their singing the Christian prisoners were transported to another world; and it was the newcomer who brought them the invisible wings. The criminals and warders asked each other:

"What is it he tells them? What does he say? He shows them something that we cannot see, he makes them hear something that we cannot hear."

"Enter with us!" cried Paul. "The doors stand open for everyone! Come to the arms of the lord, his love awaits you too!"

"What? For us strangers? For us who tormented you?"

"God's grace is boundless, His grace is like the sun. For Him there is neither stranger nor kin. Those that believe in Him shall not be shamed. So the Holy Script tells us. He is the same Lord for all. Whosoever calls on Him shall be blessed. Come, all of you, the doors stand wipe open!"

The Sheol of that immemorial prison, where the darkness of despair had made itself secure, was transformed into a radiant threshold on which white-clad souls waited for admittance to the inmost sanctuary of God's eternal presence. And those whose eyes were closed to the radiance were filled with deepest envy. Not the criminals alone, they who were condemned to death, but the warders, too, drew close, in wonder and desire, to those whom yesterday they had tortured.

A new spirit came into the Tullianum. Of the water brought to the prisoners, the first drops were used to baptize those who had been unbelievers until now. The dry bread which was their sole food was transformed into the flesh of the Messiah; and in the darkness, heavy with death, the banquet of the living faith was spread.

"We were naked and God clothed us in the raiment of His love," sang Paul from his corner. "The grace of the Christ Messiah shines over us."

The converts, new and old, sang with him. They clanked their chains in rhythm with the chant.

"Naked and bare we were, and God clothes us with His love. The grace of the Christ Messiah shines over us. '

The seeing of visions became common among them. They called

742

out names, laughed in sheer joy, stretched out their arms. They saw help approaching:

"A fiery horse comes down through the rocks. It is winged and saddled, and it waits for me. It flies up with me to the lord, who will save me."

So the life-line of the name of Yeshua was thrown out, not alone to those for whom death was already prepared, but to those who were set to watch them, the soldiers and warders on the upper levels of the prison. In old Gabelus, the faith which had been flickering toward extinction was kindled anew, and he addressed himself to the task of winning completely those whose comrade-in-arms he had once been; old Gabelus, who had once led the cohorts of Caesar to victory on the field of battle, now led the soldiers of Caesar—those who were stationed in the Tullianum—to victory on the field of faith.

It was, indeed, the soldiers stationed in the prison who arranged to rescue the two apostles on the eve of their execution.

In the darkness a lamp appears. The warders are at the lower door. There is a whispering, an unlocking of chains.

"Begone! The gates above are open!"

Simon bar Jonah is ready to see in this offer the hand of God. The Messiah still needs him. And he is overwhelmed by sudden longing for the quiet waters of Kineret, where first he served the Messiah; his heart yearns for the old places, tugs him toward the congregations of the Holy Land, where he would spend his last days, telling them of the deeds and words of the Messiah, as in time past. He catches joyfully at the hands of his liberators. Has this not happened once before? Was it not in Jerusalem that God sent a slumber to seal the eyelids of the guards? Now, not in slumber, but still under the guidance of God, his guards will co-operate in his escape. His old limbs, scarred and bleeding, gain sudden strength. He rises, fired by the hope which has come at the last moment, when the sword is already on his throat, and he cries to his comrade:

"Come, Paul, the congregations need us."

"No, thou first of the disciples! The congregations need our death more than our life. The child has grown to manhood, has become a giant in the faith. From this day on he will do battle alone."

The first of the disciples has not the time to bethink himself of the meaning of Paul's words. He has not the time to hear them properly.

743

He is all haste. He is lifted from shoulder to shoulder, he is passed upward to the opening.

On the uppermost ledge he realizes suddenly that he is alone. He shouts down into the pit:

"Come, brother. We must be the last!" And there flashes through his memory the words he used when he had left the congregation of Rome.

"No, Khaifa," Paul cries up from the pit. "We must be the first!"

But still, in the haste of his flight, Peter cannot catch the meaning of Paul's cry. His liberators thrust him onward. One warder, beneath, lifts him, one, above, draws him into the open. Avoiding the Palatine, they conduct him through the valley at the foot of the Coelian hill, out to the Porta Capena. There, providing him with a bag containing bread and a few copper coins, they leave him in the dewy fields about the Via Appia.

Chapter Twenty-one

"L'ON?"

SLOWLY the blackness around him yielded to a dim, milky whiteness, which concealed the world from him not less than the night had done. It was as though he were still in the prison. Night had departed, but her hand was still on the bolt of the gate, and morning could not enter. The wanderer knew where he was—on the Via Appia. The thick white mist, though he could not penetrate it, was sweet to his eyes. He stooped, wetted his hands with the dew, and washed his eyes, which had learned to see better in darkness than in light. It was not easy to walk. His legs were racked by the ague, and every step was a hell of pain. Yet he walked, supported by his will, guided by instinct. He walked, or rather swam, through the nebula of space. He was free— and that was what mattered! He would live to carry the tidings of the Messiah through the world! He saw as in a vision his brothers in Puteoli, whither he was now making his way. They would send him

744

on, farther, farther. They would supply his needs, they would put him on a ship which would bring him to the shores of Asia, to Ephesus. Perhaps he would even see once more his beloved Antioch, where the congregation waited for him. He would send word to his dearest son, to Marcus, who was assuredly in one of the Asiatic cities. And then he would go on—O God!—to K'far Nahum on the shores of Kineret. No, no, his time has not yet come. The congregations needed him. The lord had work for him on earth and had saved him from the clutches of Edom to send him on new missions.

These were the thoughts of the first of the disciples, as he dragged himself heavily on his sick legs through the heavy white mist which lay on the Via Appia. His robe was torn into a thousand tatters, and the naked flesh showed through the rents. In those nine months of imprisonment the rats and the vermin had eaten his clothes and even his flesh. His beard, clotted with blood and filth, clung to his cheeks and throat. The bag with the supply of bread and the handful of copper coins was slung over his shoulder. And as he stumbled forward his mind at last began to catch up with the words which the apostle to the gentiles had called up to him from the blackness of the pit: "We must be the first. The congregations need our death more than our life. . . ." He repeated the phrases, a little impatiently. Brother Paul had always been hard to understand.

Just the same, a queer discomfort took hold of him, as he thought of himself, rescued thus, alone. He had become set in the vision of his own death—a sacrifice for the Messiah; and often he had meditated on the coming encounter, when his lord would draw him up sweetly to a place beside him on the cross, as he had done with Reb Jacob, and as he would do with the younger apostle, Paul, and with all the others. Yes, it was an odd feeling that invaded Khaifa, who had turned away his lips from the cup held out to him by the Messiah—the cup with the common drink. But—had not the lord himself implored God: "Take away the cup from me?" Did not Simon bar Jonah remember now, and did he not see, in the white thickness of the mist, the Messiah in the garden of Gat Shemen, the Messiah among the lengthening shadows of the olive trees, on that spring evening? For the lord had taken him along, and with him Jacob and Jochanan. The lord had been waiting for something, and he had become afraid. He had said to them: "My spirit is heavy within me. Stay here and wait for me." And he had

745

withdrawn from them a little space and had kneeled and prayed. He had fallen to the earth, and he had said: "If it may be, let this hour pass over me." And Simon bar Jonah, stumbling through the white mist, heard the words, as in a dream. Yes, he remembered now to his shame that he had become sleepy with the meat and wine which he had eaten at the Passover meal with the lord; he had become heavy, like the other disciples, and had fallen asleep. He had not waited for the lord, as the latter had beseeched him. He, the first of the disciples, had slept away the agonies of the Messiah. "Simon, sleepest thou?" his lord had asked him. "Couldst thou not stay awake one hour?" And the lord had said: "Watch and pray, that ye may not be tempted. The spirit is willing, but the flesh is weak." Had not the lord intended this for all time to come, including the present occasion? Had not Khaifa now failed the lord again, falling as it were into a neglectful sleep in regard to his own trial? Another utterance of the lord rose sharply in his memory: "Ere the cock shall have crowed twice thou shalt have denied me three times." What was he doing here, on the road to Puteoli, but denying the lord? He had abandoned the flock entrusted to him by the lord and was saving himself. Simon's heart stirred uneasily. He shivered, but it was not with cold. His teeth chattered, his hands trembled, his old, rheumy eyes were bathed in tears. Where was he? What had he done? What door was open to him now? Had he indeed done well to flee, telling himself he was doing so for the sake of future service?

He knelt down, lifted his arms to heaven, and cried out: "*Abba,* Father! All things are possible with Thee. Take away the cup from me; but according to Thy desire, not according to mine!"

He rose. The tears welling from his eyes seemed to have frozen into a heavy layer, and a stabbing pain shot through them unceasingly. The mist shrouding road and field began to lift, and morning sunlight broke through upon the wide earth. A freshening, liberating wind moved lightly about him, as though all the world had issued, like himself, from long imprisonment. He could not bear the light. He opened his eyes for an instant, closed them again, and wondered. It seemed to him that the radiance was streaming upward from the earth. Above him fragments of cloud, woolly, disordered, fled before the wind like abandoned sheep. Simon plodded on hopelessly. At this hour the road was deserted save for himself. The world was silent, but the silence was alive, like some tremendous spirit holding in its joy. Half blinded, confused between self-pity and remorse, Simon prayed passionately.

Then suddenly it was as if his sight had been restored to him. He saw a man coming toward him on the road. The man was barefoot, his robe was luminously white, his face.... Whose face was that? Those pale, long cheeks framed in a graying, black beard, those quivering lips, the eyes filled with sadness and pain, the shining forehead.... Simon's heart stood still, and his throat was constricted, so that he could not breathe. Awed, he drew to one side and made obeisance as the figure passed. There was no greeting, no sign of recognition. The man passed silently, absorbed in thought; the dreamy face was set, the hands hung down, the feet moved rhythmically. Simon turned, watching the figure grow smaller as it moved cityward. And now Simon seemed to waken. It is he! It is his Rabbi! His Rabbi!

Drenched in perspiration Simon forced himself into a run, crying breathlessly:

"*Rabbenu! Rabbenu!* Our Rabbi!"

The figure suspended its slow, rhythmic walk, waiting for Simon to draw near. And Simon, flooded with bliss, confronted his Rabbi and cried:

"*L'on ath azil?*"—"Whither goest thou?"

"*Romah, l'hitlot sheinit.*"—"To Rome, to be crucified again," his Rabbi answered in a low voice, and, lifting his arm sadly from underneath his white robe, pointed to the city awakening under the sunlight. Simon saw the bloody mark of the nail on the hand of his Rabbi. Shame paralyzed Simon. He stood as one forlorn, not knowing what he was to do. Then he sank on his knees, and broke into a bitter cry:

"*S'lach li, adoni.*"—"Lord, lord, forgive me, I pray thee."

Thus he stayed awhile, kneeling, his head sunk on his breast. A breath passed over his head, as though a dove's wing had touched him. When he opened his eyes road and field were empty again. Simon bent down and kissed the spot on which his Rabbi had stood, saying to himself:

"Why forgivest thou me so often, lord?"

Then he rose to his feet, turned cityward, and set out for the Tullianum prison.

Terrified and yet filled with joy, humbled and yet exalted, Simon

747

retraced his steps. One longing filled him now : to be near his lord, to see again his white robe, to hear again his voice, from this moment on and for evermore; and if the road to eternal reunion led through the gates of death, then death was welcome, too.

In the guard house of the Tullianum Simon came upon the squad which was leading Paul to his execution. Simon approached, fell into Paul's arms, and said:

"I have seen the lord, brother Paul. O Paul, thou knewest the will of the lord better than I."

"My teacher! My Rabbi!" answered Paul. "Thou first of the disciples!"

They turned to the guard, saying :

"Let us be led to our death together."

The centurion in command, who had of late evinced a certain friendliness toward the Christians, said to his men: "Let them go together as far as the Porta Ostiensis. There they must be separated. The old man goes to the Trans-Tiber, thence to the Vaticanum, to be crucified. But this one, being a Roman citizen, lead out by the Via Ostiensis to the Cesti Pyramid, where he is to be beheaded."

Before the two apostles were led away, Paul bent down over the opening in the ground, and called out to the prisoners in the dungeons :

"The grace of our lord, Yeshua the Messiah, be with your spirit! Amen!"

After him Simon called down :

"Peace be with you who are in the lord Messiah! Amen!"

From the depths below there floated up a chorus of voices, the strong, the weak, the firm, the tremulous:

"Peter and Paul! Pray for our souls!"

For the first time the two names were intertwined in a single cord of salvation.

Chapter Twenty-two

THE MEETING OF THE WAYS

IN the midst of a wall of shields, chained on either side to a soldier the two apostles walked, hand in hand. Walking, they murmured constantly: "The Lord is my shepherd, I shall not want. He maketh me to lie down in green pastures, He leadeth me beside the still waters. . . ." Part of the way Peter retraced the path of his flight; but when the procession reached the Via Sacra, it did not make for the Porta Capena, but turned toward the Via Ostiensis. At the beginning of the road the apostles were separated.

"Peace be with thee, my brother Paul!"

"Peace be with thee, my teacher and guide in the faith."

Paul gazed a moment at the older apostle. He saw the bloody feet, bruised by the stones, and he would have kneeled down. For he said:

"Let me kiss the feet which accompanied the lord when he was in the flesh."

But Peter restrained him, saying: "Nay, it is for me to kiss the feet which have carried the tidings of the lord to the nations of the world."

They embraced for the last time, and as they were led away from each other they turned their heads backward.

"I shall see thee soon in the presence of the lord," cried Peter.

"Pray for me, apostle to the Jews."

They led old Simon, with his bloodied feet, uphill again. Beyond the Porta Trigemina lay the Sublicius bridge. How often he had been conducted this way by the faithful, to the assemblies in the house of Priscilla on the Aventine hill! Simon looked up the slope. A few passersby stopped. Were they of the faithful? Yes! They paused! They turned back. Their lips were moving unmistakably in prayer. And as the procession drew through the narrow streets of the Jewish quarter the cortege grew. An inaudible proclamation seemed to run before it, for at the windows of the high houses heads appeared. "They are leading the apostle to the cross!" Mothers hastened down to the street level, carrying their little ones. Simon beheld the multitude of sad faces; he thought he caught the murmur of the prayers issuing from their lips. He smiled to them, and they, mastering their sorrow, tried to smile back. "Weep not for me," murmured Simon. "Soon I shall be with the lord. I shall see him, as I saw him this morning, but now he will never leave me again. I shall be with him for ever. And you, you too, shall be with him for ever. .... This I promise, in the Name of our Father in heaven, who is the God of all grace! I rejoiced when they said to me, Come, let us go up to the house of the lord. Peace be with you, my children, near and far." He inclined his head to right and left, smiling at the men and women and children crowding about the doors.

When he had passed through the Jewish quarter, he began the ascent of the Janiculum and came at last to the place of execution, where his cross waited for him. But before they nailed him to the cross, they scourged him, for it was the law that a man condemned to crucifixion had to be scourged first. They bound him to a wooden block, and two soldiers wielded the lead-loaded whip over him. The last drops of his blood started out under the lashes, but no sound came from the old man. His lips moved silently, as he uttered a prayer of thanks for the privilege of suffering like the lord. Like the lord? Peter started in fright at the tenor of his thoughts. Who was he that he should compare himself with the lord? Had he indeed suffered like the lord? Was he not a runaway slave? How often he had denied the lord, how often fled from the lord's fate! He had put away the cup held out to him, again and again, until the lord himself had appeared, with a last admonition. How could he say of himself that he was dying the death of his lord?

They unbound him at last from the block and half led, half carried him, toward the cross. They asked him if he had a last request. He could have a cup of sour wine, the right of any slave who was about to be crucified.

Yes, he had a last request, which he uttered in the broken Greek which he had picked up in the years of his wandering. He wanted them to nail him to the cross head down.

The soldier executioners did not understand him, or thought that they did not understand him. "Head down?" The old man nodded and moved his hands feebly, to indicate his meaning. "Head down. Nail me to the cross head down."

750

It was a strange request, but they fulfilled it. They lifted up the lean, bruised body, still covered with tattered sackcloth, and nailed the two feet to the arms of the cross, and the hands to the upright.

Two naked feet looked down from the cross-piece; the toes were twisted and broken, like the roots of an old olive tree; but they were mighty limbs, broadboned, gnarled like tree trunks. And suddenly it seemed that the feet had taken on the likeness of human faces, cut and battered. The blood ran from the wounds, which were like open mouths. And as the bleeding feet looked heavenward, the gray, mighty head with its short, tangled beard, hung earthward. But still the eyes smiled, seeking the little group of men and women who stood at a distance, and still the lips moved in last greeting and prayer. Then his voice was raised, and they heard him, distinctly: "Lord take me to thee!" And a few moments later his voice rang clearly:

"Hear, O Israel, the Lord our God, the Lord is One."

The men and women lifted their faces heavenward and repeated:

"Hear, O Israel, the Lord our God, the Lord is One."

A moment of silence. The blood descended, pulse by pulse, into the head. The feet on the cross-piece were now as white as snow, but the face was crimson, like a flame. And now the old man pulled his head violently away from the cross. His bloodshot eyes were wide open. In the hoarse, joyous voice with which he had greeted the lord on the Via Appia, he called now:

"*Rabban! Rabban! Rabban!*"

The head fell back on the cross, and was motionless.

* * *

While at one end of Rome, on the Vaticanum, the apostle to the Jews was being nailed to the cross, sentence of death was being carried out on the apostle to the gentiles on the Via Ostiensis, at the other end of Rome. Paul too was accompanied on his last earthly journey by a little group of the faithful. They walked behind him, at a distance. Lukas the physician and Eubulus the soldier were among them; also Pudens, and Linus, strong, faithful Linus, on whom Peter counted most, consigning into his hands the leadership of the congregation of Rome. Two or three women were there too, and Paul greeted them with his last looks and commended them to God with his last thoughts. There was no fear in him now for the future of the congregations.

He had planted their roots deep; and the storm would only drive the roots deeper. He had done his work well, and after him strong hands would continue it. "I have fought a good fight," he said to himself again, as he stood on the place of execution. And again he reviewed, swiftly, the years that linked Saul with Paul. There was nothing that he would have otherwise; the errors and the sins he had committed when he was Saul he brought to nothing; he had cleansed them with his blood, sweat, and sorrows; and Saul too had sought God, in his own way, and according to his own light, with all his heart and soul. Everything had been as it had to be, in its own time. He had done that which it had seemed right for him to do in the eyes of God, and he had done nothing with a view to his own advantage. His life had been a sacrifice laid on the altar of God. Even that part of it which had been without the Messiah, yes, against the Messiah, he had consecrated to God. It had been one long pursuit of the divinity. Now the pursuit was over, he had come to the end of the course, he had reached God. His life was whole, because throughout he had kept the faith. His death would be part of his mission. All was as it ought to be. His whole being was filled with the perfection of righteousness, and this he regarded as a special grant of grace from God; it was a special miracle of grace that the sense of righteousness should sustain him in the last moment. He had discharged his obligations, and now a crown of righteousness was laid up for him, was held for him by the right judge.

Firm in the bond of peace between him and the Lord of the world, he approached with unfaltering steps the block on which his head would be severed from his body by the executioner's sword.

A Roman citizen, he was spared the final humiliation and torture of the lash; nor could he be made to suffer death by crucifixion. Paul did not regard his own impending death as martyrdom. His death was but a necessary part of his mission, a rounding out of his life. The peace of his spirit imparted to his body, in those last moments, an unwonted majesty. He threw a last glance at his companions, who bore themselves with the same tranquil dignity. A soldier approached him, to bind his eyes. "Must this be done?" he asked, wordlessly. "It is the law," said the soldier. Paul submitted. His respect for the law did not desert him even then. One of the women approached the soldier and gave him her veil. Paul thanked her with a look. The soldier

752

bound his eyes. Now he was ready. He kneeled and placed his head on the block.

"The grace of our lord, Yeshua the Messiah, be with you all," he blessed them.

In the few dark moments which preceded his death, Paul saw again the vision which had come to him so often after the martyrdom of Reb Istephan: the white, radiant angel, with body steeped in stones, with wings uplifted for flight. And now Paul felt himself transformed into the angel. He felt the wings lifting him, he was in flight, the world was below him.

"Hear, O Israel, the Lord our God, the Lord is One."

These were the last words of the apostle to the gentiles.

* * *

On the Sabbath morning a fierce restlessness reigned among the worshipers of the crowded Augustus Synagogue in the Trans-Tiber. Word had come from Jerusalem that the storm which had so long been gathering in Judaea against the might of Rome had at last broken out. The Jews had risen in rebellion; they had defeated the troops of the Procurator Festus and once again, after so many years, Jerusalem was in Jewish hands, Jerusalem was free! In Rome the Jewish congregation received the news with mixed feelings. There was joy; there was uncertainty, and fear. They trembled not only for themselves, who lived in the capital of the Empire but—much more—for the fate of the Temple. They trembled for that ultimate symbol of Jewish unity, more important in their eyes even than national independence. It was the young people who rejoiced, though they were well aware that the final issue was still in doubt; it was the older people who, remembering many rebellions and many triumphal processions of captured rebels passing through the streets of Rome, were filled with forebodings for the Holy City and its shrine.

But they talked, that Sabbath, of another portentous event—the execution of the two apostles. The martyrdom of the Christians had healed the breach between the two sections of the congregation even before the death of the apostles; and if any bitterness had survived the common sorrow of the long persecutions, it was wiped away now. Somehow the worshipers connected the two events—the uprising in Jerusalem and the martyrdom of the apostles.

753

The old Rabbi of the congregation, Reb Sabbatai Zadoc, sought, in his sermon of that morning, to restore calm:

"We know not whether the hand of Israel can overcome the sword of Edom. Assuredly all things are possible with God, but what is the earthly power of Israel against the earthly power of Edom? Is it not as a thorn bush against a mighty forest? But I say to you that the spirit of God has already overcome the power of Edom—here in the city of Rome."

The congregation looked at the preacher in wonder.

"All things are possible with God!" cried a voice.

"All things are possible with God!" repeated Reb Sabbatai Zadoc. "I say to you that Edom has already been overthrown!"

"What mean you, Rabbi?" someone asked.

"See you not what has happened in Rome? The more they burn the believers in the Messiah, the more they fling them to the beasts, the mightier grow their numbers. Behold! Rome went forth against Jerusalem with the sword, and Jerusalem went forth against Rome with the spirit. The sword conquered for a while, but the spirit conquers for ever!"

* * *

The writer adds:

I thank Thee and praise Thee, Lord of the world, that thou hast given
me the strength to withstand all temptations and overcome all obstacles, those of my own making and those made by others,
and to complete the two works, "The Nazarene" and
"The Apostle," which are one work; so that I might
set forth in them the merit of Israel, whom
Thou hast elected to bring the light of
the faith to the nations of the
world, for Thy glory
and out of Thy
love of man-
kind.

754